the
PLAIN
Janes

Cecil Castellucci and Jim Rugg

LITTLE, BROWN AND COMPANY
New York Boston

Copyright © 2020 by Cecil Castellucci and Jim Rugg
Foreword copyright © 2020 by Mariko Tamaki
Lettering of parts 1 and 2 by Jared Fletcher; lettering of part 3 by Ching N. Chan

Cover art copyright © 2020 by Jim Rugg. Cover design by Ching N. Chan.
Cover copyright © 2020 by Hachette Book Group, Inc.

Little, Brown and Company
Hachette Book Group
1290 Avenue of the Americas, New York, NY 10104
Visit us at LBYR.com

First Edition: January 2020
The Plain Janes originally published in 2007 by DC Comics
Janes in Love originally published in 2008 by DC Comics

Little, Brown and Company is a division of Hachette Book Group, Inc.
The Little, Brown name and logo are trademarks of Hachette Book Group, Inc.

Library of Congress Cataloging-in-Publication Data
Names: Castellucci, Cecil, 1969– author. | Rugg, Jim, illustrator.
Title: The plain Janes / Cecil Castellucci and Jim Rugg.
Description: First edition. | New York ; Boston : Little, Brown and Company, 2020. | "The Plain Janes originally published in 2007 by DC Comics. Janes in Love originally published in 2008 by DC Comics." | Presents the full text of Plain Janes and Janes in Love, plus bonus content such as the evolution of the graphic novel and original cover sketches. | Summary: When Jane moves to the suburbs and thinks her life is over, she and three new friends form a club to make public art but are soon distracted by romance.
Identifiers: LCCN 2018050077| ISBN 9780316522724 (hardcover) | ISBN 9780316522816 (trade pbk.) | ISBN 9780316522748 (ebook) | ISBN 9780316522786 (library ebook edition)
Subjects: LCSH: Graphic novels. | CYAC: Graphic novels. | Friendship—Fiction. | Clubs—Fiction. | Street art—Fiction. | Dating (Social customs)—Fiction. | Schools—Fiction.
Classification: LCC PZ7.7.C375 Pp 2020 | DDC 741.5/973—dc23
LC record available at https://lccn.loc.gov/2018050077

ISBNs: 978-0-316-52272-4 (hardcover), 978-0-316-52281-6 (pbk.),
978-0-316-52274-8 (ebook), 978-0-316-52280-9 (ebook), 978-0-316-52279-3 (ebook)

PRINTED IN CHINA

IM

Hardcover: 10 9 8 7 6 5 4 3 2 1
Paperback: 10 9 8 7 6 5 4 3 2 1

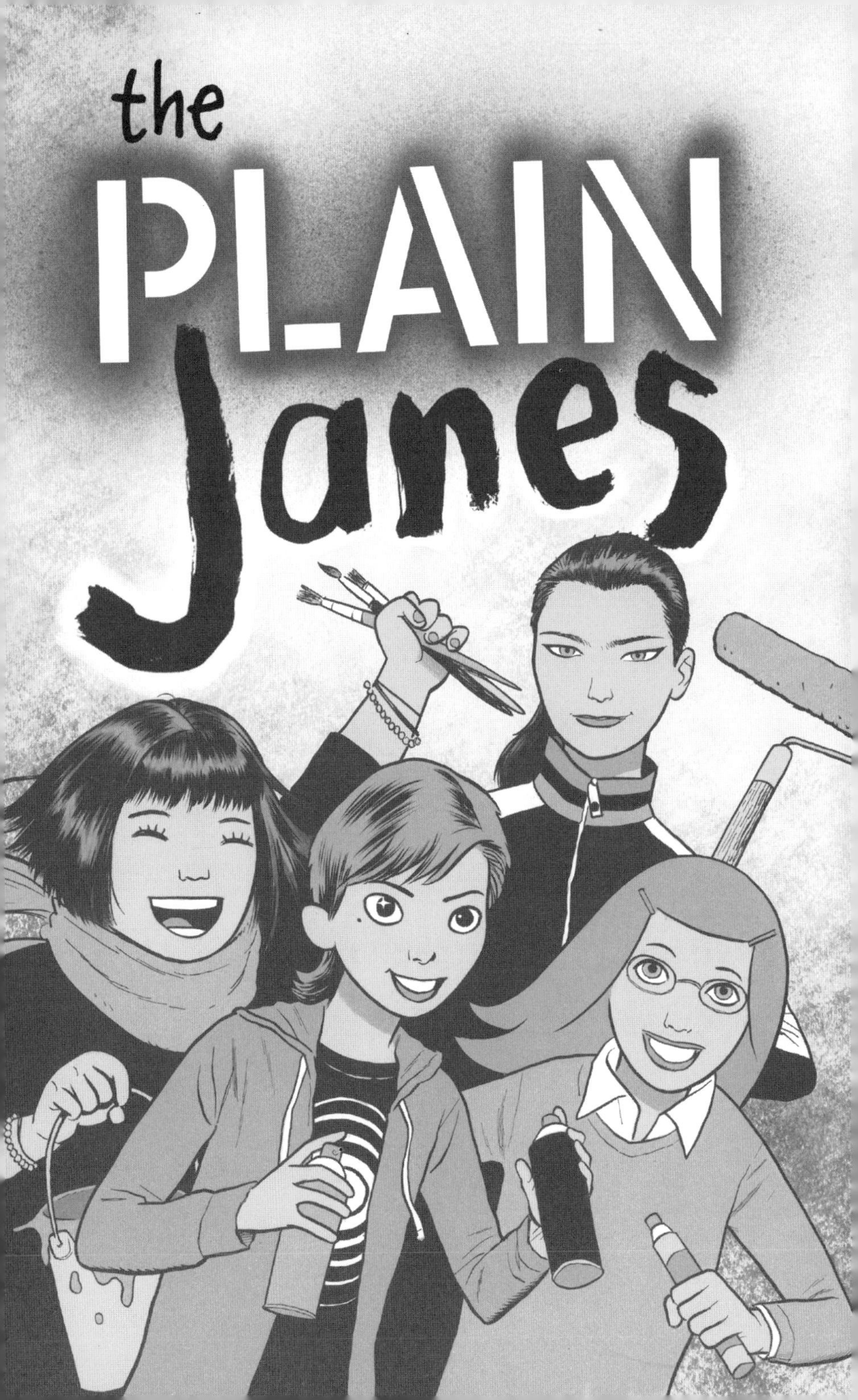
the PLAIN Janes

ART SAVES

Foreword

It's possible that my love of *The PLAIN Janes* has something to do with the fact that I have no doubt that when I was a teenager, being an art nerd saved my life.

Before I was an art nerd, I was a weird kid. Before I was an art nerd, I was the kid who didn't like most people's music and was bad at parties. Before I was an art nerd, my culture was *Entertainment Tonight* every night at 7 P.M.

Then in tenth grade everything changed. I had a cool friend, Jen, who knew way more than I did about pretty much everything. She introduced me to improv theater, documentary films, music not produced by major labels, and, crucially, *The Rocky Horror Picture Show*. I discovered dressing up as a form of self-expression. Eyeliner as lipstick.

I discovered the joy of obsessing over the work of an artist who inspires you to make your own work, however rough that might be in the beginning.

I came to this book through Cecil Castellucci. The first time I ever saw Cecil, it was 1995 (ish), and she was rocking out on her guitar in a freezing, bare concrete warehouse in Montreal, in front of a crowd of college art geeks, with her band Nerdy Girl. I remember thinking that she was cool the way so much of Montreal seemed impossibly cool to me then. Cool like a pair of Doc Martens weathered to the perfect shade of worn. I immediately bought her CD and played it endlessly.

A decade later, I got to actually meet Cecil at a comic convention in Toronto. She was over the moon about her new graphic novel with artist Jim Rugg: The PLAIN Janes. Jim would bring the Janes to life with expressive style and impeccable detail (which you can also see in his other works, including Street Angel), capturing the glory and frustration of these characters. Jim rules.

The PLAIN Janes is the story of budding artist and suburban transfer Jane Beckles, who creates a community of friends and fellow artists (all also named Jane) to change the face of their part of the world.

I finished the book a giant fan of Cecil and Jim. It exemplifies and celebrates the power of collaboration, the coming together of minds, channeling inspirations and experiences into a story for young artists-to-be in the middle of that strange journey of being a teenager.

The PLAIN Janes is about finding your people, finding your voice, finding your future. It dives into art as expression, art as activism, art as resistance.

Art celebrates: the work of the nerds who came before us and the work of the nerds who are just now putting pen to paper.

Art saves. It saves you and me in little ways every day. We pass it forward to the people caught in torment and hope it shines a light.

Thank you, Cecil and Jim, for these incredible stories!

—Mariko Tamaki

Part 1
The PLAIN Janes

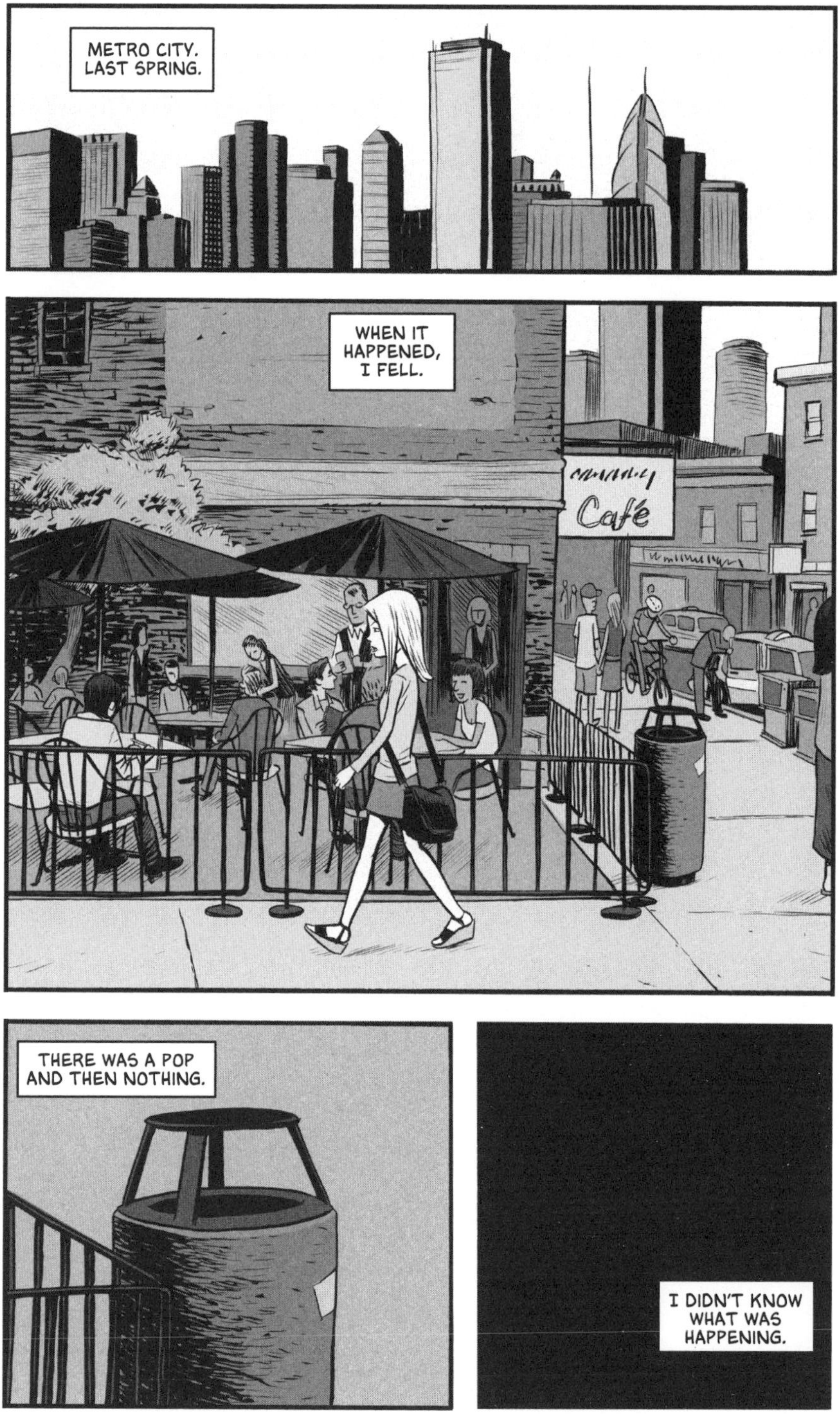
METRO CITY.
LAST SPRING.
WHEN IT HAPPENED, I FELL.
Café
THERE WAS A POP AND THEN NOTHING.
I DIDN'T KNOW WHAT WAS HAPPENING.

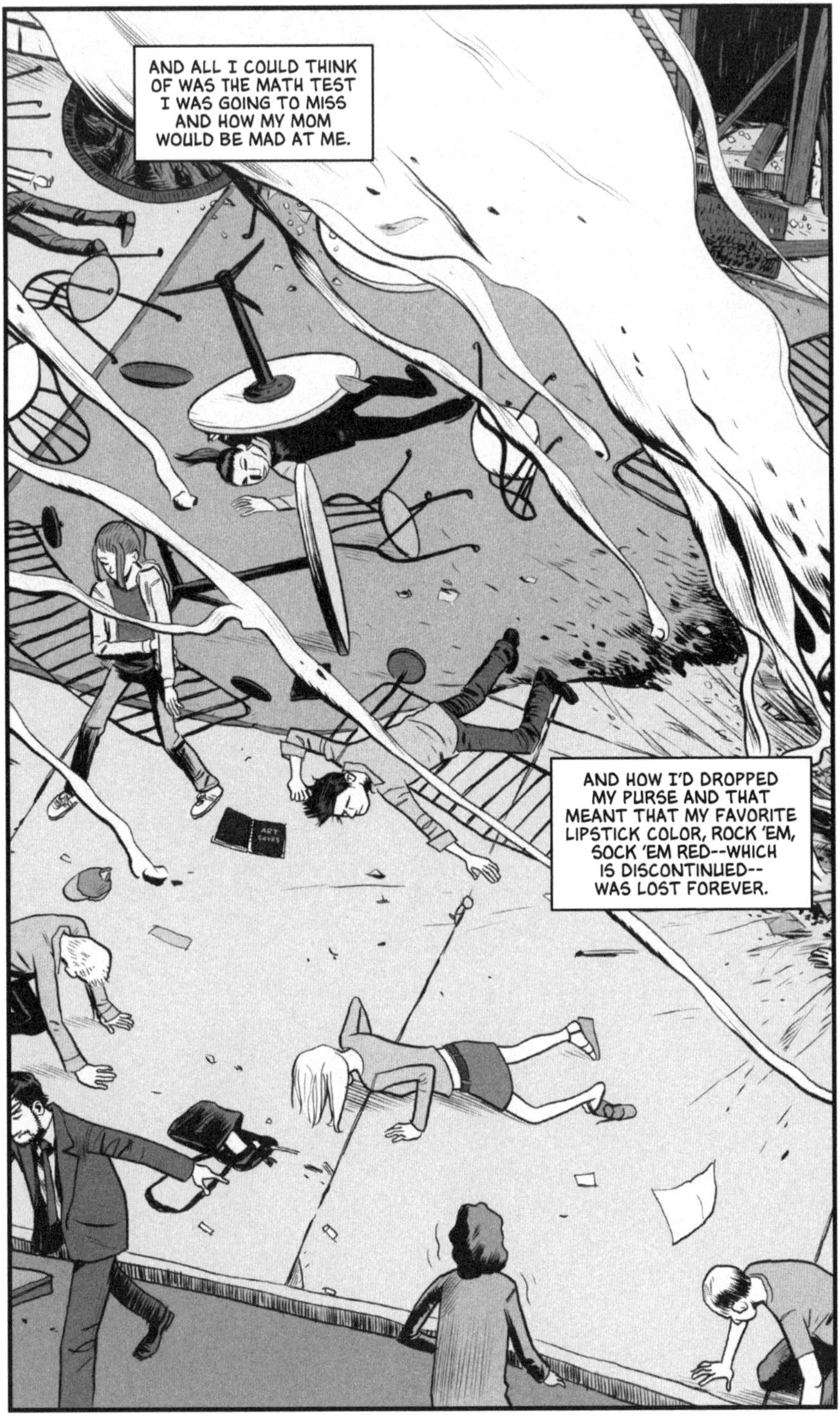
AND ALL I COULD THINK OF WAS THE MATH TEST I WAS GOING TO MISS AND HOW MY MOM WOULD BE MAD AT ME.
AND HOW I'D DROPPED MY PURSE AND THAT MEANT THAT MY FAVORITE LIPSTICK COLOR, ROCK 'EM, SOCK 'EM RED--WHICH IS DISCONTINUED--WAS LOST FOREVER.

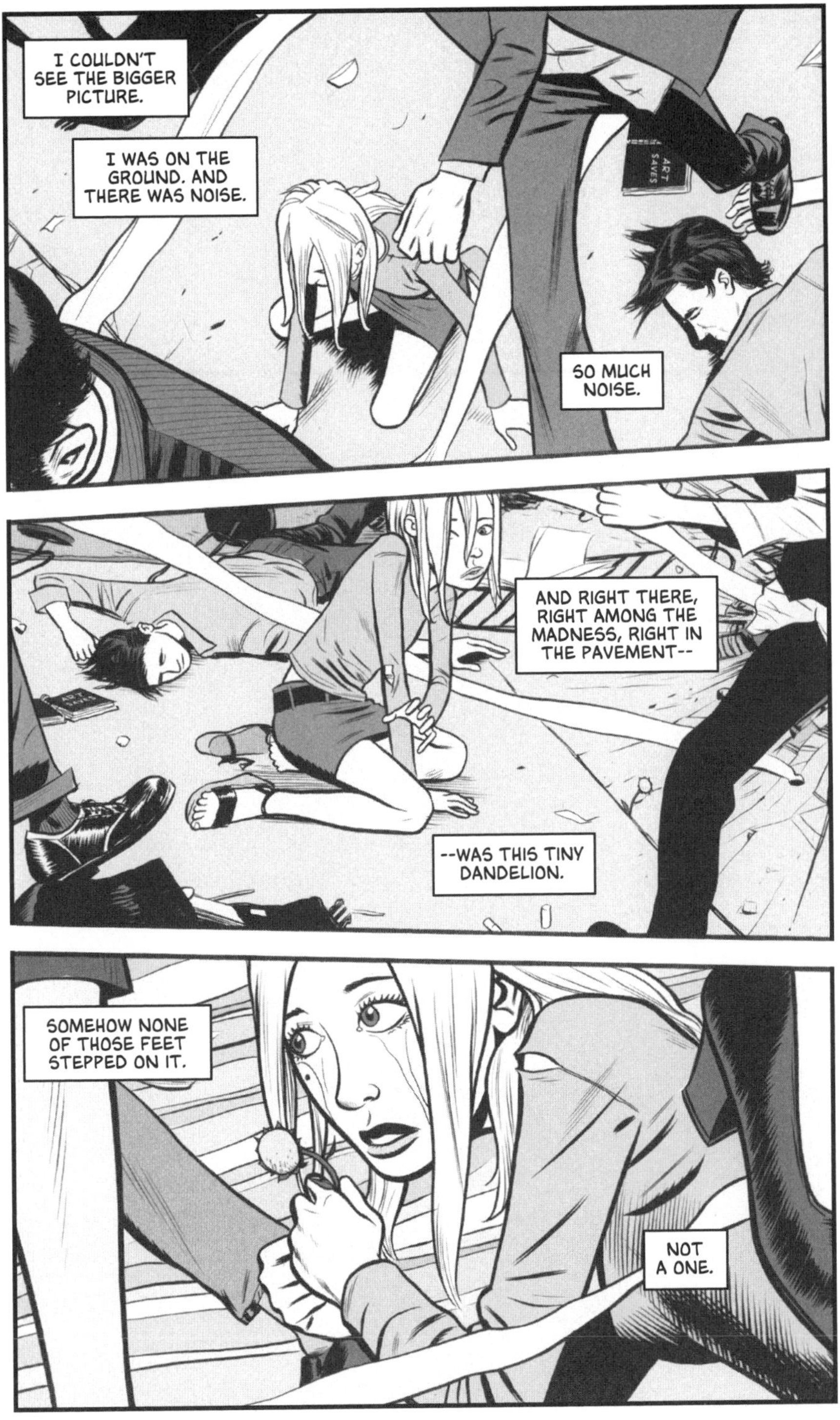
I COULDN'T SEE THE BIGGER PICTURE.
I WAS ON THE GROUND. AND THERE WAS NOISE.
SO MUCH NOISE.
ART SAVES
AND RIGHT THERE, RIGHT AMONG THE MADNESS, RIGHT IN THE PAVEMENT--
--WAS THIS TINY DANDELION.
SOMEHOW NONE OF THOSE FEET STEPPED ON IT.
NOT A ONE.

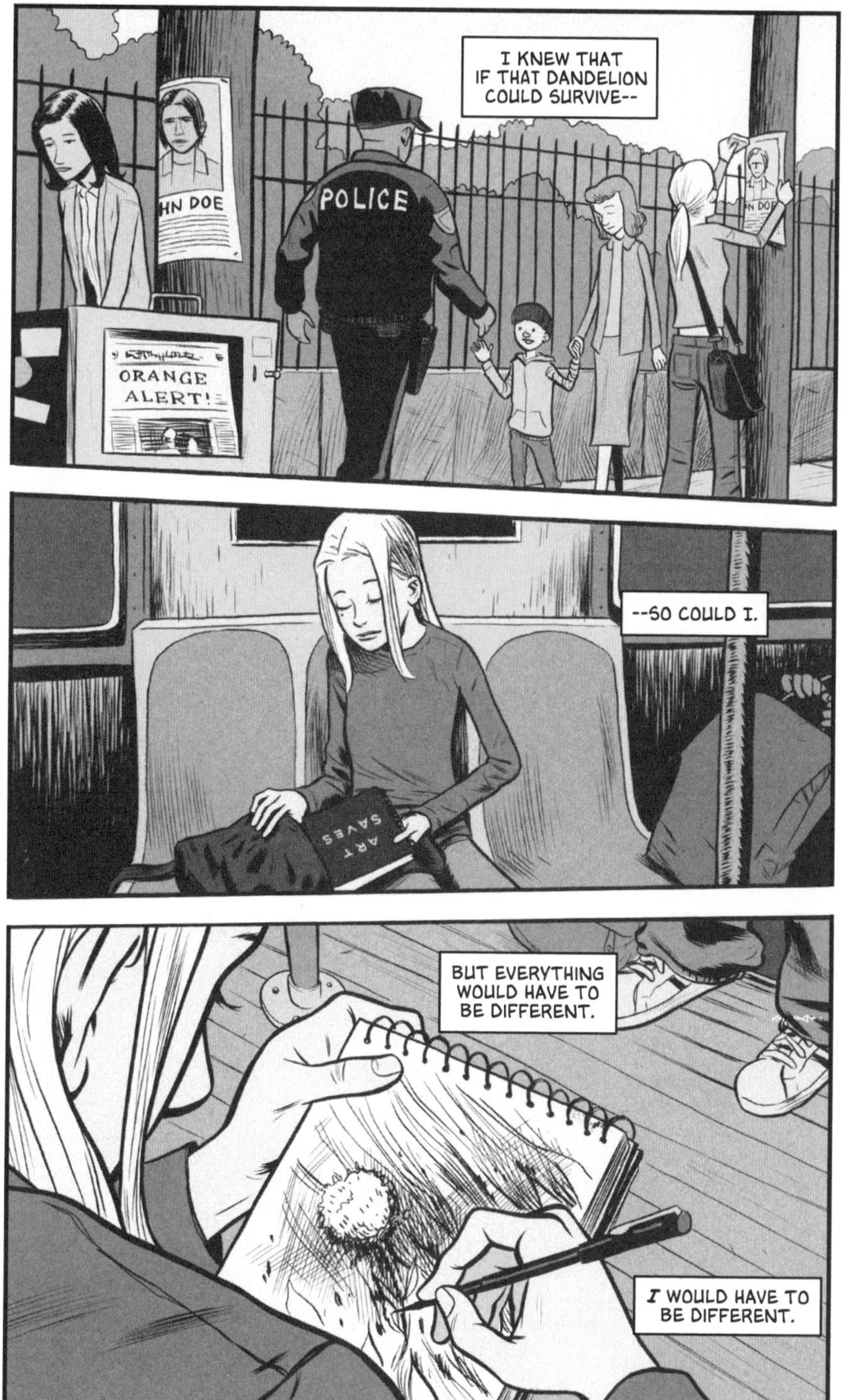

I KNEW THAT IF THAT DANDELION COULD SURVIVE--
HN DOE
POLICE
ORANGE ALERT!
--SO COULD I.
ART SAVES
BUT EVERYTHING WOULD HAVE TO BE DIFFERENT.
I WOULD HAVE TO BE DIFFERENT.

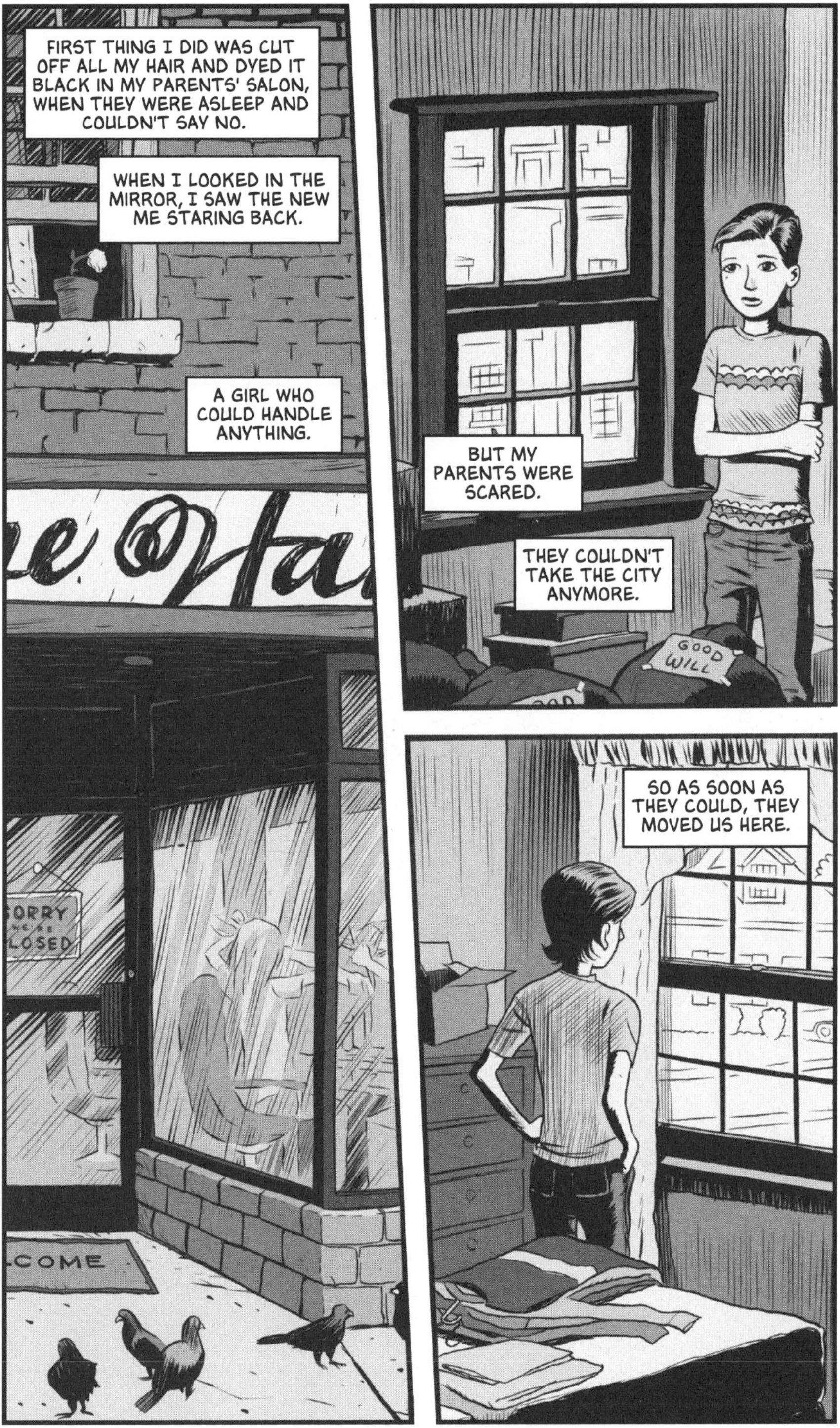
FIRST THING I DID WAS CUT OFF ALL MY HAIR AND DYED IT BLACK IN MY PARENTS' SALON, WHEN THEY WERE ASLEEP AND COULDN'T SAY NO.
WHEN I LOOKED IN THE MIRROR, I SAW THE NEW ME STARING BACK.
A GIRL WHO COULD HANDLE ANYTHING.
BUT MY PARENTS WERE SCARED.
THEY COULDN'T TAKE THE CITY ANYMORE.
GOOD WILL
SO AS SOON AS THEY COULD, THEY MOVED US HERE.

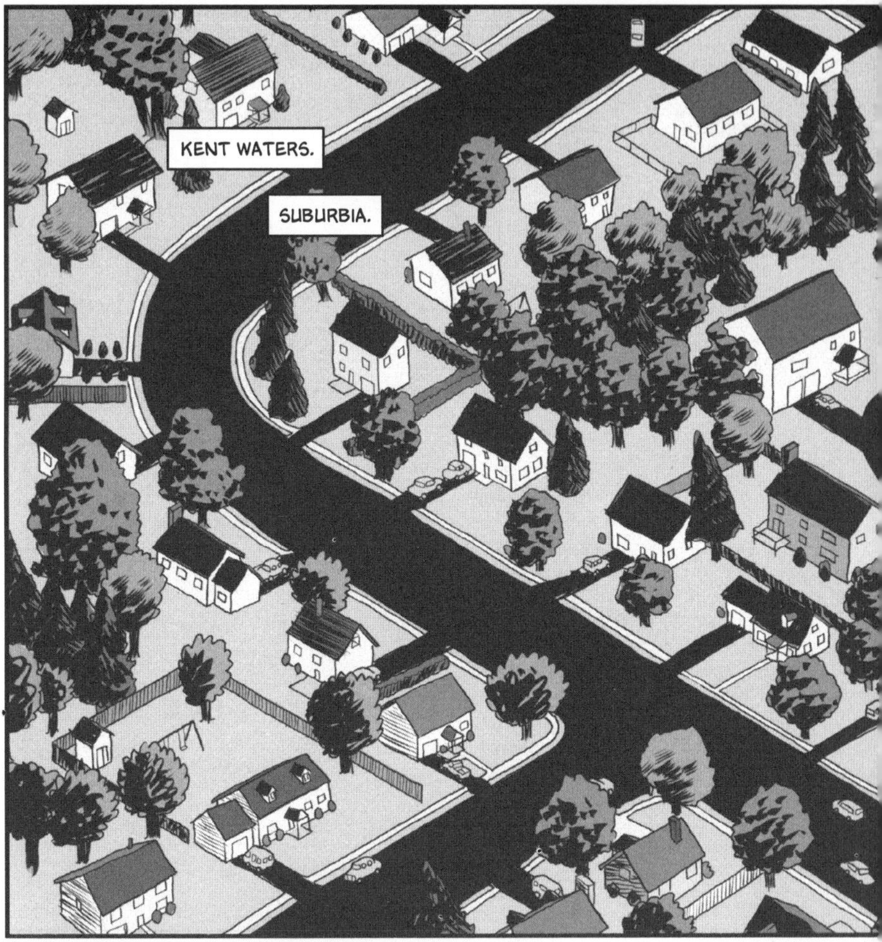
KENT WATERS.
SUBURBIA.

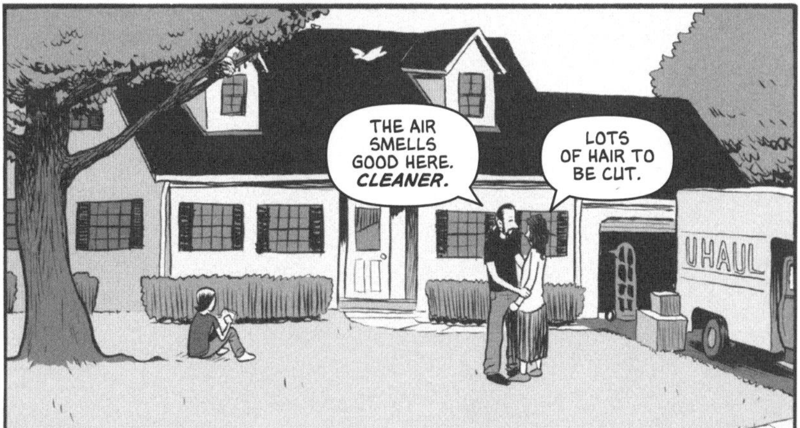
THE AIR SMELLS GOOD HERE. CLEANER.
LOTS OF HAIR TO BE CUT.
UHAUL

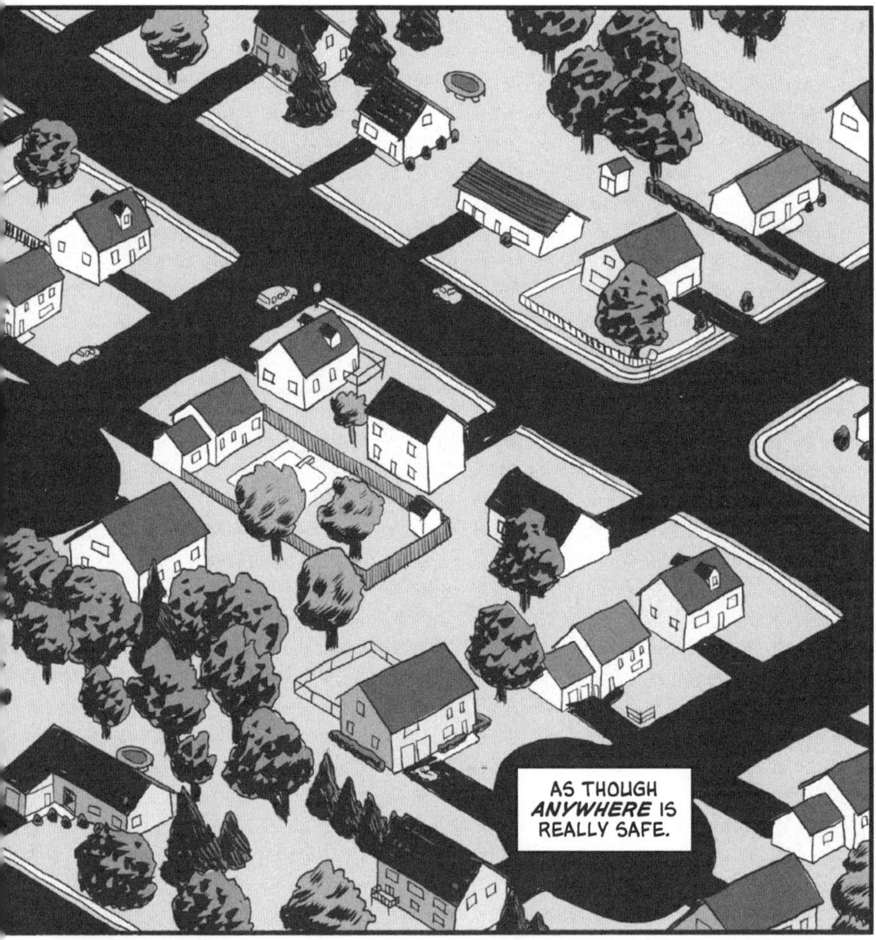
AS THOUGH *ANYWHERE* IS REALLY SAFE.

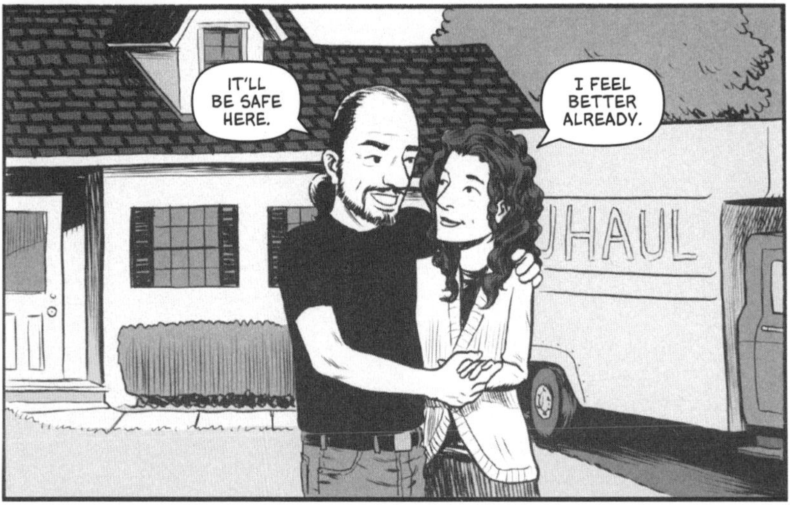
IT'LL BE SAFE HERE.
I FEEL BETTER ALREADY.
UHAUL

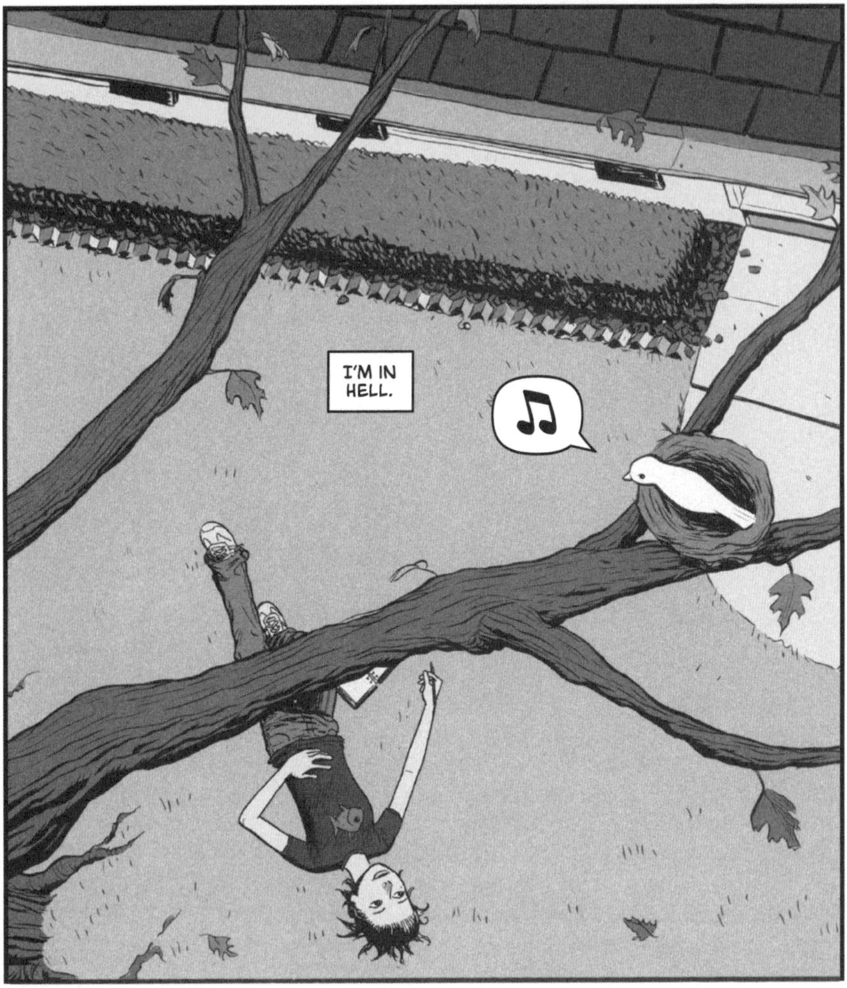
I'M IN
HELL.
♫

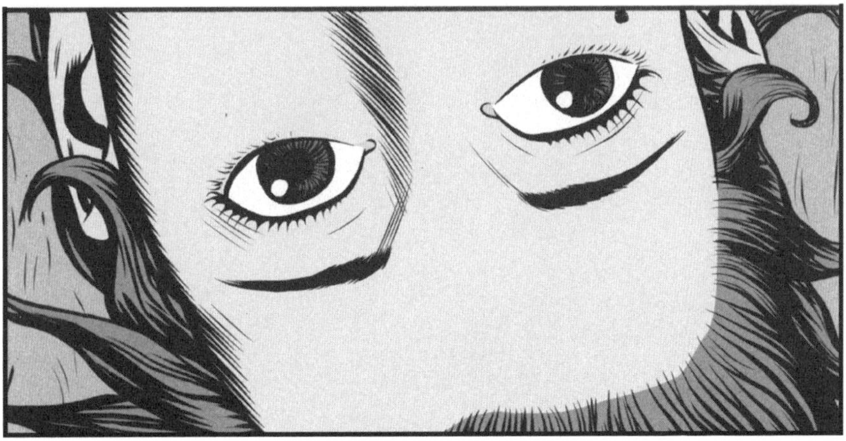

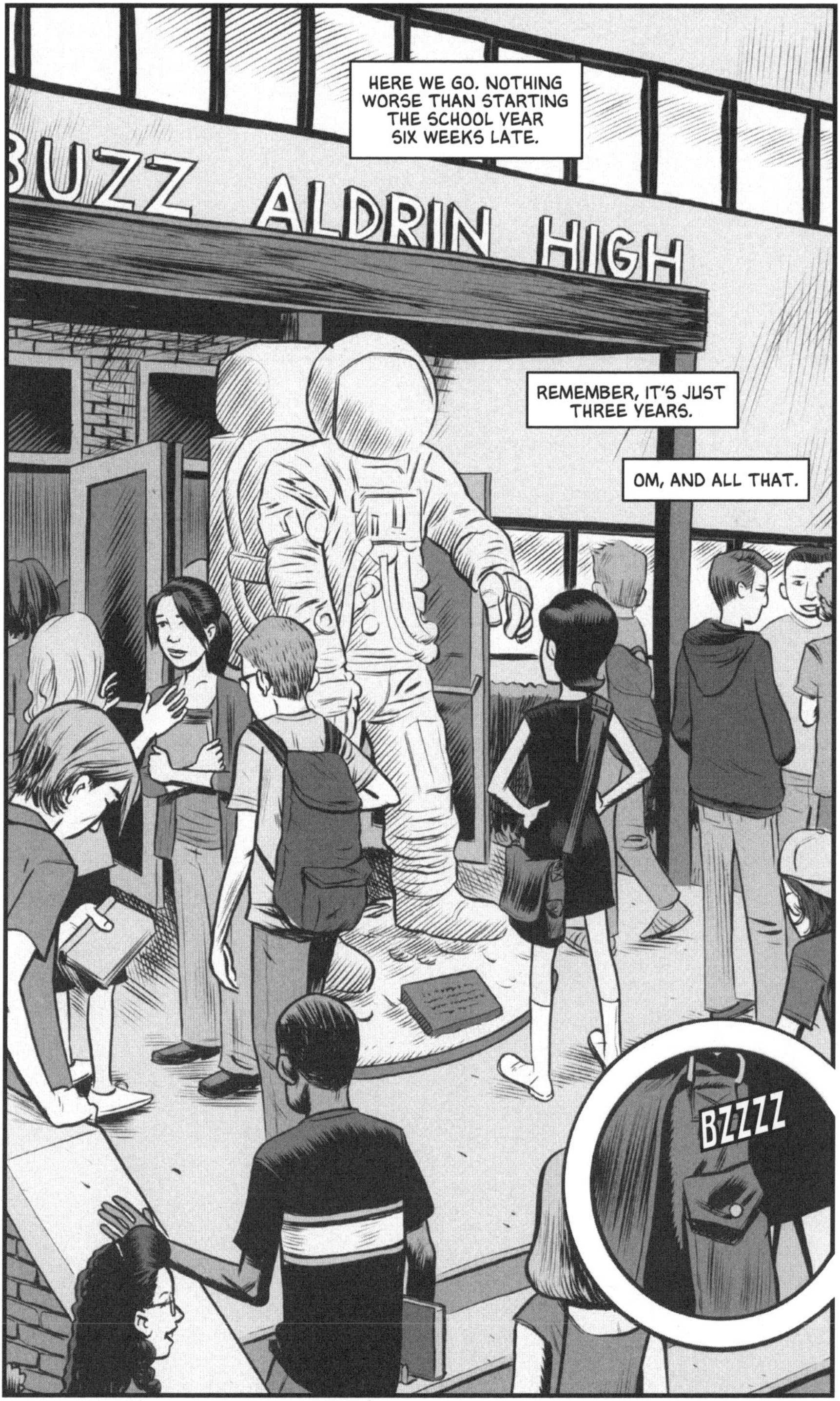
HERE WE GO. NOTHING WORSE THAN STARTING THE SCHOOL YEAR SIX WEEKS LATE.
BUZZ ALDRIN HIGH
REMEMBER, IT'S JUST THREE YEARS.
OM, AND ALL THAT.
BZZZZ

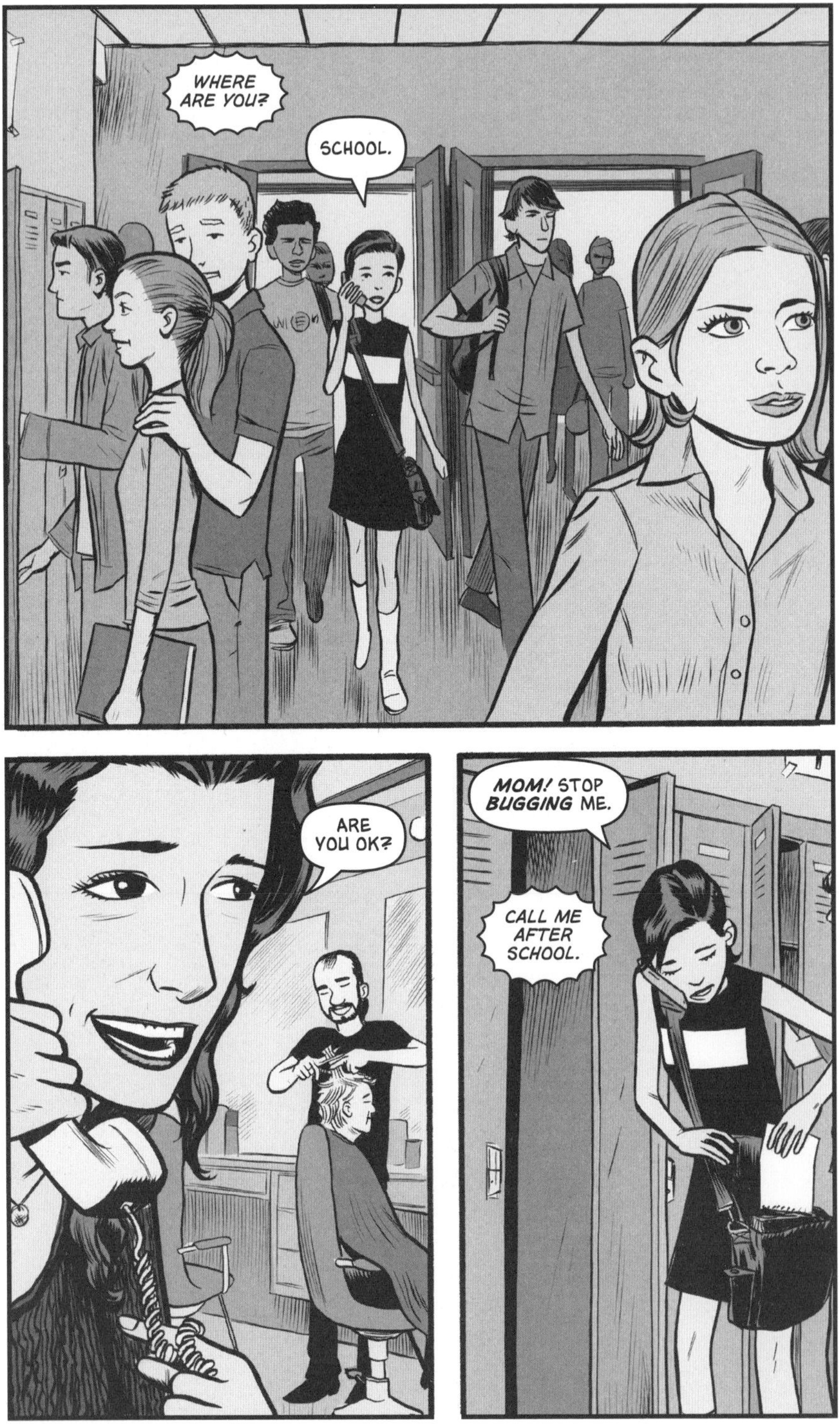
WHERE ARE YOU?
SCHOOL.
ARE YOU OK?
MOM! STOP BUGGING ME.
CALL ME AFTER SCHOOL.

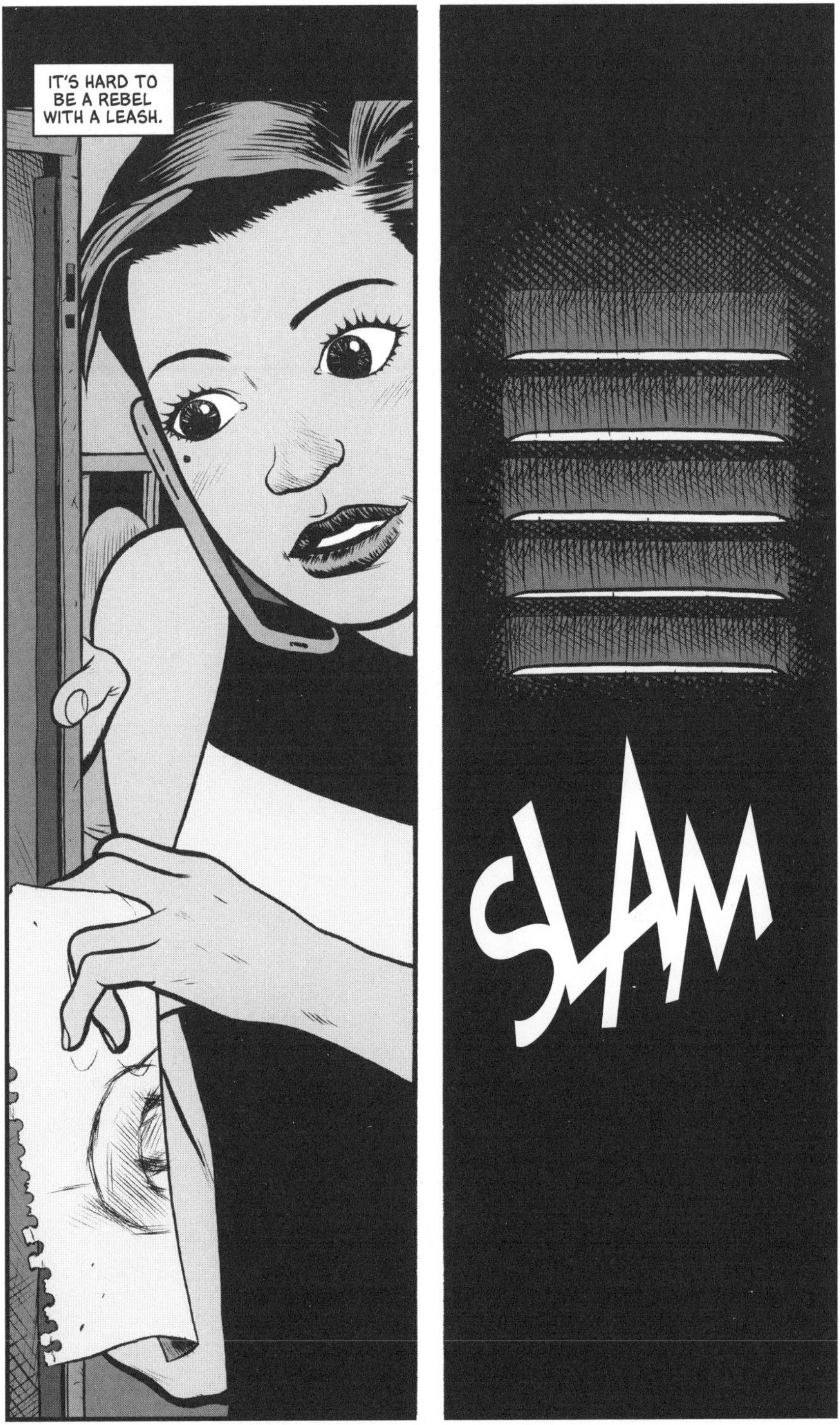
IT'S HARD TO BE A REBEL WITH A LEASH.
SLAM

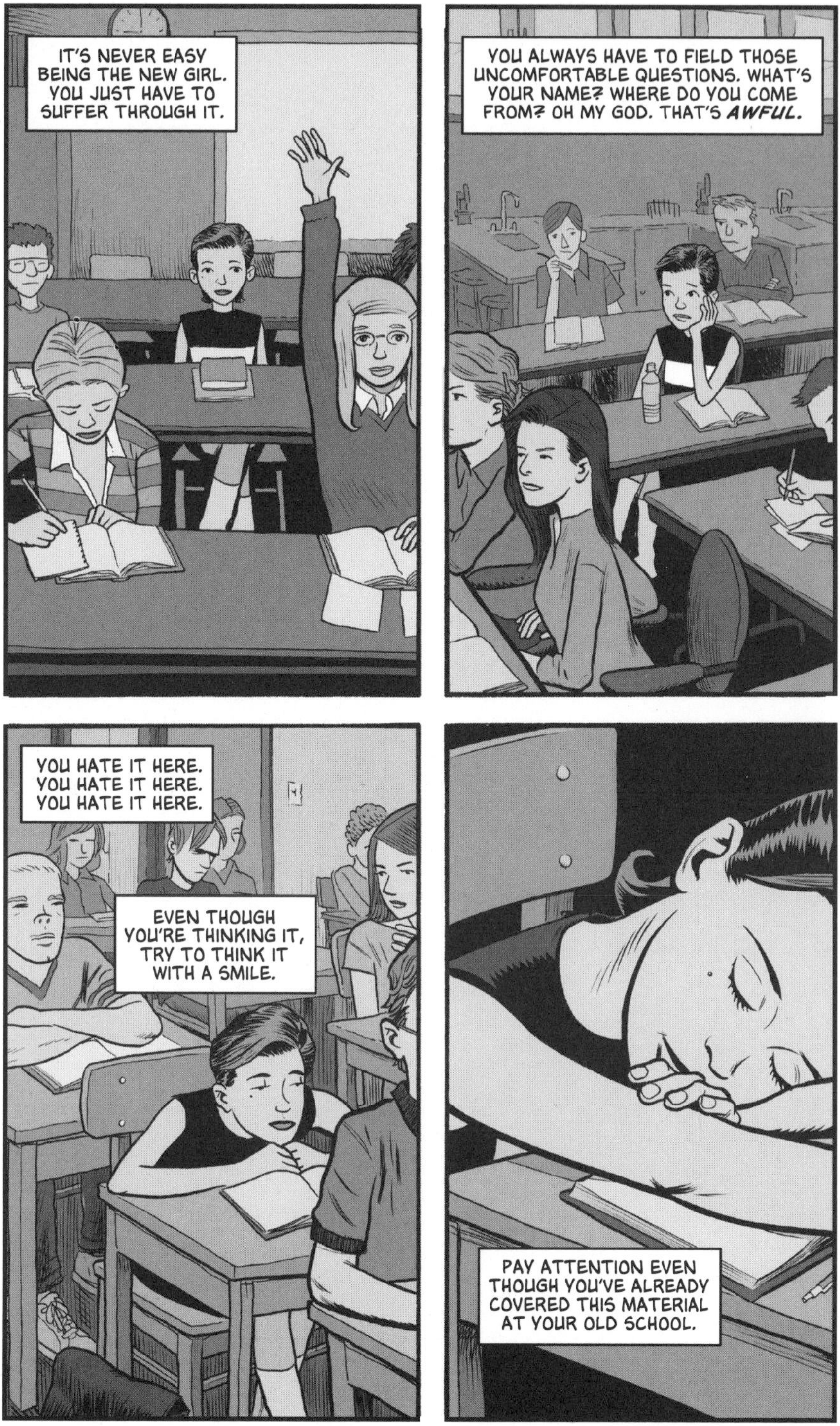
IT'S NEVER EASY BEING THE NEW GIRL. YOU JUST HAVE TO SUFFER THROUGH IT.
YOU ALWAYS HAVE TO FIELD THOSE UNCOMFORTABLE QUESTIONS. WHAT'S YOUR NAME? WHERE DO YOU COME FROM? OH MY GOD. THAT'S AWFUL.
YOU HATE IT HERE. YOU HATE IT HERE. YOU HATE IT HERE.
EVEN THOUGH YOU'RE THINKING IT, TRY TO THINK IT WITH A SMILE.
PAY ATTENTION EVEN THOUGH YOU'VE ALREADY COVERED THIS MATERIAL AT YOUR OLD SCHOOL.

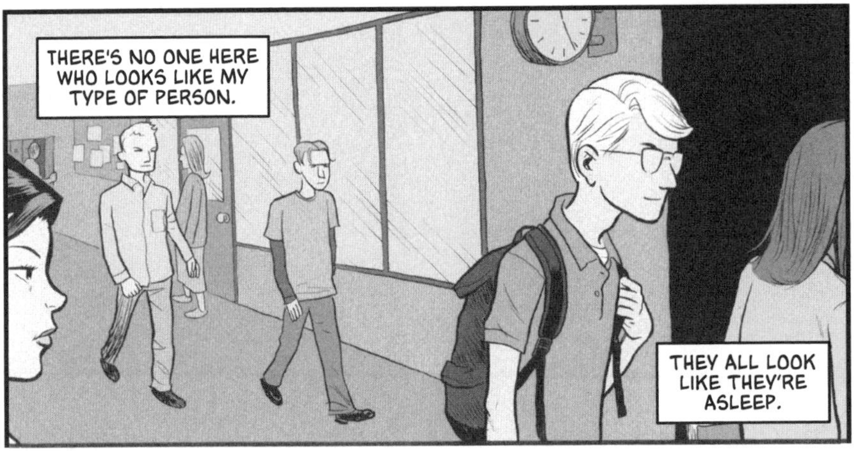
THERE'S NO ONE HERE WHO LOOKS LIKE MY TYPE OF PERSON.
THEY ALL LOOK LIKE THEY'RE ASLEEP.

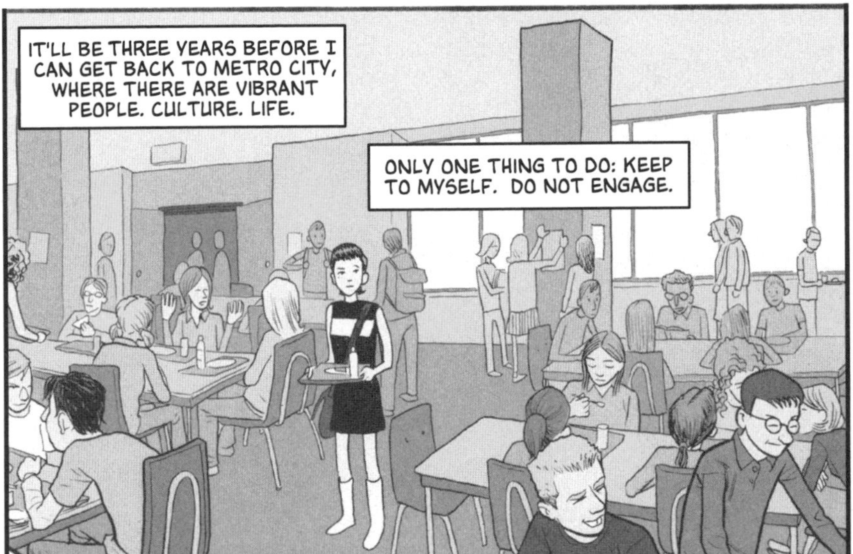
IT'LL BE THREE YEARS BEFORE I CAN GET BACK TO METRO CITY, WHERE THERE ARE VIBRANT PEOPLE. CULTURE. LIFE.
ONLY ONE THING TO DO: KEEP TO MYSELF. DO NOT ENGAGE.

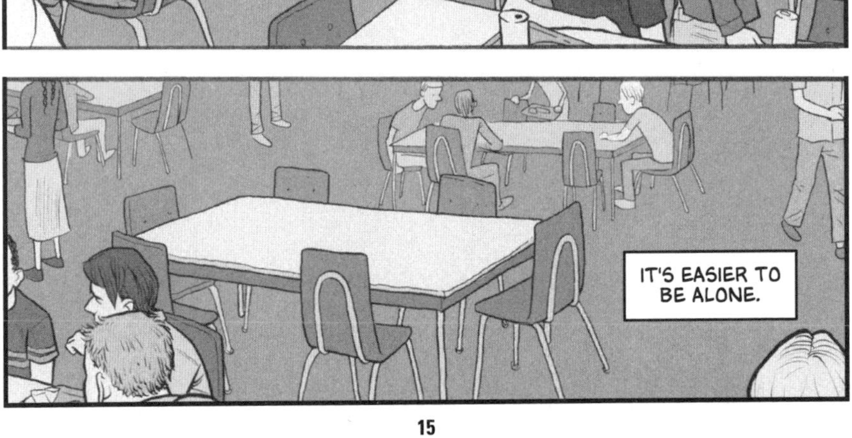
IT'S EASIER TO BE ALONE.

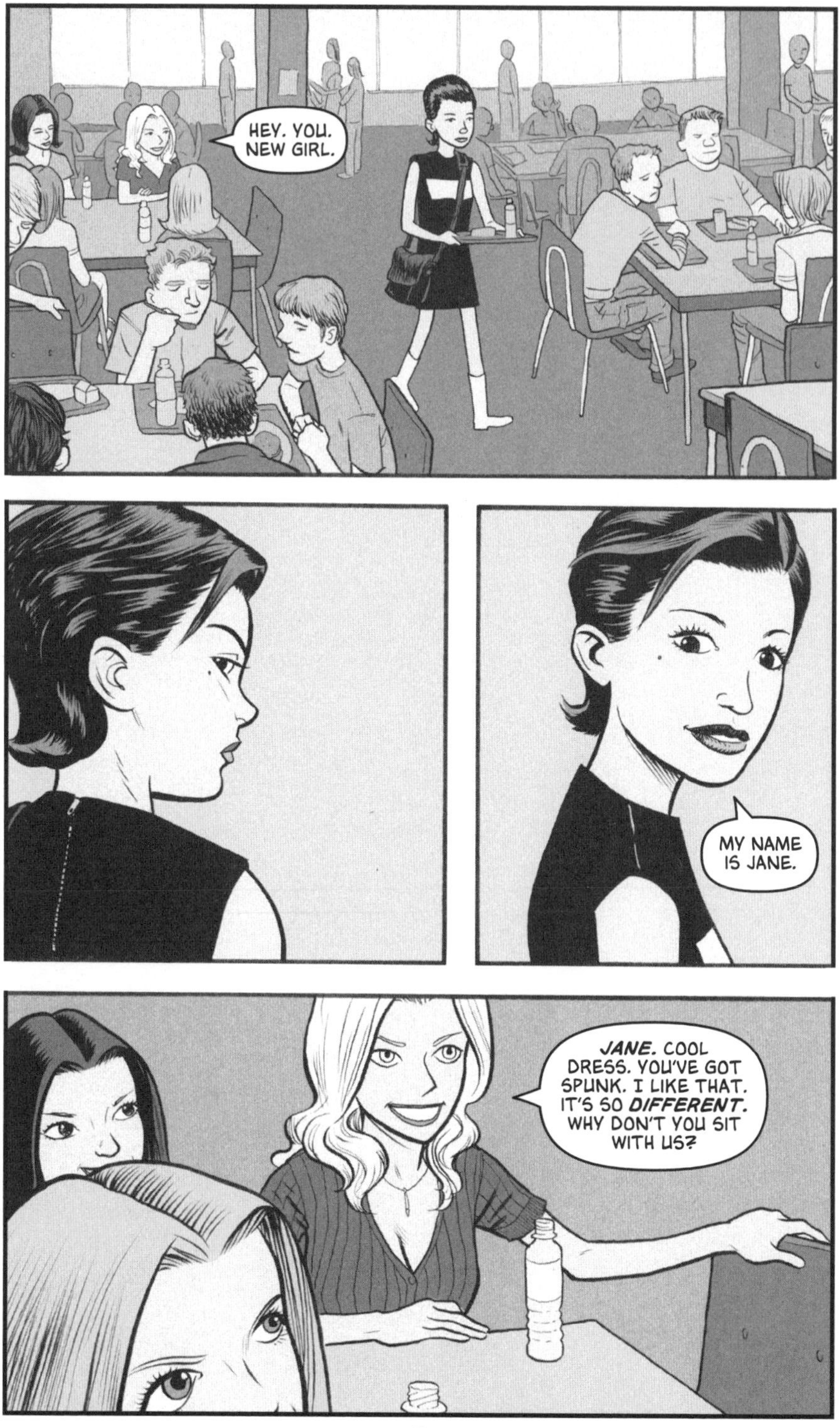
HEY. YOU. NEW GIRL.
MY NAME IS JANE.
JANE. COOL DRESS. YOU'VE GOT SPUNK. I LIKE THAT. IT'S SO DIFFERENT. WHY DON'T YOU SIT WITH US?

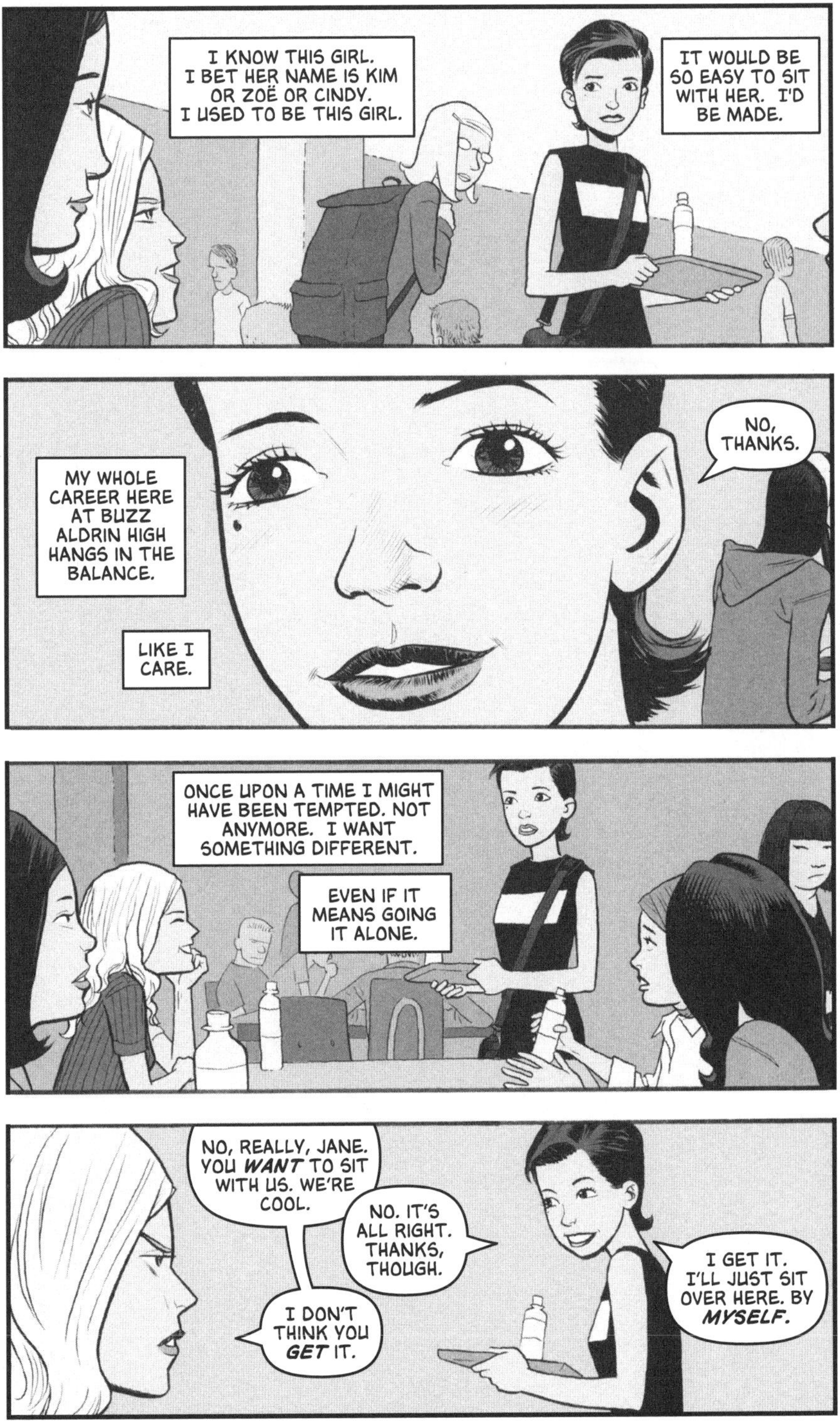
I KNOW THIS GIRL. I BET HER NAME IS KIM OR ZOË OR CINDY. I USED TO BE THIS GIRL.
IT WOULD BE SO EASY TO SIT WITH HER. I'D BE MADE.
MY WHOLE CAREER HERE AT BUZZ ALDRIN HIGH HANGS IN THE BALANCE.
LIKE I CARE.
NO, THANKS.
ONCE UPON A TIME I MIGHT HAVE BEEN TEMPTED. NOT ANYMORE. I WANT SOMETHING DIFFERENT.
EVEN IF IT MEANS GOING IT ALONE.
NO, REALLY, JANE. YOU *WANT* TO SIT WITH US. WE'RE COOL.
NO. IT'S ALL RIGHT. THANKS, THOUGH.
I DON'T THINK YOU *GET* IT.
I GET IT. I'LL JUST SIT OVER HERE. BY *MYSELF*.

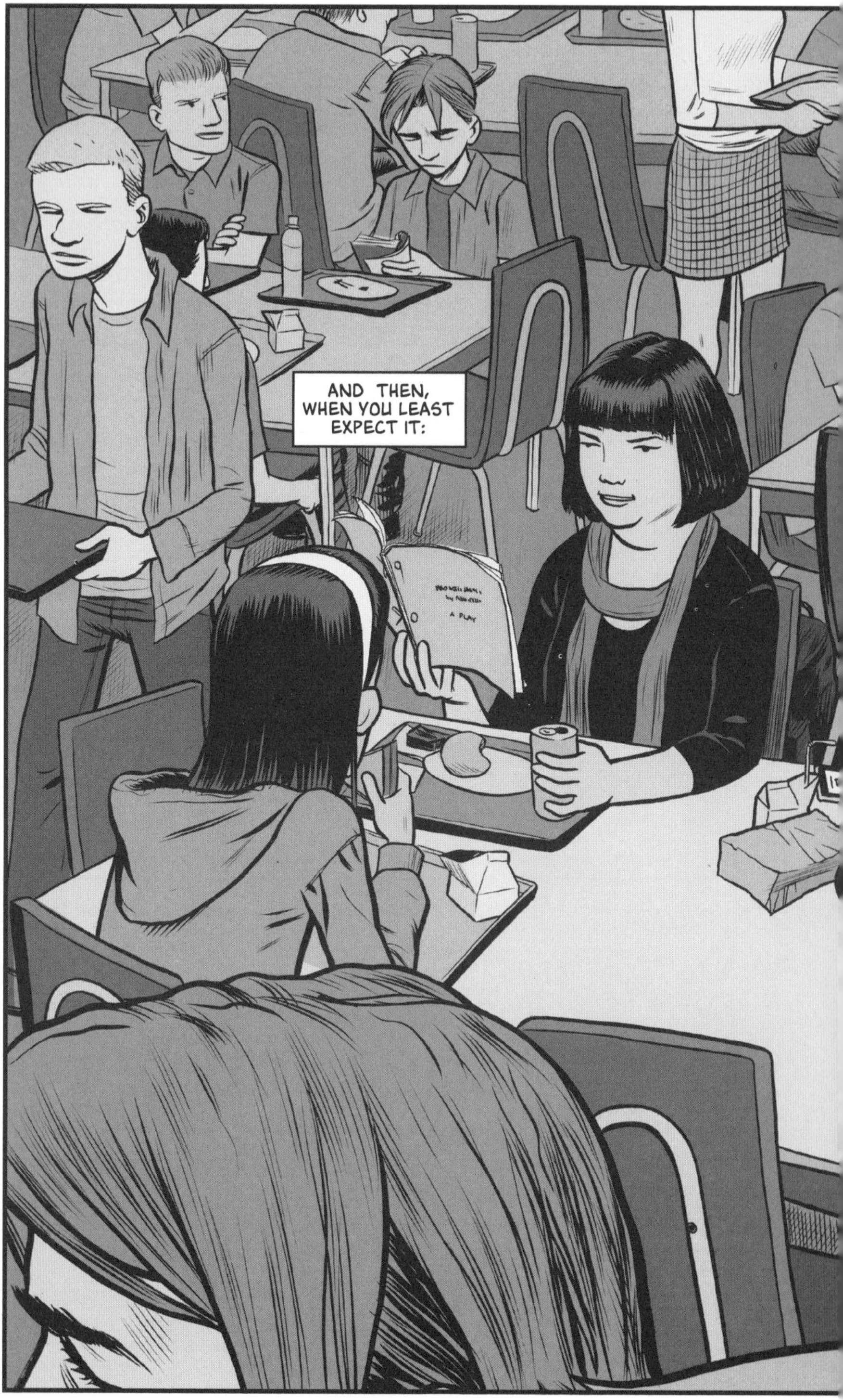
AND THEN, WHEN YOU LEAST EXPECT IT:

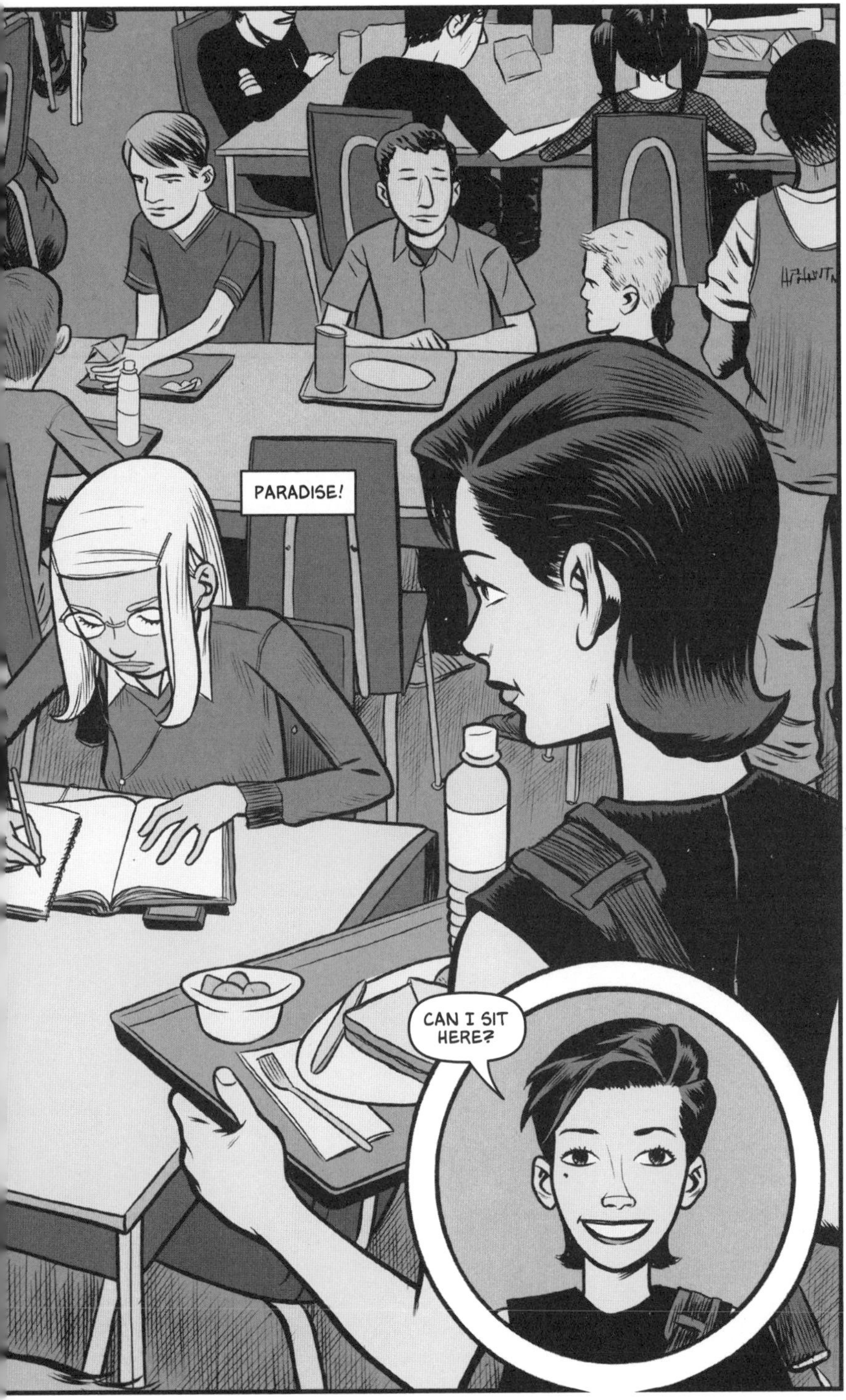
PARADISE!
CAN I SIT HERE?

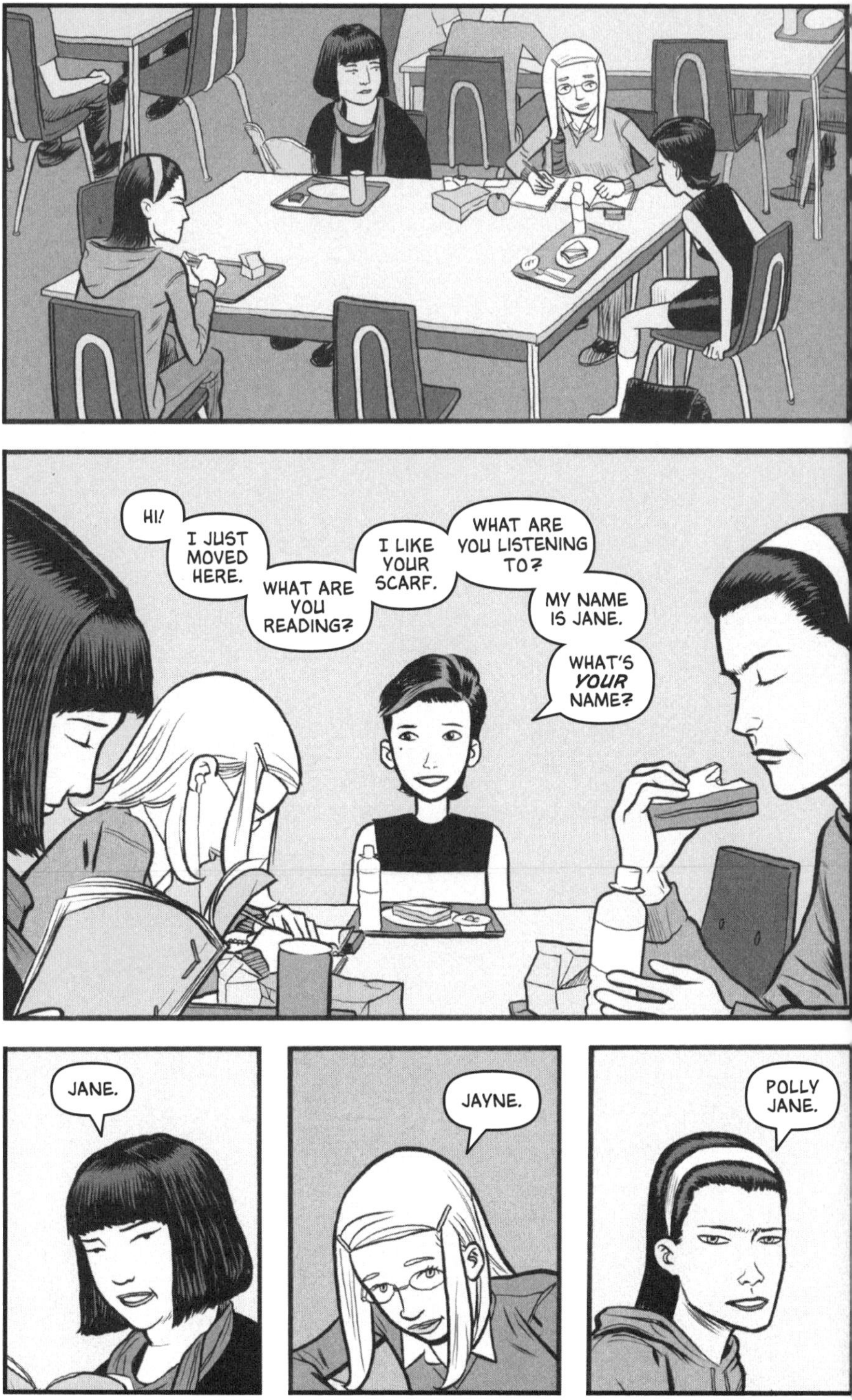
HI!
I JUST MOVED HERE.
WHAT ARE YOU READING?
I LIKE YOUR SCARF.
WHAT ARE YOU LISTENING TO?
MY NAME IS JANE.
WHAT'S *YOUR* NAME?
JANE.
JAYNE.
POLLY JANE.

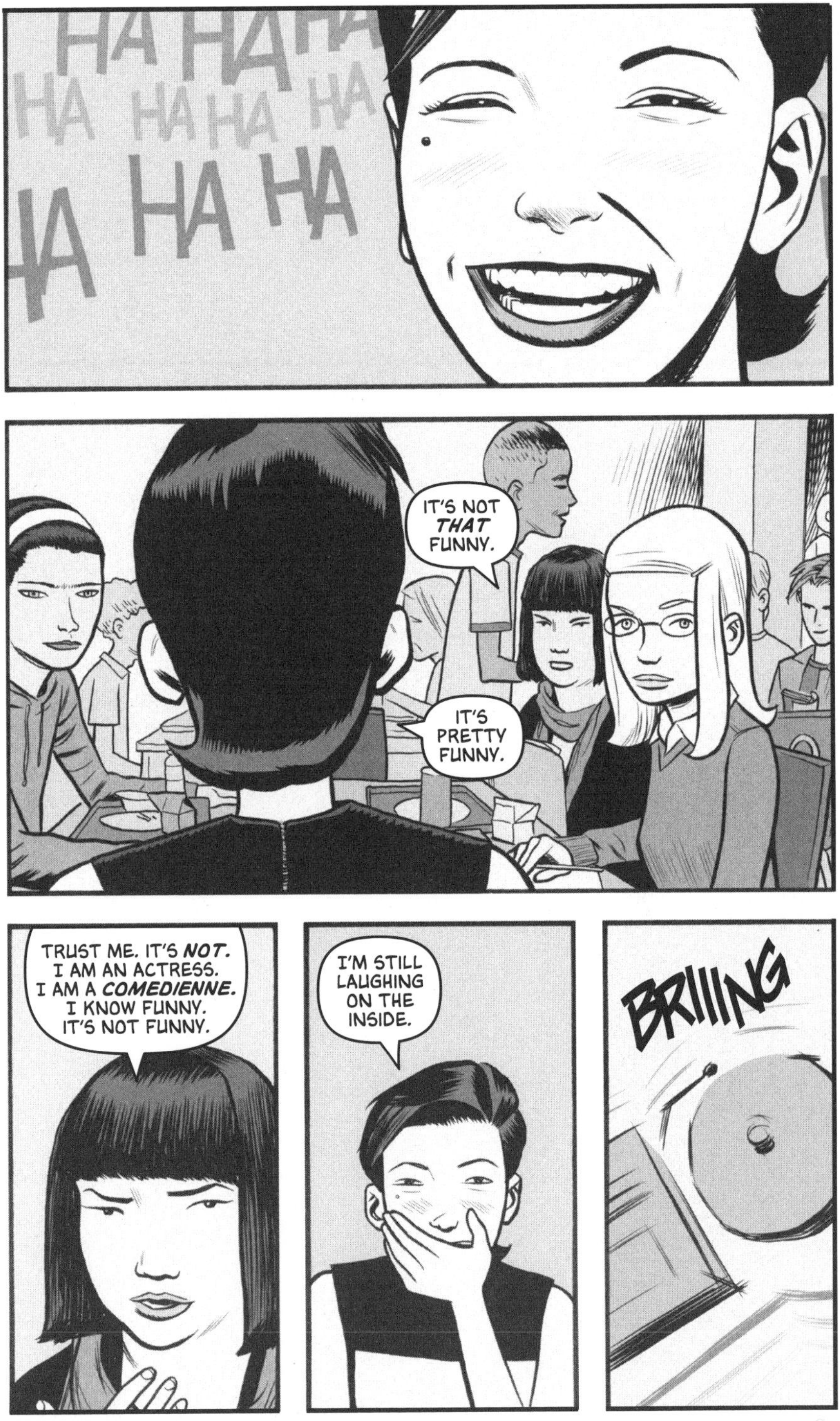
HA HA HA HA HA HA HA HA HA HA
IT'S NOT *THAT* FUNNY.
IT'S PRETTY FUNNY.
TRUST ME. IT'S *NOT.* I AM AN ACTRESS. I AM A *COMEDIENNE.* I KNOW FUNNY. IT'S NOT FUNNY.
I'M STILL LAUGHING ON THE INSIDE.
BRIIING

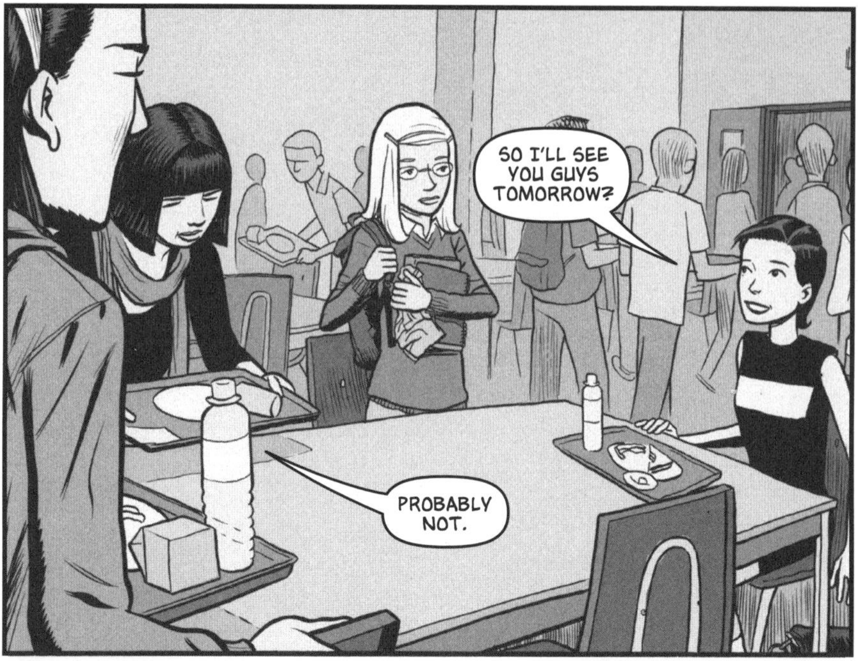
SO I'LL SEE YOU GUYS TOMORROW?
PROBABLY NOT.

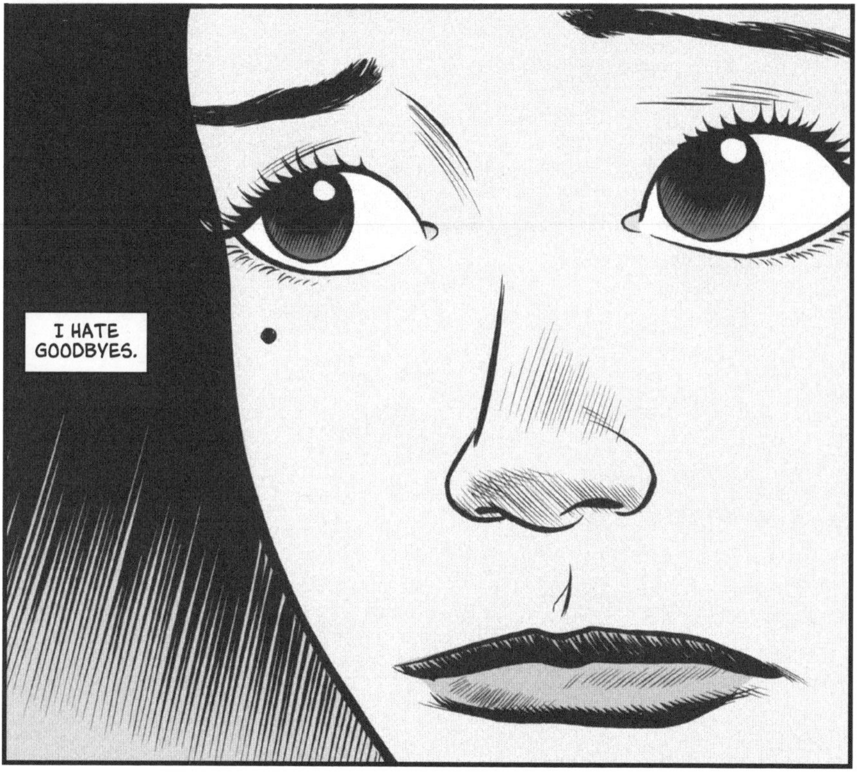
I HATE GOODBYES.

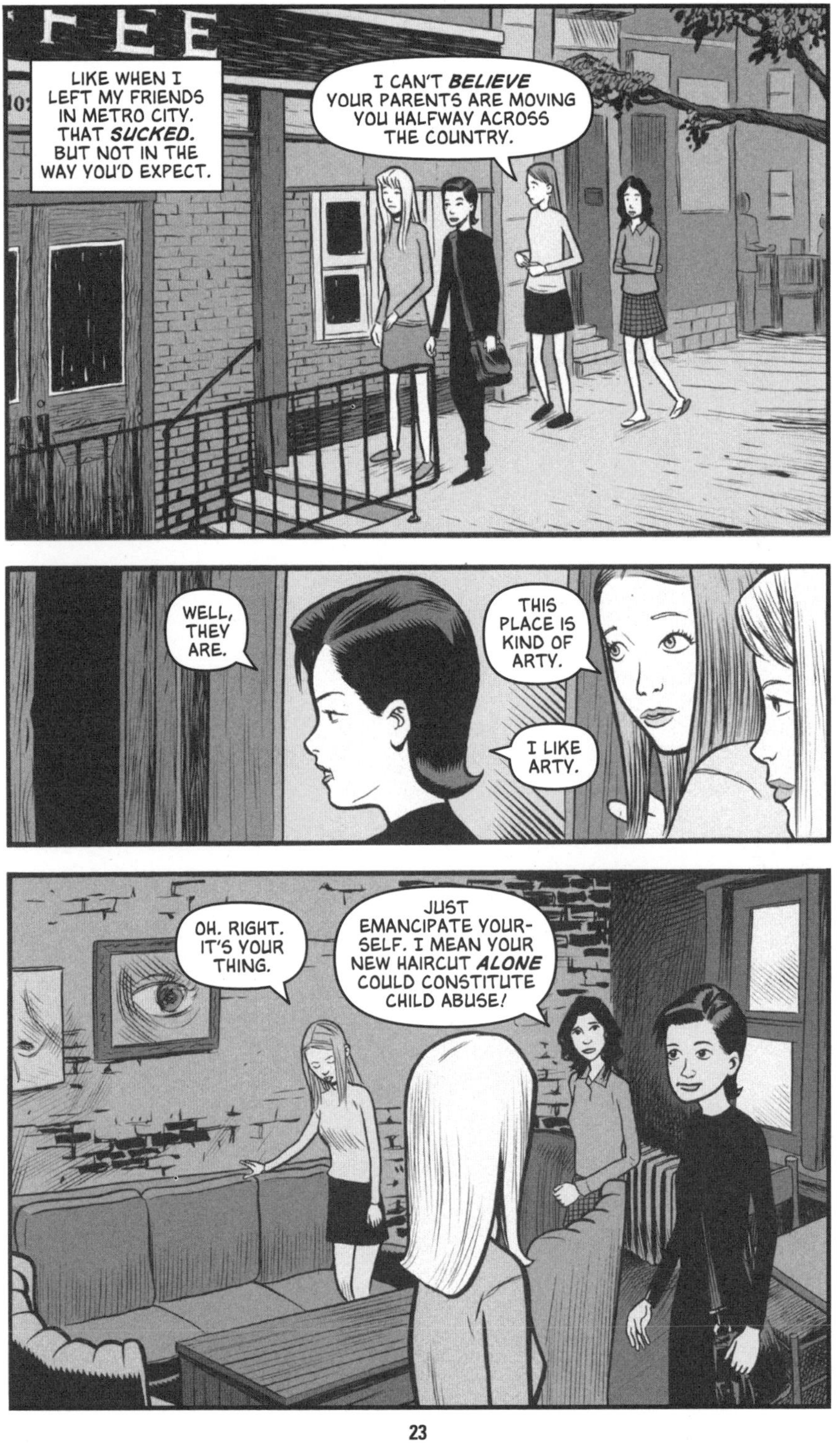
FEE
LIKE WHEN I LEFT MY FRIENDS IN METRO CITY. THAT ***SUCKED.*** BUT NOT IN THE WAY YOU'D EXPECT.
I CAN'T ***BELIEVE*** YOUR PARENTS ARE MOVING YOU HALFWAY ACROSS THE COUNTRY.
WELL, THEY ARE.
THIS PLACE IS KIND OF ARTY.
I LIKE ARTY.
OH. RIGHT. IT'S YOUR THING.
JUST EMANCIPATE YOURSELF. I MEAN YOUR NEW HAIRCUT ***ALONE*** COULD CONSTITUTE CHILD ABUSE!

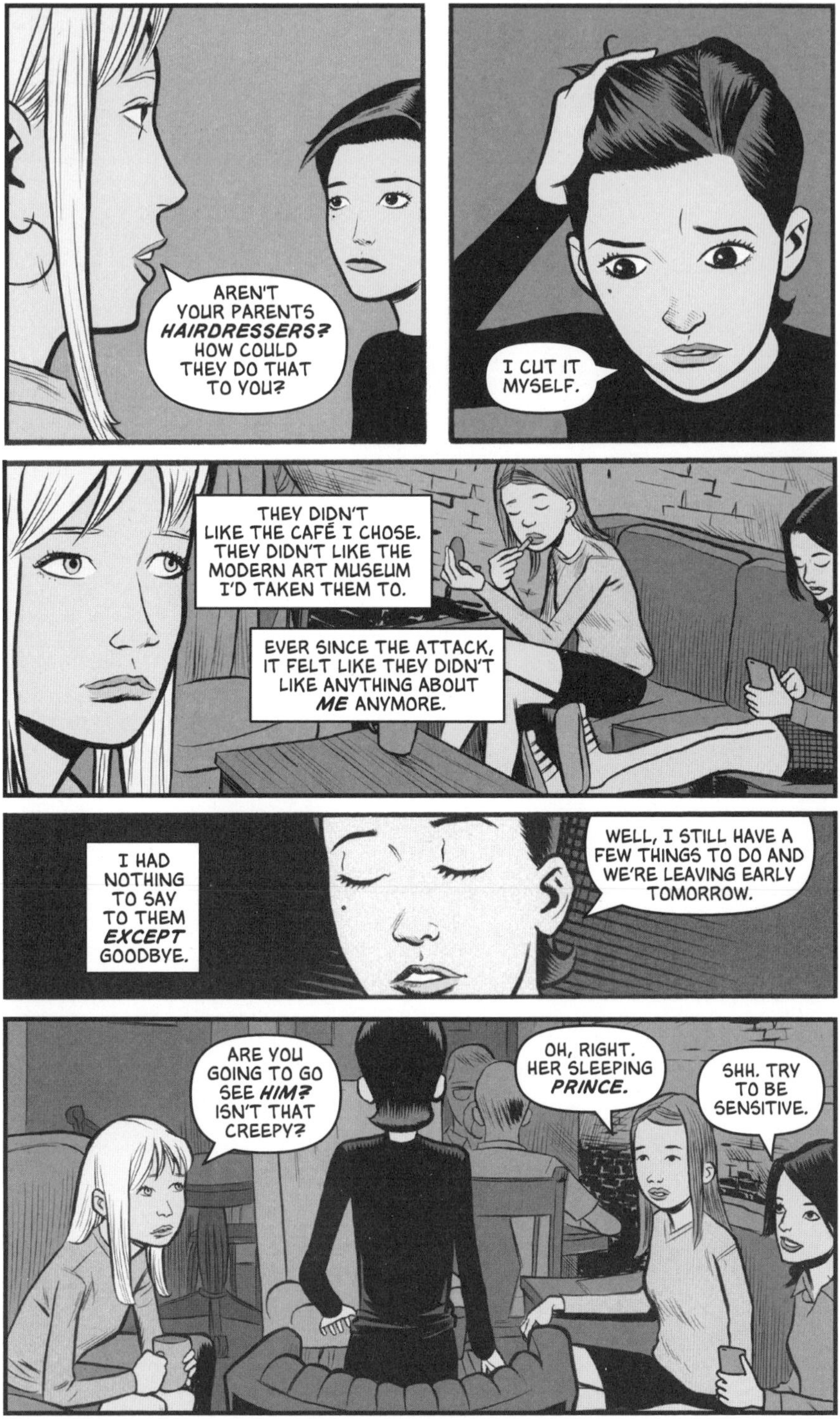
AREN'T YOUR PARENTS *HAIRDRESSERS?* HOW COULD THEY DO THAT TO YOU?
I CUT IT MYSELF.
THEY DIDN'T LIKE THE CAFÉ I CHOSE. THEY DIDN'T LIKE THE MODERN ART MUSEUM I'D TAKEN THEM TO.
EVER SINCE THE ATTACK, IT FELT LIKE THEY DIDN'T LIKE ANYTHING ABOUT *ME* ANYMORE.
I HAD NOTHING TO SAY TO THEM *EXCEPT* GOODBYE.
WELL, I STILL HAVE A FEW THINGS TO DO AND WE'RE LEAVING EARLY TOMORROW.
ARE YOU GOING TO GO SEE *HIM?* ISN'T THAT CREEPY?
OH, RIGHT. HER SLEEPING *PRINCE.*
SHH. TRY TO BE SENSITIVE.

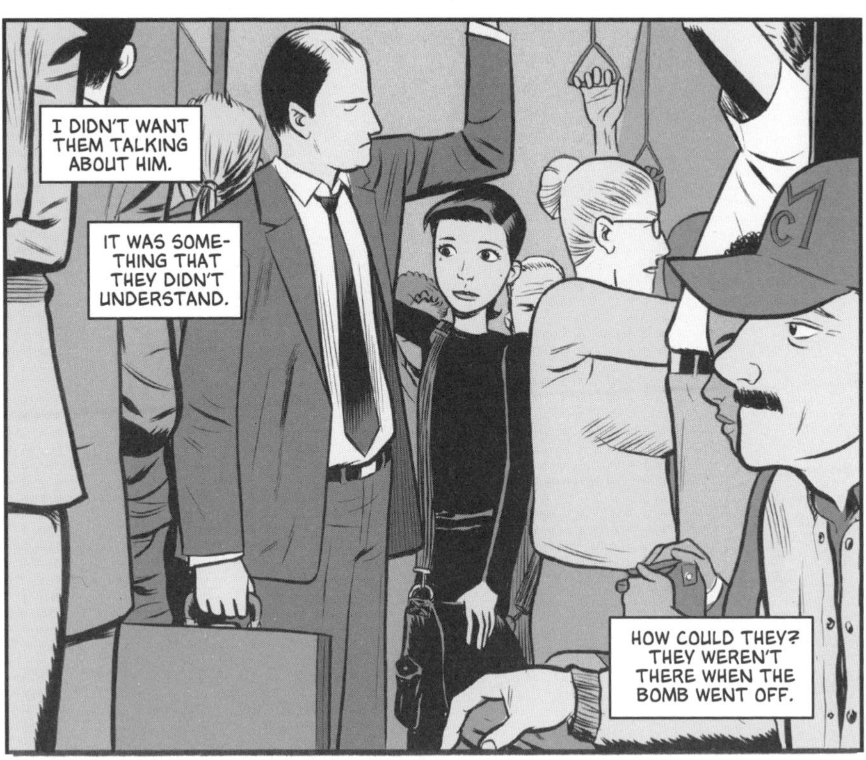
I DIDN'T WANT THEM TALKING ABOUT HIM.
IT WAS SOMETHING THAT THEY DIDN'T UNDERSTAND.
HOW COULD THEY? THEY WEREN'T THERE WHEN THE BOMB WENT OFF.

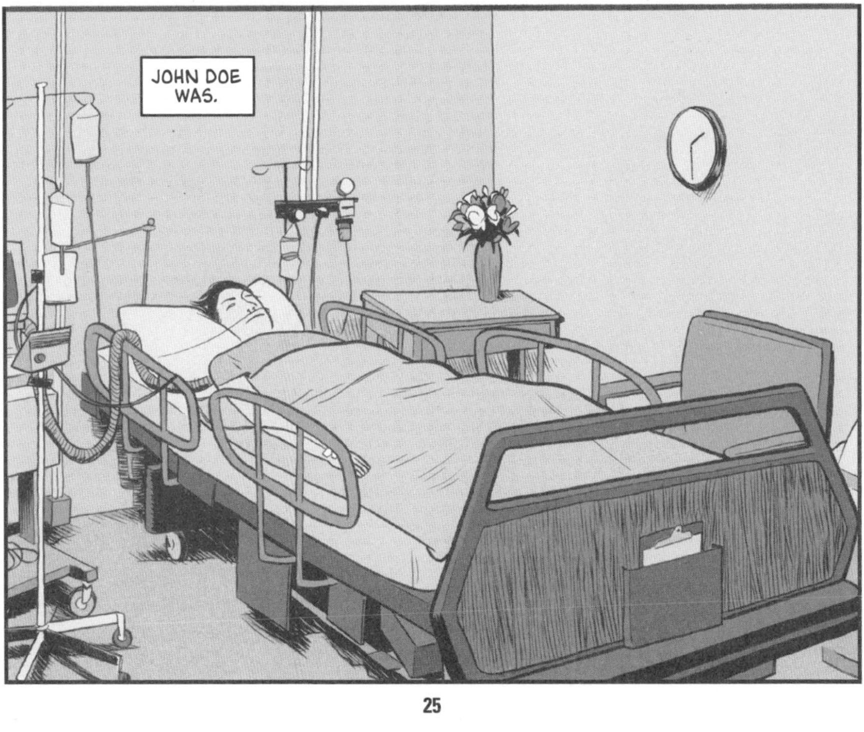
JOHN DOE WAS.

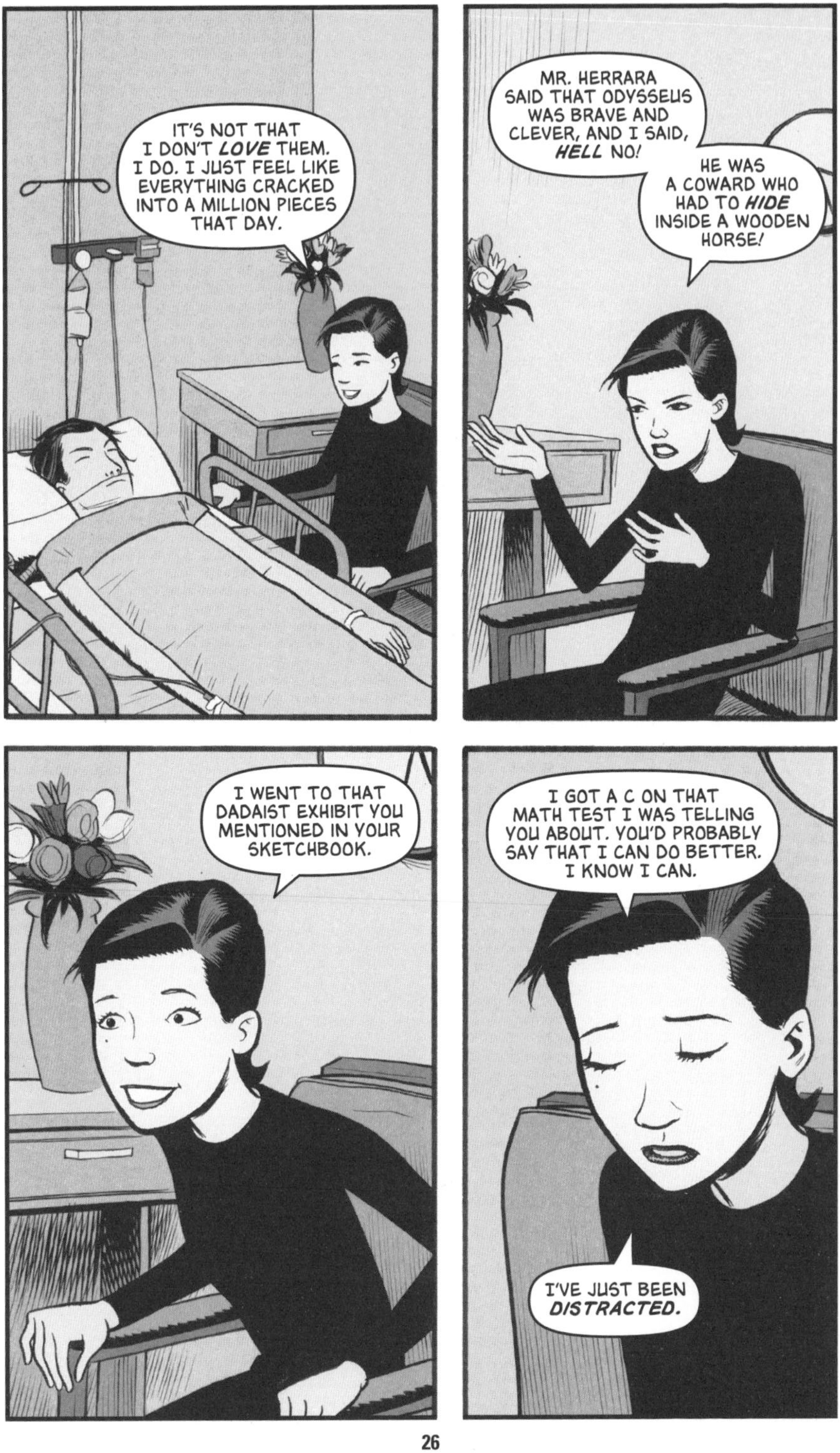
IT'S NOT THAT I DON'T LOVE THEM. I DO. I JUST FEEL LIKE EVERYTHING CRACKED INTO A MILLION PIECES THAT DAY.
MR. HERRARA SAID THAT ODYSSEUS WAS BRAVE AND CLEVER, AND I SAID, HELL NO!
HE WAS A COWARD WHO HAD TO HIDE INSIDE A WOODEN HORSE!
I WENT TO THAT DADAIST EXHIBIT YOU MENTIONED IN YOUR SKETCHBOOK.
I GOT A C ON THAT MATH TEST I WAS TELLING YOU ABOUT. YOU'D PROBABLY SAY THAT I CAN DO BETTER. I KNOW I CAN.
I'VE JUST BEEN DISTRACTED.

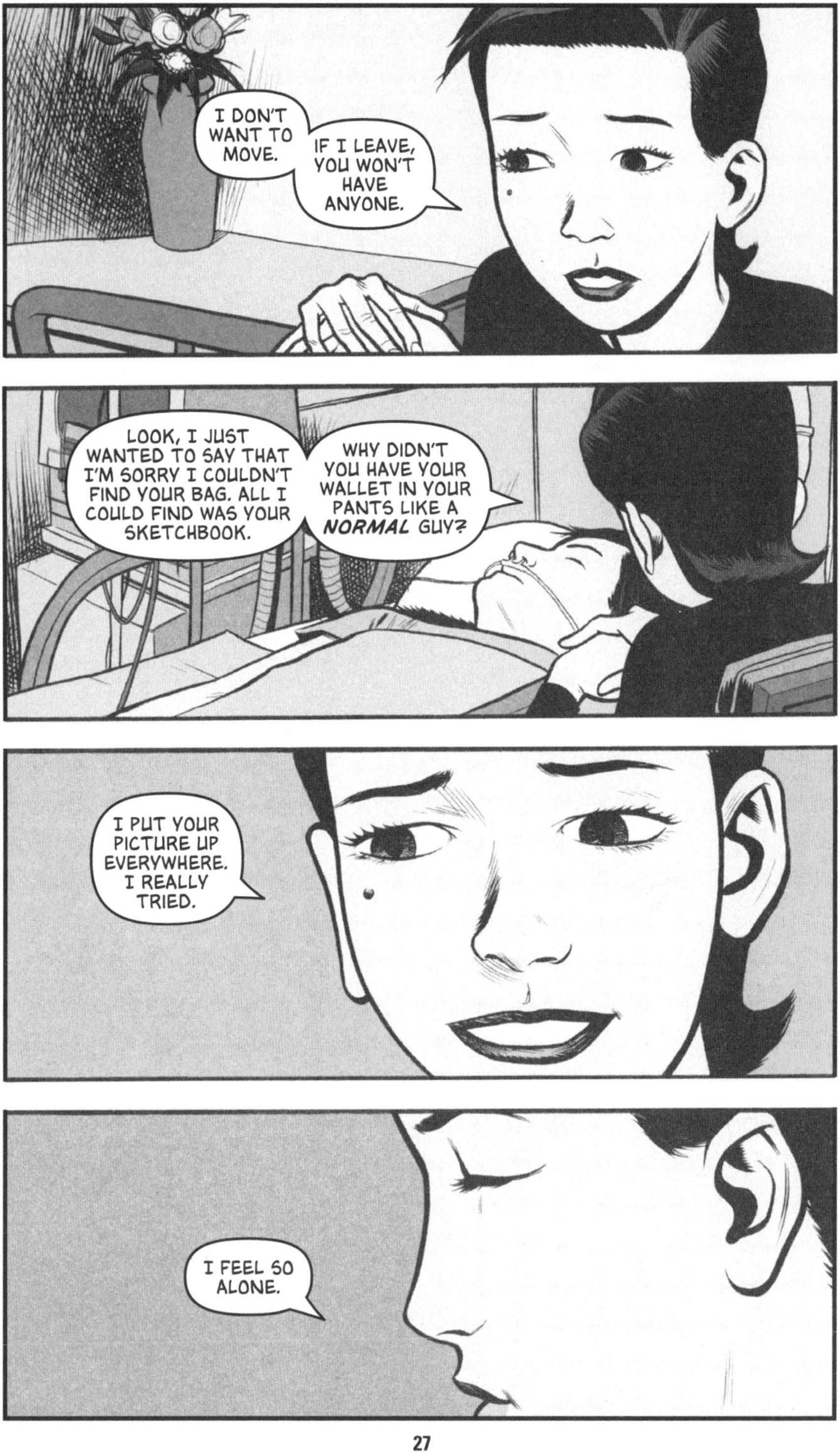
I DON'T WANT TO MOVE.
IF I LEAVE, YOU WON'T HAVE ANYONE.
LOOK, I JUST WANTED TO SAY THAT I'M SORRY I COULDN'T FIND YOUR BAG. ALL I COULD FIND WAS YOUR SKETCHBOOK.
WHY DIDN'T YOU HAVE YOUR WALLET IN YOUR PANTS LIKE A NORMAL GUY?
I PUT YOUR PICTURE UP EVERYWHERE. I REALLY TRIED.
I FEEL SO ALONE.

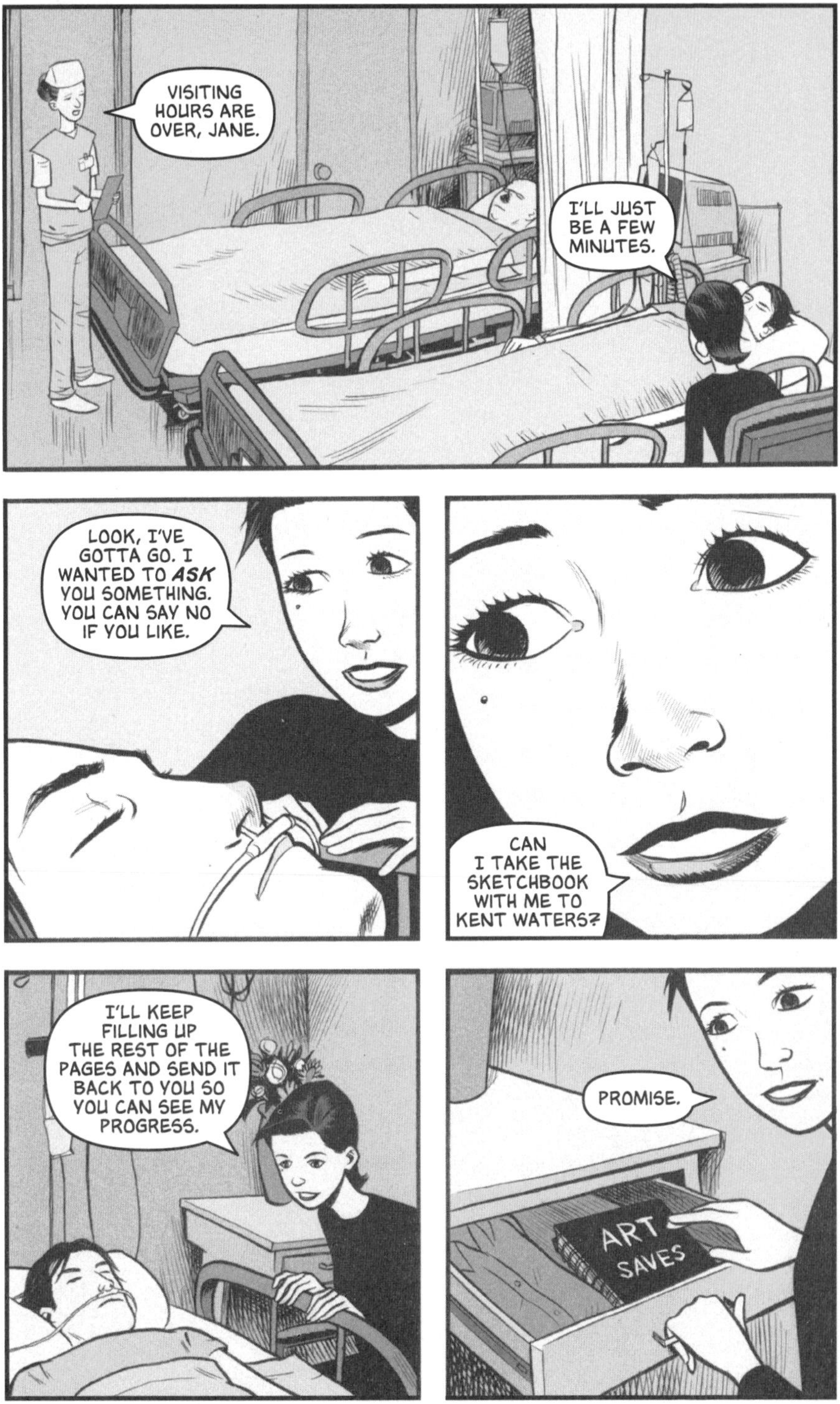
VISITING HOURS ARE OVER, JANE.
I'LL JUST BE A FEW MINUTES.
LOOK, I'VE GOTTA GO. I WANTED TO *ASK* YOU SOMETHING. YOU CAN SAY NO IF YOU LIKE.
CAN I TAKE THE SKETCHBOOK WITH ME TO KENT WATERS?
I'LL KEEP FILLING UP THE REST OF THE PAGES AND SEND IT BACK TO YOU SO YOU CAN SEE MY PROGRESS.
PROMISE.
ART SAVES

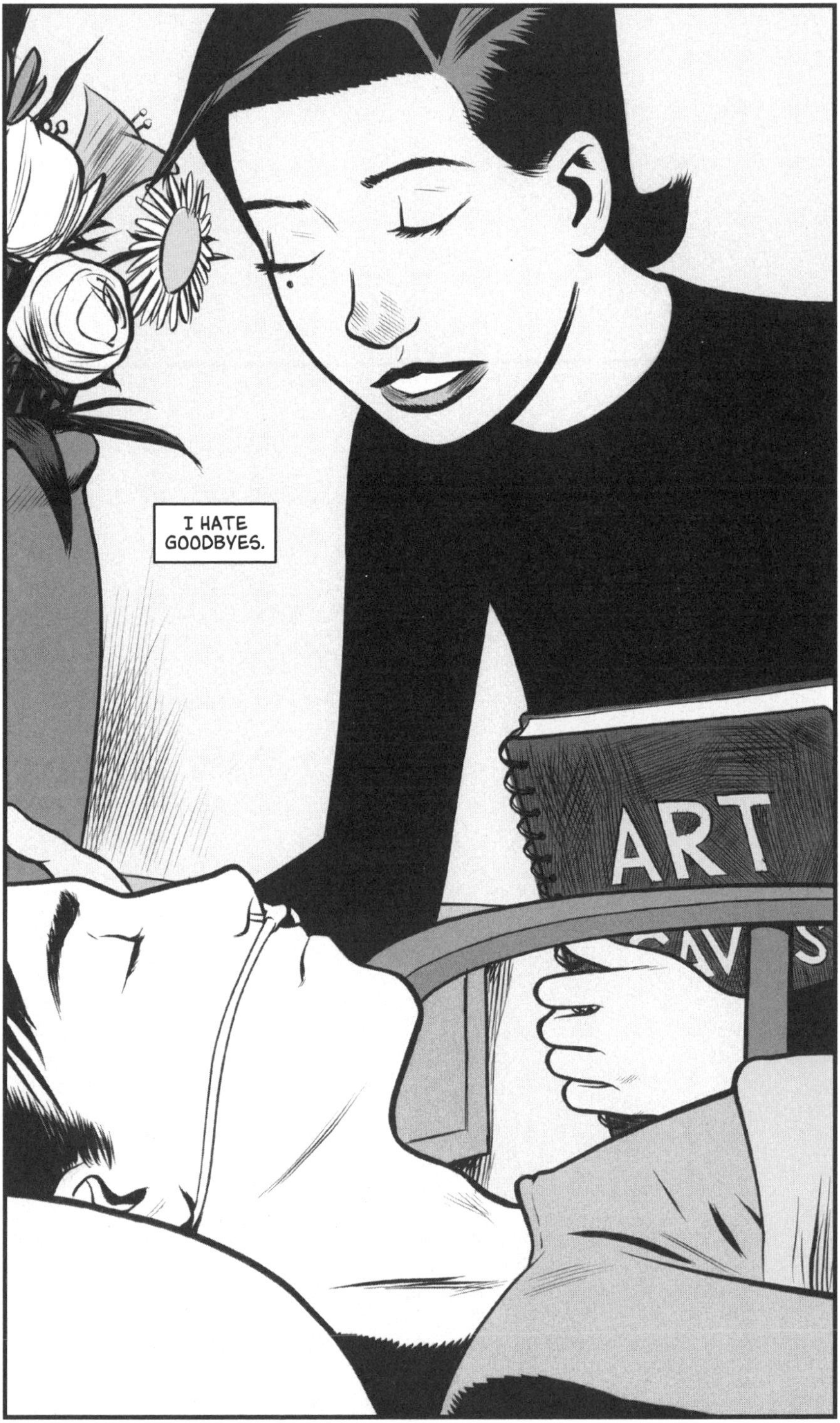
I HATE
GOODBYES.
ART

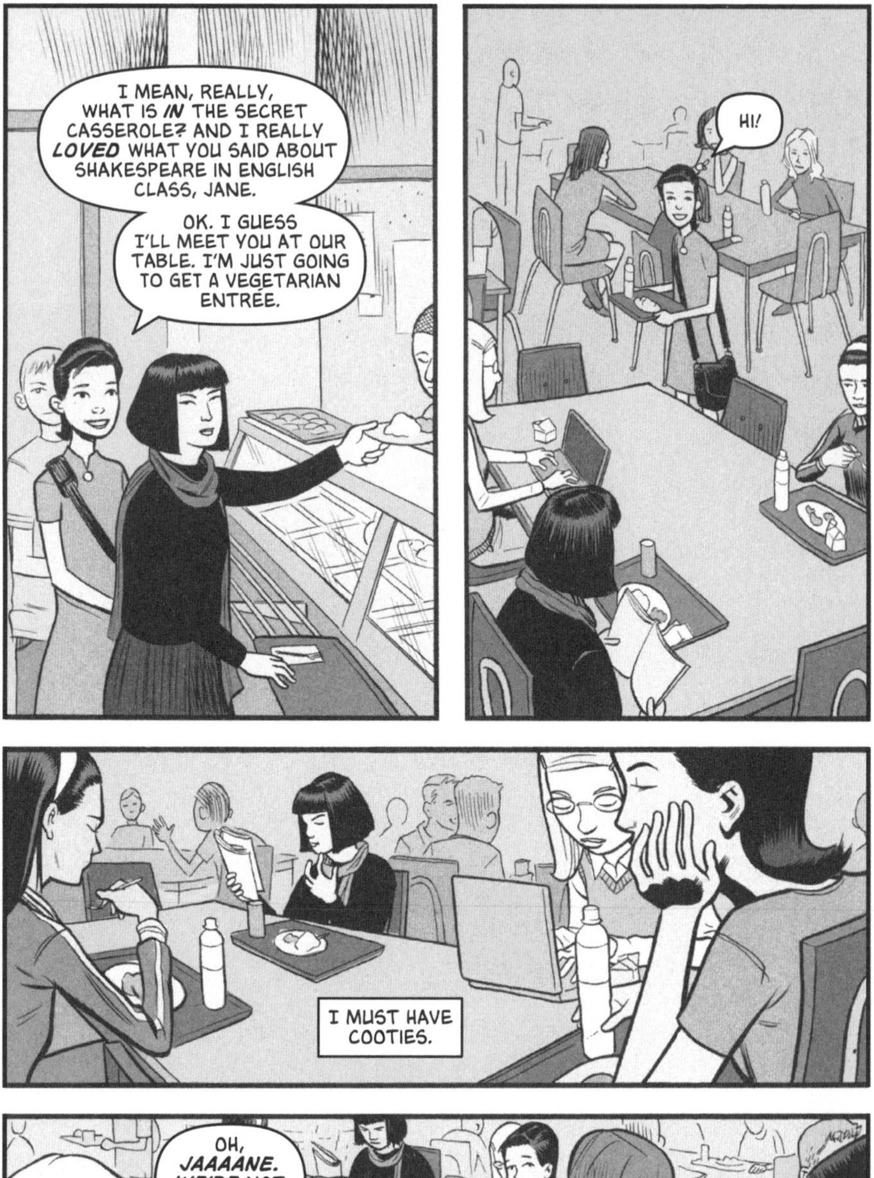
I MEAN, REALLY, WHAT IS *IN* THE SECRET CASSEROLE? AND I REALLY *LOVED* WHAT YOU SAID ABOUT SHAKESPEARE IN ENGLISH CLASS, JANE.
OK. I GUESS I'LL MEET YOU AT OUR TABLE. I'M JUST GOING TO GET A VEGETARIAN ENTRÉE.
HI!
I MUST HAVE COOTIES.
OH, *JAAAANE. WE'RE* NOT DOING HOME-WORK.
I'M GOOD HERE, THANKS.

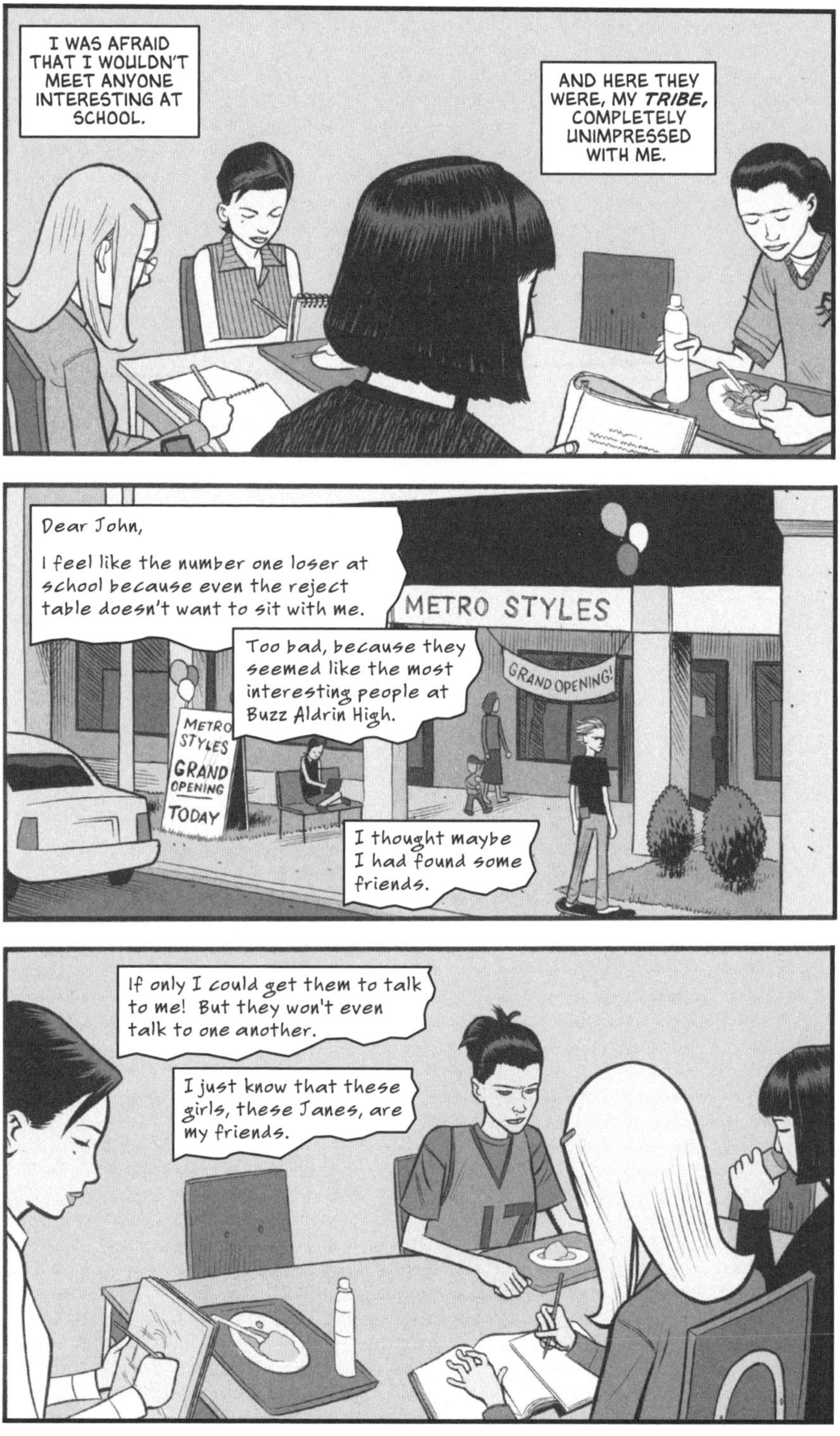

I WAS AFRAID THAT I WOULDN'T MEET ANYONE INTERESTING AT SCHOOL.
AND HERE THEY WERE, MY *TRIBE,* COMPLETELY UNIMPRESSED WITH ME.
Dear John,
I feel like the number one loser at school because even the reject table doesn't want to sit with me.
METRO STYLES
Too bad, because they seemed like the most interesting people at Buzz Aldrin High.
GRAND OPENING!
METRO STYLES GRAND OPENING TODAY
I thought maybe I had found some friends.
If only I could get them to talk to me! But they won't even talk to one another.
I just know that these girls, these Janes, are my friends.

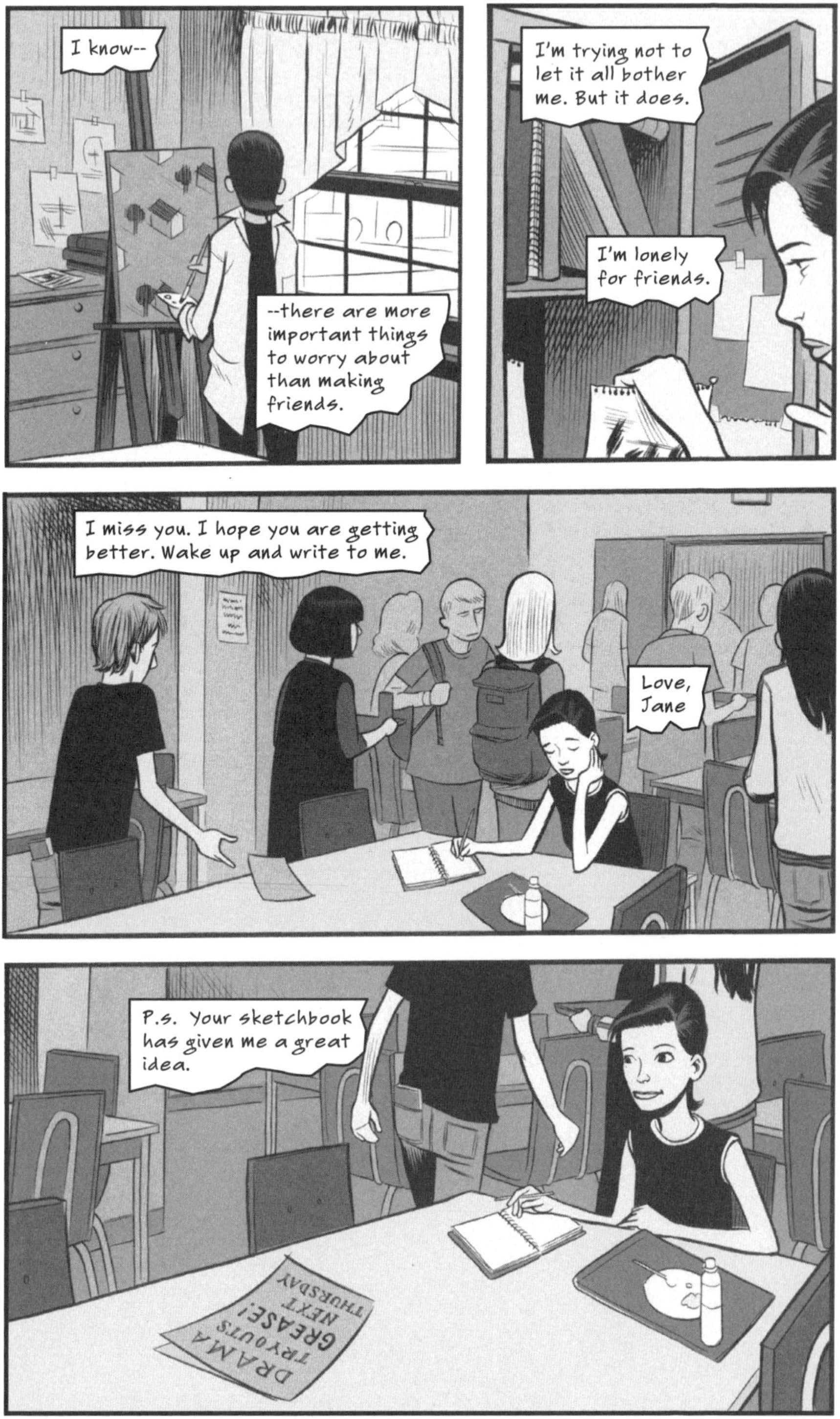
I know--
--there are more important things to worry about than making friends.
I'm trying not to let it all bother me. But it does.
I'm lonely for friends.
I miss you. I hope you are getting better. Wake up and write to me.
Love, Jane
P.s. Your sketchbook has given me a great idea.
DRAMA TRYOUTS: GREASE! NEXT THURSDAY

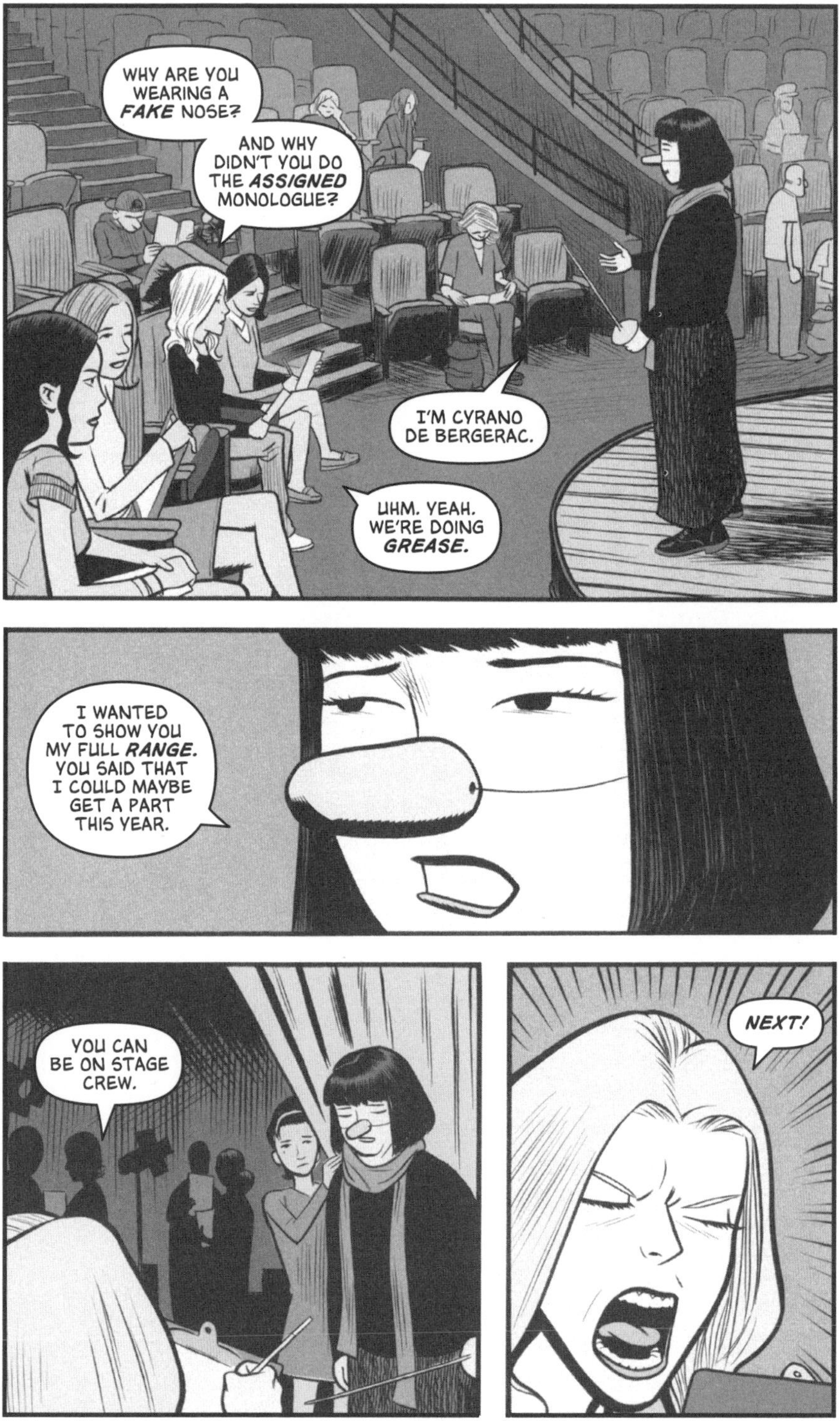
WHY ARE YOU WEARING A *FAKE* NOSE?
AND WHY DIDN'T YOU DO THE *ASSIGNED* MONOLOGUE?
I'M CYRANO DE BERGERAC.
UHM. YEAH. WE'RE DOING ***GREASE.***
I WANTED TO SHOW YOU MY FULL *RANGE.* YOU SAID THAT I COULD MAYBE GET A PART THIS YEAR.
YOU CAN BE ON STAGE CREW.
NEXT!

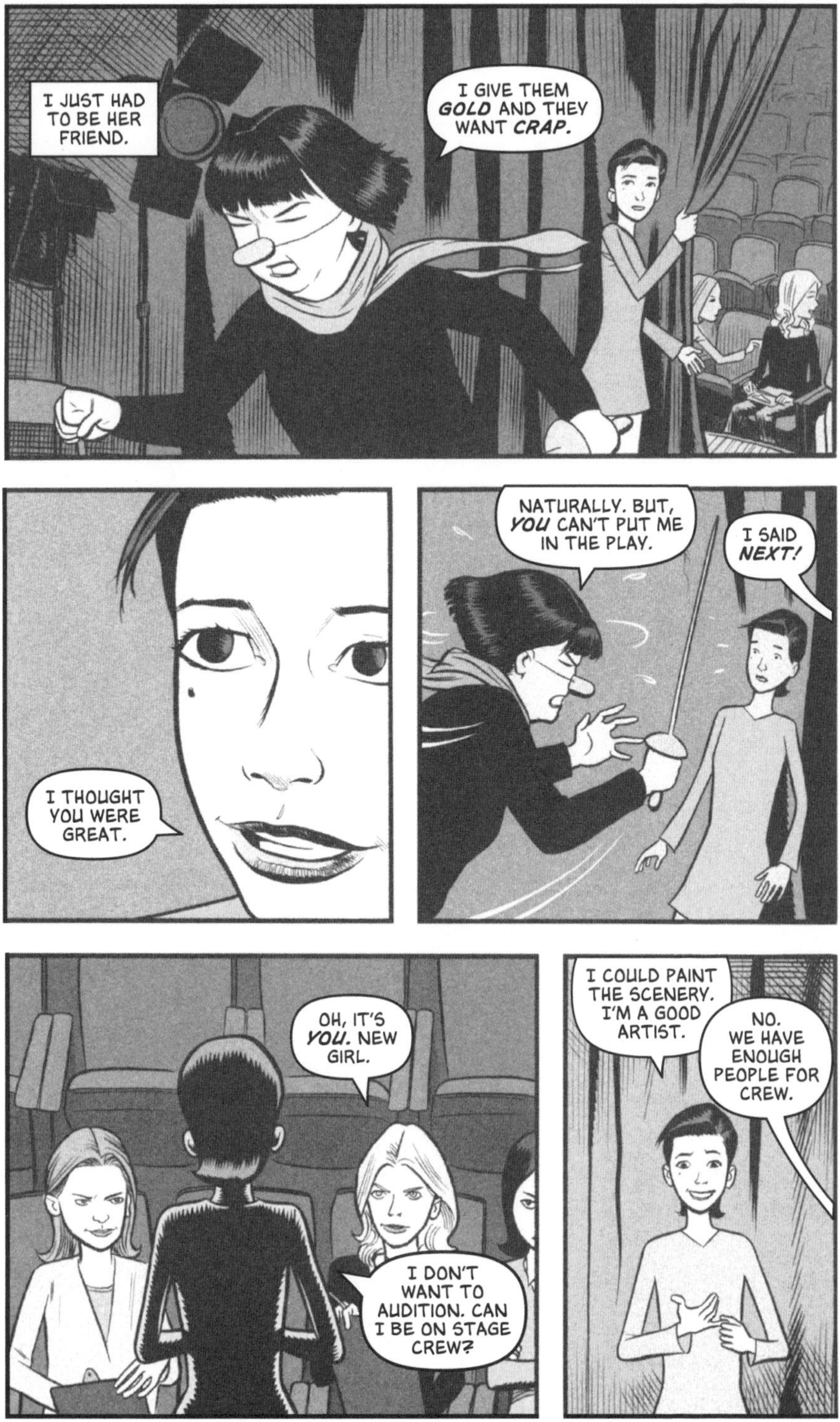
I JUST HAD TO BE HER FRIEND.
I GIVE THEM GOLD AND THEY WANT CRAP.
I THOUGHT YOU WERE GREAT.
NATURALLY. BUT, YOU CAN'T PUT ME IN THE PLAY.
I SAID NEXT!
OH, IT'S YOU. NEW GIRL.
I DON'T WANT TO AUDITION. CAN I BE ON STAGE CREW?
I COULD PAINT THE SCENERY. I'M A GOOD ARTIST.
NO. WE HAVE ENOUGH PEOPLE FOR CREW.

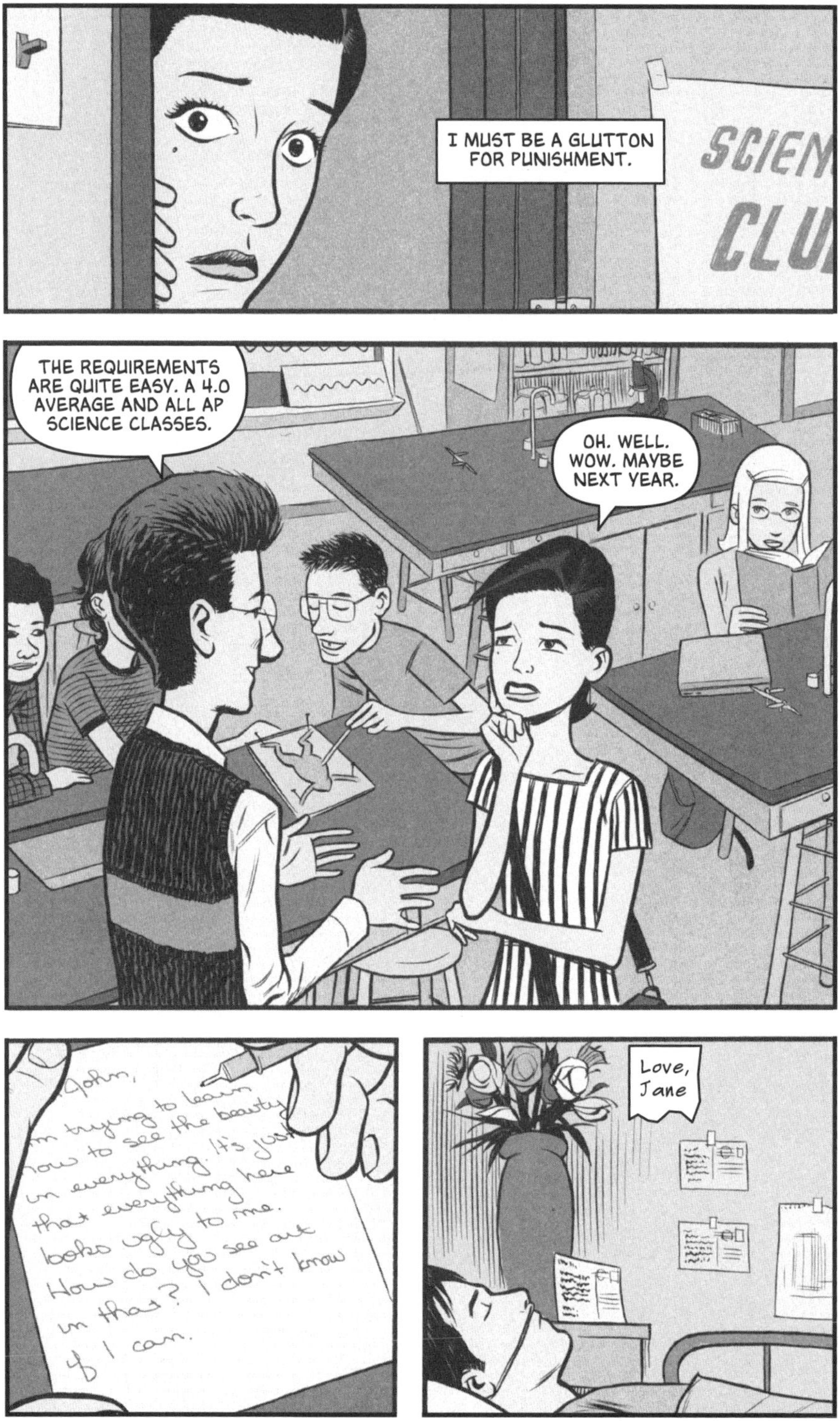
I MUST BE A GLUTTON FOR PUNISHMENT.
SCIEN
CLU
THE REQUIREMENTS ARE QUITE EASY. A 4.0 AVERAGE AND ALL AP SCIENCE CLASSES.
OH. WELL. WOW. MAYBE NEXT YEAR.
John,
m trying to learn
ow to see the beauty
n everything. It's just
that everything here
looks ugly to me.
How do you see art
in that? I don't know
if I can.
Love, Jane

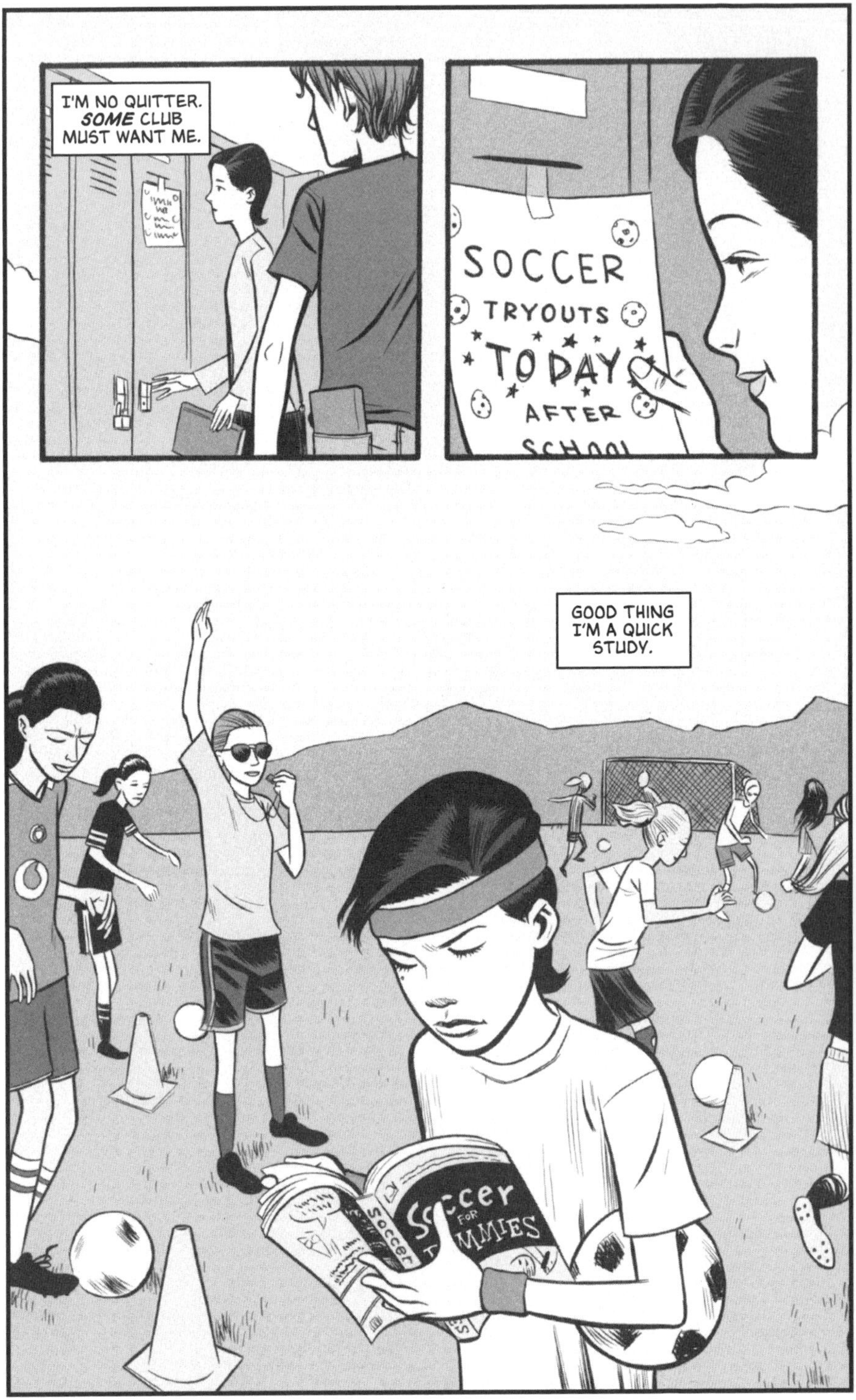
I'M NO QUITTER. *SOME* CLUB MUST WANT ME.
SOCCER
TRYOUTS
TODAY
AFTER
GOOD THING I'M A QUICK STUDY.
Soccer
FOR

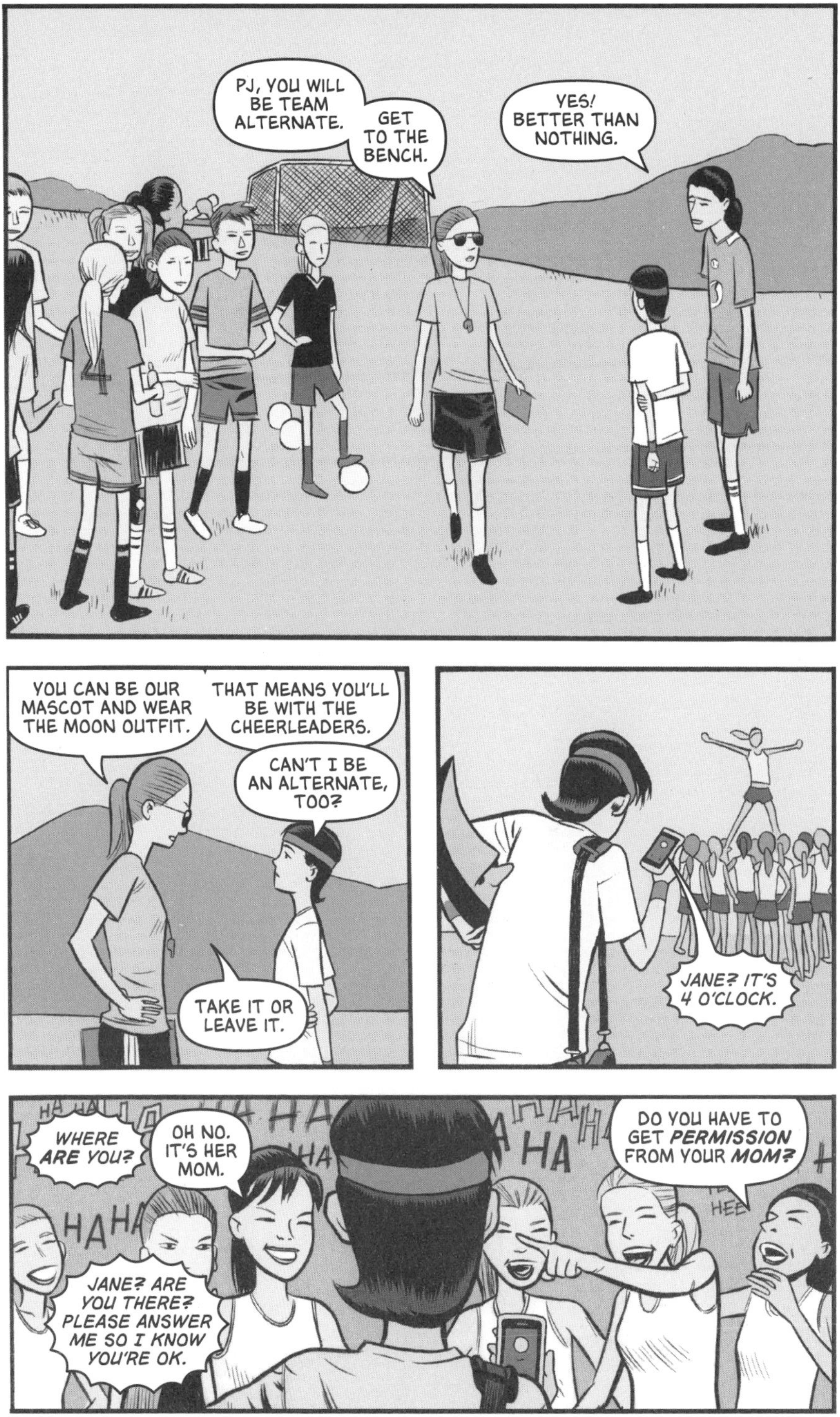
PJ, YOU WILL BE TEAM ALTERNATE.
GET TO THE BENCH.
YES! BETTER THAN NOTHING.
YOU CAN BE OUR MASCOT AND WEAR THE MOON OUTFIT.
THAT MEANS YOU'LL BE WITH THE CHEERLEADERS.
CAN'T I BE AN ALTERNATE, TOO?
TAKE IT OR LEAVE IT.
JANE? IT'S 4 O'CLOCK.
HA HA HA HA HA
WHERE ARE YOU?
OH NO. IT'S HER MOM.
DO YOU HAVE TO GET PERMISSION FROM YOUR MOM?
HEE
HA HA
JANE? ARE YOU THERE? PLEASE ANSWER ME SO I KNOW YOU'RE OK.

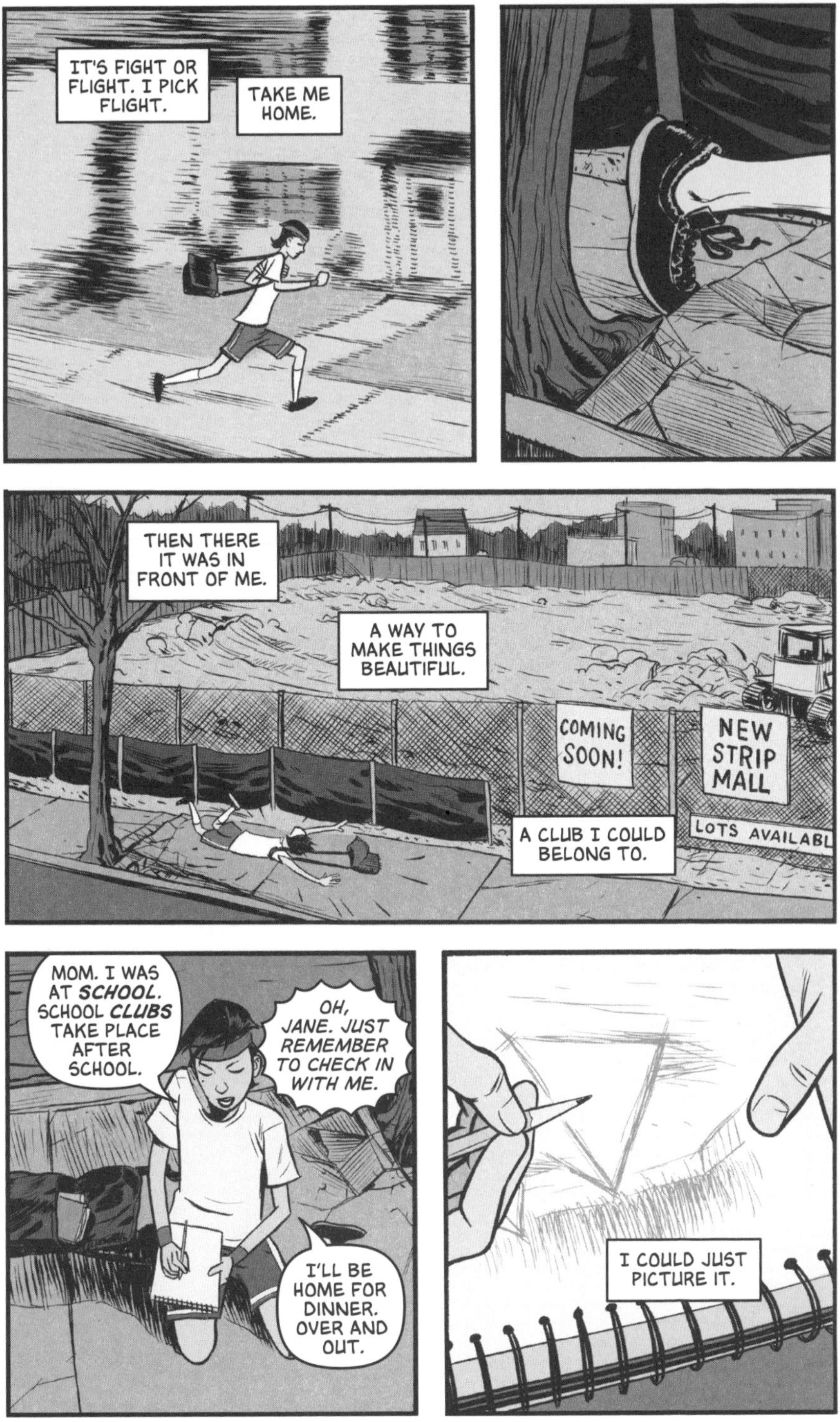
IT'S FIGHT OR FLIGHT. I PICK FLIGHT.
TAKE ME HOME.
THEN THERE IT WAS IN FRONT OF ME.
A WAY TO MAKE THINGS BEAUTIFUL.
COMING SOON!
NEW STRIP MALL
LOTS AVAILABL
A CLUB I COULD BELONG TO.
MOM. I WAS AT *SCHOOL*. SCHOOL *CLUBS* TAKE PLACE AFTER SCHOOL.
OH, JANE. JUST REMEMBER TO CHECK IN WITH ME.
I'LL BE HOME FOR DINNER. OVER AND OUT.
I COULD JUST PICTURE IT.

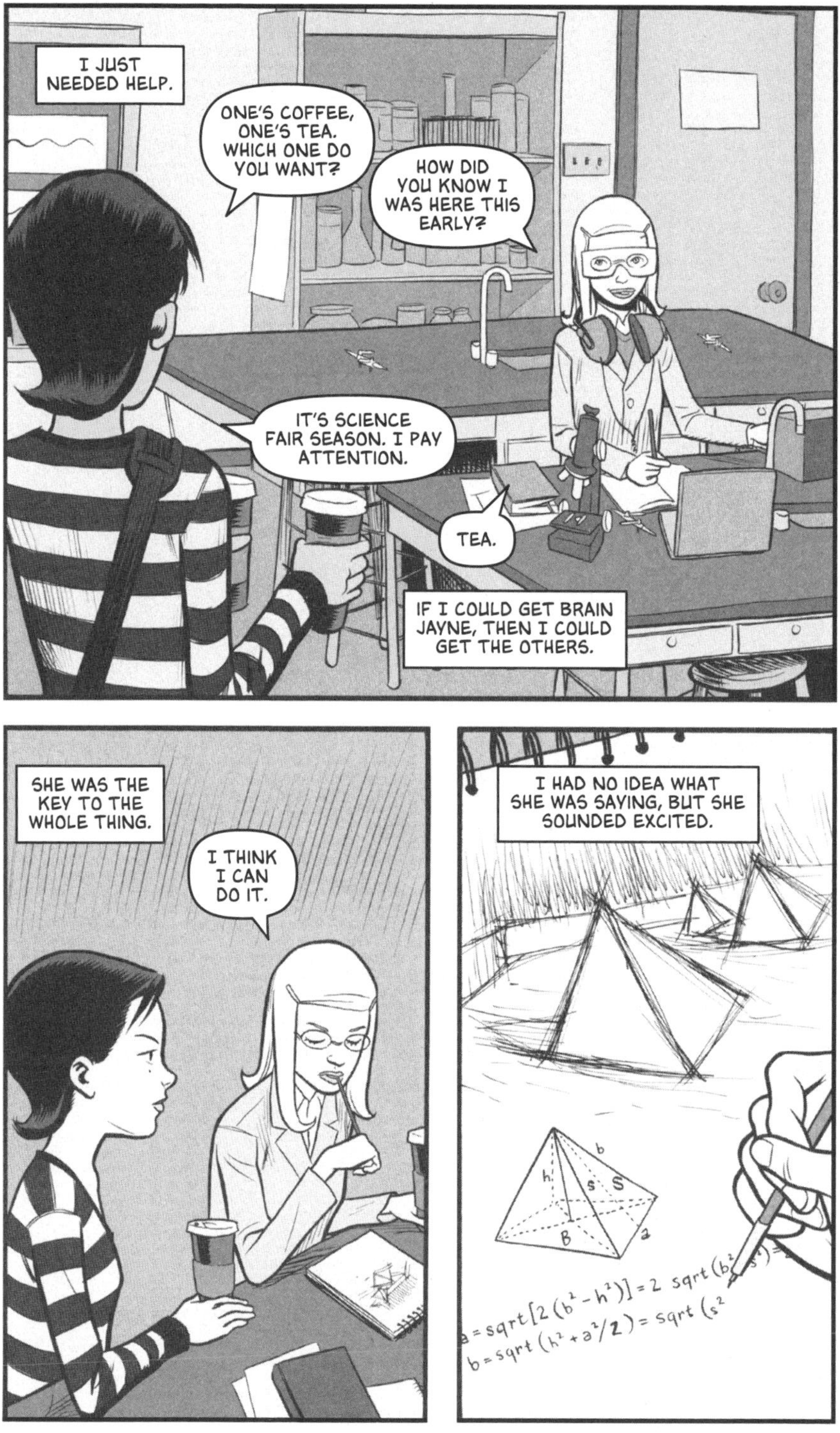
I JUST NEEDED HELP.
ONE'S COFFEE, ONE'S TEA. WHICH ONE DO YOU WANT?
HOW DID YOU KNOW I WAS HERE THIS EARLY?
IT'S SCIENCE FAIR SEASON. I PAY ATTENTION.
TEA.
IF I COULD GET BRAIN JAYNE, THEN I COULD GET THE OTHERS.
SHE WAS THE KEY TO THE WHOLE THING.
I THINK I CAN DO IT.
I HAD NO IDEA WHAT SHE WAS SAYING, BUT SHE SOUNDED EXCITED.

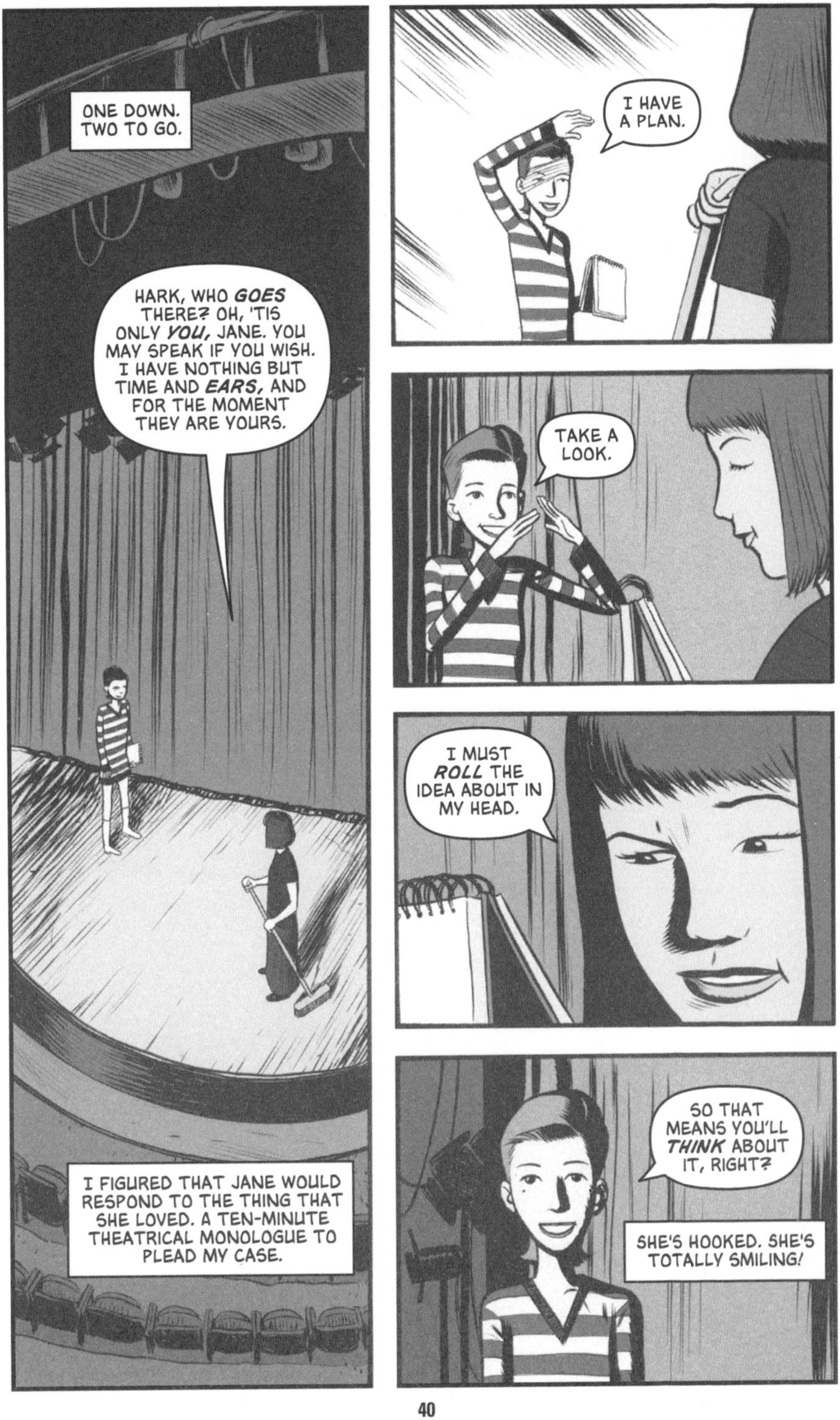
ONE DOWN. TWO TO GO.
HARK, WHO *GOES* THERE? OH, 'TIS ONLY *YOU,* JANE. YOU MAY SPEAK IF YOU WISH. I HAVE NOTHING BUT TIME AND *EARS,* AND FOR THE MOMENT THEY ARE YOURS.
I FIGURED THAT JANE WOULD RESPOND TO THE THING THAT SHE LOVED. A TEN-MINUTE THEATRICAL MONOLOGUE TO PLEAD MY CASE.
I HAVE A PLAN.
TAKE A LOOK.
I MUST *ROLL* THE IDEA ABOUT IN MY HEAD.
SO THAT MEANS YOU'LL *THINK* ABOUT IT, RIGHT?
SHE'S HOOKED. SHE'S TOTALLY SMILING!

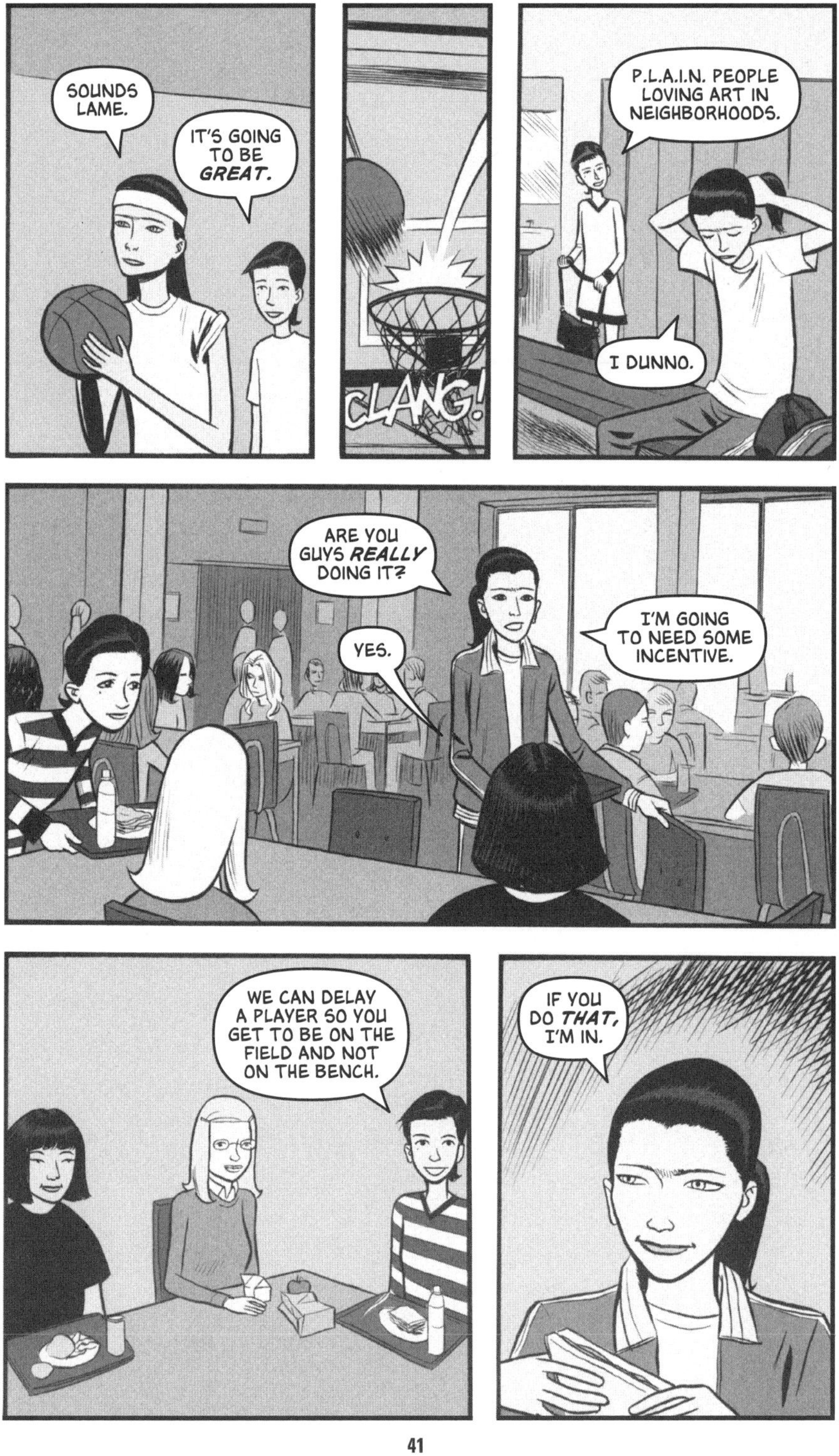
SOUNDS LAME.
IT'S GOING TO BE GREAT.
CLANG!
P.L.A.I.N. PEOPLE LOVING ART IN NEIGHBORHOODS.
I DUNNO.
ARE YOU GUYS REALLY DOING IT?
YES.
I'M GOING TO NEED SOME INCENTIVE.
WE CAN DELAY A PLAYER SO YOU GET TO BE ON THE FIELD AND NOT ON THE BENCH.
IF YOU DO THAT, I'M IN.

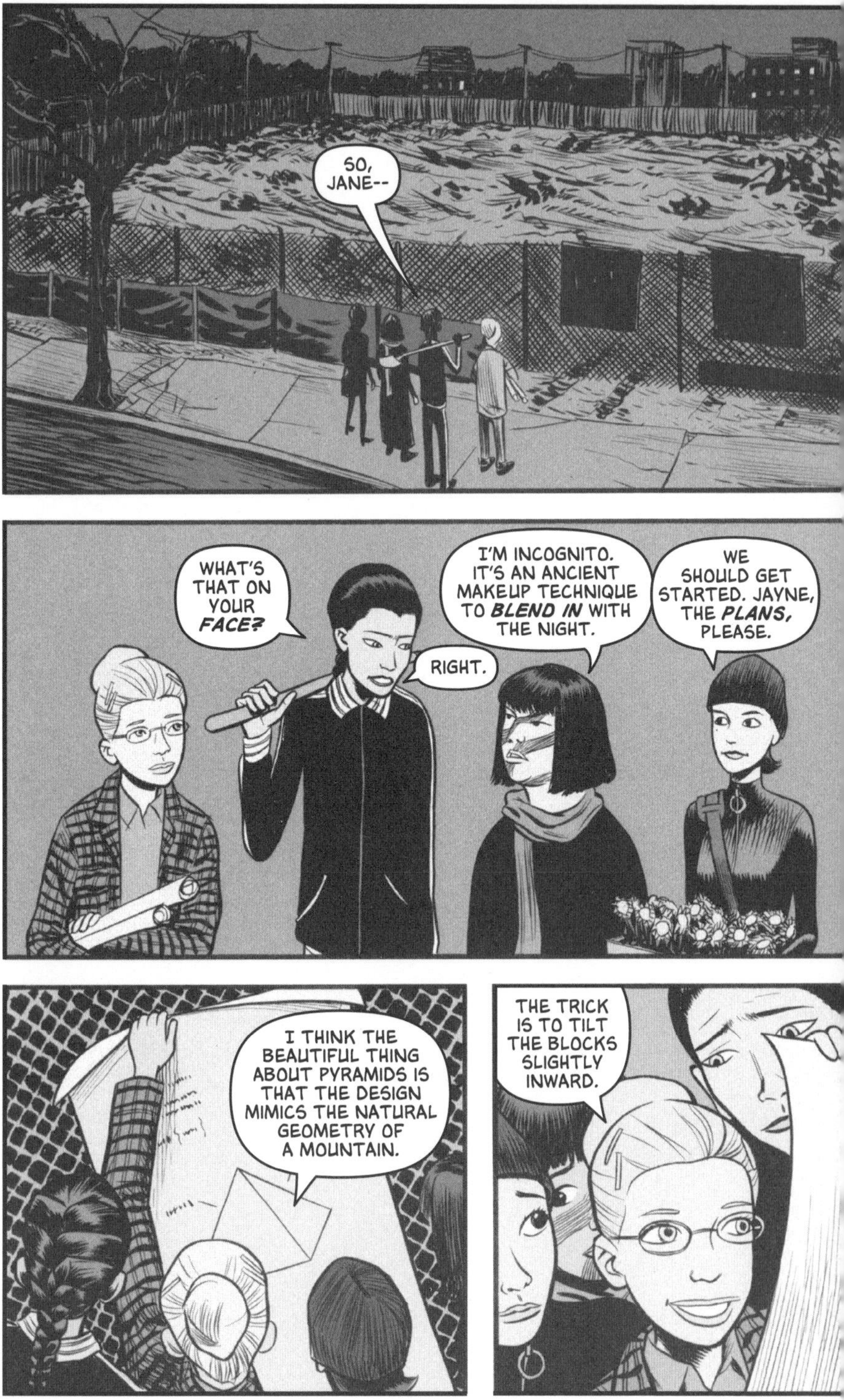
SO, JANE--
WHAT'S THAT ON YOUR FACE?
RIGHT.
I'M INCOGNITO. IT'S AN ANCIENT MAKEUP TECHNIQUE TO BLEND IN WITH THE NIGHT.
WE SHOULD GET STARTED. JAYNE, THE PLANS, PLEASE.
I THINK THE BEAUTIFUL THING ABOUT PYRAMIDS IS THAT THE DESIGN MIMICS THE NATURAL GEOMETRY OF A MOUNTAIN.
THE TRICK IS TO TILT THE BLOCKS SLIGHTLY INWARD.

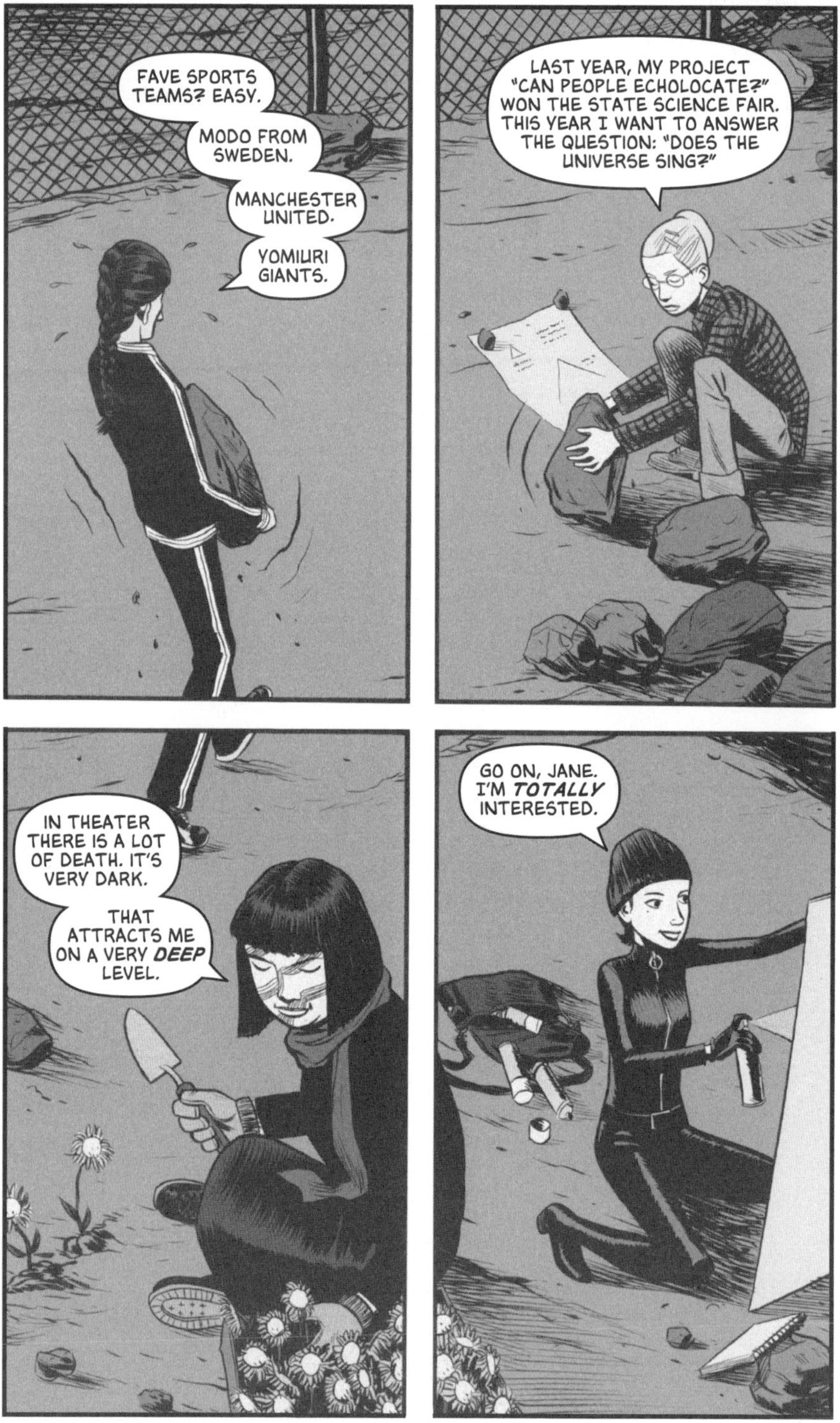

FAVE SPORTS TEAMS? EASY.
MODO FROM SWEDEN.
MANCHESTER UNITED.
YOMIURI GIANTS.
LAST YEAR, MY PROJECT "CAN PEOPLE ECHOLOCATE?" WON THE STATE SCIENCE FAIR. THIS YEAR I WANT TO ANSWER THE QUESTION: "DOES THE UNIVERSE SING?"
IN THEATER THERE IS A LOT OF DEATH. IT'S VERY DARK.
THAT ATTRACTS ME ON A VERY *DEEP* LEVEL.
GO ON, JANE. I'M ***TOTALLY*** INTERESTED.

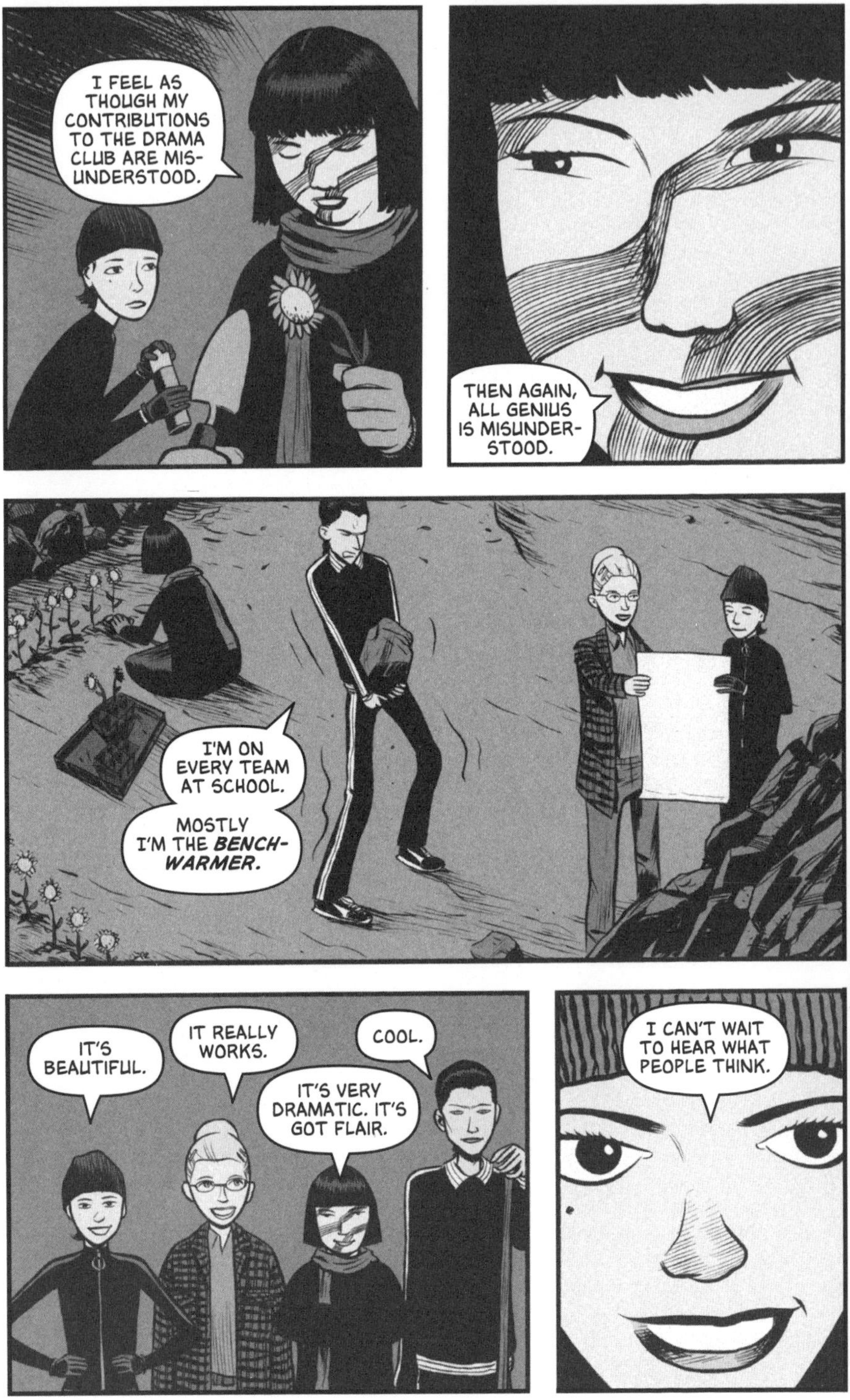
I FEEL AS THOUGH MY CONTRIBUTIONS TO THE DRAMA CLUB ARE MIS-UNDERSTOOD.
THEN AGAIN, ALL GENIUS IS MISUNDER-STOOD.
I'M ON EVERY TEAM AT SCHOOL.
MOSTLY I'M THE *BENCH-WARMER.*
IT'S BEAUTIFUL.
IT REALLY WORKS.
COOL.
IT'S VERY DRAMATIC. IT'S GOT FLAIR.
I CAN'T WAIT TO HEAR WHAT PEOPLE THINK.

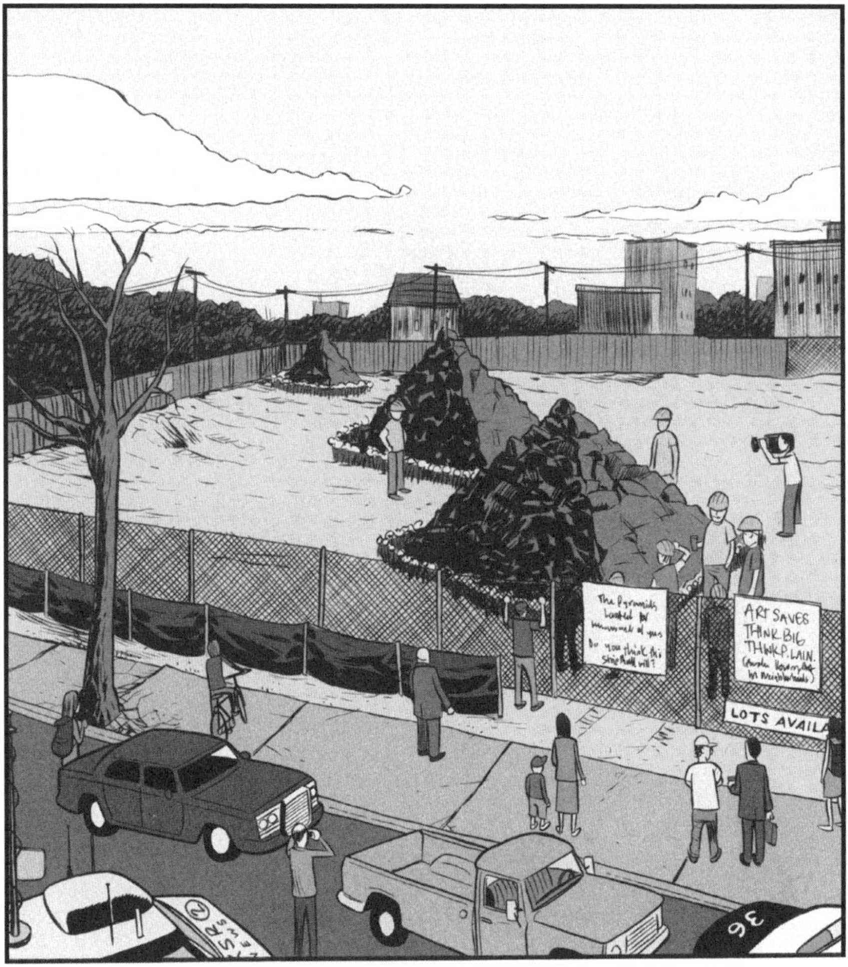
ART SAVES
THINK BIG
THINK P.LAIN.
LOTS AVAILA

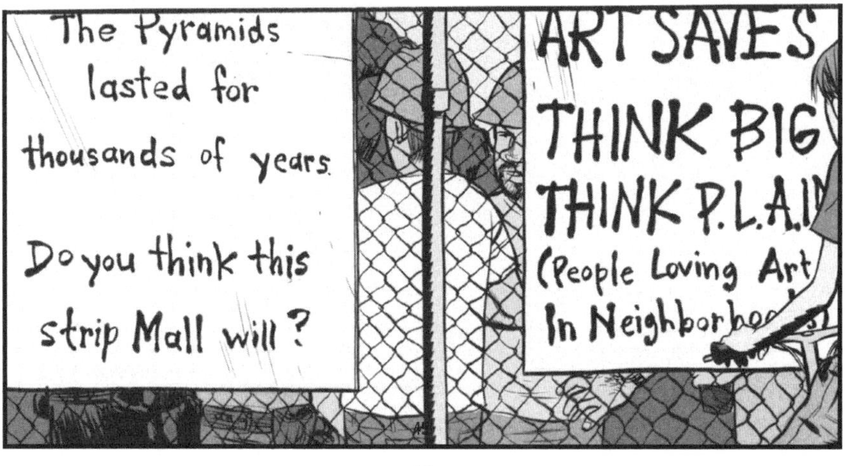
The Pyramids
lasted for
thousands of years.
Do you think this
strip Mall will?
ART SAVES
THINK BIG
THINK P.L.A.I
(People Loving Art
In Neighborho

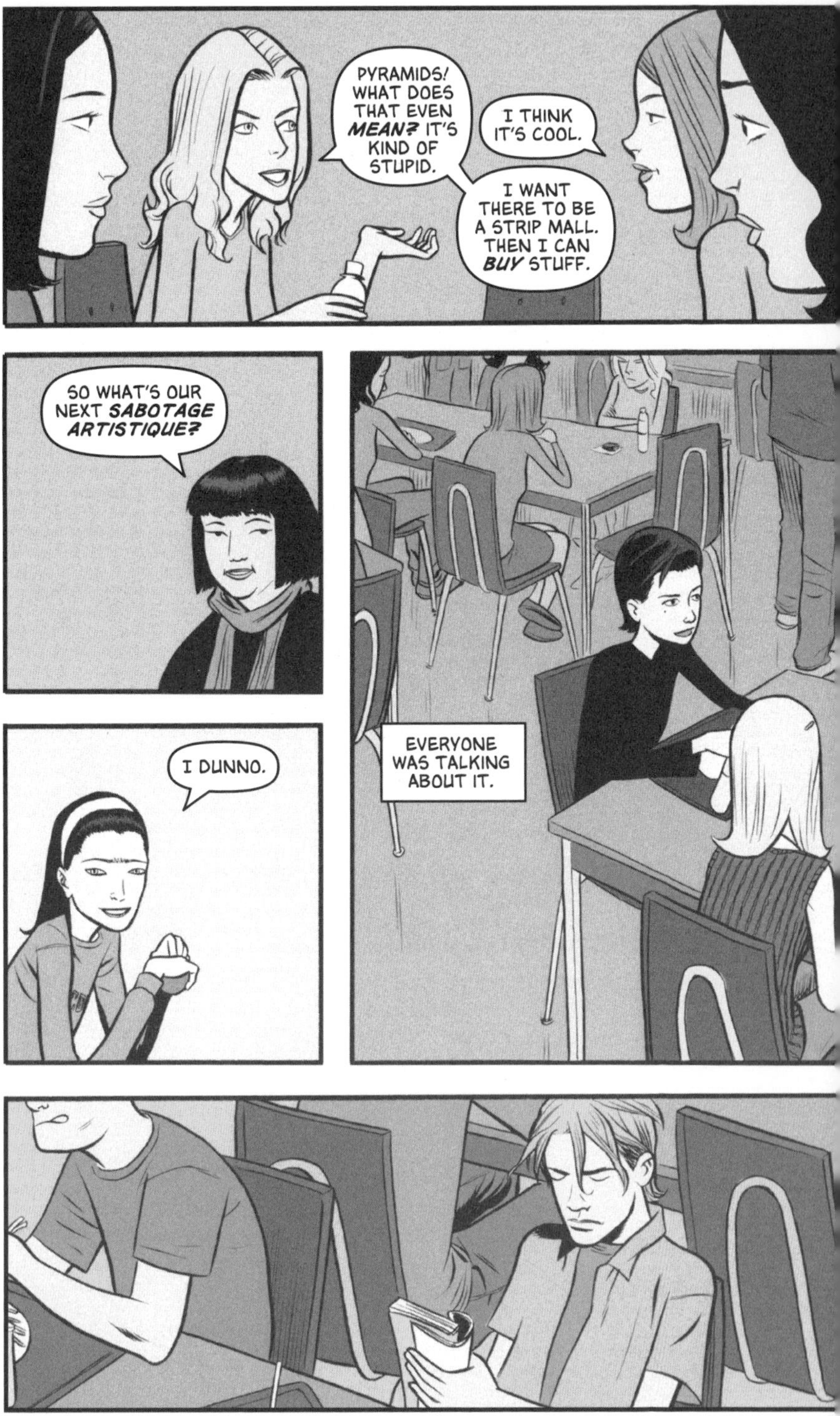
PYRAMIDS! WHAT DOES THAT EVEN *MEAN?* IT'S KIND OF STUPID.
I THINK IT'S COOL.
I WANT THERE TO BE A STRIP MALL. THEN I CAN *BUY* STUFF.
SO WHAT'S OUR NEXT *SABOTAGE ARTISTIQUE?*
I DUNNO.
EVERYONE WAS TALKING ABOUT IT.

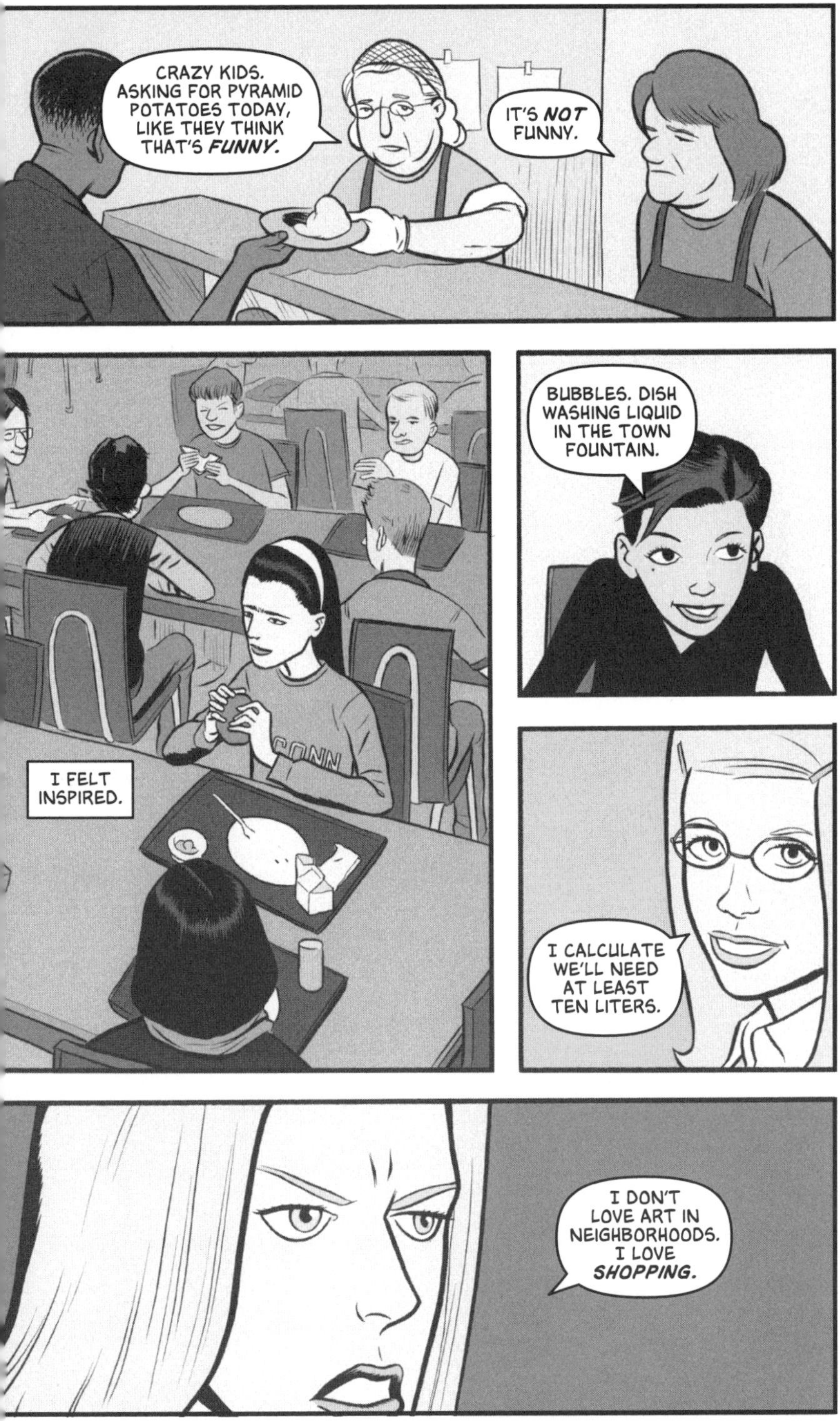
CRAZY KIDS. ASKING FOR PYRAMID POTATOES TODAY, LIKE THEY THINK THAT'S *FUNNY.*
IT'S *NOT* FUNNY.
I FELT INSPIRED.
BUBBLES. DISH WASHING LIQUID IN THE TOWN FOUNTAIN.
I CALCULATE WE'LL NEED AT LEAST TEN LITERS.
I DON'T LOVE ART IN NEIGHBORHOODS. I LOVE *SHOPPING.*

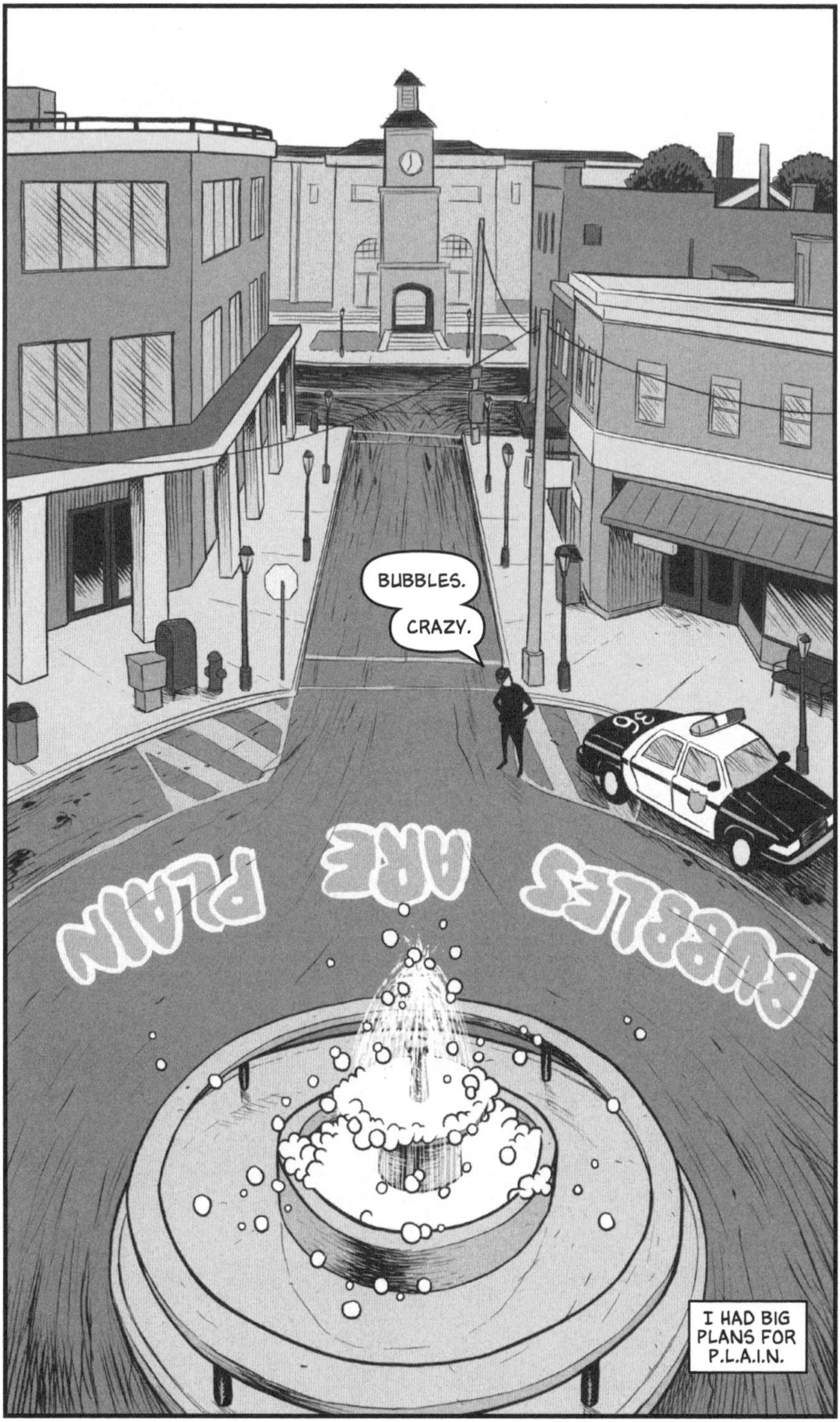
BUBBLES.
CRAZY.
BUBBLES ARE PLAIN
I HAD BIG PLANS FOR P.L.A.I.N.

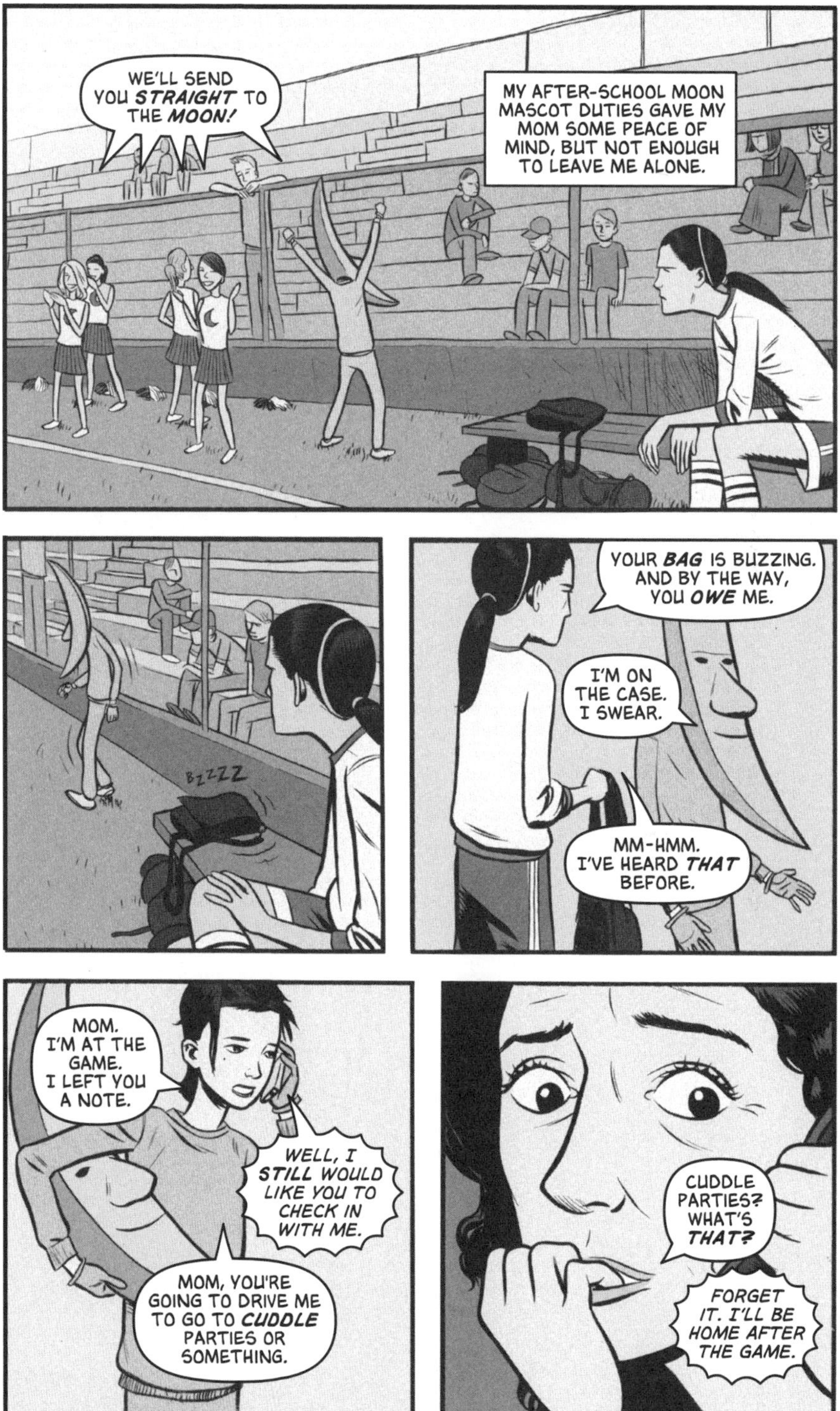
WE'LL SEND YOU STRAIGHT TO THE MOON!
MY AFTER-SCHOOL MOON MASCOT DUTIES GAVE MY MOM SOME PEACE OF MIND, BUT NOT ENOUGH TO LEAVE ME ALONE.
BZZZZ
YOUR BAG IS BUZZING. AND BY THE WAY, YOU OWE ME.
I'M ON THE CASE. I SWEAR.
MM-HMM. I'VE HEARD THAT BEFORE.
MOM. I'M AT THE GAME. I LEFT YOU A NOTE.
WELL, I STILL WOULD LIKE YOU TO CHECK IN WITH ME.
MOM, YOU'RE GOING TO DRIVE ME TO GO TO CUDDLE PARTIES OR SOMETHING.
CUDDLE PARTIES? WHAT'S THAT?
FORGET IT. I'LL BE HOME AFTER THE GAME.

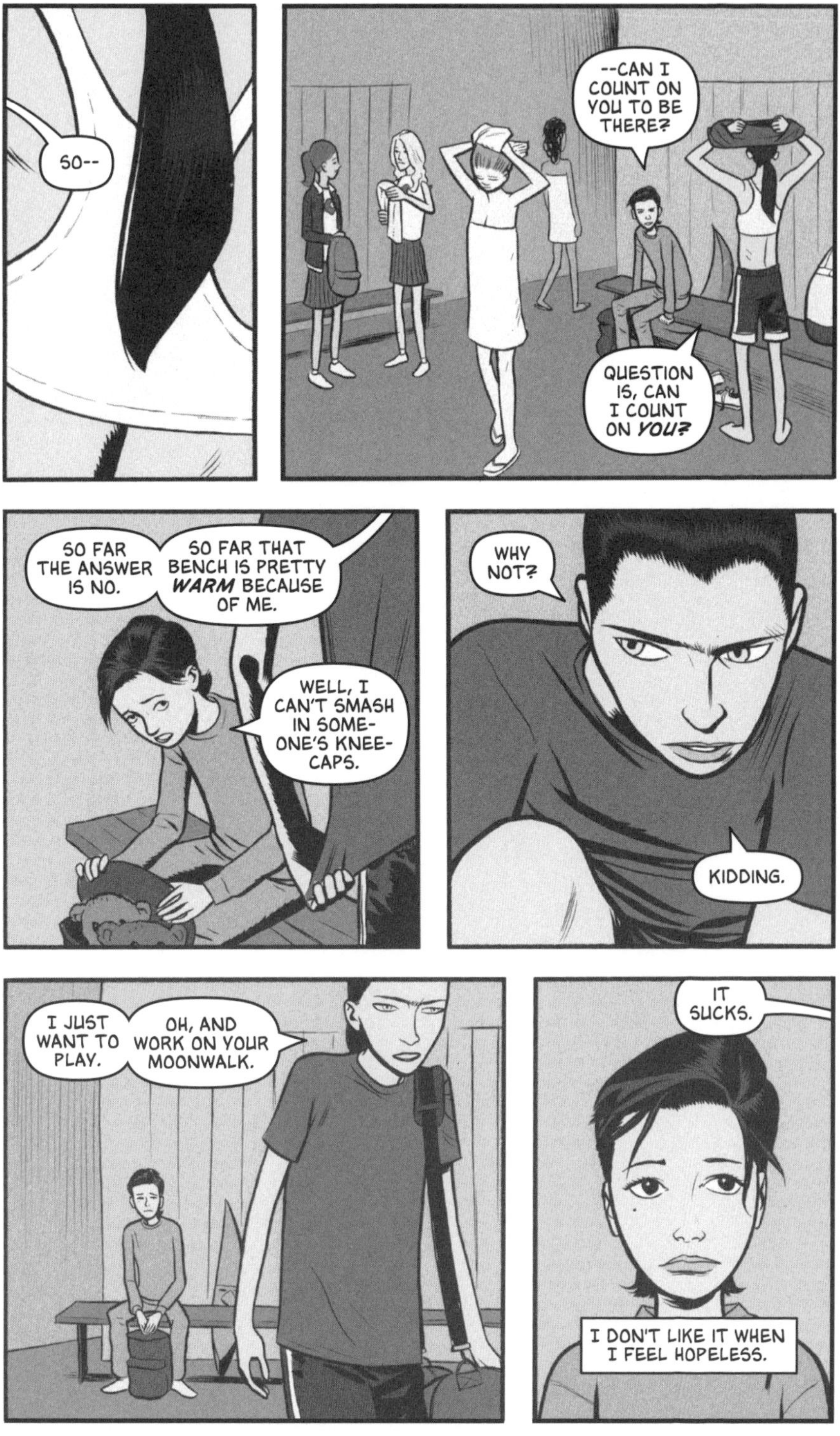
SO--
--CAN I COUNT ON YOU TO BE THERE?
QUESTION IS, CAN I COUNT ON *YOU?*
SO FAR THE ANSWER IS NO.
SO FAR THAT BENCH IS PRETTY *WARM* BECAUSE OF ME.
WELL, I CAN'T SMASH IN SOME-ONE'S KNEE-CAPS.
WHY NOT?
KIDDING.
I JUST WANT TO PLAY.
OH, AND WORK ON YOUR MOONWALK.
IT SUCKS.
I DON'T LIKE IT WHEN I FEEL HOPELESS.

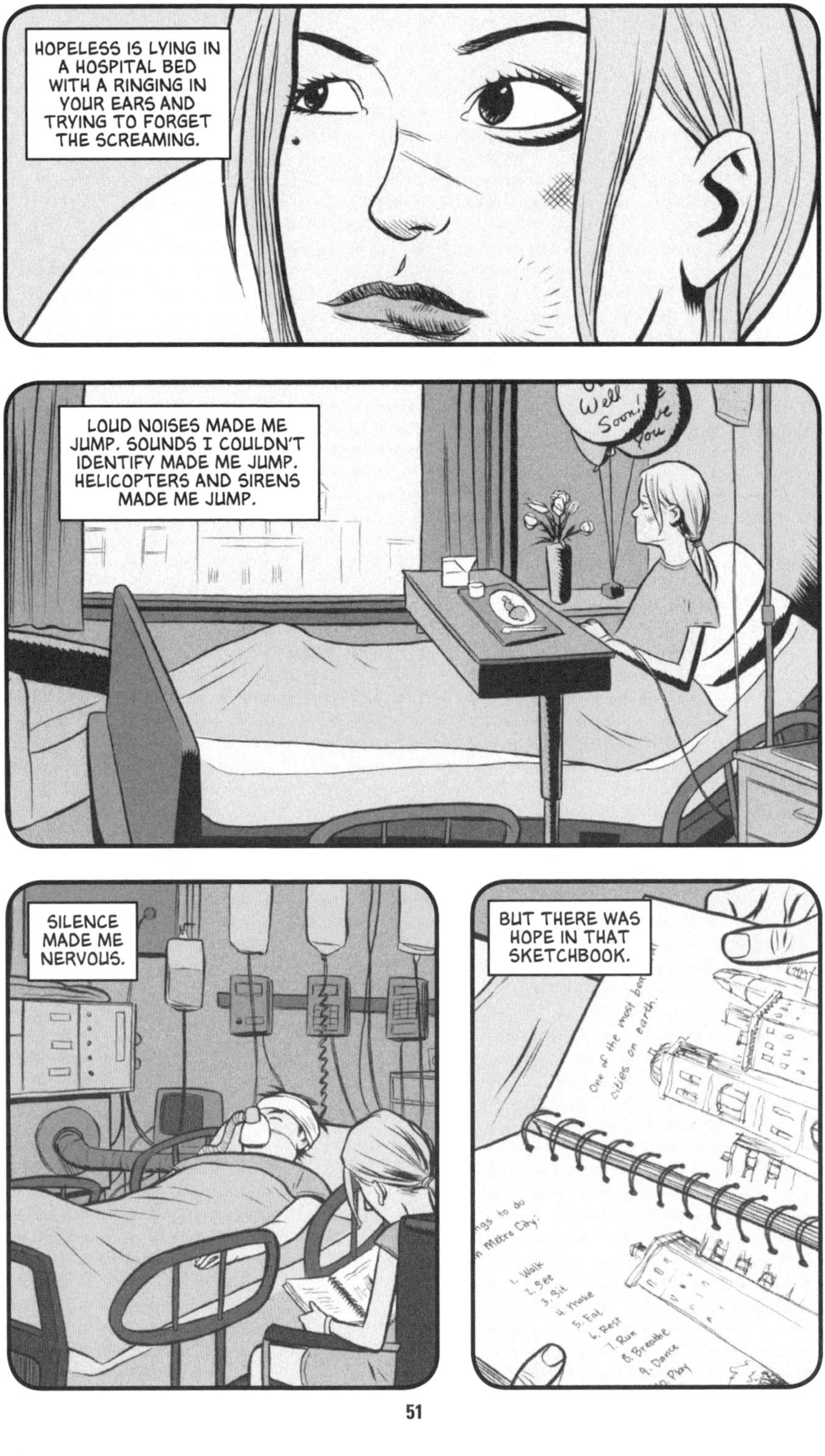
HOPELESS IS LYING IN A HOSPITAL BED WITH A RINGING IN YOUR EARS AND TRYING TO FORGET THE SCREAMING.
LOUD NOISES MADE ME JUMP. SOUNDS I COULDN'T IDENTIFY MADE ME JUMP. HELICOPTERS AND SIRENS MADE ME JUMP.
Well Soon!
SILENCE MADE ME NERVOUS.
BUT THERE WAS HOPE IN THAT SKETCHBOOK.
One of the most
cities on earth.
Metro City:
1. Walk
2. See
3. Sit
4. Make
5. Eat
6. Rest
7. Run
8. Breathe
9. Dance

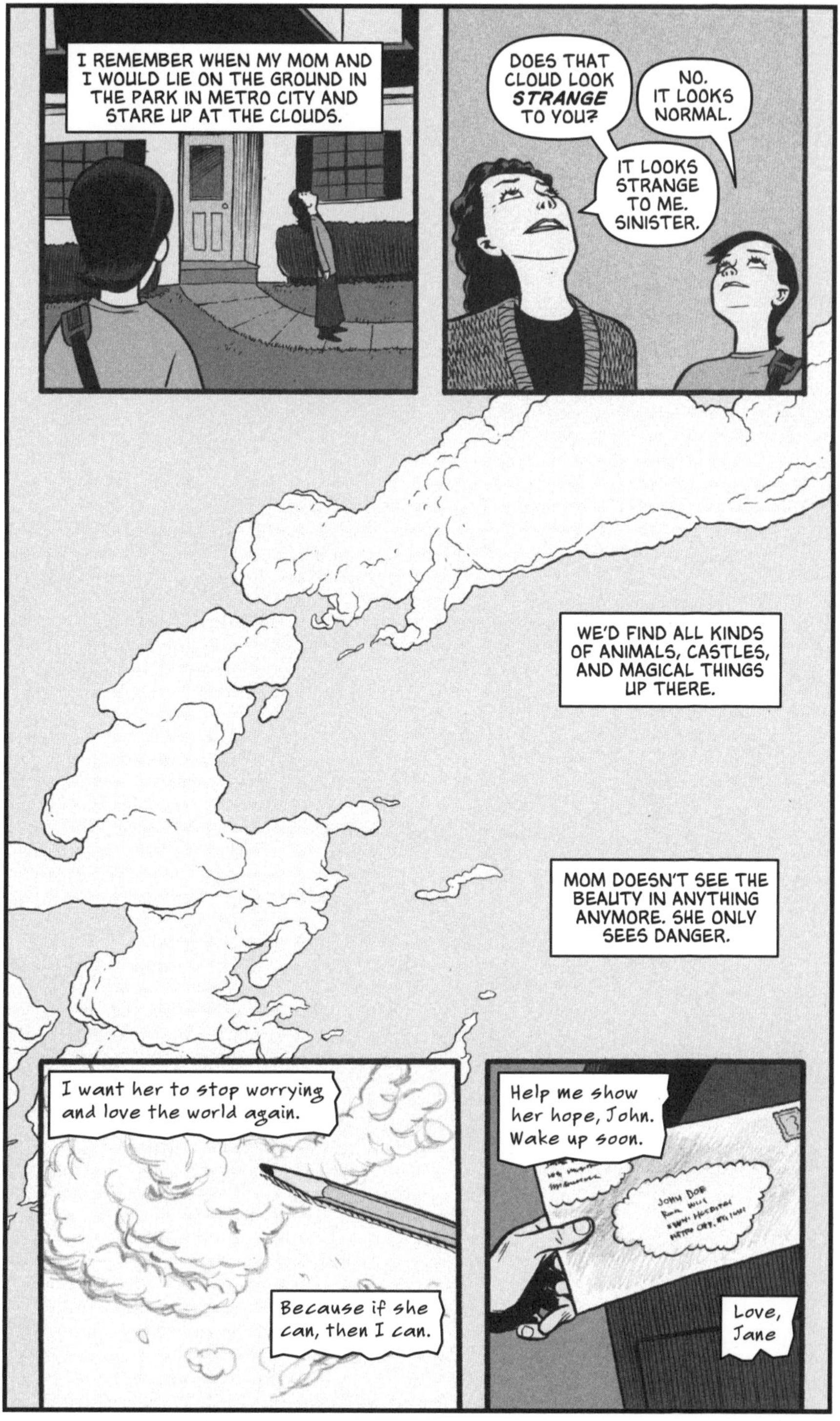

I REMEMBER WHEN MY MOM AND I WOULD LIE ON THE GROUND IN THE PARK IN METRO CITY AND STARE UP AT THE CLOUDS.
DOES THAT CLOUD LOOK STRANGE TO YOU?
NO. IT LOOKS NORMAL.
IT LOOKS STRANGE TO ME. SINISTER.
WE'D FIND ALL KINDS OF ANIMALS, CASTLES, AND MAGICAL THINGS UP THERE.
MOM DOESN'T SEE THE BEAUTY IN ANYTHING ANYMORE. SHE ONLY SEES DANGER.
I want her to stop worrying and love the world again.
Because if she can, then I can.
Help me show her hope, John. Wake up soon.
JOHN DOE
Love, Jane

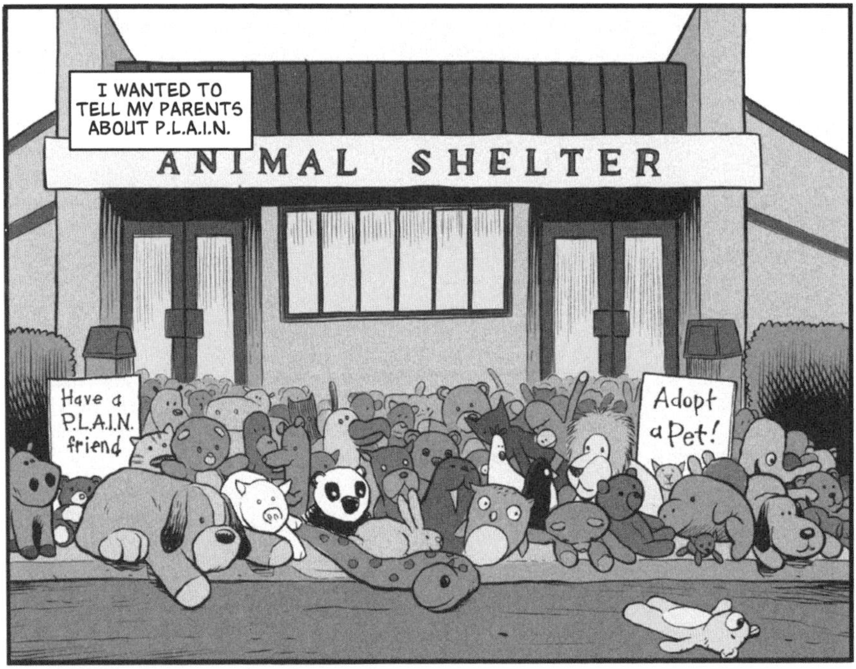
I WANTED TO TELL MY PARENTS ABOUT P.L.A.I.N.
ANIMAL SHELTER
Have a P.L.A.I.N. friend
Adopt a Pet!

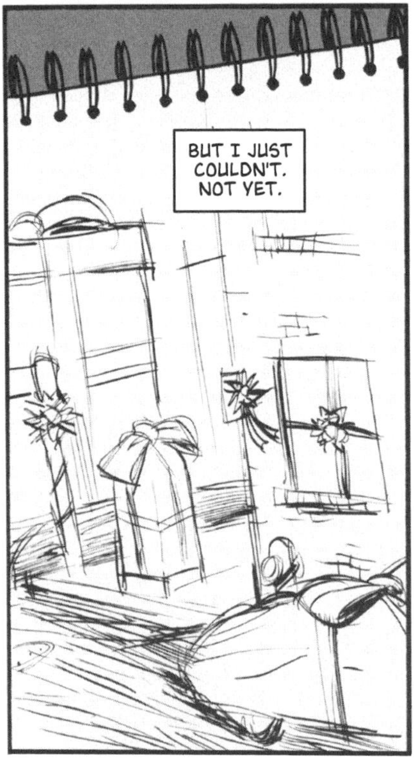
BUT I JUST COULDN'T. NOT YET.

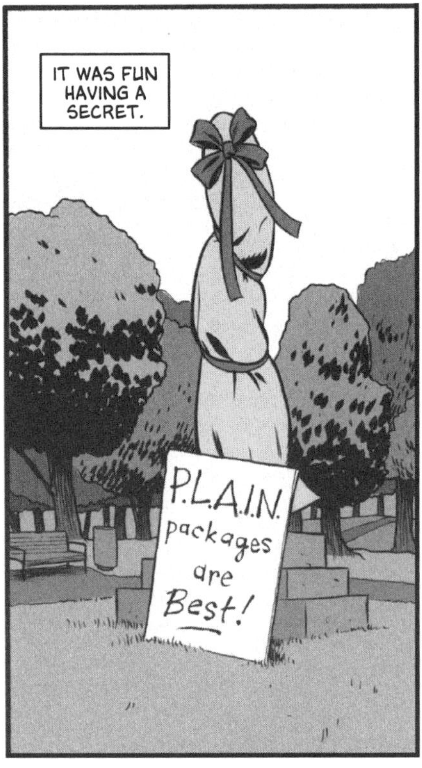
IT WAS FUN HAVING A SECRET.
P.L.A.I.N. packages are Best!

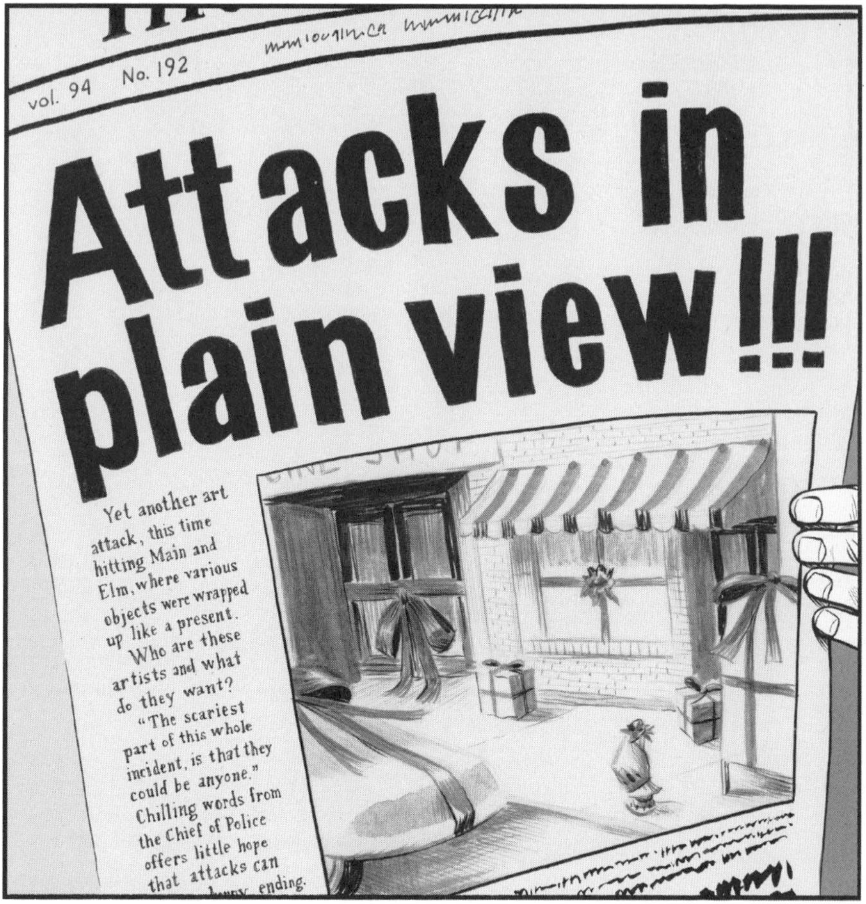
vol. 94 No. 192
Attacks in plain view!!!
Yet another art attack, this time hitting Main and Elm, where various objects were wrapped up like a present.
Who are these artists and what do they want?
"The scariest part of this whole incident, is that they could be anyone."
Chilling words from the Chief of Police offers little hope that attacks can
ending.

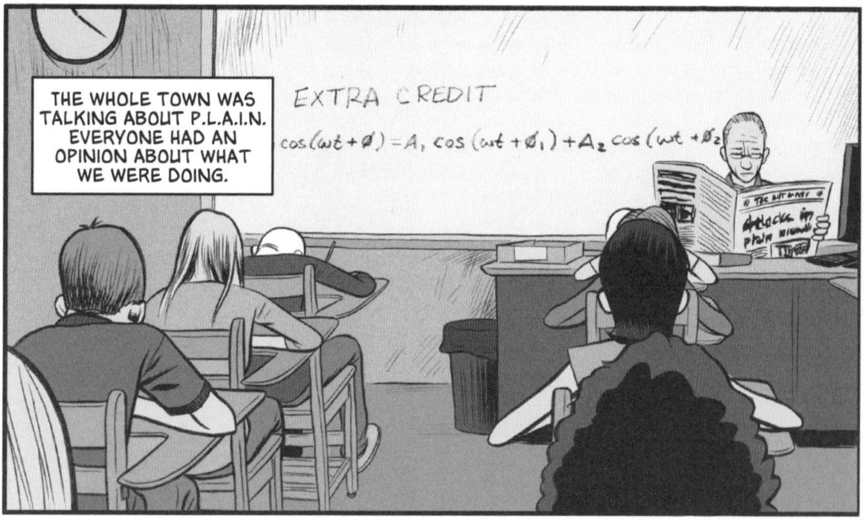
THE WHOLE TOWN WAS TALKING ABOUT P.L.A.I.N. EVERYONE HAD AN OPINION ABOUT WHAT WE WERE DOING.
EXTRA CREDIT
cos(ωt+∅)=A₁ cos(ωt+∅₁)+A₂ cos(ωt+∅₂

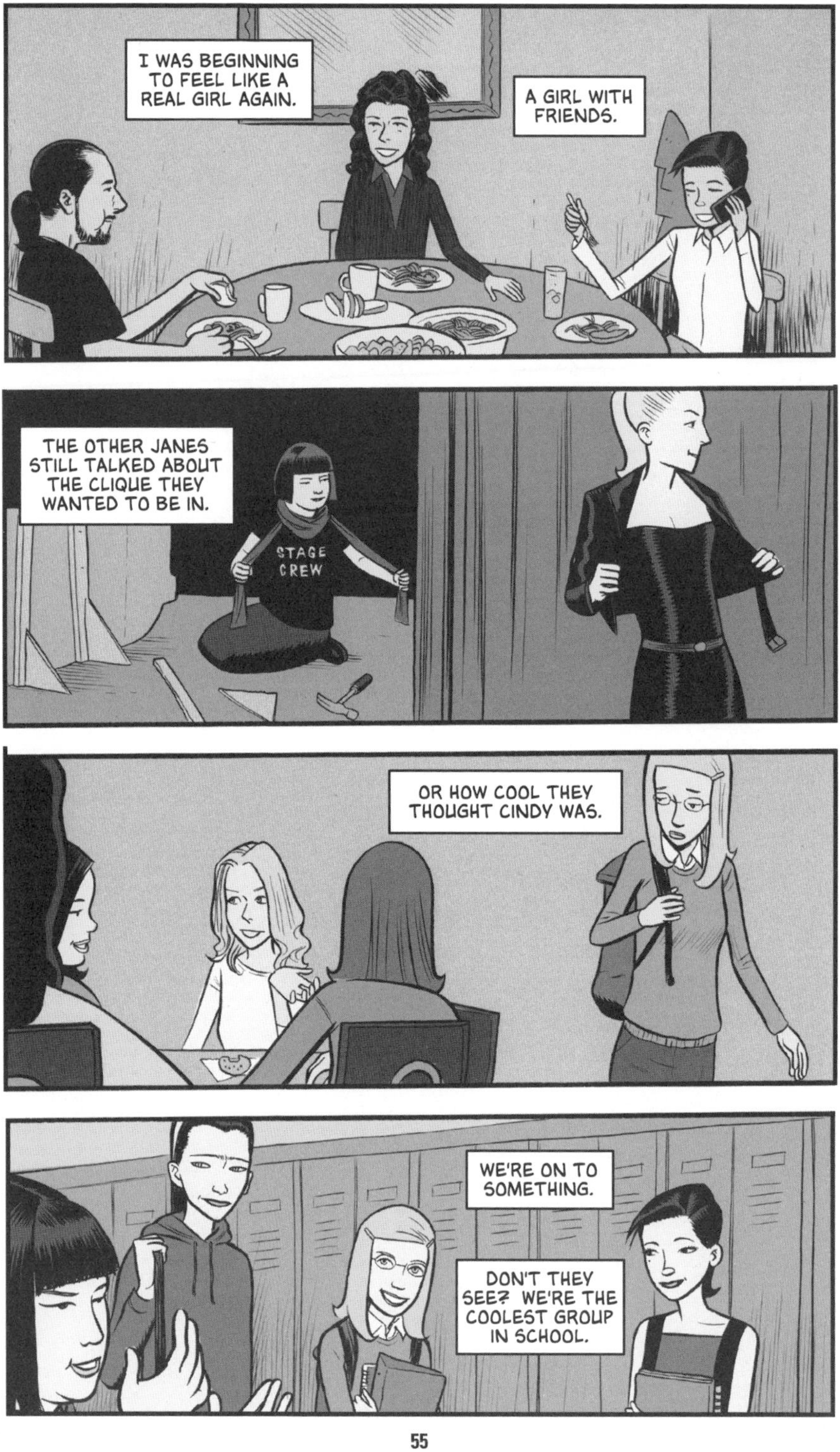
I WAS BEGINNING TO FEEL LIKE A REAL GIRL AGAIN.
A GIRL WITH FRIENDS.
THE OTHER JANES STILL TALKED ABOUT THE CLIQUE THEY WANTED TO BE IN.
STAGE CREW
OR HOW COOL THEY THOUGHT CINDY WAS.
WE'RE ON TO SOMETHING.
DON'T THEY SEE? WE'RE THE COOLEST GROUP IN SCHOOL.

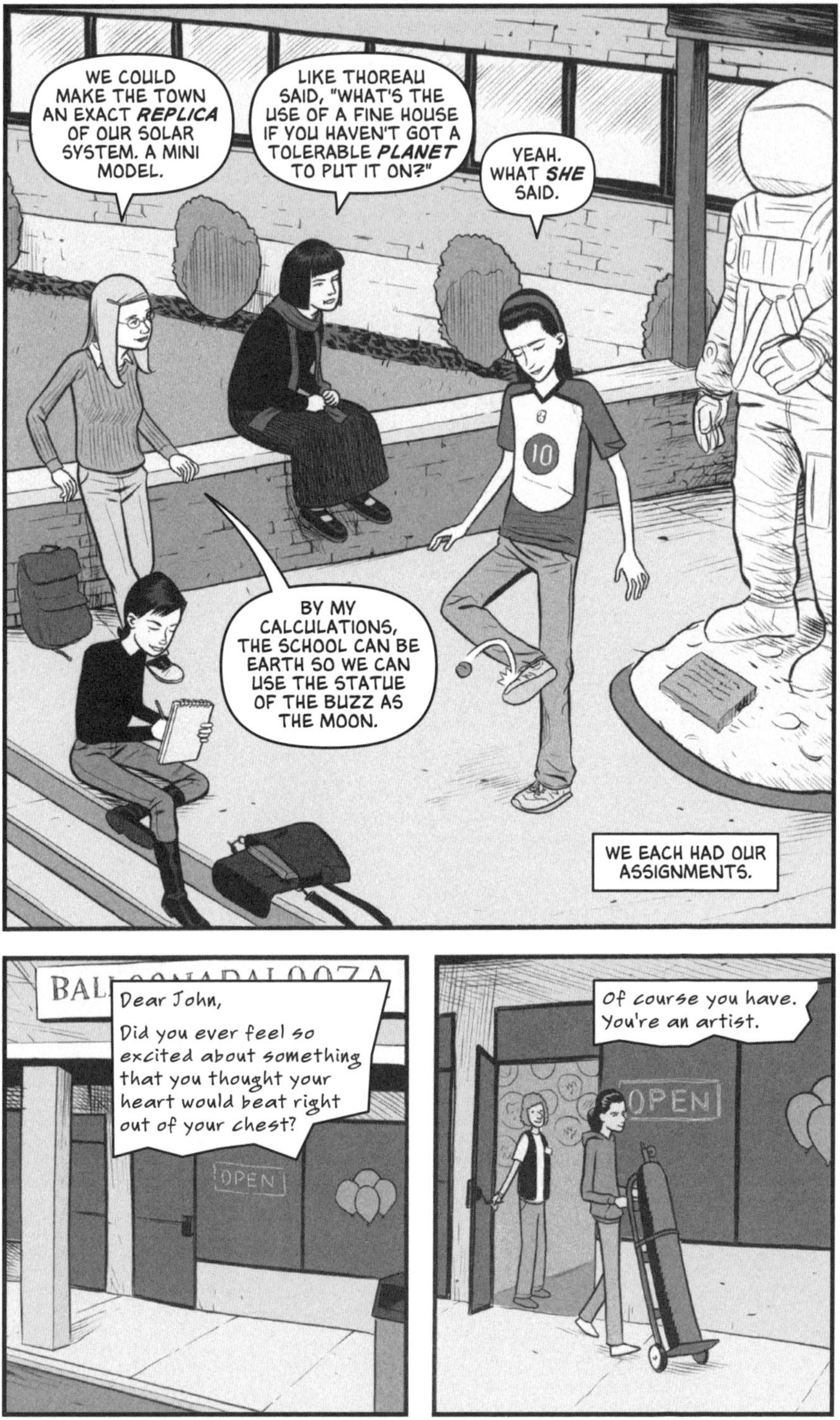
WE COULD MAKE THE TOWN AN EXACT *REPLICA* OF OUR SOLAR SYSTEM. A MINI MODEL.
LIKE THOREAU SAID, "WHAT'S THE USE OF A FINE HOUSE IF YOU HAVEN'T GOT A TOLERABLE *PLANET* TO PUT IT ON?"
YEAH. WHAT *SHE* SAID.
10
BY MY CALCULATIONS, THE SCHOOL CAN BE EARTH SO WE CAN USE THE STATUE OF THE BUZZ AS THE MOON.
WE EACH HAD OUR ASSIGNMENTS.
Dear John,
Did you ever feel so excited about something that you thought your heart would beat right out of your chest?
OPEN
Of course you have. You're an artist.
OPEN

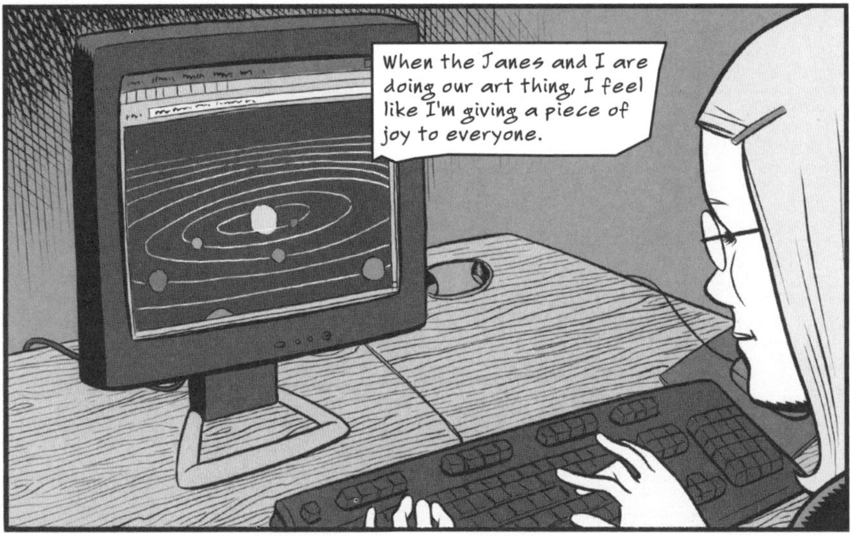
When the Janes and I are doing our art thing, I feel like I'm giving a piece of joy to everyone.

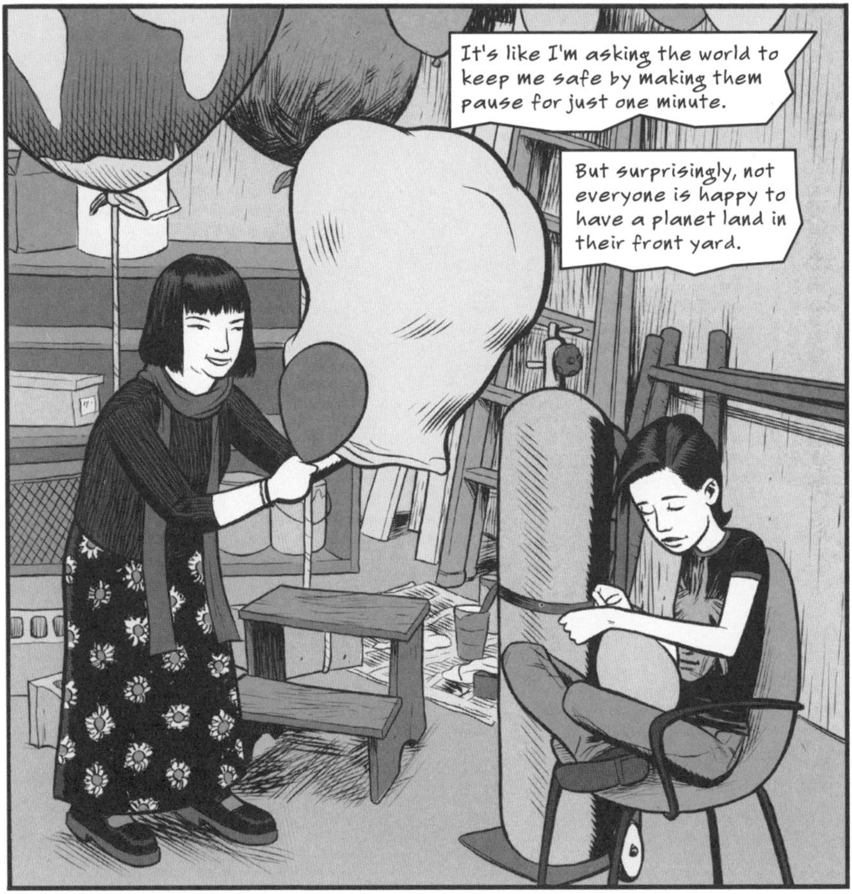
It's like I'm asking the world to keep me safe by making them pause for just one minute.
But surprisingly, not everyone is happy to have a planet land in their front yard.

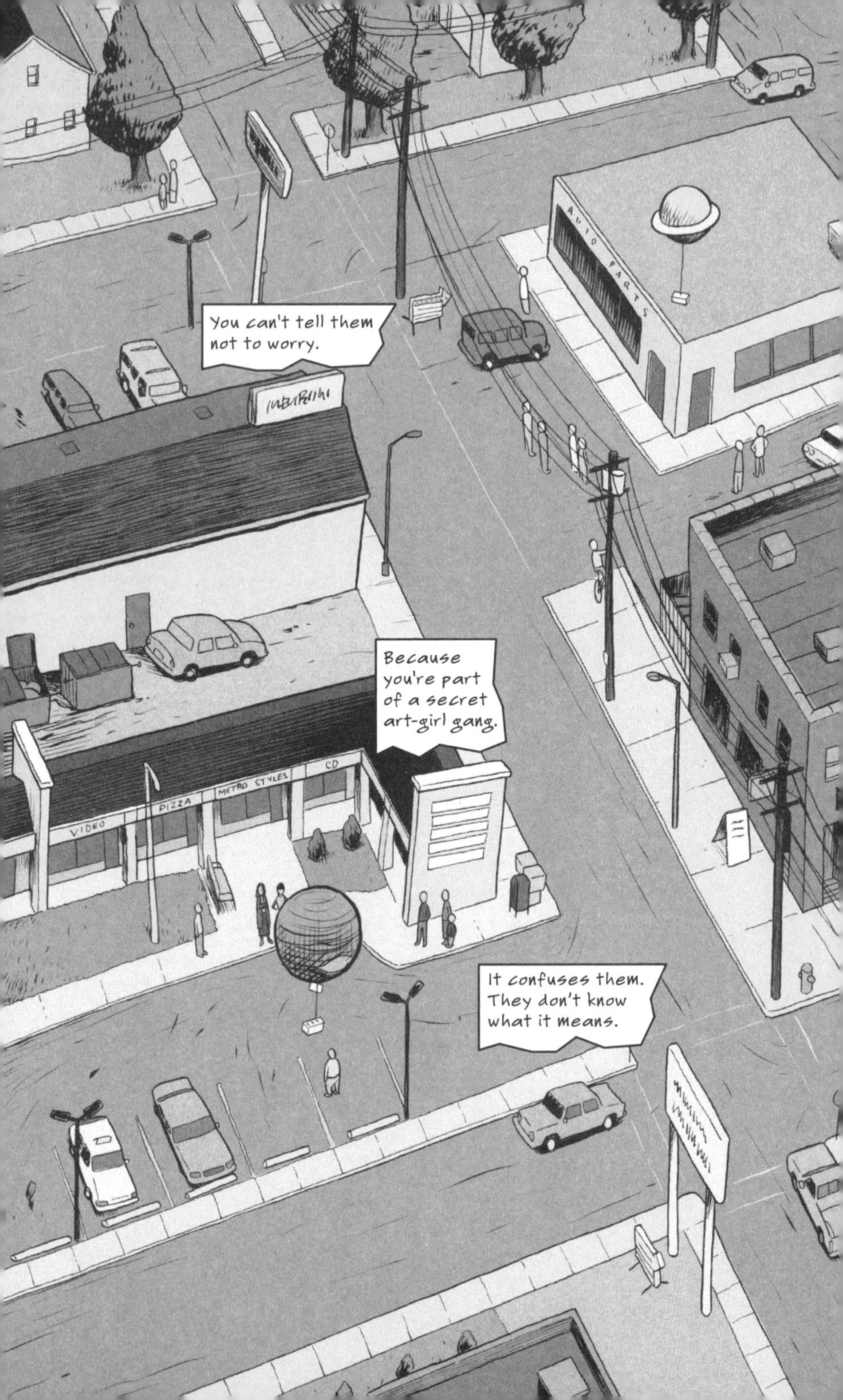
You can't tell them not to worry.
Because you're part of a secret art-girl gang.
It confuses them. They don't know what it means.
AUTO PARTS
VIDEO
PIZZA
METRO STYLES
CD

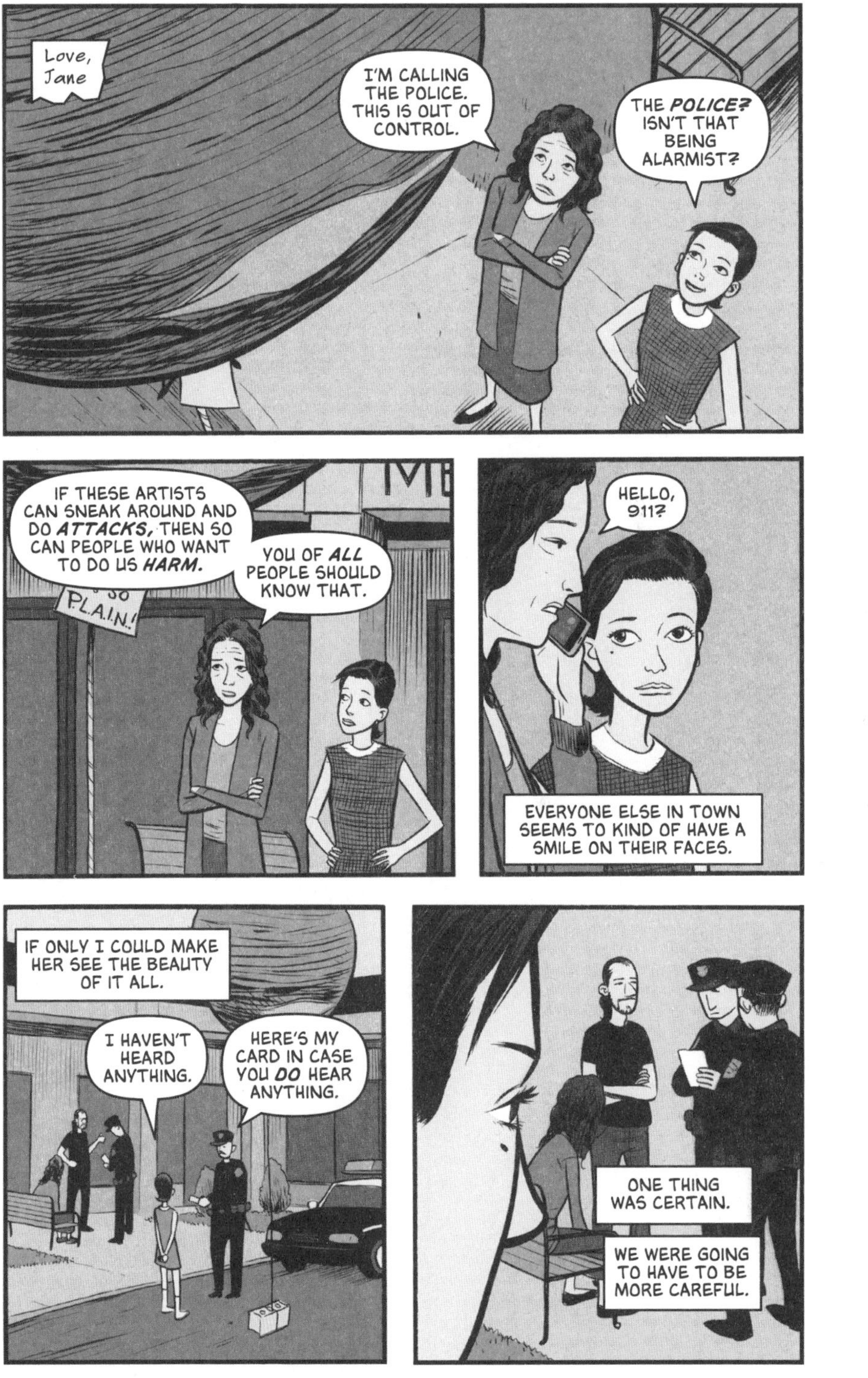
Love, Jane
I'M CALLING THE POLICE. THIS IS OUT OF CONTROL.
THE POLICE? ISN'T THAT BEING ALARMIST?
IF THESE ARTISTS CAN SNEAK AROUND AND DO ATTACKS, THEN SO CAN PEOPLE WHO WANT TO DO US HARM.
YOU OF ALL PEOPLE SHOULD KNOW THAT.
P.L.A.I.N.!
HELLO, 911?
EVERYONE ELSE IN TOWN SEEMS TO KIND OF HAVE A SMILE ON THEIR FACES.
IF ONLY I COULD MAKE HER SEE THE BEAUTY OF IT ALL.
I HAVEN'T HEARD ANYTHING.
HERE'S MY CARD IN CASE YOU DO HEAR ANYTHING.
ONE THING WAS CERTAIN.
WE WERE GOING TO HAVE TO BE MORE CAREFUL.

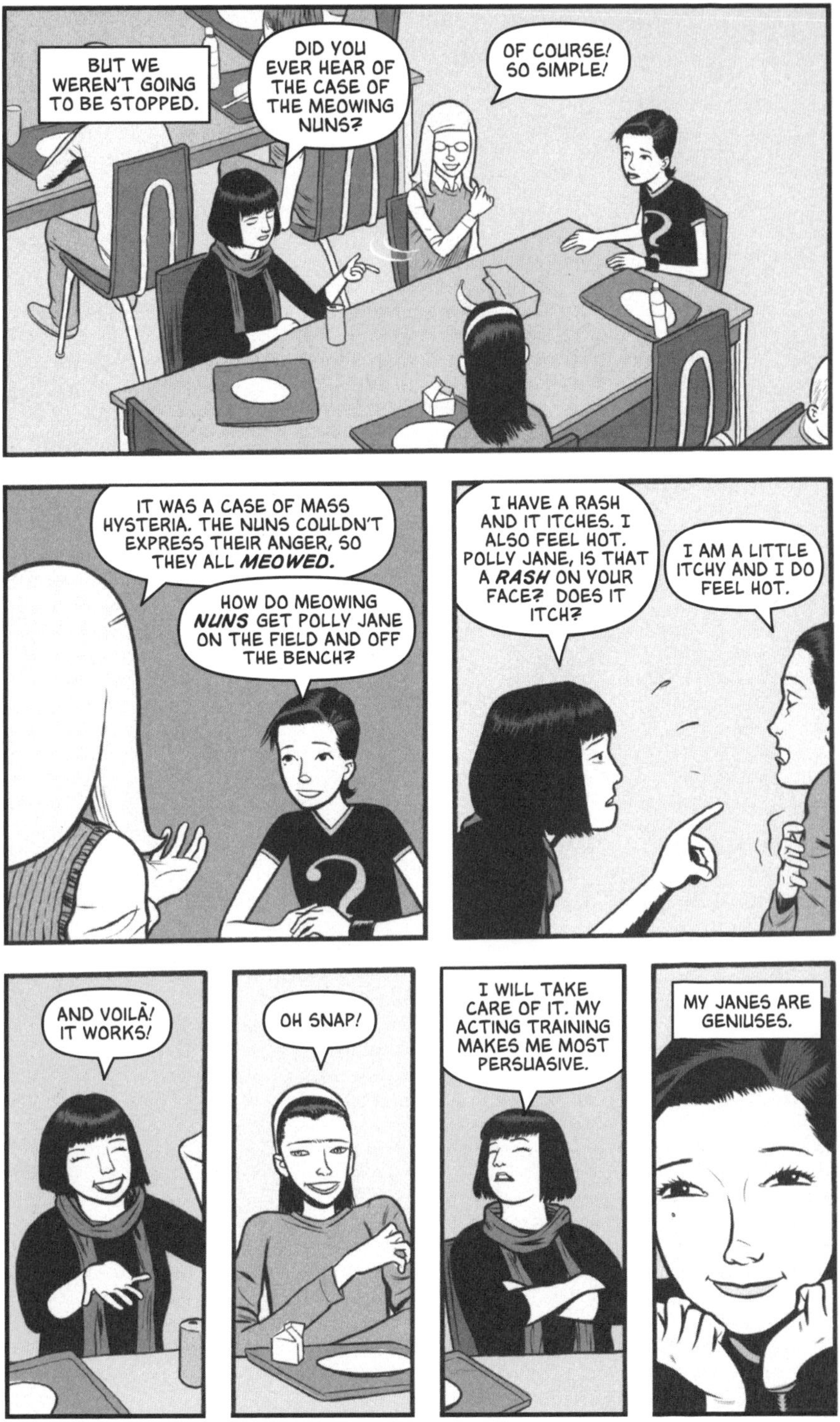
BUT WE WEREN'T GOING TO BE STOPPED.
DID YOU EVER HEAR OF THE CASE OF THE MEOWING NUNS?
OF COURSE! SO SIMPLE!
IT WAS A CASE OF MASS HYSTERIA. THE NUNS COULDN'T EXPRESS THEIR ANGER, SO THEY ALL *MEOWED.*
HOW DO MEOWING *NUNS* GET POLLY JANE ON THE FIELD AND OFF THE BENCH?
I HAVE A RASH AND IT ITCHES. I ALSO FEEL HOT. POLLY JANE, IS THAT A *RASH* ON YOUR FACE? DOES IT ITCH?
I AM A LITTLE ITCHY AND I DO FEEL HOT.
AND VOILÀ! IT WORKS!
OH SNAP!
I WILL TAKE CARE OF IT. MY ACTING TRAINING MAKES ME MOST PERSUASIVE.
MY JANES ARE GENIUSES.

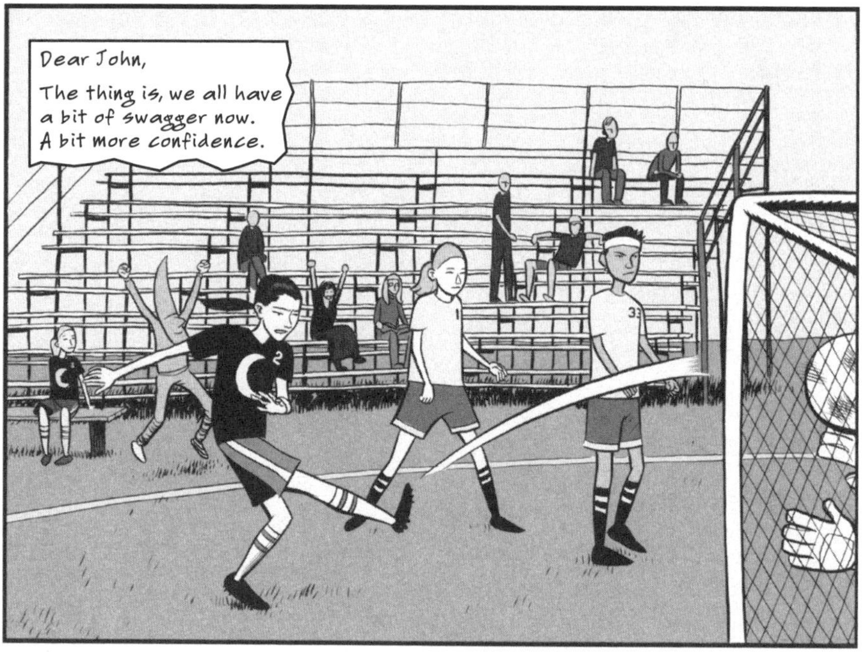
Dear John,
The thing is, we all have a bit of swagger now. A bit more confidence.

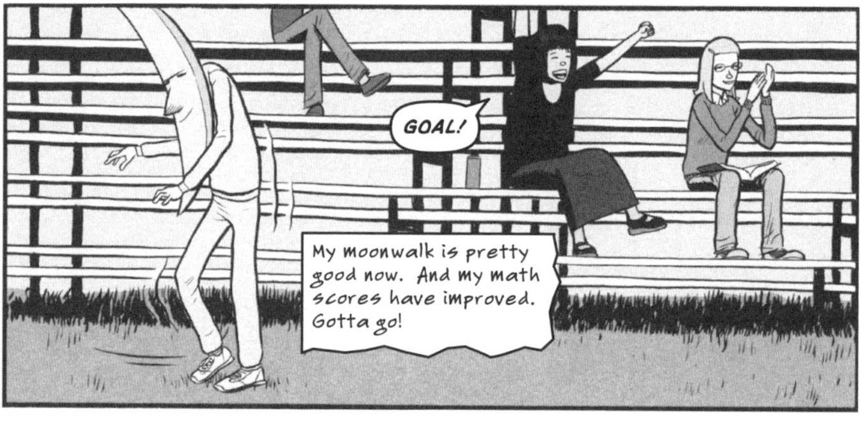
GOAL!
My moonwalk is pretty good now. And my math scores have improved. Gotta go!

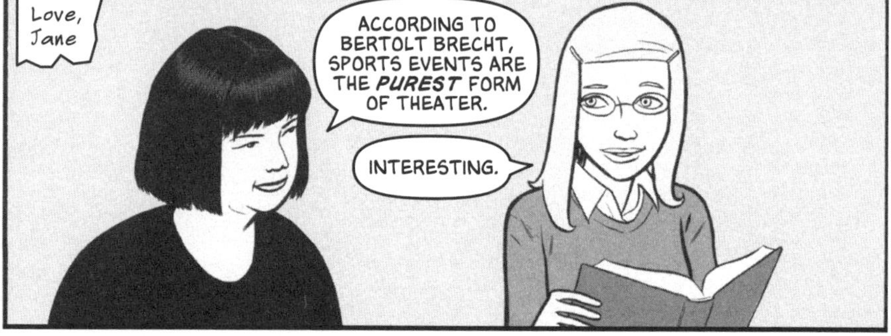
Love, Jane
ACCORDING TO BERTOLT BRECHT, SPORTS EVENTS ARE THE PUREST FORM OF THEATER.
INTERESTING.

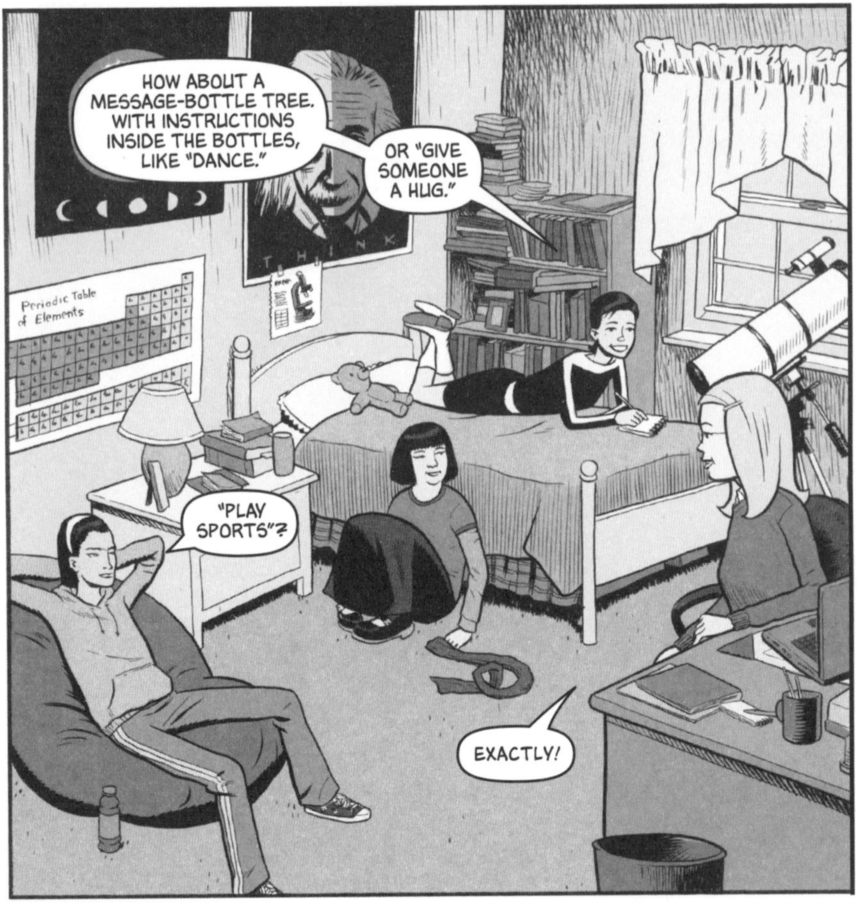
HOW ABOUT A MESSAGE-BOTTLE TREE. WITH INSTRUCTIONS INSIDE THE BOTTLES, LIKE "DANCE."
OR "GIVE SOMEONE A HUG."
Periodic Table of Elements
THINK
"PLAY SPORTS"?
EXACTLY!

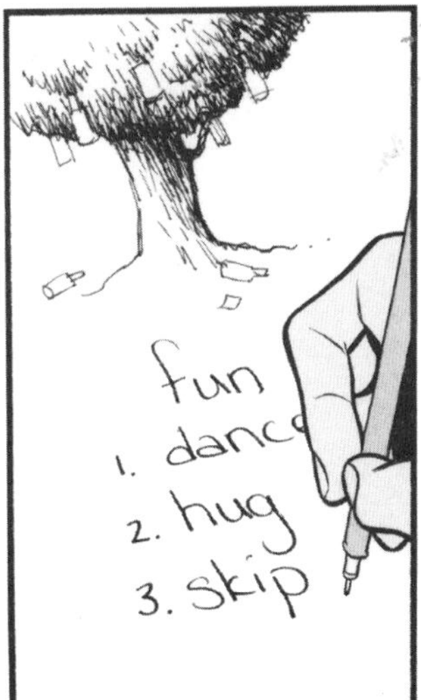
fun
1. dance
2. hug
3. skip

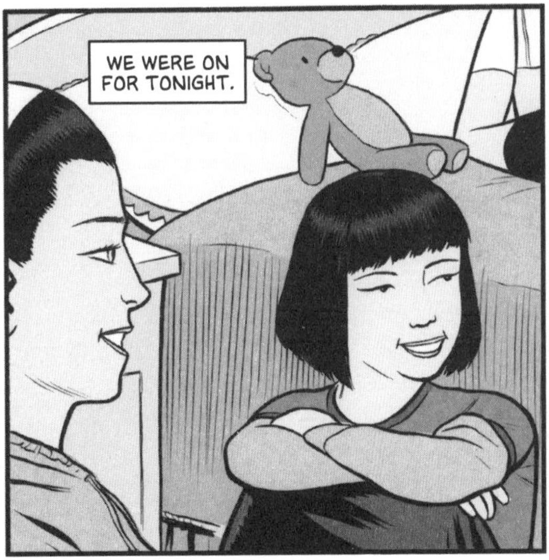
WE WERE ON FOR TONIGHT.

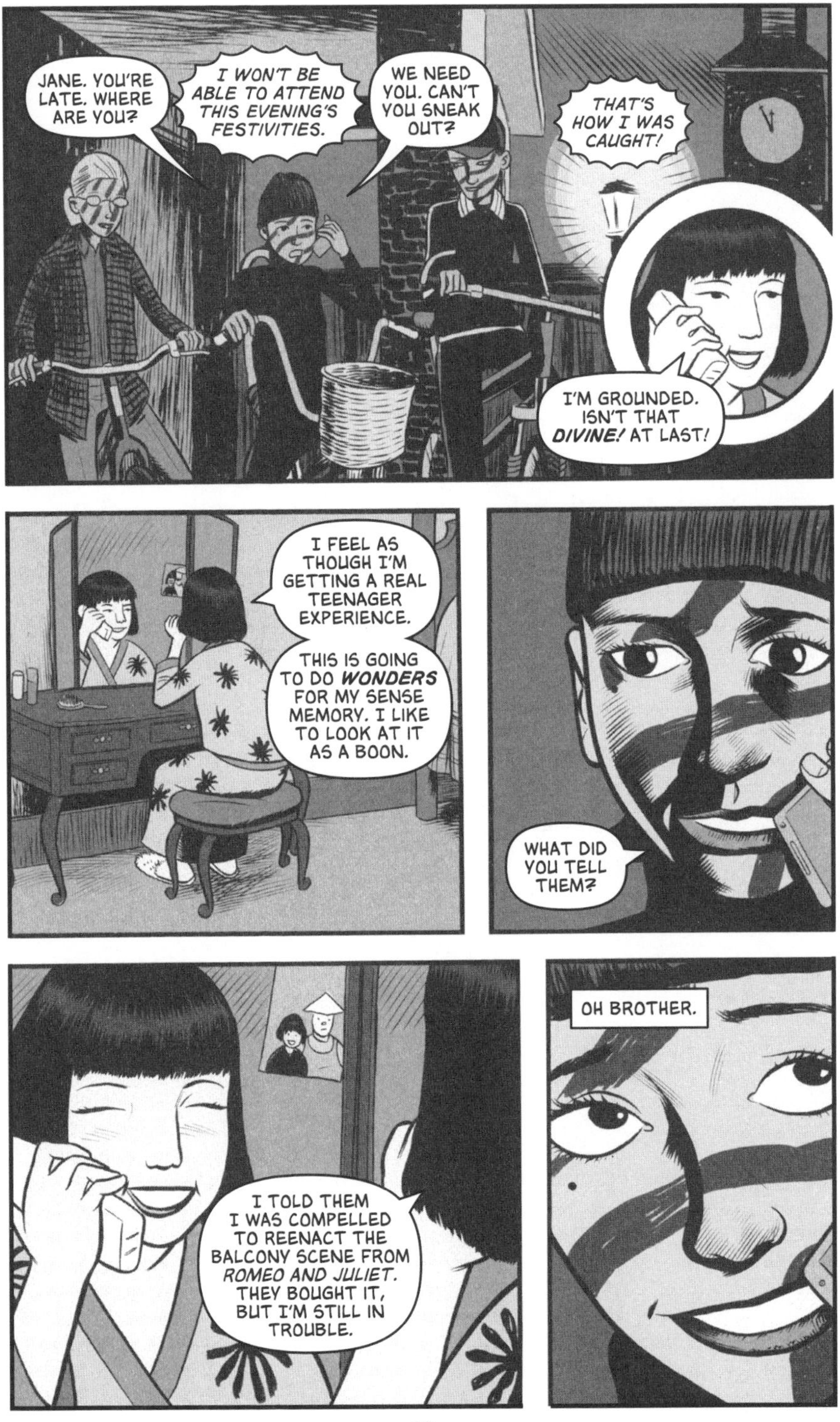
JANE. YOU'RE LATE. WHERE ARE YOU?
I WON'T BE ABLE TO ATTEND THIS EVENING'S FESTIVITIES.
WE NEED YOU. CAN'T YOU SNEAK OUT?
THAT'S HOW I WAS CAUGHT!
I'M GROUNDED. ISN'T THAT DIVINE! AT LAST!
I FEEL AS THOUGH I'M GETTING A REAL TEENAGER EXPERIENCE.
THIS IS GOING TO DO WONDERS FOR MY SENSE MEMORY. I LIKE TO LOOK AT IT AS A BOON.
WHAT DID YOU TELL THEM?
I TOLD THEM I WAS COMPELLED TO REENACT THE BALCONY SCENE FROM ROMEO AND JULIET. THEY BOUGHT IT, BUT I'M STILL IN TROUBLE.
OH BROTHER.

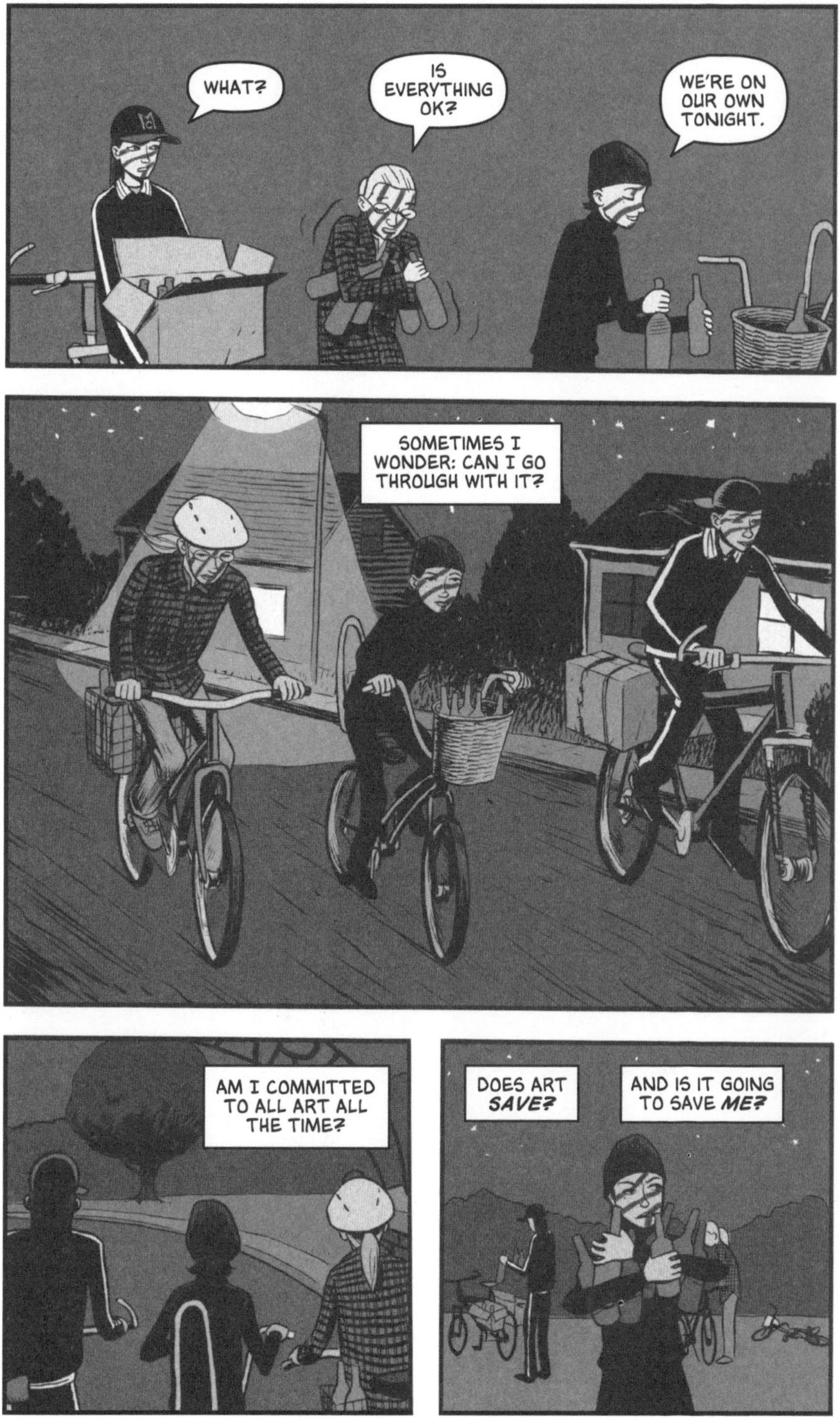
WHAT?
IS EVERYTHING OK?
WE'RE ON OUR OWN TONIGHT.
SOMETIMES I WONDER: CAN I GO THROUGH WITH IT?
AM I COMMITTED TO ALL ART ALL THE TIME?
DOES ART *SAVE?*
AND IS IT GOING TO SAVE *ME?*

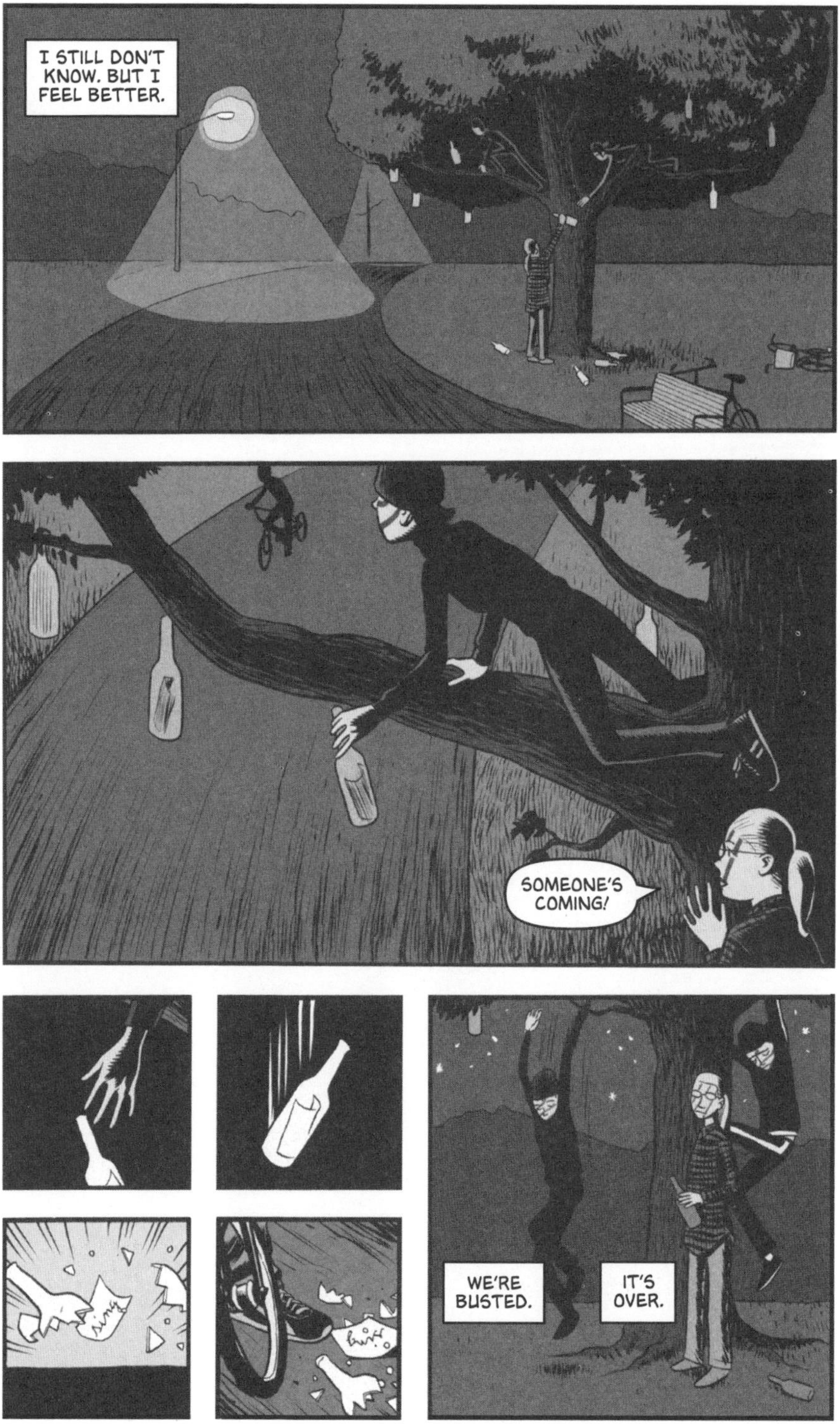
I STILL DON'T KNOW. BUT I FEEL BETTER.
SOMEONE'S COMING!
WE'RE BUSTED.
IT'S OVER.

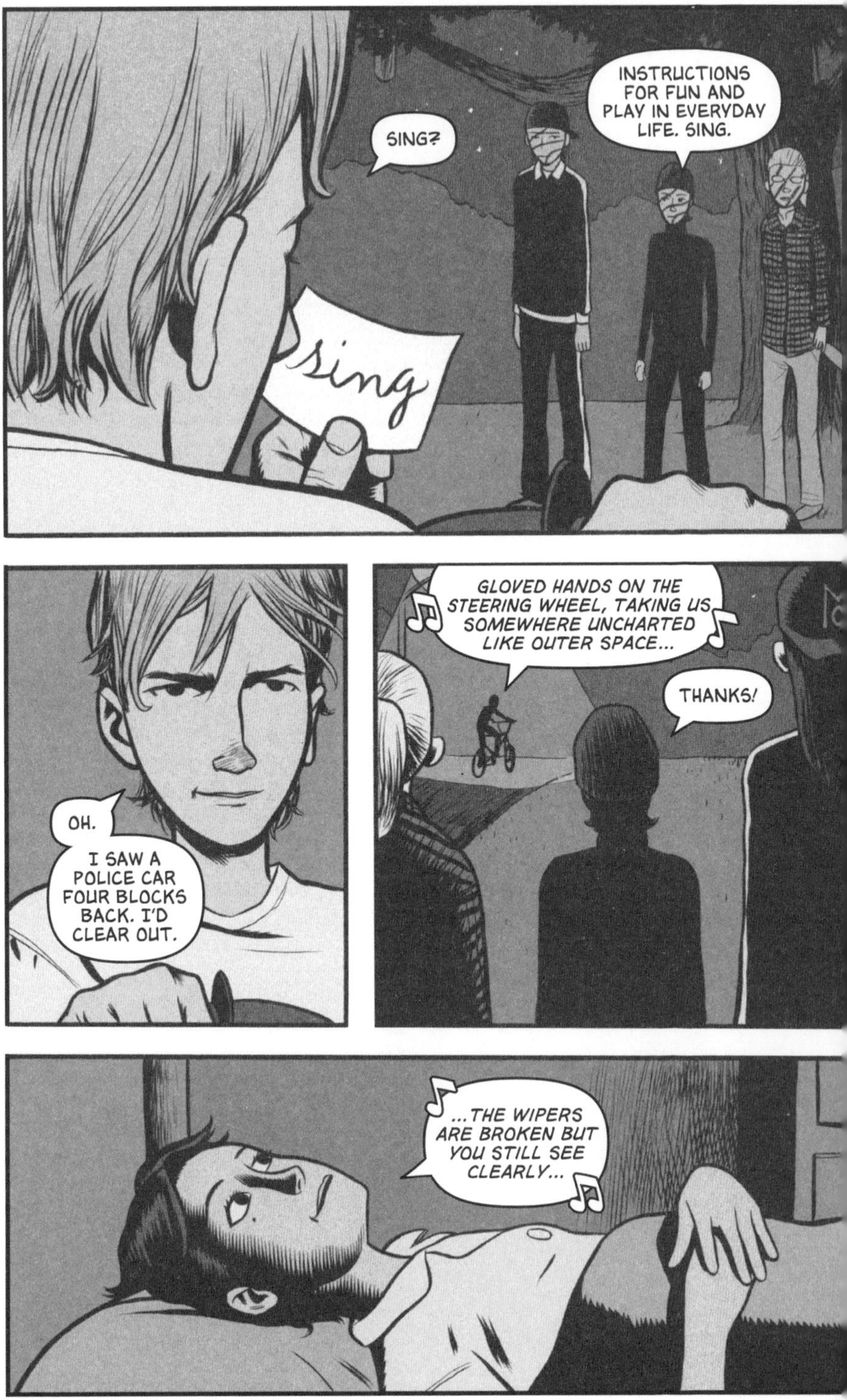
sing
SING?
INSTRUCTIONS FOR FUN AND PLAY IN EVERYDAY LIFE. SING.
OH.
I SAW A POLICE CAR FOUR BLOCKS BACK. I'D CLEAR OUT.
GLOVED HANDS ON THE STEERING WHEEL, TAKING US SOMEWHERE UNCHARTED LIKE OUTER SPACE...
THANKS!
...THE WIPERS ARE BROKEN BUT YOU STILL SEE CLEARLY...

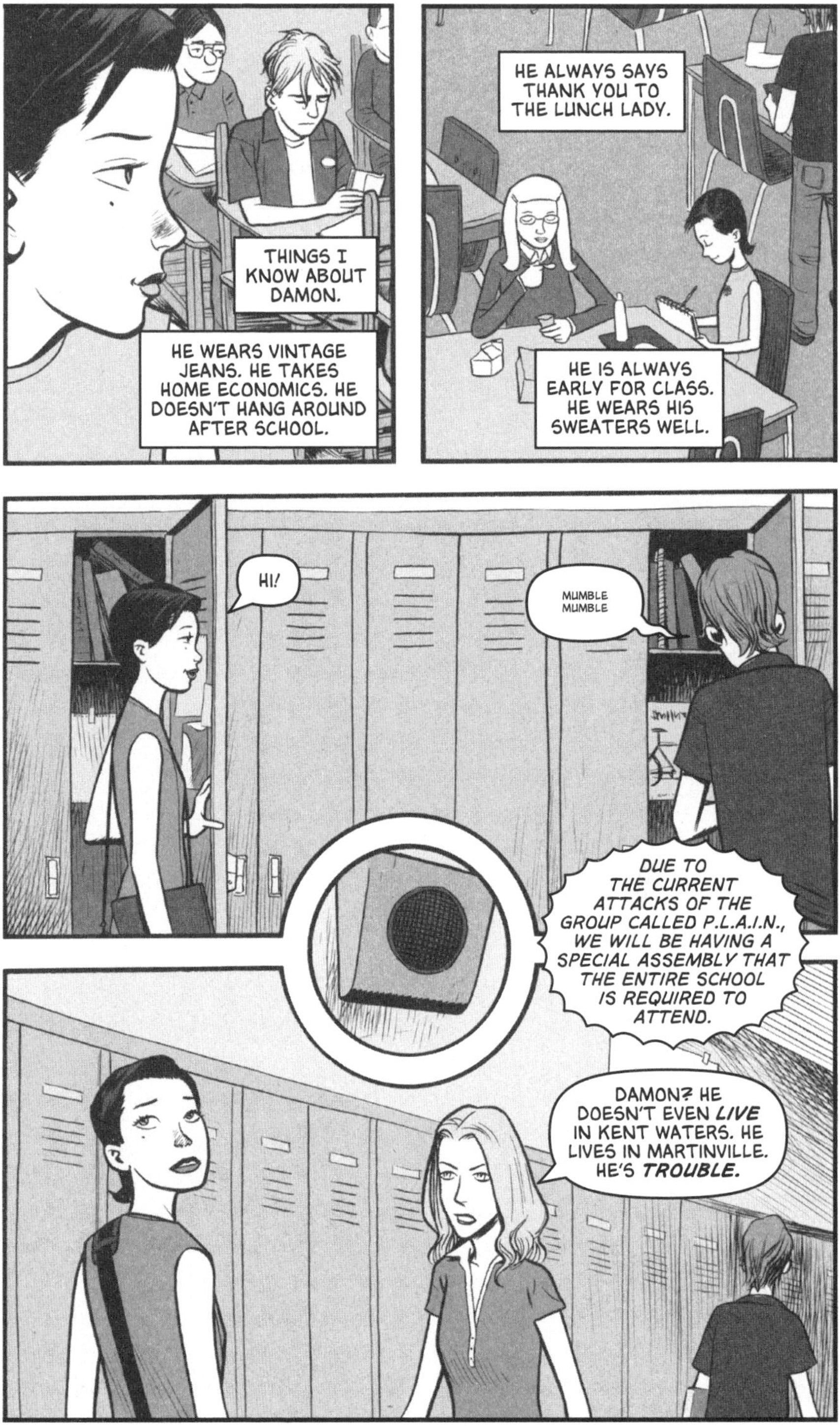
THINGS I KNOW ABOUT DAMON.
HE WEARS VINTAGE JEANS. HE TAKES HOME ECONOMICS. HE DOESN'T HANG AROUND AFTER SCHOOL.
HE ALWAYS SAYS THANK YOU TO THE LUNCH LADY.
HE IS ALWAYS EARLY FOR CLASS. HE WEARS HIS SWEATERS WELL.
HI!
MUMBLE MUMBLE
DUE TO THE CURRENT ATTACKS OF THE GROUP CALLED P.L.A.I.N., WE WILL BE HAVING A SPECIAL ASSEMBLY THAT THE ENTIRE SCHOOL IS REQUIRED TO ATTEND.
DAMON? HE DOESN'T EVEN *LIVE* IN KENT WATERS. HE LIVES IN MARTINVILLE. HE'S ***TROUBLE.***

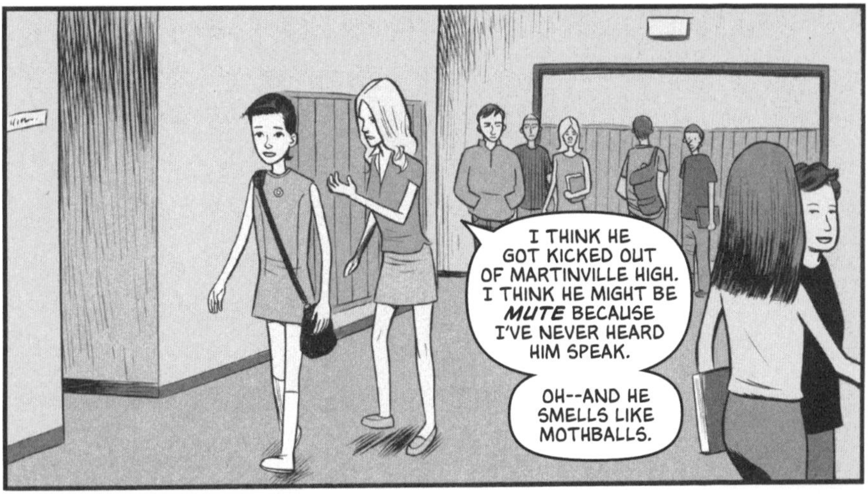
I THINK HE GOT KICKED OUT OF MARTINVILLE HIGH. I THINK HE MIGHT BE ***MUTE*** BECAUSE I'VE NEVER HEARD HIM SPEAK.
OH--AND HE SMELLS LIKE MOTHBALLS.

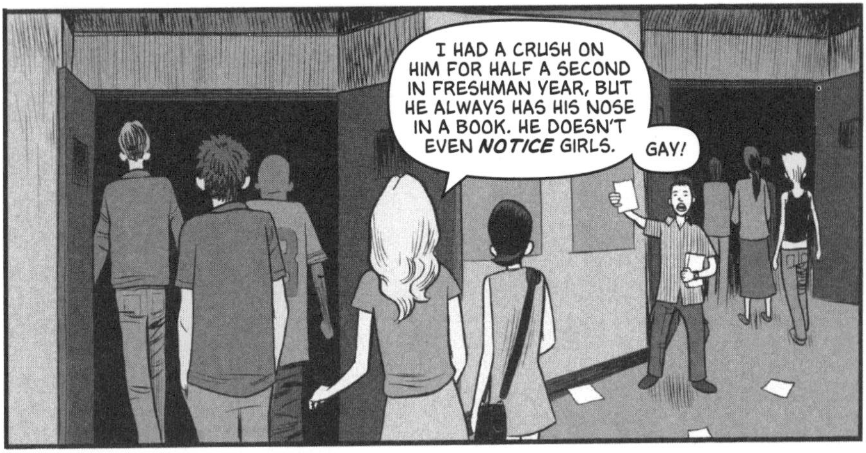
I HAD A CRUSH ON HIM FOR HALF A SECOND IN FRESHMAN YEAR, BUT HE ALWAYS HAS HIS NOSE IN A BOOK. HE DOESN'T EVEN ***NOTICE*** GIRLS.
GAY!

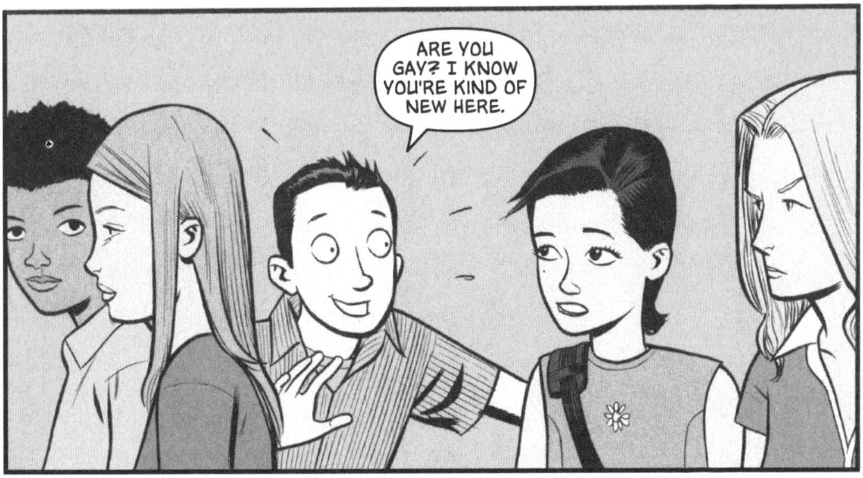
ARE YOU GAY? I KNOW YOU'RE KIND OF NEW HERE.

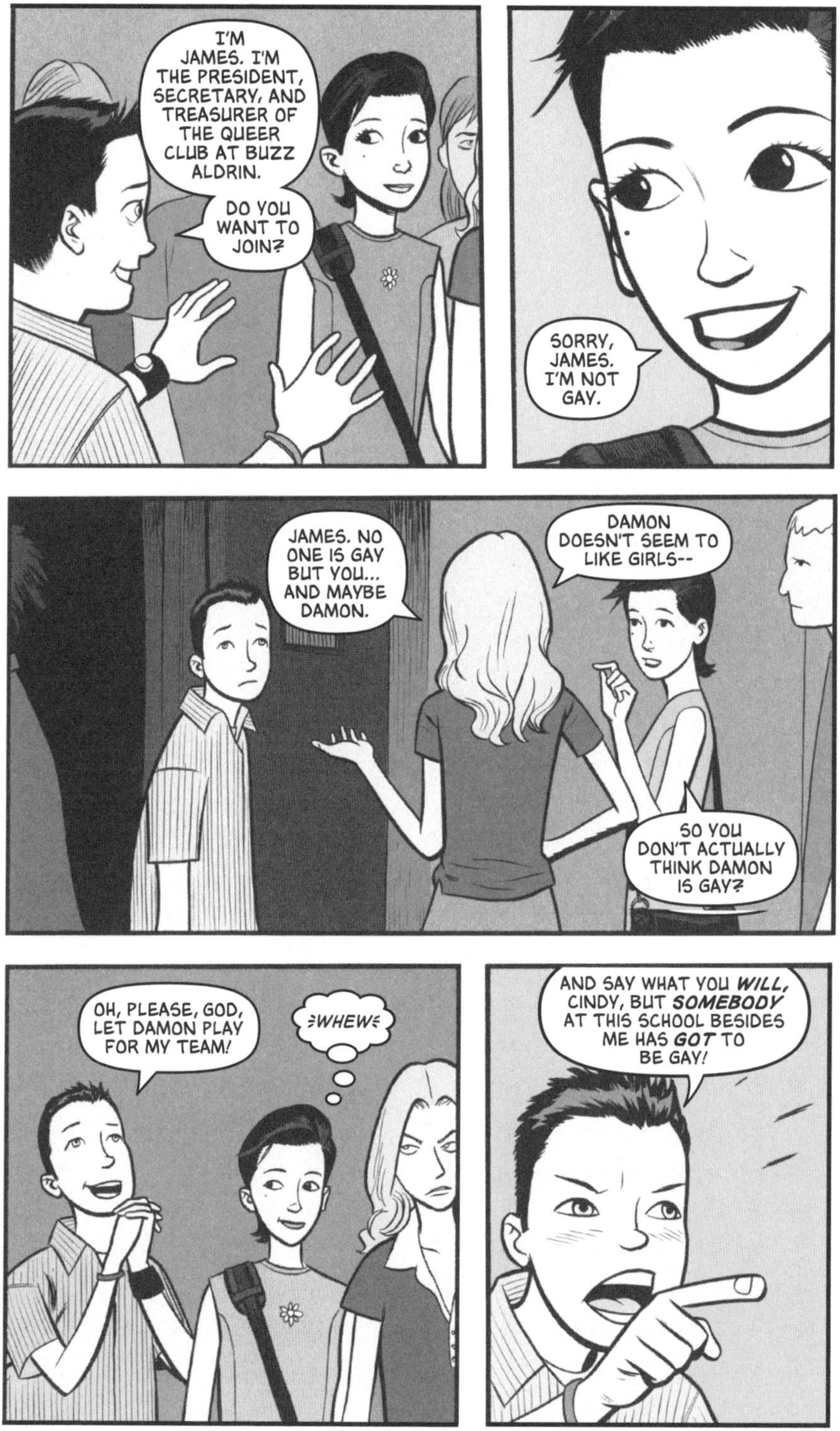
I'M JAMES. I'M THE PRESIDENT, SECRETARY, AND TREASURER OF THE QUEER CLUB AT BUZZ ALDRIN.
DO YOU WANT TO JOIN?
SORRY, JAMES. I'M NOT GAY.
JAMES. NO ONE IS GAY BUT YOU... AND MAYBE DAMON.
DAMON DOESN'T SEEM TO LIKE GIRLS--
SO YOU DON'T ACTUALLY THINK DAMON IS GAY?
OH, PLEASE, GOD, LET DAMON PLAY FOR MY TEAM!
WHEW
AND SAY WHAT YOU *WILL*, CINDY, BUT *SOMEBODY* AT THIS SCHOOL BESIDES ME HAS *GOT* TO BE GAY!

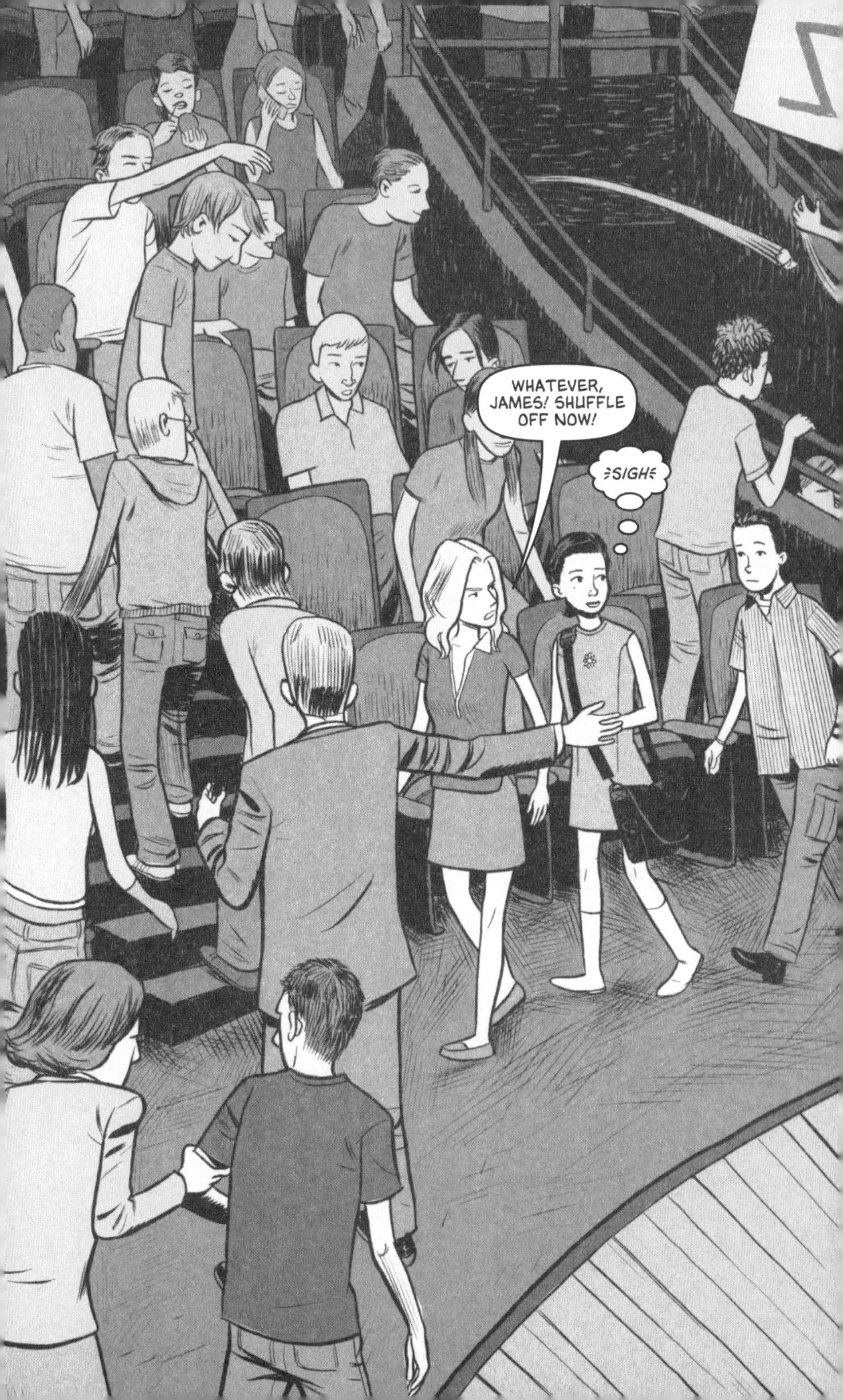
WHATEVER, JAMES! SHUFFLE OFF NOW!
SIGH

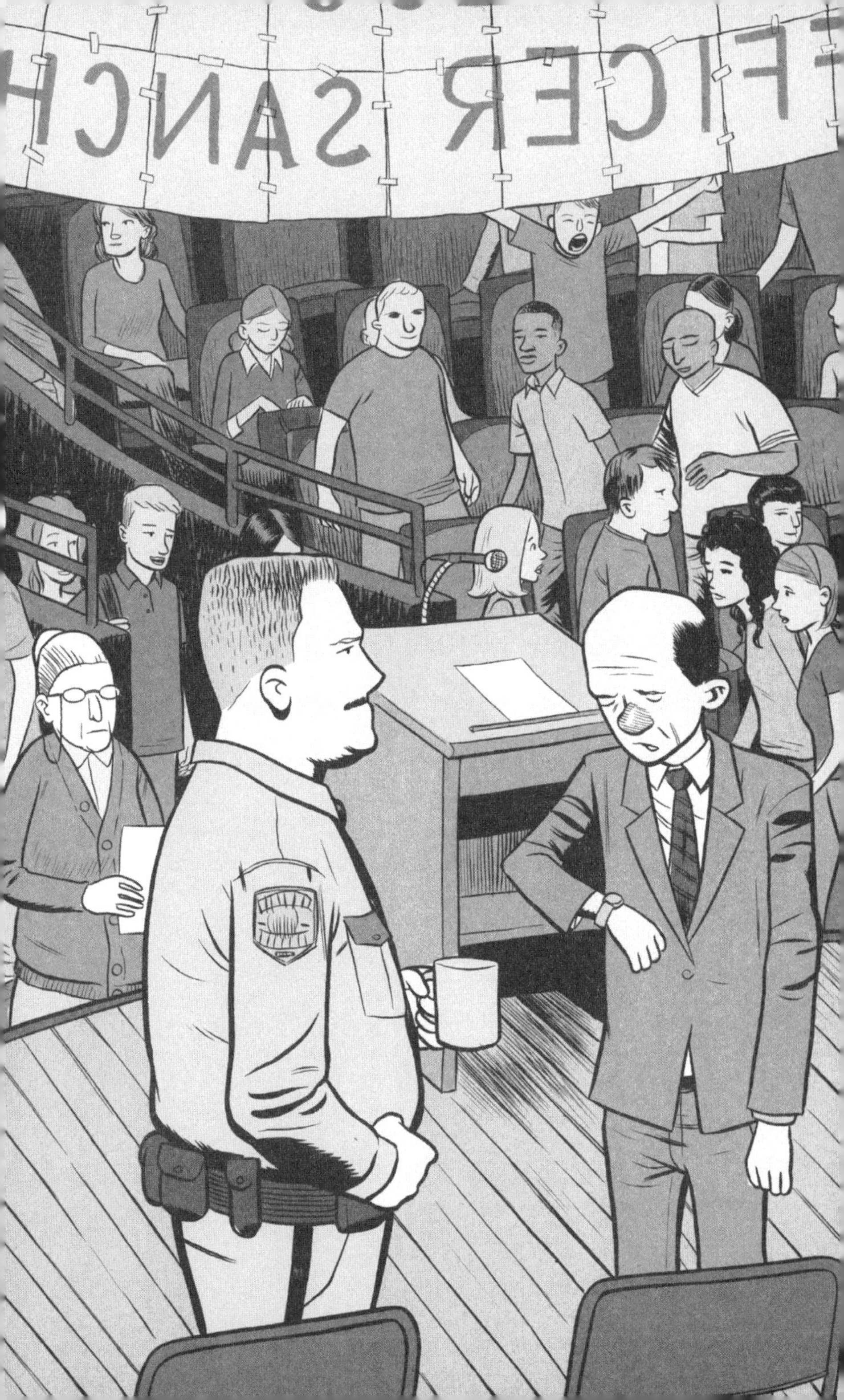

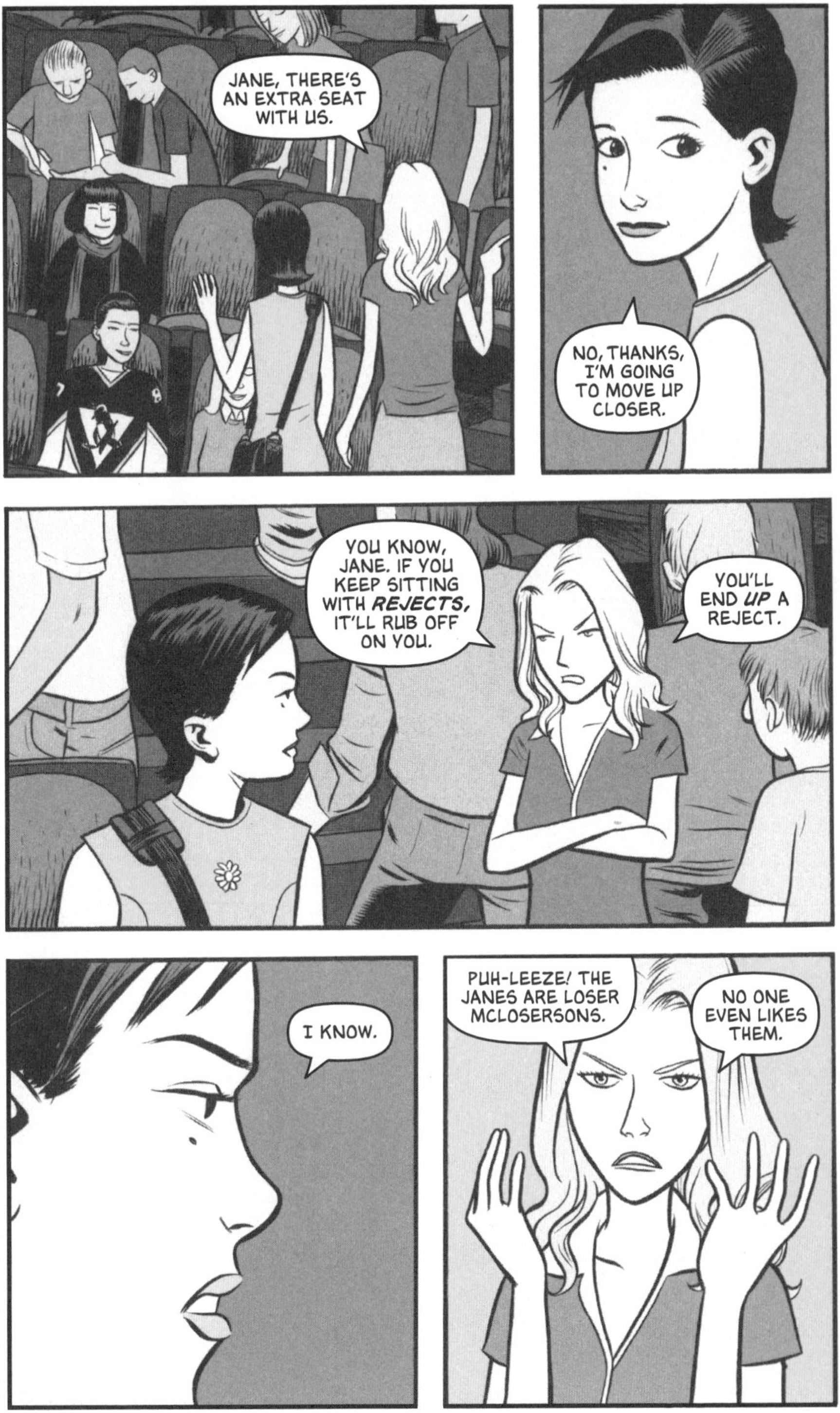
JANE, THERE'S AN EXTRA SEAT WITH US.
NO, THANKS, I'M GOING TO MOVE UP CLOSER.
YOU KNOW, JANE. IF YOU KEEP SITTING WITH *REJECTS,* IT'LL RUB OFF ON YOU.
YOU'LL END *UP* A REJECT.
I KNOW.
PUH-LEEZE! THE JANES ARE LOSER MCLOSERSONS.
NO ONE EVEN LIKES THEM.

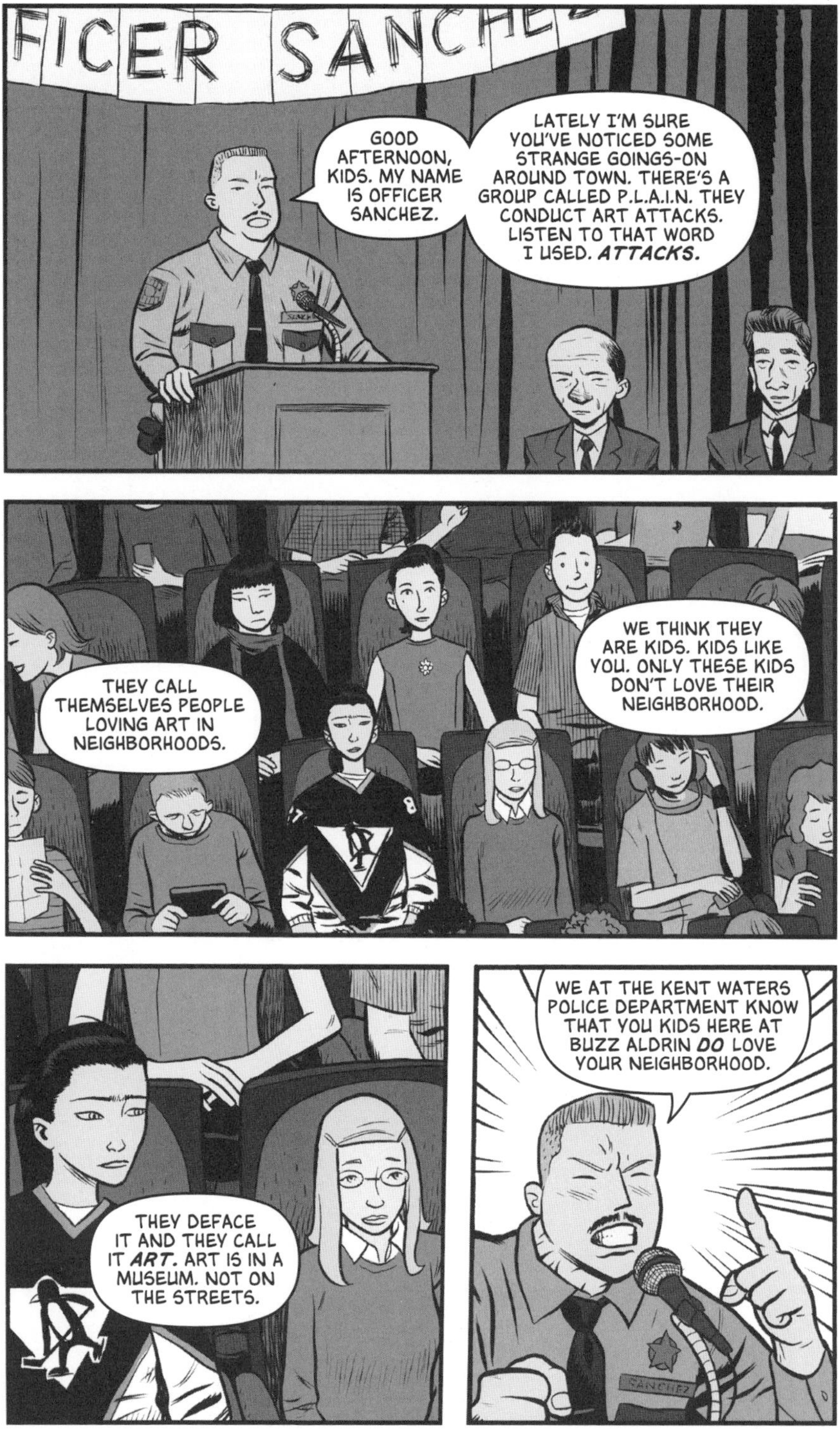
FICER SANCHE
GOOD AFTERNOON, KIDS. MY NAME IS OFFICER SANCHEZ.
LATELY I'M SURE YOU'VE NOTICED SOME STRANGE GOINGS-ON AROUND TOWN. THERE'S A GROUP CALLED P.L.A.I.N. THEY CONDUCT ART ATTACKS. LISTEN TO THAT WORD I USED. *ATTACKS.*
THEY CALL THEMSELVES PEOPLE LOVING ART IN NEIGHBORHOODS.
WE THINK THEY ARE KIDS. KIDS LIKE YOU. ONLY THESE KIDS DON'T LOVE THEIR NEIGHBORHOOD.
THEY DEFACE IT AND THEY CALL IT *ART.* ART IS IN A MUSEUM. NOT ON THE STREETS.
WE AT THE KENT WATERS POLICE DEPARTMENT KNOW THAT YOU KIDS HERE AT BUZZ ALDRIN *DO* LOVE YOUR NEIGHBORHOOD.
SANCHEZ

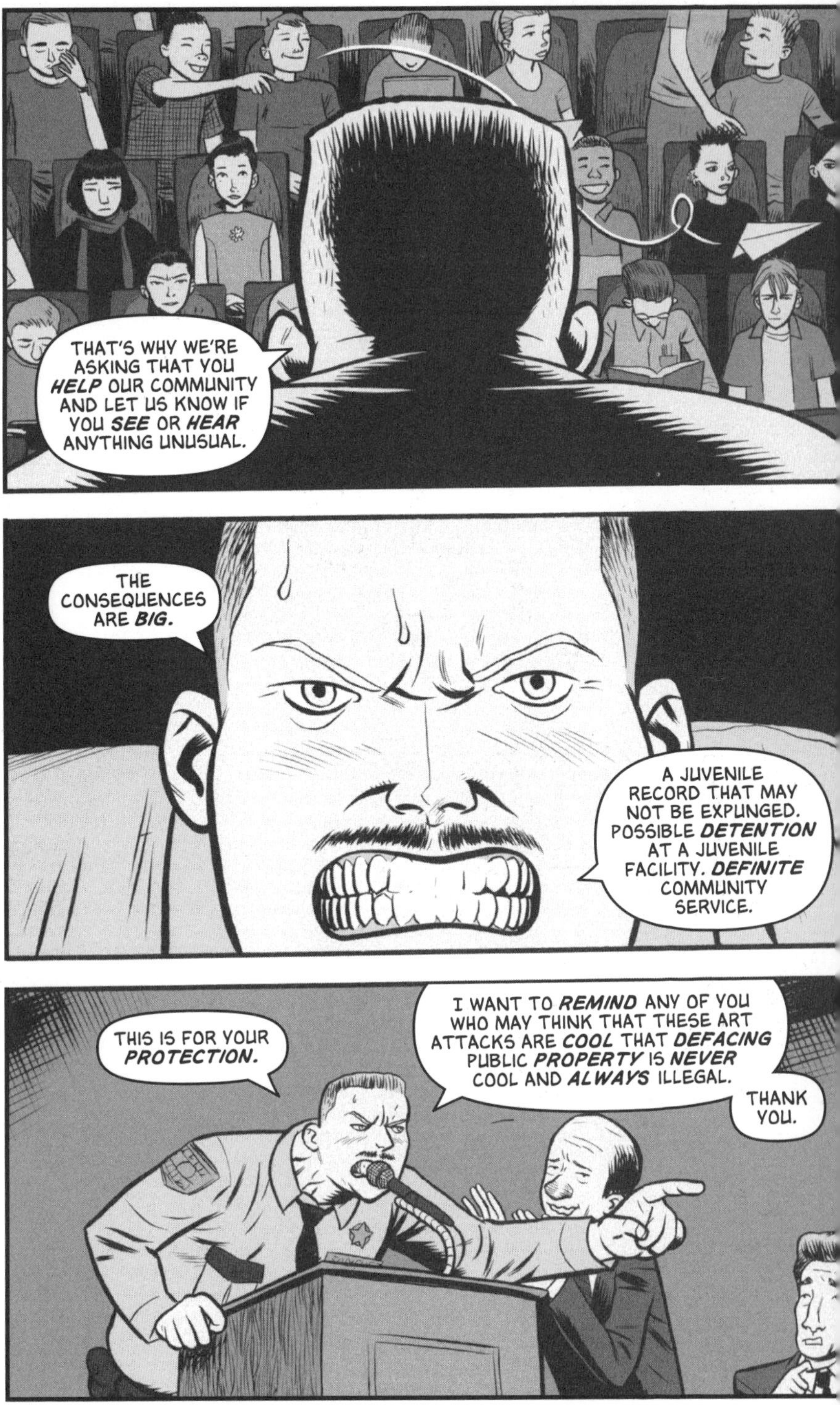
THAT'S WHY WE'RE ASKING THAT YOU *HELP* OUR COMMUNITY AND LET US KNOW IF YOU *SEE* OR *HEAR* ANYTHING UNUSUAL.
THE CONSEQUENCES ARE *BIG*.
A JUVENILE RECORD THAT MAY NOT BE EXPUNGED. POSSIBLE *DETENTION* AT A JUVENILE FACILITY. *DEFINITE* COMMUNITY SERVICE.
THIS IS FOR YOUR *PROTECTION*.
I WANT TO *REMIND* ANY OF YOU WHO MAY THINK THAT THESE ART ATTACKS ARE *COOL* THAT *DEFACING* PUBLIC *PROPERTY* IS *NEVER* COOL AND *ALWAYS* ILLEGAL.
THANK YOU.

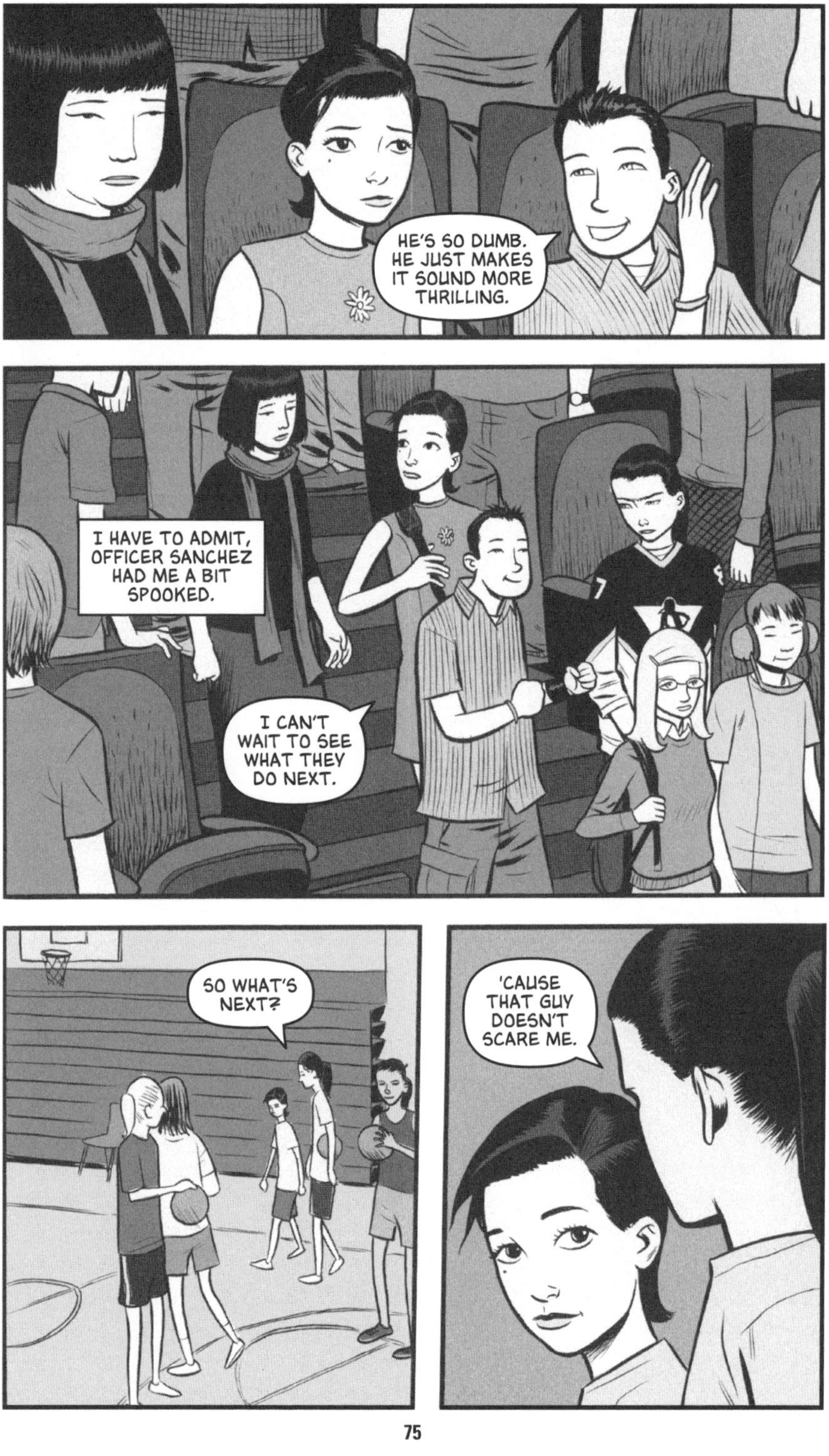
HE'S SO DUMB. HE JUST MAKES IT SOUND MORE THRILLING.
I HAVE TO ADMIT, OFFICER SANCHEZ HAD ME A BIT SPOOKED.
I CAN'T WAIT TO SEE WHAT THEY DO NEXT.
SO WHAT'S NEXT?
'CAUSE THAT GUY DOESN'T SCARE ME.

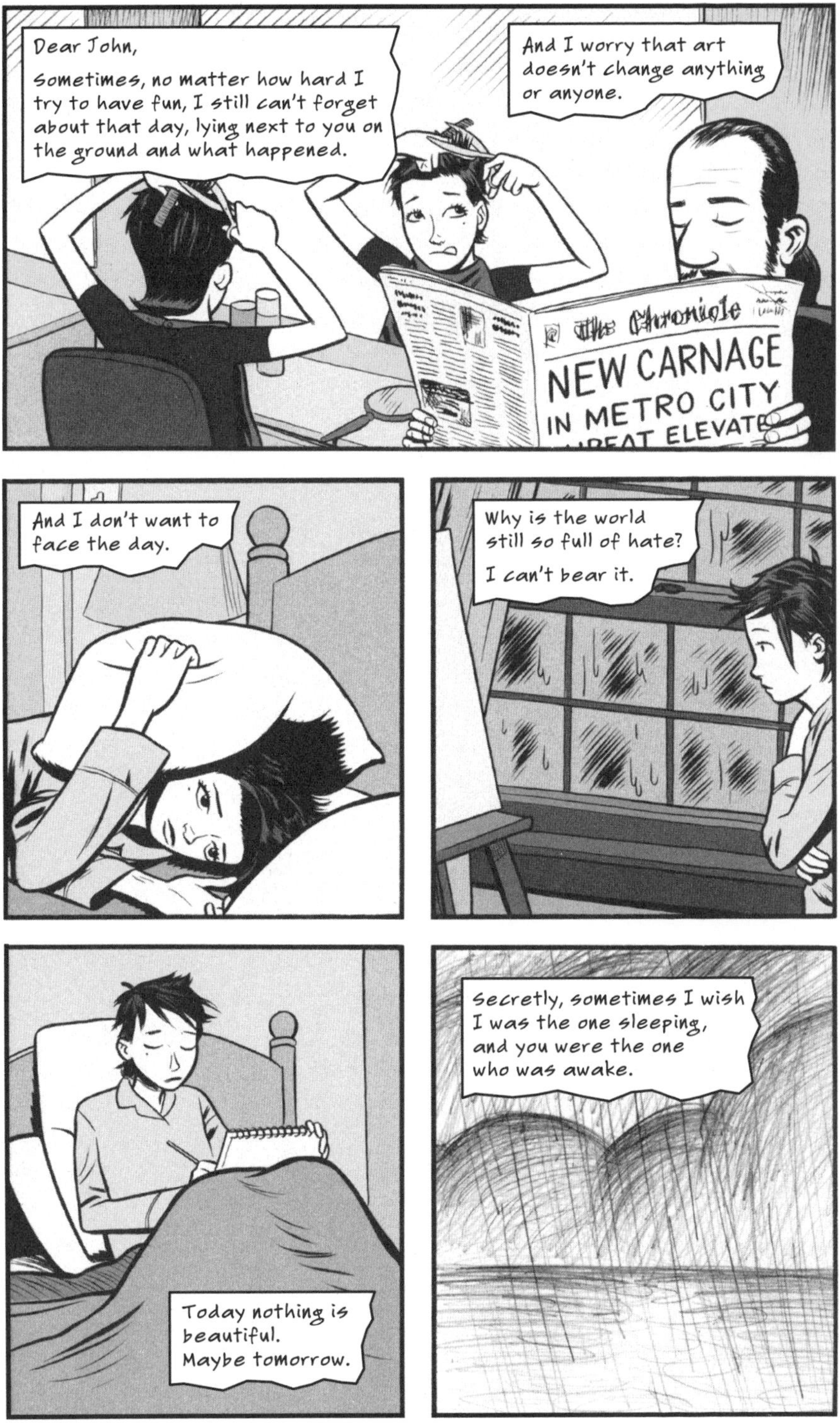

Dear John,
Sometimes, no matter how hard I try to have fun, I still can't forget about that day, lying next to you on the ground and what happened.
And I worry that art doesn't change anything or anyone.
The Chronicle
NEW CARNAGE IN METRO CITY
And I don't want to face the day.
Why is the world still so full of hate?
I can't bear it.
Today nothing is beautiful.
Maybe tomorrow.
Secretly, sometimes I wish I was the one sleeping, and you were the one who was awake.

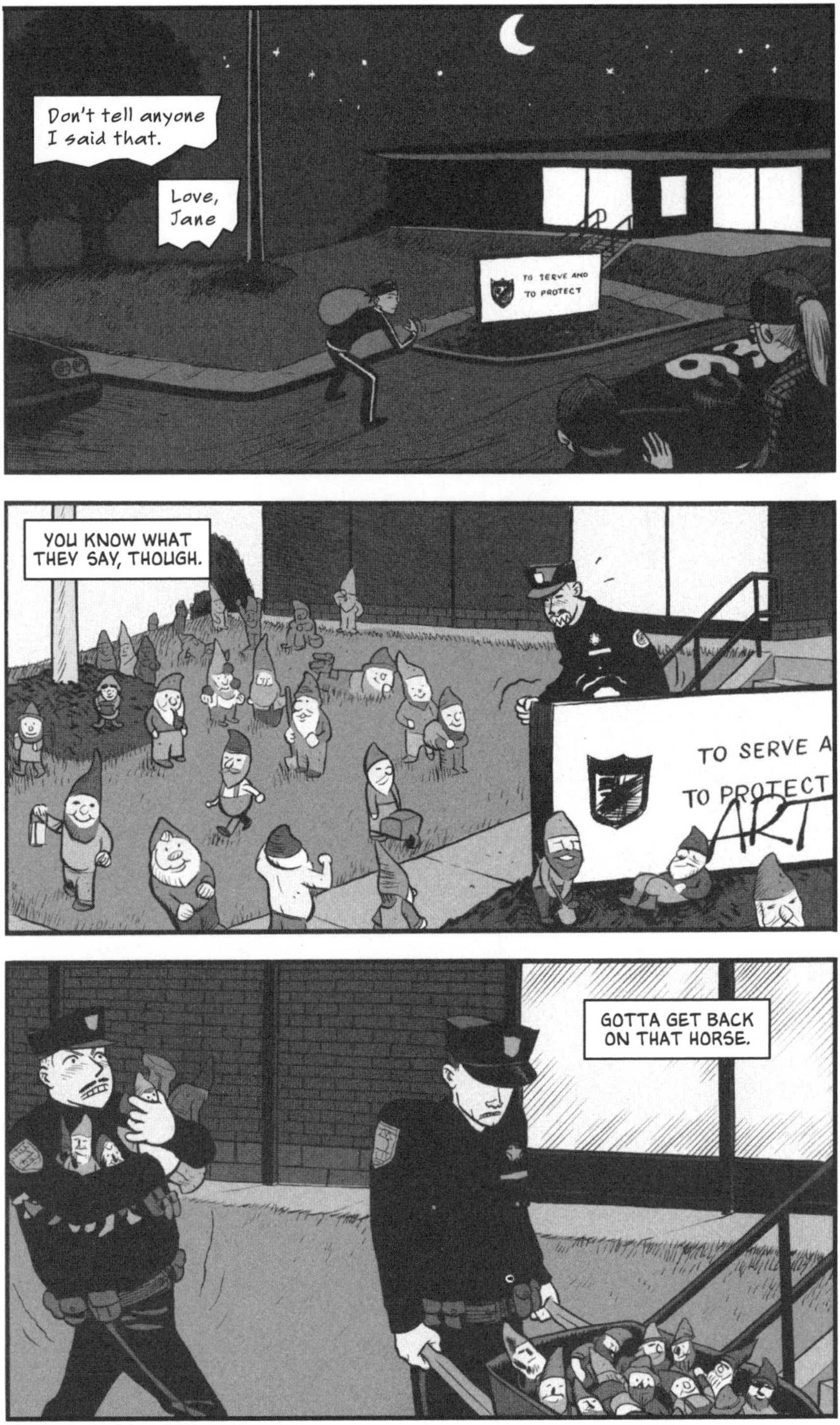
Don't tell anyone I said that.
Love, Jane
TO SERVE AND TO PROTECT
YOU KNOW WHAT THEY SAY, THOUGH.
TO PROTECT
ART
GOTTA GET BACK ON THAT HORSE.

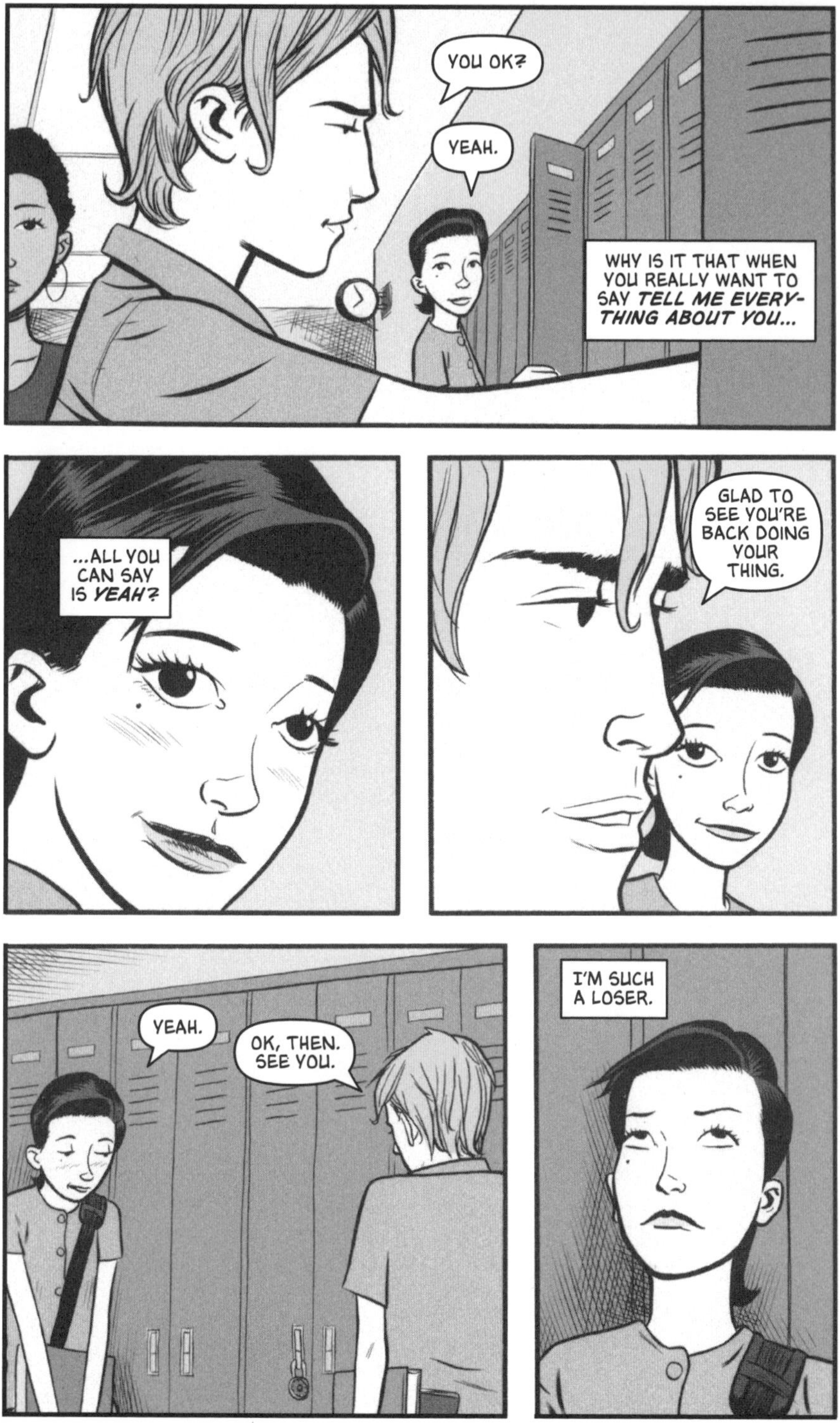
YOU OK?
YEAH.
WHY IS IT THAT WHEN YOU REALLY WANT TO SAY TELL ME EVERYTHING ABOUT YOU...
...ALL YOU CAN SAY IS YEAH?
GLAD TO SEE YOU'RE BACK DOING YOUR THING.
YEAH.
OK, THEN. SEE YOU.
I'M SUCH A LOSER.

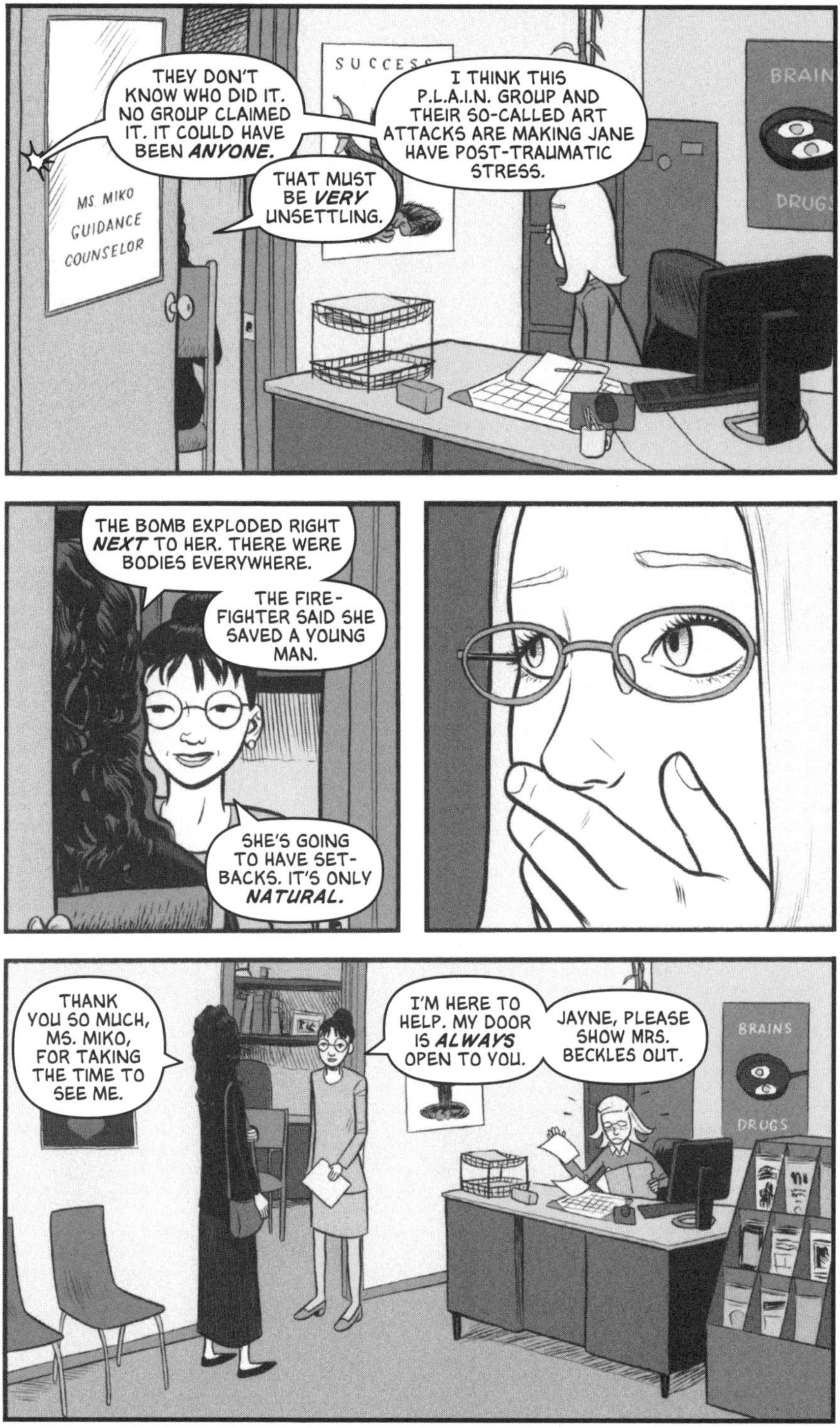
MS. MIKO
GUIDANCE
COUNSELOR
SUCCESS
BRAIN
DRUGS
THEY DON'T KNOW WHO DID IT. NO GROUP CLAIMED IT. IT COULD HAVE BEEN ANYONE.
I THINK THIS P.L.A.I.N. GROUP AND THEIR SO-CALLED ART ATTACKS ARE MAKING JANE HAVE POST-TRAUMATIC STRESS.
THAT MUST BE VERY UNSETTLING.
THE BOMB EXPLODED RIGHT NEXT TO HER. THERE WERE BODIES EVERYWHERE.
THE FIRE-FIGHTER SAID SHE SAVED A YOUNG MAN.
SHE'S GOING TO HAVE SET-BACKS. IT'S ONLY NATURAL.
THANK YOU SO MUCH, MS. MIKO, FOR TAKING THE TIME TO SEE ME.
I'M HERE TO HELP. MY DOOR IS ALWAYS OPEN TO YOU.
JAYNE, PLEASE SHOW MRS. BECKLES OUT.
BRAINS
DRUGS

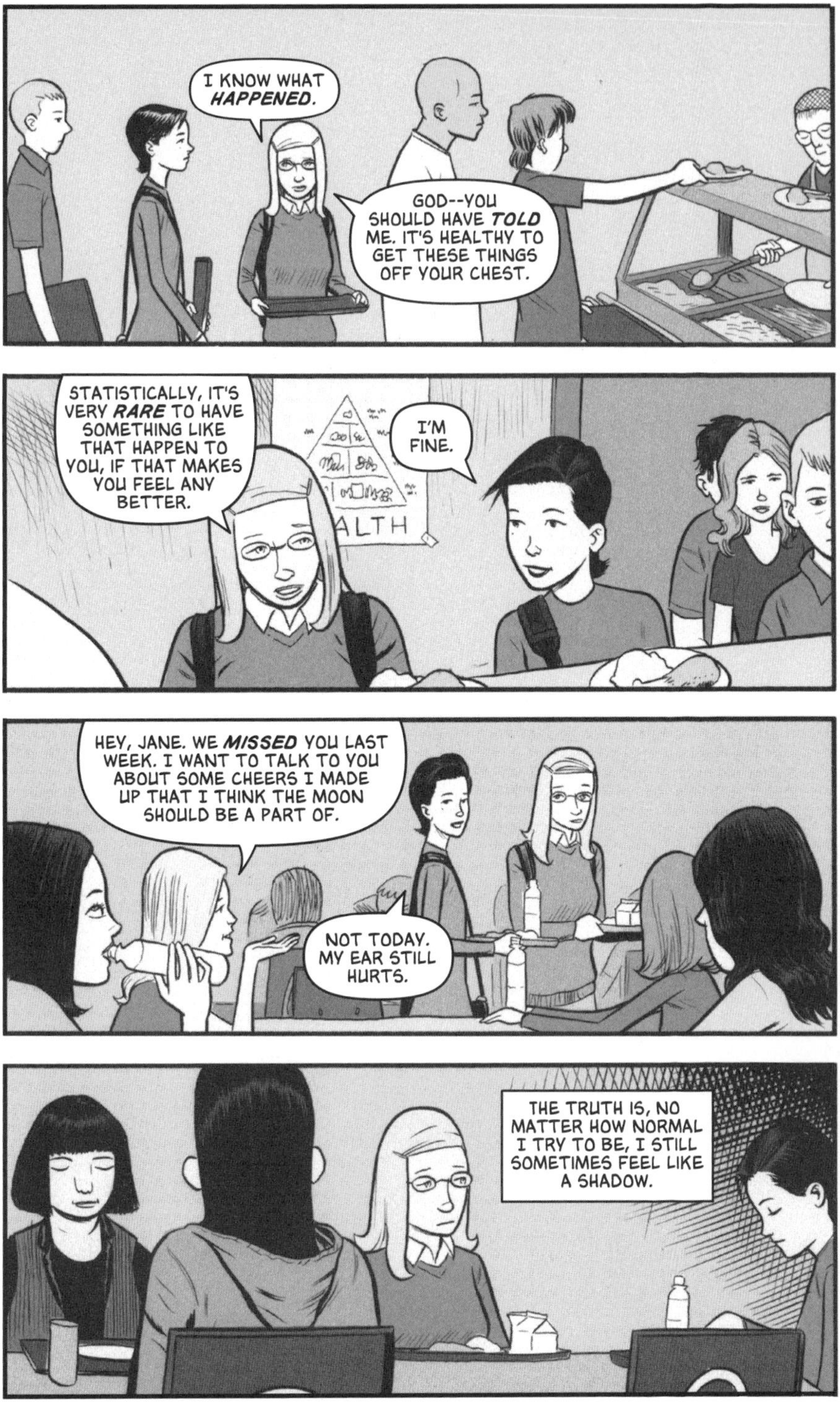
I KNOW WHAT *HAPPENED*.
GOD--YOU SHOULD HAVE *TOLD* ME. IT'S HEALTHY TO GET THESE THINGS OFF YOUR CHEST.
STATISTICALLY, IT'S VERY *RARE* TO HAVE SOMETHING LIKE THAT HAPPEN TO YOU, IF THAT MAKES YOU FEEL ANY BETTER.
I'M FINE.
HEY, JANE. WE *MISSED* YOU LAST WEEK. I WANT TO TALK TO YOU ABOUT SOME CHEERS I MADE UP THAT I THINK THE MOON SHOULD BE A PART OF.
NOT TODAY. MY EAR STILL HURTS.
THE TRUTH IS, NO MATTER HOW NORMAL I TRY TO BE, I STILL SOMETIMES FEEL LIKE A SHADOW.

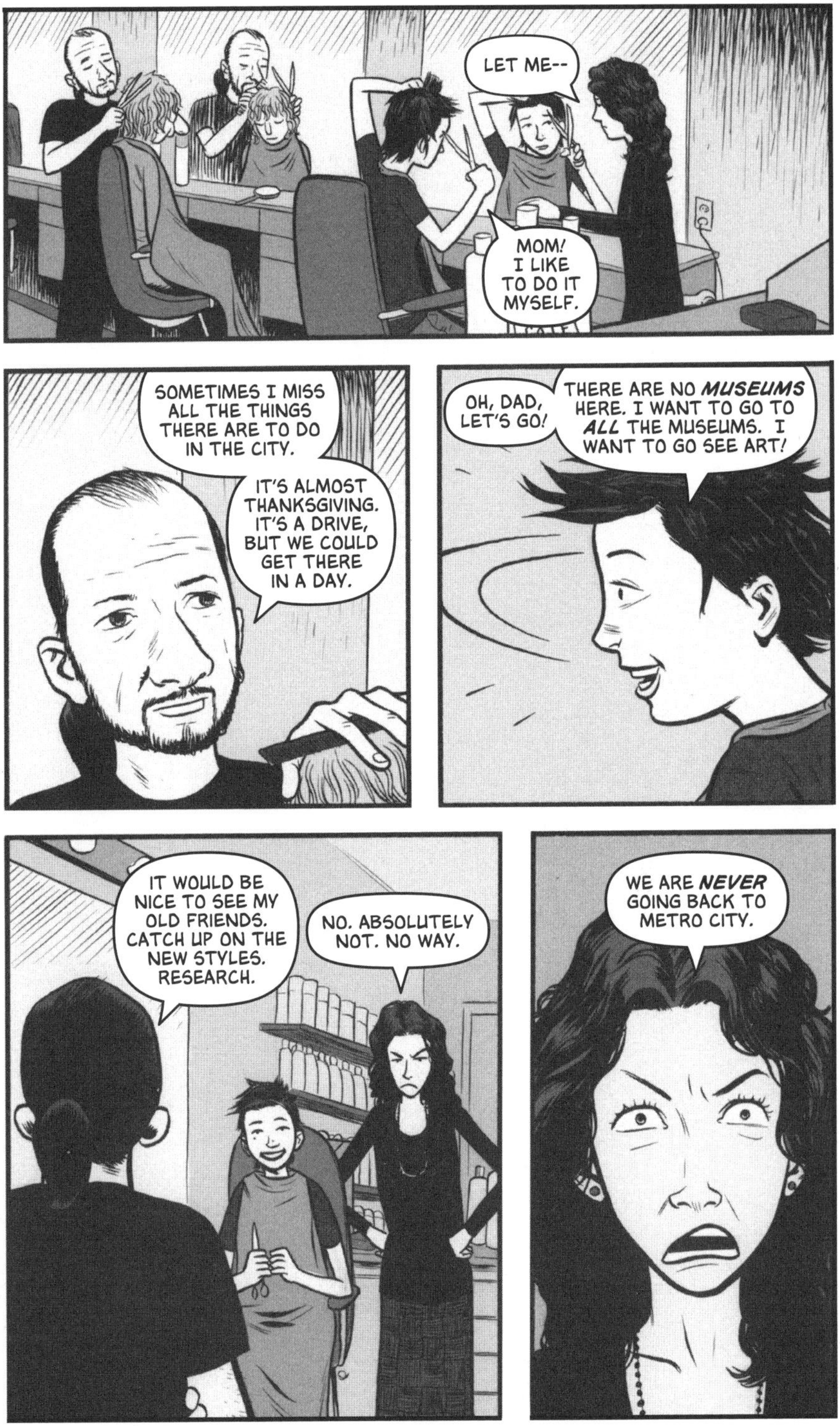
LET ME--
MOM! I LIKE TO DO IT MYSELF.
SOMETIMES I MISS ALL THE THINGS THERE ARE TO DO IN THE CITY.
IT'S ALMOST THANKSGIVING. IT'S A DRIVE, BUT WE COULD GET THERE IN A DAY.
OH, DAD, LET'S GO!
THERE ARE NO *MUSEUMS* HERE. I WANT TO GO TO *ALL* THE MUSEUMS. I WANT TO GO SEE ART!
IT WOULD BE NICE TO SEE MY OLD FRIENDS. CATCH UP ON THE NEW STYLES. RESEARCH.
NO. ABSOLUTELY NOT. NO WAY.
WE ARE *NEVER* GOING BACK TO METRO CITY.

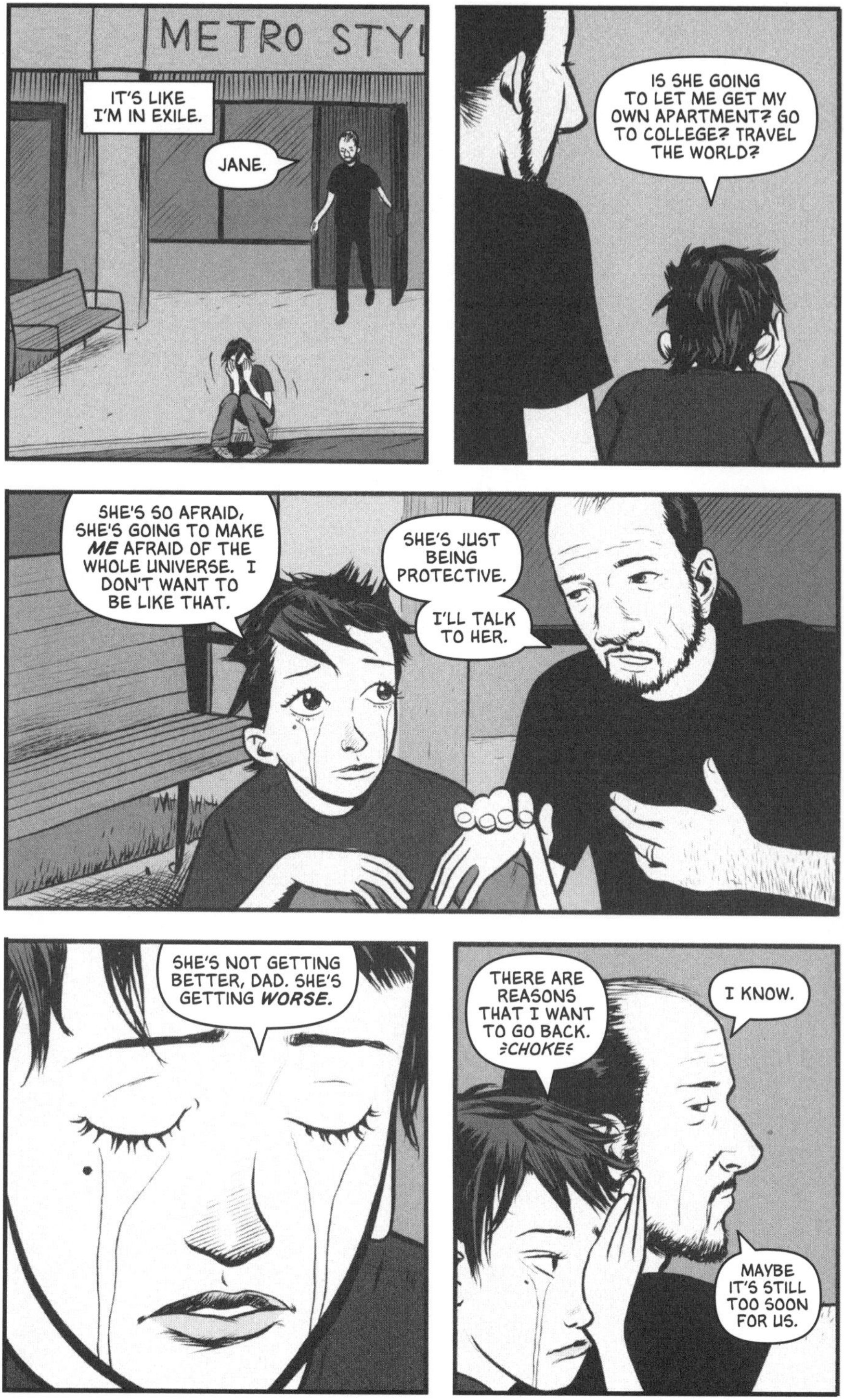
METRO STY
IT'S LIKE I'M IN EXILE.
JANE.
IS SHE GOING TO LET ME GET MY OWN APARTMENT? GO TO COLLEGE? TRAVEL THE WORLD?
SHE'S SO AFRAID, SHE'S GOING TO MAKE *ME* AFRAID OF THE WHOLE UNIVERSE. I DON'T WANT TO BE LIKE THAT.
SHE'S JUST BEING PROTECTIVE.
I'LL TALK TO HER.
SHE'S NOT GETTING BETTER, DAD. SHE'S GETTING *WORSE.*
THERE ARE REASONS THAT I WANT TO GO BACK. *CHOKE*
I KNOW.
MAYBE IT'S STILL TOO SOON FOR US.

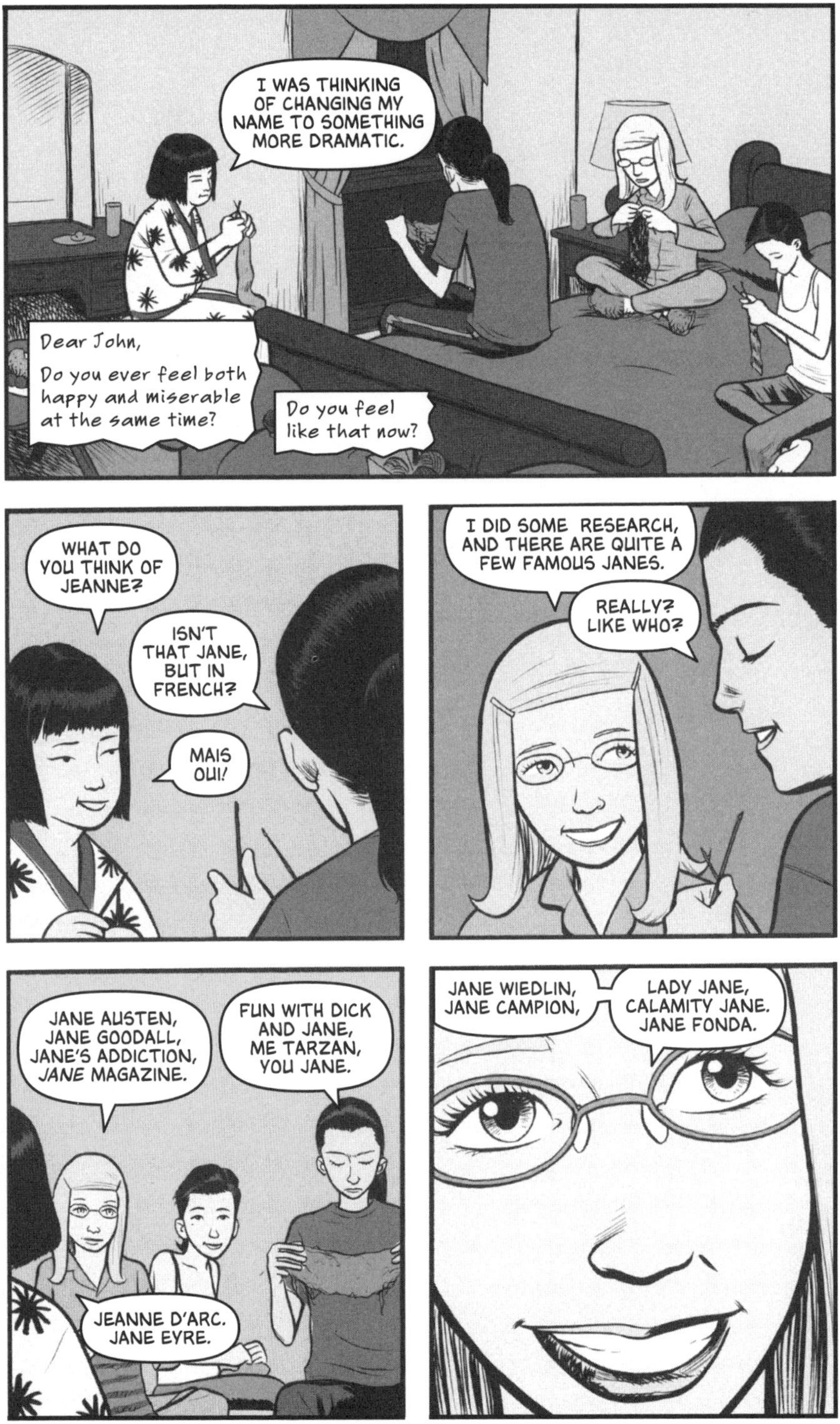
I WAS THINKING OF CHANGING MY NAME TO SOMETHING MORE DRAMATIC.
Dear John,
Do you ever feel both happy and miserable at the same time?
Do you feel like that now?
WHAT DO YOU THINK OF JEANNE?
ISN'T THAT JANE, BUT IN FRENCH?
MAIS OUI!
I DID SOME RESEARCH, AND THERE ARE QUITE A FEW FAMOUS JANES.
REALLY? LIKE WHO?
JANE AUSTEN, JANE GOODALL, JANE'S ADDICTION, *JANE* MAGAZINE.
FUN WITH DICK AND JANE, ME TARZAN, YOU JANE.
JEANNE D'ARC. JANE EYRE.
JANE WIEDLIN, JANE CAMPION,
LADY JANE, CALAMITY JANE. JANE FONDA.

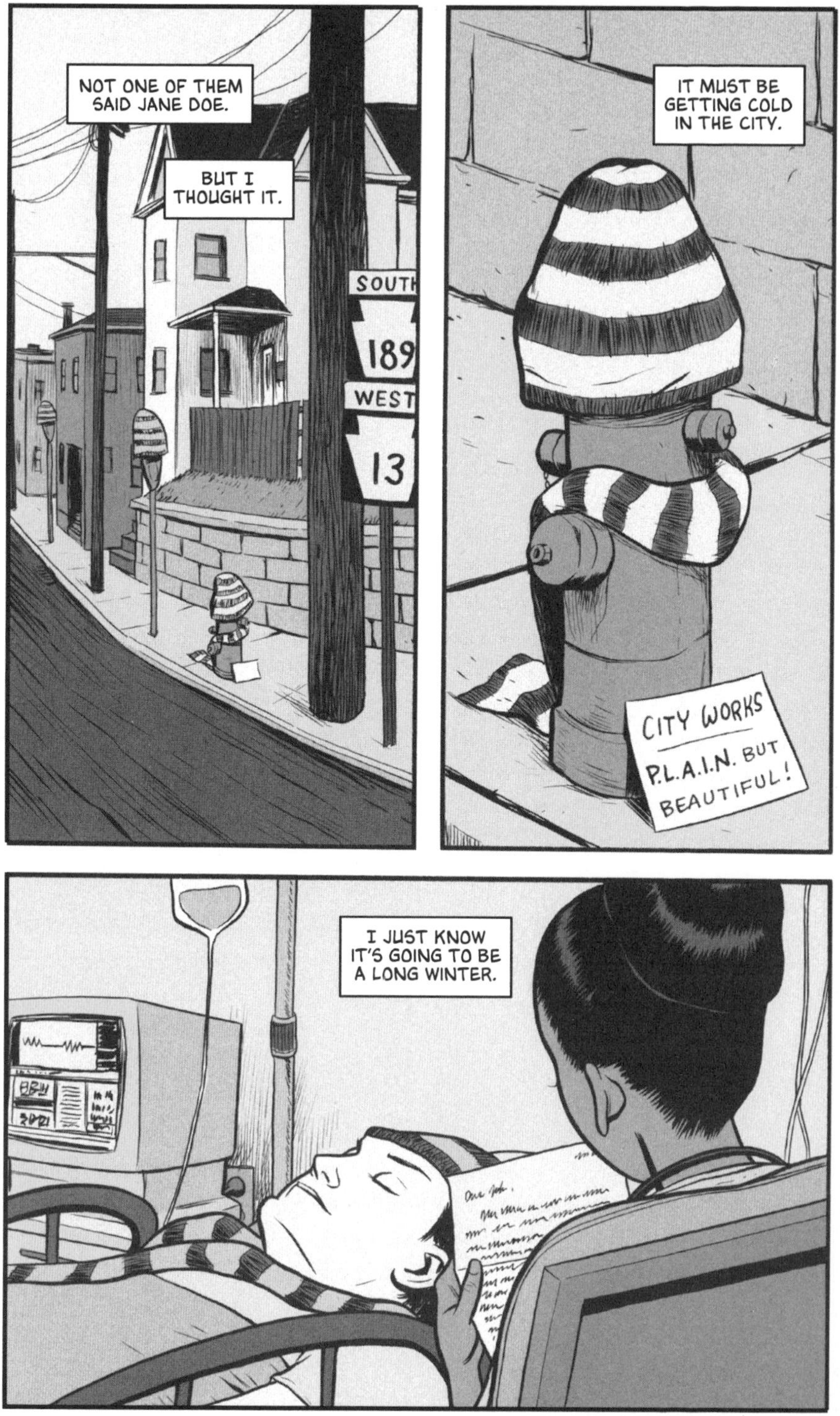
NOT ONE OF THEM SAID JANE DOE.
BUT I THOUGHT IT.
SOUTH
189
WEST
13
IT MUST BE GETTING COLD IN THE CITY.
CITY WORKS
P.L.A.I.N. BUT BEAUTIFUL!
I JUST KNOW IT'S GOING TO BE A LONG WINTER.

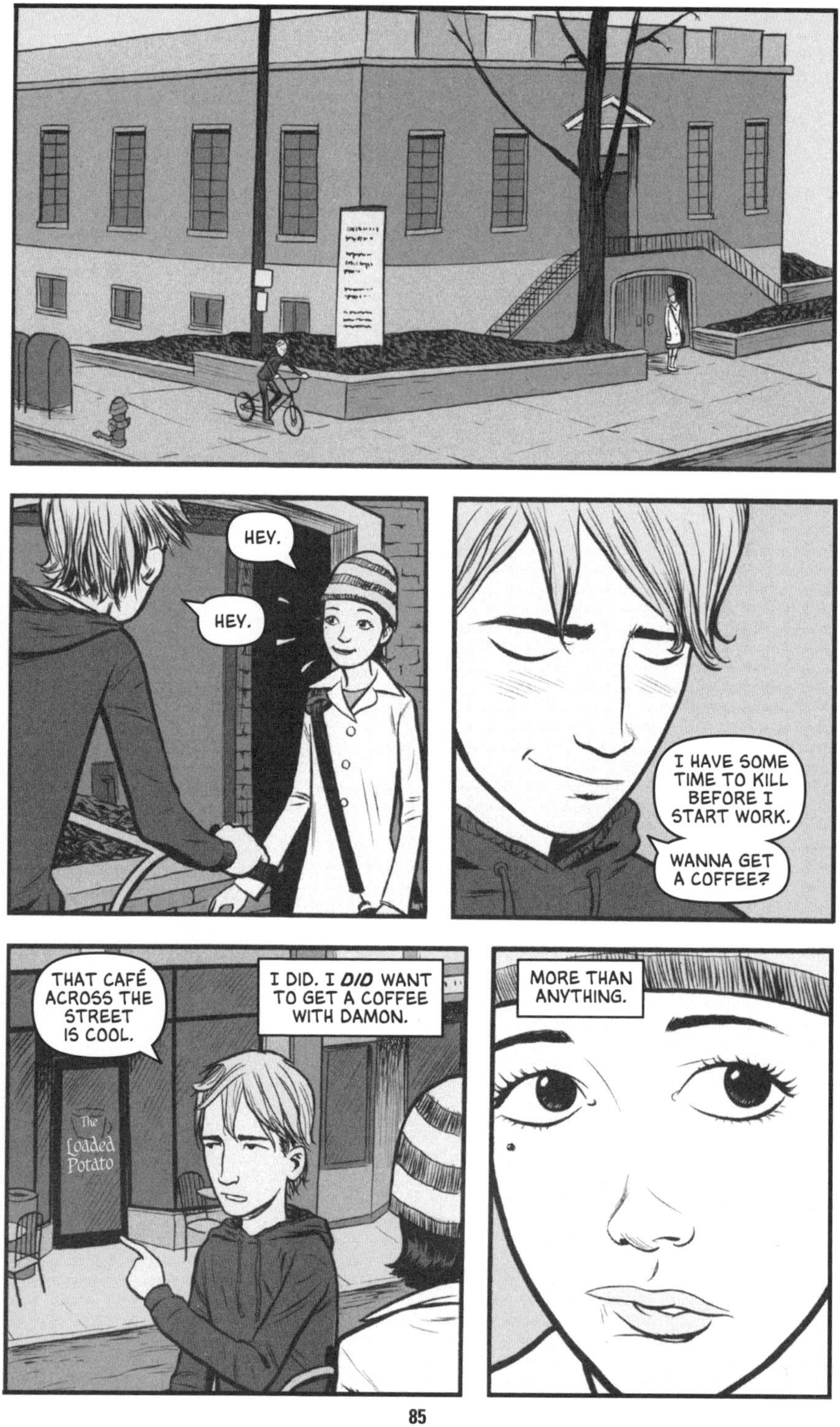
HEY.
HEY.
I HAVE SOME TIME TO KILL BEFORE I START WORK.
WANNA GET A COFFEE?
THAT CAFÉ ACROSS THE STREET IS COOL.
I DID. I *DID* WANT TO GET A COFFEE WITH DAMON.
The Loaded Potato
MORE THAN ANYTHING.

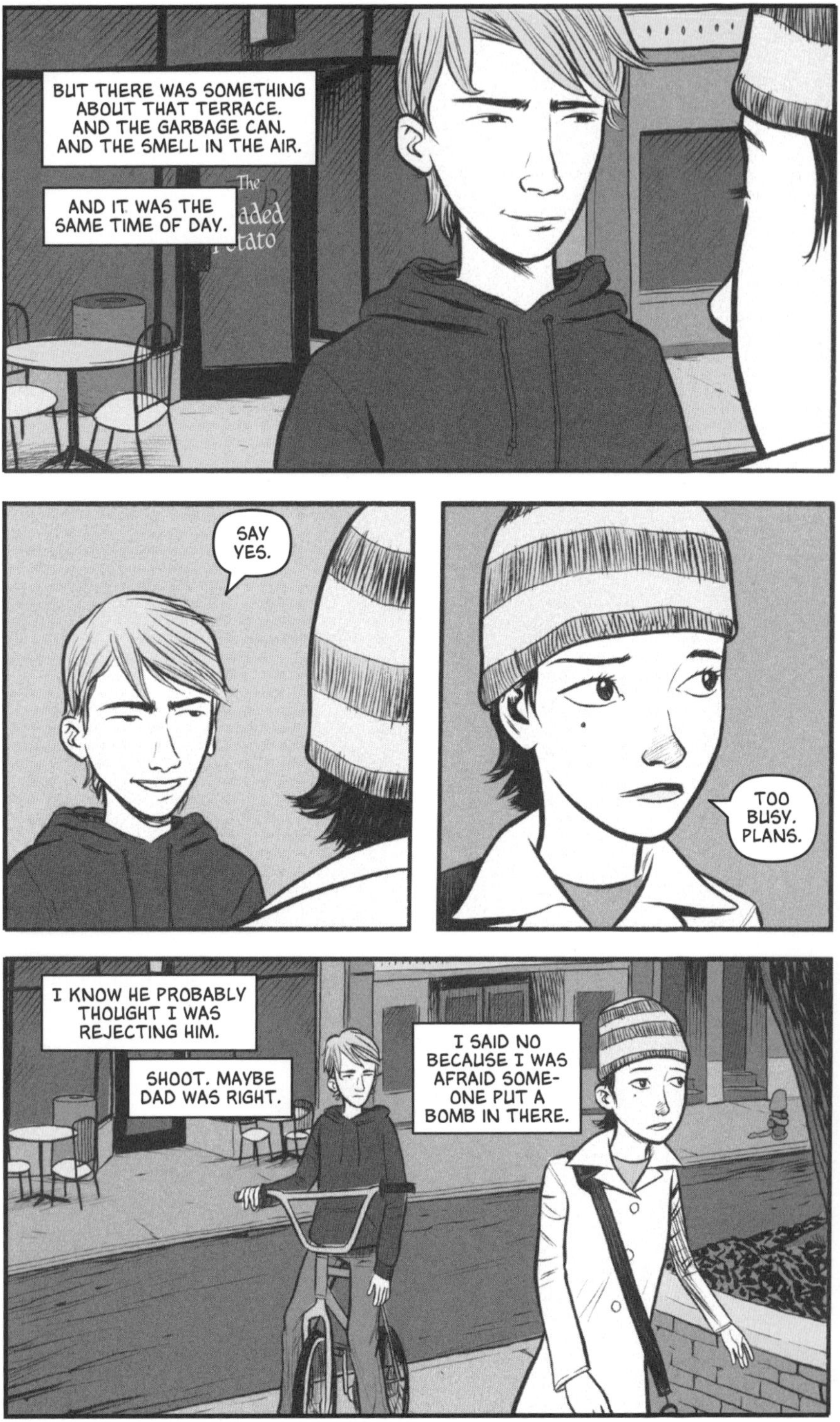
BUT THERE WAS SOMETHING ABOUT THAT TERRACE. AND THE GARBAGE CAN. AND THE SMELL IN THE AIR.
AND IT WAS THE SAME TIME OF DAY.
SAY YES.
TOO BUSY. PLANS.
I KNOW HE PROBABLY THOUGHT I WAS REJECTING HIM.
SHOOT. MAYBE DAD WAS RIGHT.
I SAID NO BECAUSE I WAS AFRAID SOME-ONE PUT A BOMB IN THERE.

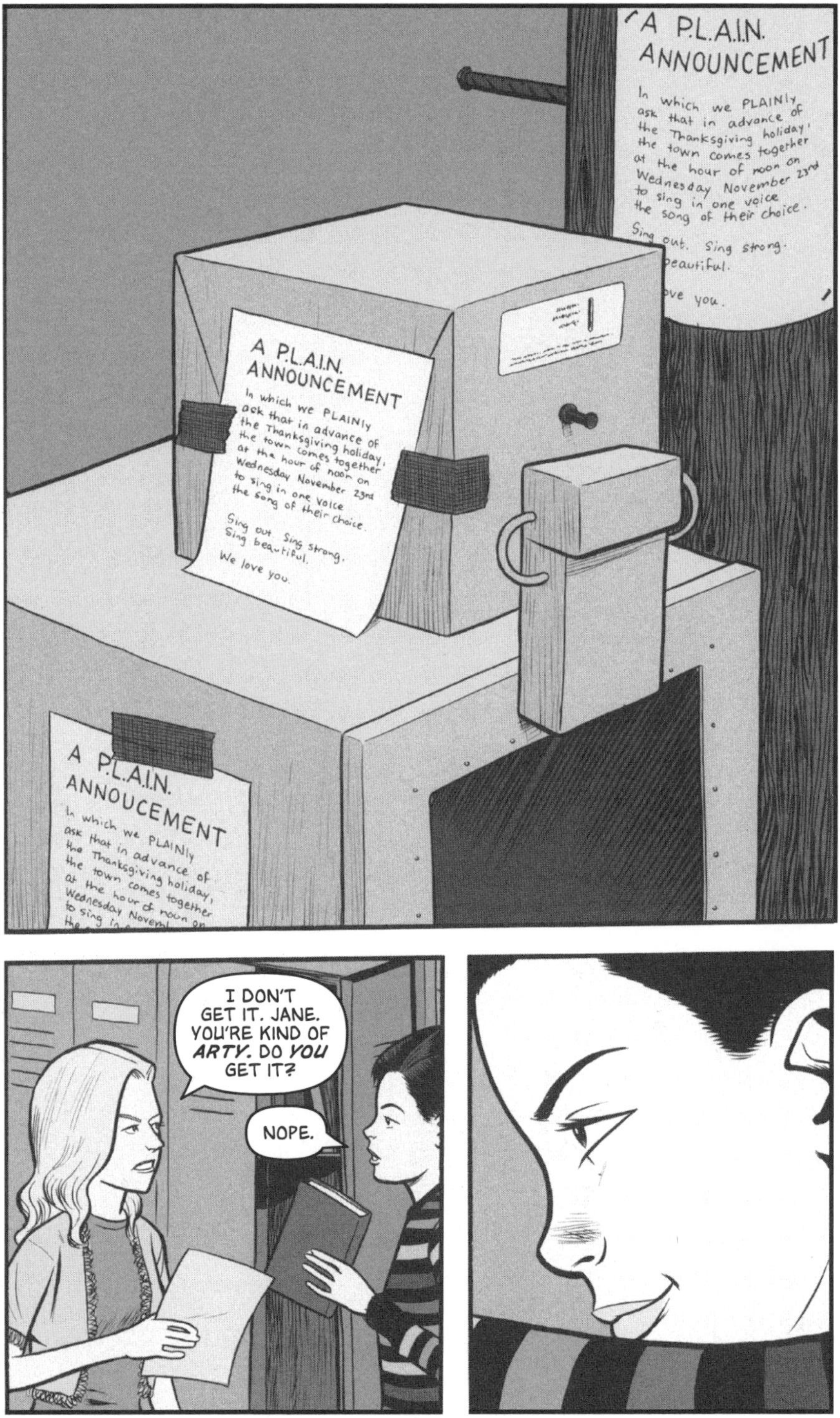
A P.L.A.I.N. ANNOUNCEMENT
In which we PLAINly ask that in advance of the Thanksgiving holiday, the town comes together at the hour of noon on Wednesday November 23rd to sing in one voice the song of their choice.
Sing out. Sing strong. Sing beautiful.
We love you.
I DON'T GET IT. JANE. YOU'RE KIND OF *ARTY*. DO *YOU* GET IT?
NOPE.

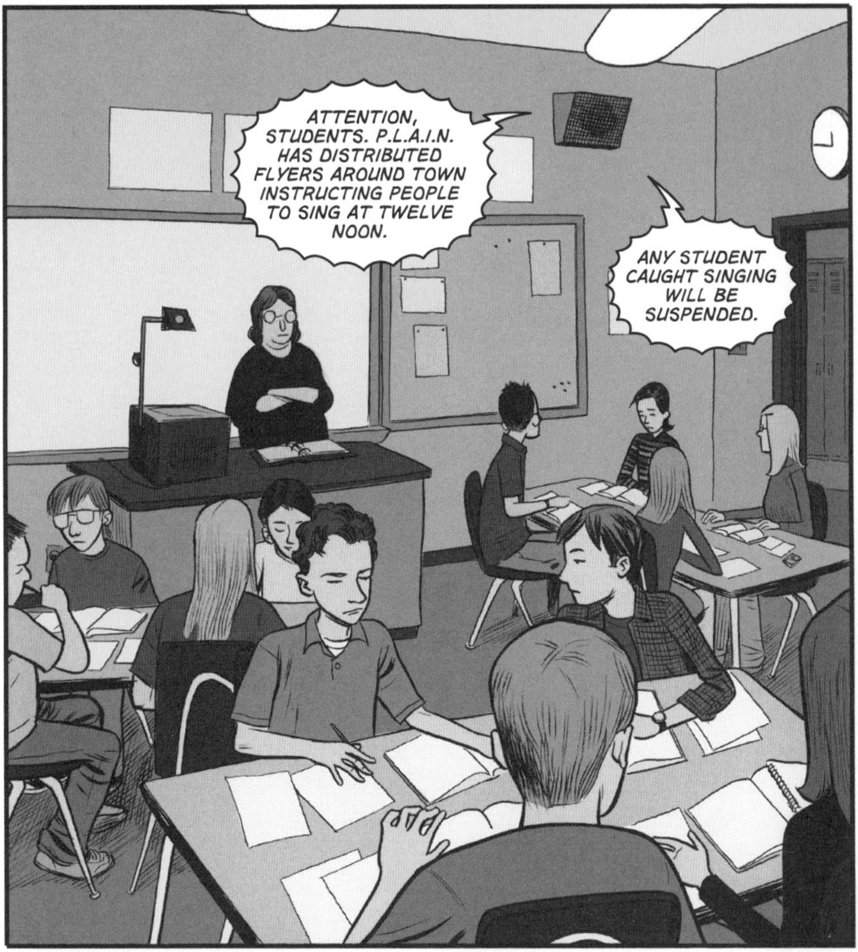
ATTENTION, STUDENTS. P.L.A.I.N. HAS DISTRIBUTED FLYERS AROUND TOWN INSTRUCTING PEOPLE TO SING AT TWELVE NOON.
ANY STUDENT CAUGHT SINGING WILL BE SUSPENDED.

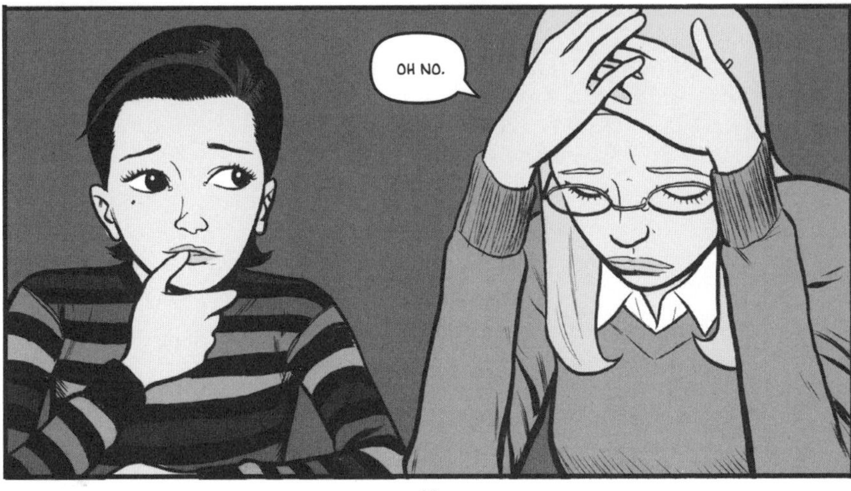
OH NO.

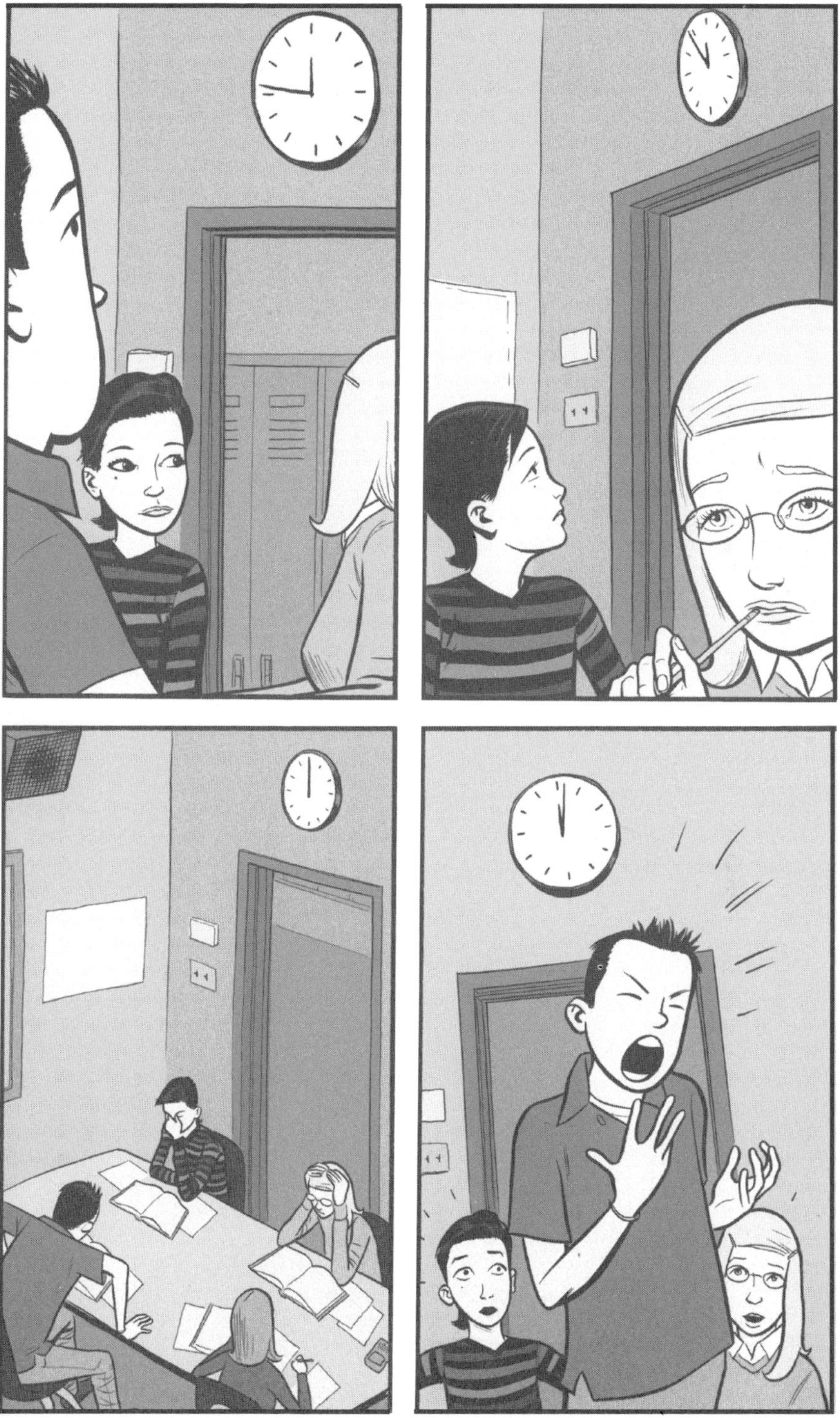

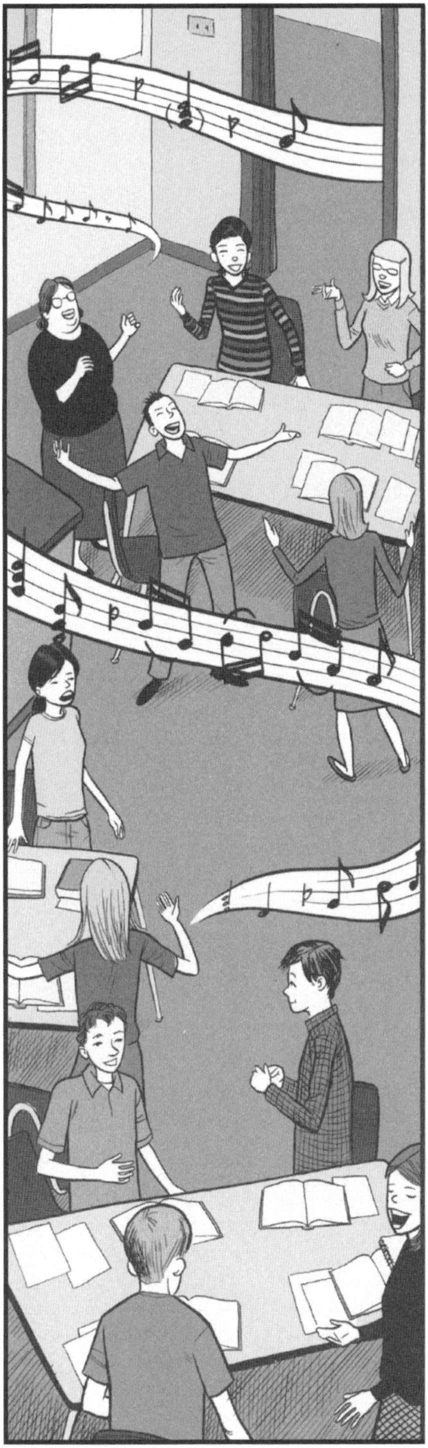

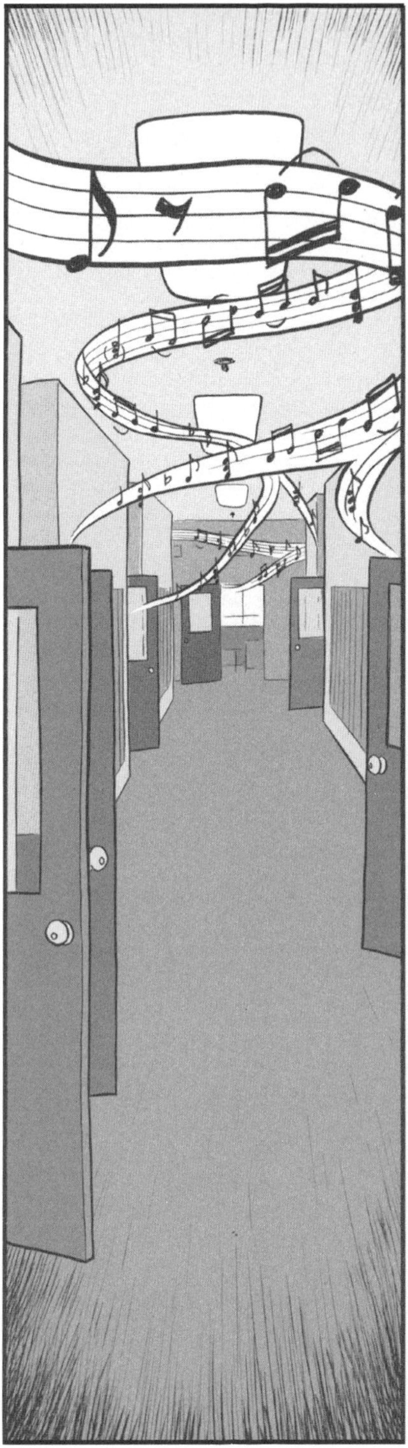

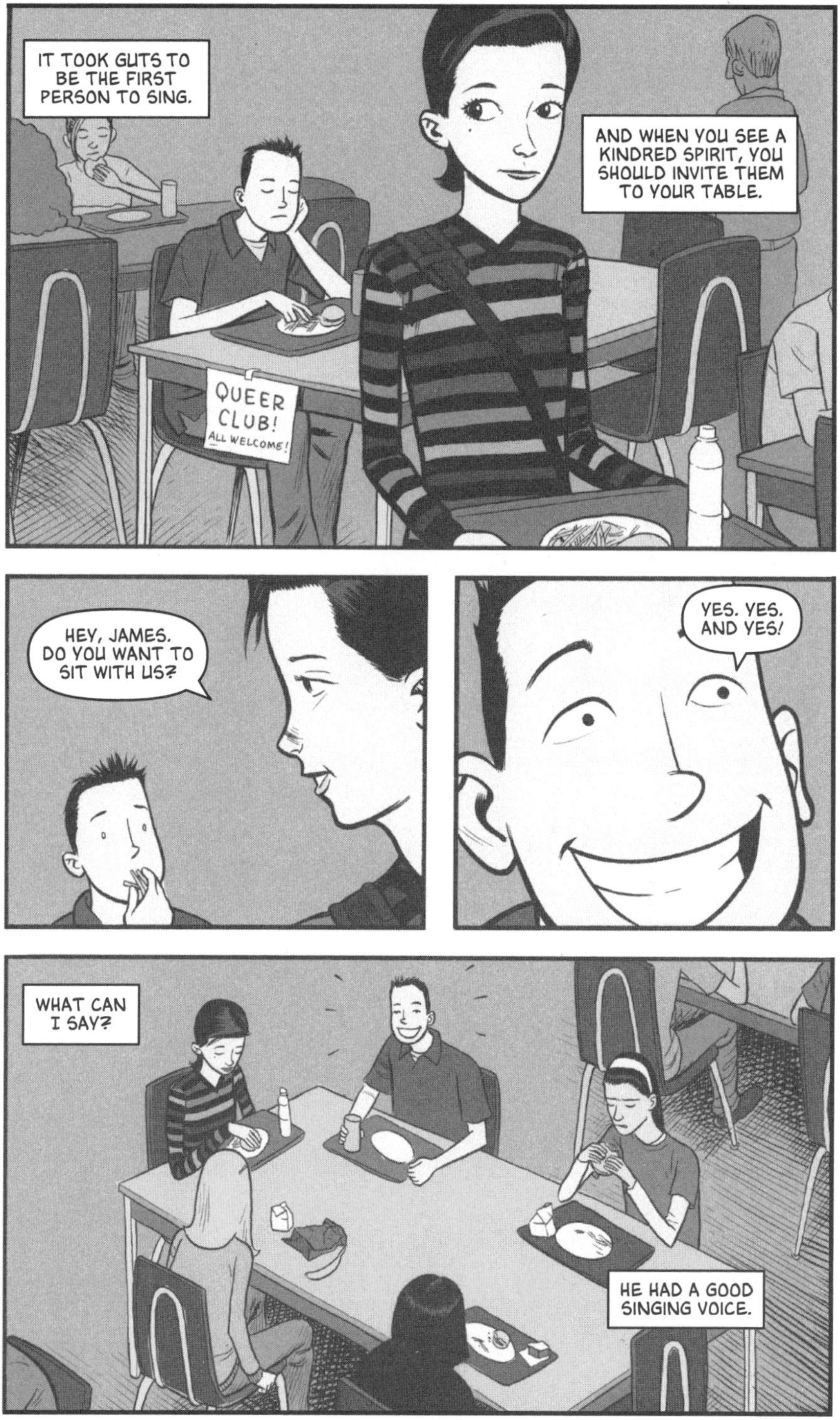
IT TOOK GUTS TO BE THE FIRST PERSON TO SING.
AND WHEN YOU SEE A KINDRED SPIRIT, YOU SHOULD INVITE THEM TO YOUR TABLE.
QUEER CLUB! ALL WELCOME!
HEY, JAMES. DO YOU WANT TO SIT WITH US?
YES. YES. AND YES!
WHAT CAN I SAY?
HE HAD A GOOD SINGING VOICE.

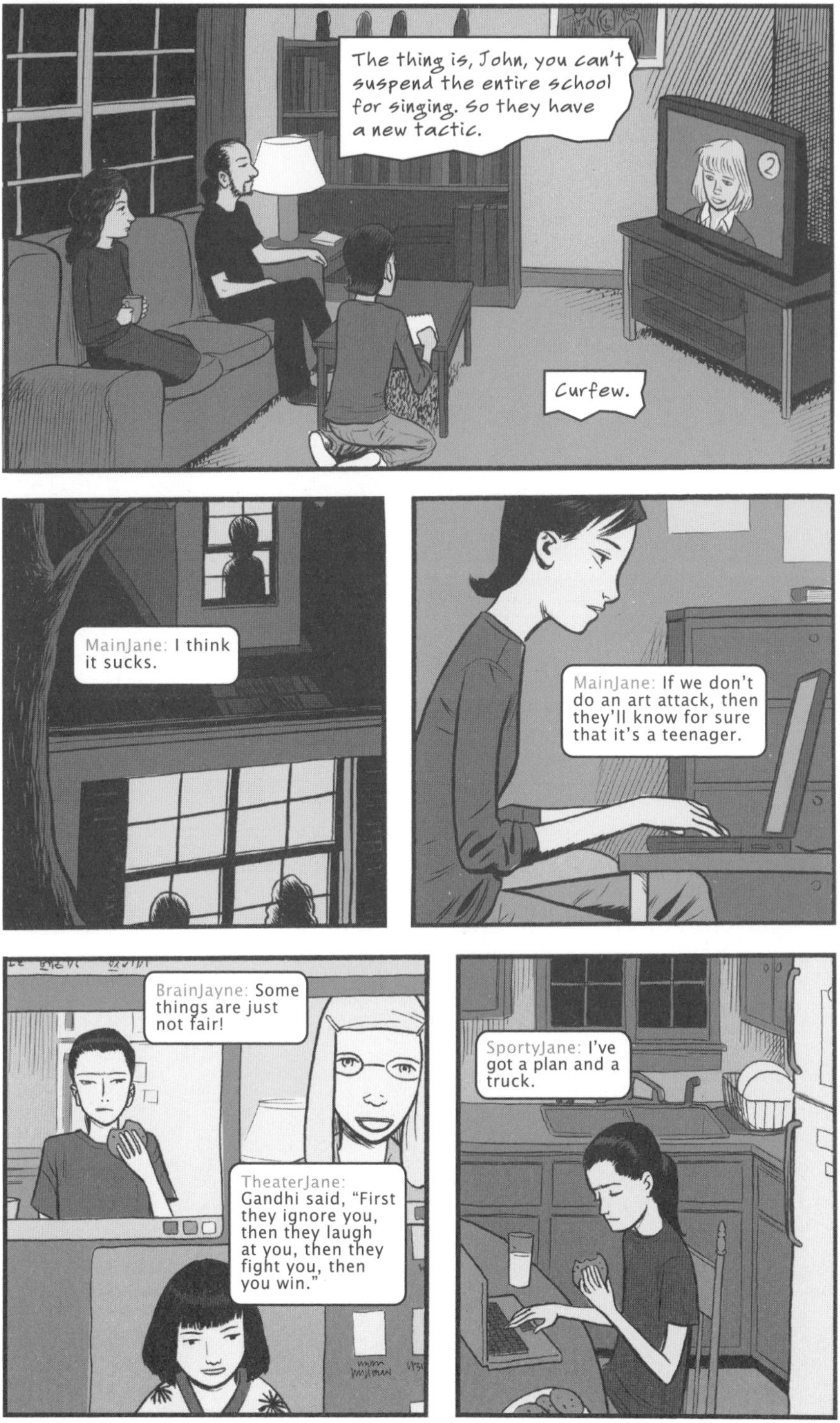

The thing is, John, you can't suspend the entire school for singing. So they have a new tactic.
Curfew.
MainJane: I think it sucks.
MainJane: If we don't do an art attack, then they'll know for sure that it's a teenager.
BrainJayne: Some things are just not fair!
TheaterJane: Gandhi said, "First they ignore you, then they laugh at you, then they fight you, then you win."
SportyJane: I've got a plan and a truck.

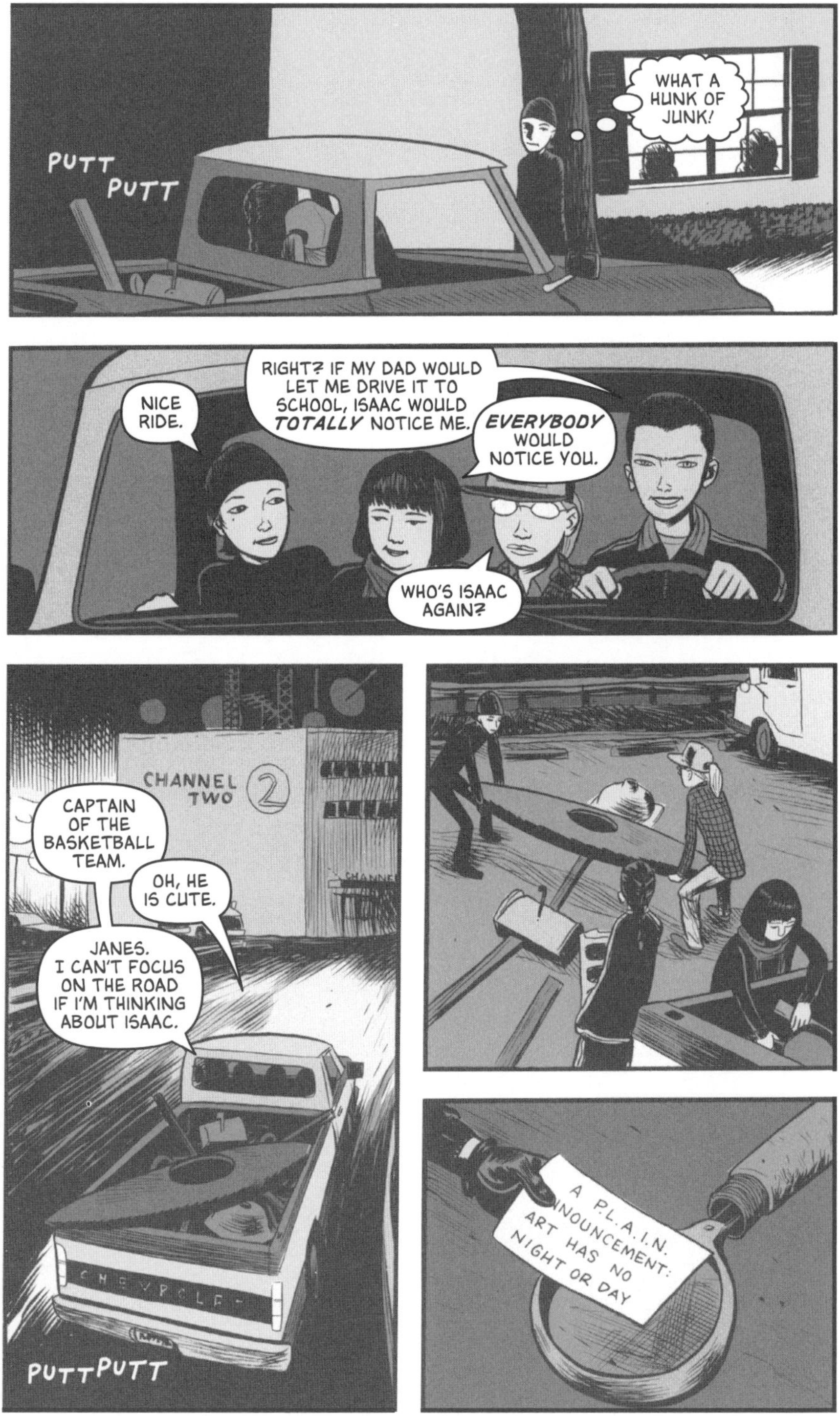
PUTT
PUTT
WHAT A HUNK OF JUNK!
NICE RIDE.
RIGHT? IF MY DAD WOULD LET ME DRIVE IT TO SCHOOL, ISAAC WOULD TOTALLY NOTICE ME.
EVERYBODY WOULD NOTICE YOU.
WHO'S ISAAC AGAIN?
CHANNEL TWO
2
CAPTAIN OF THE BASKETBALL TEAM.
OH, HE IS CUTE.
JANES. I CAN'T FOCUS ON THE ROAD IF I'M THINKING ABOUT ISAAC.
CHEVROLET
PUTT PUTT
A P.L.A.I.N. ANNOUNCEMENT: ART HAS NO NIGHT OR DAY

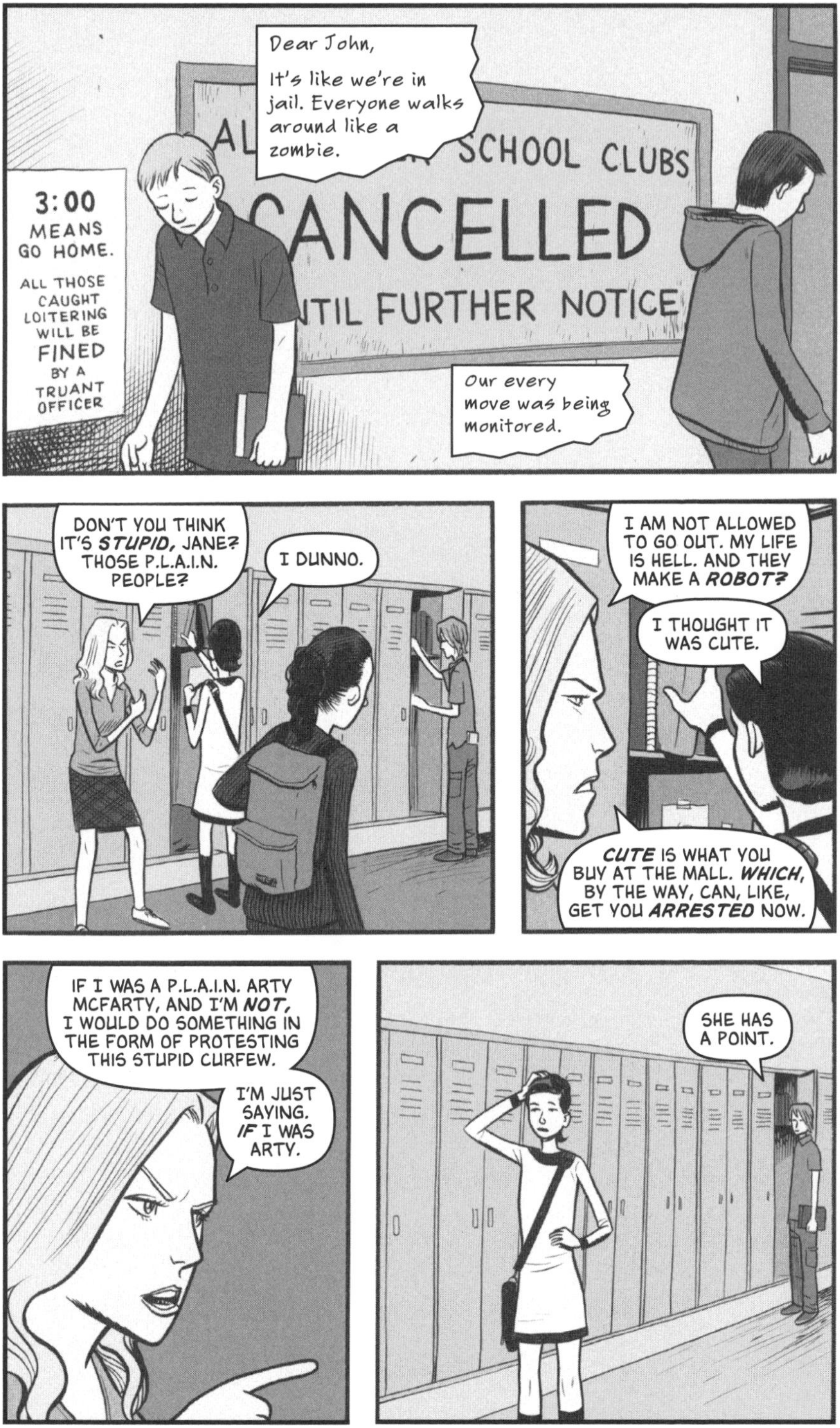
Dear John,
It's like we're in jail. Everyone walks around like a zombie.
AL SCHOOL CLUBS CANCELLED NTIL FURTHER NOTICE
3:00 MEANS GO HOME. ALL THOSE CAUGHT LOITERING WILL BE FINED BY A TRUANT OFFICER
Our every move was being monitored.
DON'T YOU THINK IT'S STUPID, JANE? THOSE P.L.A.I.N. PEOPLE?
I DUNNO.
I AM NOT ALLOWED TO GO OUT. MY LIFE IS HELL. AND THEY MAKE A ROBOT?
I THOUGHT IT WAS CUTE.
CUTE IS WHAT YOU BUY AT THE MALL. WHICH, BY THE WAY, CAN, LIKE, GET YOU ARRESTED NOW.
IF I WAS A P.L.A.I.N. ARTY MCFARTY, AND I'M NOT, I WOULD DO SOMETHING IN THE FORM OF PROTESTING THIS STUPID CURFEW.
I'M JUST SAYING. IF I WAS ARTY.
SHE HAS A POINT.

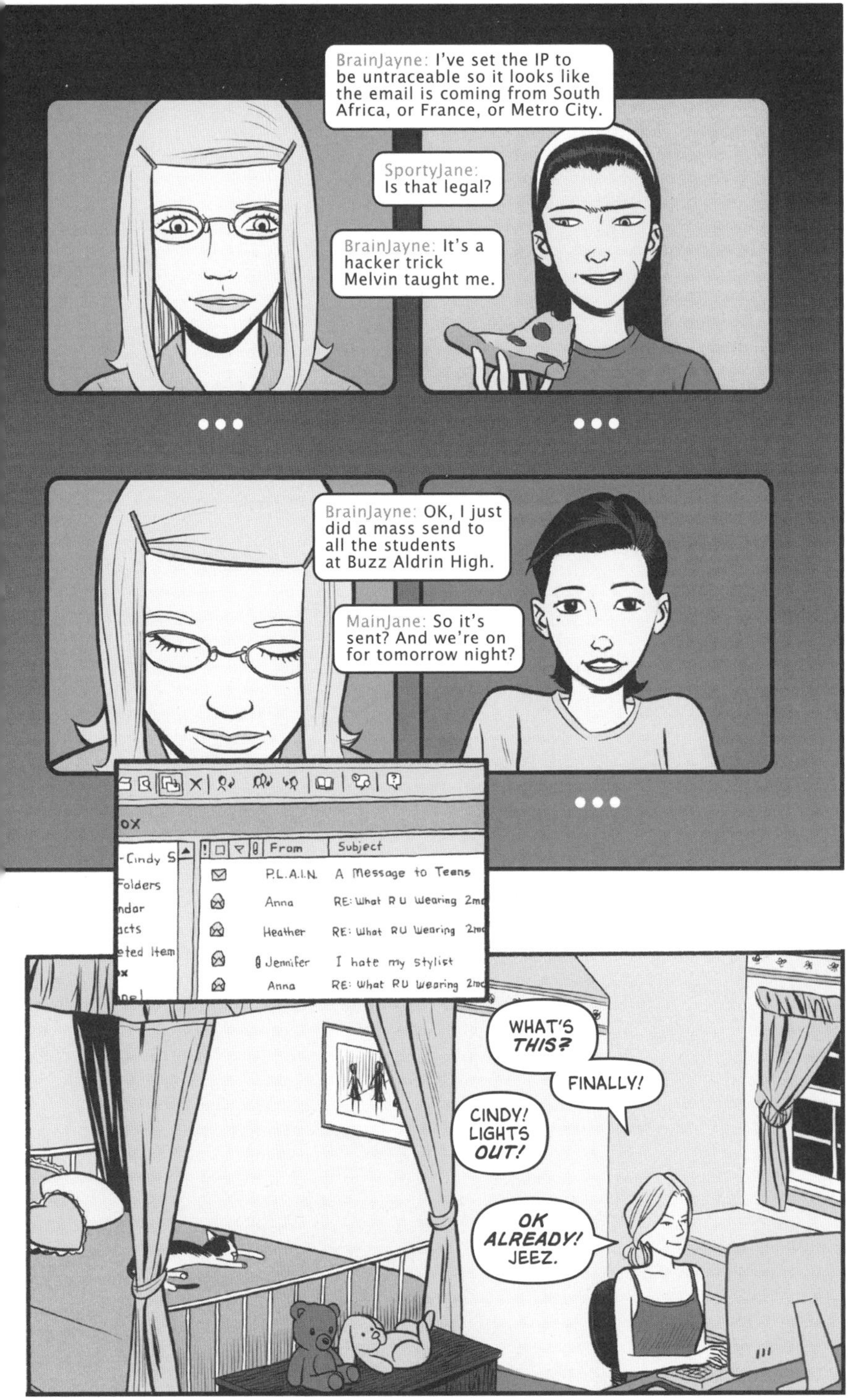
BrainJayne: I've set the IP to be untraceable so it looks like the email is coming from South Africa, or France, or Metro City.
SportyJane: Is that legal?
BrainJayne: It's a hacker trick Melvin taught me.
BrainJayne: OK, I just did a mass send to all the students at Buzz Aldrin High.
MainJane: So it's sent? And we're on for tomorrow night?
From
Subject
P.L.A.I.N. A Message to Teens
Anna RE: What R U Wearing
Heather RE: What RU Wearing
Jennifer I hate my stylist
Anna RE: What RU Wearing
WHAT'S THIS?
FINALLY!
CINDY! LIGHTS OUT!
OK ALREADY! JEEZ.

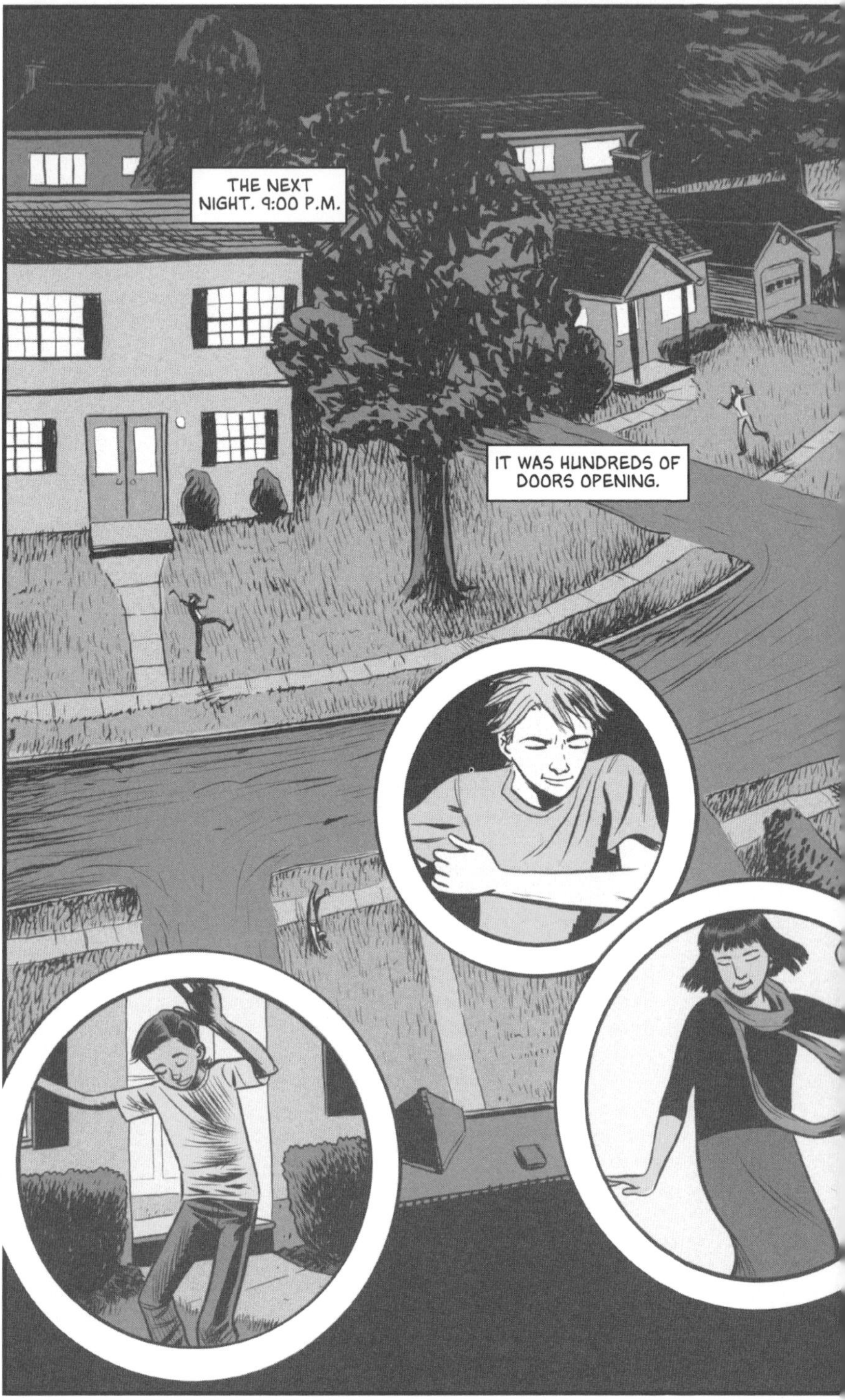
THE NEXT NIGHT. 9:00 P.M.
IT WAS HUNDREDS OF DOORS OPENING.

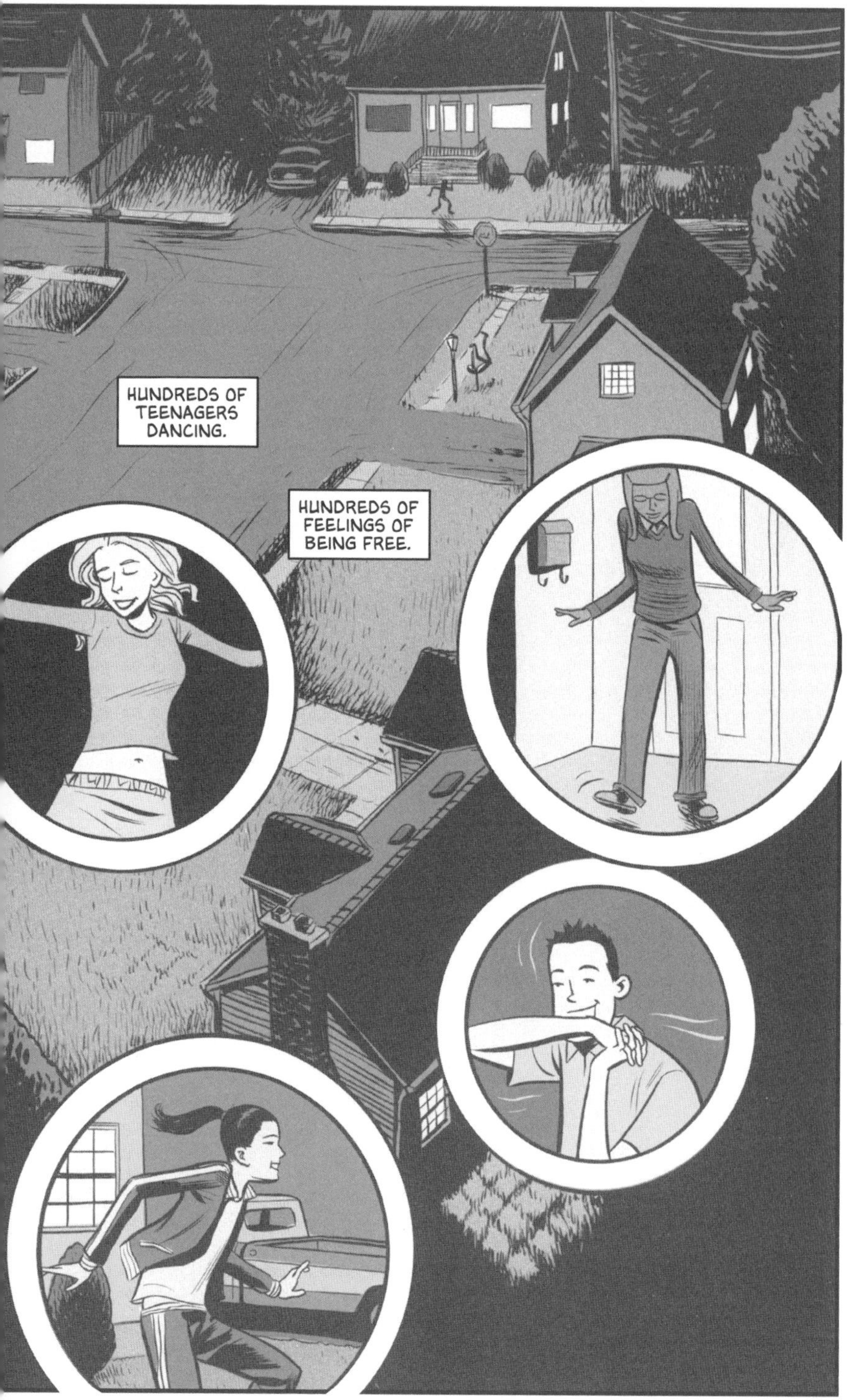
HUNDREDS OF TEENAGERS DANCING.
HUNDREDS OF FEELINGS OF BEING FREE.

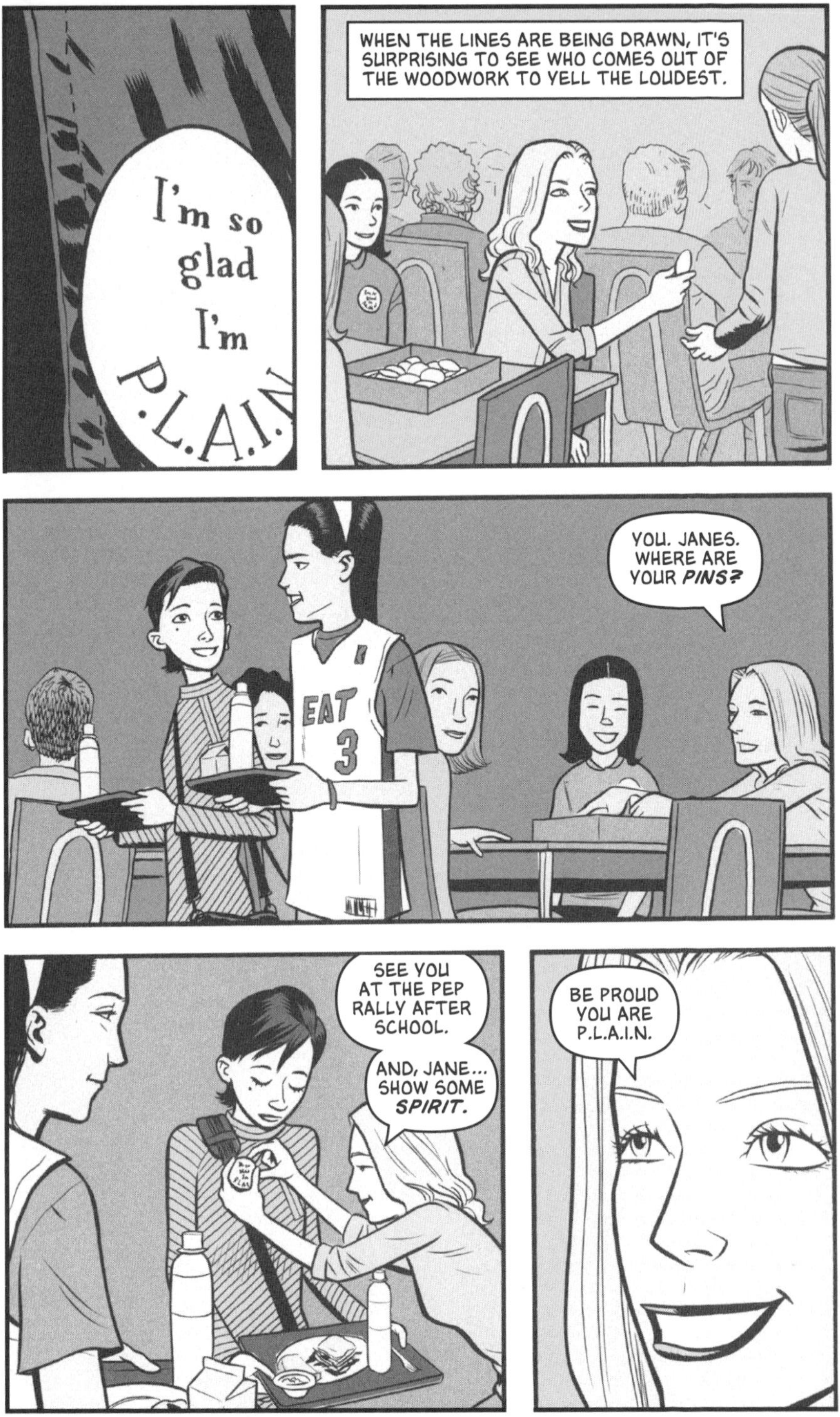
I'm so glad I'm P.L.A.I.N
WHEN THE LINES ARE BEING DRAWN, IT'S SURPRISING TO SEE WHO COMES OUT OF THE WOODWORK TO YELL THE LOUDEST.
YOU. JANES. WHERE ARE YOUR *PINS?*
EAT 3
SEE YOU AT THE PEP RALLY AFTER SCHOOL.
AND, JANE... SHOW SOME *SPIRIT*.
BE PROUD YOU ARE P.L.A.I.N.

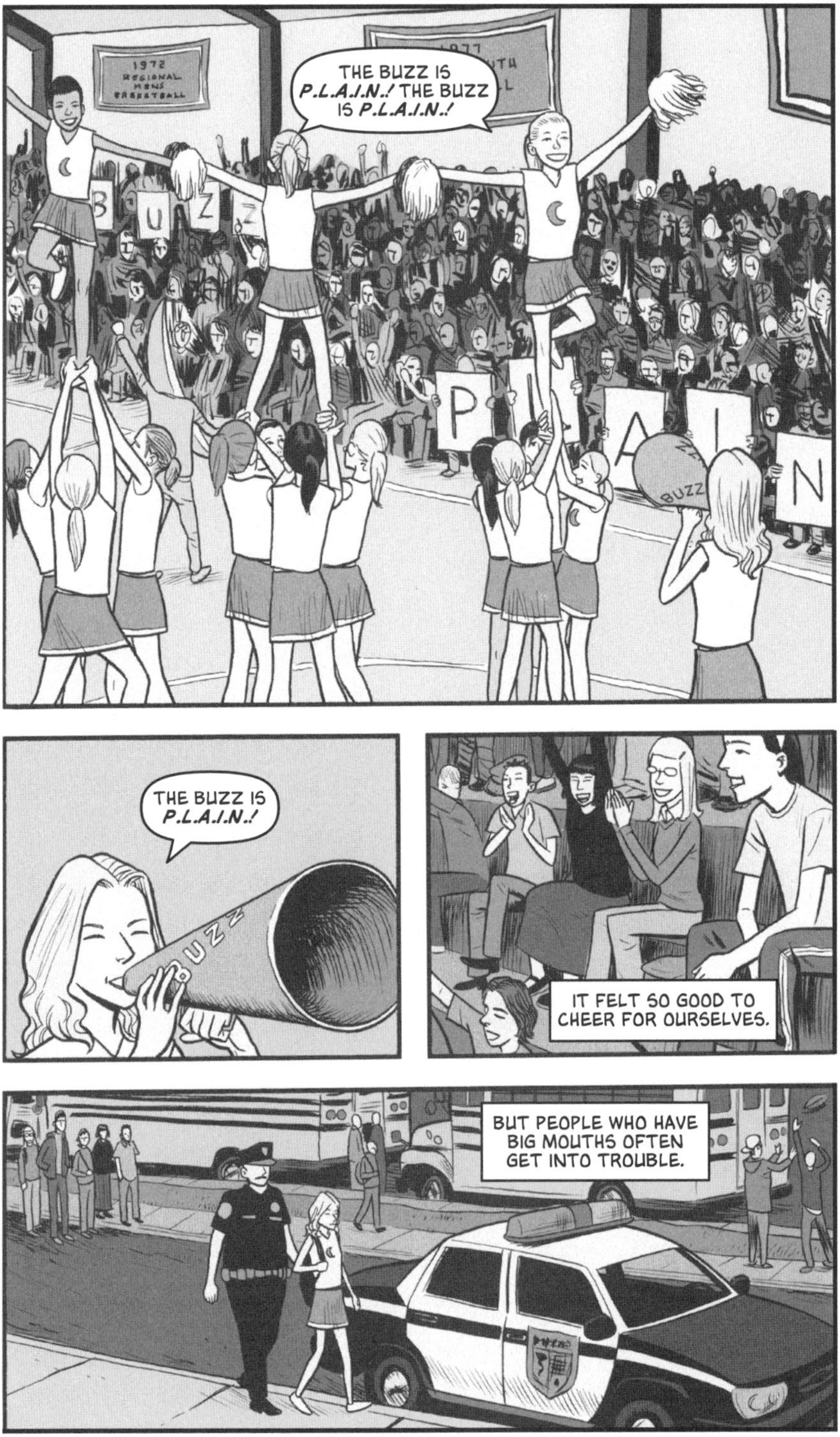
1972 REGIONAL MENS BASKETBALL
THE BUZZ IS P.L.A.I.N.! THE BUZZ IS P.L.A.I.N.!
B U Z Z
P L A I N
BUZZ
THE BUZZ IS P.L.A.I.N.!
BUZZ
IT FELT SO GOOD TO CHEER FOR OURSELVES.
BUT PEOPLE WHO HAVE BIG MOUTHS OFTEN GET INTO TROUBLE.

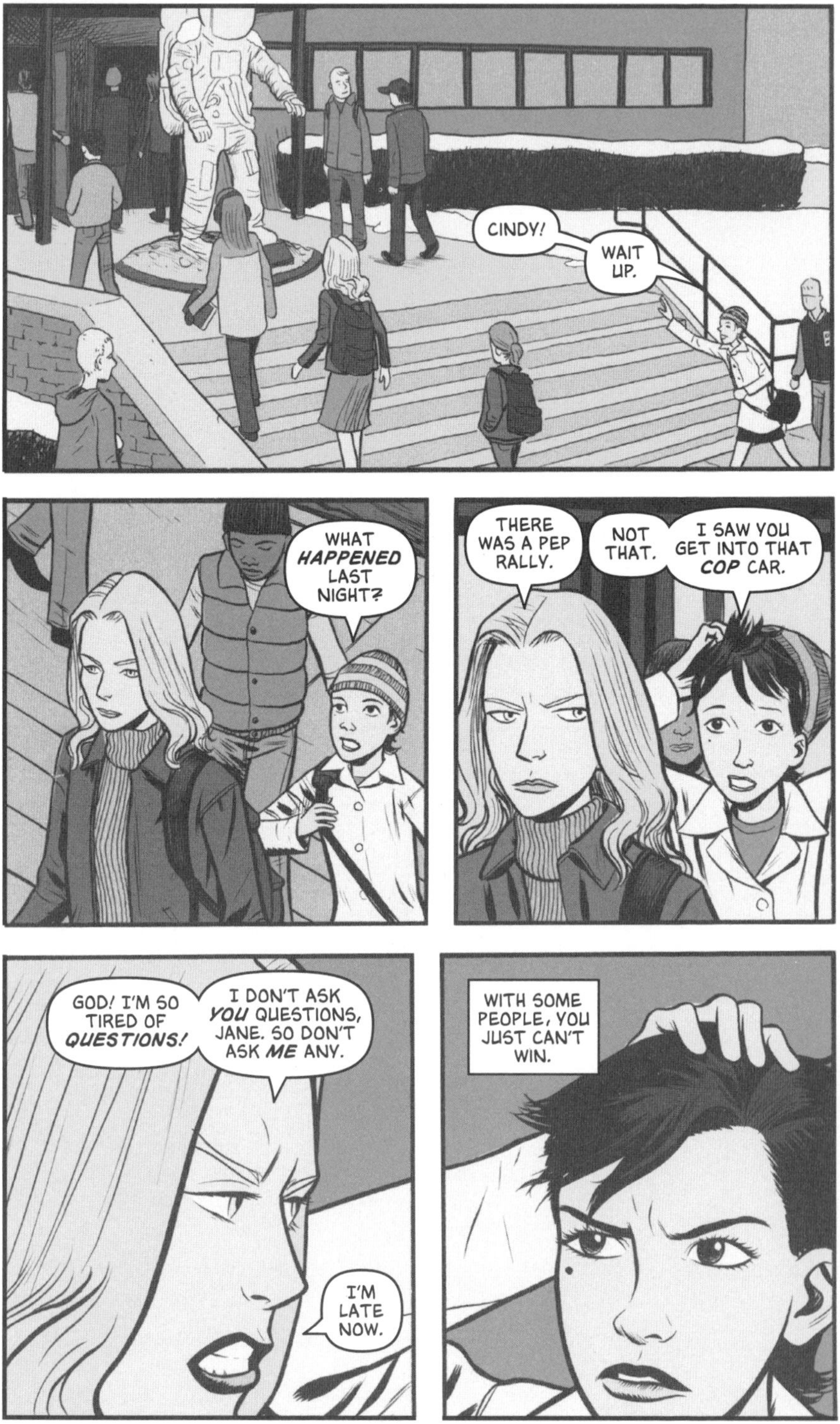
CINDY!
WAIT UP.
WHAT HAPPENED LAST NIGHT?
THERE WAS A PEP RALLY.
NOT THAT.
I SAW YOU GET INTO THAT COP CAR.
GOD! I'M SO TIRED OF QUESTIONS!
I DON'T ASK YOU QUESTIONS, JANE. SO DON'T ASK ME ANY.
I'M LATE NOW.
WITH SOME PEOPLE, YOU JUST CAN'T WIN.

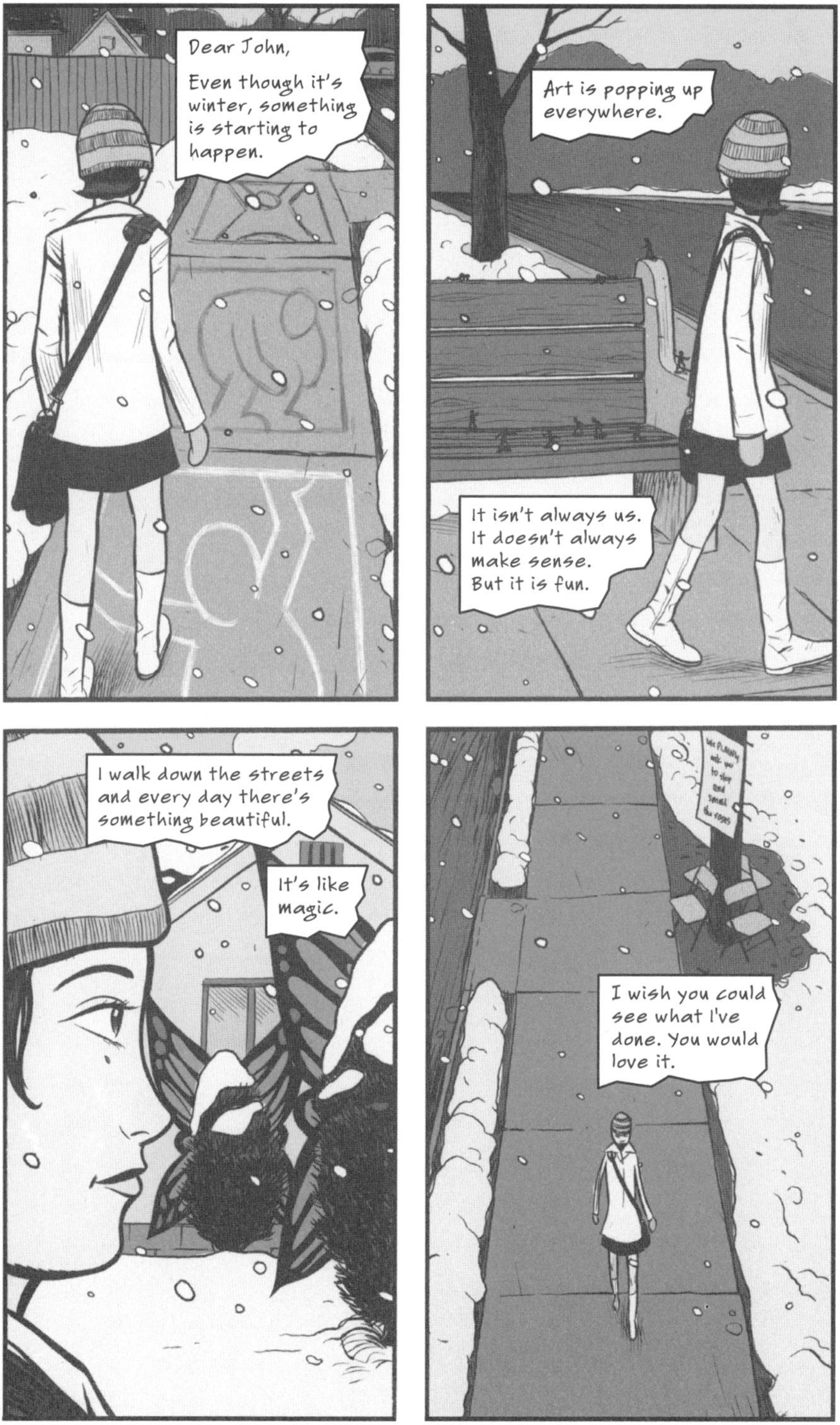

Dear John,
Even though it's winter, something is starting to happen.
Art is popping up everywhere.
It isn't always us. It doesn't always make sense. But it is fun.
I walk down the streets and every day there's something beautiful.
It's like magic.
We PLAINLY ask you to stop and smell the roses
I wish you could see what I've done. You would love it.

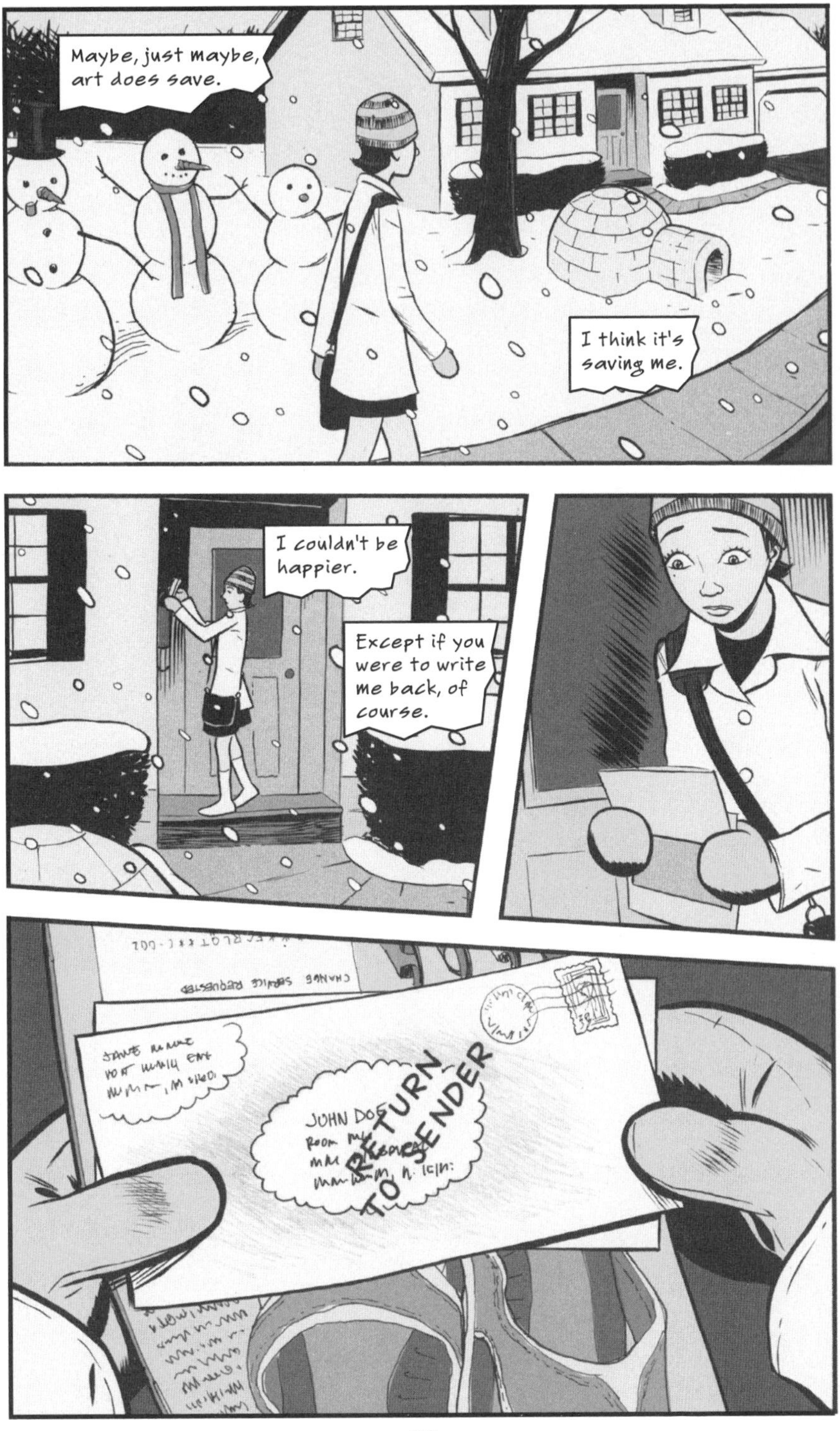
Maybe, just maybe, art does save.
I think it's saving me.
I couldn't be happier.
Except if you were to write me back, of course.
JOHN DOE
RETURN TO SENDER

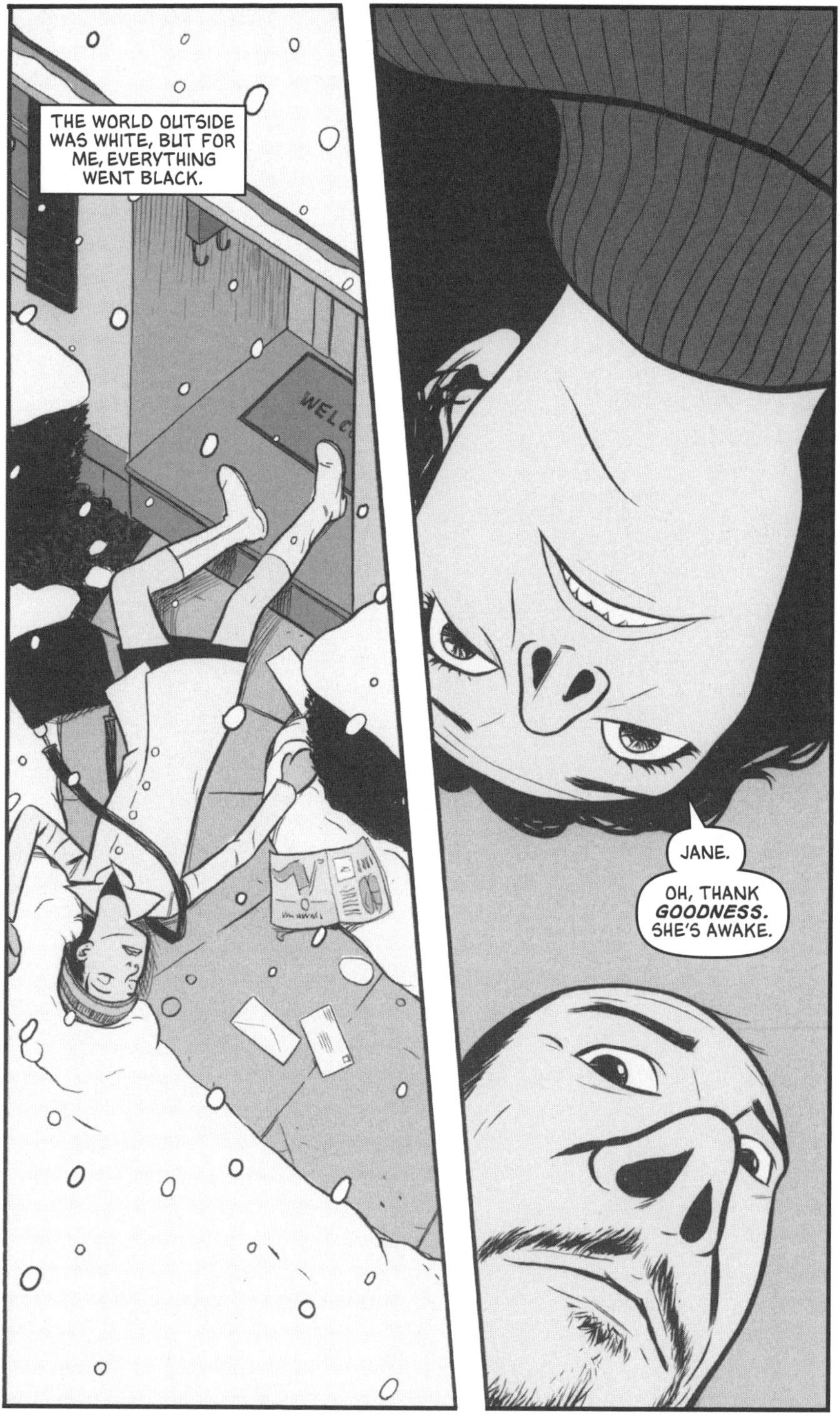
THE WORLD OUTSIDE WAS WHITE, BUT FOR ME, EVERYTHING WENT BLACK.
WELC
JANE.
OH, THANK *GOODNESS.* SHE'S AWAKE.

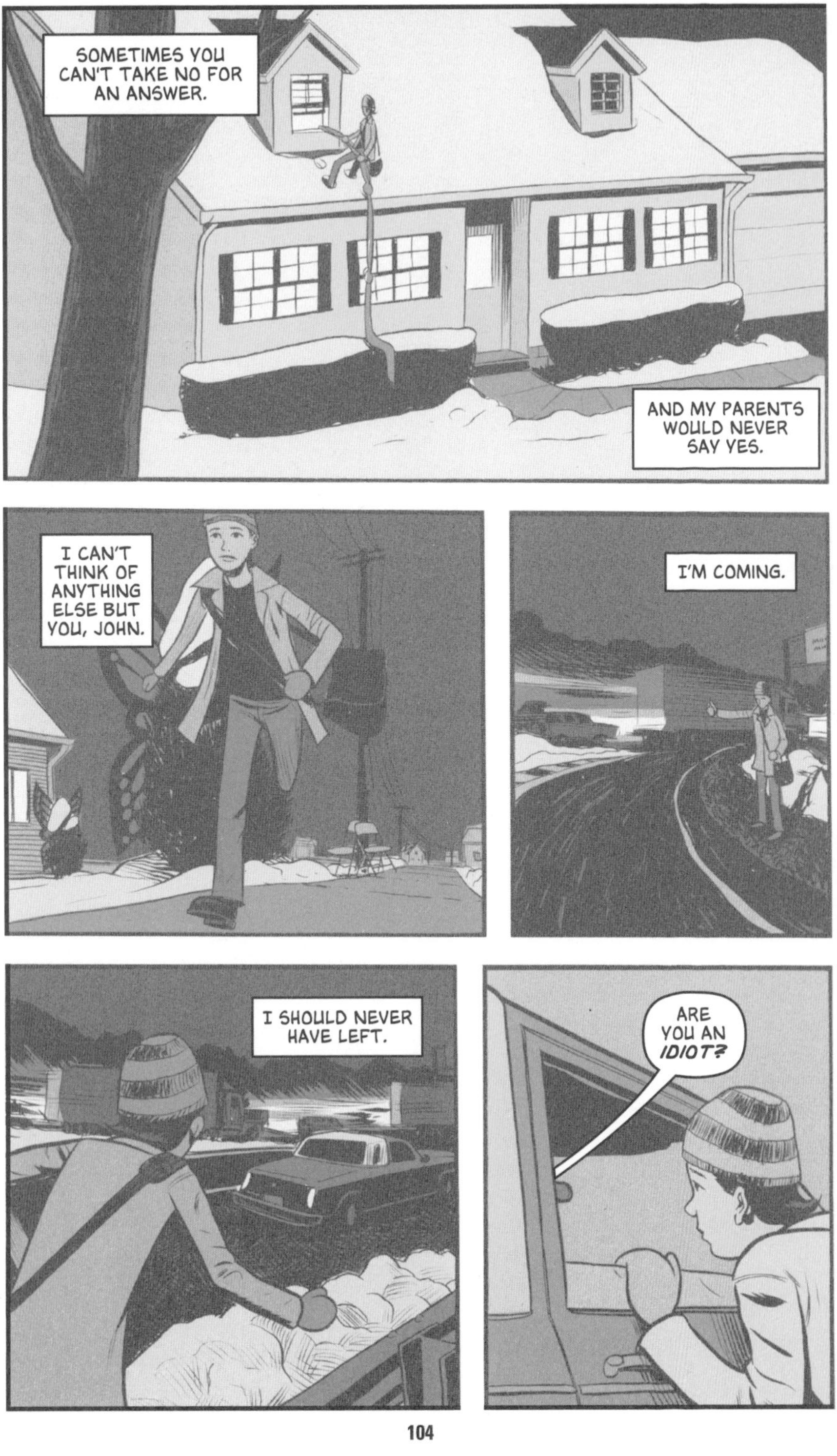
SOMETIMES YOU CAN'T TAKE NO FOR AN ANSWER.
AND MY PARENTS WOULD NEVER SAY YES.
I CAN'T THINK OF ANYTHING ELSE BUT YOU, JOHN.
I'M COMING.
I SHOULD NEVER HAVE LEFT.
ARE YOU AN *IDIOT?*

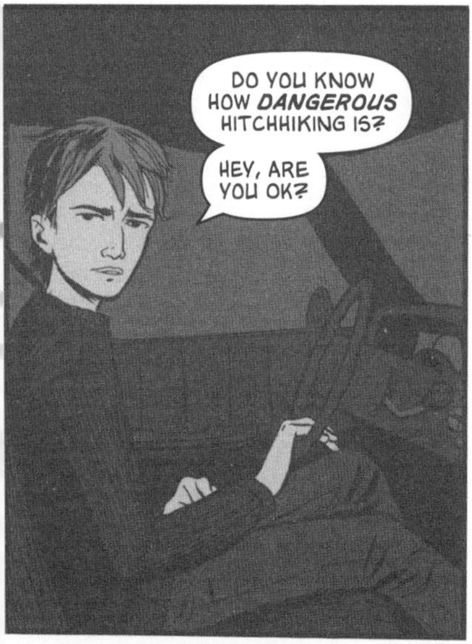
DO YOU KNOW HOW *DANGEROUS* HITCHHIKING IS?
HEY, ARE YOU OK?

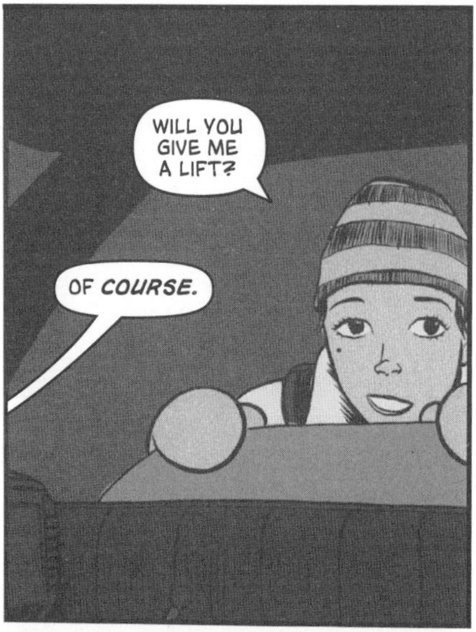
WILL YOU GIVE ME A LIFT?
OF *COURSE.*

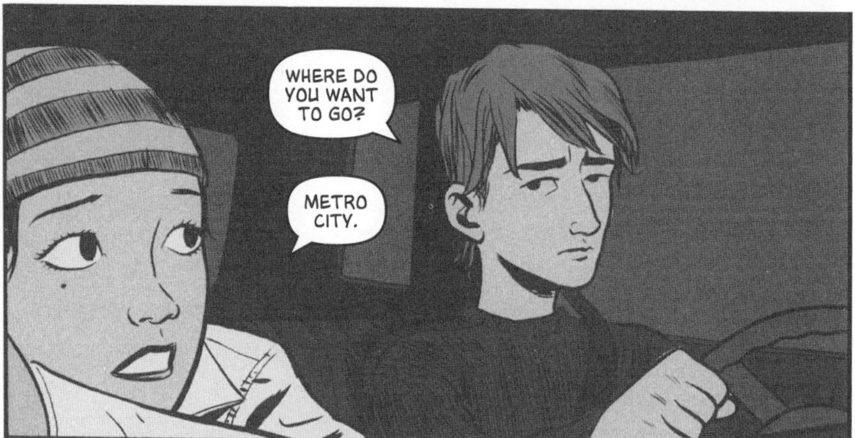
WHERE DO YOU WANT TO GO?
METRO CITY.

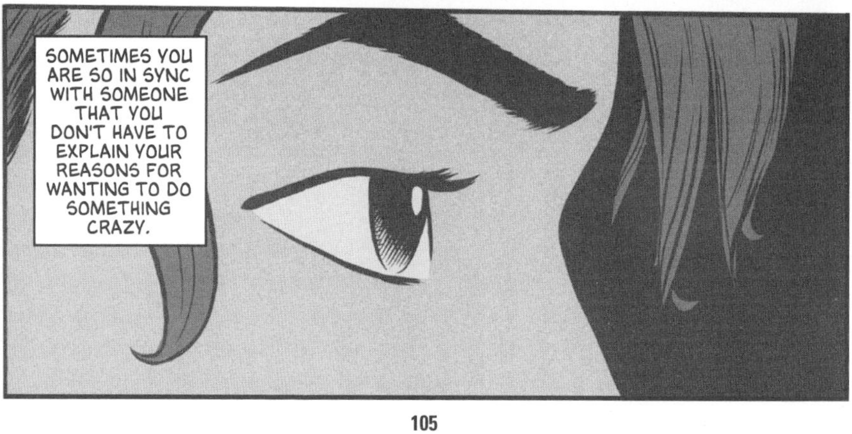
SOMETIMES YOU ARE SO IN SYNC WITH SOMEONE THAT YOU DON'T HAVE TO EXPLAIN YOUR REASONS FOR WANTING TO DO SOMETHING CRAZY.

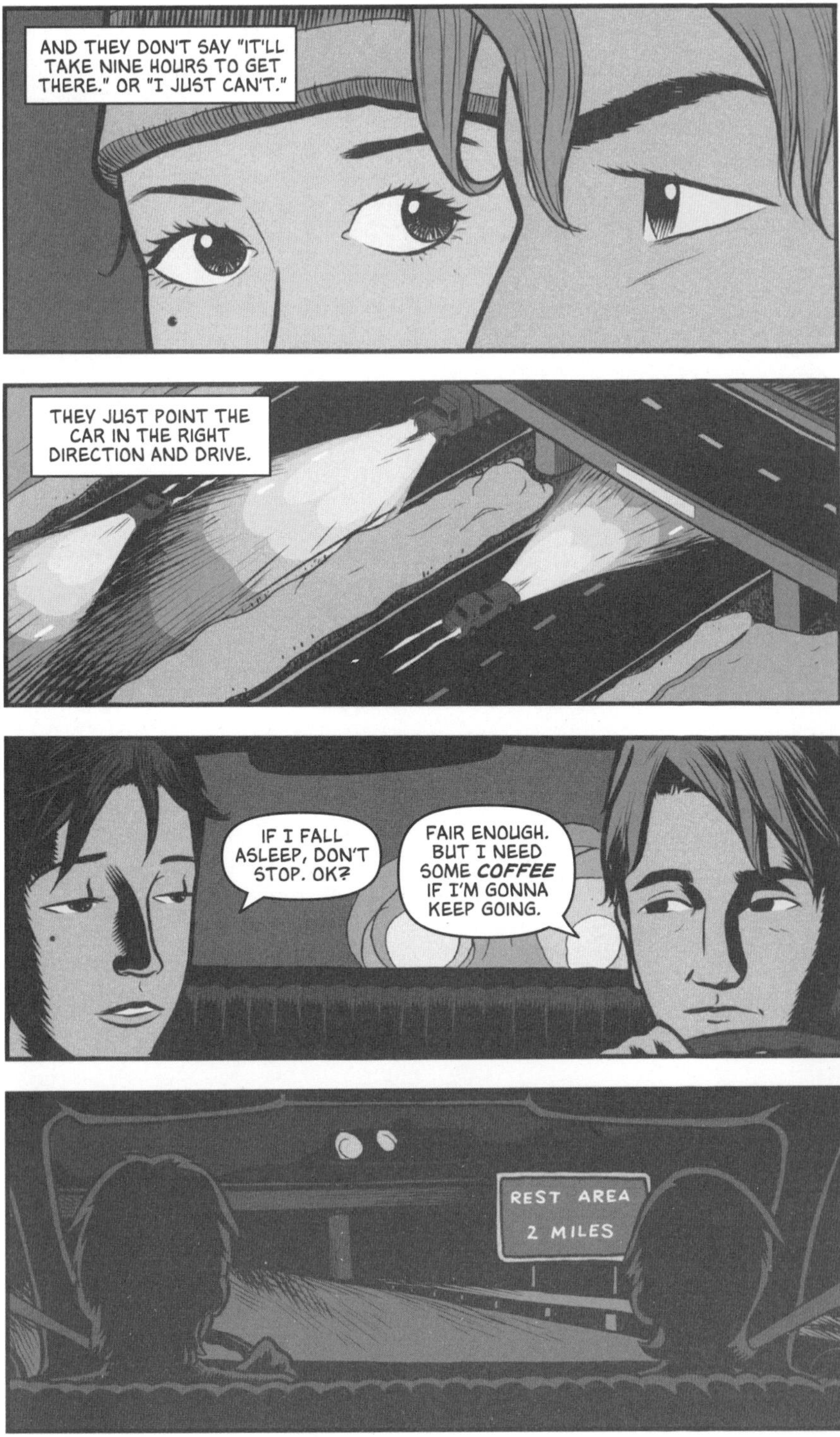
AND THEY DON'T SAY "IT'LL TAKE NINE HOURS TO GET THERE." OR "I JUST CAN'T."
THEY JUST POINT THE CAR IN THE RIGHT DIRECTION AND DRIVE.
IF I FALL ASLEEP, DON'T STOP. OK?
FAIR ENOUGH. BUT I NEED SOME COFFEE IF I'M GONNA KEEP GOING.
REST AREA 2 MILES

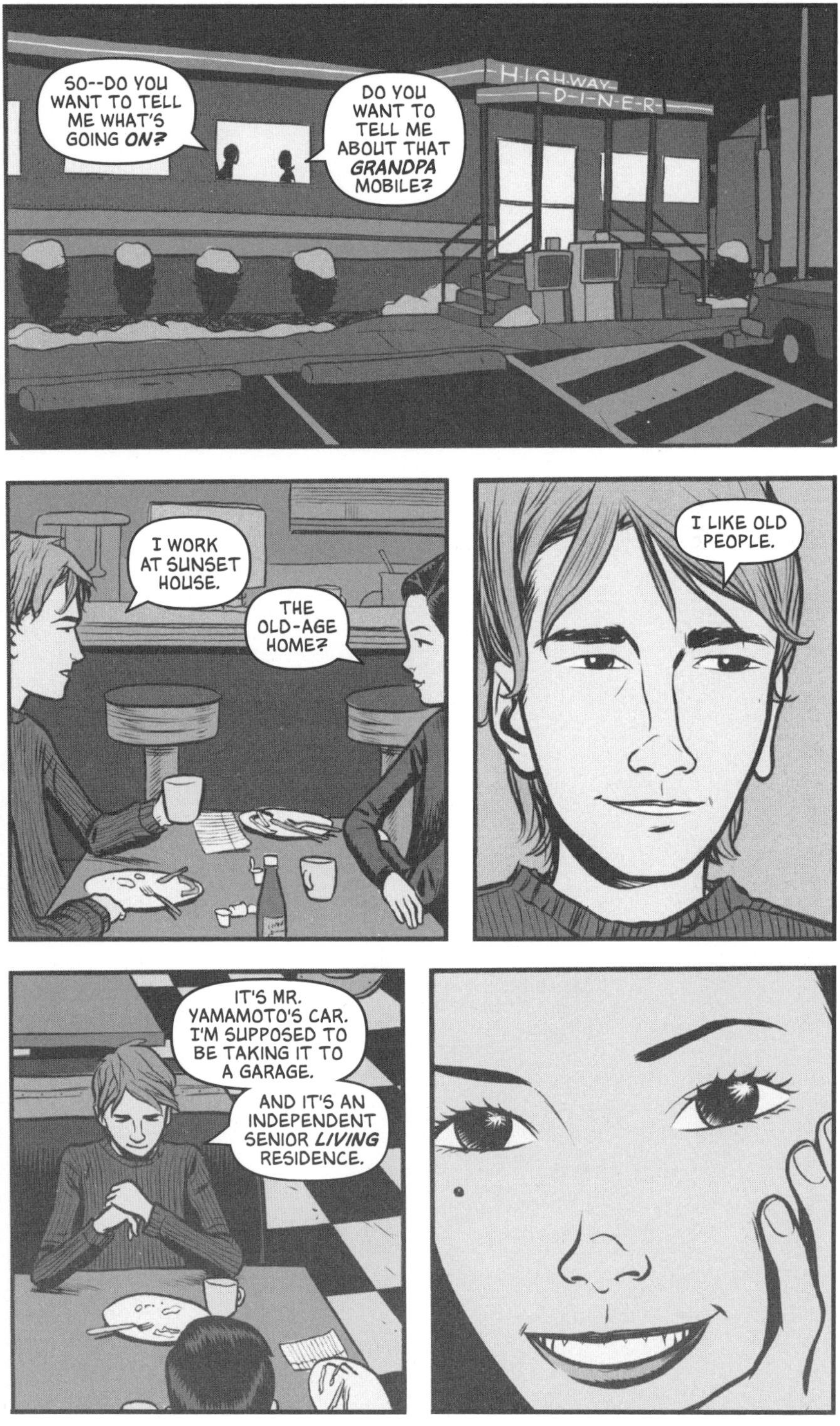
HIGHWAY DINER
SO--DO YOU WANT TO TELL ME WHAT'S GOING *ON?*
DO YOU WANT TO TELL ME ABOUT THAT *GRANDPA* MOBILE?
I WORK AT SUNSET HOUSE.
THE OLD-AGE HOME?
I LIKE OLD PEOPLE.
IT'S MR. YAMAMOTO'S CAR. I'M SUPPOSED TO BE TAKING IT TO A GARAGE.
AND IT'S AN INDEPENDENT SENIOR *LIVING* RESIDENCE.

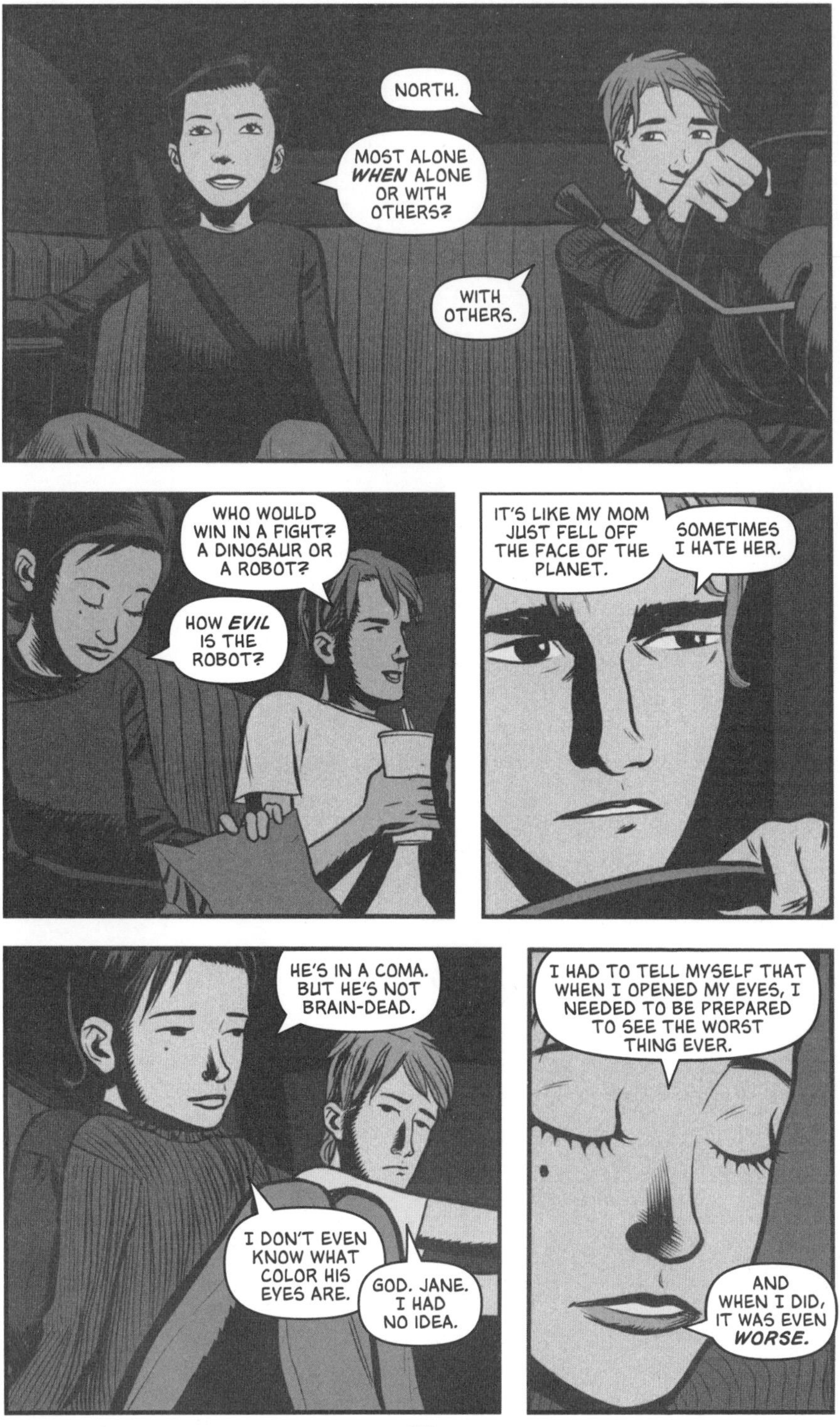
NORTH.
MOST ALONE *WHEN* ALONE OR WITH OTHERS?
WITH OTHERS.
WHO WOULD WIN IN A FIGHT? A DINOSAUR OR A ROBOT?
HOW *EVIL* IS THE ROBOT?
IT'S LIKE MY MOM JUST FELL OFF THE FACE OF THE PLANET.
SOMETIMES I HATE HER.
HE'S IN A COMA. BUT HE'S NOT BRAIN-DEAD.
I DON'T EVEN KNOW WHAT COLOR HIS EYES ARE.
GOD. JANE. I HAD NO IDEA.
I HAD TO TELL MYSELF THAT WHEN I OPENED MY EYES, I NEEDED TO BE PREPARED TO SEE THE WORST THING EVER.
AND WHEN I DID, IT WAS EVEN *WORSE.*

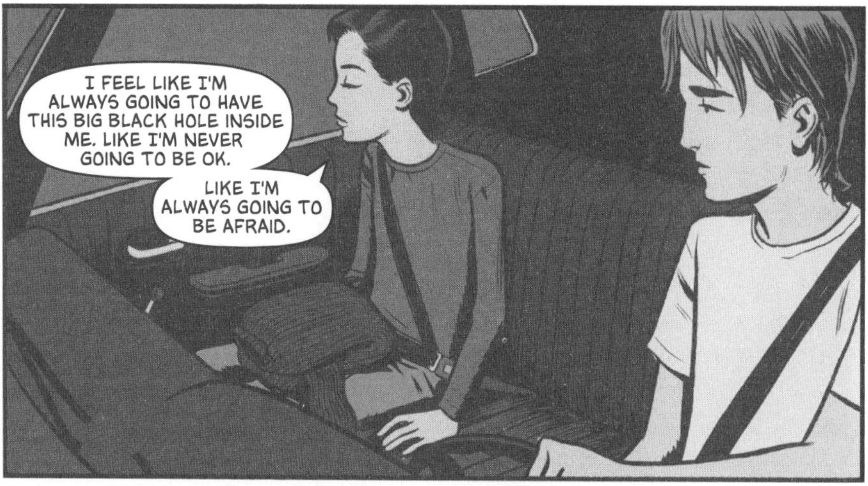
I FEEL LIKE I'M ALWAYS GOING TO HAVE THIS BIG BLACK HOLE INSIDE ME. LIKE I'M NEVER GOING TO BE OK.
LIKE I'M ALWAYS GOING TO BE AFRAID.

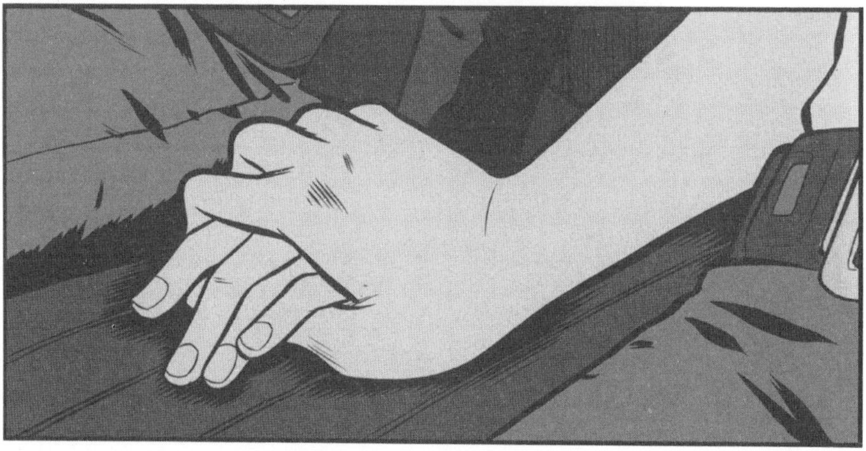

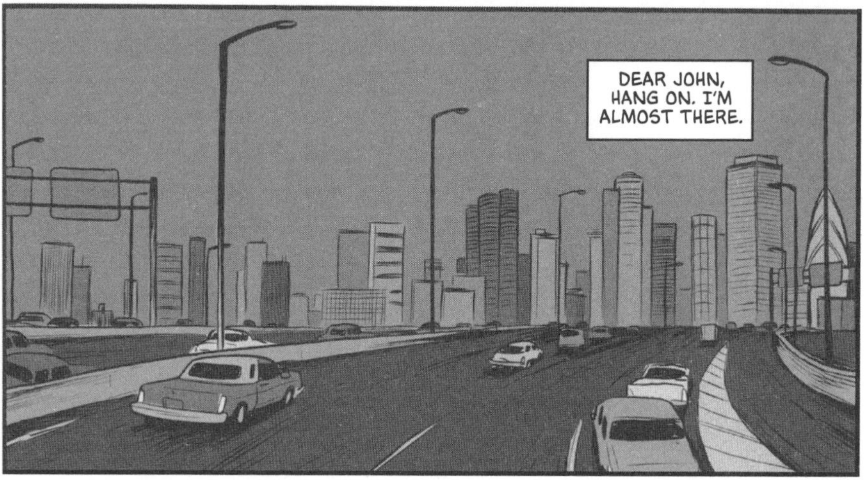
DEAR JOHN, HANG ON. I'M ALMOST THERE.

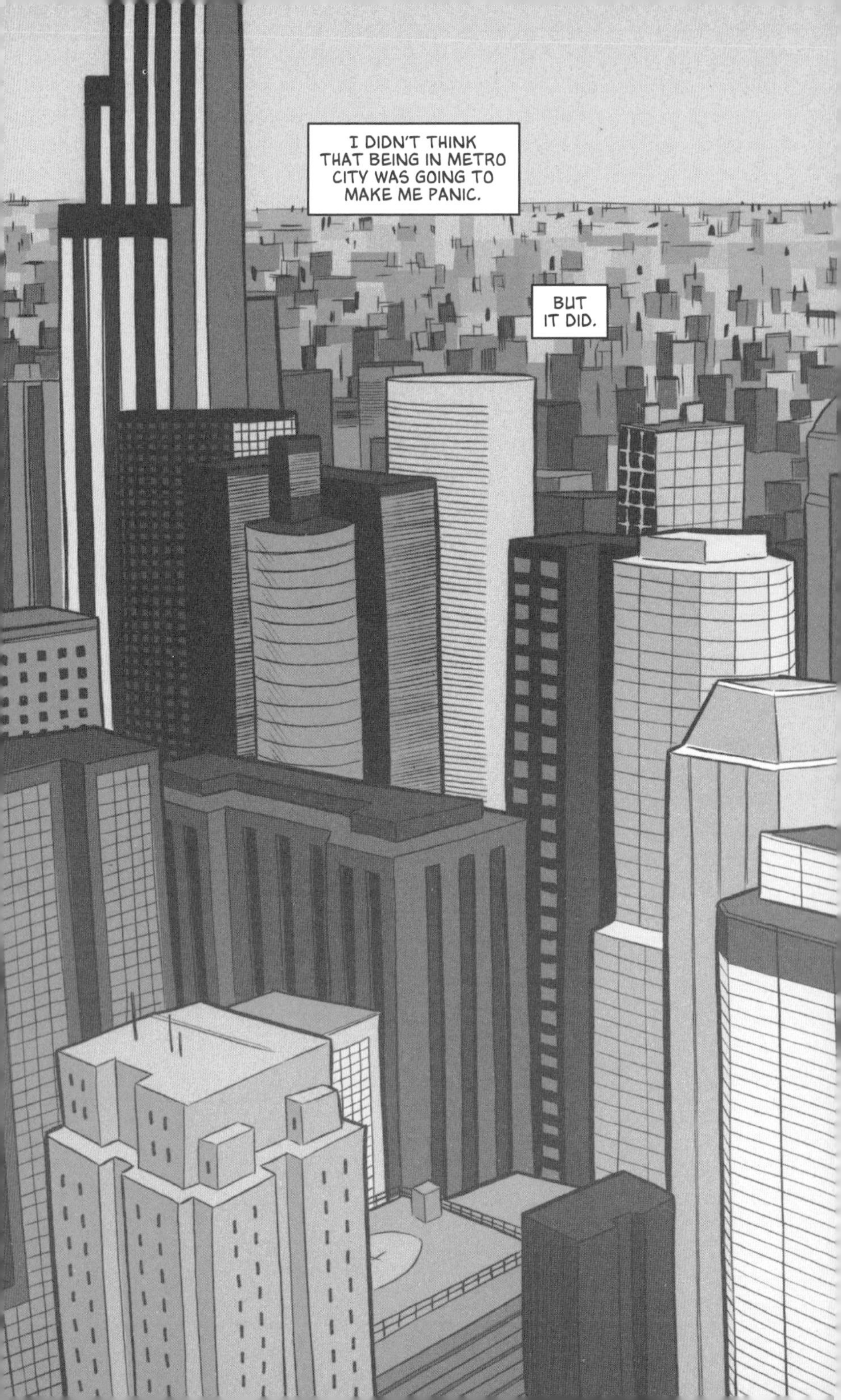
I DIDN'T THINK THAT BEING IN METRO CITY WAS GOING TO MAKE ME PANIC.
BUT IT DID.

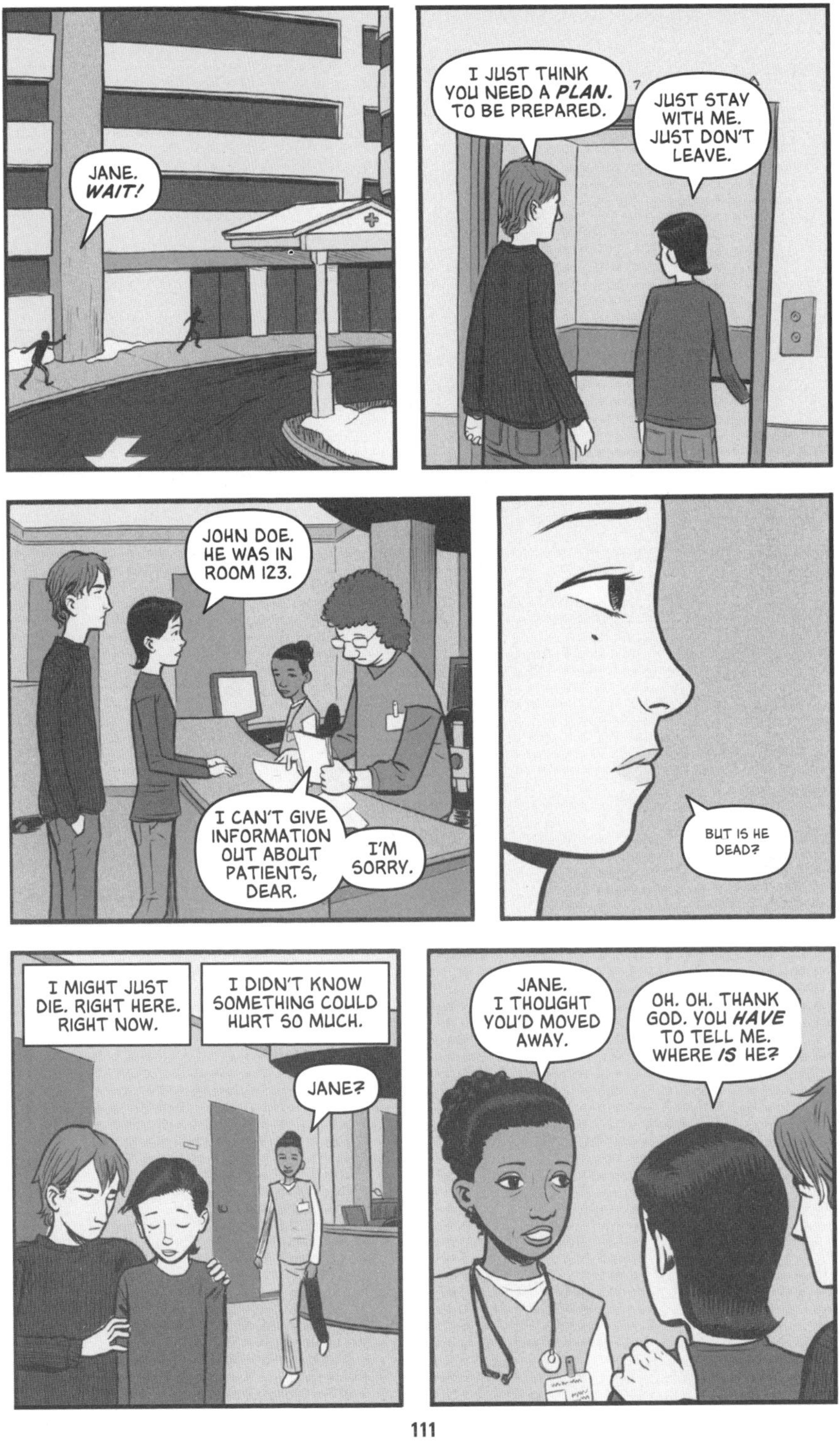
JANE. WAIT!
I JUST THINK YOU NEED A PLAN. TO BE PREPARED.
JUST STAY WITH ME. JUST DON'T LEAVE.
JOHN DOE. HE WAS IN ROOM 123.
I CAN'T GIVE INFORMATION OUT ABOUT PATIENTS, DEAR.
I'M SORRY.
BUT IS HE DEAD?
I MIGHT JUST DIE. RIGHT HERE. RIGHT NOW.
I DIDN'T KNOW SOMETHING COULD HURT SO MUCH.
JANE?
JANE. I THOUGHT YOU'D MOVED AWAY.
OH. OH. THANK GOD. YOU HAVE TO TELL ME. WHERE IS HE?

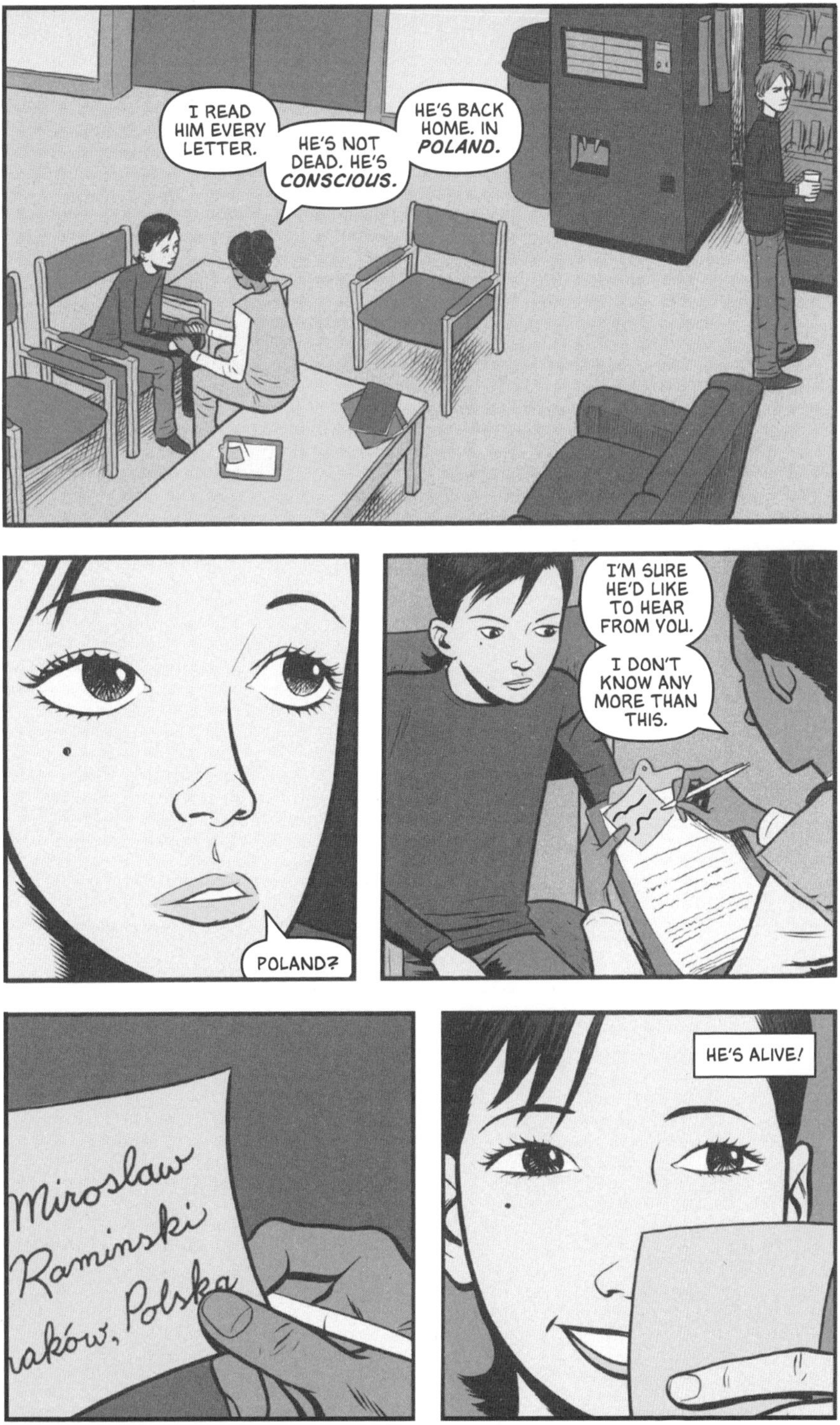
I READ HIM EVERY LETTER.
HE'S NOT DEAD. HE'S *CONSCIOUS.*
HE'S BACK HOME. IN *POLAND.*
POLAND?
I'M SURE HE'D LIKE TO HEAR FROM YOU.
I DON'T KNOW ANY MORE THAN THIS.
Miroslaw
Raminski
raków, Polska
HE'S ALIVE!

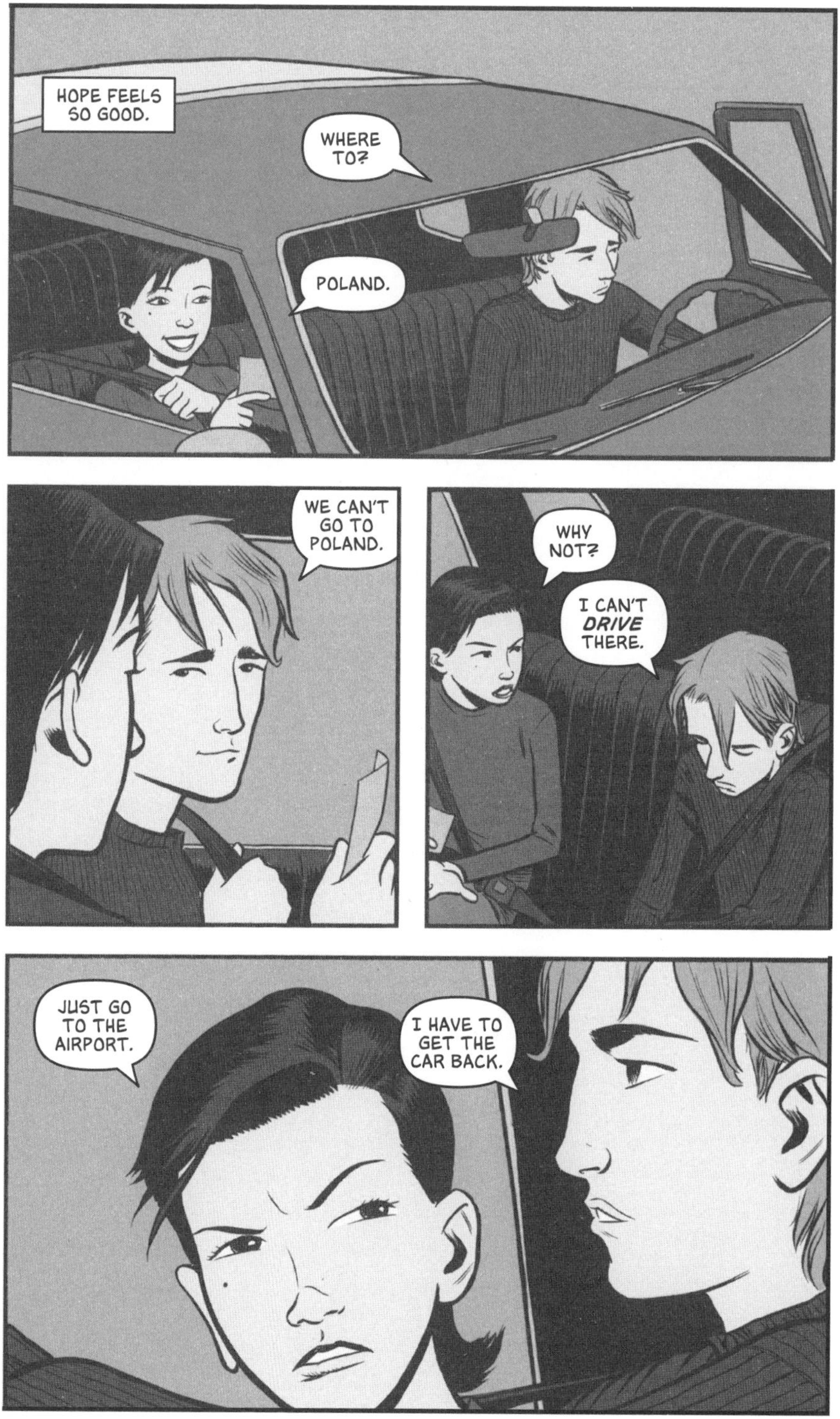
HOPE FEELS SO GOOD.
WHERE TO?
POLAND.
WE CAN'T GO TO POLAND.
WHY NOT?
I CAN'T *DRIVE* THERE.
JUST GO TO THE AIRPORT.
I HAVE TO GET THE CAR BACK.

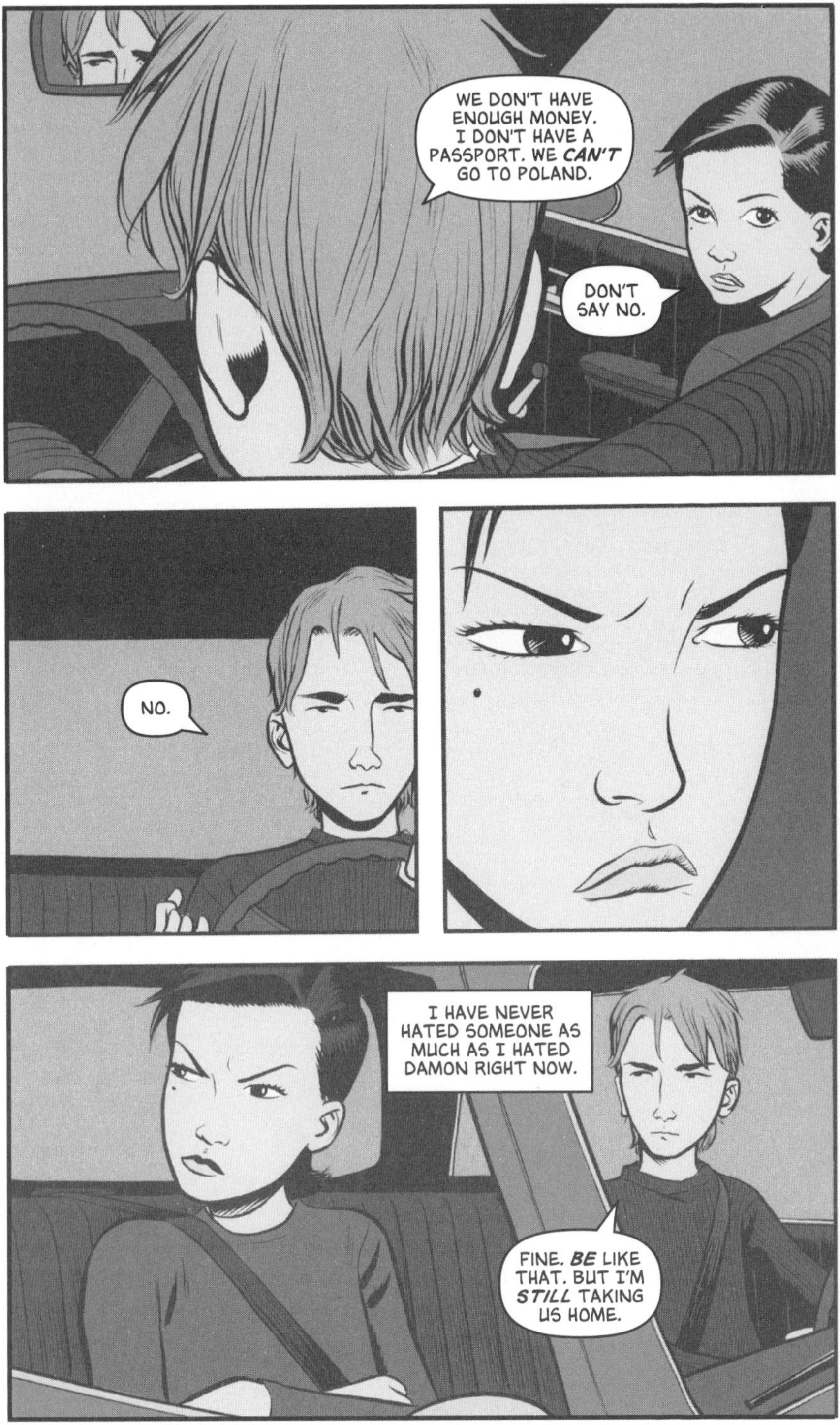

WE DON'T HAVE ENOUGH MONEY. I DON'T HAVE A PASSPORT. WE *CAN'T* GO TO POLAND.
DON'T SAY NO.
NO.
I HAVE NEVER HATED SOMEONE AS MUCH AS I HATED DAMON RIGHT NOW.
FINE. *BE* LIKE THAT. BUT I'M *STILL* TAKING US HOME.

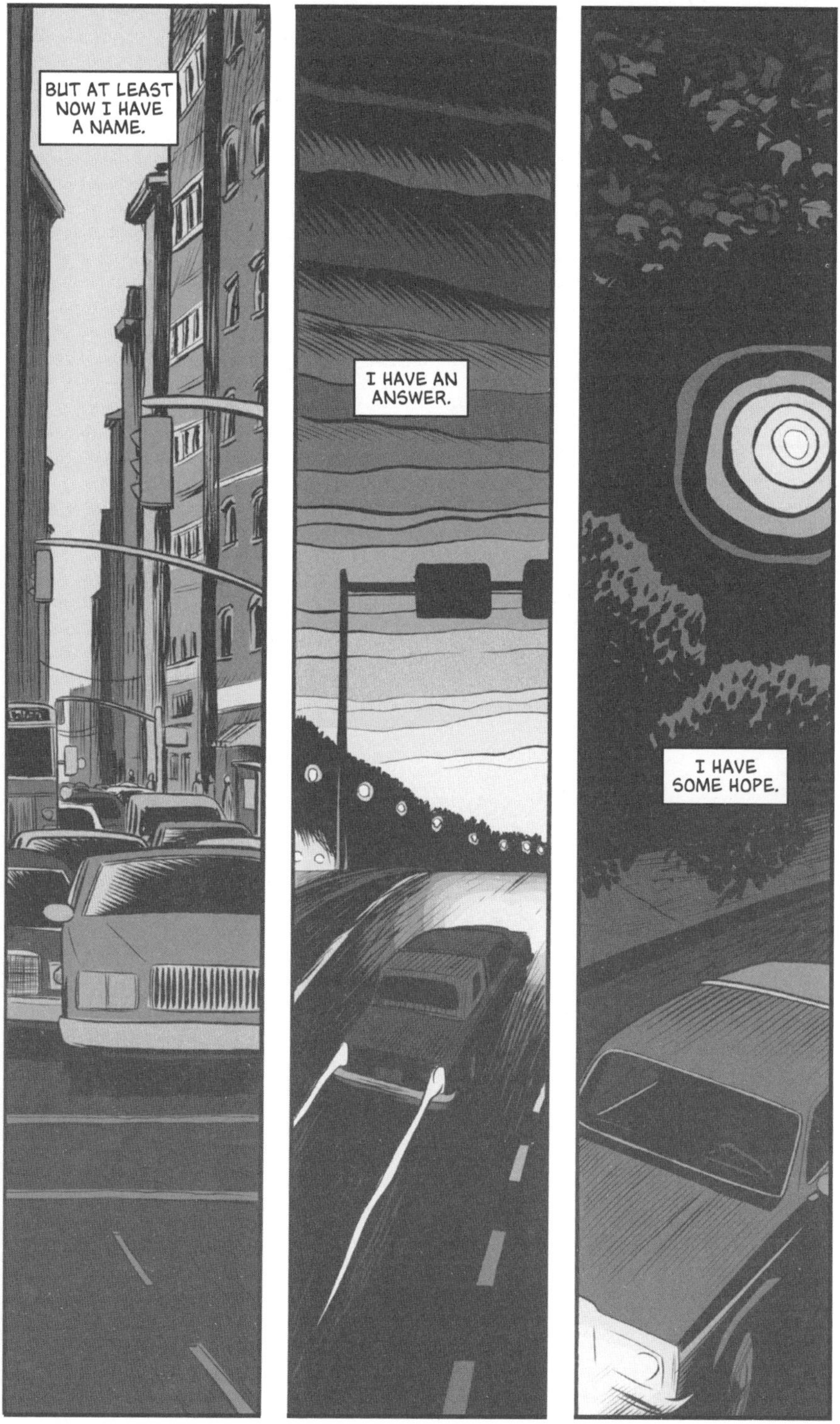
BUT AT LEAST NOW I HAVE A NAME.
I HAVE AN ANSWER.
I HAVE SOME HOPE.

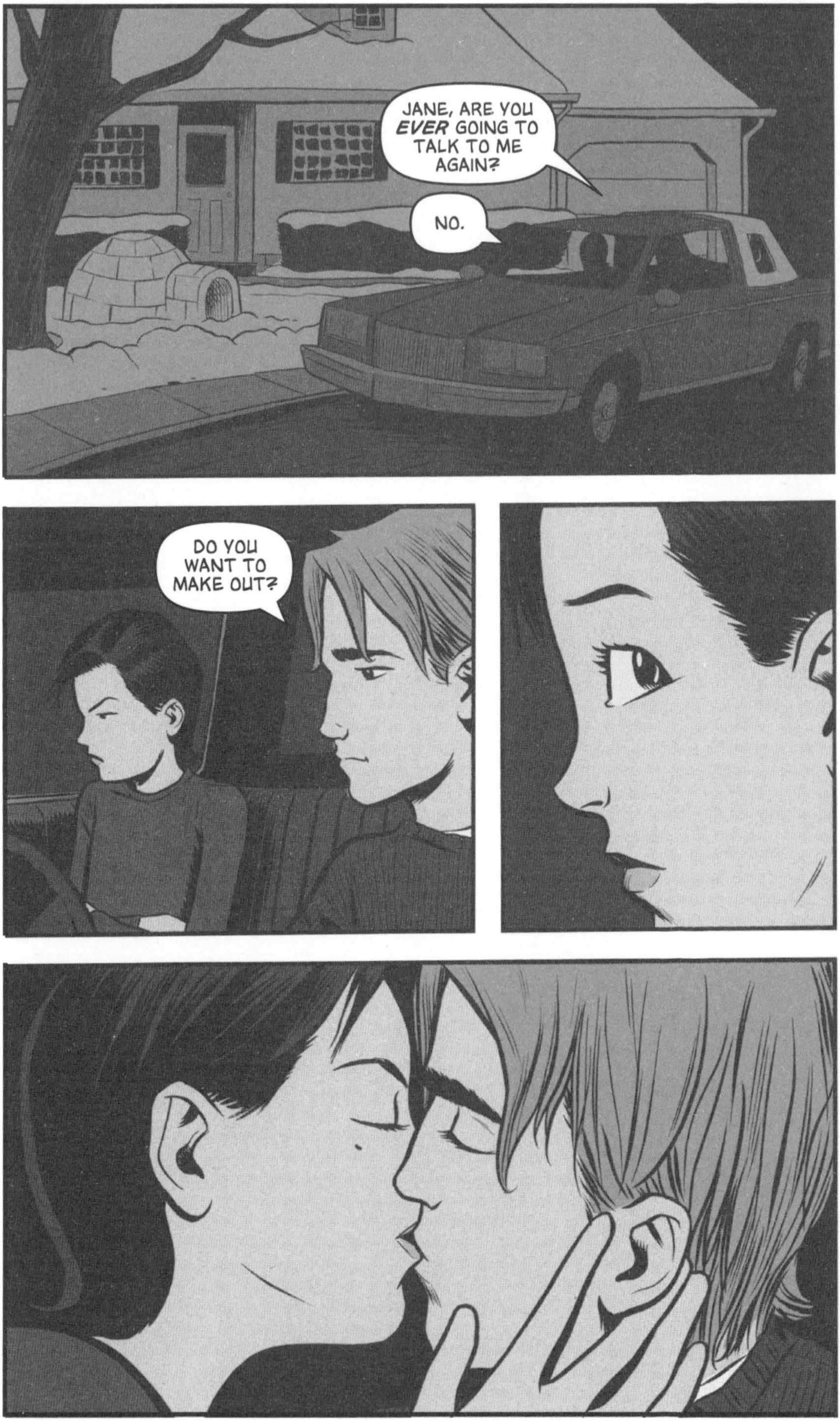
JANE, ARE YOU *EVER* GOING TO TALK TO ME AGAIN?
NO.
DO YOU WANT TO MAKE OUT?

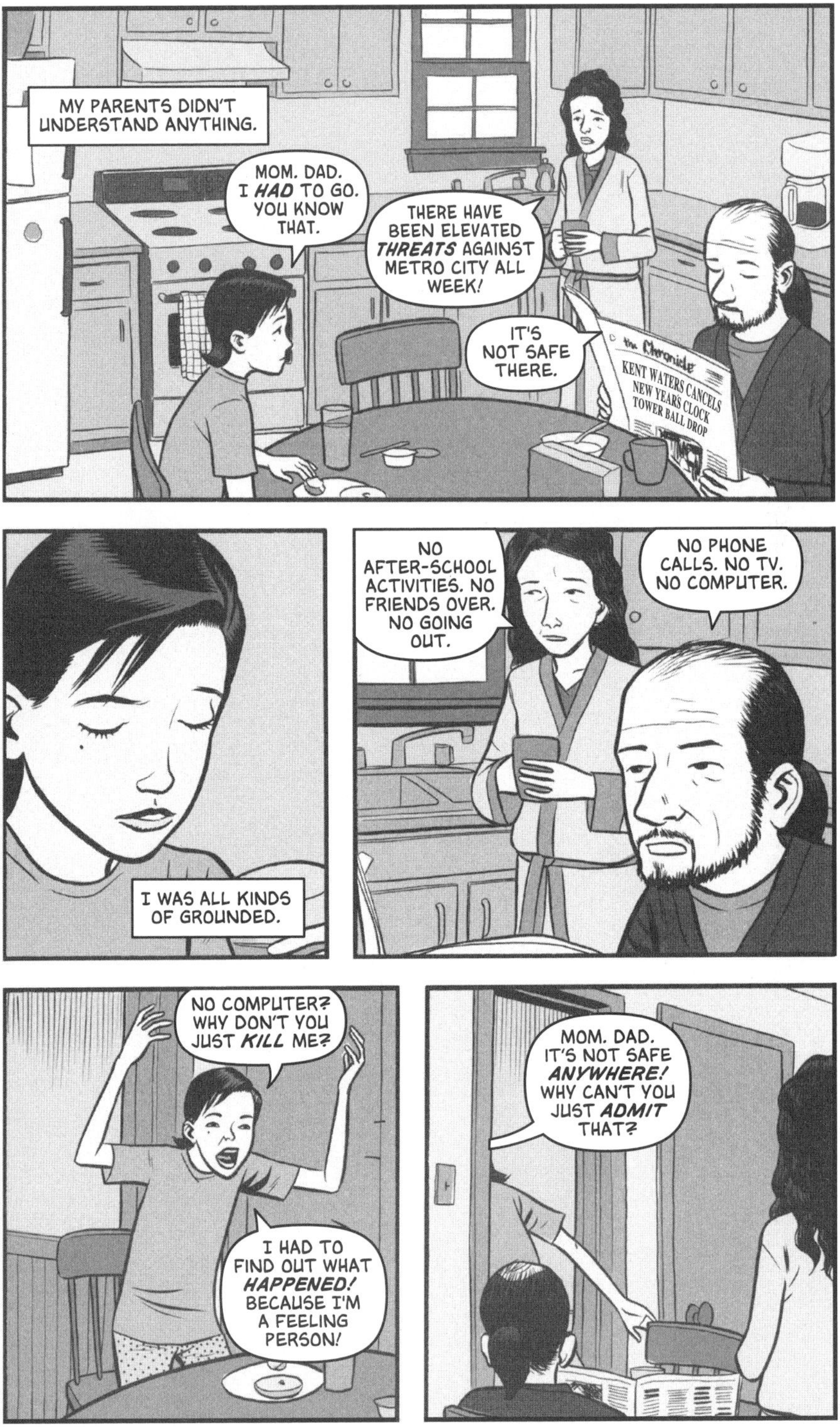
MY PARENTS DIDN'T UNDERSTAND ANYTHING.
MOM. DAD. I *HAD* TO GO. YOU KNOW THAT.
THERE HAVE BEEN ELEVATED *THREATS* AGAINST METRO CITY ALL WEEK!
IT'S NOT SAFE THERE.
the Chronicle
KENT WATERS CANCELS NEW YEAR'S CLOCK TOWER BALL DROP
I WAS ALL KINDS OF GROUNDED.
NO AFTER-SCHOOL ACTIVITIES. NO FRIENDS OVER. NO GOING OUT.
NO PHONE CALLS. NO TV. NO COMPUTER.
NO COMPUTER? WHY DON'T YOU JUST *KILL* ME?
I HAD TO FIND OUT WHAT *HAPPENED!* BECAUSE I'M A FEELING PERSON!
MOM. DAD. IT'S NOT SAFE *ANYWHERE!* WHY CAN'T YOU JUST *ADMIT* THAT?

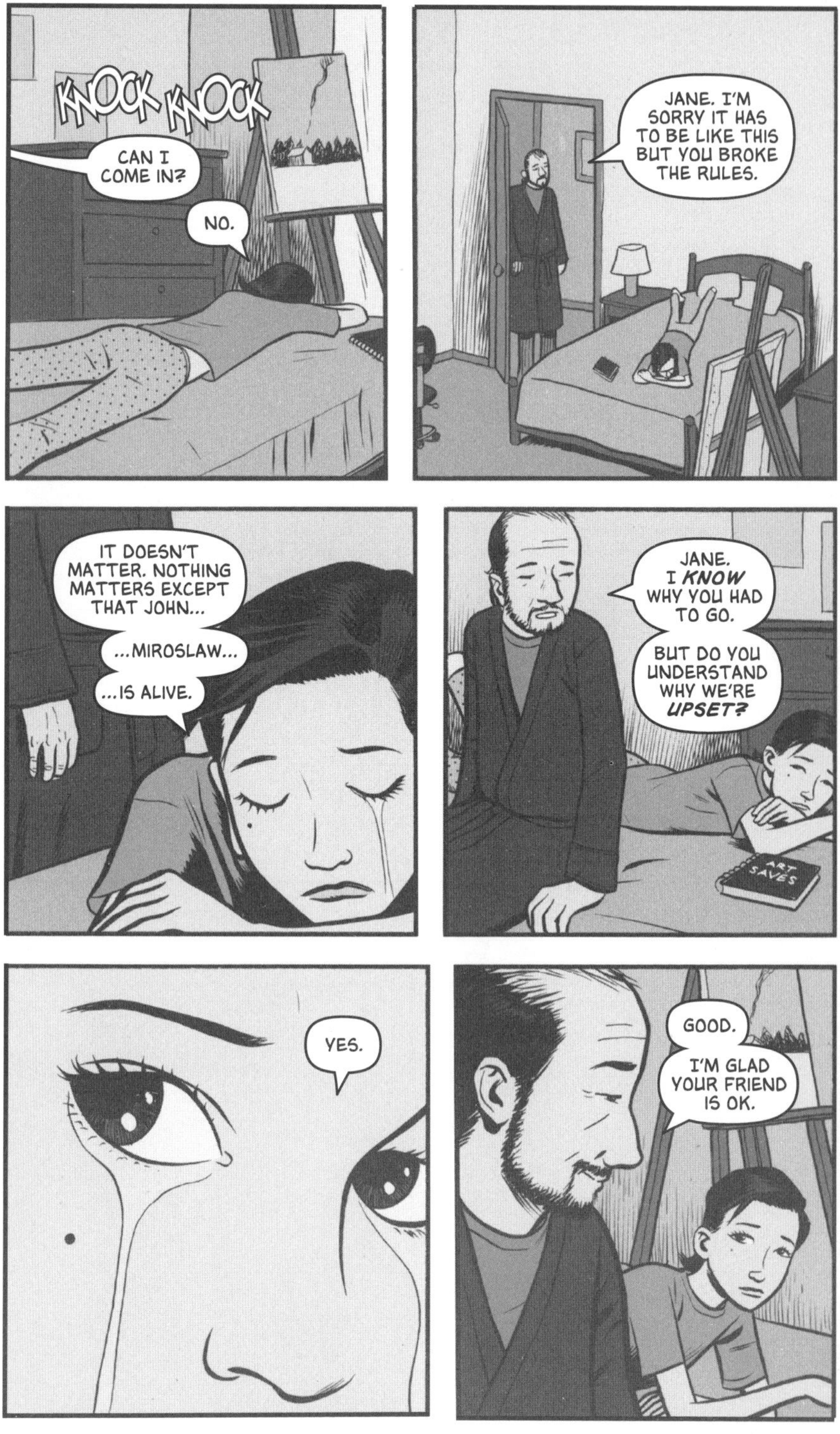
KNOCK KNOCK
CAN I COME IN?
NO.
JANE. I'M SORRY IT HAS TO BE LIKE THIS BUT YOU BROKE THE RULES.
IT DOESN'T MATTER. NOTHING MATTERS EXCEPT THAT JOHN...
...MIROSLAW...
...IS ALIVE.
JANE. I *KNOW* WHY YOU HAD TO GO.
BUT DO YOU UNDERSTAND WHY WE'RE *UPSET?*
ART SAVES
YES.
GOOD.
I'M GLAD YOUR FRIEND IS OK.

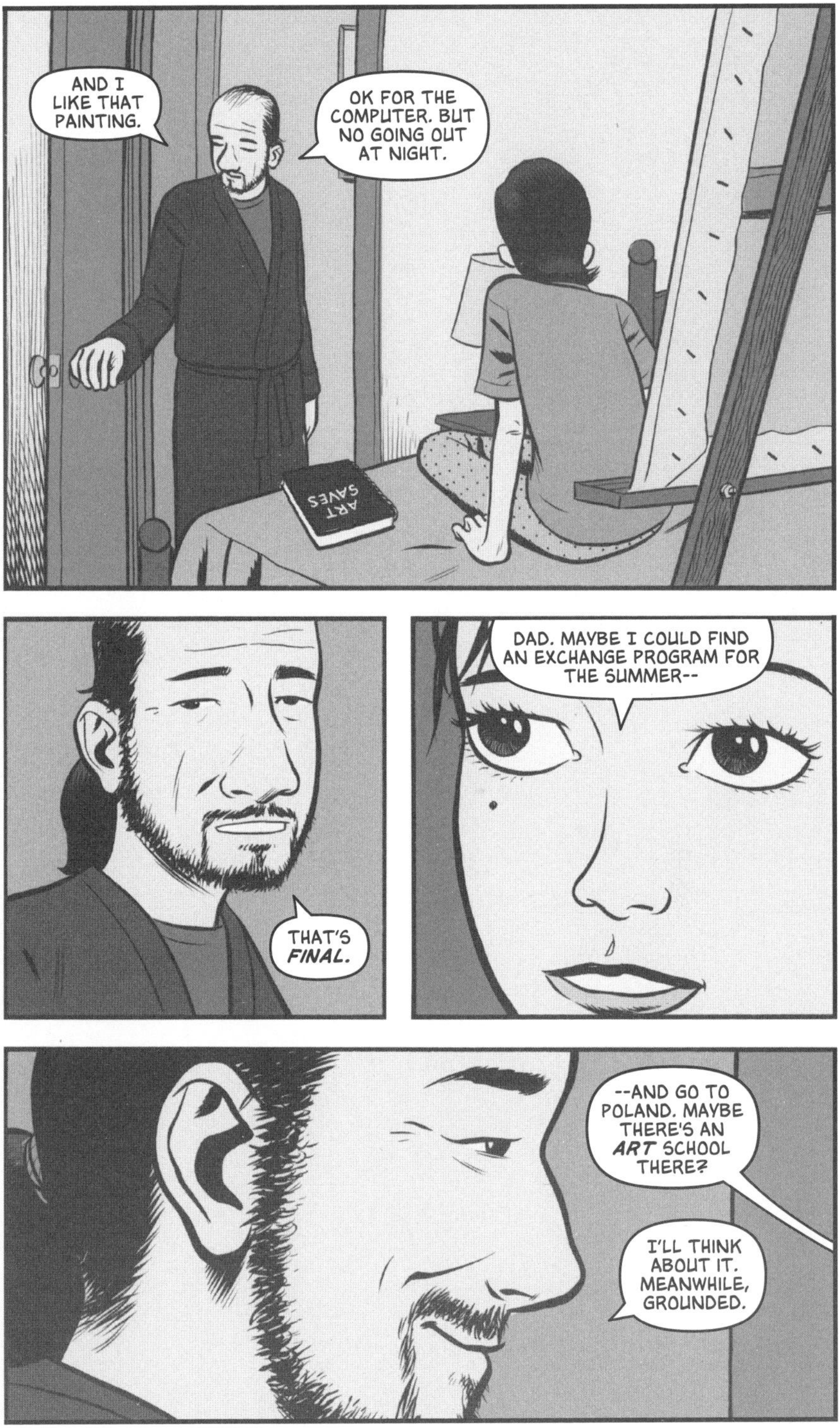
AND I LIKE THAT PAINTING.
OK FOR THE COMPUTER. BUT NO GOING OUT AT NIGHT.
ART SAVES
THAT'S *FINAL*.
DAD. MAYBE I COULD FIND AN EXCHANGE PROGRAM FOR THE SUMMER--
--AND GO TO POLAND. MAYBE THERE'S AN *ART* SCHOOL THERE?
I'LL THINK ABOUT IT. MEANWHILE, GROUNDED.

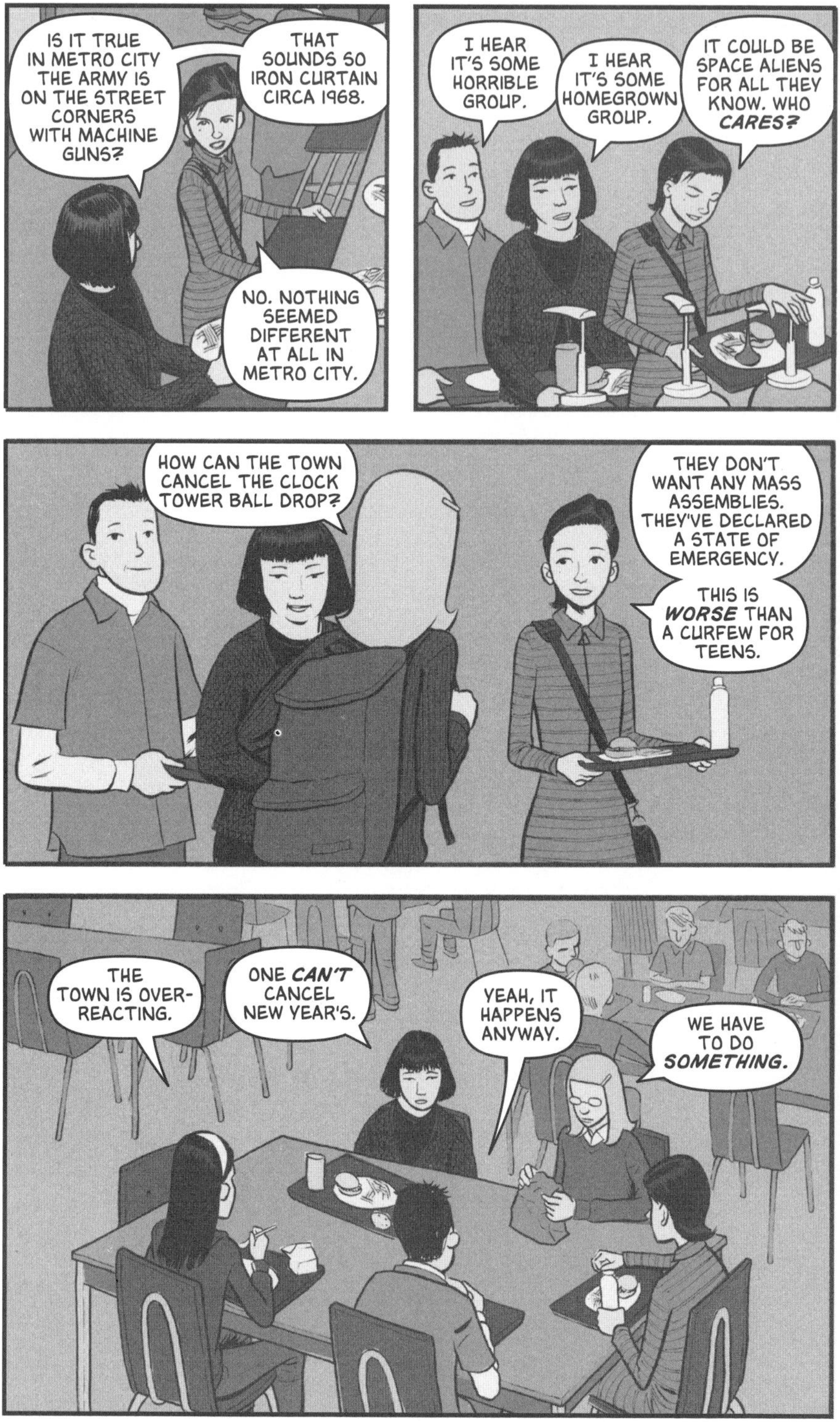
IS IT TRUE IN METRO CITY THE ARMY IS ON THE STREET CORNERS WITH MACHINE GUNS?
THAT SOUNDS SO IRON CURTAIN CIRCA 1968.
NO. NOTHING SEEMED DIFFERENT AT ALL IN METRO CITY.
I HEAR IT'S SOME HORRIBLE GROUP.
I HEAR IT'S SOME HOMEGROWN GROUP.
IT COULD BE SPACE ALIENS FOR ALL THEY KNOW. WHO CARES?
HOW CAN THE TOWN CANCEL THE CLOCK TOWER BALL DROP?
THEY DON'T WANT ANY MASS ASSEMBLIES. THEY'VE DECLARED A STATE OF EMERGENCY.
THIS IS WORSE THAN A CURFEW FOR TEENS.
THE TOWN IS OVER-REACTING.
ONE CAN'T CANCEL NEW YEAR'S.
YEAH, IT HAPPENS ANYWAY.
WE HAVE TO DO SOMETHING.

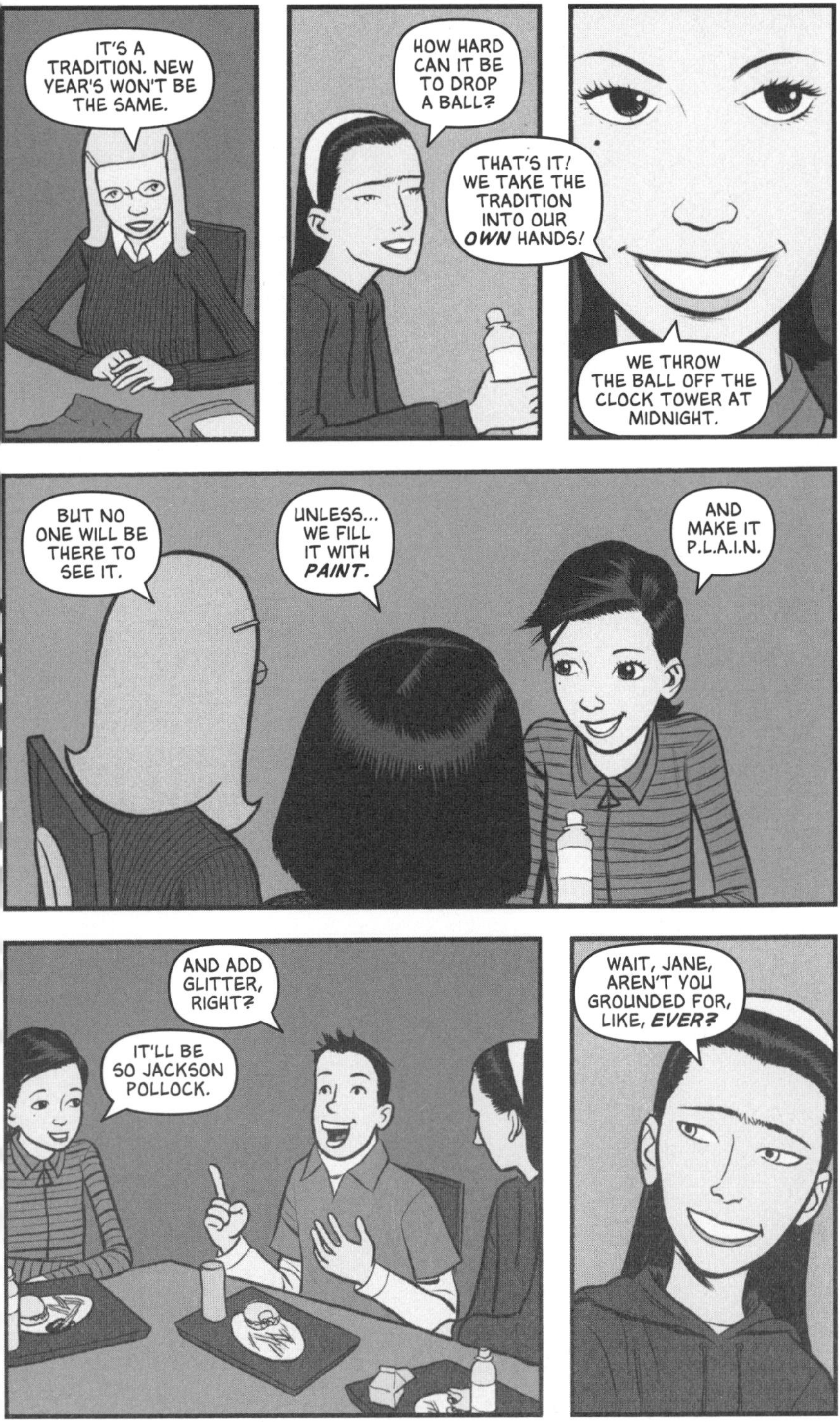
IT'S A TRADITION. NEW YEAR'S WON'T BE THE SAME.
HOW HARD CAN IT BE TO DROP A BALL?
THAT'S IT! WE TAKE THE TRADITION INTO OUR *OWN* HANDS!
WE THROW THE BALL OFF THE CLOCK TOWER AT MIDNIGHT.
BUT NO ONE WILL BE THERE TO SEE IT.
UNLESS... WE FILL IT WITH *PAINT*.
AND MAKE IT P.L.A.I.N.
AND ADD GLITTER, RIGHT?
IT'LL BE SO JACKSON POLLOCK.
WAIT, JANE, AREN'T YOU GROUNDED FOR, LIKE, *EVER*?

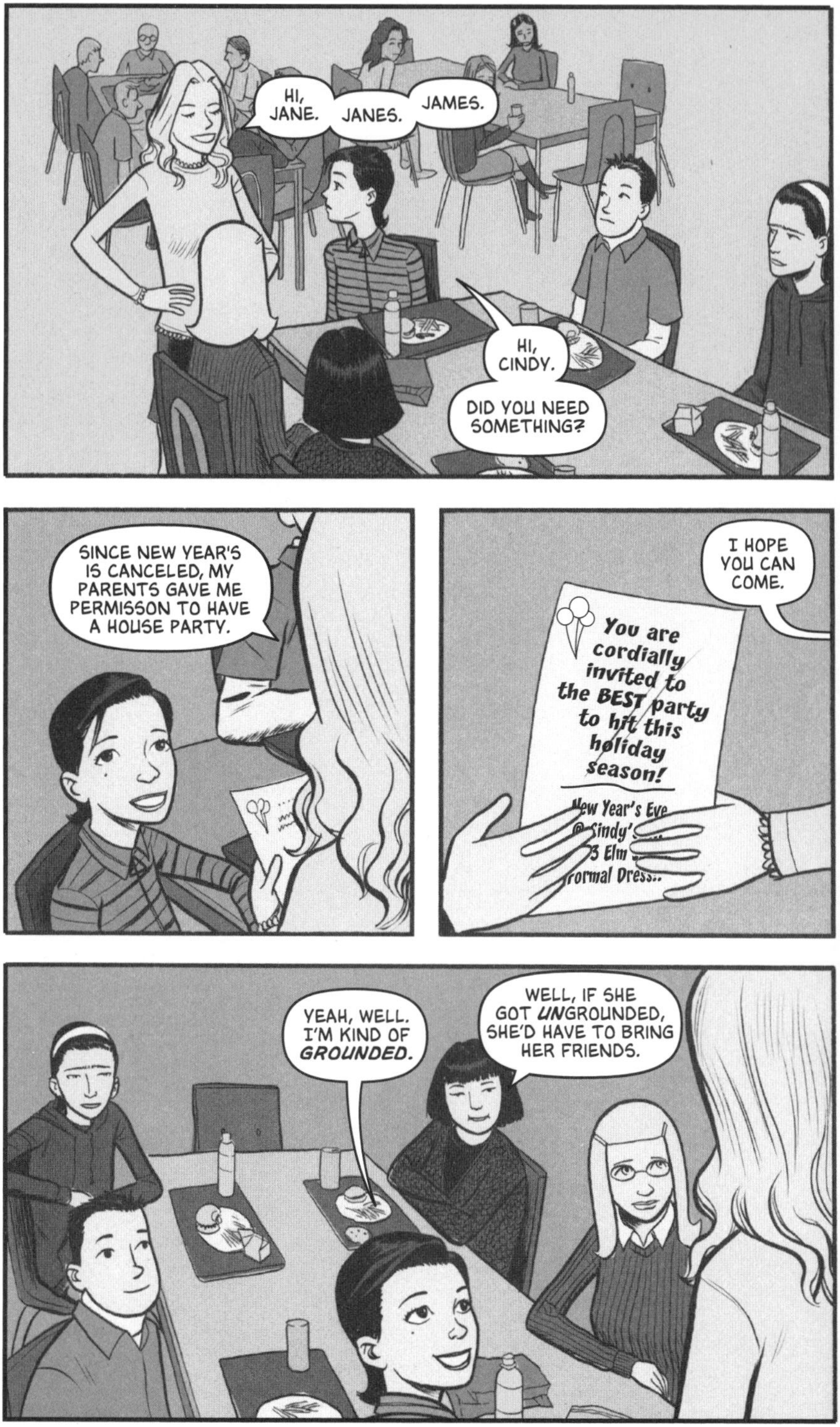
HI, JANE.
JANES.
JAMES.
HI, CINDY.
DID YOU NEED SOMETHING?
SINCE NEW YEAR'S IS CANCELED, MY PARENTS GAVE ME PERMISSON TO HAVE A HOUSE PARTY.
You are cordially invited to the BEST party to hit this holiday season!
I HOPE YOU CAN COME.
YEAH, WELL. I'M KIND OF GROUNDED.
WELL, IF SHE GOT UNGROUNDED, SHE'D HAVE TO BRING HER FRIENDS.

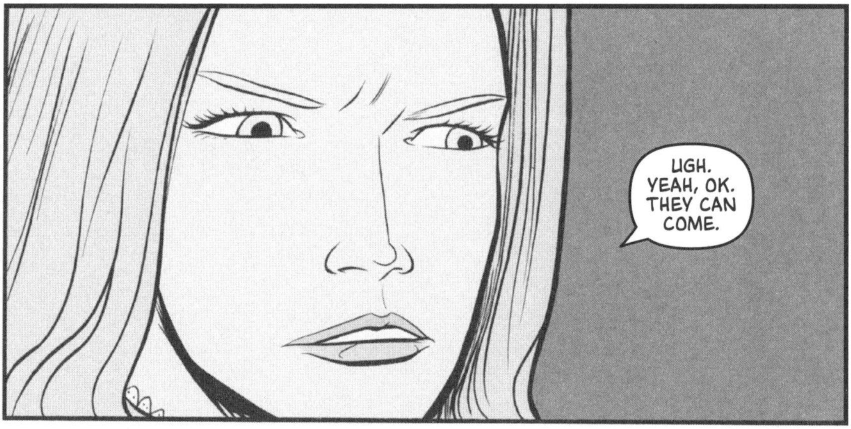
UGH.
YEAH, OK.
THEY CAN
COME.

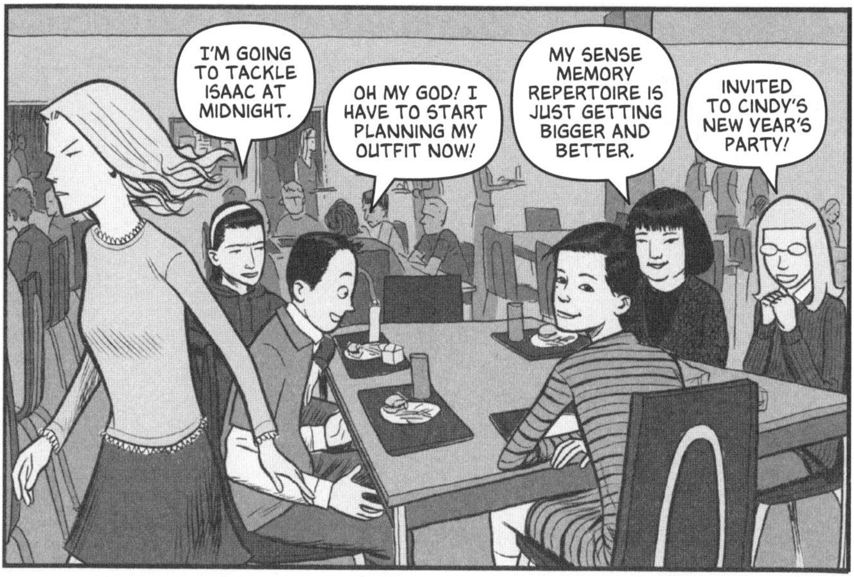
I'M GOING TO TACKLE ISAAC AT MIDNIGHT.
OH MY GOD! I HAVE TO START PLANNING MY OUTFIT NOW!
MY SENSE MEMORY REPERTOIRE IS JUST GETTING BIGGER AND BETTER.
INVITED TO CINDY'S NEW YEAR'S PARTY!

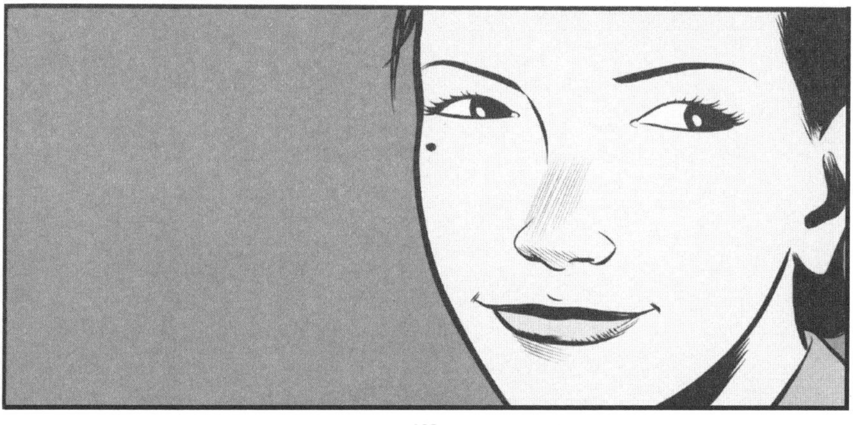

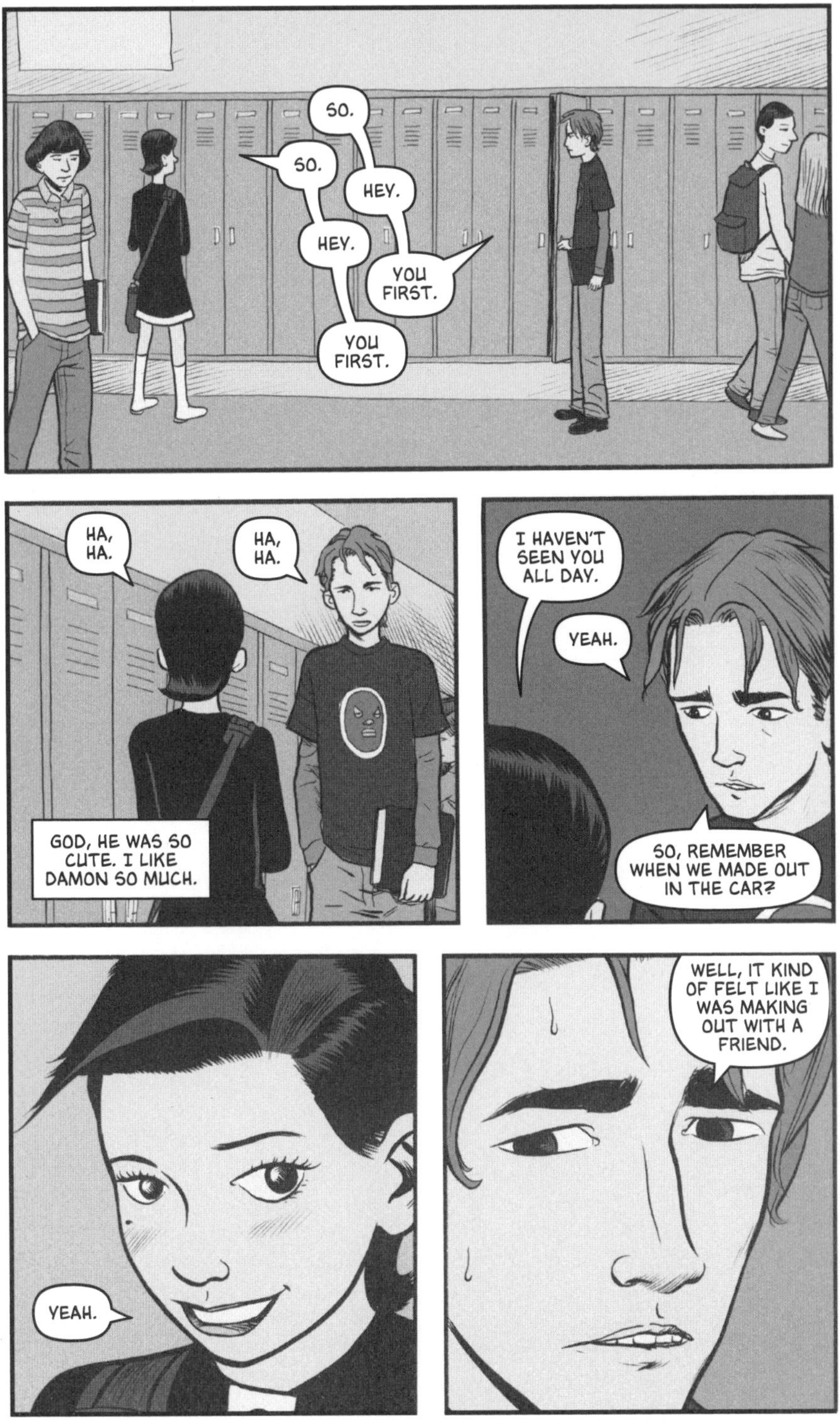
SO.
SO.
HEY.
HEY.
YOU FIRST.
YOU FIRST.
HA, HA.
HA, HA.
GOD, HE WAS SO CUTE. I LIKE DAMON SO MUCH.
I HAVEN'T SEEN YOU ALL DAY.
YEAH.
SO, REMEMBER WHEN WE MADE OUT IN THE CAR?
YEAH.
WELL, IT KIND OF FELT LIKE I WAS MAKING OUT WITH A FRIEND.

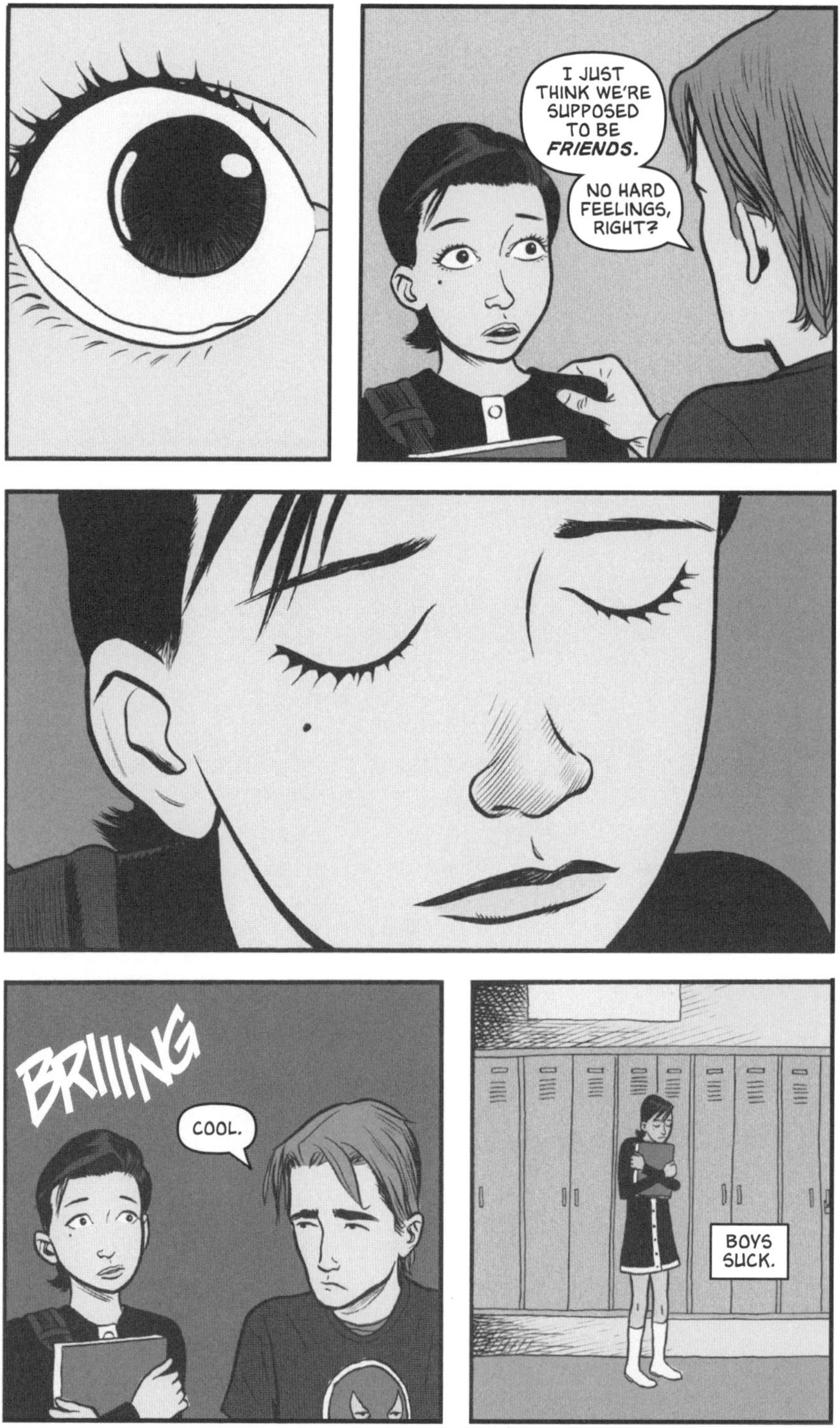
I JUST THINK WE'RE SUPPOSED TO BE FRIENDS.
NO HARD FEELINGS, RIGHT?
BRIIING
COOL.
BOYS SUCK.

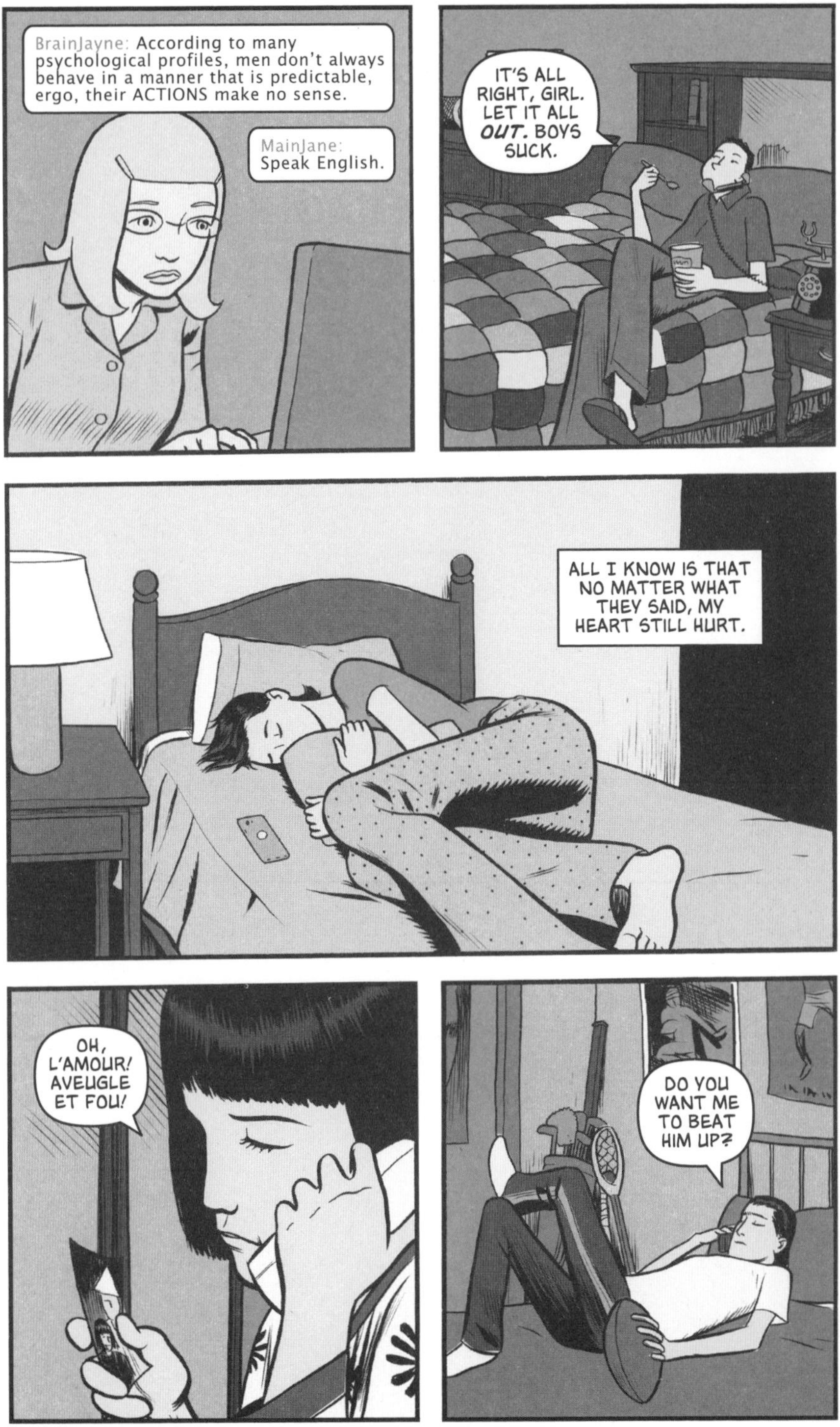
BrainJayne: According to many psychological profiles, men don't always behave in a manner that is predictable, ergo, their ACTIONS make no sense.
MainJane: Speak English.
IT'S ALL RIGHT, GIRL. LET IT ALL OUT. BOYS SUCK.
ALL I KNOW IS THAT NO MATTER WHAT THEY SAID, MY HEART STILL HURT.
OH, L'AMOUR! AVEUGLE ET FOU!
DO YOU WANT ME TO BEAT HIM UP?

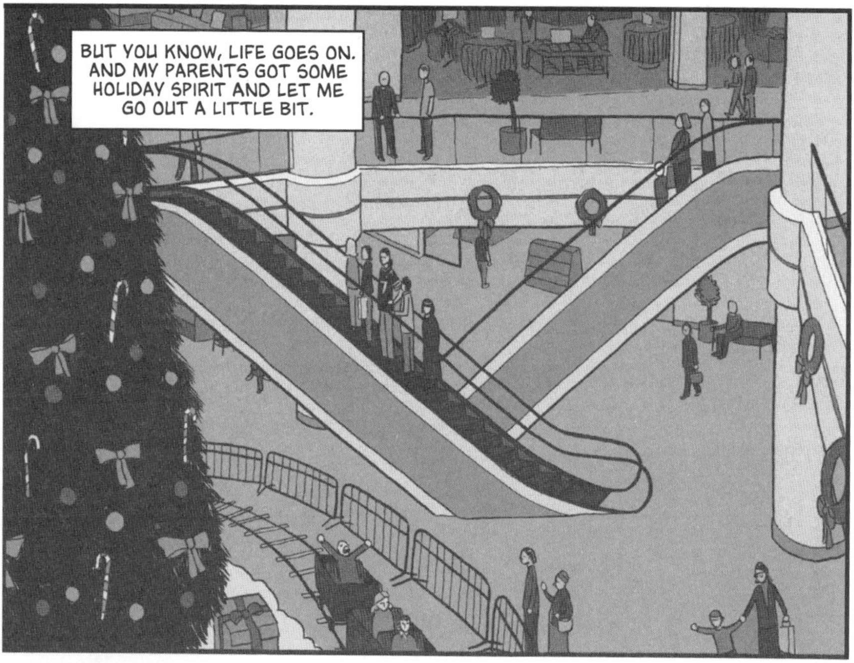
BUT YOU KNOW, LIFE GOES ON. AND MY PARENTS GOT SOME HOLIDAY SPIRIT AND LET ME GO OUT A LITTLE BIT.

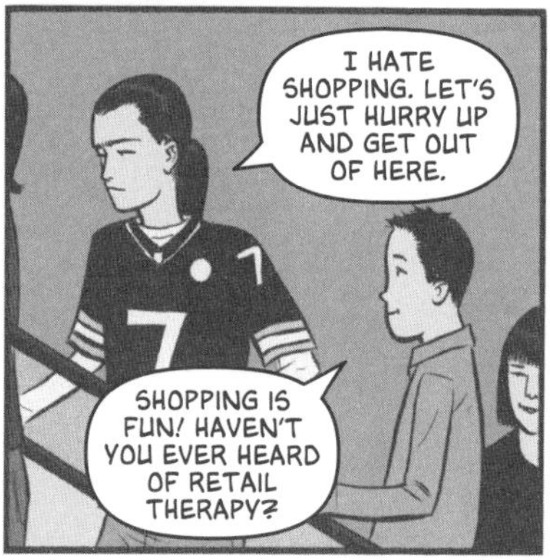
I HATE SHOPPING. LET'S JUST HURRY UP AND GET OUT OF HERE.
SHOPPING IS FUN! HAVEN'T YOU EVER HEARD OF RETAIL THERAPY?

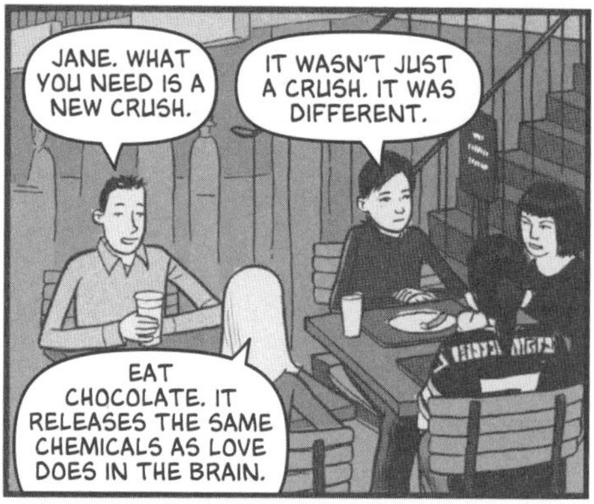
JANE. WHAT YOU NEED IS A NEW CRUSH.
IT WASN'T JUST A CRUSH. IT WAS DIFFERENT.
EAT CHOCOLATE. IT RELEASES THE SAME CHEMICALS AS LOVE DOES IN THE BRAIN.

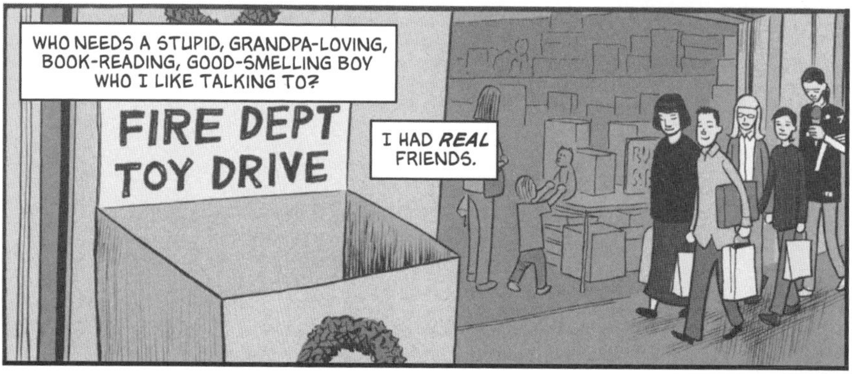
WHO NEEDS A STUPID, GRANDPA-LOVING, BOOK-READING, GOOD-SMELLING BOY WHO I LIKE TALKING TO?
FIRE DEPT TOY DRIVE
I HAD *REAL* FRIENDS.

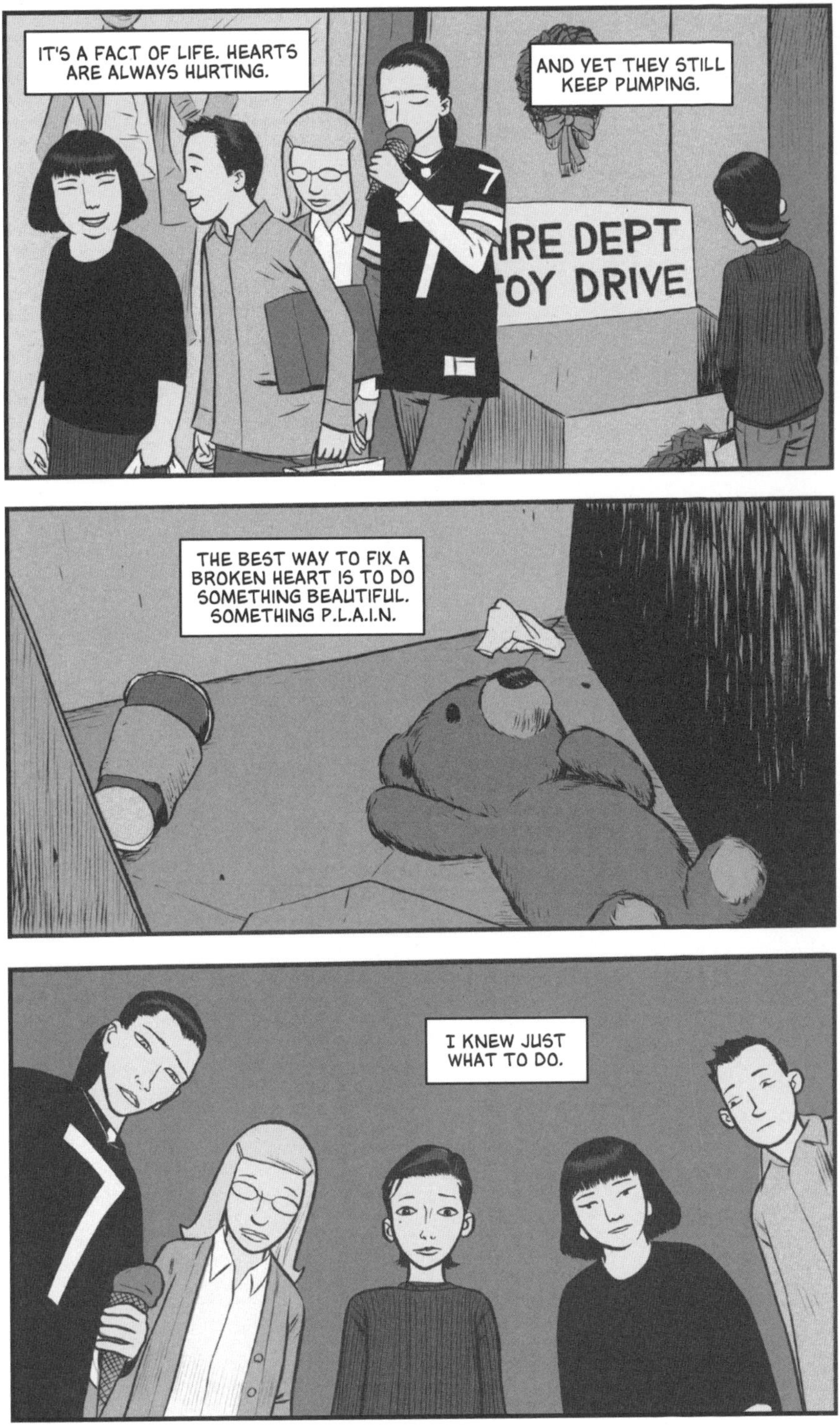
IT'S A FACT OF LIFE. HEARTS ARE ALWAYS HURTING.
AND YET THEY STILL KEEP PUMPING.
IRE DEPT TOY DRIVE
THE BEST WAY TO FIX A BROKEN HEART IS TO DO SOMETHING BEAUTIFUL. SOMETHING P.L.A.I.N.
I KNEW JUST WHAT TO DO.

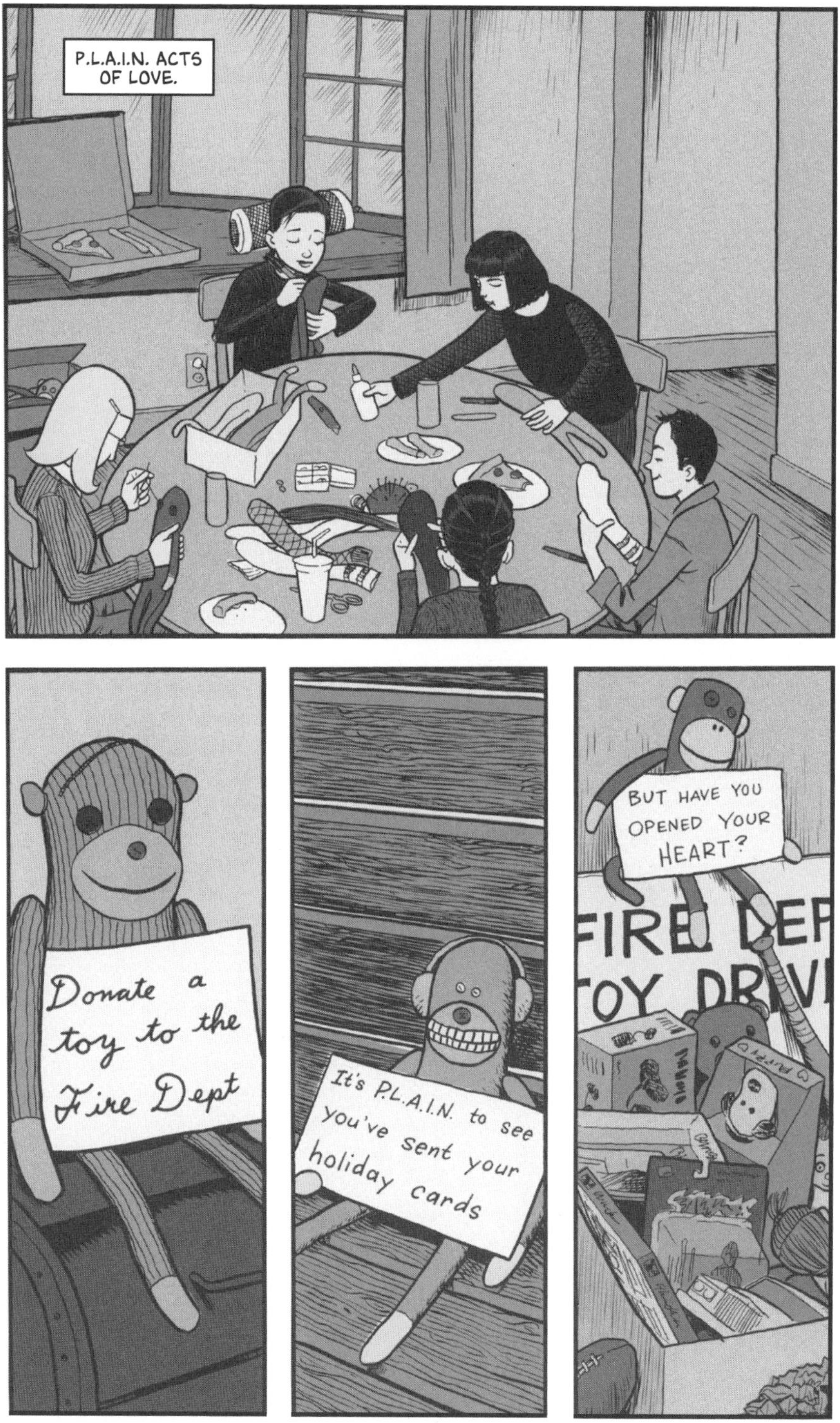
P.L.A.I.N. ACTS OF LOVE.
Donate a toy to the Fire Dept
It's P.L.A.I.N. to see you've sent your holiday cards
BUT HAVE YOU OPENED YOUR HEART?
FIRE DEP
TOY DRIV

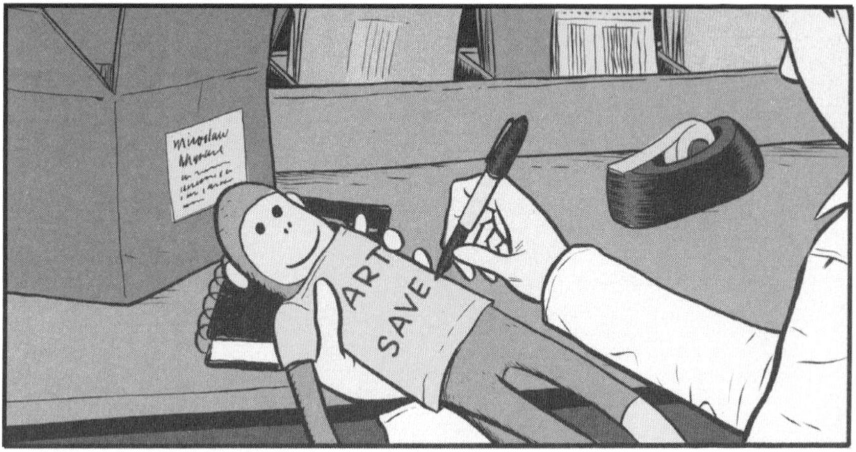
ART SAVE

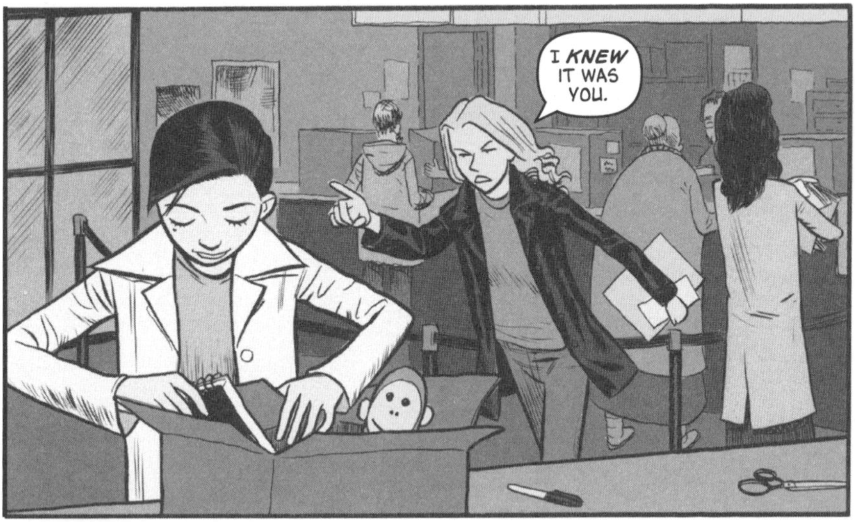
I **KNEW** IT WAS YOU.

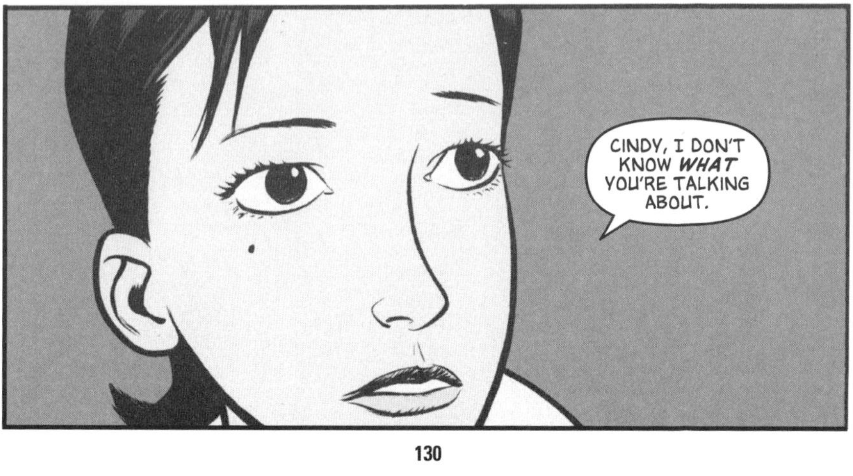
CINDY, I DON'T KNOW ***WHAT*** YOU'RE TALKING ABOUT.

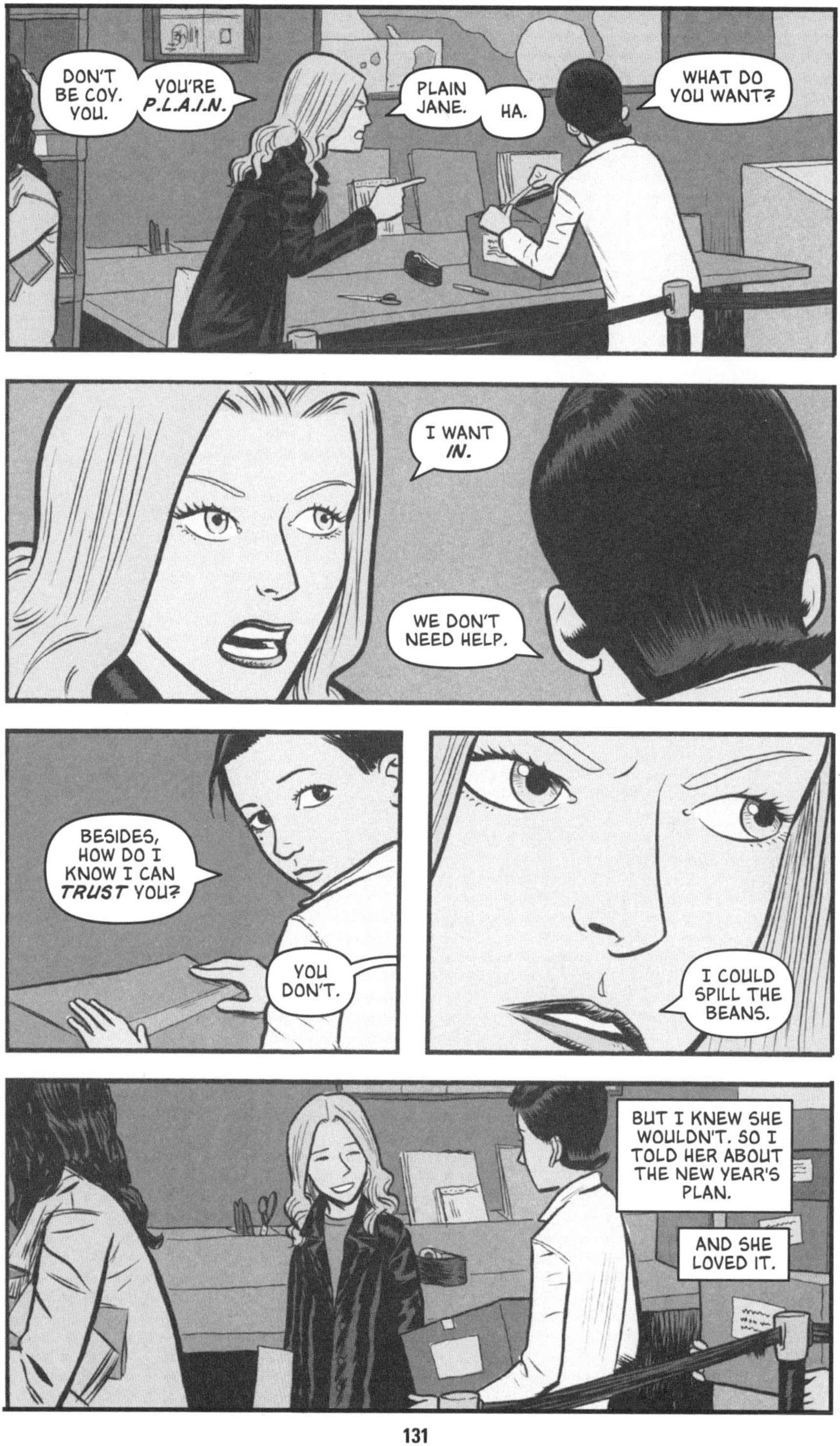
DON'T BE COY. YOU.
YOU'RE *P.L.A.I.N.*
PLAIN JANE.
HA.
WHAT DO YOU WANT?
I WANT *IN.*
WE DON'T NEED HELP.
BESIDES, HOW DO I KNOW I CAN *TRUST* YOU?
YOU DON'T.
I COULD SPILL THE BEANS.
BUT I KNEW SHE WOULDN'T. SO I TOLD HER ABOUT THE NEW YEAR'S PLAN.
AND SHE LOVED IT.

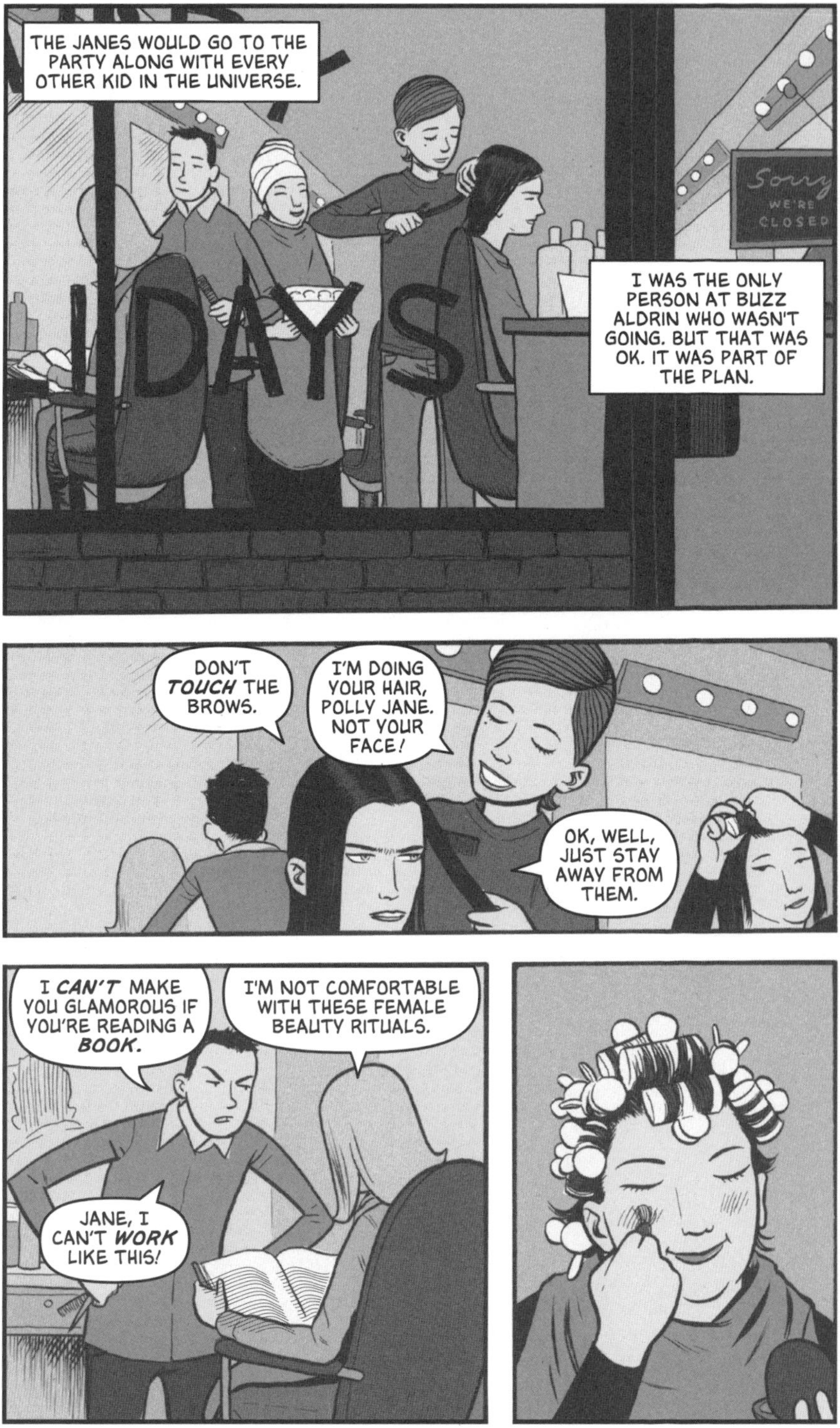
THE JANES WOULD GO TO THE PARTY ALONG WITH EVERY OTHER KID IN THE UNIVERSE.
DAYS
Sorry WE'RE CLOSED
I WAS THE ONLY PERSON AT BUZZ ALDRIN WHO WASN'T GOING. BUT THAT WAS OK. IT WAS PART OF THE PLAN.
DON'T TOUCH THE BROWS.
I'M DOING YOUR HAIR, POLLY JANE. NOT YOUR FACE!
OK, WELL, JUST STAY AWAY FROM THEM.
I CAN'T MAKE YOU GLAMOROUS IF YOU'RE READING A BOOK.
I'M NOT COMFORTABLE WITH THESE FEMALE BEAUTY RITUALS.
JANE, I CAN'T WORK LIKE THIS!

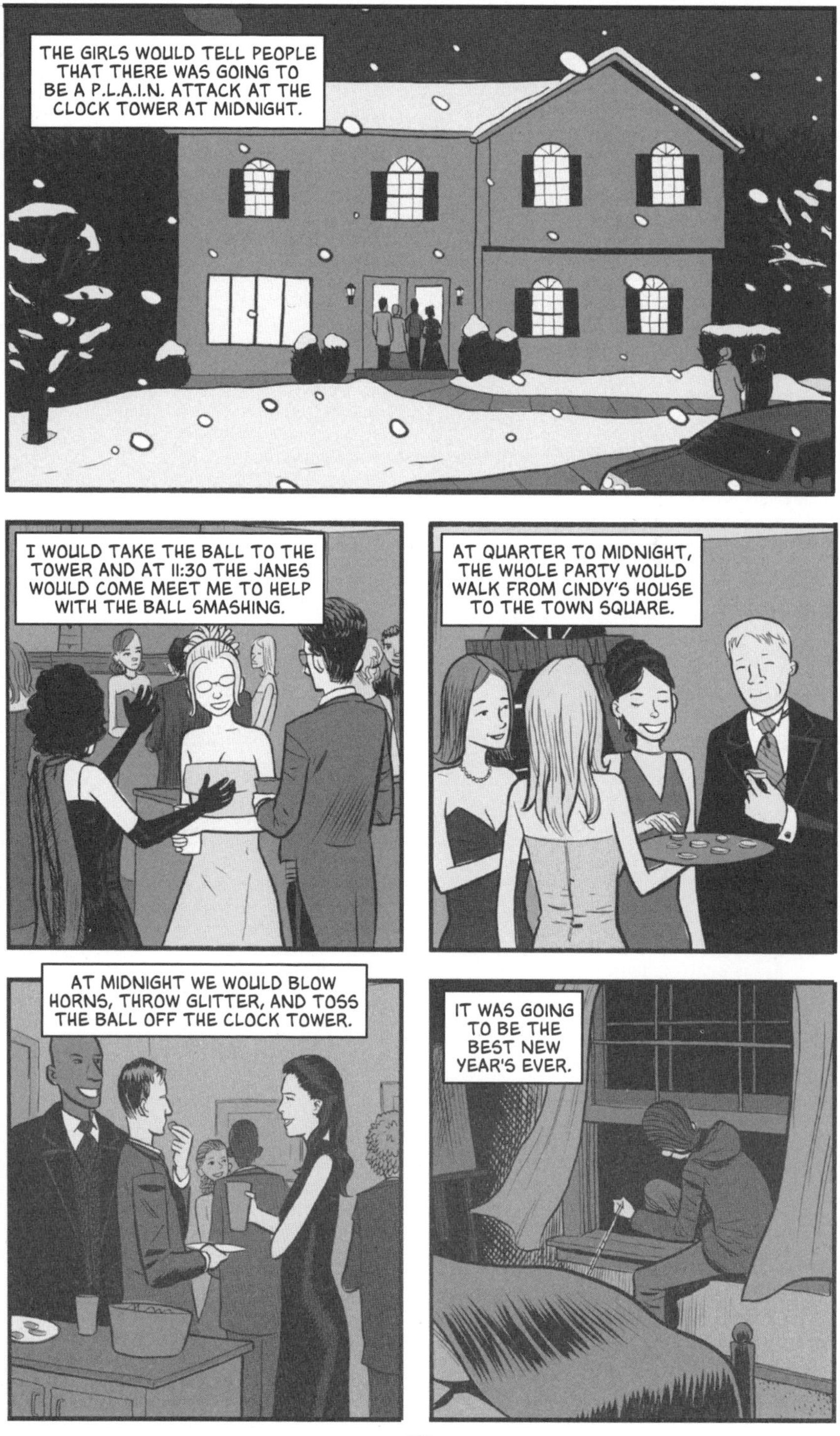
THE GIRLS WOULD TELL PEOPLE THAT THERE WAS GOING TO BE A P.L.A.I.N. ATTACK AT THE CLOCK TOWER AT MIDNIGHT.
I WOULD TAKE THE BALL TO THE TOWER AND AT 11:30 THE JANES WOULD COME MEET ME TO HELP WITH THE BALL SMASHING.
AT QUARTER TO MIDNIGHT, THE WHOLE PARTY WOULD WALK FROM CINDY'S HOUSE TO THE TOWN SQUARE.
AT MIDNIGHT WE WOULD BLOW HORNS, THROW GLITTER, AND TOSS THE BALL OFF THE CLOCK TOWER.
IT WAS GOING TO BE THE BEST NEW YEAR'S EVER.

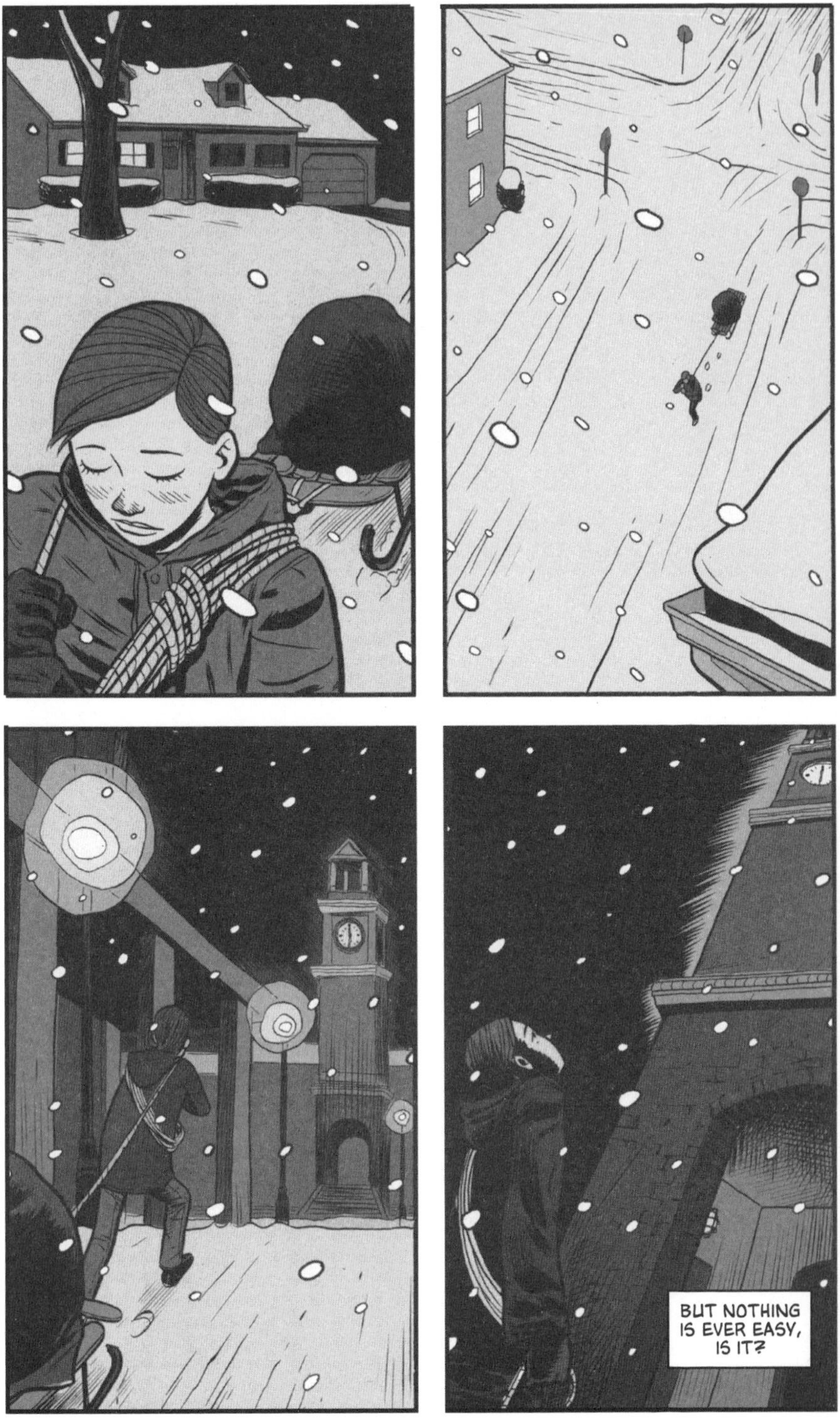
BUT NOTHING IS EVER EASY, IS IT?

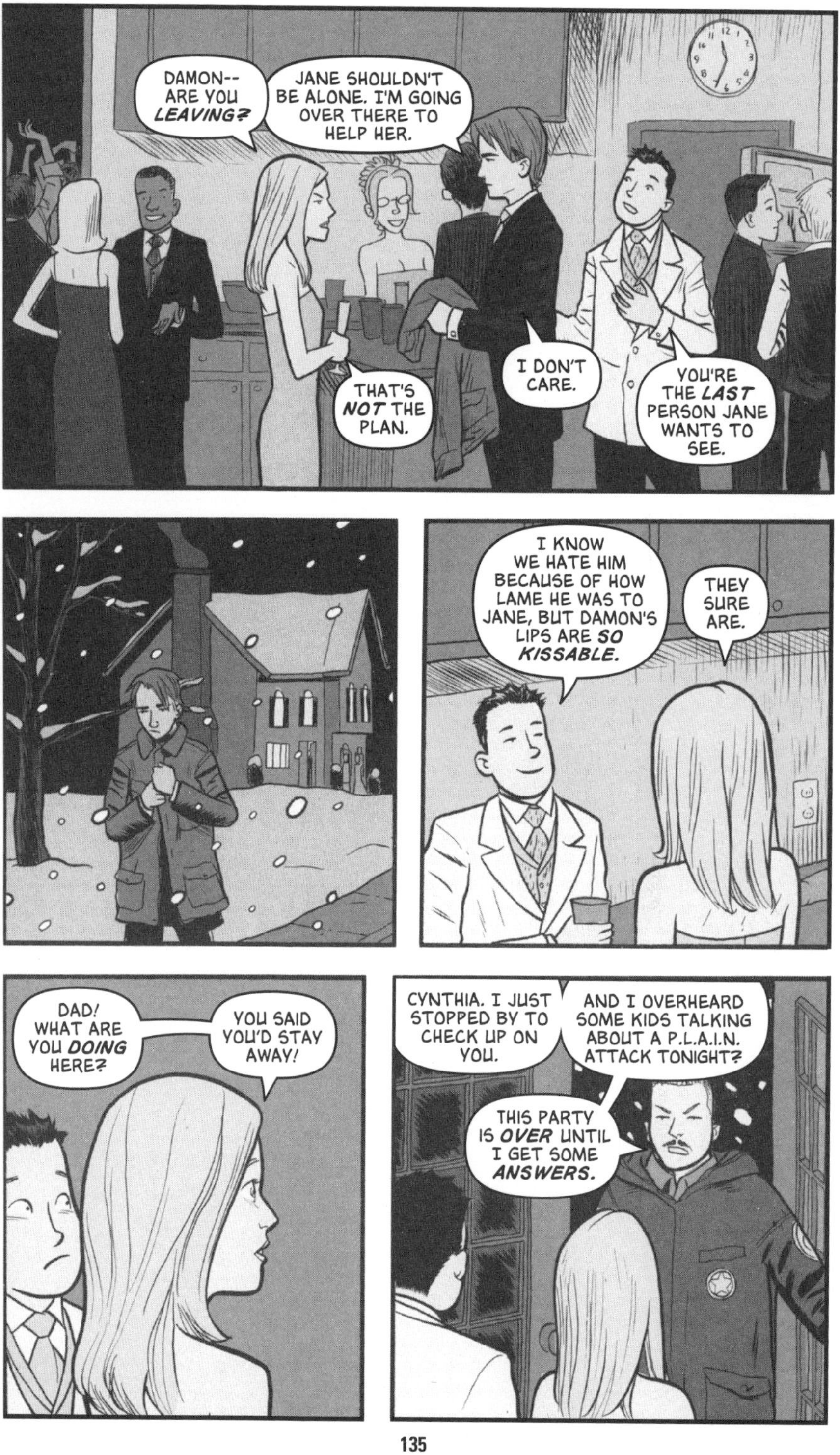
DAMON-- ARE YOU LEAVING?
JANE SHOULDN'T BE ALONE. I'M GOING OVER THERE TO HELP HER.
THAT'S NOT THE PLAN.
I DON'T CARE.
YOU'RE THE LAST PERSON JANE WANTS TO SEE.
I KNOW WE HATE HIM BECAUSE OF HOW LAME HE WAS TO JANE, BUT DAMON'S LIPS ARE SO KISSABLE.
THEY SURE ARE.
DAD! WHAT ARE YOU DOING HERE?
YOU SAID YOU'D STAY AWAY!
CYNTHIA. I JUST STOPPED BY TO CHECK UP ON YOU.
AND I OVERHEARD SOME KIDS TALKING ABOUT A P.L.A.I.N. ATTACK TONIGHT?
THIS PARTY IS OVER UNTIL I GET SOME ANSWERS.

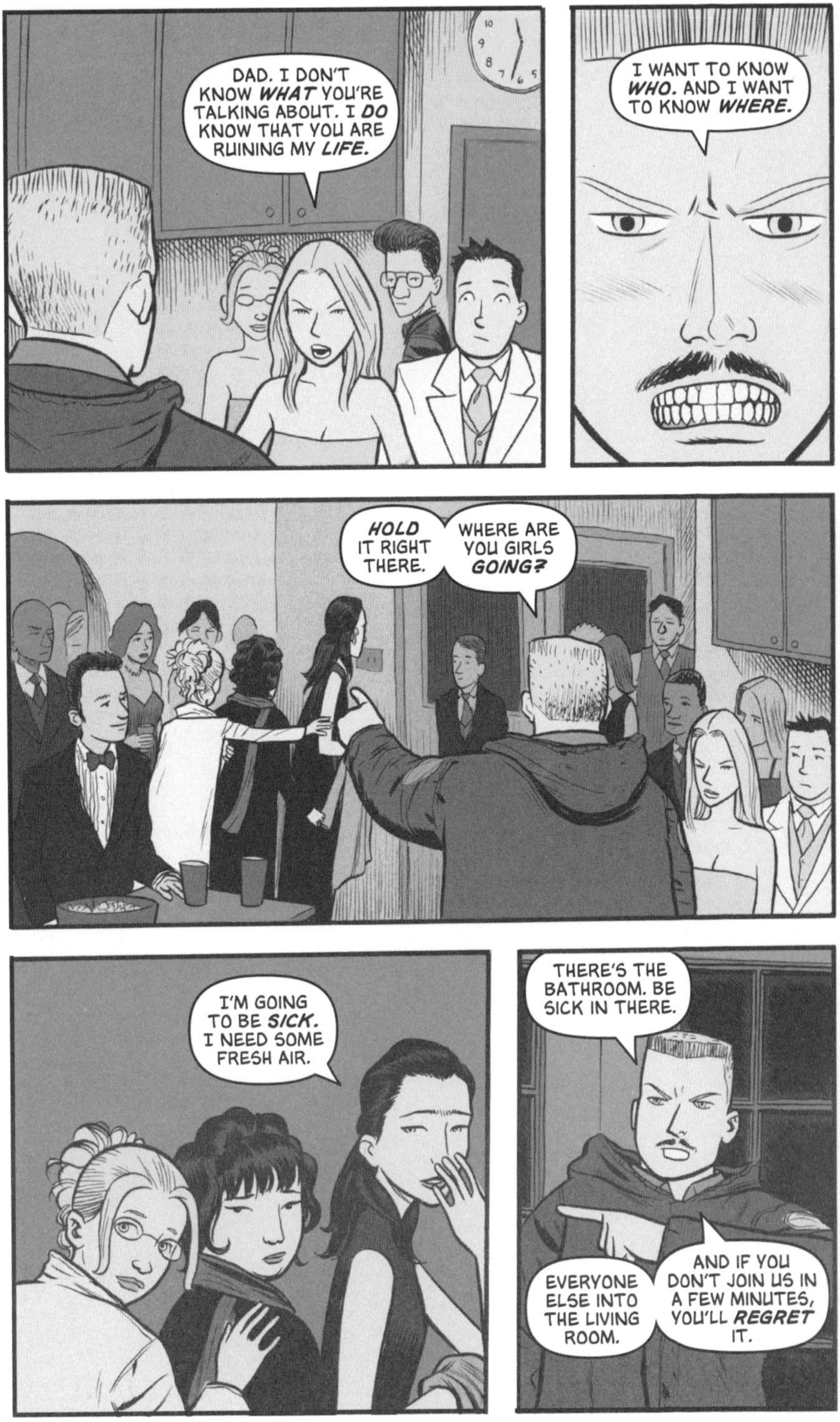
DAD. I DON'T KNOW WHAT YOU'RE TALKING ABOUT. I DO KNOW THAT YOU ARE RUINING MY LIFE.
I WANT TO KNOW WHO. AND I WANT TO KNOW WHERE.
HOLD IT RIGHT THERE.
WHERE ARE YOU GIRLS GOING?
I'M GOING TO BE SICK. I NEED SOME FRESH AIR.
THERE'S THE BATHROOM. BE SICK IN THERE.
EVERYONE ELSE INTO THE LIVING ROOM.
AND IF YOU DON'T JOIN US IN A FEW MINUTES, YOU'LL REGRET IT.

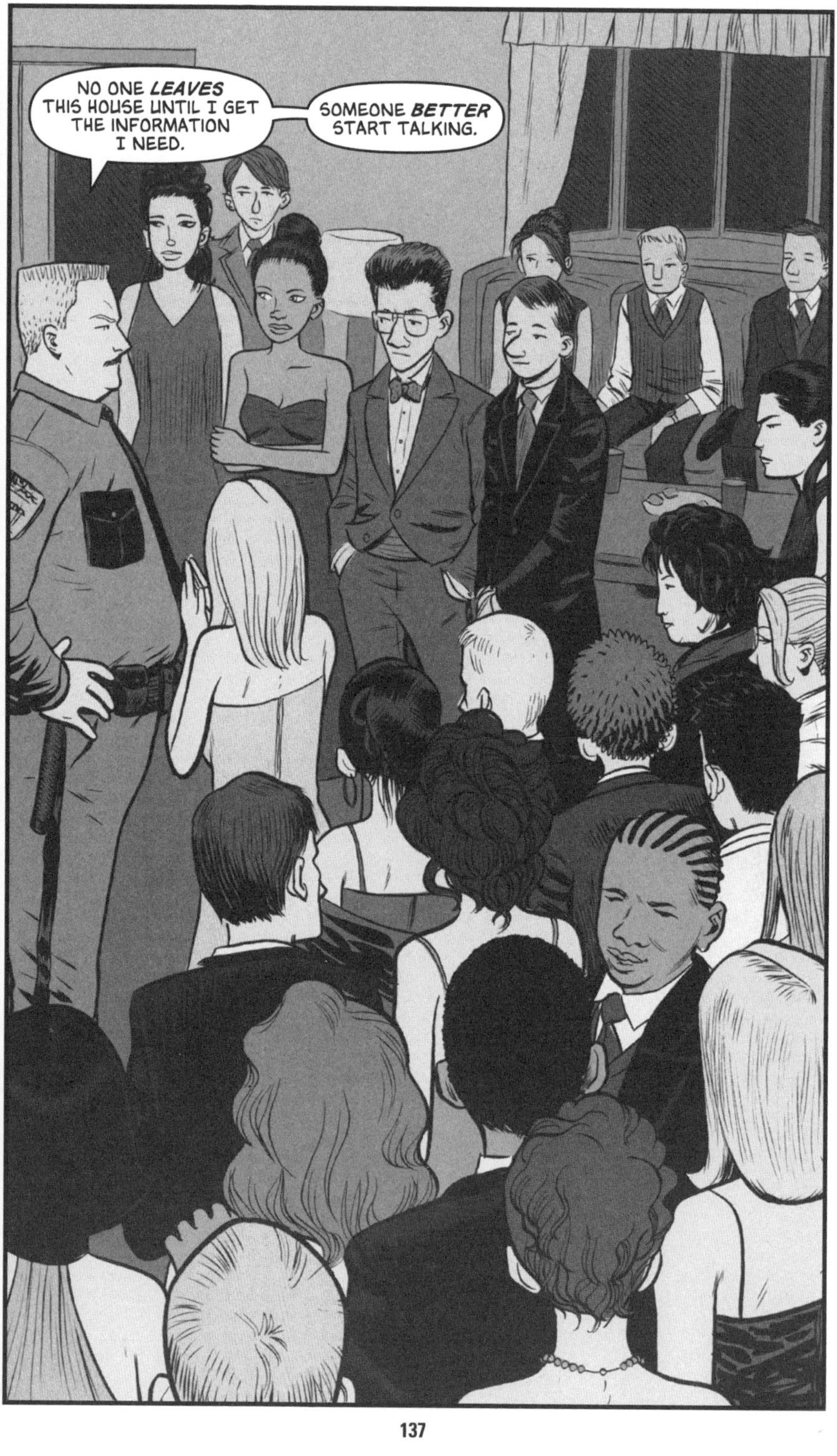
NO ONE *LEAVES* THIS HOUSE UNTIL I GET THE INFORMATION I NEED.
SOMEONE *BETTER* START TALKING.

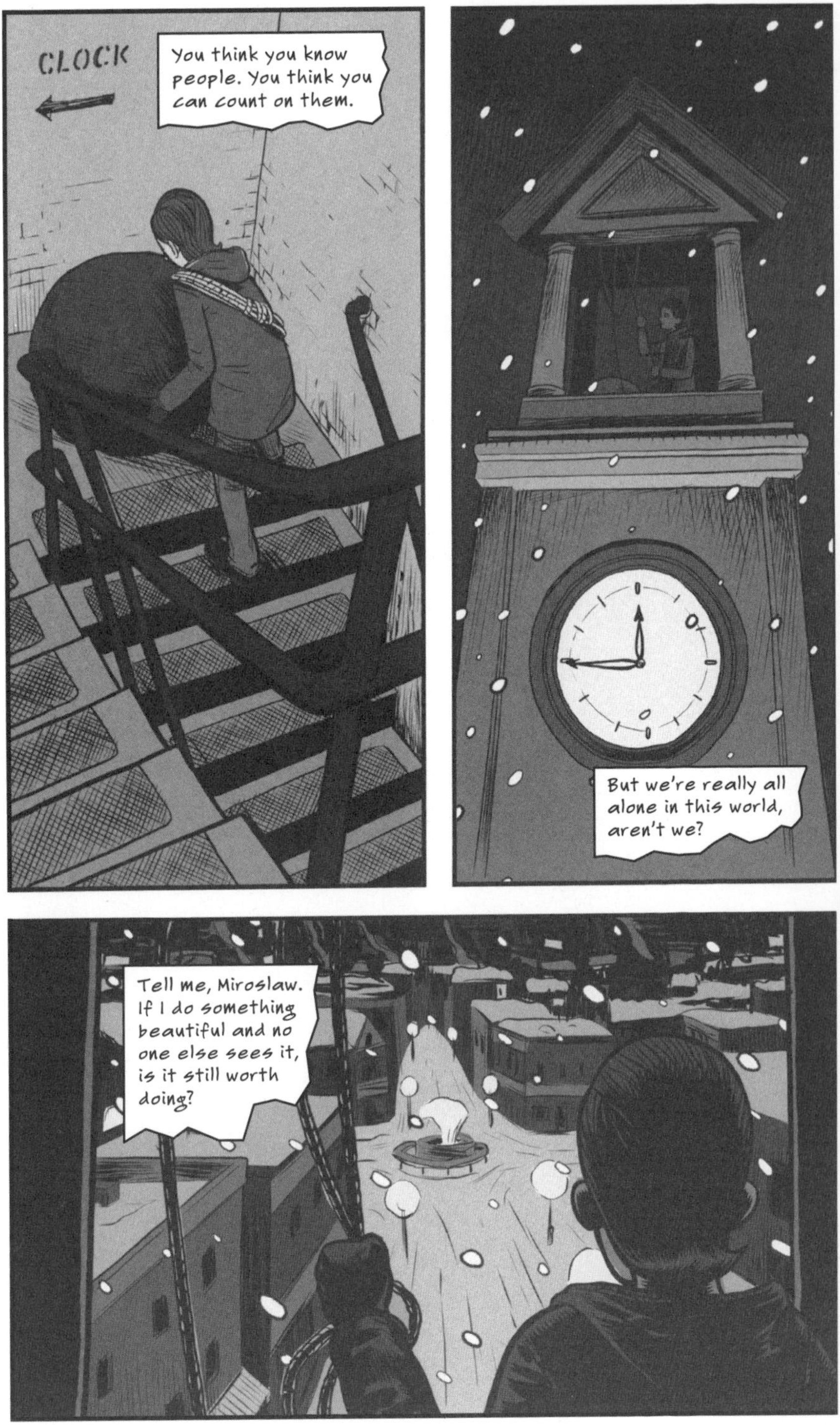
CLOCK
You think you know people. You think you can count on them.
But we're really all alone in this world, aren't we?
Tell me, Miroslaw. If I do something beautiful and no one else sees it, is it still worth doing?

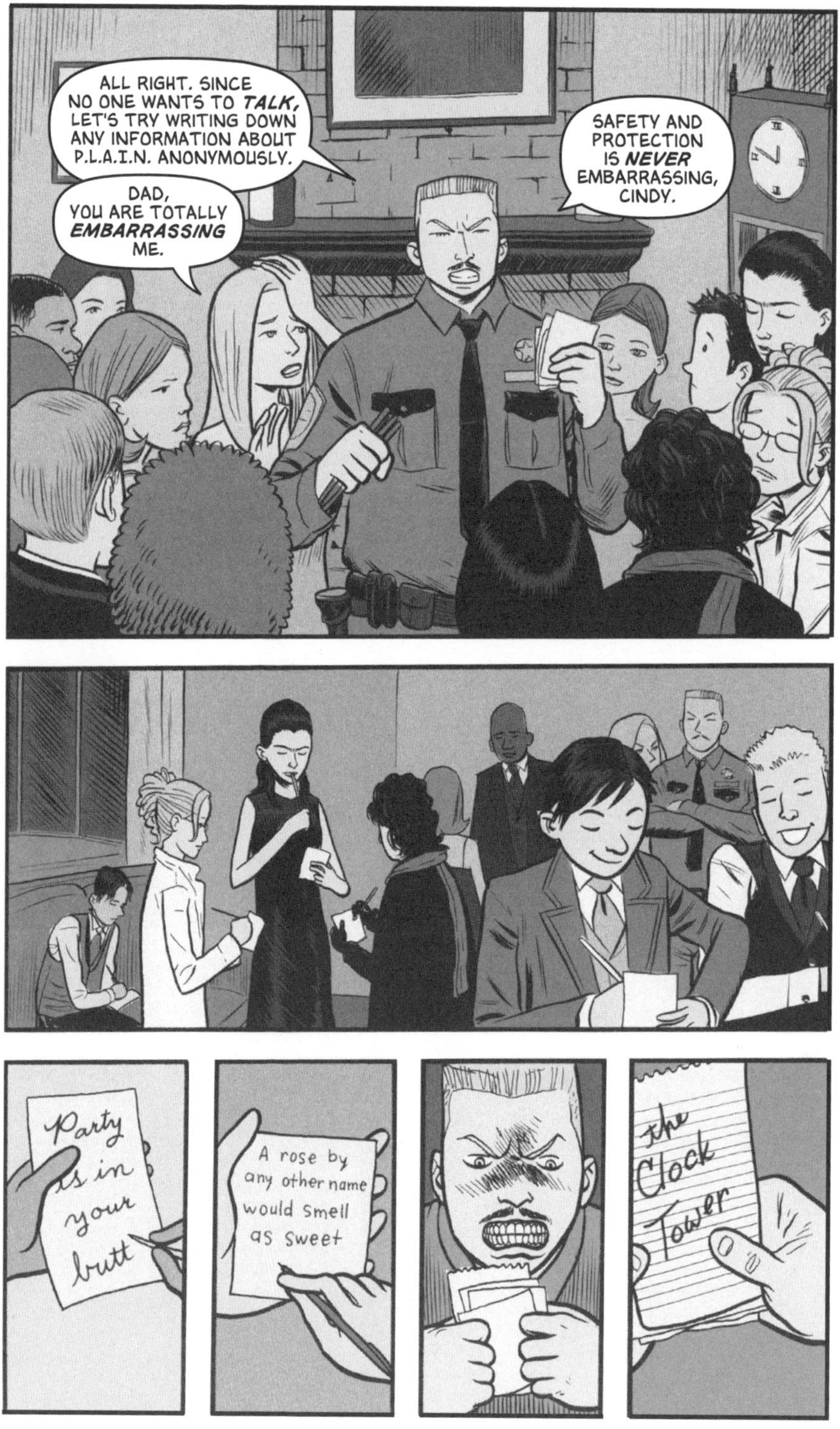
ALL RIGHT. SINCE NO ONE WANTS TO *TALK,* LET'S TRY WRITING DOWN ANY INFORMATION ABOUT P.L.A.I.N. ANONYMOUSLY.
DAD, YOU ARE TOTALLY *EMBARRASSING* ME.
SAFETY AND PROTECTION IS *NEVER* EMBARRASSING, CINDY.
Party is in your butt
A rose by any other name would smell as sweet
the Clock Tower

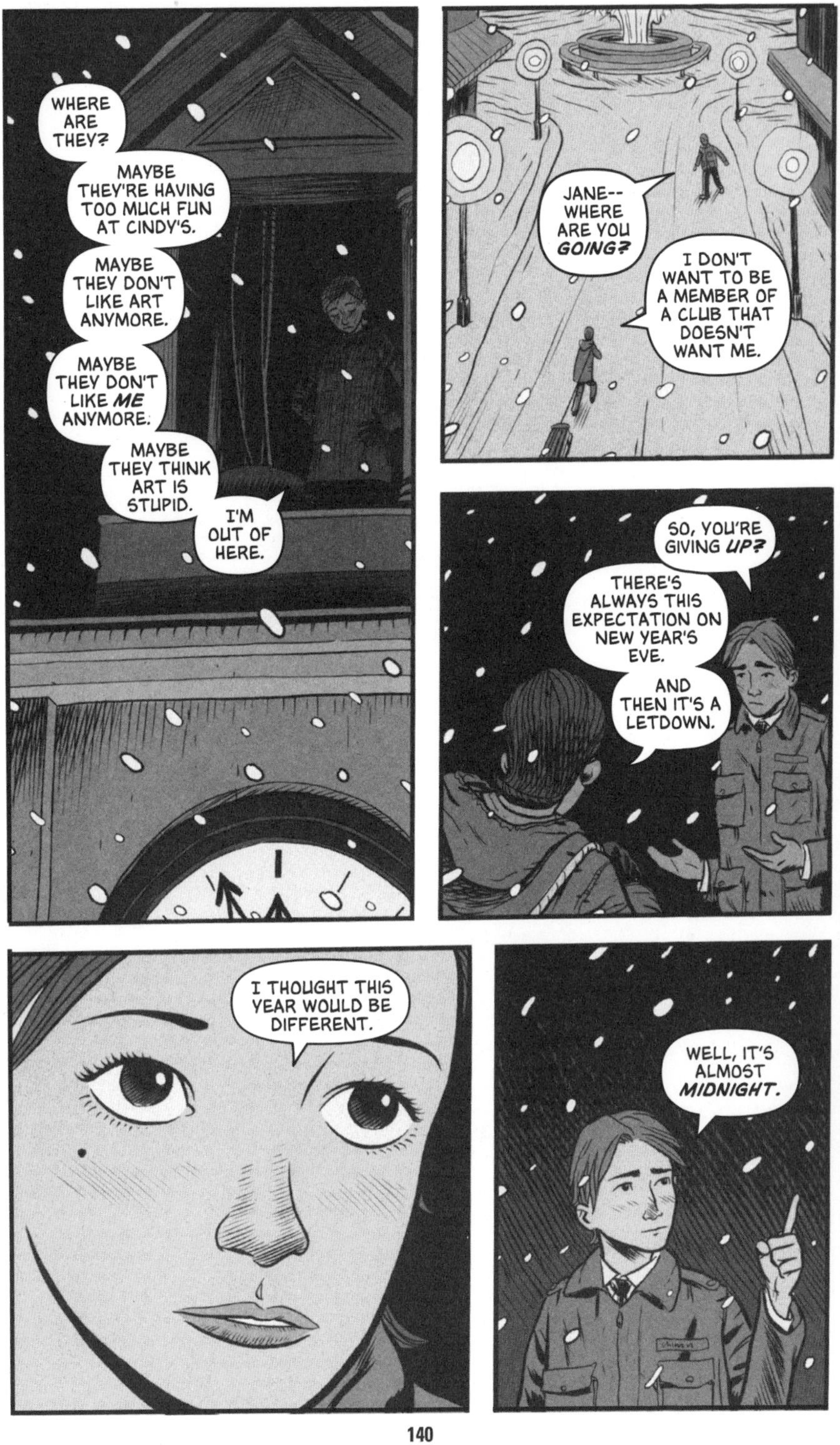
WHERE ARE THEY?
MAYBE THEY'RE HAVING TOO MUCH FUN AT CINDY'S.
MAYBE THEY DON'T LIKE ART ANYMORE.
MAYBE THEY DON'T LIKE *ME* ANYMORE.
MAYBE THEY THINK ART IS STUPID.
I'M OUT OF HERE.
JANE--WHERE ARE YOU *GOING?*
I DON'T WANT TO BE A MEMBER OF A CLUB THAT DOESN'T WANT ME.
SO, YOU'RE GIVING *UP?*
THERE'S ALWAYS THIS EXPECTATION ON NEW YEAR'S EVE.
AND THEN IT'S A LETDOWN.
I THOUGHT THIS YEAR WOULD BE DIFFERENT.
WELL, IT'S ALMOST *MIDNIGHT*.

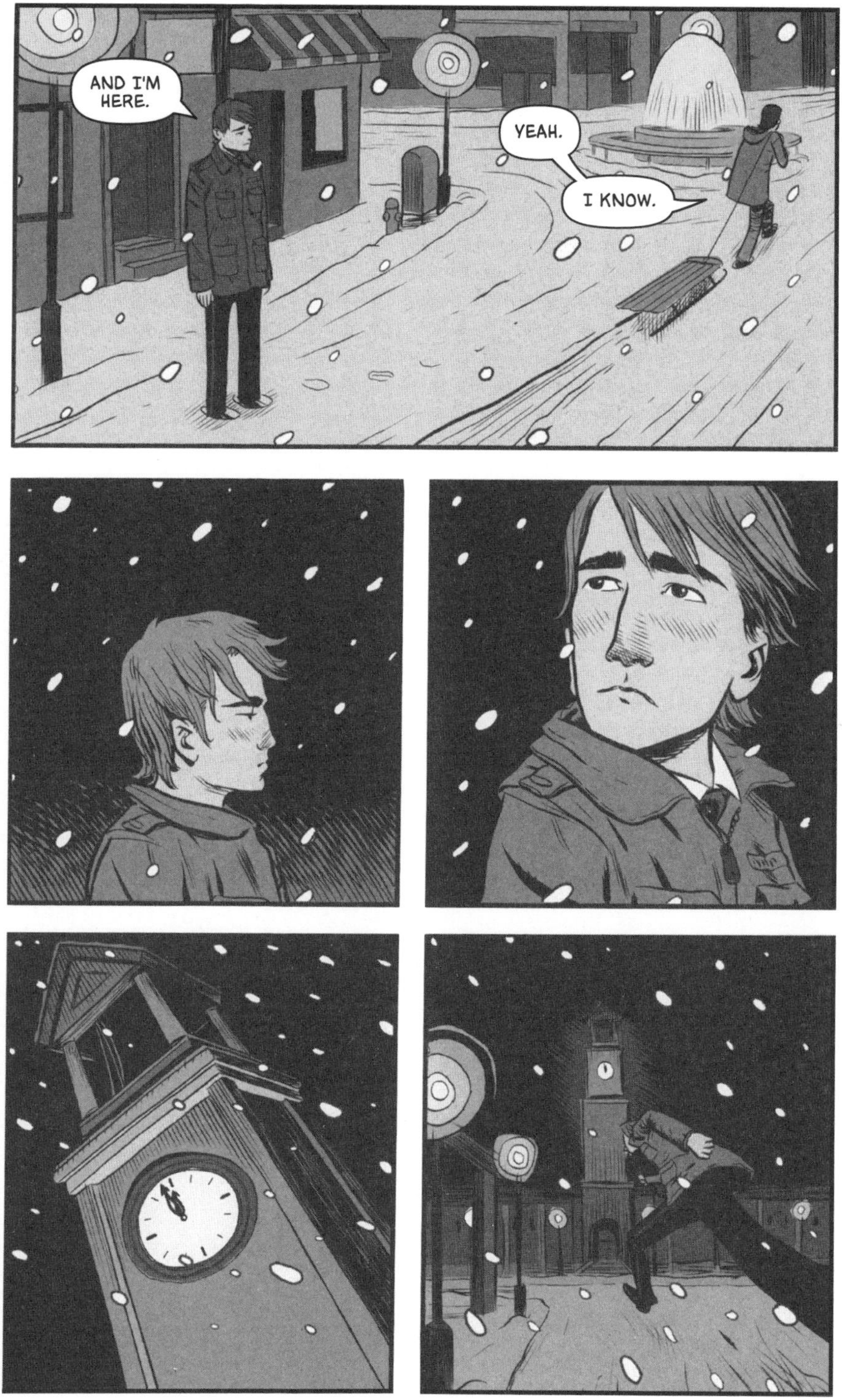
AND I'M HERE.
YEAH.
I KNOW.

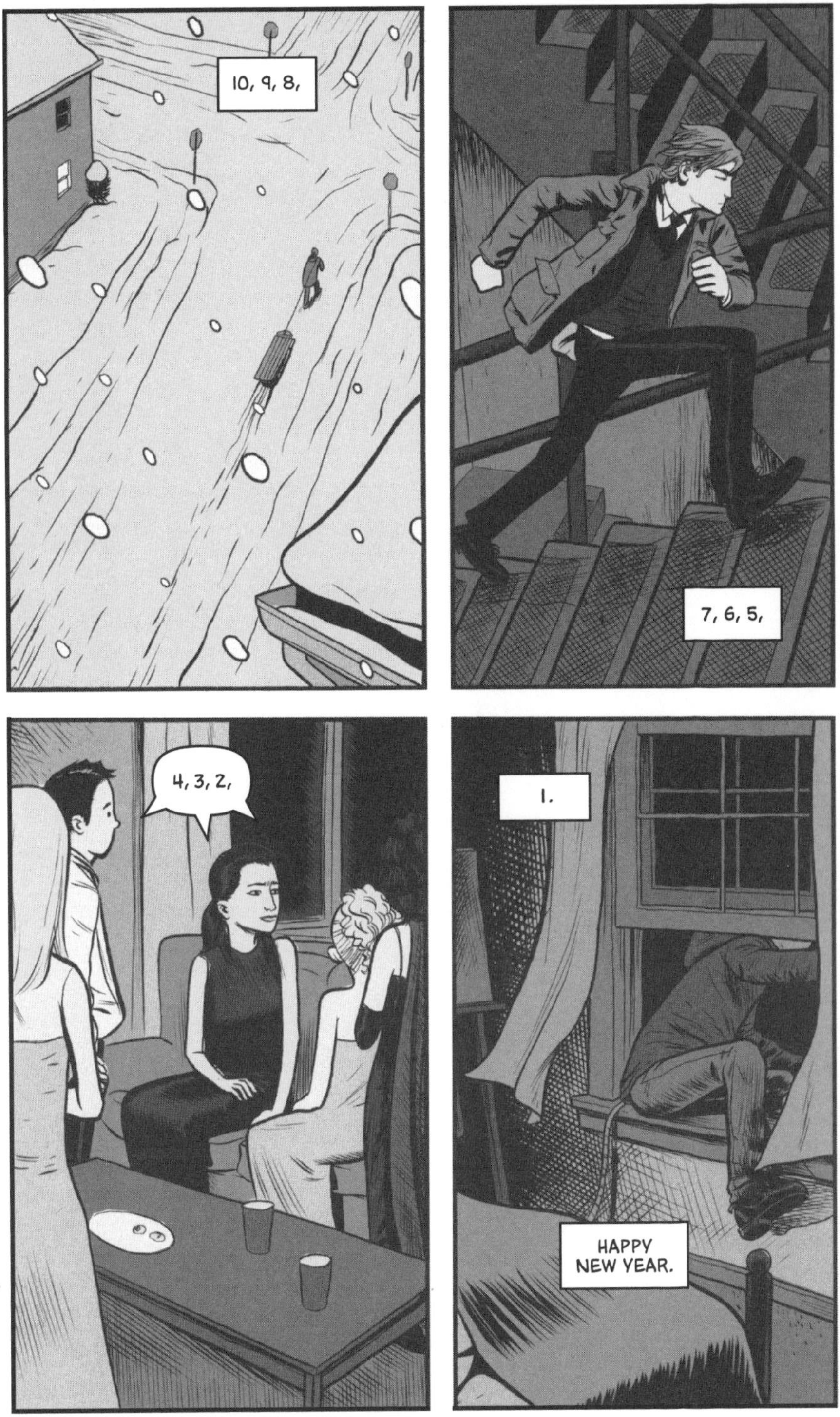
10, 9, 8,
7, 6, 5,
4, 3, 2,
1.
HAPPY NEW YEAR.

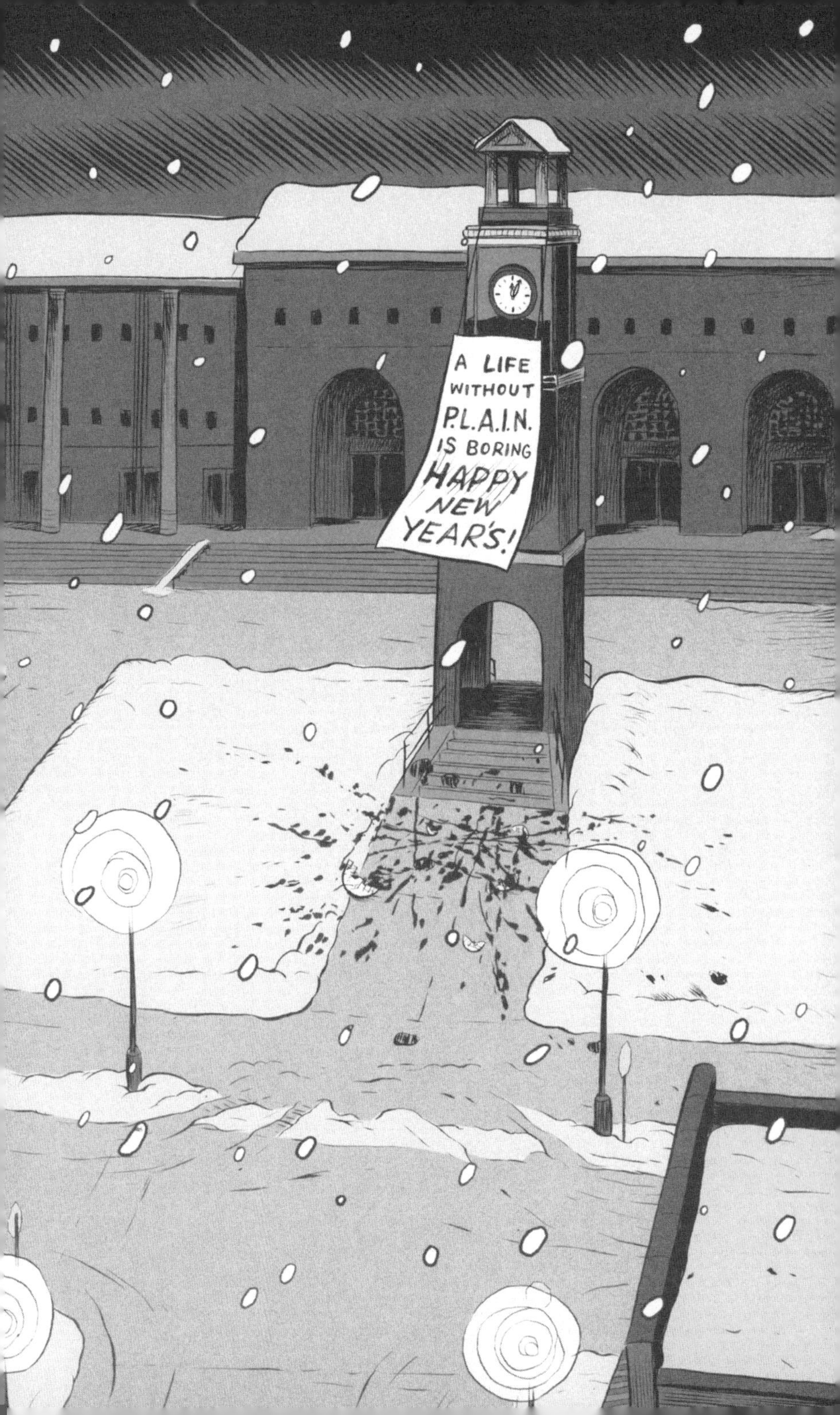
A LIFE WITHOUT P.L.A.I.N. IS BORING
HAPPY NEW YEAR'S!

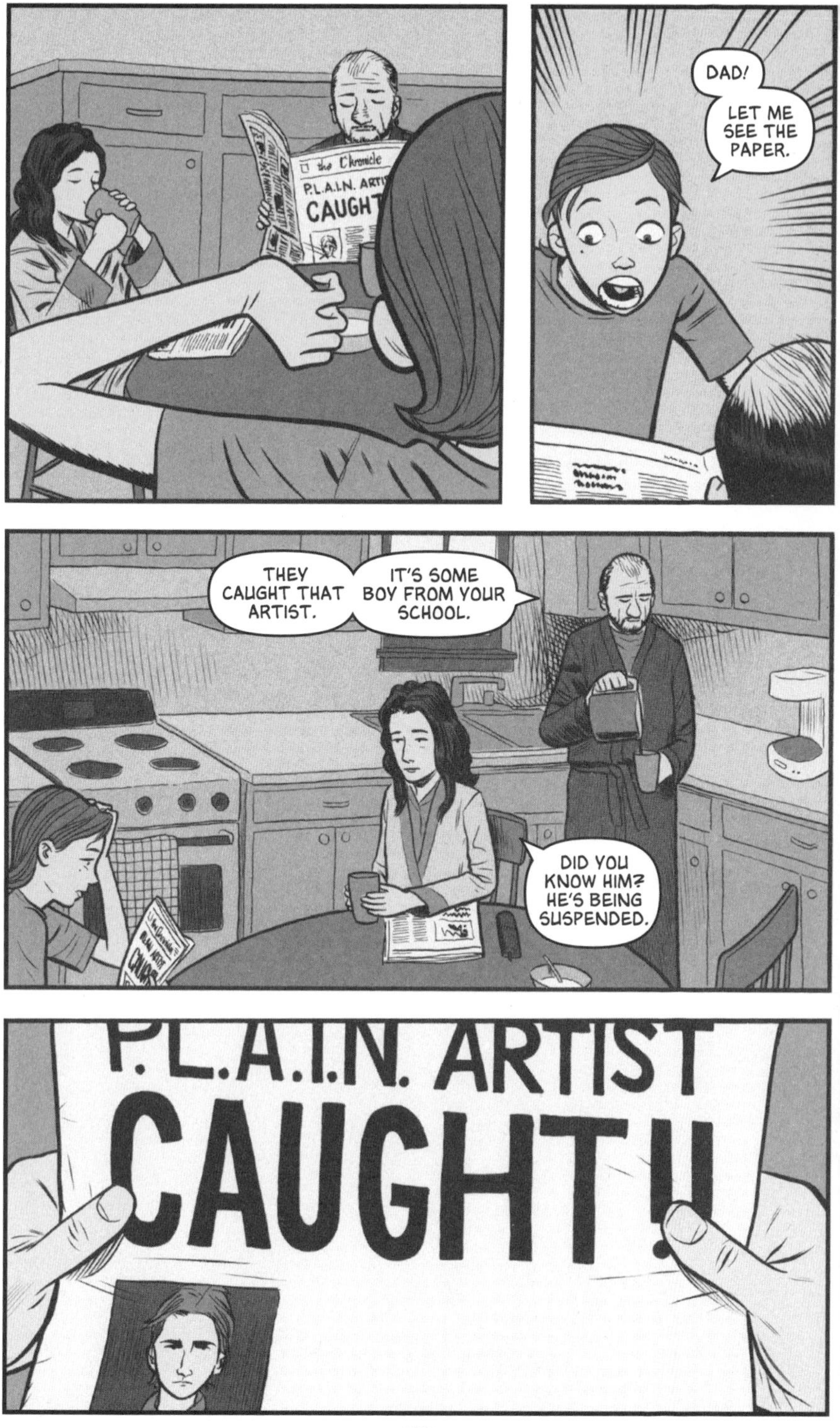
the Chronicle
P.L.A.I.N. ARTI
CAUGHT
DAD!
LET ME SEE THE PAPER.
THEY CAUGHT THAT ARTIST.
IT'S SOME BOY FROM YOUR SCHOOL.
DID YOU KNOW HIM? HE'S BEING SUSPENDED.
P.L.A.I.N. ARTIST
CAUGHT!!

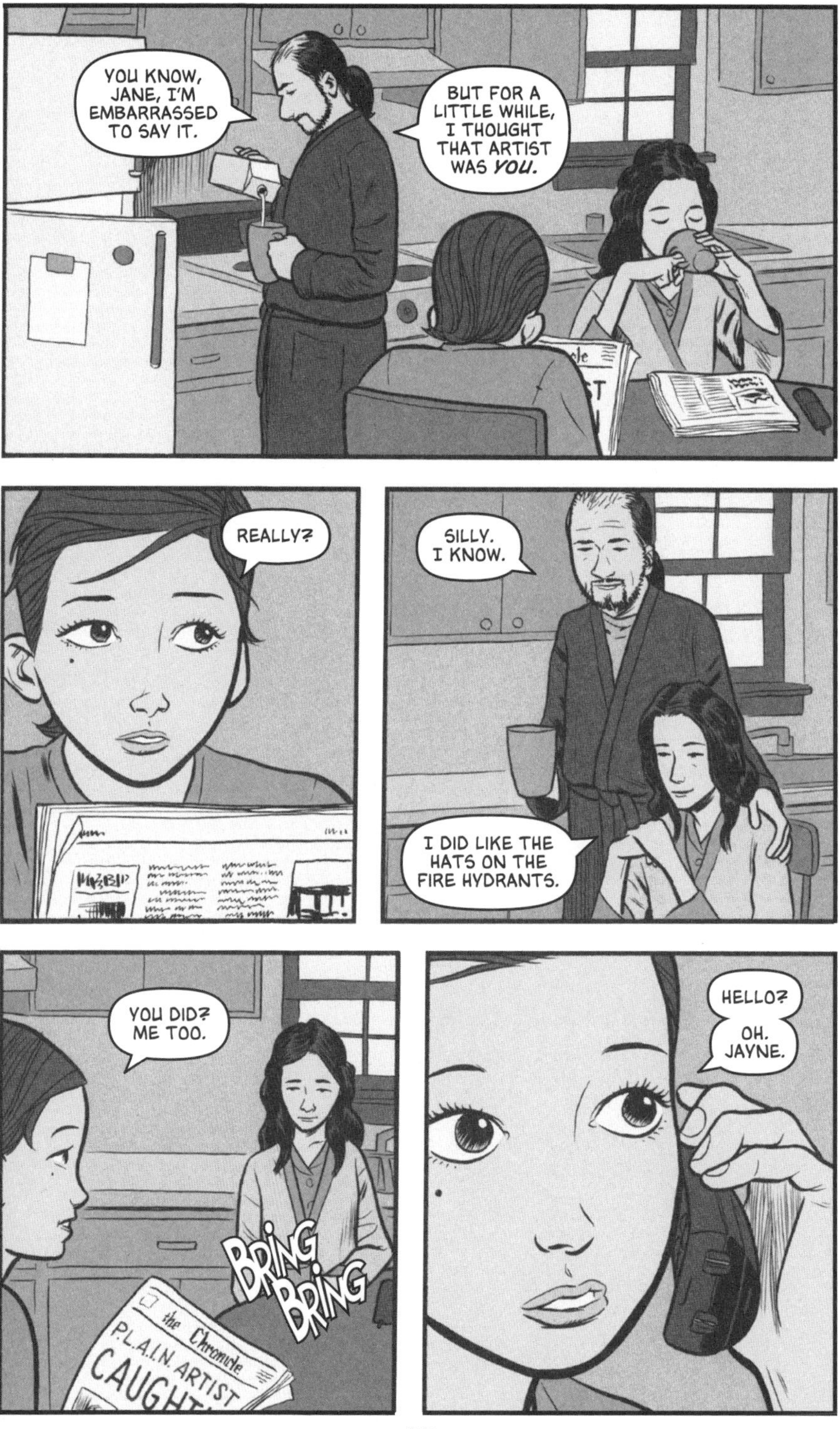
YOU KNOW, JANE, I'M EMBARRASSED TO SAY IT.
BUT FOR A LITTLE WHILE, I THOUGHT THAT ARTIST WAS *YOU.*
REALLY?
SILLY. I KNOW.
I DID LIKE THE HATS ON THE FIRE HYDRANTS.
YOU DID? ME TOO.
BRING BRING
the Chronicle
P.L.A.I.N. ARTIST CAUGHT
HELLO?
OH. JAYNE.

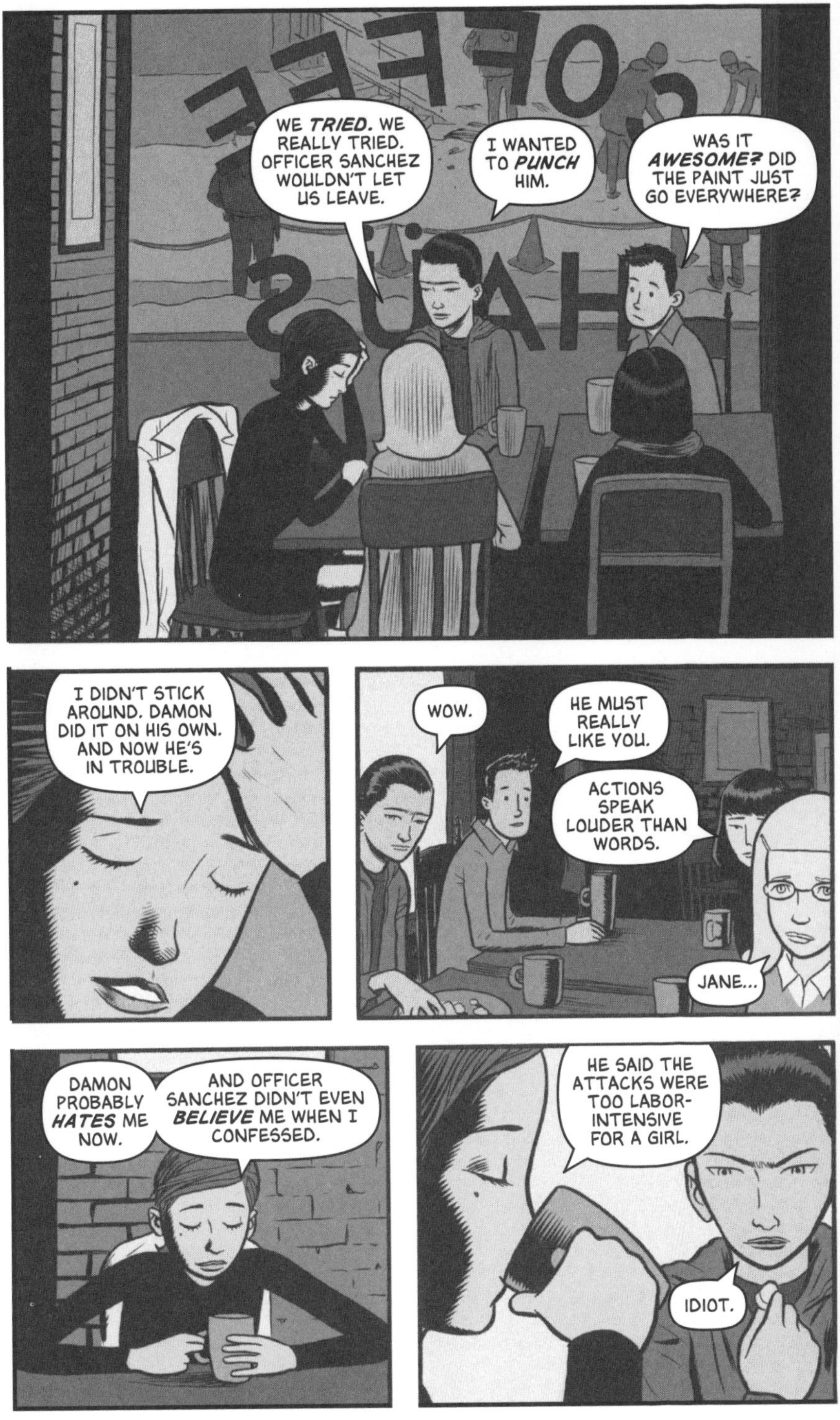
COFFEE HAUS
WE *TRIED.* WE REALLY TRIED. OFFICER SANCHEZ WOULDN'T LET US LEAVE.
I WANTED TO *PUNCH* HIM.
WAS IT *AWESOME?* DID THE PAINT JUST GO EVERYWHERE?
I DIDN'T STICK AROUND. DAMON DID IT ON HIS OWN. AND NOW HE'S IN TROUBLE.
WOW.
HE MUST REALLY LIKE YOU.
ACTIONS SPEAK LOUDER THAN WORDS.
JANE...
DAMON PROBABLY *HATES* ME NOW.
AND OFFICER SANCHEZ DIDN'T EVEN *BELIEVE* ME WHEN I CONFESSED.
HE SAID THE ATTACKS WERE TOO LABOR-INTENSIVE FOR A GIRL.
IDIOT.

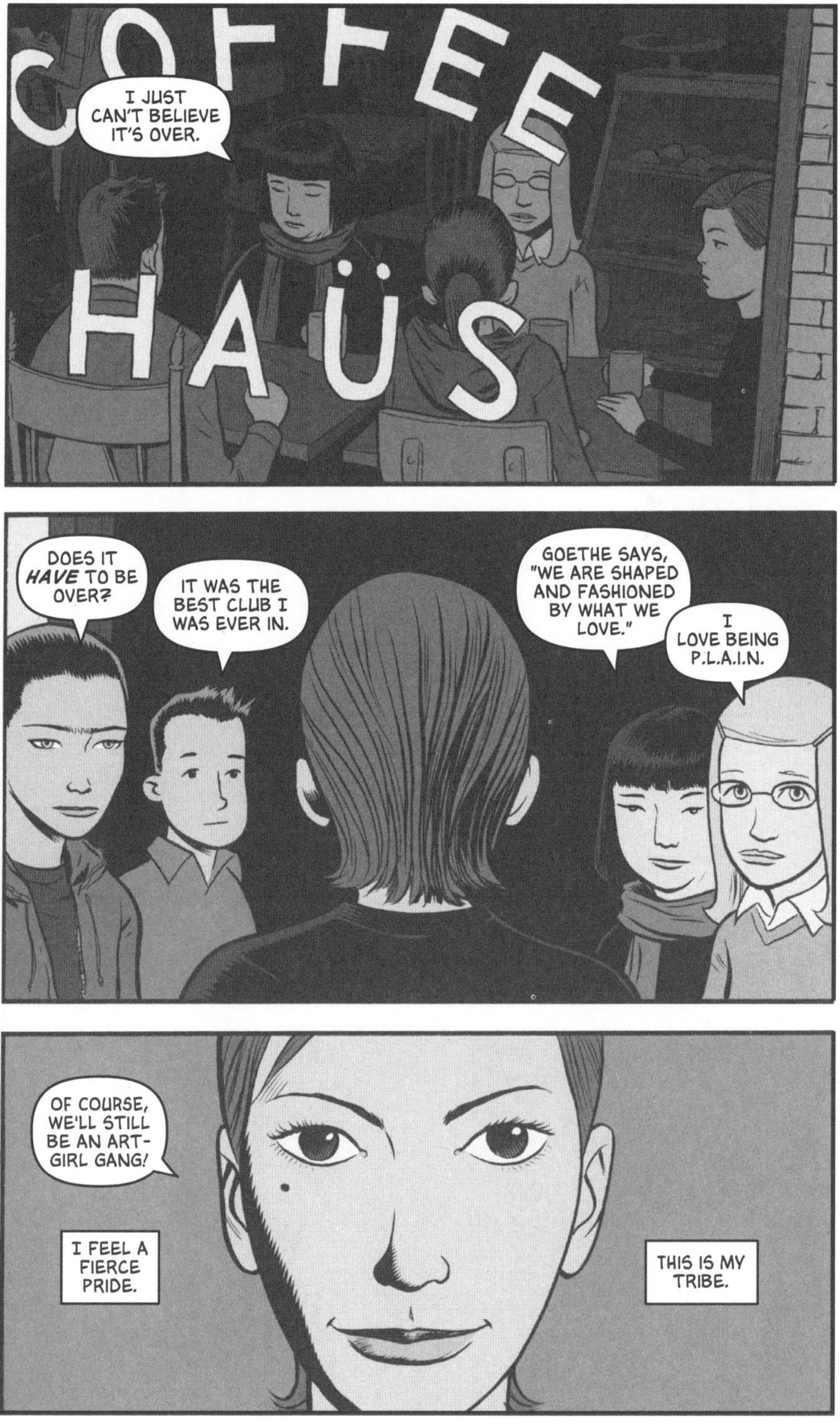
COFFEE
I JUST CAN'T BELIEVE IT'S OVER.
HAÜS
DOES IT *HAVE* TO BE OVER?
IT WAS THE BEST CLUB I WAS EVER IN.
GOETHE SAYS, "WE ARE SHAPED AND FASHIONED BY WHAT WE LOVE."
I LOVE BEING P.L.A.I.N.
OF COURSE, WE'LL STILL BE AN ART-GIRL GANG!
I FEEL A FIERCE PRIDE.
THIS IS MY TRIBE.

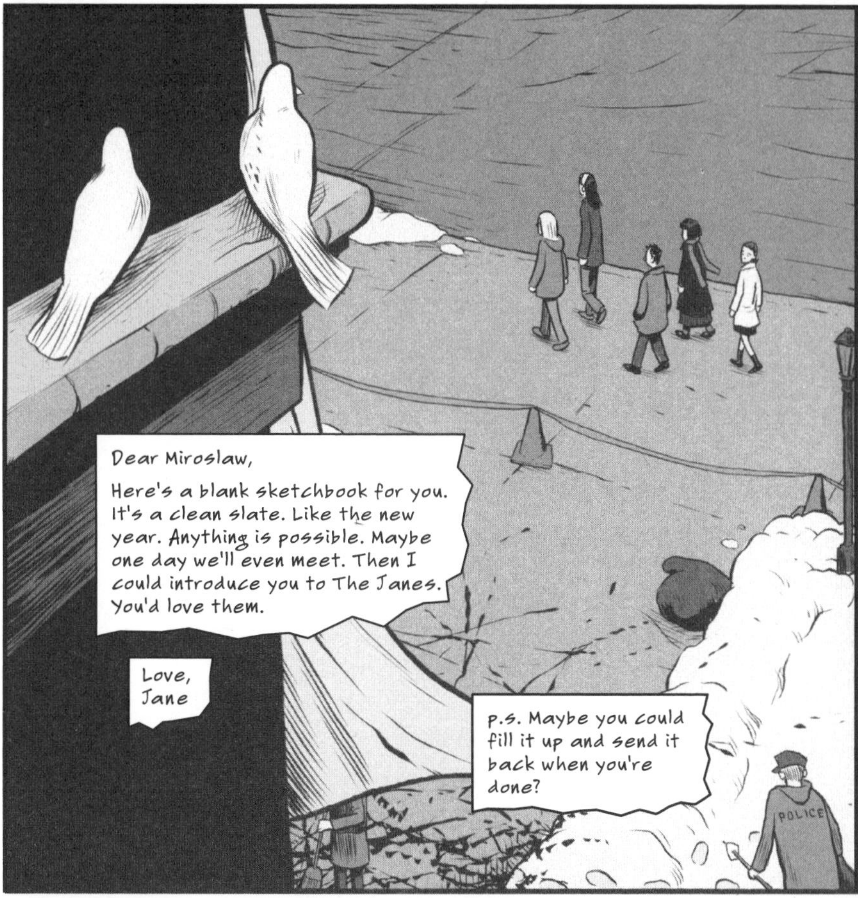
Dear Miroslaw,
Here's a blank sketchbook for you. It's a clean slate. Like the new year. Anything is possible. Maybe one day we'll even meet. Then I could introduce you to The Janes. You'd love them.
Love, Jane
p.s. Maybe you could fill it up and send it back when you're done?
POLICE

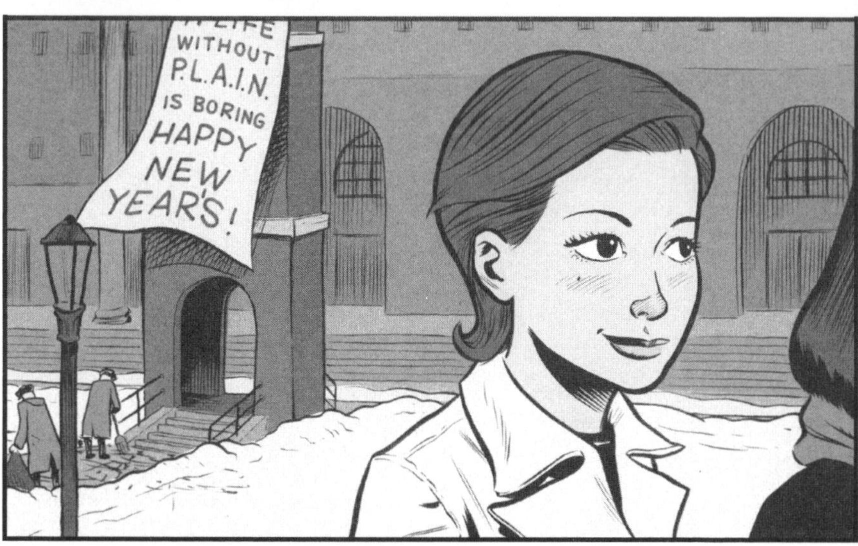
WITHOUT P.L.A.I.N. IS BORING HAPPY NEW YEAR'S!

Early Concepts for Main Jane

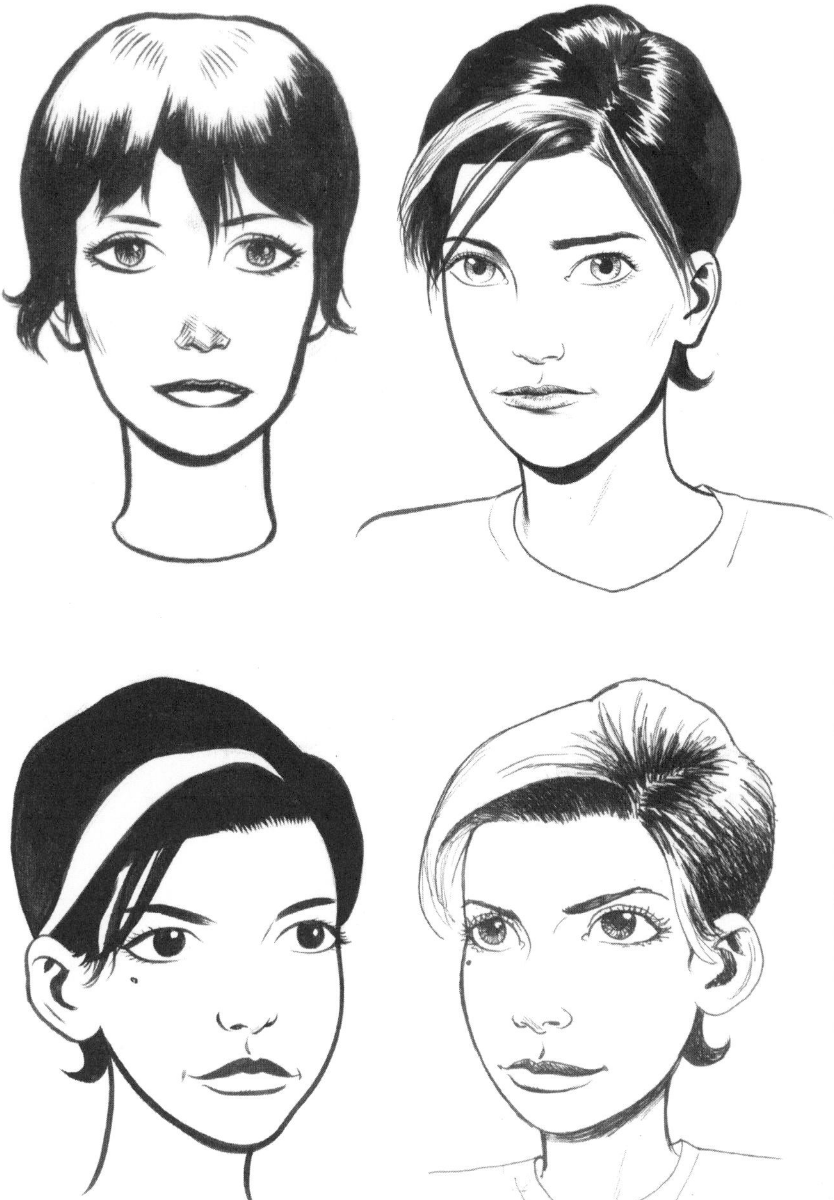

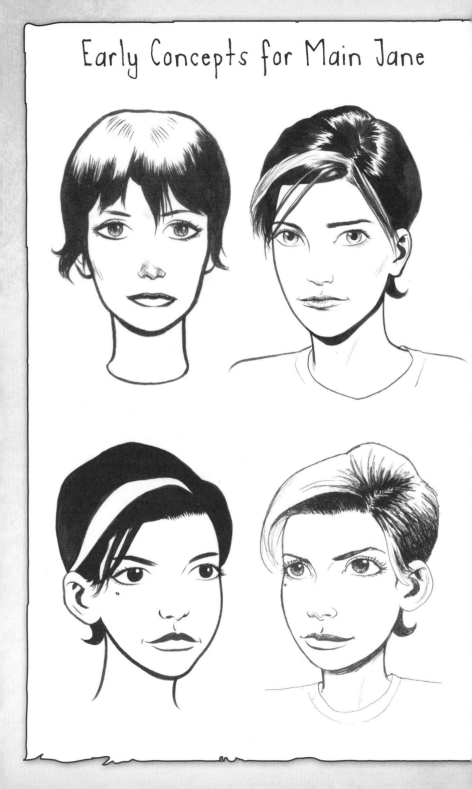

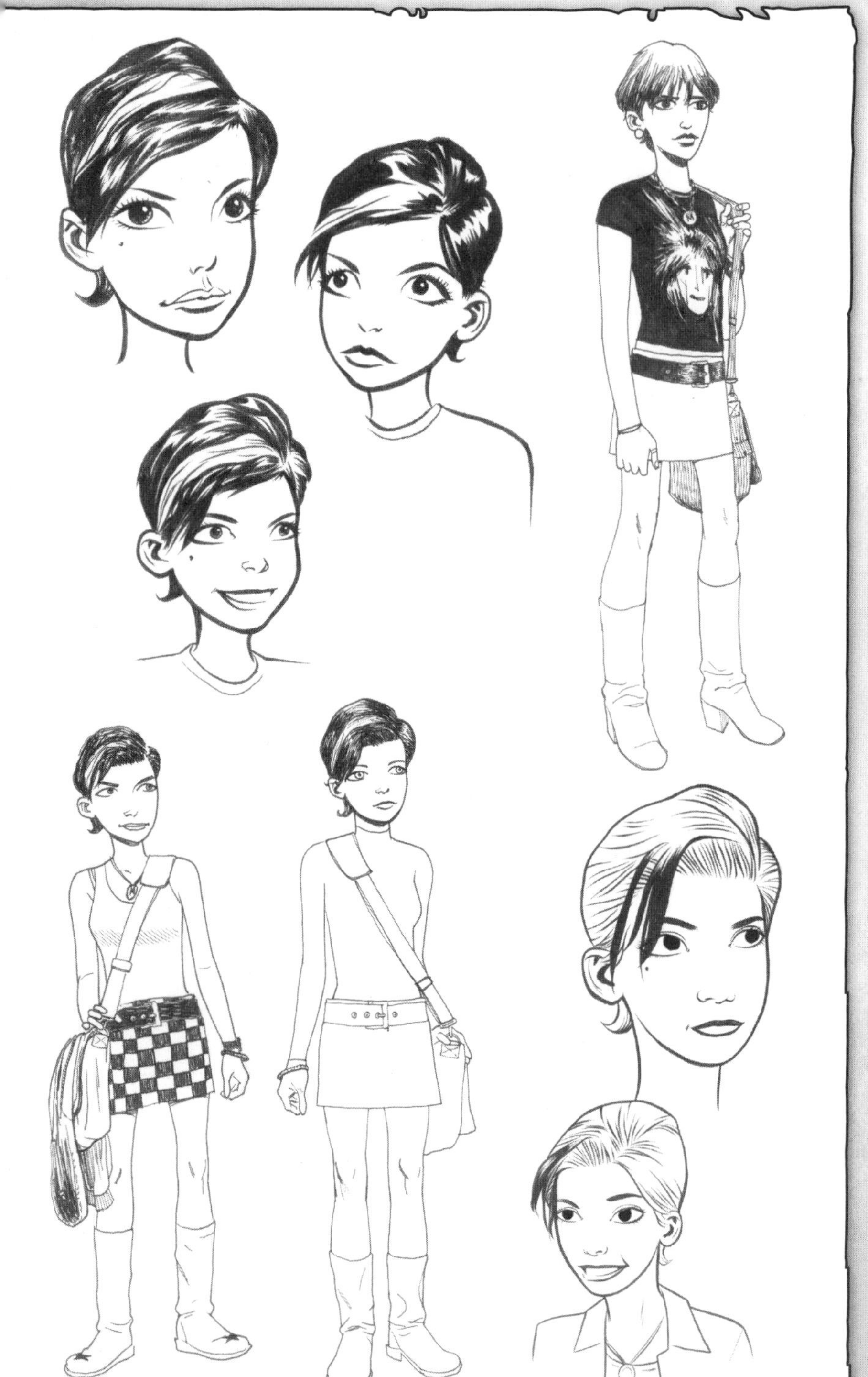

Part 2
Janes in Love

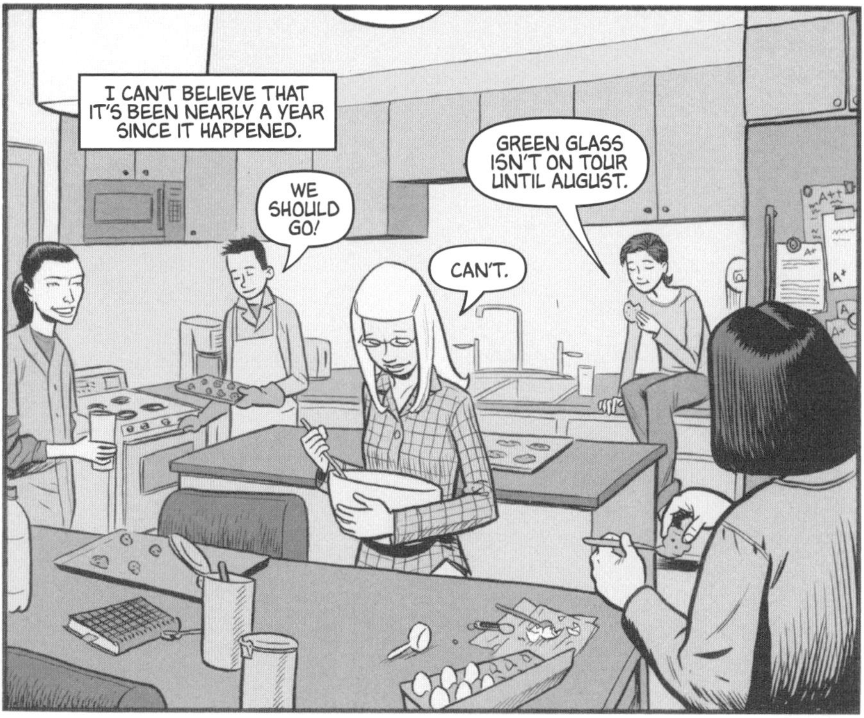
I CAN'T BELIEVE THAT IT'S BEEN NEARLY A YEAR SINCE IT HAPPENED.
WE SHOULD GO!
GREEN GLASS ISN'T ON TOUR UNTIL AUGUST.
CAN'T.

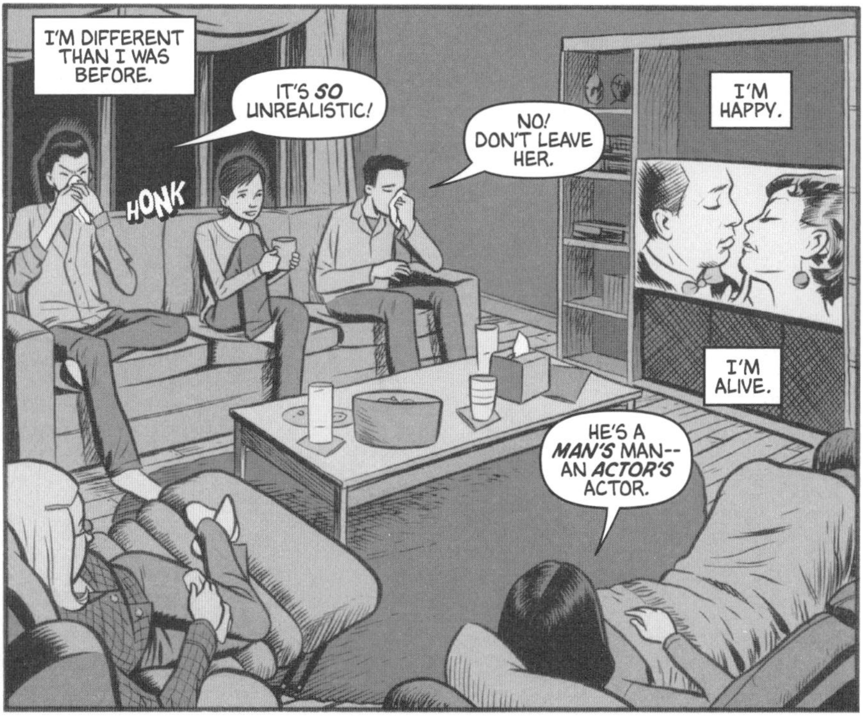
I'M DIFFERENT THAN I WAS BEFORE.
IT'S *SO* UNREALISTIC!
NO! DON'T LEAVE HER.
HONK
I'M HAPPY.
I'M ALIVE.
HE'S A *MAN'S* MAN-- AN *ACTOR'S* ACTOR.

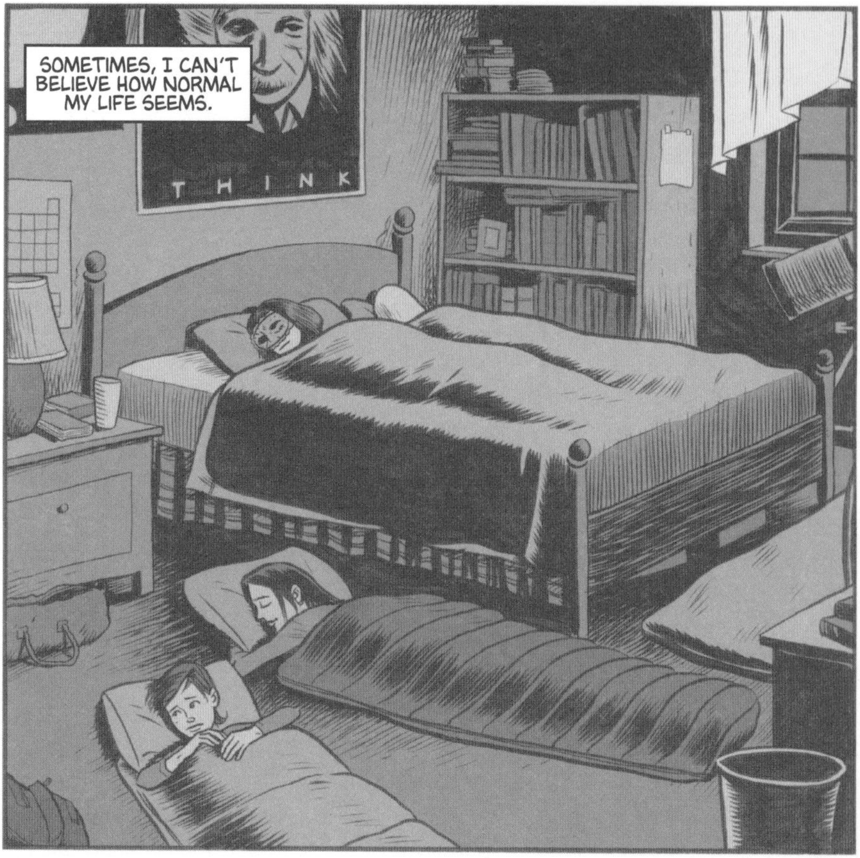
SOMETIMES, I CAN'T BELIEVE HOW NORMAL MY LIFE SEEMS.
THINK

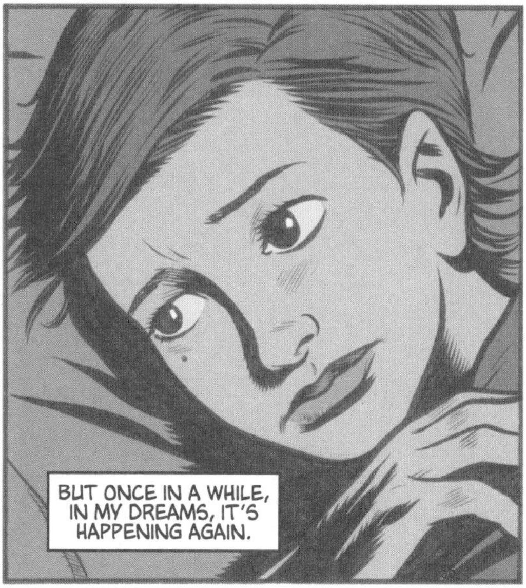
BUT ONCE IN A WHILE, IN MY DREAMS, IT'S HAPPENING AGAIN.

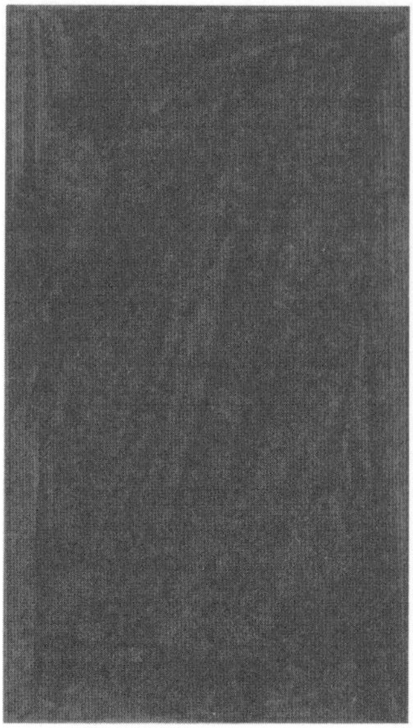

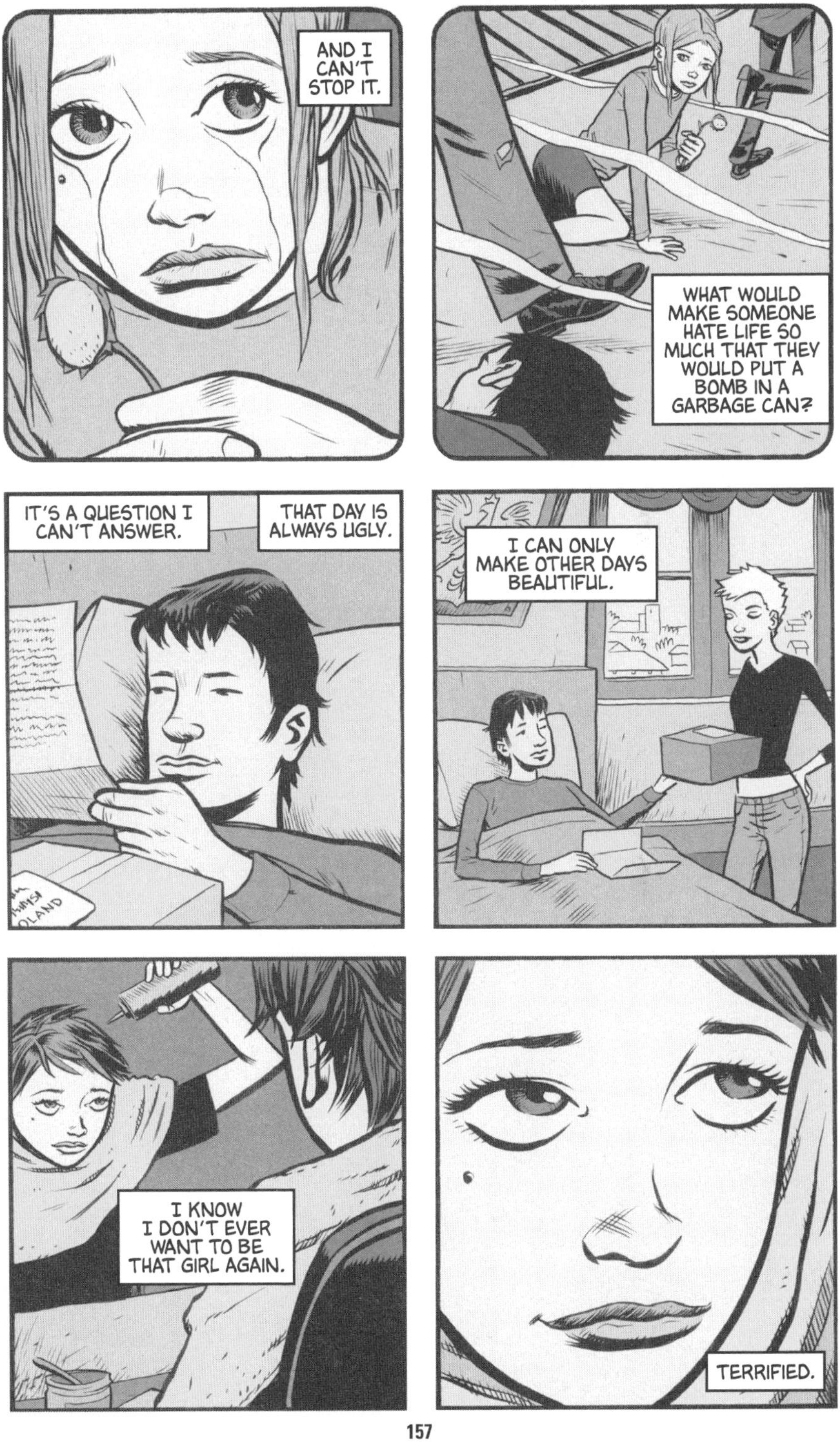
AND I CAN'T STOP IT.
WHAT WOULD MAKE SOMEONE HATE LIFE SO MUCH THAT THEY WOULD PUT A BOMB IN A GARBAGE CAN?
IT'S A QUESTION I CAN'T ANSWER.
THAT DAY IS ALWAYS UGLY.
I CAN ONLY MAKE OTHER DAYS BEAUTIFUL.
I KNOW I DON'T EVER WANT TO BE THAT GIRL AGAIN.
TERRIFIED.

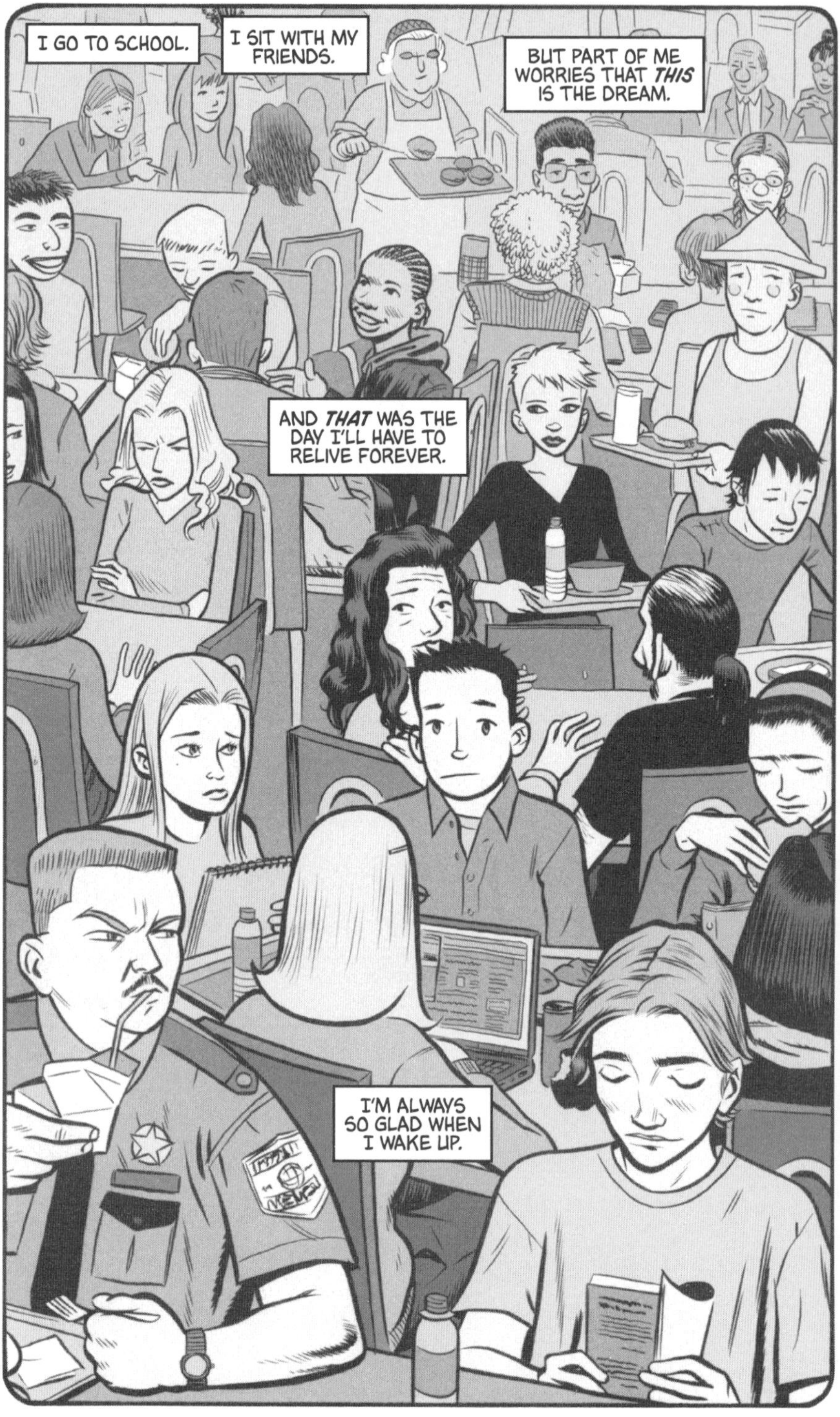
I GO TO SCHOOL.
I SIT WITH MY FRIENDS.
BUT PART OF ME WORRIES THAT *THIS* IS THE DREAM.
AND *THAT* WAS THE DAY I'LL HAVE TO RELIVE FOREVER.
I'M ALWAYS SO GLAD WHEN I WAKE UP.

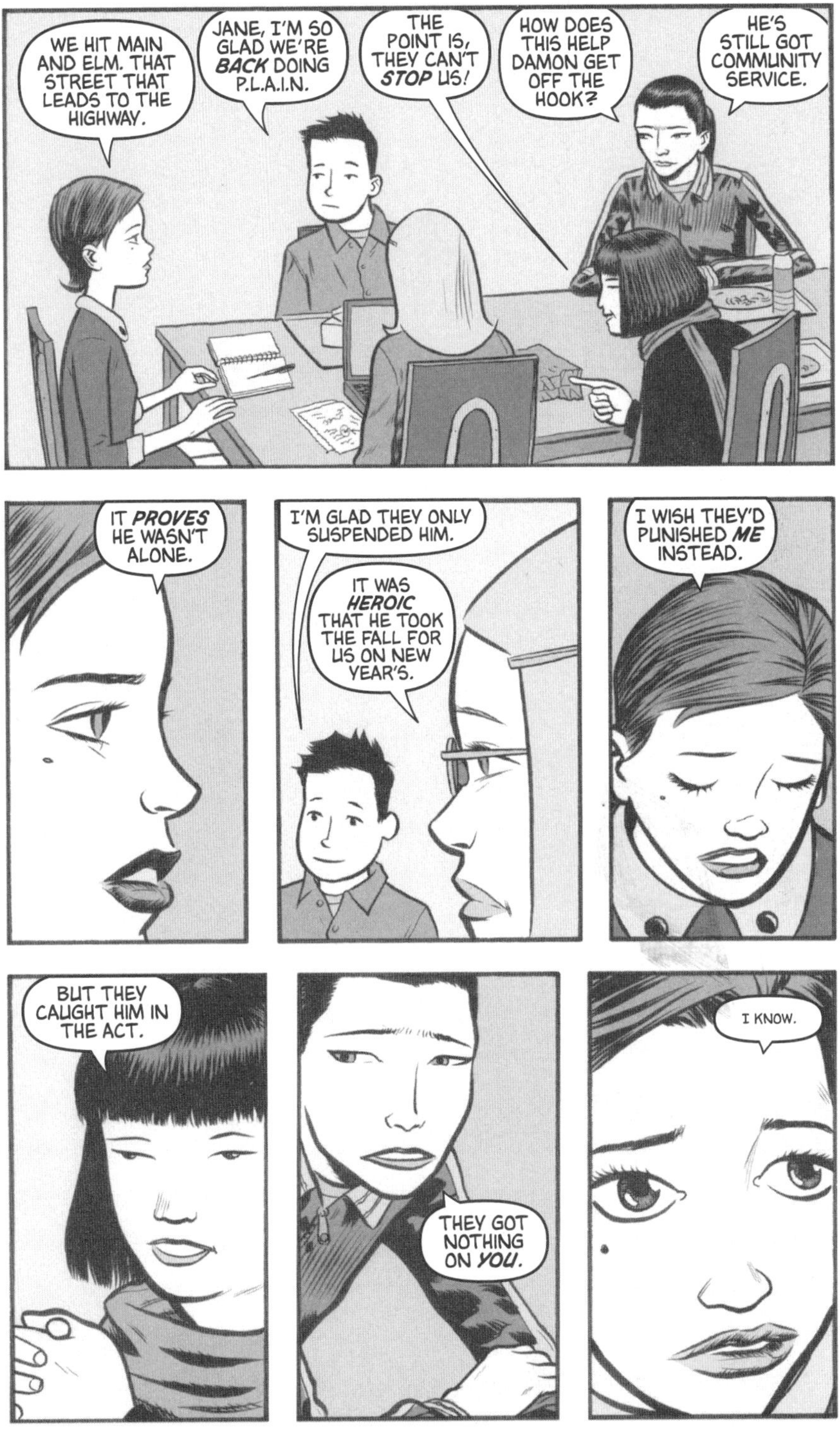
WE HIT MAIN AND ELM. THAT STREET THAT LEADS TO THE HIGHWAY.
JANE, I'M SO GLAD WE'RE BACK DOING P.L.A.I.N.
THE POINT IS, THEY CAN'T STOP US!
HOW DOES THIS HELP DAMON GET OFF THE HOOK?
HE'S STILL GOT COMMUNITY SERVICE.
IT PROVES HE WASN'T ALONE.
I'M GLAD THEY ONLY SUSPENDED HIM.
IT WAS HEROIC THAT HE TOOK THE FALL FOR US ON NEW YEAR'S.
I WISH THEY'D PUNISHED ME INSTEAD.
BUT THEY CAUGHT HIM IN THE ACT.
THEY GOT NOTHING ON YOU.
I KNOW.

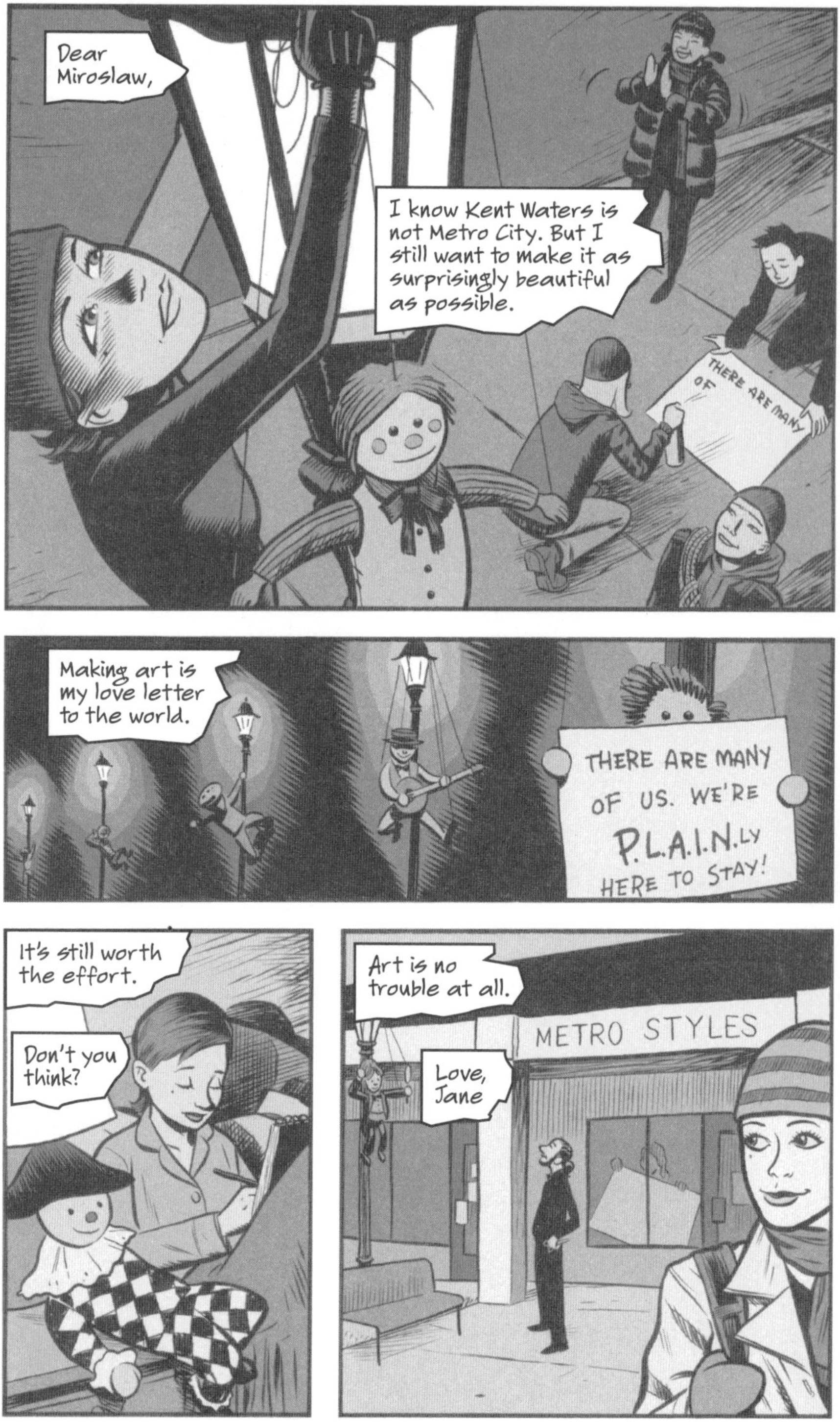
Dear Miroslaw,
I know Kent Waters is not Metro City. But I still want to make it as surprisingly beautiful as possible.
THERE ARE MANY OF
Making art is my love letter to the world.
THERE ARE MANY OF US. WE'RE P.L.A.I.N.LY HERE TO STAY!
It's still worth the effort.
Don't you think?
Art is no trouble at all.
METRO STYLES
Love, Jane

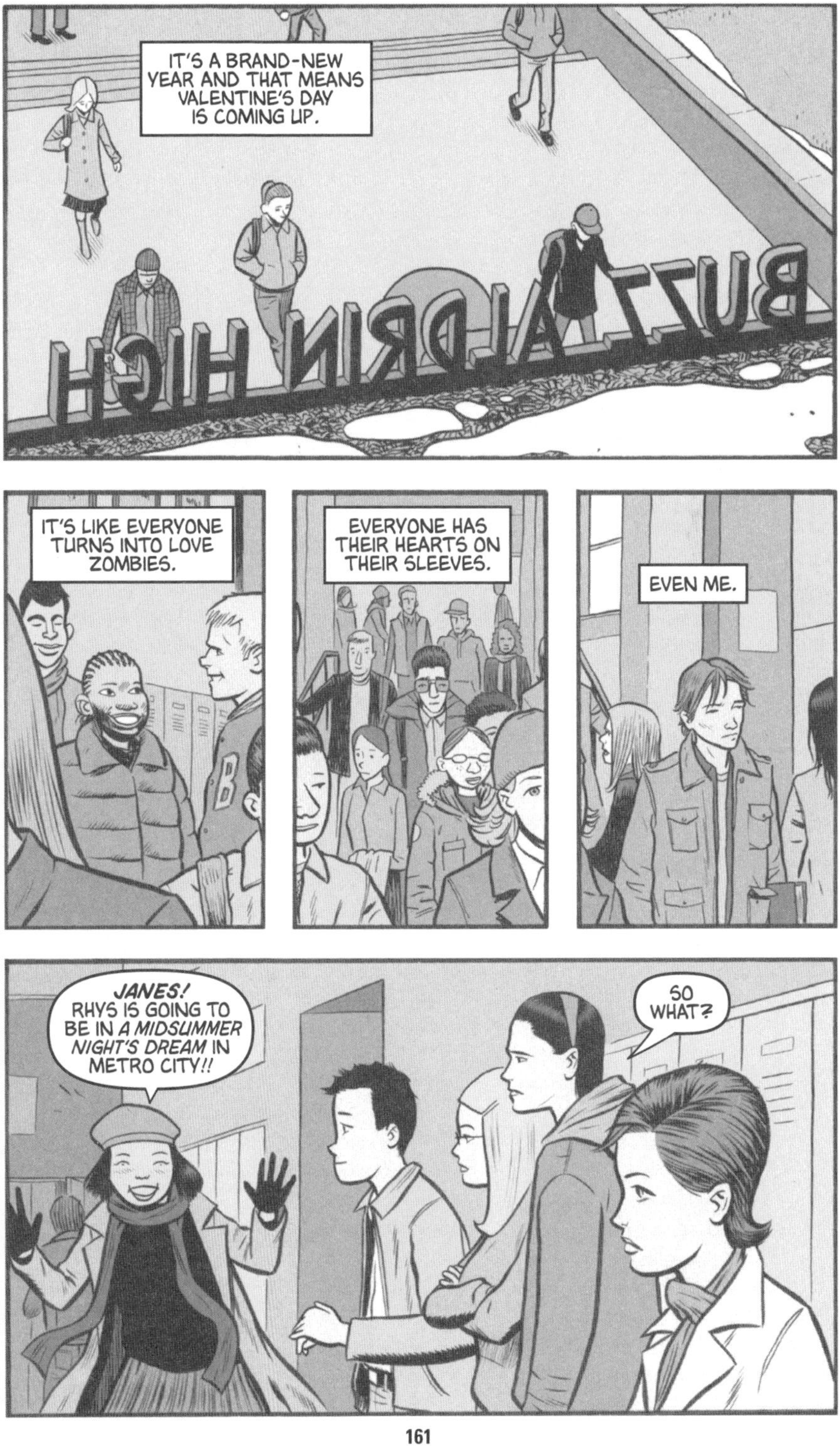
IT'S A BRAND-NEW YEAR AND THAT MEANS VALENTINE'S DAY IS COMING UP.
BUZZ ALDRIN HIGH
IT'S LIKE EVERYONE TURNS INTO LOVE ZOMBIES.
EVERYONE HAS THEIR HEARTS ON THEIR SLEEVES.
EVEN ME.
JANES! RHYS IS GOING TO BE IN A *MIDSUMMER NIGHT'S DREAM* IN METRO CITY!!
SO WHAT?

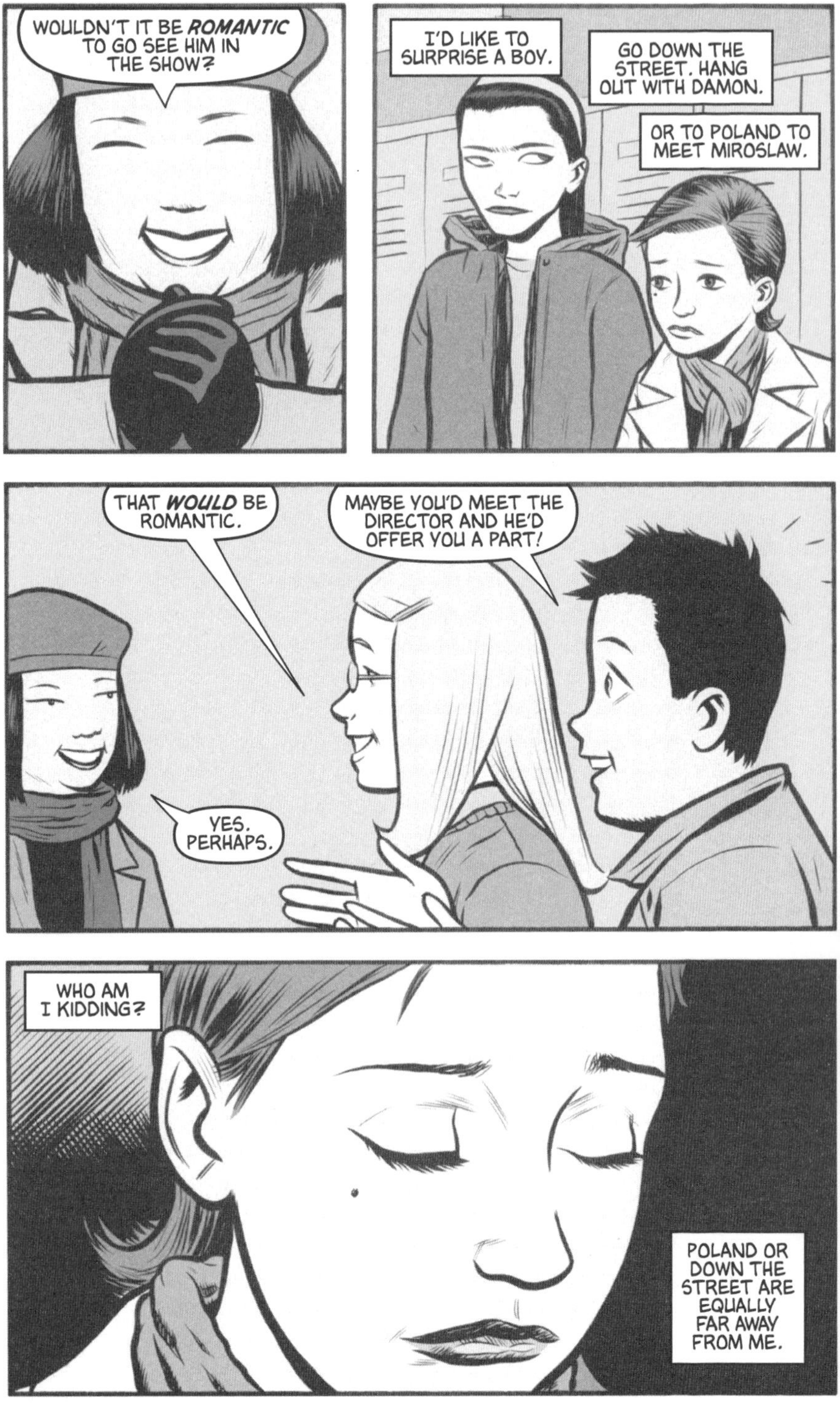
WOULDN'T IT BE *ROMANTIC* TO GO SEE HIM IN THE SHOW?
I'D LIKE TO SURPRISE A BOY.
GO DOWN THE STREET. HANG OUT WITH DAMON.
OR TO POLAND TO MEET MIROSLAW.
THAT *WOULD* BE ROMANTIC.
MAYBE YOU'D MEET THE DIRECTOR AND HE'D OFFER YOU A PART!
YES. PERHAPS.
WHO AM I KIDDING?
POLAND OR DOWN THE STREET ARE EQUALLY FAR AWAY FROM ME.

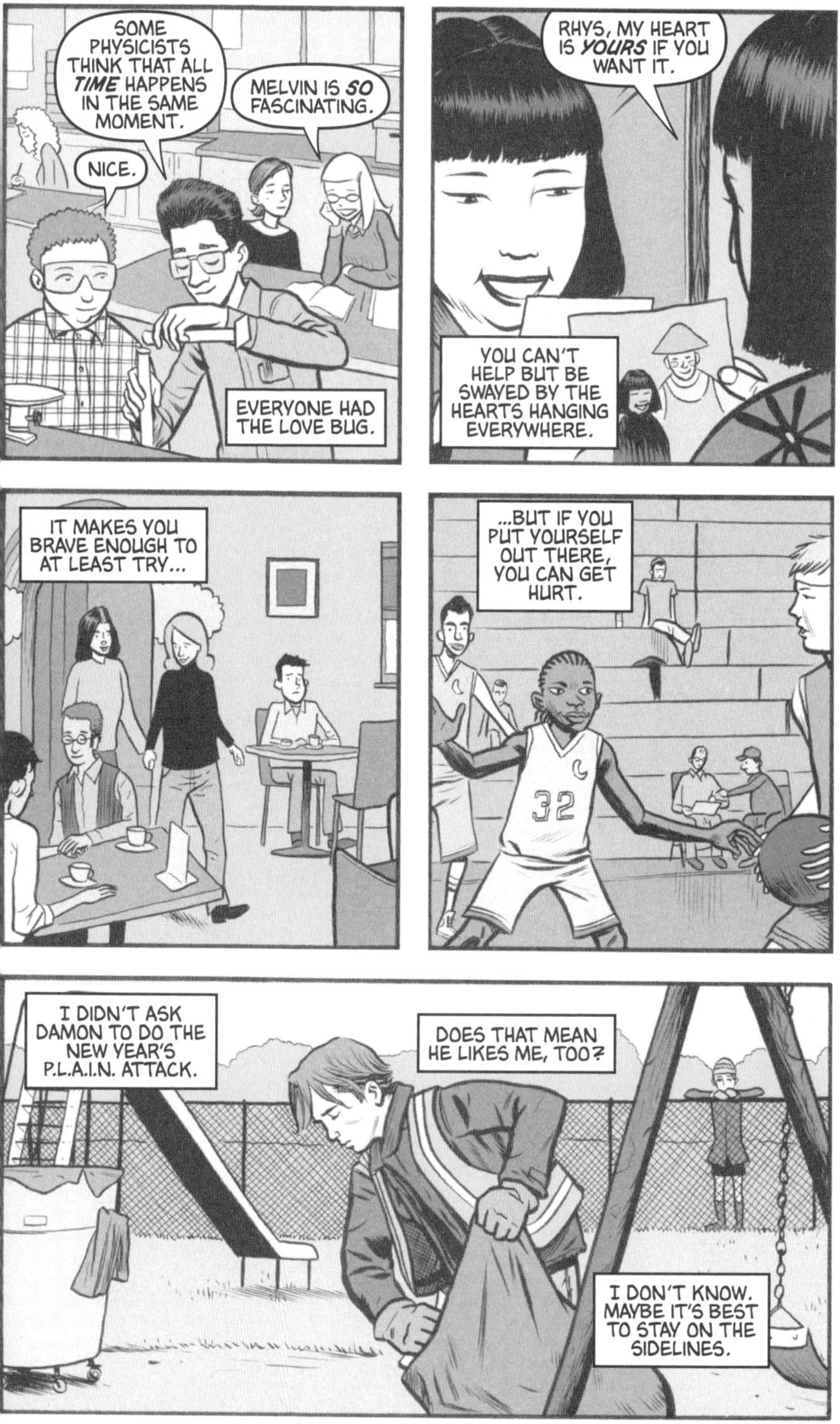
SOME PHYSICISTS THINK THAT ALL TIME HAPPENS IN THE SAME MOMENT.
NICE.
MELVIN IS SO FASCINATING.
EVERYONE HAD THE LOVE BUG.
RHYS, MY HEART IS YOURS IF YOU WANT IT.
YOU CAN'T HELP BUT BE SWAYED BY THE HEARTS HANGING EVERYWHERE.
IT MAKES YOU BRAVE ENOUGH TO AT LEAST TRY...
...BUT IF YOU PUT YOURSELF OUT THERE, YOU CAN GET HURT.
32
I DIDN'T ASK DAMON TO DO THE NEW YEAR'S P.L.A.I.N. ATTACK.
DOES THAT MEAN HE LIKES ME, TOO?
I DON'T KNOW. MAYBE IT'S BEST TO STAY ON THE SIDELINES.

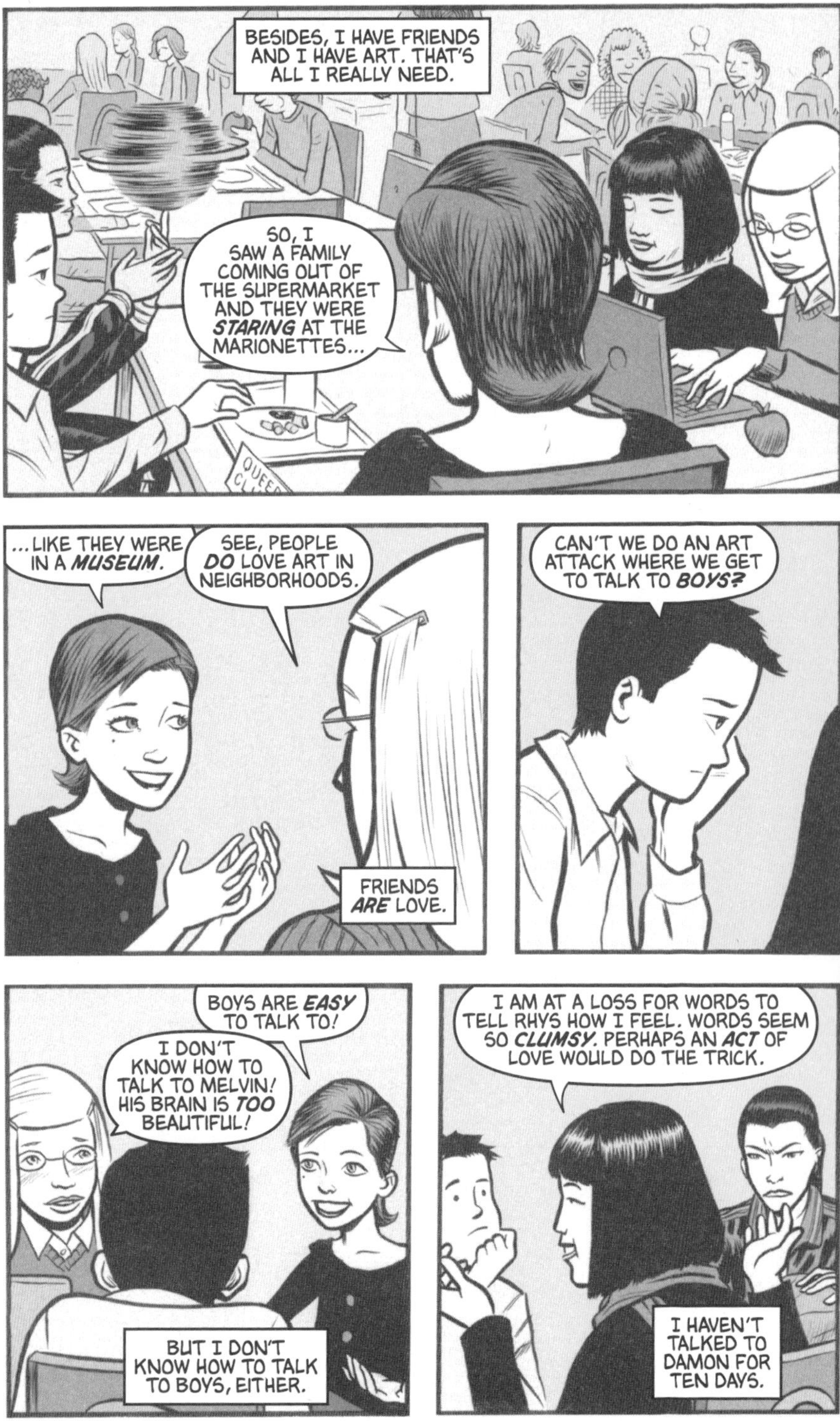
BESIDES, I HAVE FRIENDS AND I HAVE ART. THAT'S ALL I REALLY NEED.
SO, I SAW A FAMILY COMING OUT OF THE SUPERMARKET AND THEY WERE STARING AT THE MARIONETTES...
...LIKE THEY WERE IN A MUSEUM.
SEE, PEOPLE DO LOVE ART IN NEIGHBORHOODS.
FRIENDS ARE LOVE.
CAN'T WE DO AN ART ATTACK WHERE WE GET TO TALK TO BOYS?
BOYS ARE EASY TO TALK TO!
I DON'T KNOW HOW TO TALK TO MELVIN! HIS BRAIN IS TOO BEAUTIFUL!
BUT I DON'T KNOW HOW TO TALK TO BOYS, EITHER.
I AM AT A LOSS FOR WORDS TO TELL RHYS HOW I FEEL. WORDS SEEM SO CLUMSY. PERHAPS AN ACT OF LOVE WOULD DO THE TRICK.
I HAVEN'T TALKED TO DAMON FOR TEN DAYS.

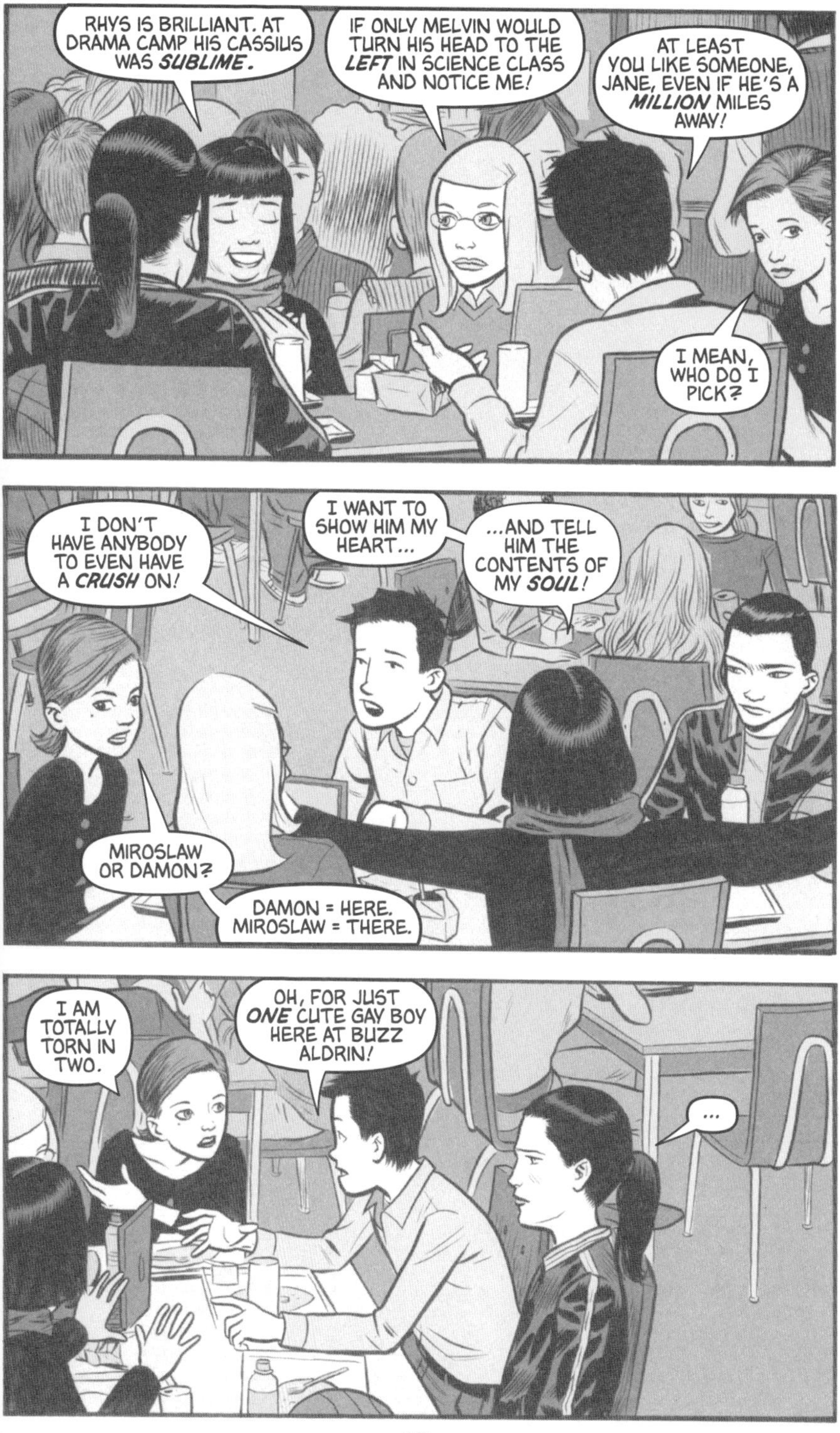

RHYS IS BRILLIANT. AT DRAMA CAMP HIS CASSIUS WAS SUBLIME.
IF ONLY MELVIN WOULD TURN HIS HEAD TO THE LEFT IN SCIENCE CLASS AND NOTICE ME!
AT LEAST YOU LIKE SOMEONE, JANE, EVEN IF HE'S A MILLION MILES AWAY!
I MEAN, WHO DO I PICK?
I DON'T HAVE ANYBODY TO EVEN HAVE A CRUSH ON!
I WANT TO SHOW HIM MY HEART...
...AND TELL HIM THE CONTENTS OF MY SOUL!
MIROSLAW OR DAMON?
DAMON = HERE. MIROSLAW = THERE.
I AM TOTALLY TORN IN TWO.
OH, FOR JUST ONE CUTE GAY BOY HERE AT BUZZ ALDRIN!
...

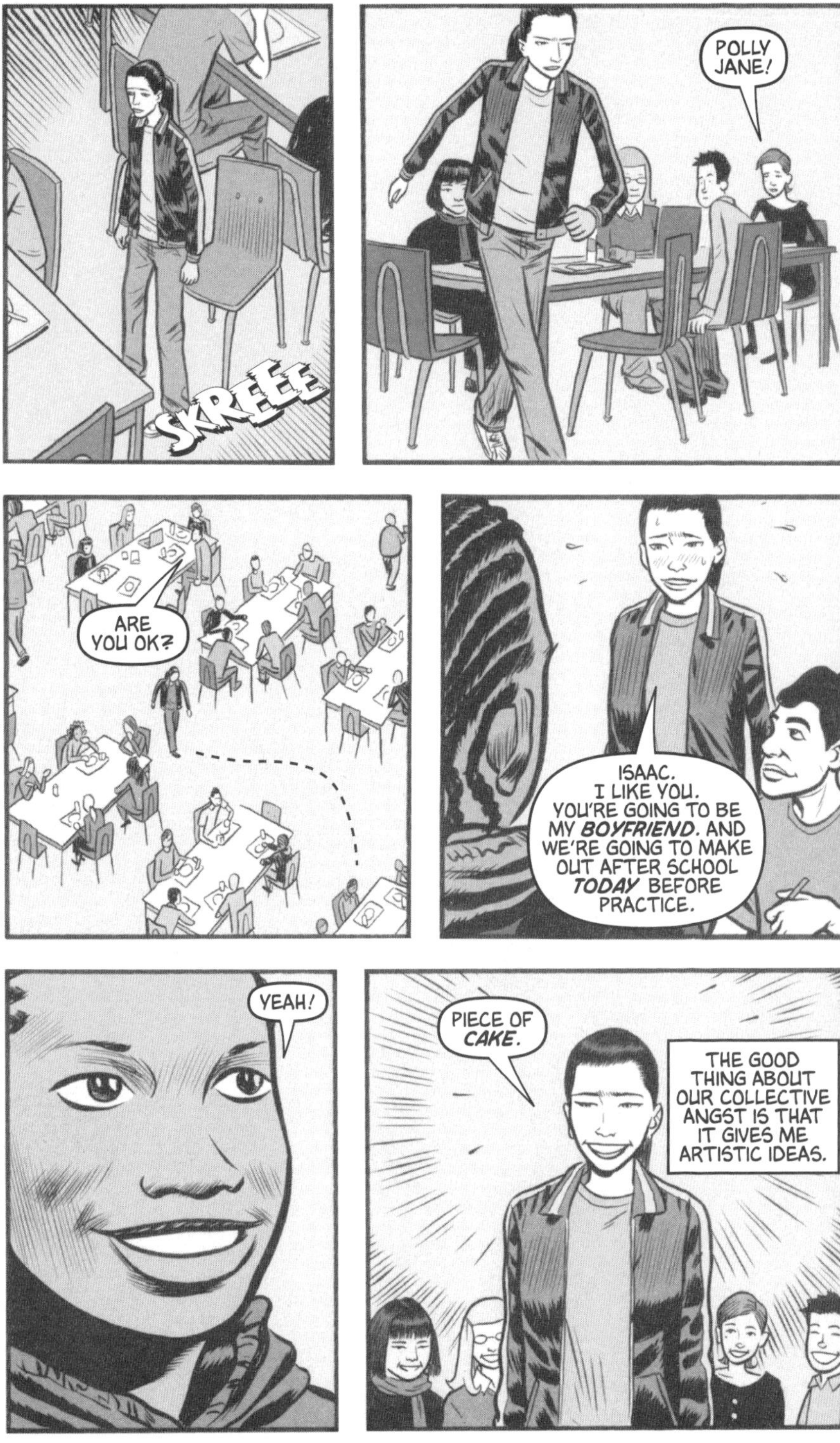
SKREEE
POLLY JANE!
ARE YOU OK?
ISAAC. I LIKE YOU. YOU'RE GOING TO BE MY **BOYFRIEND**. AND WE'RE GOING TO MAKE OUT AFTER SCHOOL **TODAY** BEFORE PRACTICE.
YEAH!
PIECE OF **CAKE**.
THE GOOD THING ABOUT OUR COLLECTIVE ANGST IS THAT IT GIVES ME ARTISTIC IDEAS.

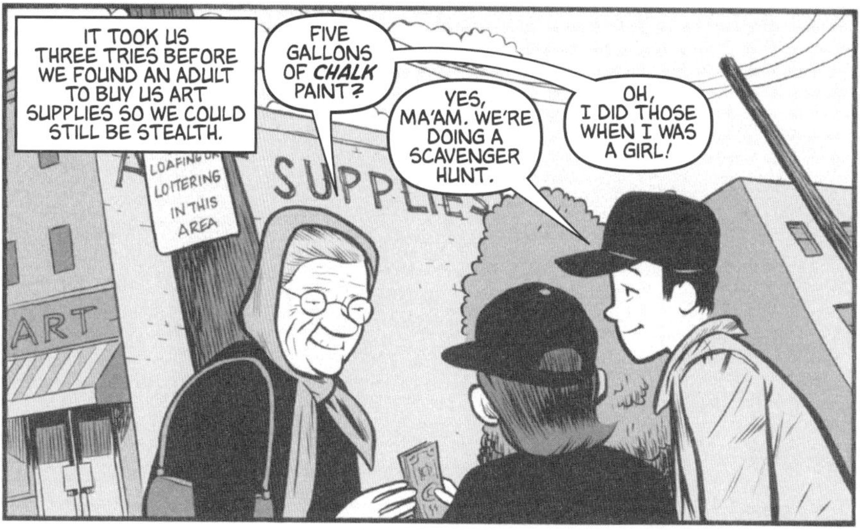
IT TOOK US THREE TRIES BEFORE WE FOUND AN ADULT TO BUY US ART SUPPLIES SO WE COULD STILL BE STEALTH.
FIVE GALLONS OF CHALK PAINT?
YES, MA'AM. WE'RE DOING A SCAVENGER HUNT.
OH, I DID THOSE WHEN I WAS A GIRL!
SUPPLIES
LOAFING OR LOITERING IN THIS AREA
ART

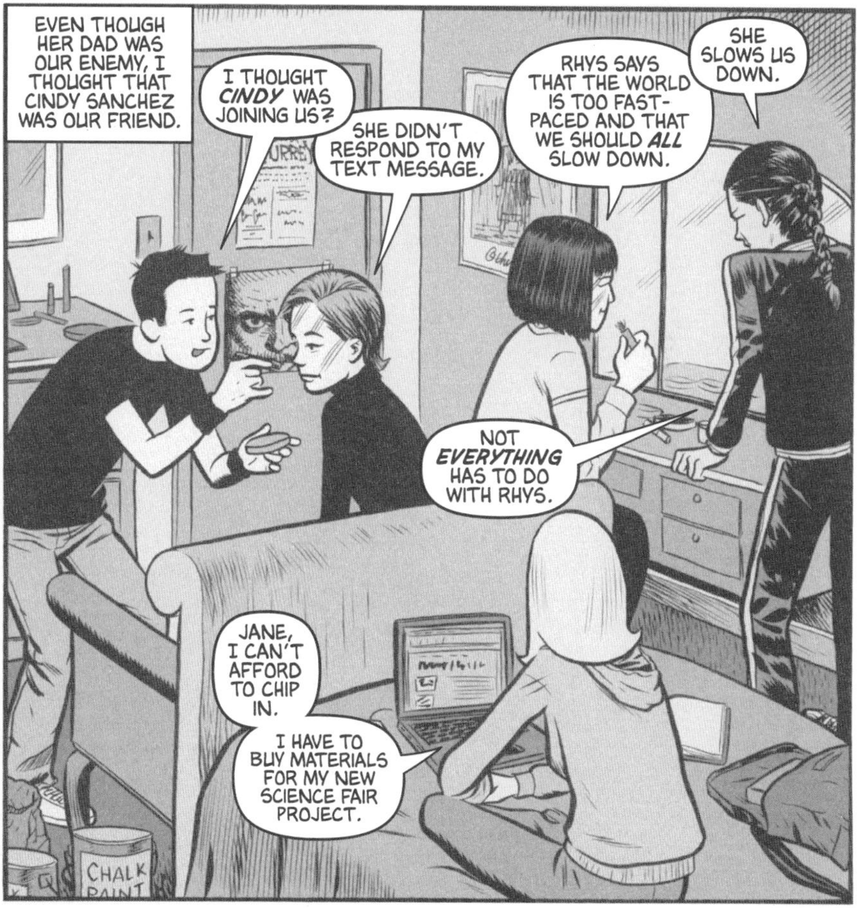
EVEN THOUGH HER DAD WAS OUR ENEMY, I THOUGHT THAT CINDY SANCHEZ WAS OUR FRIEND.
I THOUGHT CINDY WAS JOINING US?
SHE DIDN'T RESPOND TO MY TEXT MESSAGE.
RHYS SAYS THAT THE WORLD IS TOO FAST-PACED AND THAT WE SHOULD ALL SLOW DOWN.
SHE SLOWS US DOWN.
NOT EVERYTHING HAS TO DO WITH RHYS.
JANE, I CAN'T AFFORD TO CHIP IN.
I HAVE TO BUY MATERIALS FOR MY NEW SCIENCE FAIR PROJECT.
CHALK PAINT

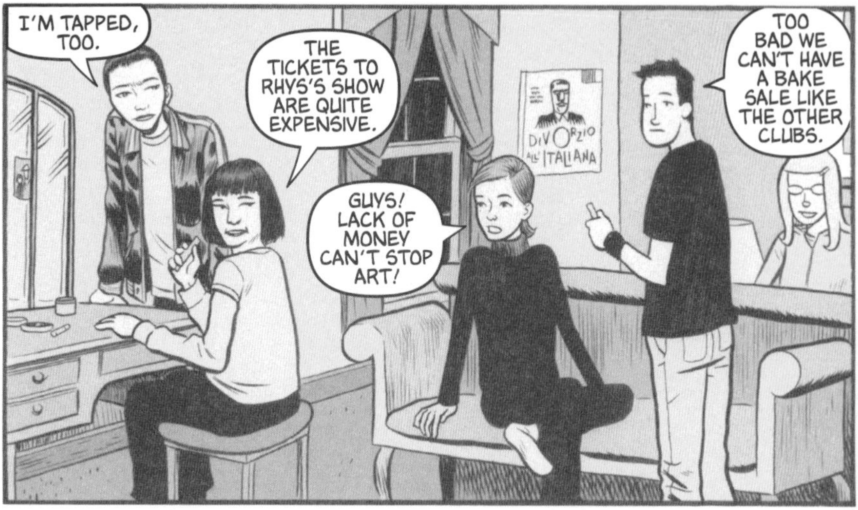
I'M TAPPED, TOO.
THE TICKETS TO RHYS'S SHOW ARE QUITE EXPENSIVE.
GUYS! LACK OF MONEY CAN'T STOP ART!
TOO BAD WE CAN'T HAVE A BAKE SALE LIKE THE OTHER CLUBS.
DIVORZIO ALL'ITALIANA

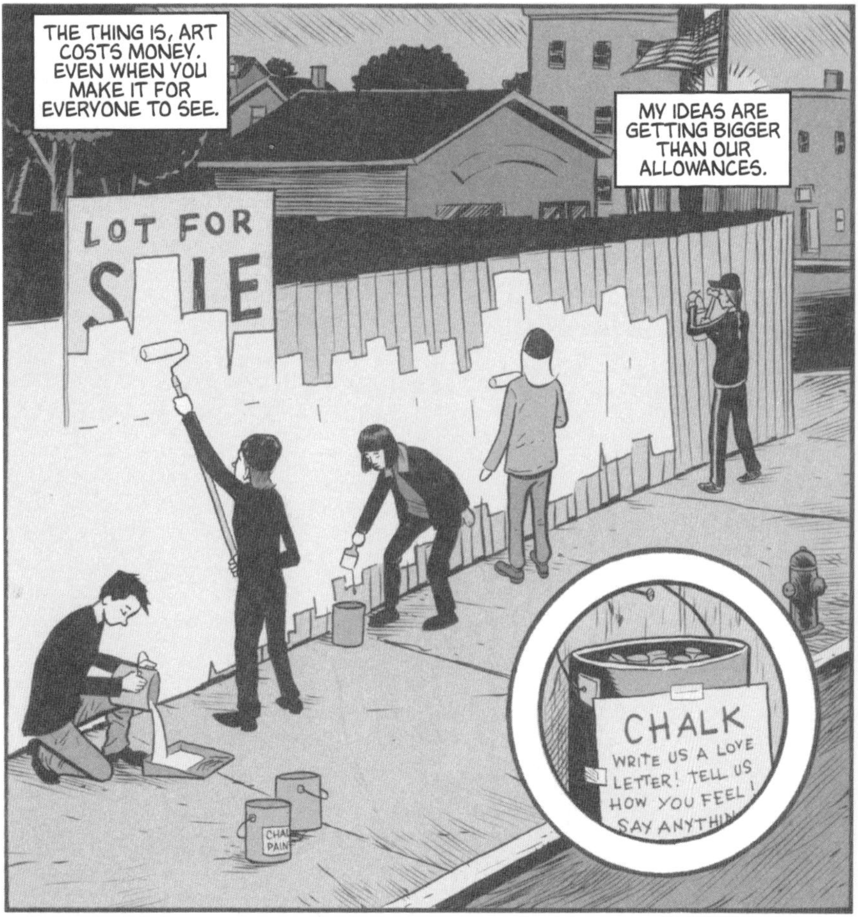
THE THING IS, ART COSTS MONEY. EVEN WHEN YOU MAKE IT FOR EVERYONE TO SEE.
MY IDEAS ARE GETTING BIGGER THAN OUR ALLOWANCES.
LOT FOR S IE
CHALK
WRITE US A LOVE LETTER! TELL US HOW YOU FEEL!
SAY ANYTHIN

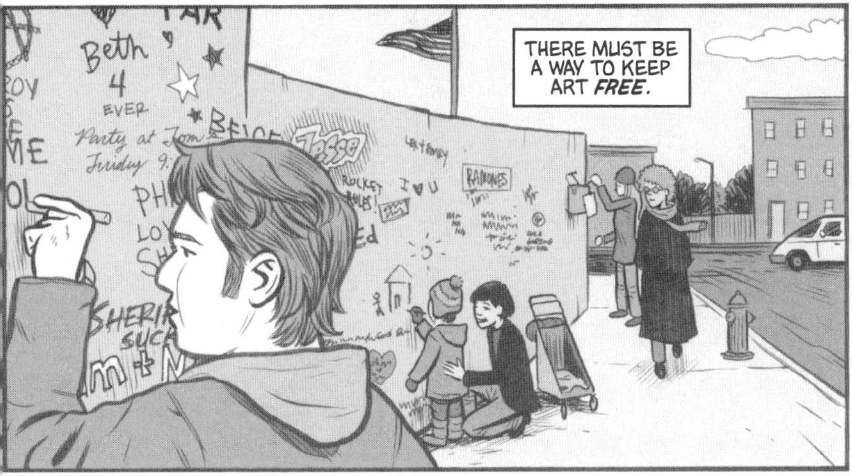
THERE MUST BE A WAY TO KEEP ART *FREE*.

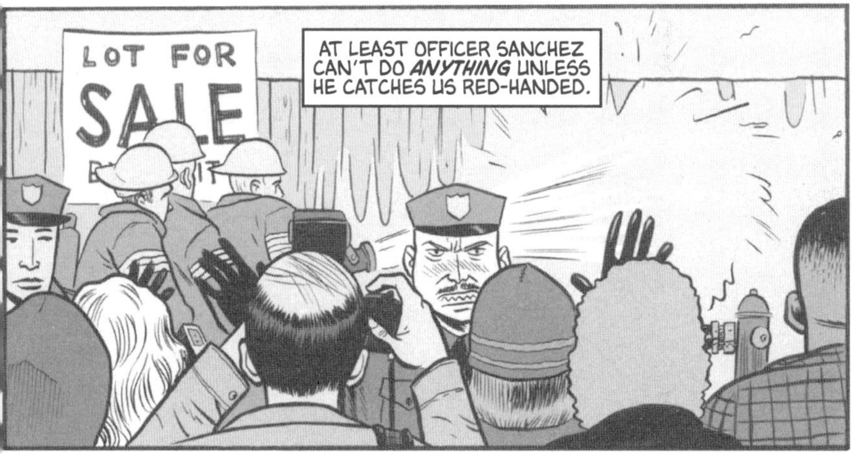
LOT FOR SALE
AT LEAST OFFICER SANCHEZ CAN'T DO *ANYTHING* UNLESS HE CATCHES US RED-HANDED.

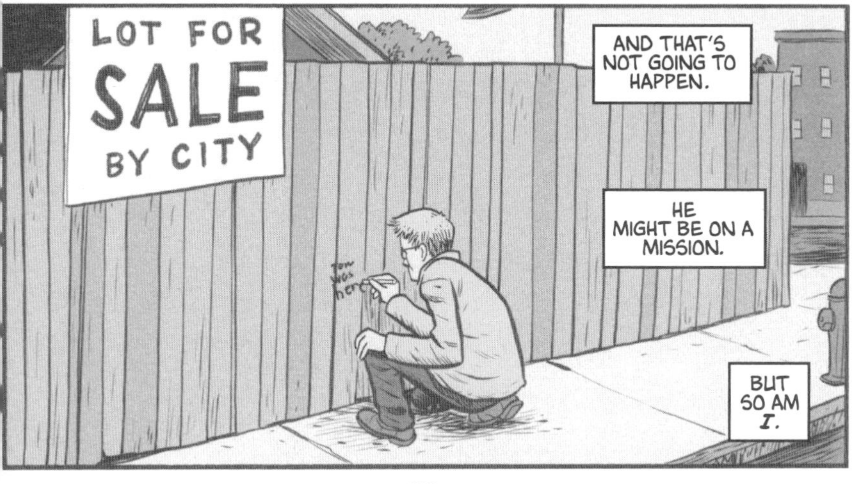
LOT FOR SALE BY CITY
AND THAT'S NOT GOING TO HAPPEN.
HE MIGHT BE ON A MISSION.
BUT SO AM *I*.

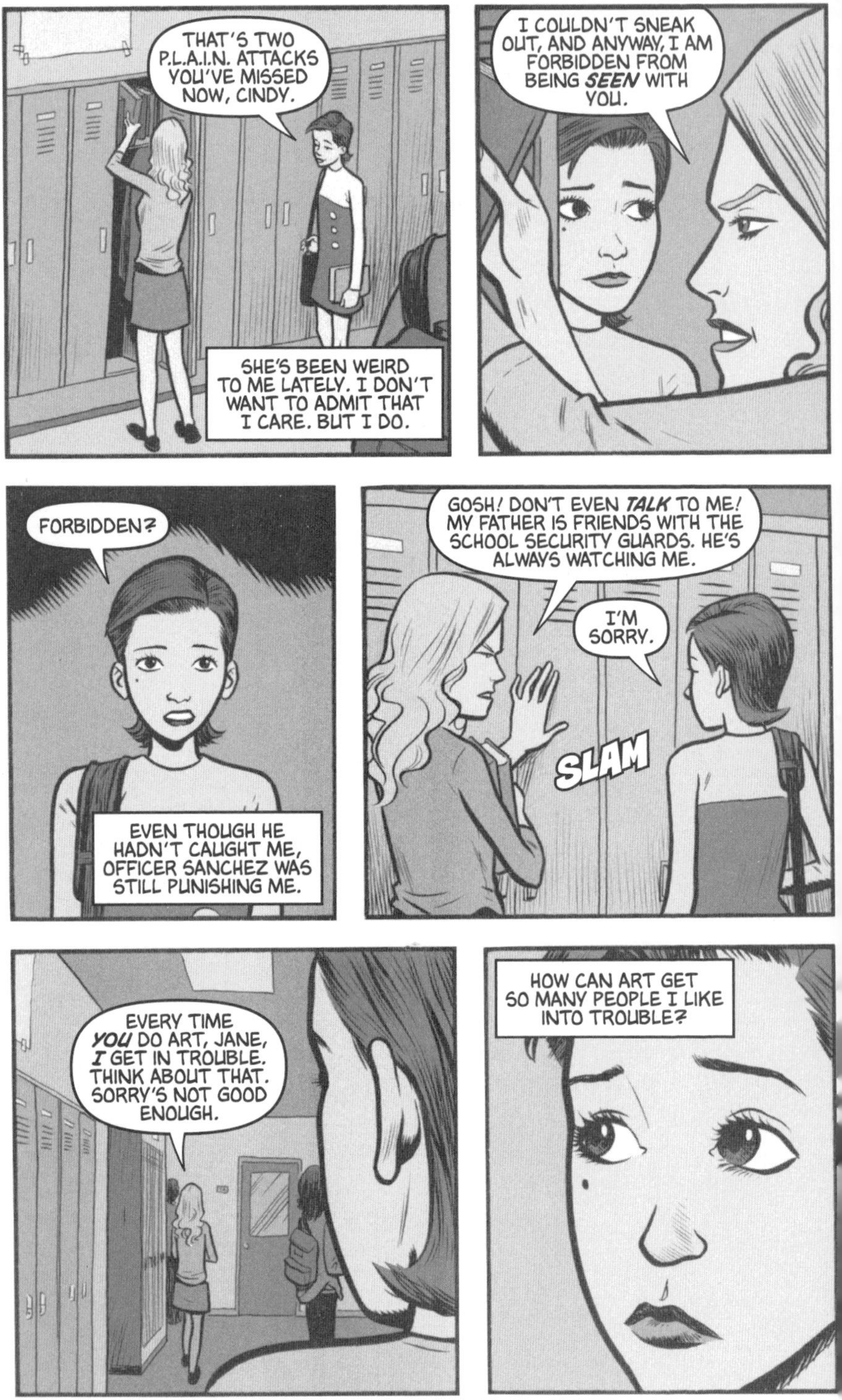
THAT'S TWO P.L.A.I.N. ATTACKS YOU'VE MISSED NOW, CINDY.
SHE'S BEEN WEIRD TO ME LATELY. I DON'T WANT TO ADMIT THAT I CARE. BUT I DO.
I COULDN'T SNEAK OUT, AND ANYWAY, I AM FORBIDDEN FROM BEING *SEEN* WITH YOU.
FORBIDDEN?
EVEN THOUGH HE HADN'T CAUGHT ME, OFFICER SANCHEZ WAS STILL PUNISHING ME.
GOSH! DON'T EVEN *TALK* TO ME! MY FATHER IS FRIENDS WITH THE SCHOOL SECURITY GUARDS. HE'S ALWAYS WATCHING ME.
I'M SORRY.
SLAM
EVERY TIME *YOU* DO ART, JANE, *I* GET IN TROUBLE. THINK ABOUT THAT. SORRY'S NOT GOOD ENOUGH.
HOW CAN ART GET SO MANY PEOPLE I LIKE INTO TROUBLE?

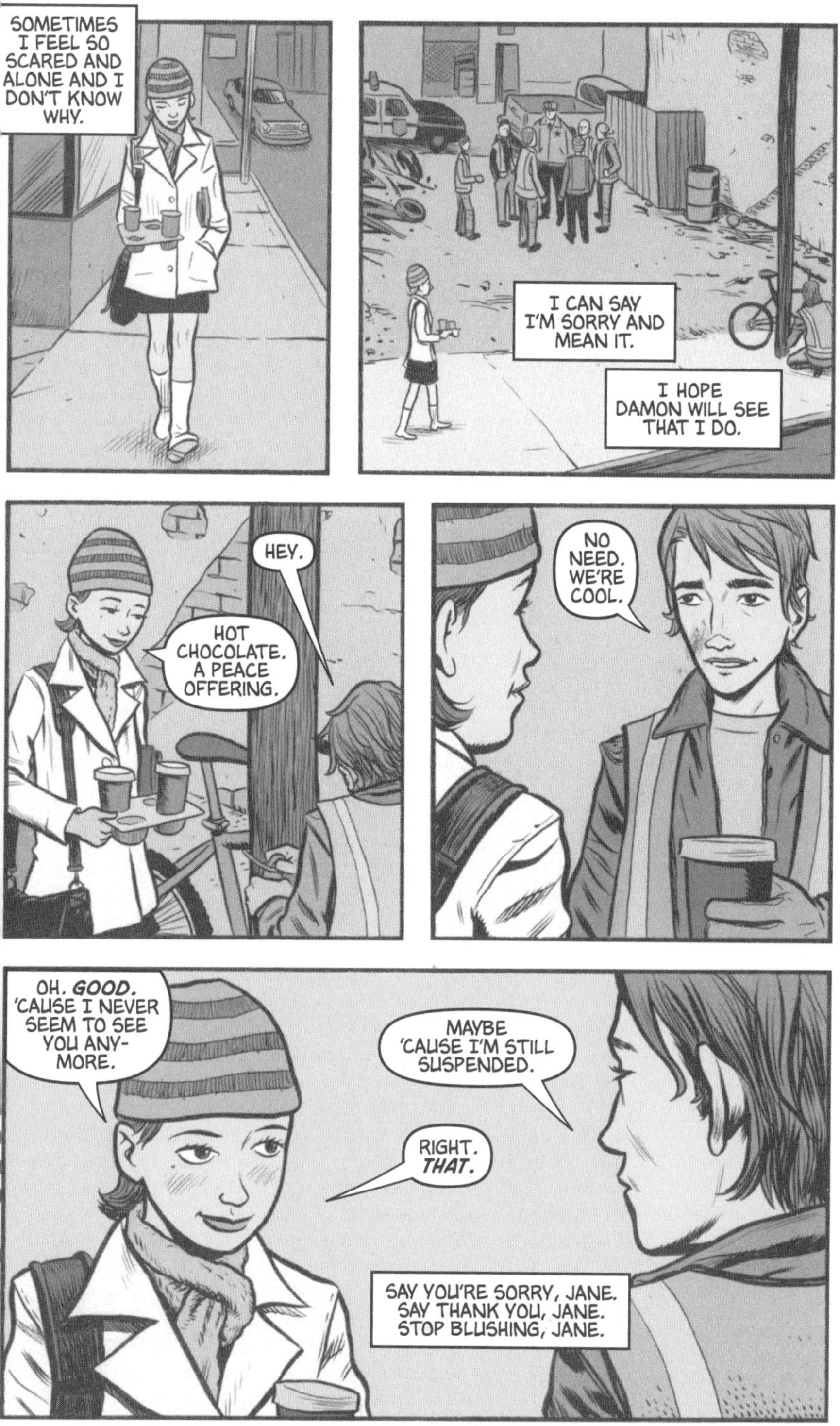
SOMETIMES I FEEL SO SCARED AND ALONE AND I DON'T KNOW WHY.
I CAN SAY I'M SORRY AND MEAN IT.
I HOPE DAMON WILL SEE THAT I DO.
HEY.
HOT CHOCOLATE. A PEACE OFFERING.
NO NEED. WE'RE COOL.
OH. *GOOD.* 'CAUSE I NEVER SEEM TO SEE YOU ANY-MORE.
MAYBE 'CAUSE I'M STILL SUSPENDED.
RIGHT. *THAT.*
SAY YOU'RE SORRY, JANE. SAY THANK YOU, JANE. STOP BLUSHING, JANE.

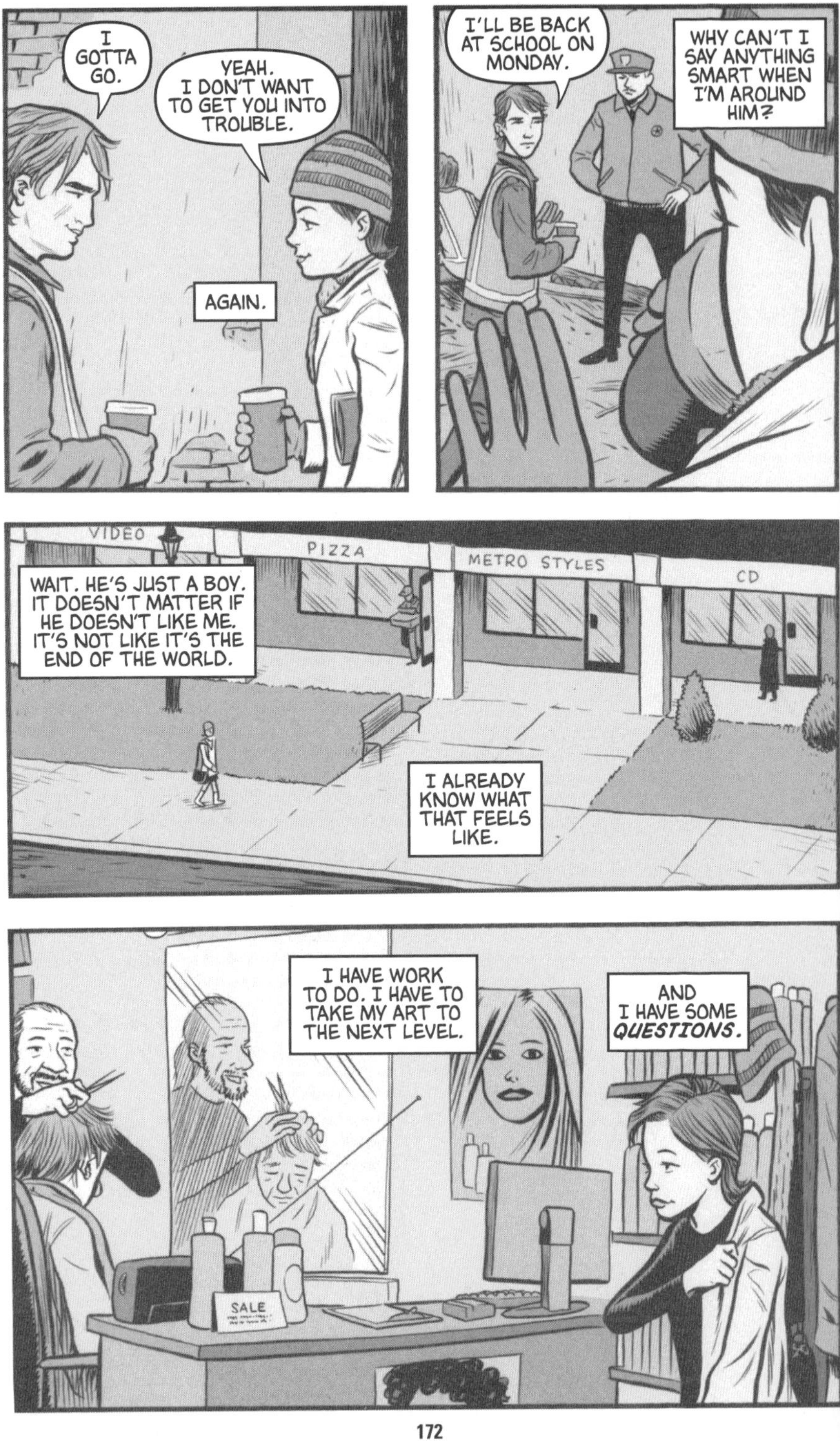

I GOTTA GO.
YEAH. I DON'T WANT TO GET YOU INTO TROUBLE.
AGAIN.
I'LL BE BACK AT SCHOOL ON MONDAY.
WHY CAN'T I SAY ANYTHING SMART WHEN I'M AROUND HIM?
VIDEO
PIZZA
METRO STYLES
CD
WAIT. HE'S JUST A BOY. IT DOESN'T MATTER IF HE DOESN'T LIKE ME. IT'S NOT LIKE IT'S THE END OF THE WORLD.
I ALREADY KNOW WHAT THAT FEELS LIKE.
I HAVE WORK TO DO. I HAVE TO TAKE MY ART TO THE NEXT LEVEL.
AND I HAVE SOME ***QUESTIONS***.
SALE

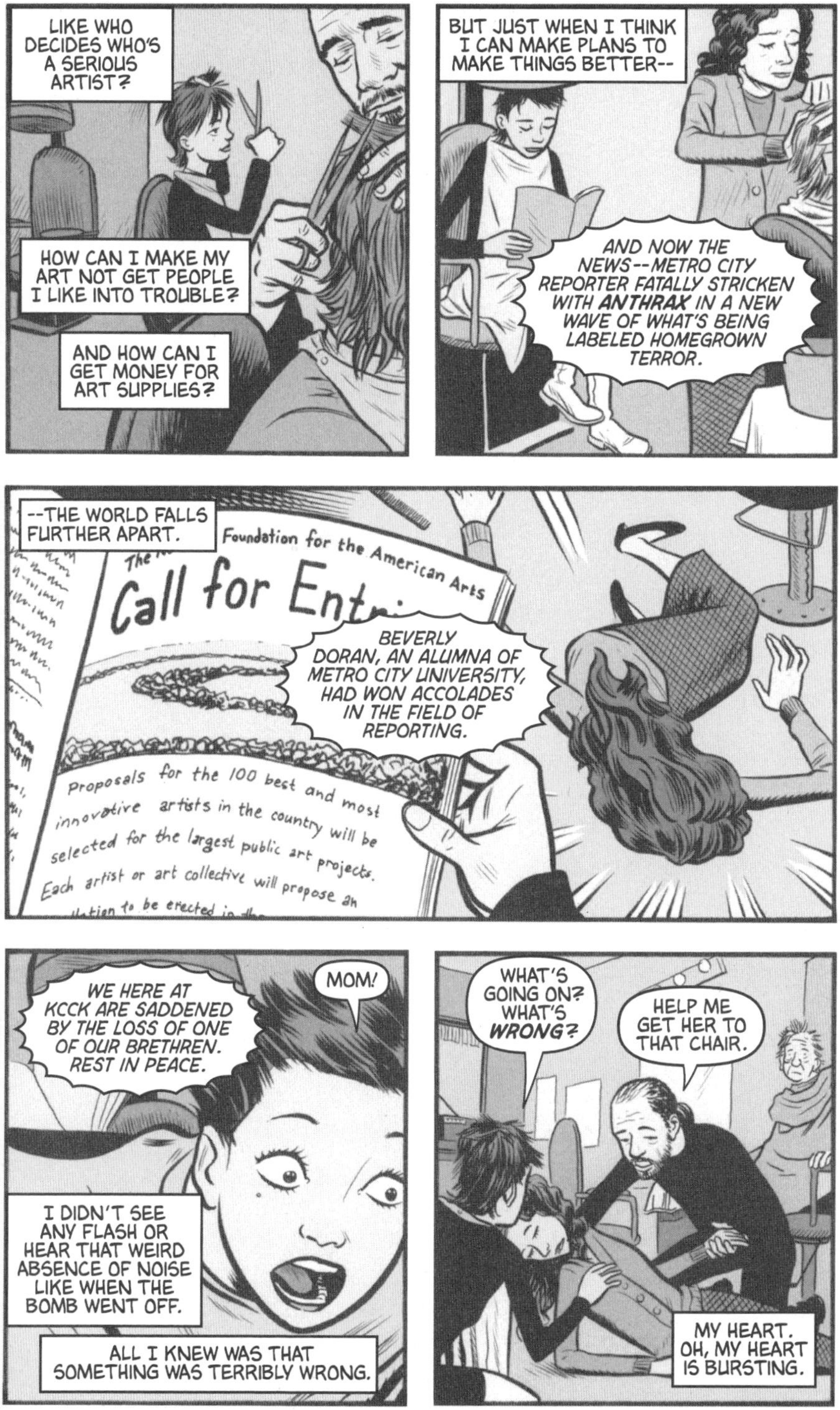
LIKE WHO DECIDES WHO'S A SERIOUS ARTIST?
HOW CAN I MAKE MY ART NOT GET PEOPLE I LIKE INTO TROUBLE?
AND HOW CAN I GET MONEY FOR ART SUPPLIES?
BUT JUST WHEN I THINK I CAN MAKE PLANS TO MAKE THINGS BETTER--
AND NOW THE NEWS--METRO CITY REPORTER FATALLY STRICKEN WITH ANTHRAX IN A NEW WAVE OF WHAT'S BEING LABELED HOMEGROWN TERROR.
--THE WORLD FALLS FURTHER APART.
Foundation for the American Arts
Call for Ent
BEVERLY DORAN, AN ALUMNA OF METRO CITY UNIVERSITY, HAD WON ACCOLADES IN THE FIELD OF REPORTING.
Proposals for the 100 best and most innovative artists in the country will be selected for the largest public art projects. Each artist or art collective will propose an
WE HERE AT KCCK ARE SADDENED BY THE LOSS OF ONE OF OUR BRETHREN. REST IN PEACE.
MOM!
I DIDN'T SEE ANY FLASH OR HEAR THAT WEIRD ABSENCE OF NOISE LIKE WHEN THE BOMB WENT OFF.
ALL I KNEW WAS THAT SOMETHING WAS TERRIBLY WRONG.
WHAT'S GOING ON? WHAT'S WRONG?
HELP ME GET HER TO THAT CHAIR.
MY HEART. OH, MY HEART IS BURSTING.

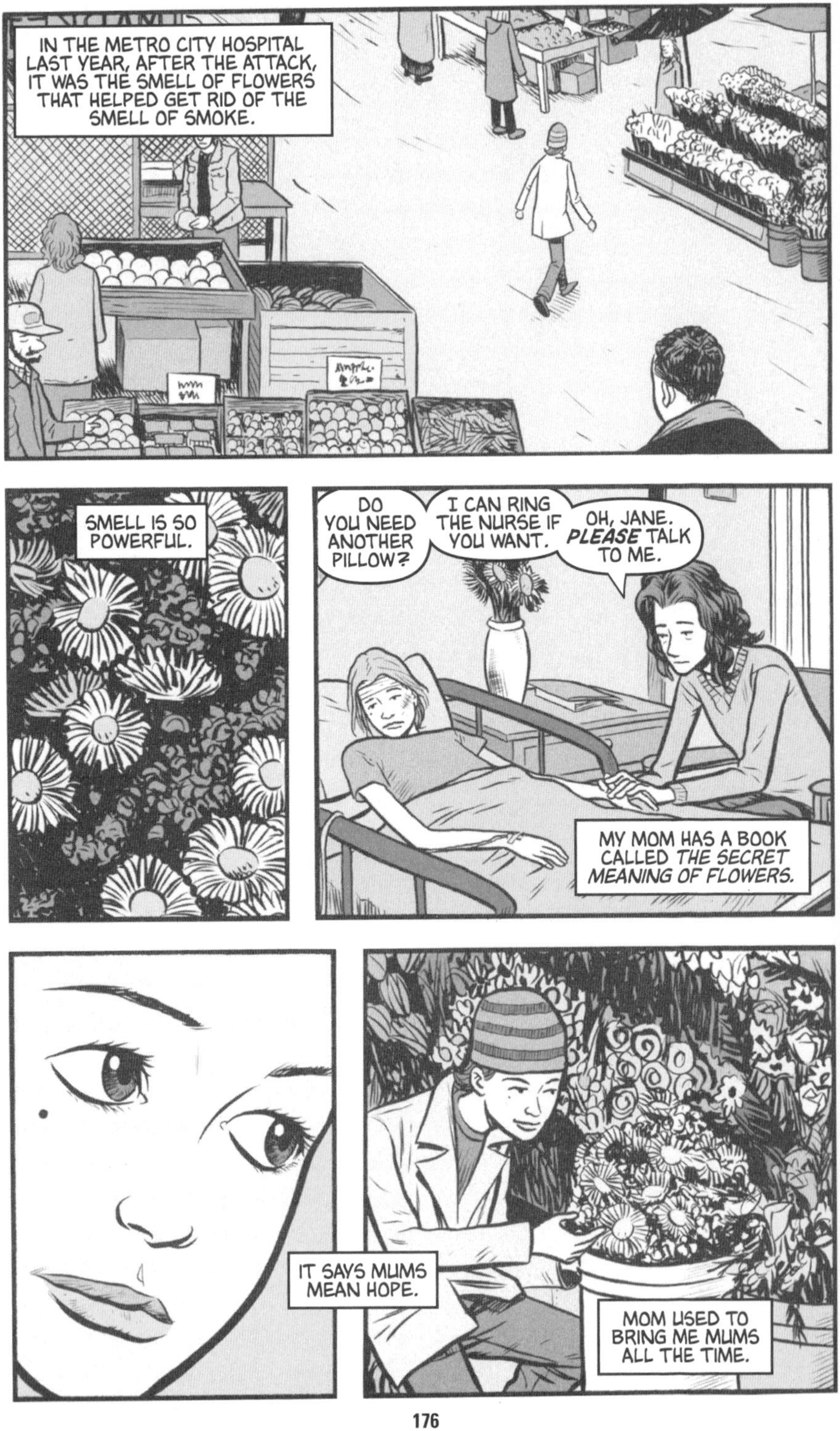
IN THE METRO CITY HOSPITAL LAST YEAR, AFTER THE ATTACK, IT WAS THE SMELL OF FLOWERS THAT HELPED GET RID OF THE SMELL OF SMOKE.
SMELL IS SO POWERFUL.
DO YOU NEED ANOTHER PILLOW?
I CAN RING THE NURSE IF YOU WANT.
OH, JANE. *PLEASE* TALK TO ME.
MY MOM HAS A BOOK CALLED *THE SECRET MEANING OF FLOWERS.*
IT SAYS MUMS MEAN HOPE.
MOM USED TO BRING ME MUMS ALL THE TIME.

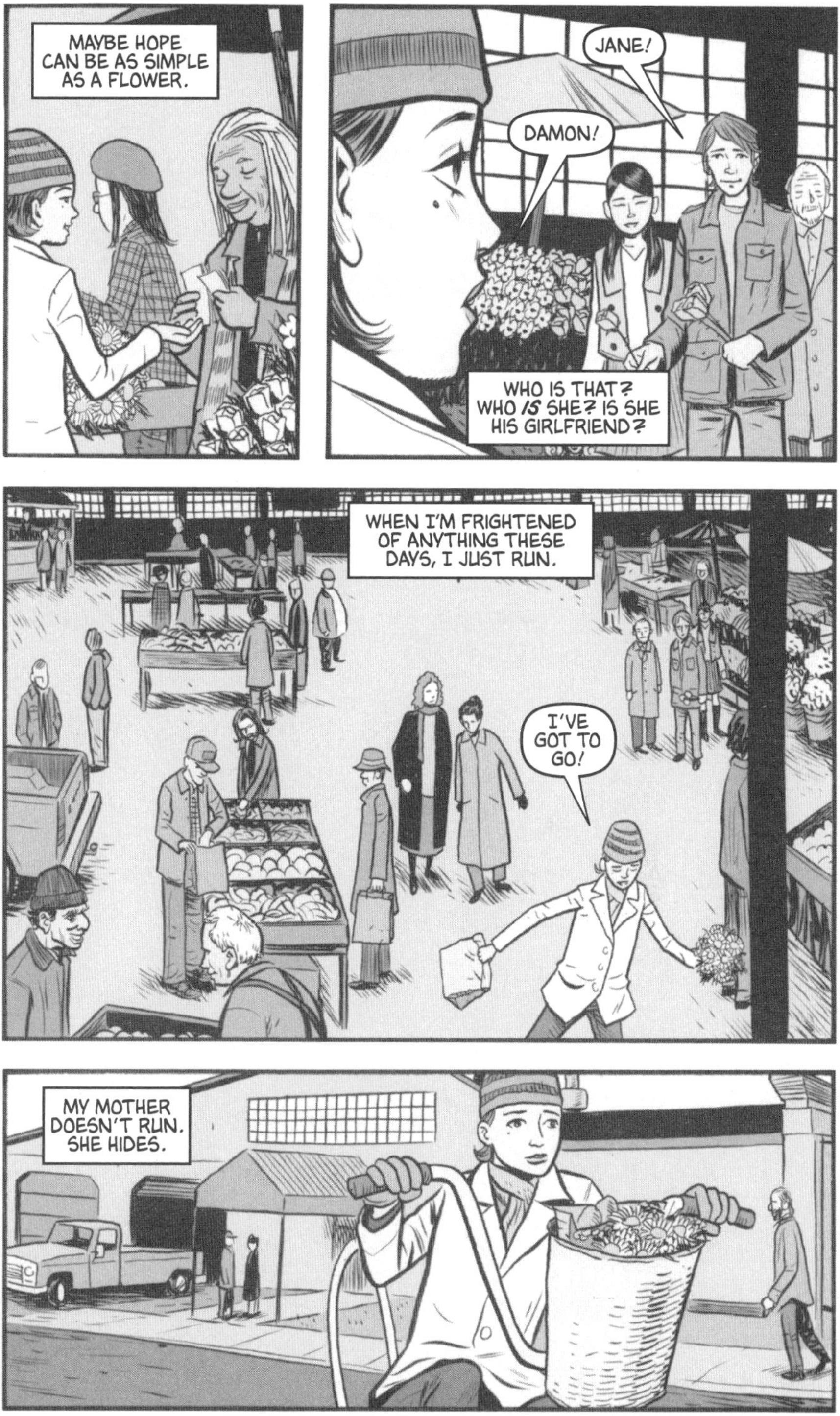
MAYBE HOPE CAN BE AS SIMPLE AS A FLOWER.
JANE!
DAMON!
WHO IS THAT? WHO *IS* SHE? IS SHE HIS GIRLFRIEND?
WHEN I'M FRIGHTENED OF ANYTHING THESE DAYS, I JUST RUN.
I'VE GOT TO GO!
MY MOTHER DOESN'T RUN. SHE HIDES.

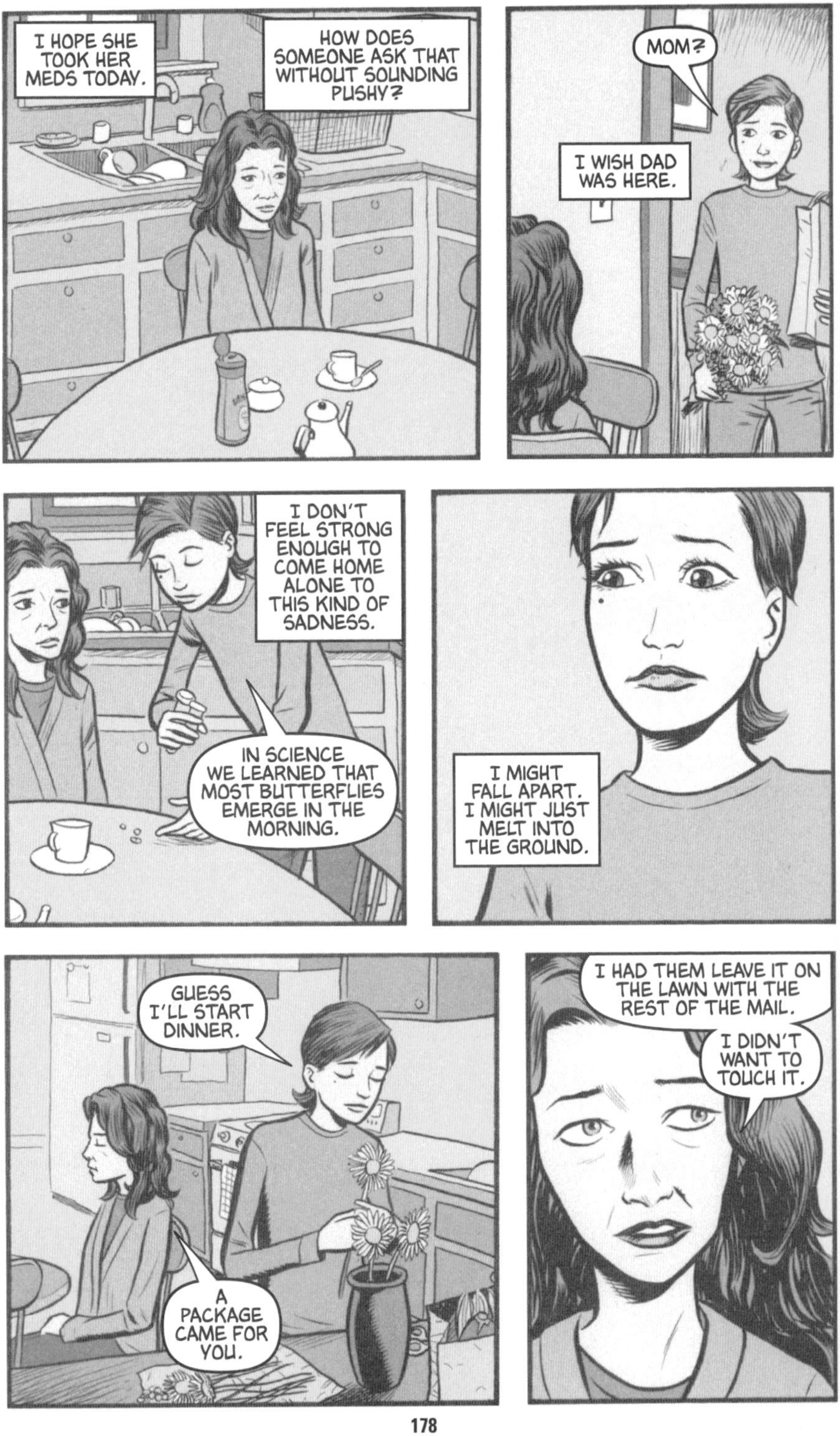
I HOPE SHE TOOK HER MEDS TODAY.
HOW DOES SOMEONE ASK THAT WITHOUT SOUNDING PUSHY?
MOM?
I WISH DAD WAS HERE.
I DON'T FEEL STRONG ENOUGH TO COME HOME ALONE TO THIS KIND OF SADNESS.
IN SCIENCE WE LEARNED THAT MOST BUTTERFLIES EMERGE IN THE MORNING.
I MIGHT FALL APART. I MIGHT JUST MELT INTO THE GROUND.
GUESS I'LL START DINNER.
A PACKAGE CAME FOR YOU.
I HAD THEM LEAVE IT ON THE LAWN WITH THE REST OF THE MAIL.
I DIDN'T WANT TO TOUCH IT.

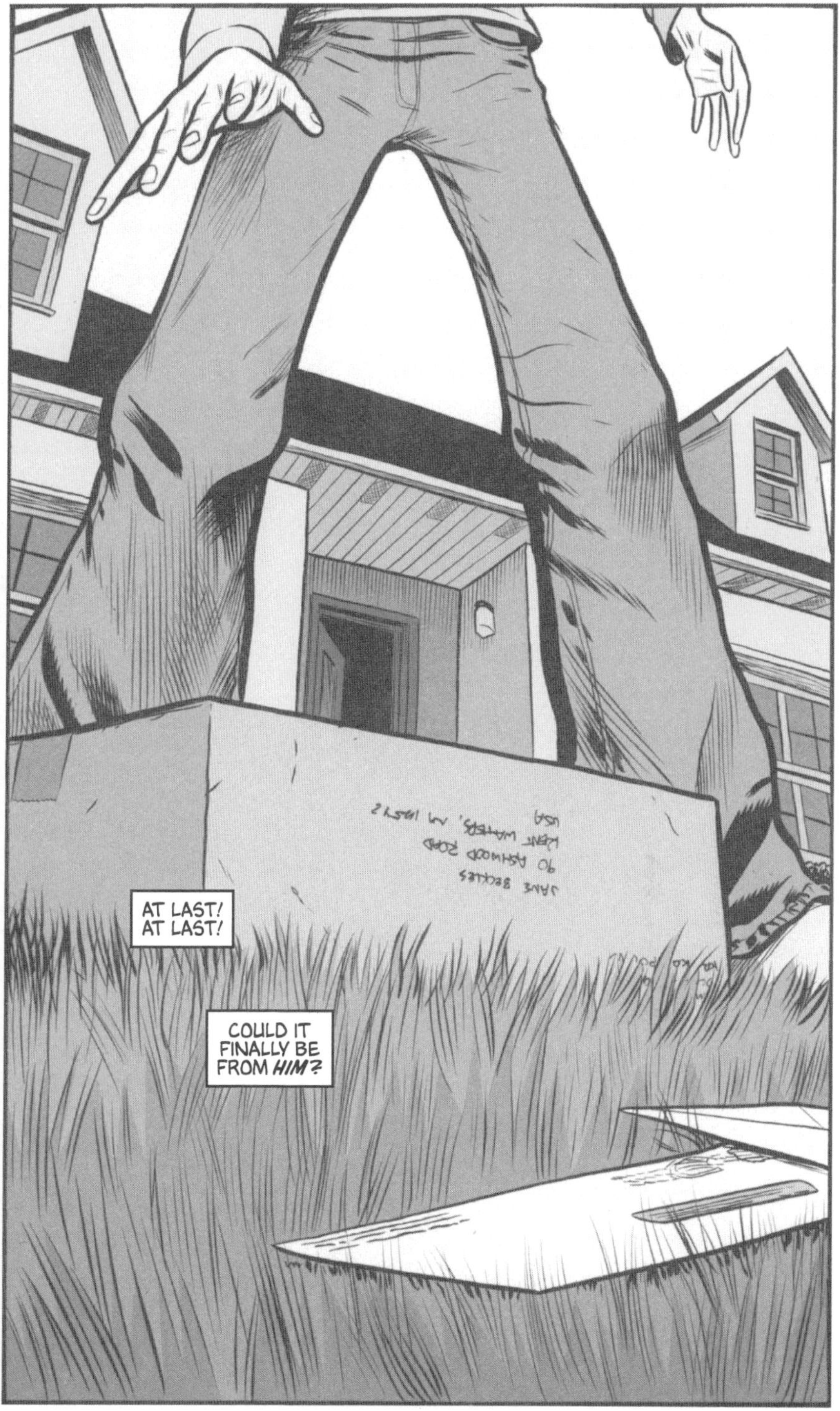
AT LAST! AT LAST!
COULD IT FINALLY BE FROM *HIM?*

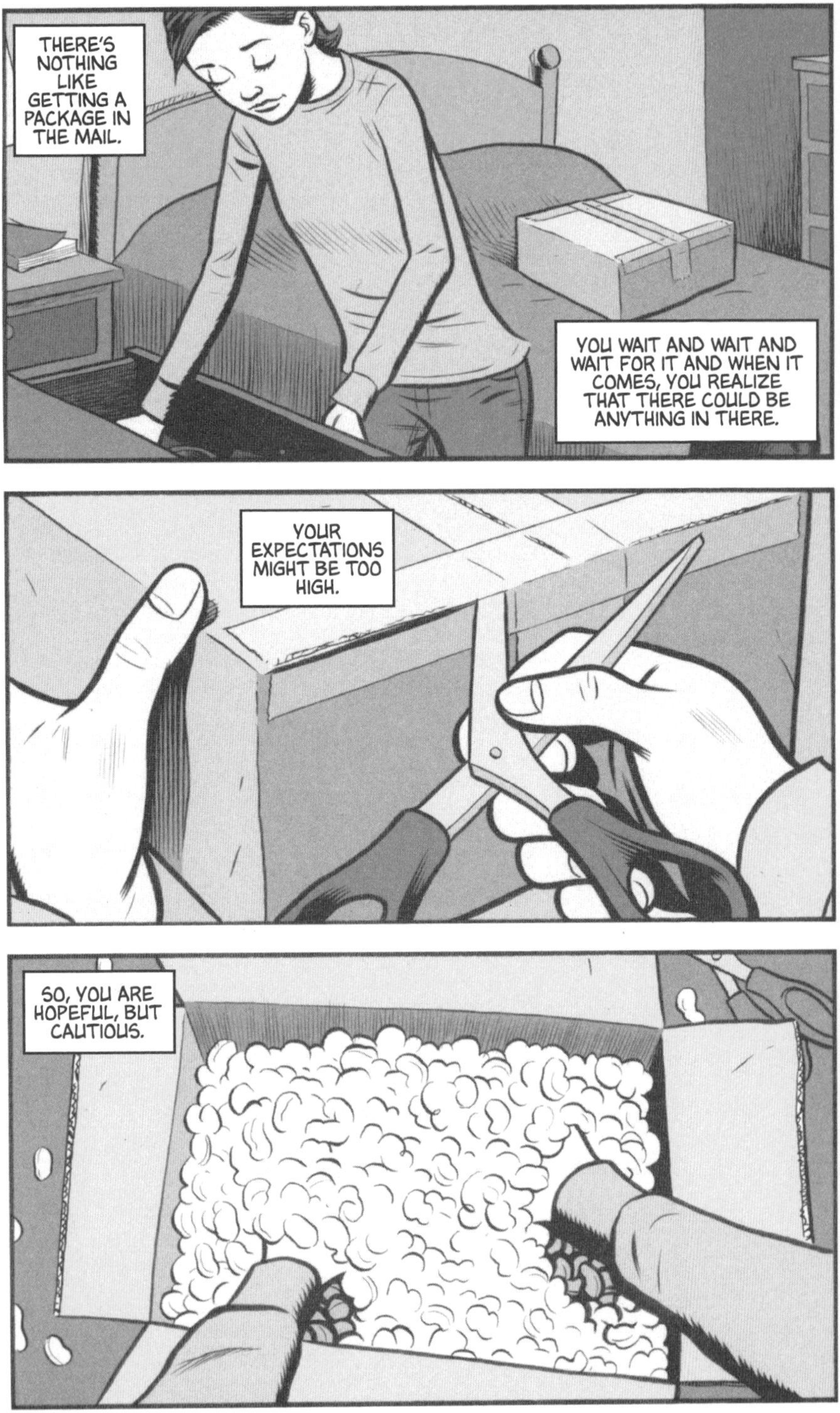
THERE'S NOTHING LIKE GETTING A PACKAGE IN THE MAIL.
YOU WAIT AND WAIT AND WAIT FOR IT AND WHEN IT COMES, YOU REALIZE THAT THERE COULD BE ANYTHING IN THERE.
YOUR EXPECTATIONS MIGHT BE TOO HIGH.
SO, YOU ARE HOPEFUL, BUT CAUTIOUS.

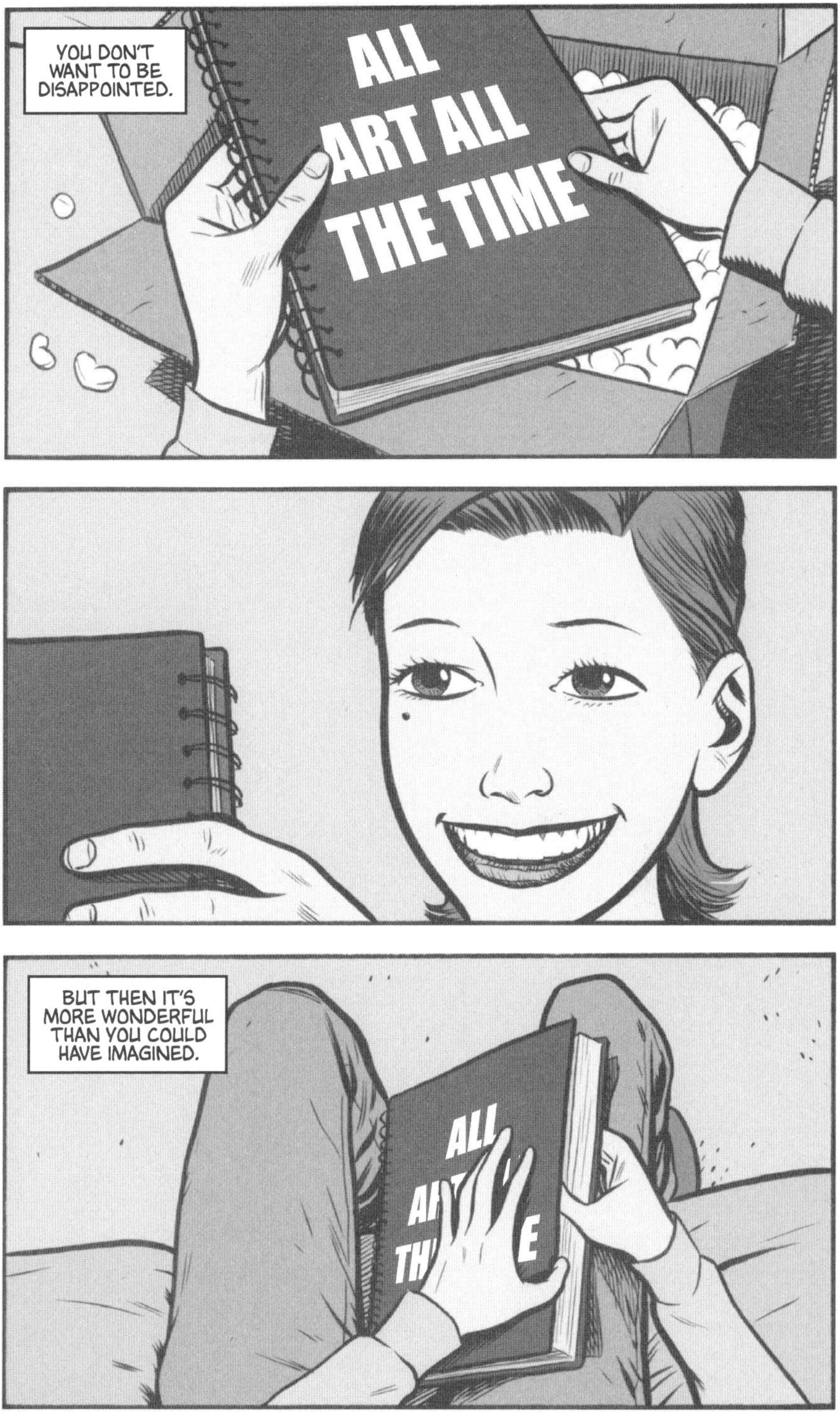

YOU DON'T WANT TO BE DISAPPOINTED.
ALL ART ALL THE TIME
BUT THEN IT'S MORE WONDERFUL THAN YOU COULD HAVE IMAGINED.

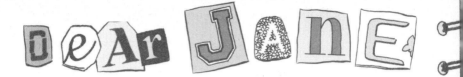

Dear Jane

Hello. How wonderful to be able to say these words to you.
Hello, dear Jane. Light of my life.

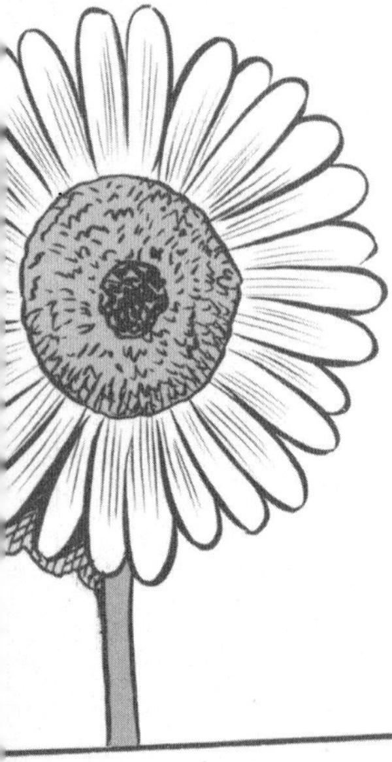

Slow is the world
I have to take things
At a slower pace
Thoughts like molasses
Careful steps
Cautious
When I speak I slur
And the soup my mother feeds me
Dribbles out the left corner of my mouth.
I am safe now
Back again in the world of light

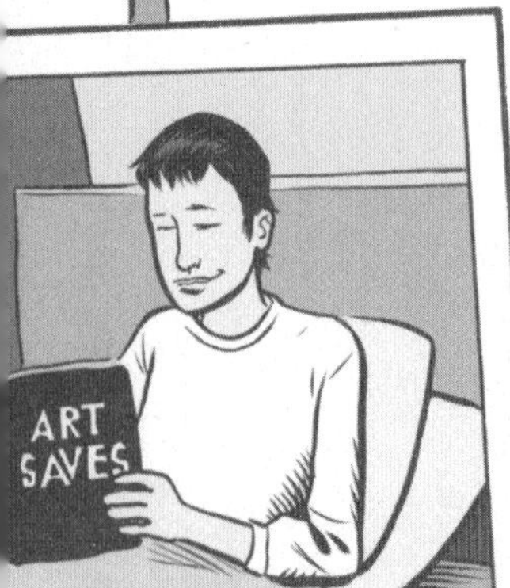
ART SAVES

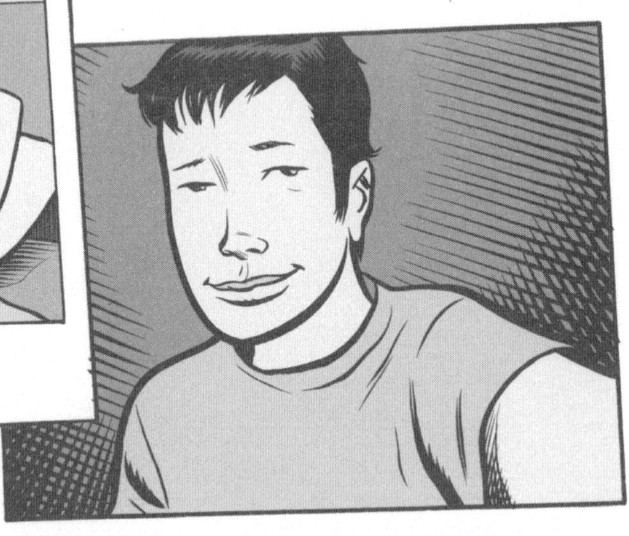

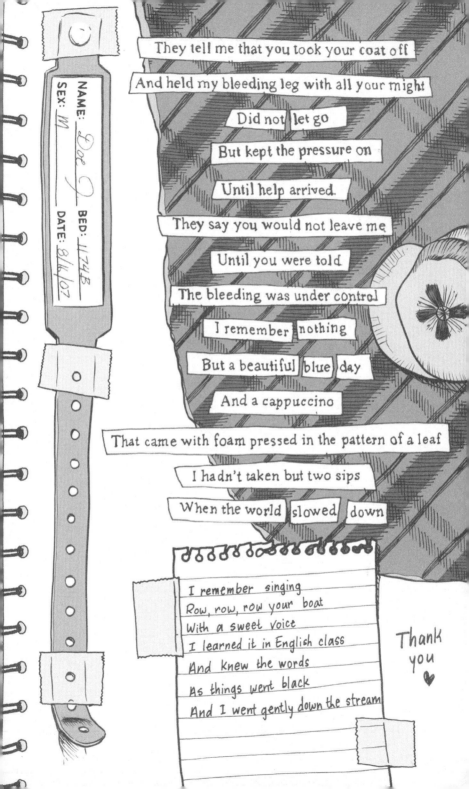

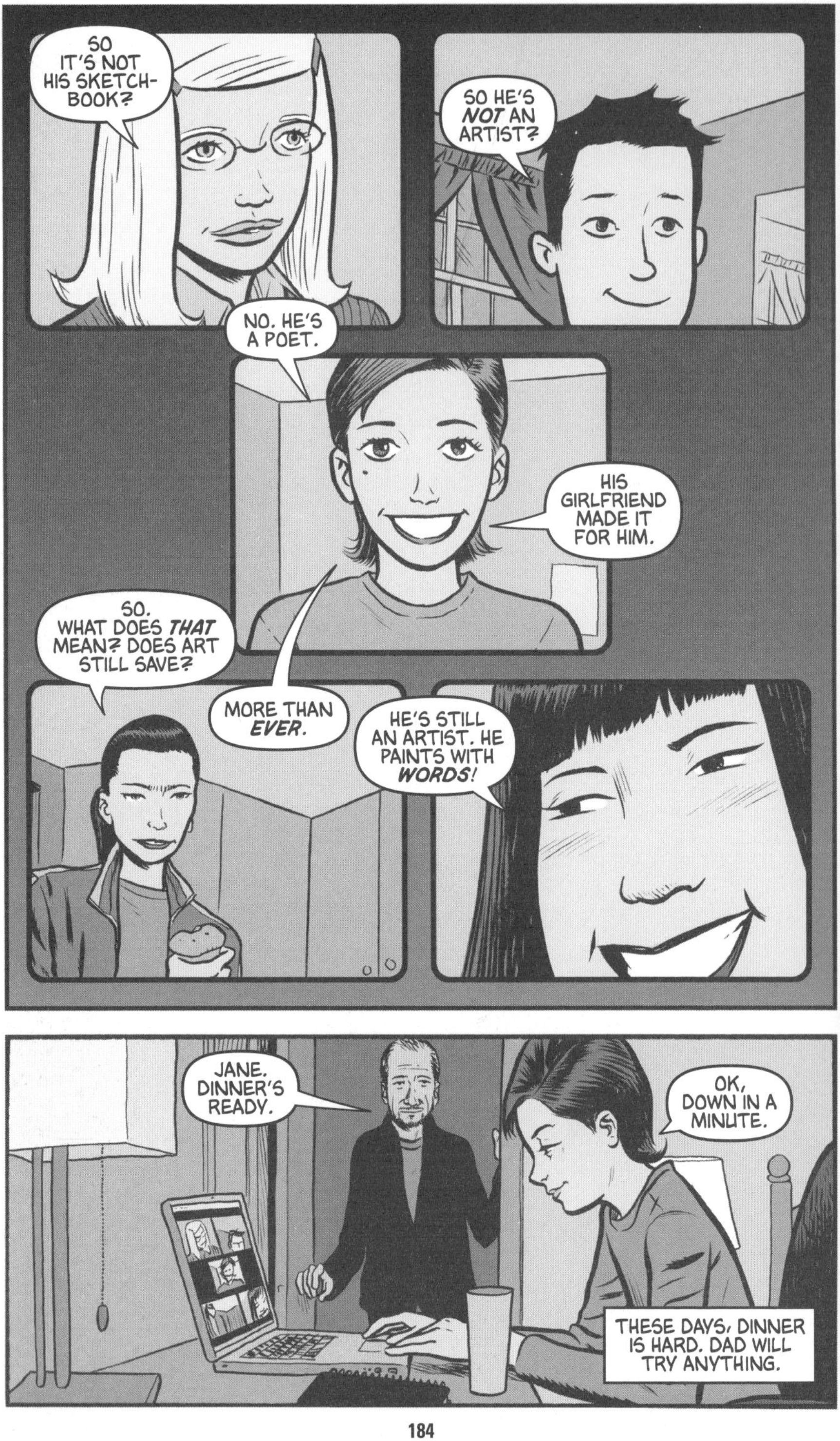
SO IT'S NOT HIS SKETCH-BOOK?
SO HE'S *NOT* AN ARTIST?
NO. HE'S A POET.
HIS GIRLFRIEND MADE IT FOR HIM.
SO. WHAT DOES *THAT* MEAN? DOES ART STILL SAVE?
MORE THAN *EVER*.
HE'S STILL AN ARTIST. HE PAINTS WITH *WORDS*!
JANE. DINNER'S READY.
OK, DOWN IN A MINUTE.
THESE DAYS, DINNER IS HARD. DAD WILL TRY ANYTHING.

185

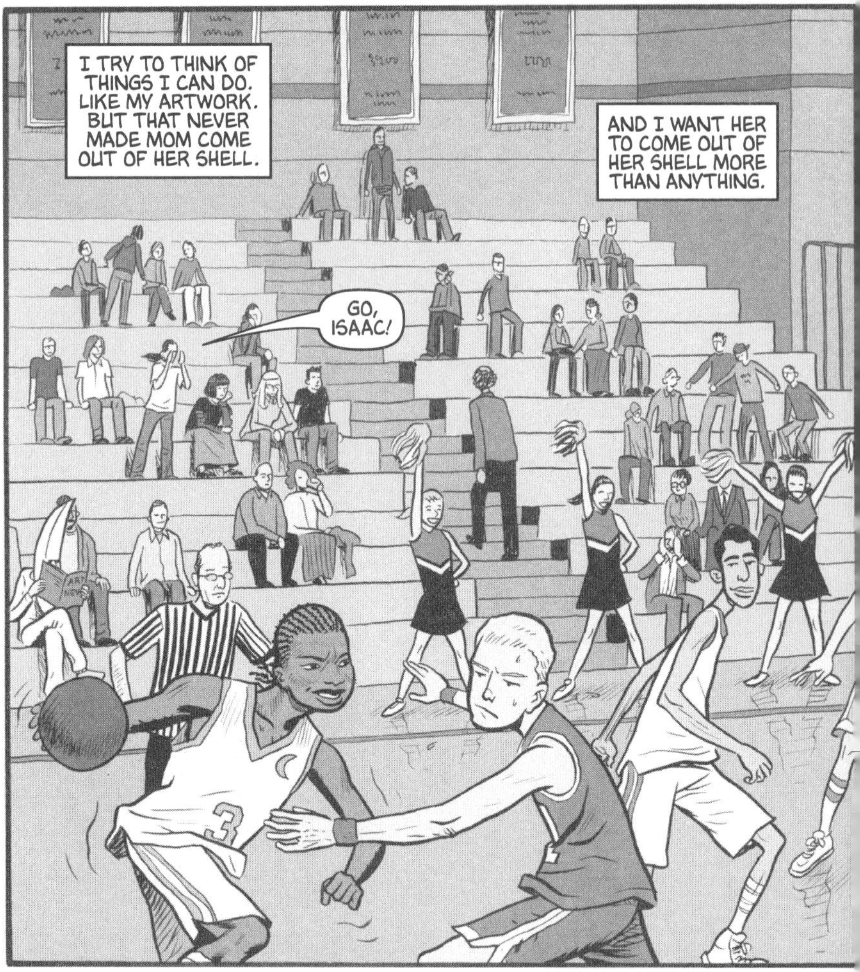
I TRY TO THINK OF THINGS I CAN DO. LIKE MY ARTWORK. BUT THAT NEVER MADE MOM COME OUT OF HER SHELL.
AND I WANT HER TO COME OUT OF HER SHELL MORE THAN ANYTHING.
GO, ISAAC!
ART NEWS

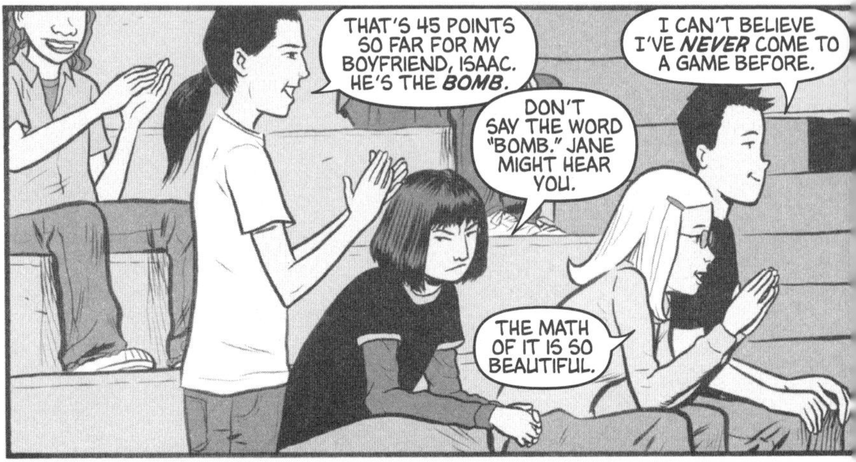
THAT'S 45 POINTS SO FAR FOR MY BOYFRIEND, ISAAC. HE'S THE *BOMB*.
I CAN'T BELIEVE I'VE *NEVER* COME TO A GAME BEFORE.
DON'T SAY THE WORD "BOMB." JANE MIGHT HEAR YOU.
THE MATH OF IT IS SO BEAUTIFUL.

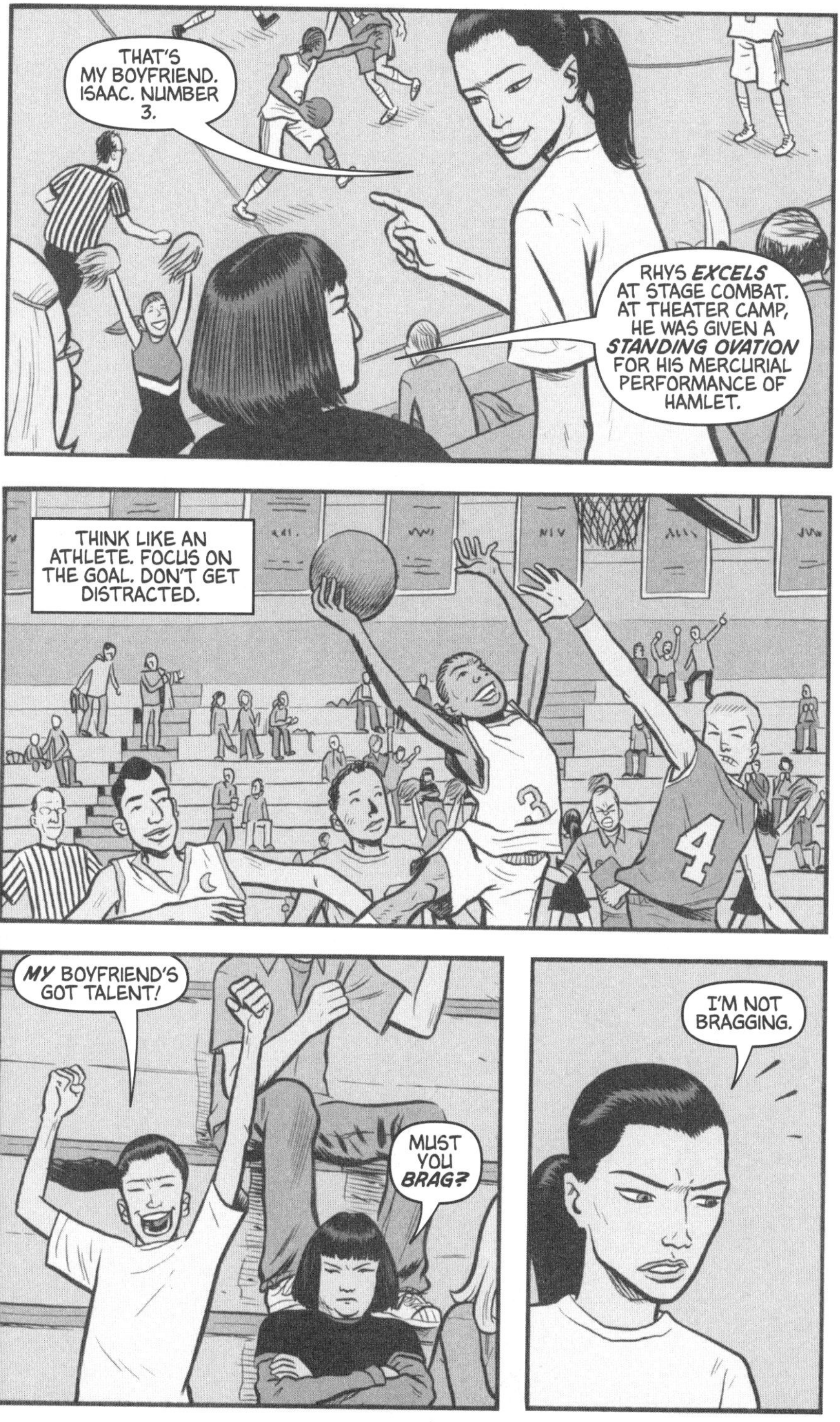

THAT'S MY BOYFRIEND. ISAAC. NUMBER 3.
RHYS *EXCELS* AT STAGE COMBAT. AT THEATER CAMP, HE WAS GIVEN A *STANDING OVATION* FOR HIS MERCURIAL PERFORMANCE OF HAMLET.
THINK LIKE AN ATHLETE. FOCUS ON THE GOAL. DON'T GET DISTRACTED.
MY BOYFRIEND'S GOT TALENT!
MUST YOU *BRAG?*
I'M NOT BRAGGING.

188

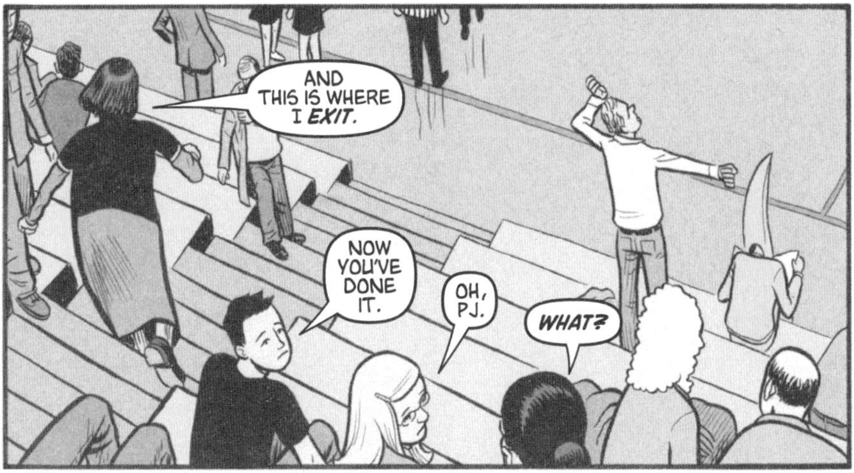
AND THIS IS WHERE I *EXIT*.
NOW YOU'VE DONE IT.
OH, PJ.
WHAT?

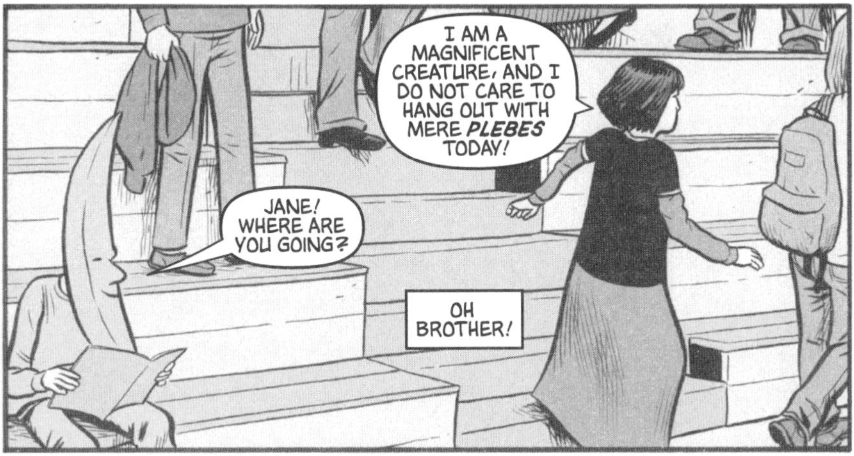
I AM A MAGNIFICENT CREATURE, AND I DO NOT CARE TO HANG OUT WITH MERE *PLEBES* TODAY!
JANE! WHERE ARE YOU GOING?
OH BROTHER!

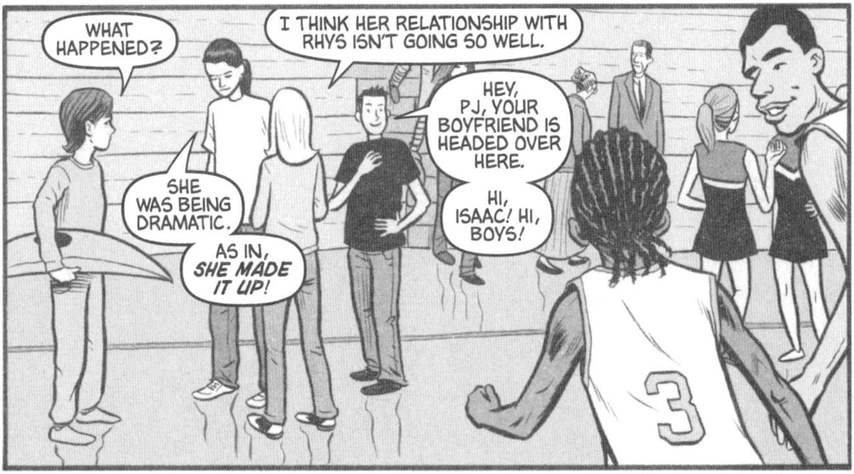
WHAT HAPPENED?
I THINK HER RELATIONSHIP WITH RHYS ISN'T GOING SO WELL.
SHE WAS BEING DRAMATIC.
AS IN, *SHE MADE IT UP*!
HEY, PJ, YOUR BOYFRIEND IS HEADED OVER HERE.
HI, ISAAC! HI, BOYS!

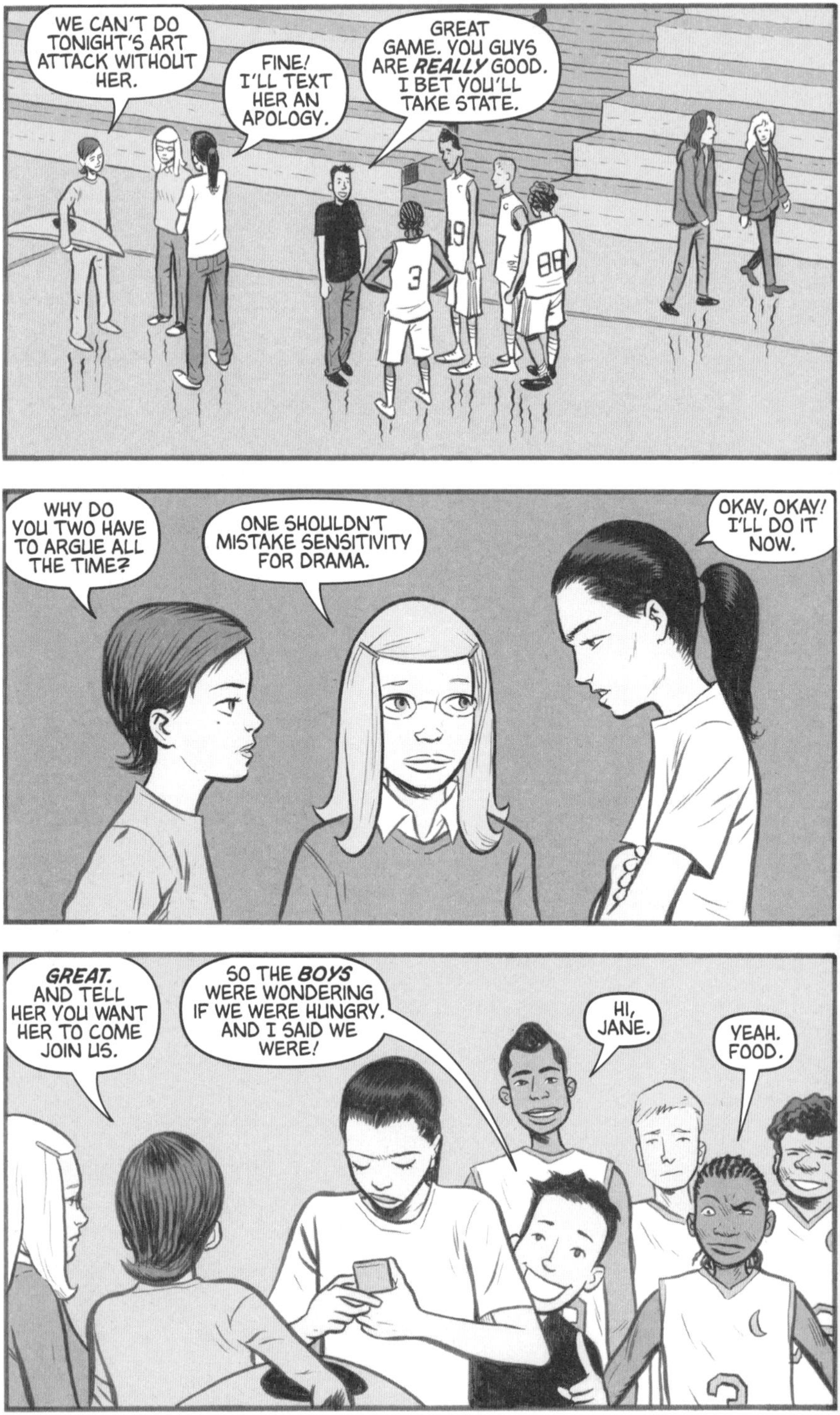
WE CAN'T DO TONIGHT'S ART ATTACK WITHOUT HER.
FINE! I'LL TEXT HER AN APOLOGY.
GREAT GAME. YOU GUYS ARE *REALLY* GOOD. I BET YOU'LL TAKE STATE.
WHY DO YOU TWO HAVE TO ARGUE ALL THE TIME?
ONE SHOULDN'T MISTAKE SENSITIVITY FOR DRAMA.
OKAY, OKAY! I'LL DO IT NOW.
GREAT. AND TELL HER YOU WANT HER TO COME JOIN US.
SO THE *BOYS* WERE WONDERING IF WE WERE HUNGRY. AND I SAID WE WERE!
HI, JANE.
YEAH. FOOD.

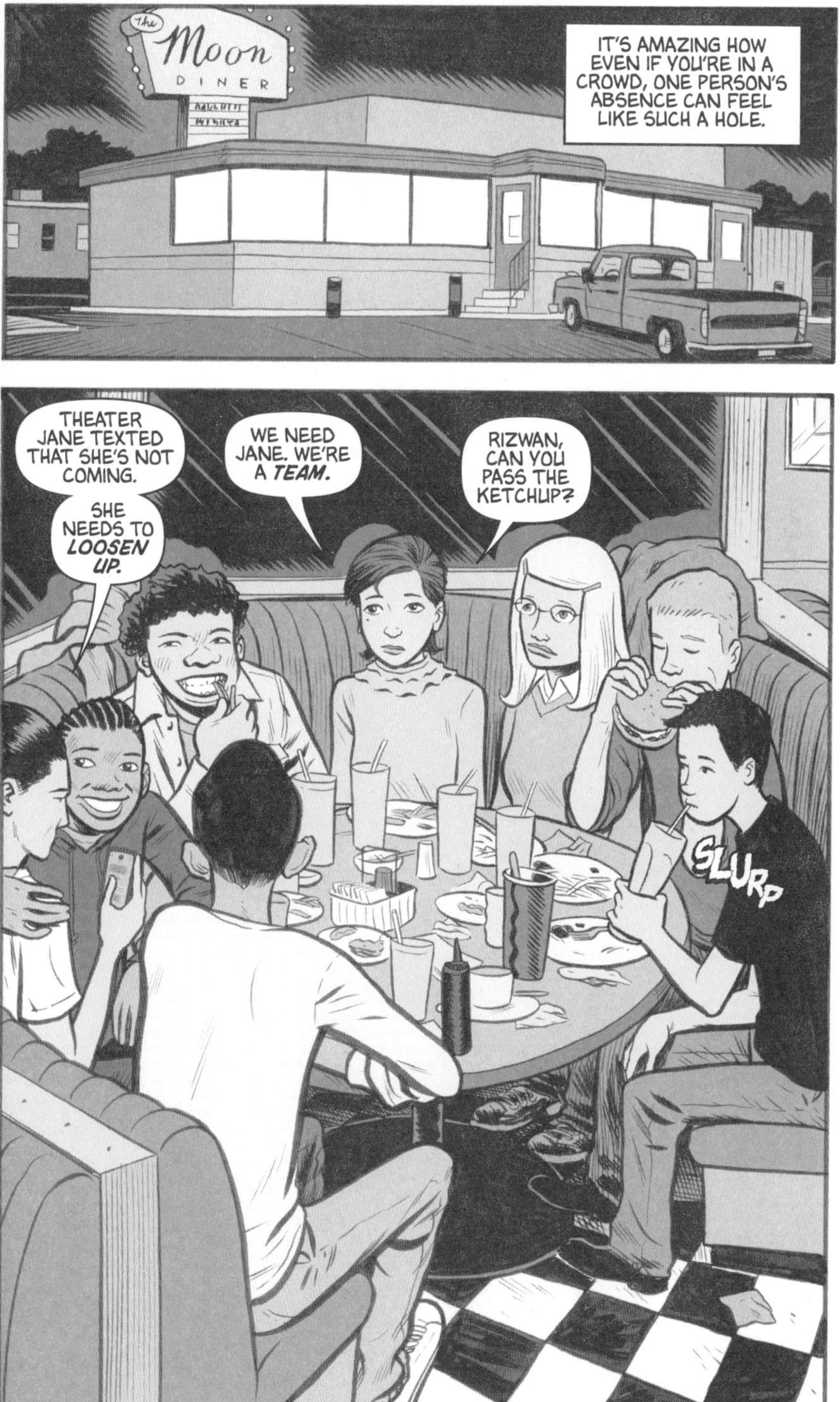
the Moon DINER
IT'S AMAZING HOW EVEN IF YOU'RE IN A CROWD, ONE PERSON'S ABSENCE CAN FEEL LIKE SUCH A HOLE.
THEATER JANE TEXTED THAT SHE'S NOT COMING.
SHE NEEDS TO *LOOSEN UP.*
WE NEED JANE. WE'RE A *TEAM.*
RIZWAN, CAN YOU PASS THE KETCHUP?
SLURP

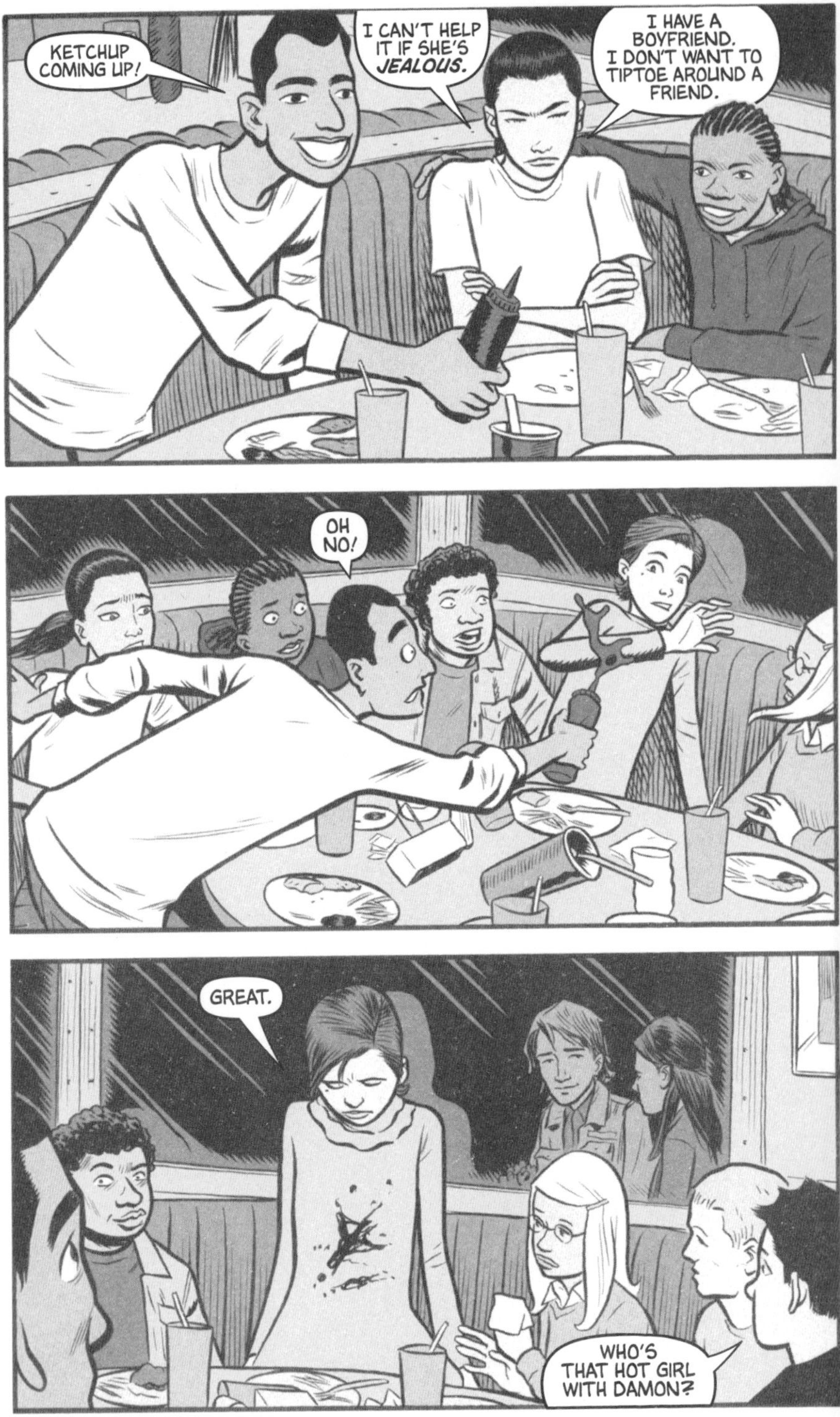
KETCHUP COMING UP!
I CAN'T HELP IT IF SHE'S JEALOUS.
I HAVE A BOYFRIEND. I DON'T WANT TO TIPTOE AROUND A FRIEND.
OH NO!
GREAT.
WHO'S THAT HOT GIRL WITH DAMON?

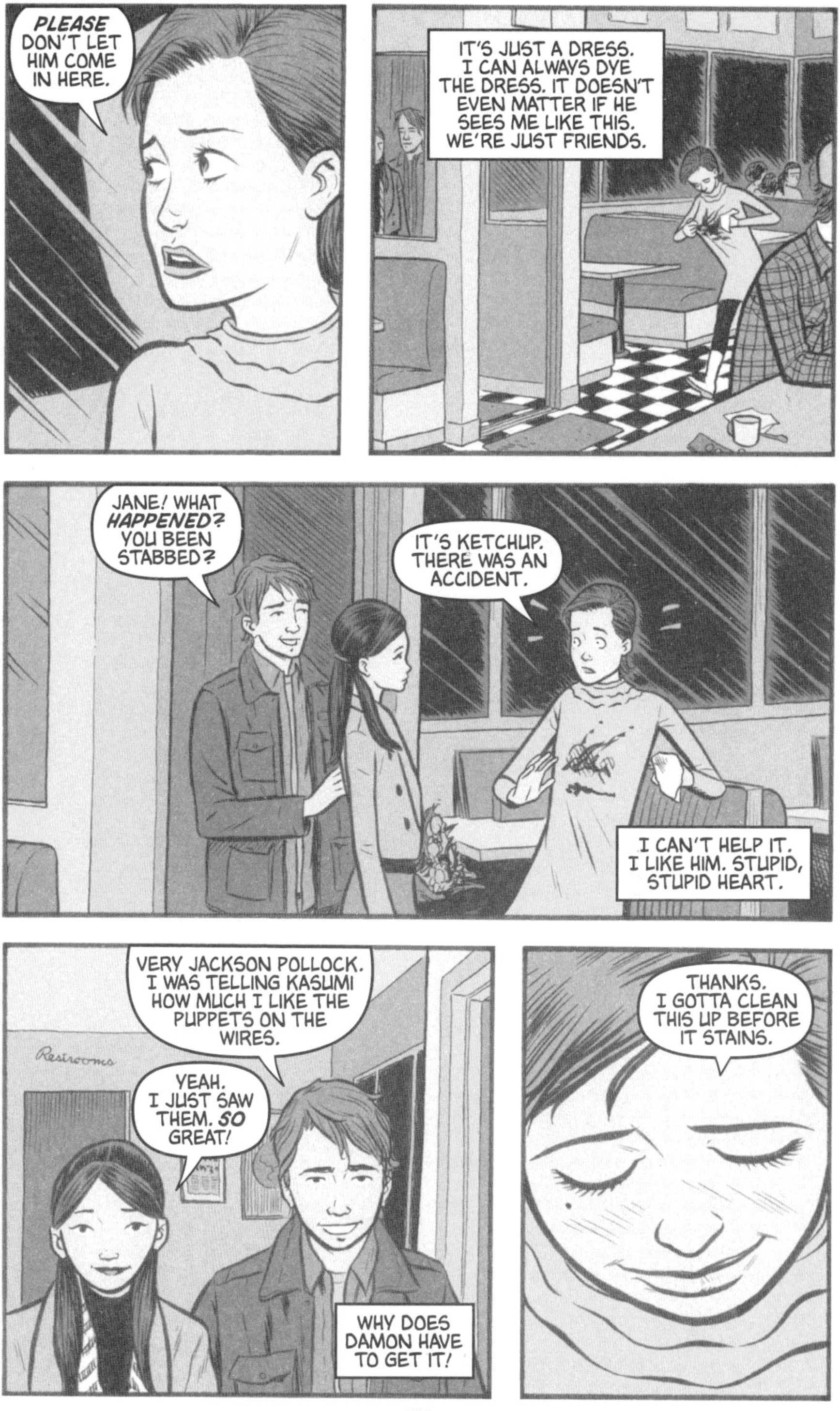
PLEASE DON'T LET HIM COME IN HERE.
IT'S JUST A DRESS. I CAN ALWAYS DYE THE DRESS. IT DOESN'T EVEN MATTER IF HE SEES ME LIKE THIS. WE'RE JUST FRIENDS.
JANE! WHAT HAPPENED? YOU BEEN STABBED?
IT'S KETCHUP. THERE WAS AN ACCIDENT.
I CAN'T HELP IT. I LIKE HIM. STUPID, STUPID HEART.
VERY JACKSON POLLOCK. I WAS TELLING KASUMI HOW MUCH I LIKE THE PUPPETS ON THE WIRES.
Restrooms
YEAH. I JUST SAW THEM. SO GREAT!
WHY DOES DAMON HAVE TO GET IT!
THANKS. I GOTTA CLEAN THIS UP BEFORE IT STAINS.

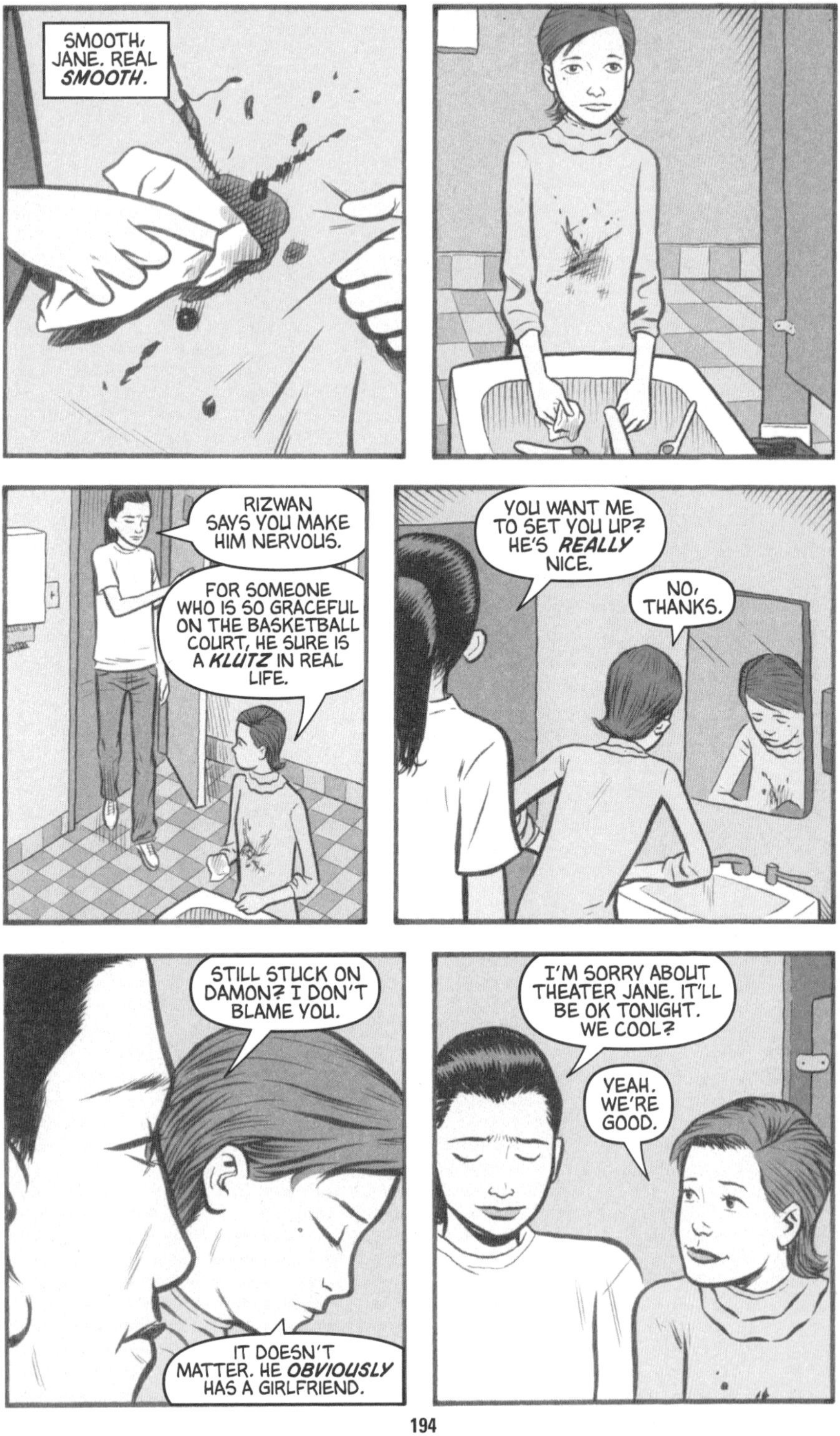
SMOOTH, JANE. REAL SMOOTH.
RIZWAN SAYS YOU MAKE HIM NERVOUS.
FOR SOMEONE WHO IS SO GRACEFUL ON THE BASKETBALL COURT, HE SURE IS A KLUTZ IN REAL LIFE.
YOU WANT ME TO SET YOU UP? HE'S REALLY NICE.
NO, THANKS.
STILL STUCK ON DAMON? I DON'T BLAME YOU.
IT DOESN'T MATTER. HE OBVIOUSLY HAS A GIRLFRIEND.
I'M SORRY ABOUT THEATER JANE. IT'LL BE OK TONIGHT. WE COOL?
YEAH. WE'RE GOOD.

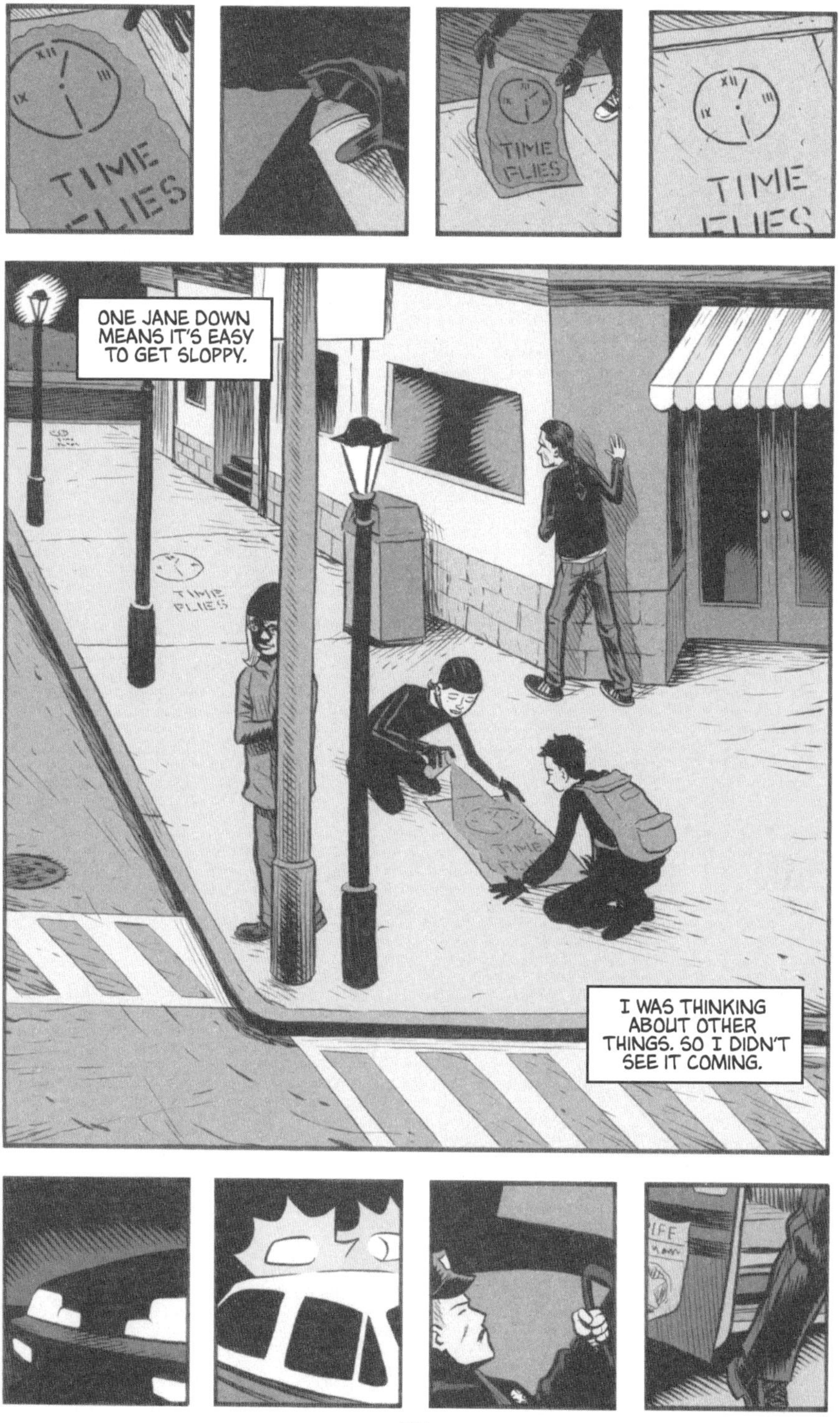
TIME FLIES
TIME FLIES
TIME FLIES
ONE JANE DOWN MEANS IT'S EASY TO GET SLOPPY.
TIME FLIES
I WAS THINKING ABOUT OTHER THINGS. SO I DIDN'T SEE IT COMING.

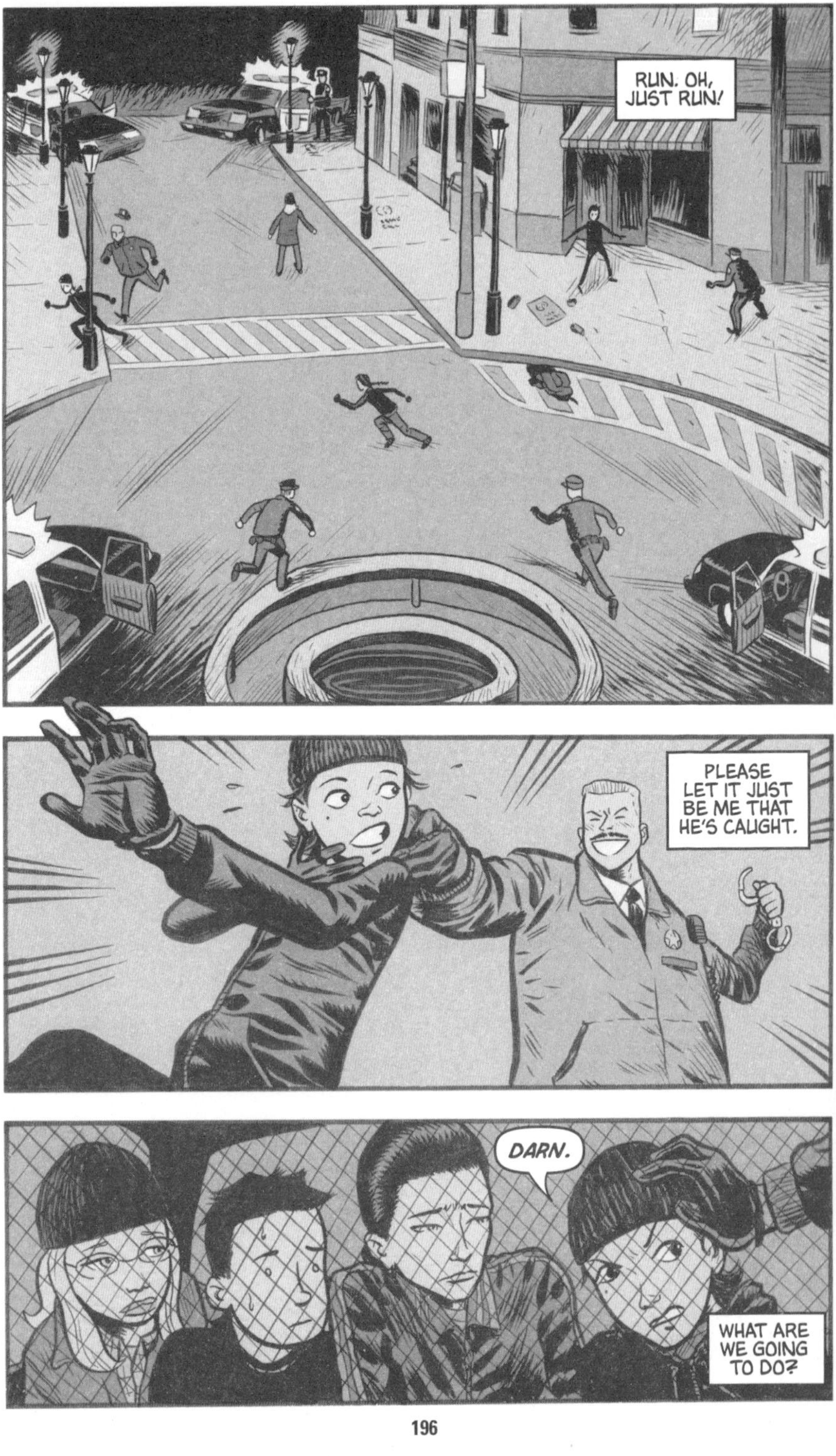
RUN. OH, JUST RUN!
PLEASE LET IT JUST BE ME THAT HE'S CAUGHT.
DARN.
WHAT ARE WE GOING TO DO?

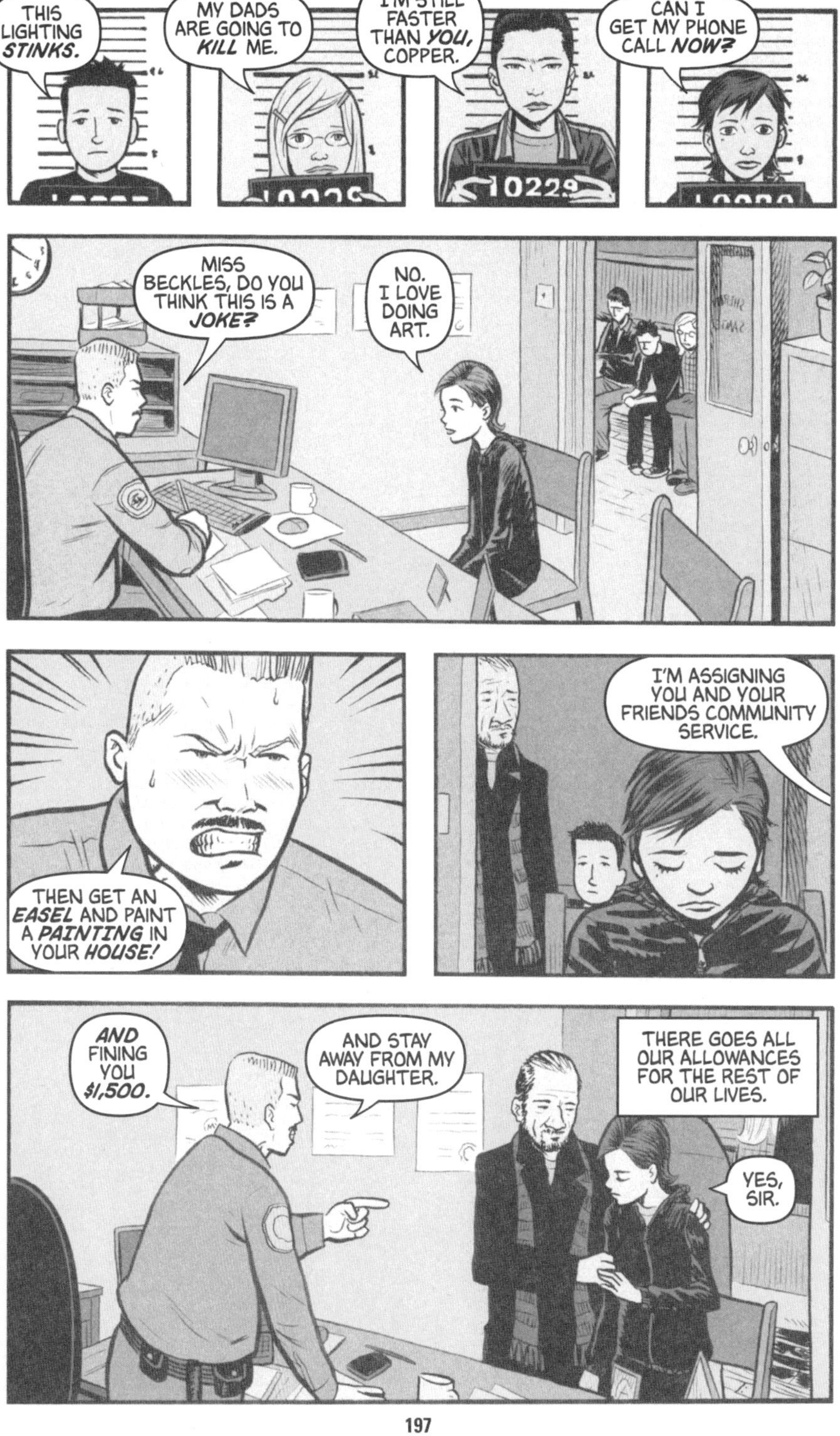
THIS LIGHTING STINKS.
MY DADS ARE GOING TO KILL ME.
I'M STILL FASTER THAN YOU, COPPER.
10229
CAN I GET MY PHONE CALL NOW?
MISS BECKLES, DO YOU THINK THIS IS A JOKE?
NO. I LOVE DOING ART.
THEN GET AN EASEL AND PAINT A PAINTING IN YOUR HOUSE!
I'M ASSIGNING YOU AND YOUR FRIENDS COMMUNITY SERVICE.
AND FINING YOU $1,500.
AND STAY AWAY FROM MY DAUGHTER.
THERE GOES ALL OUR ALLOWANCES FOR THE REST OF OUR LIVES.
YES, SIR.

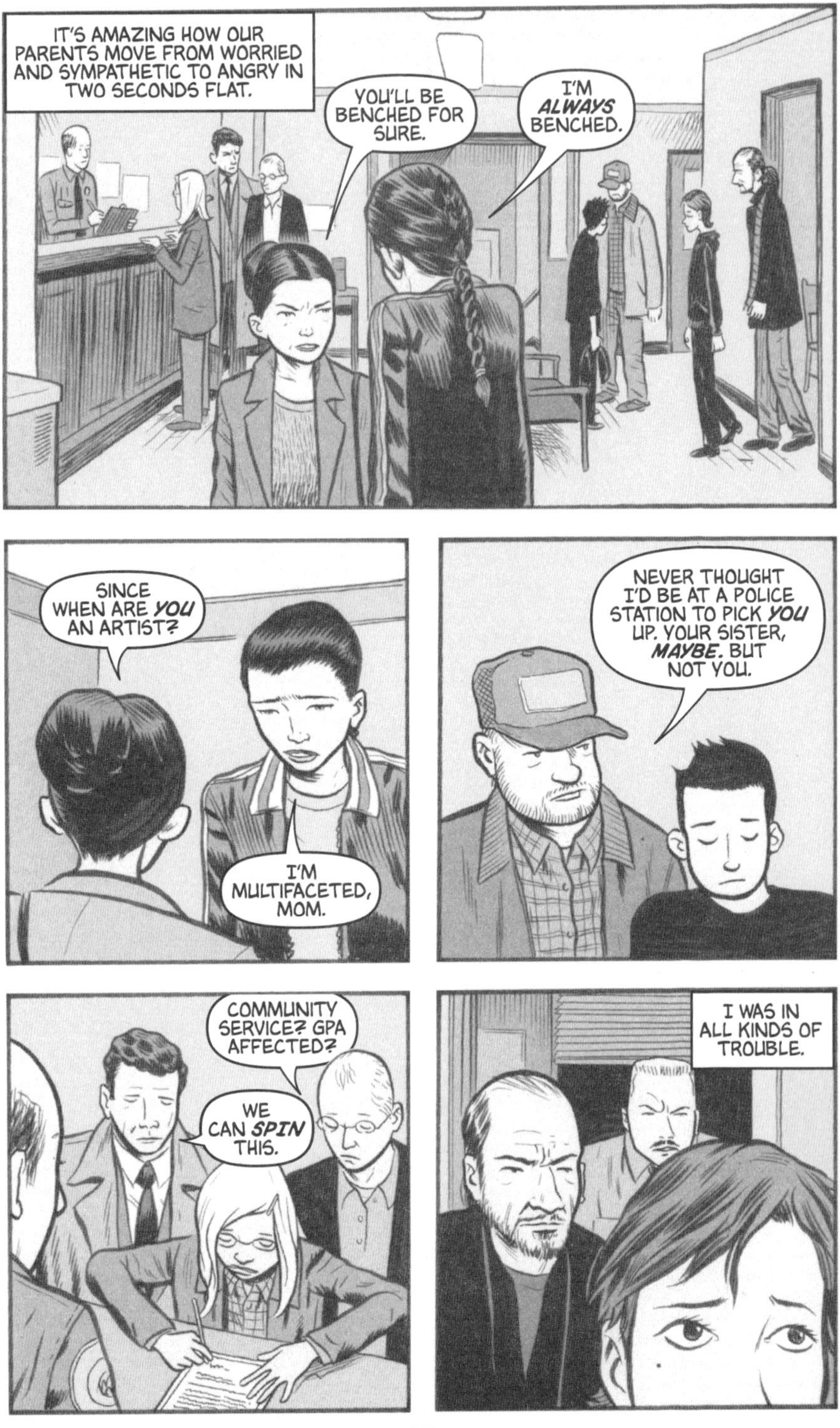

IT'S AMAZING HOW OUR PARENTS MOVE FROM WORRIED AND SYMPATHETIC TO ANGRY IN TWO SECONDS FLAT.
YOU'LL BE BENCHED FOR SURE.
I'M *ALWAYS* BENCHED.
SINCE WHEN ARE *YOU* AN ARTIST?
I'M MULTIFACETED, MOM.
NEVER THOUGHT I'D BE AT A POLICE STATION TO PICK *YOU* UP. YOUR SISTER, *MAYBE.* BUT NOT YOU.
COMMUNITY SERVICE? GPA AFFECTED?
WE CAN *SPIN* THIS.
I WAS IN ALL KINDS OF TROUBLE.

199

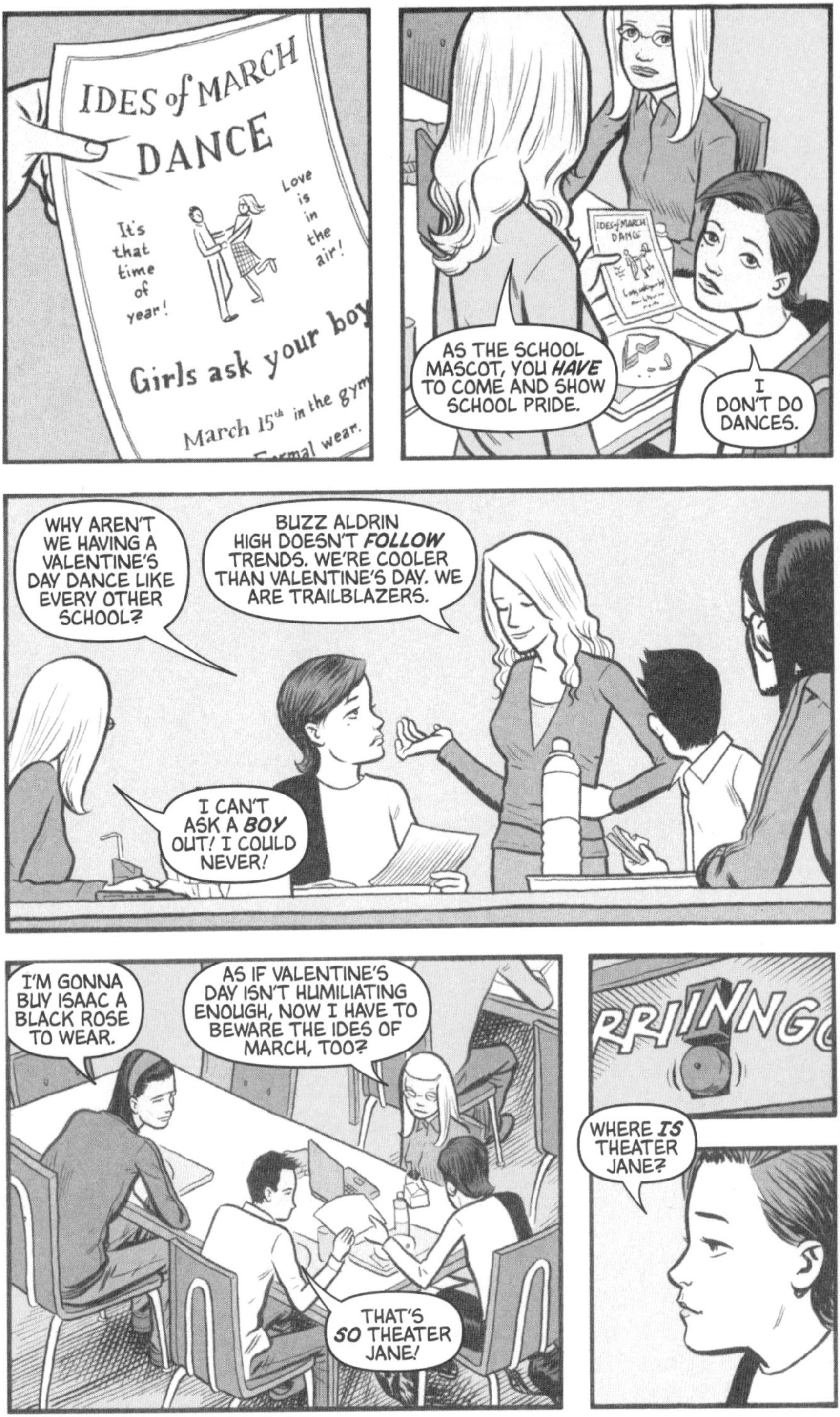
IDES of MARCH
DANCE
It's that time of year!
Love is in the air!
Girls ask your boy
March 15th in the gym
Formal wear.
AS THE SCHOOL MASCOT, YOU HAVE TO COME AND SHOW SCHOOL PRIDE.
I DON'T DO DANCES.
WHY AREN'T WE HAVING A VALENTINE'S DAY DANCE LIKE EVERY OTHER SCHOOL?
BUZZ ALDRIN HIGH DOESN'T FOLLOW TRENDS. WE'RE COOLER THAN VALENTINE'S DAY. WE ARE TRAILBLAZERS.
I CAN'T ASK A BOY OUT! I COULD NEVER!
I'M GONNA BUY ISAAC A BLACK ROSE TO WEAR.
AS IF VALENTINE'S DAY ISN'T HUMILIATING ENOUGH, NOW I HAVE TO BEWARE THE IDES OF MARCH, TOO?
THAT'S SO THEATER JANE!
RRIINNG
WHERE IS THEATER JANE?

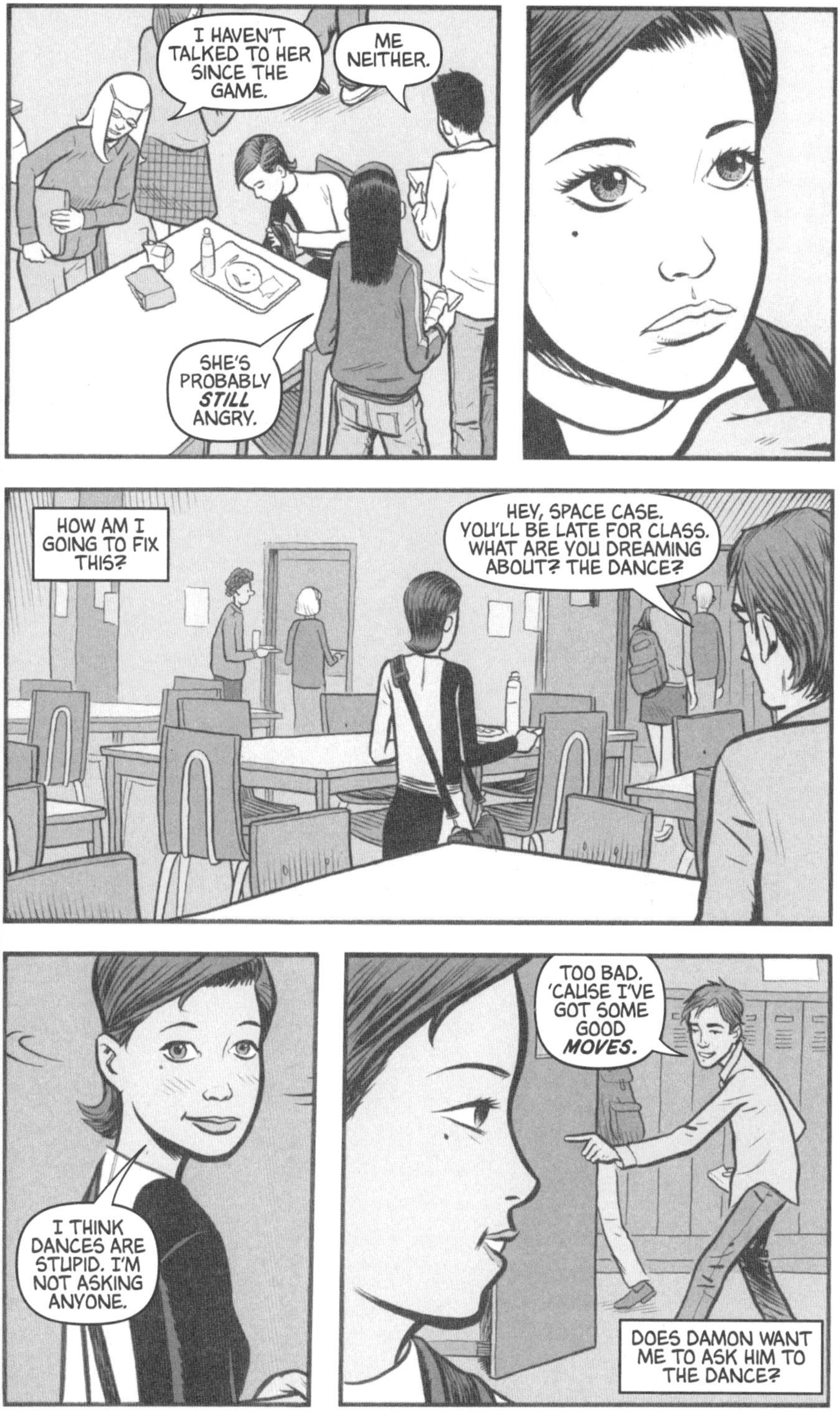
I HAVEN'T TALKED TO HER SINCE THE GAME.
ME NEITHER.
SHE'S PROBABLY *STILL* ANGRY.
HOW AM I GOING TO FIX THIS?
HEY, SPACE CASE. YOU'LL BE LATE FOR CLASS. WHAT ARE YOU DREAMING ABOUT? THE DANCE?
I THINK DANCES ARE STUPID. I'M NOT ASKING ANYONE.
TOO BAD. 'CAUSE I'VE GOT SOME GOOD *MOVES.*
DOES DAMON WANT ME TO ASK HIM TO THE DANCE?

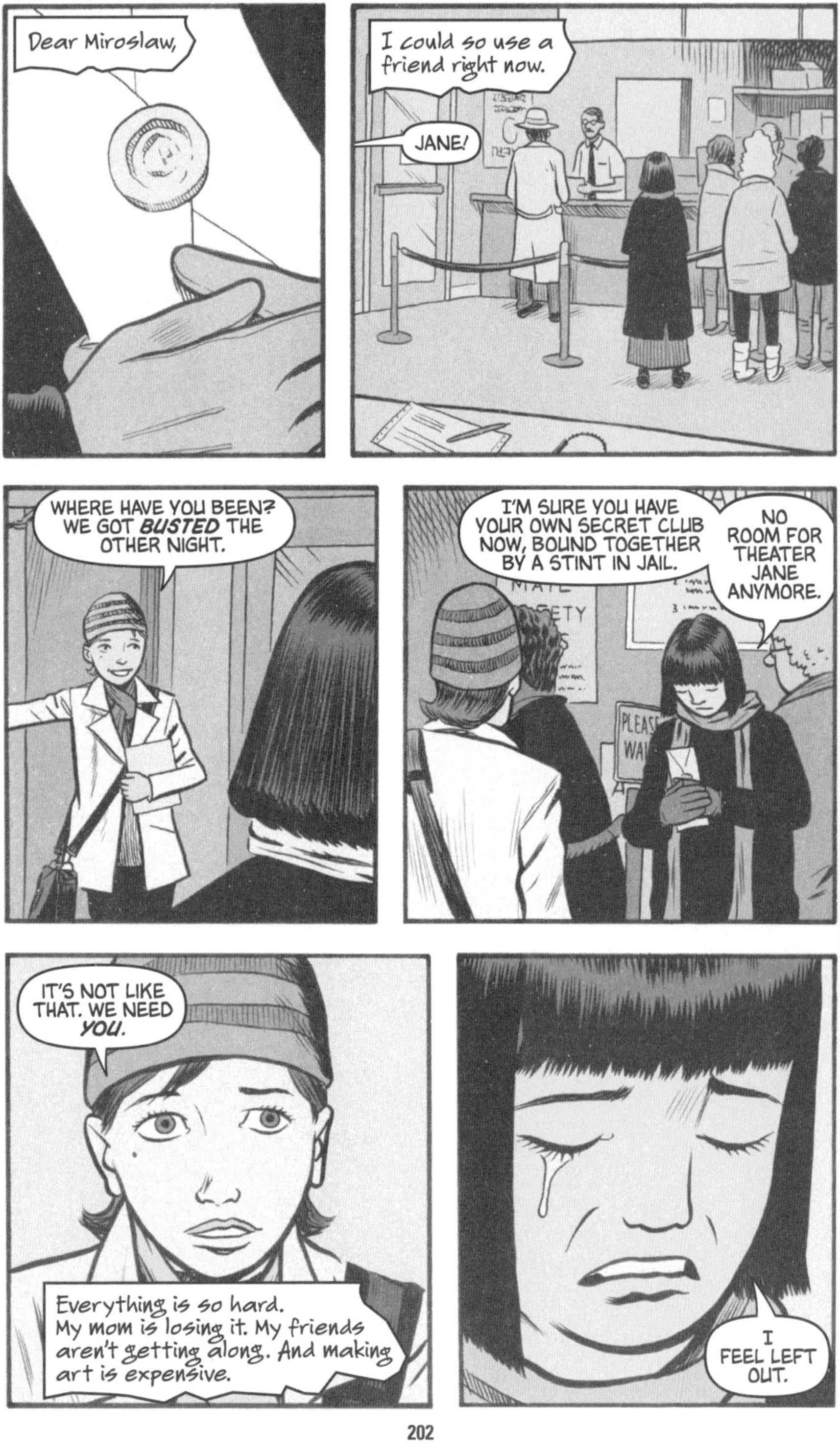
Dear Miroslaw,
I could so use a friend right now.
JANE!
WHERE HAVE YOU BEEN? WE GOT *BUSTED* THE OTHER NIGHT.
I'M SURE YOU HAVE YOUR OWN SECRET CLUB NOW, BOUND TOGETHER BY A STINT IN JAIL.
NO ROOM FOR THEATER JANE ANYMORE.
IT'S NOT LIKE THAT. WE NEED *YOU*.
Everything is so hard. My mom is losing it. My friends aren't getting along. And making art is expensive.
I FEEL LEFT OUT.

203

205

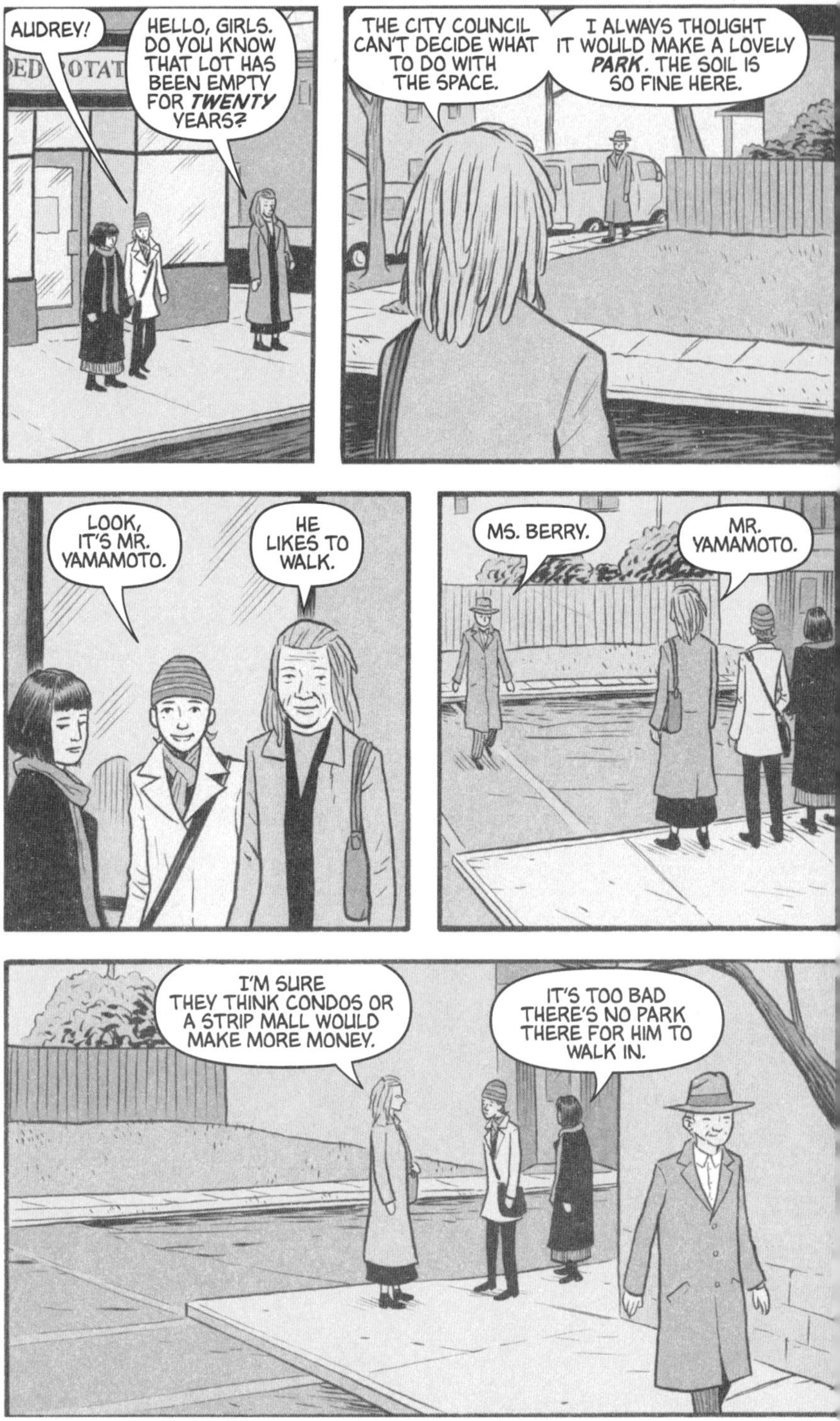
AUDREY!
HELLO, GIRLS. DO YOU KNOW THAT LOT HAS BEEN EMPTY FOR TWENTY YEARS?
THE CITY COUNCIL CAN'T DECIDE WHAT TO DO WITH THE SPACE.
I ALWAYS THOUGHT IT WOULD MAKE A LOVELY PARK. THE SOIL IS SO FINE HERE.
LOOK, IT'S MR. YAMAMOTO.
HE LIKES TO WALK.
MS. BERRY.
MR. YAMAMOTO.
I'M SURE THEY THINK CONDOS OR A STRIP MALL WOULD MAKE MORE MONEY.
IT'S TOO BAD THERE'S NO PARK THERE FOR HIM TO WALK IN.

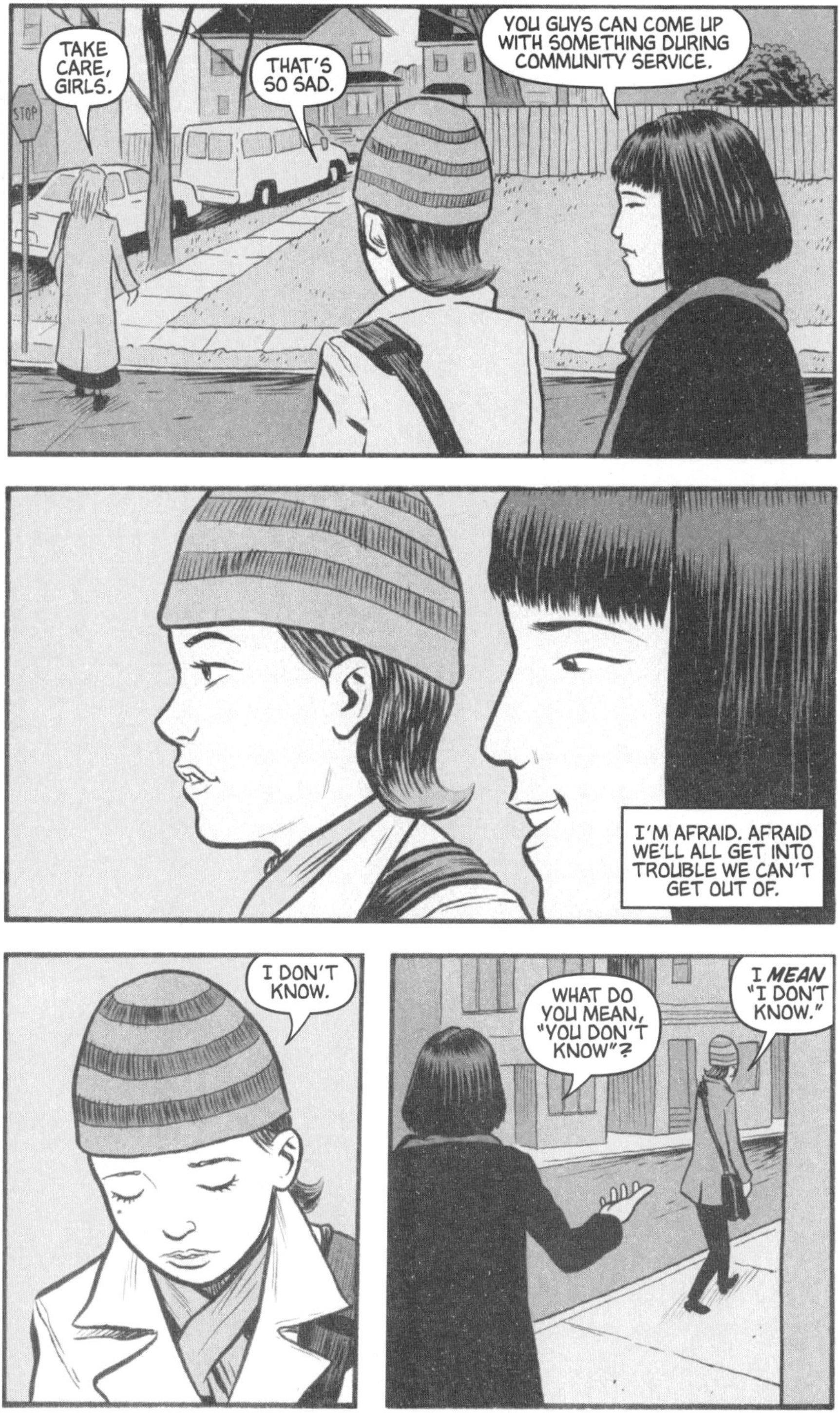
TAKE CARE, GIRLS.
THAT'S SO SAD.
YOU GUYS CAN COME UP WITH SOMETHING DURING COMMUNITY SERVICE.
I'M AFRAID. AFRAID WE'LL ALL GET INTO TROUBLE WE CAN'T GET OUT OF.
I DON'T KNOW.
WHAT DO YOU MEAN, "YOU DON'T KNOW"?
I *MEAN* "I DON'T KNOW."

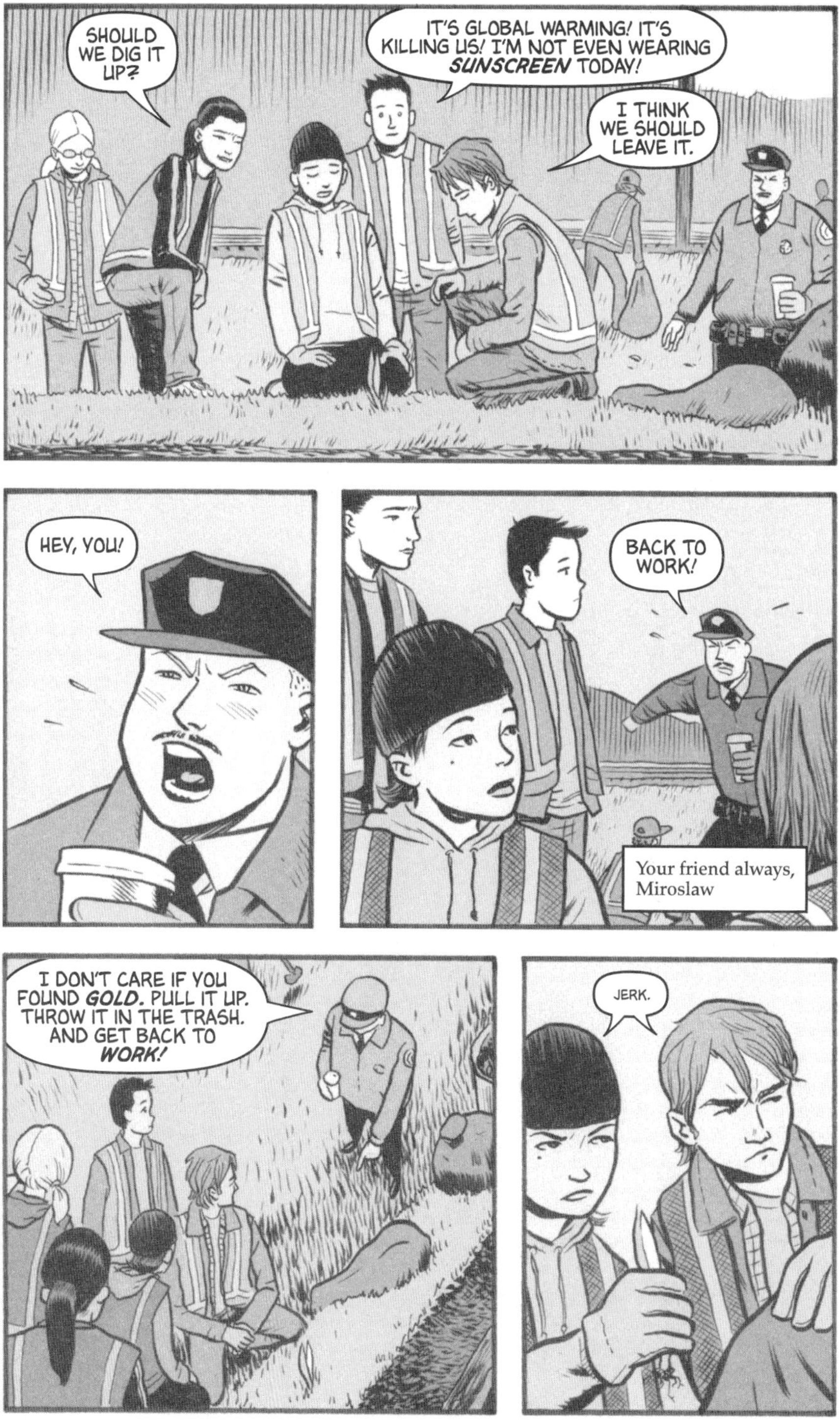
SHOULD WE DIG IT UP?
IT'S GLOBAL WARMING! IT'S KILLING US! I'M NOT EVEN WEARING SUNSCREEN TODAY!
I THINK WE SHOULD LEAVE IT.
HEY, YOU!
BACK TO WORK!
Your friend always, Miroslaw
I DON'T CARE IF YOU FOUND GOLD. PULL IT UP. THROW IT IN THE TRASH. AND GET BACK TO WORK!
JERK.

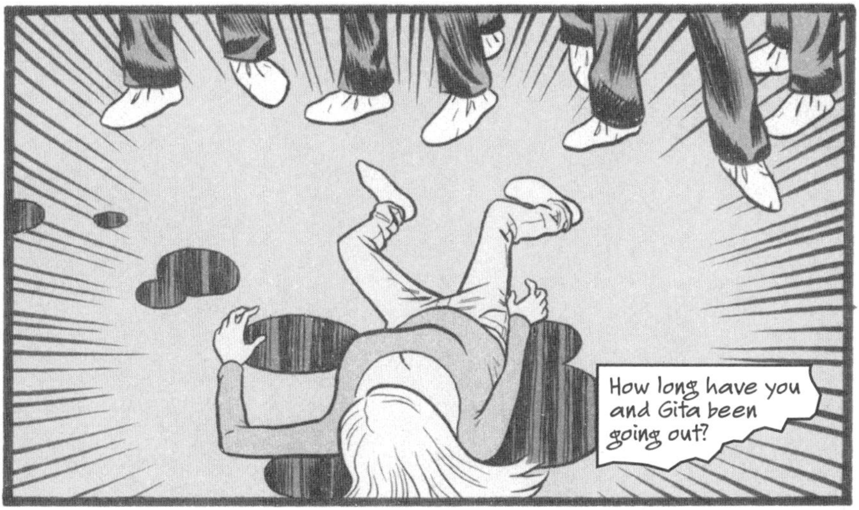
How long have you and Gita been going out?

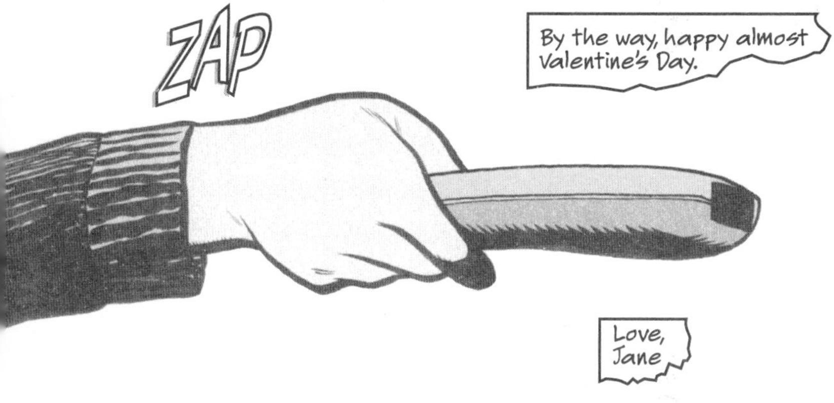
ZAP
By the way, happy almost Valentine's Day.
Love, Jane

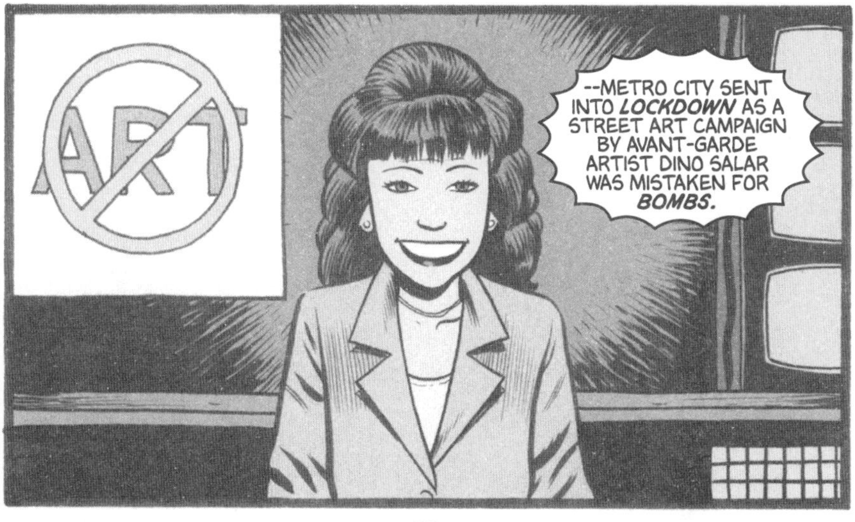
ART
--METRO CITY SENT INTO ***LOCKDOWN*** AS A STREET ART CAMPAIGN BY AVANT-GARDE ARTIST DINO SALAR WAS MISTAKEN FOR ***BOMBS.***

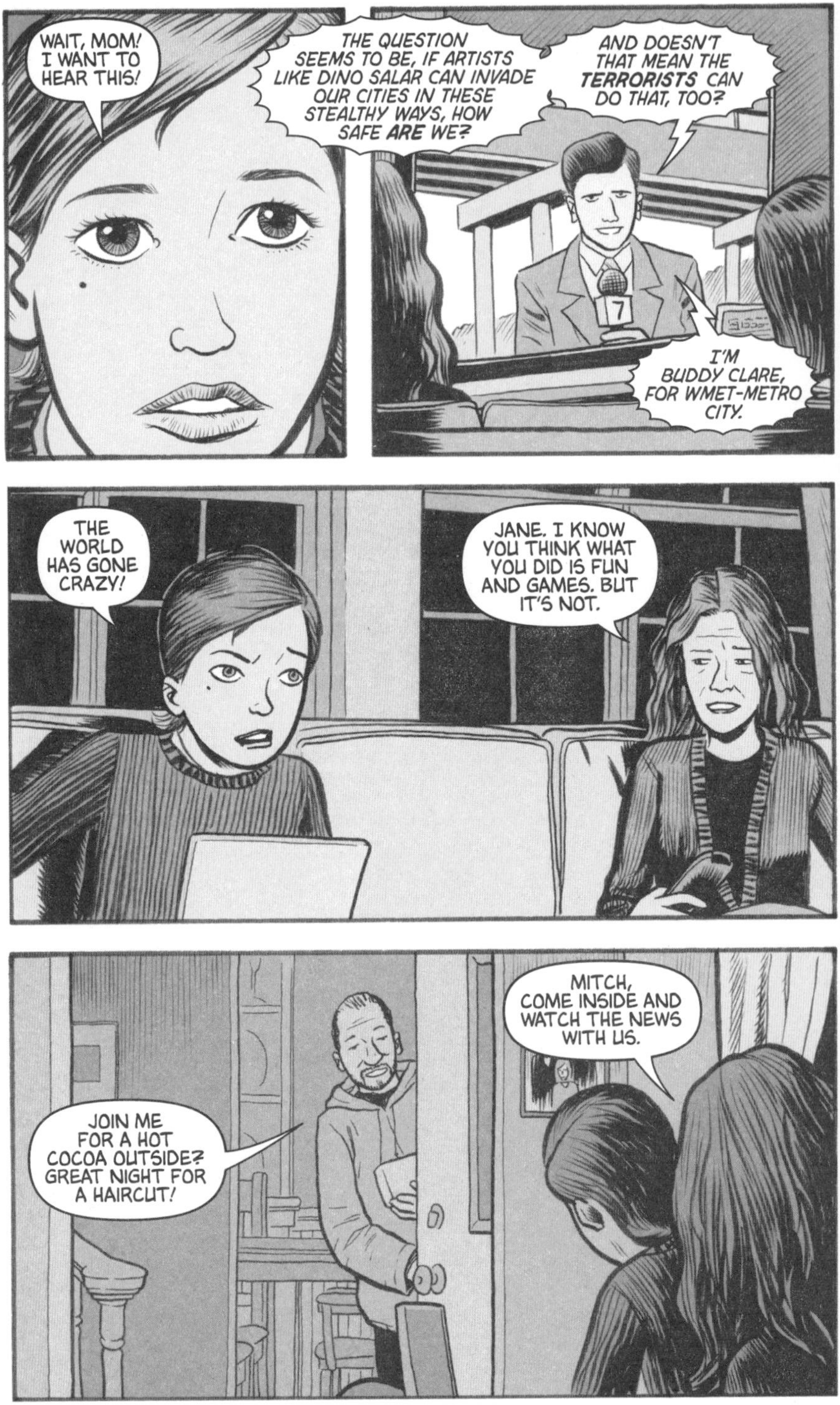
WAIT, MOM! I WANT TO HEAR THIS!
THE QUESTION SEEMS TO BE, IF ARTISTS LIKE DINO SALAR CAN INVADE OUR CITIES IN THESE STEALTHY WAYS, HOW SAFE **ARE** WE?
AND DOESN'T THAT MEAN THE **TERRORISTS** CAN DO THAT, TOO?
I'M BUDDY CLARE, FOR WMET-METRO CITY.
THE WORLD HAS GONE CRAZY!
JANE. I KNOW YOU THINK WHAT YOU DID IS FUN AND GAMES. BUT IT'S NOT.
MITCH, COME INSIDE AND WATCH THE NEWS WITH US.
JOIN ME FOR A HOT COCOA OUTSIDE? GREAT NIGHT FOR A HAIRCUT!

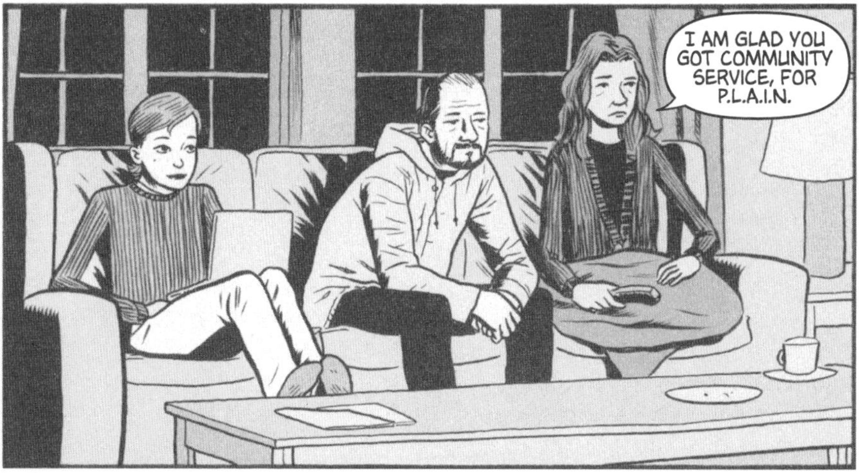
I AM GLAD YOU GOT COMMUNITY SERVICE, FOR P.L.A.I.N.

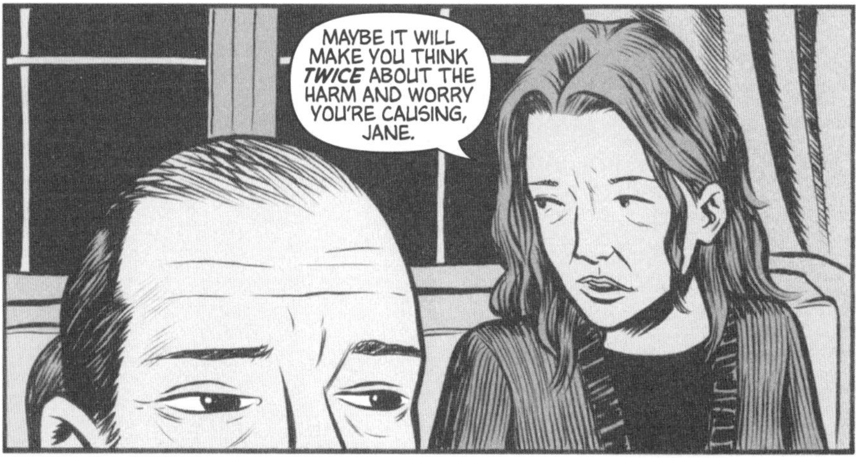
MAYBE IT WILL MAKE YOU THINK *TWICE* ABOUT THE HARM AND WORRY YOU'RE CAUSING, JANE.

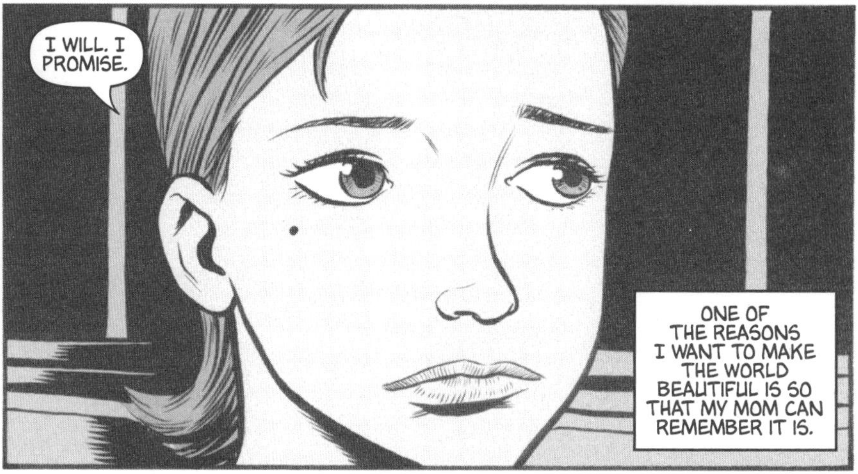
I WILL. I PROMISE.
ONE OF THE REASONS I WANT TO MAKE THE WORLD BEAUTIFUL IS SO THAT MY MOM CAN REMEMBER IT IS.

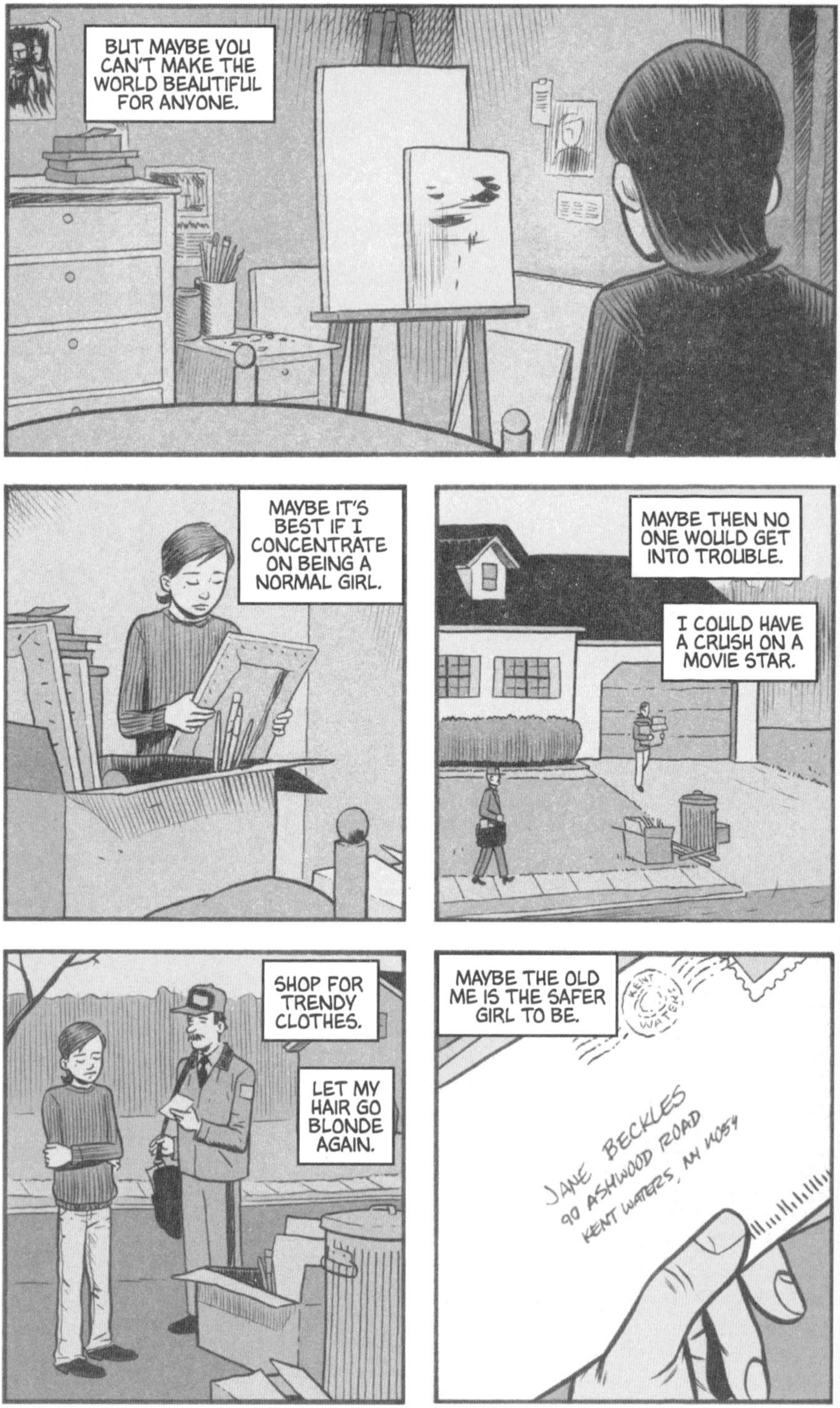

BUT MAYBE YOU CAN'T MAKE THE WORLD BEAUTIFUL FOR ANYONE.
MAYBE IT'S BEST IF I CONCENTRATE ON BEING A NORMAL GIRL.
MAYBE THEN NO ONE WOULD GET INTO TROUBLE.
I COULD HAVE A CRUSH ON A MOVIE STAR.
SHOP FOR TRENDY CLOTHES.
LET MY HAIR GO BLONDE AGAIN.
MAYBE THE OLD ME IS THE SAFER GIRL TO BE.
KENT WATERS
JANE BECKLES
90 ASHWOOD ROAD
KENT WATERS, NY 10054

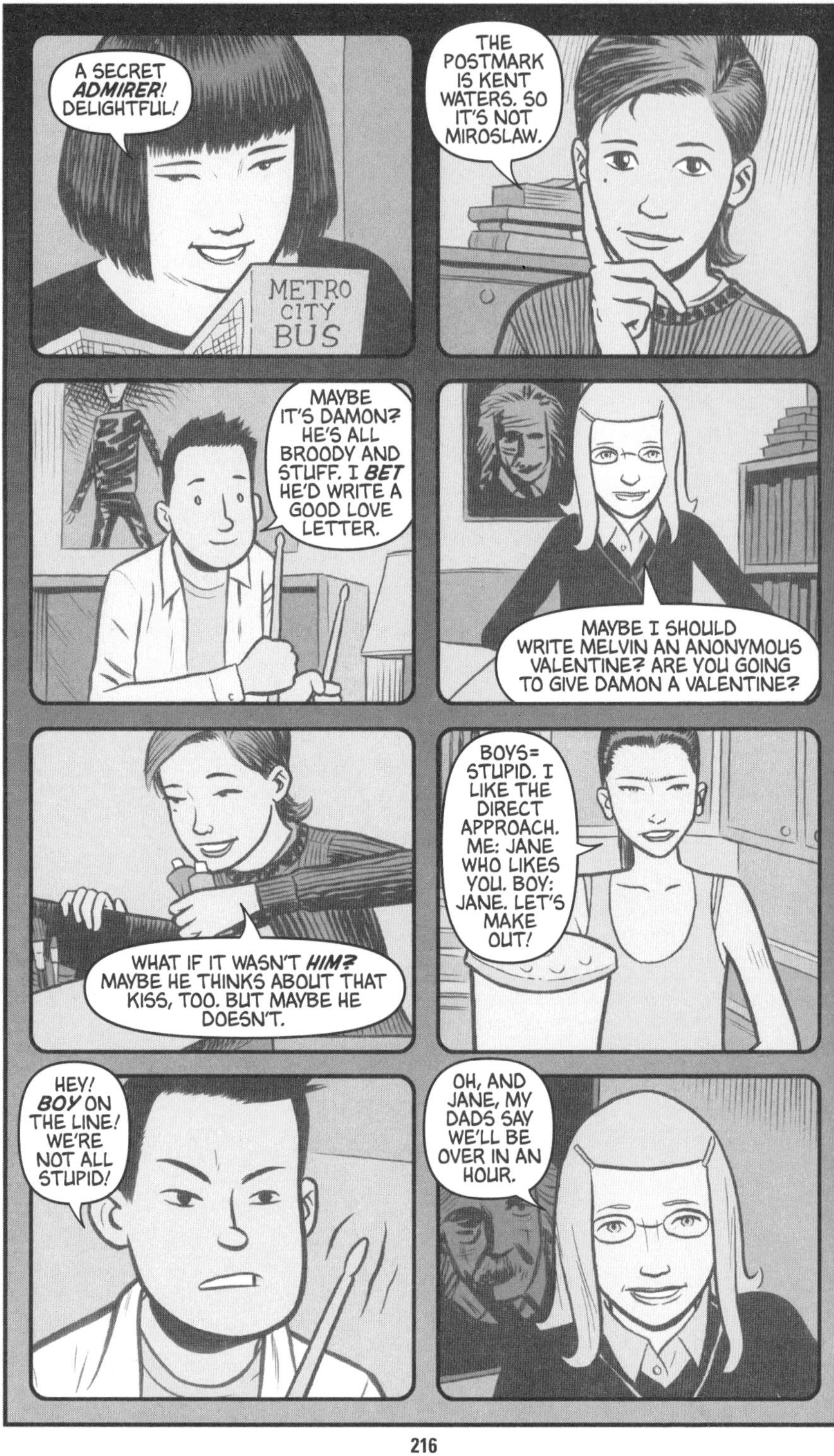
A SECRET *ADMIRER*! DELIGHTFUL!
METRO CITY BUS
THE POSTMARK IS KENT WATERS. SO IT'S NOT MIROSLAW.
MAYBE IT'S DAMON? HE'S ALL BROODY AND STUFF. I *BET* HE'D WRITE A GOOD LOVE LETTER.
MAYBE I SHOULD WRITE MELVIN AN ANONYMOUS VALENTINE? ARE YOU GOING TO GIVE DAMON A VALENTINE?
WHAT IF IT WASN'T *HIM*? MAYBE HE THINKS ABOUT THAT KISS, TOO. BUT MAYBE HE DOESN'T.
BOYS= STUPID. I LIKE THE DIRECT APPROACH. ME: JANE WHO LIKES YOU. BOY: JANE. LET'S MAKE OUT!
HEY! *BOY* ON THE LINE! WE'RE NOT ALL STUPID!
OH, AND JANE, MY DADS SAY WE'LL BE OVER IN AN HOUR.

217

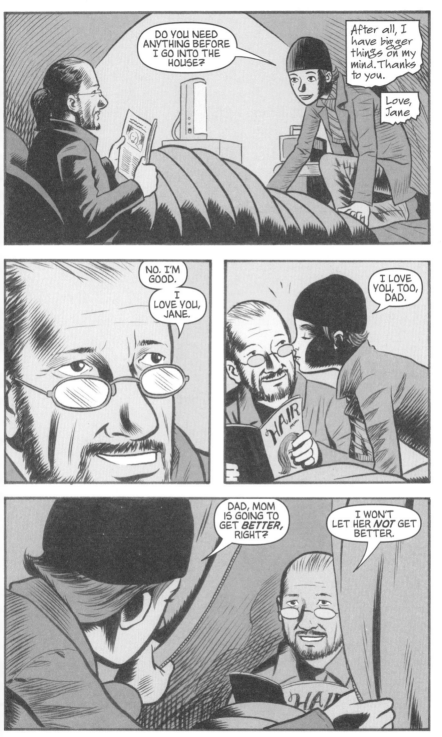

219

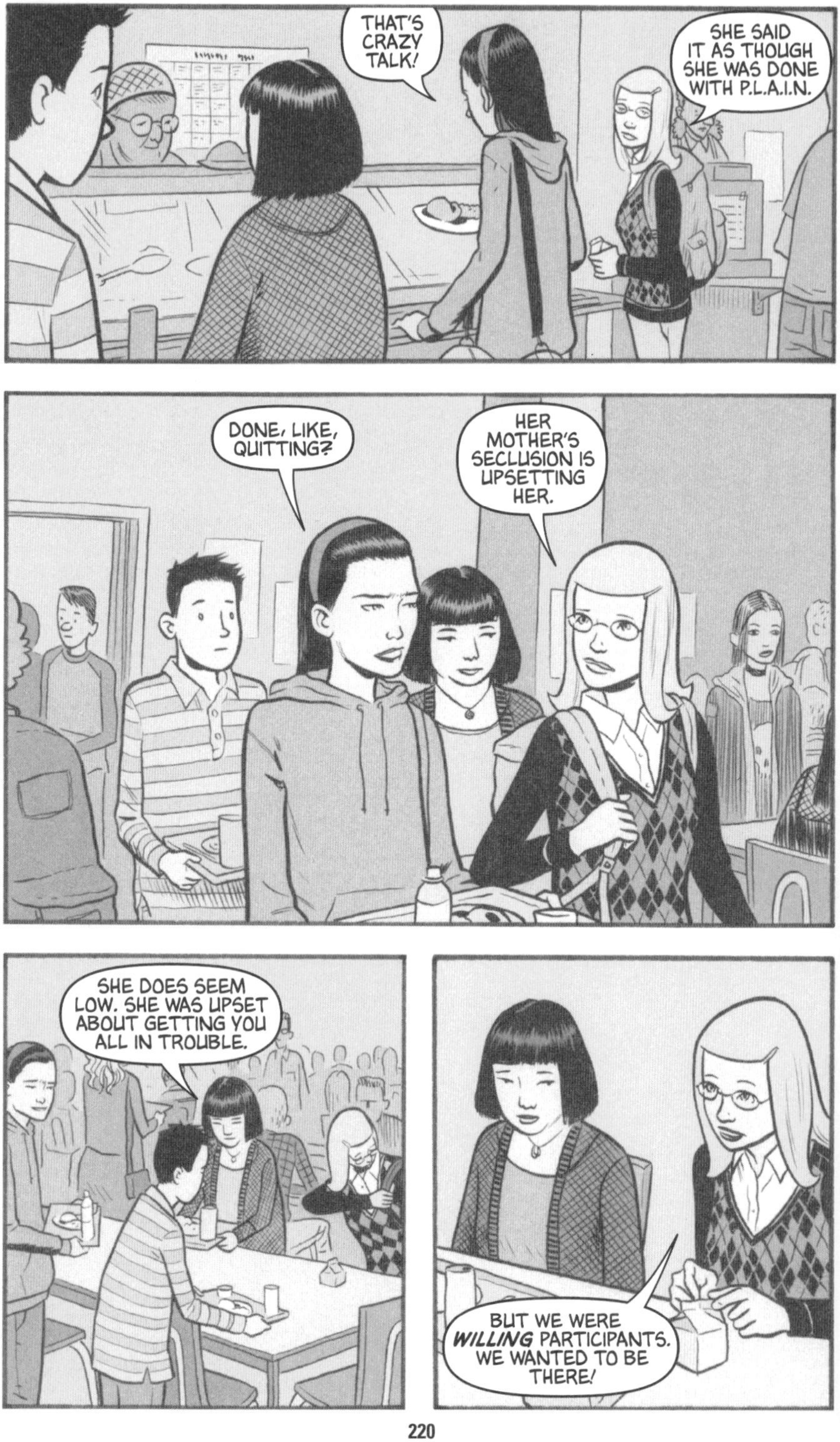
THAT'S CRAZY TALK!
SHE SAID IT AS THOUGH SHE WAS DONE WITH P.L.A.I.N.
DONE, LIKE, QUITTING?
HER MOTHER'S SECLUSION IS UPSETTING HER.
SHE DOES SEEM LOW. SHE WAS UPSET ABOUT GETTING YOU ALL IN TROUBLE.
BUT WE WERE *WILLING* PARTICIPANTS. WE WANTED TO BE THERE!

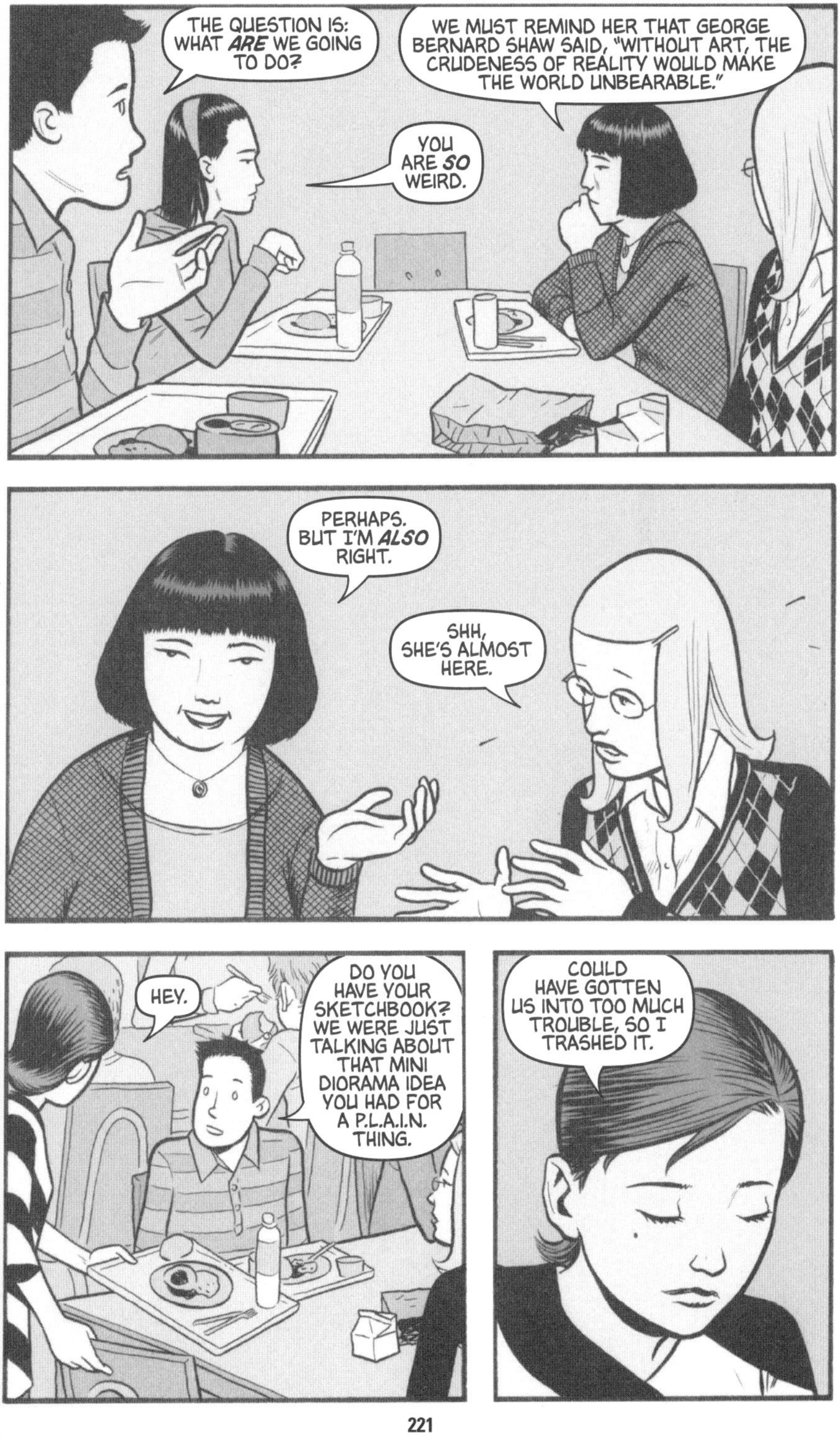

THE QUESTION IS: WHAT ARE WE GOING TO DO?
WE MUST REMIND HER THAT GEORGE BERNARD SHAW SAID, "WITHOUT ART, THE CRUDENESS OF REALITY WOULD MAKE THE WORLD UNBEARABLE."
YOU ARE SO WEIRD.
PERHAPS. BUT I'M ALSO RIGHT.
SHH, SHE'S ALMOST HERE.
HEY.
DO YOU HAVE YOUR SKETCHBOOK? WE WERE JUST TALKING ABOUT THAT MINI DIORAMA IDEA YOU HAD FOR A P.L.A.I.N. THING.
COULD HAVE GOTTEN US INTO TOO MUCH TROUBLE, SO I TRASHED IT.

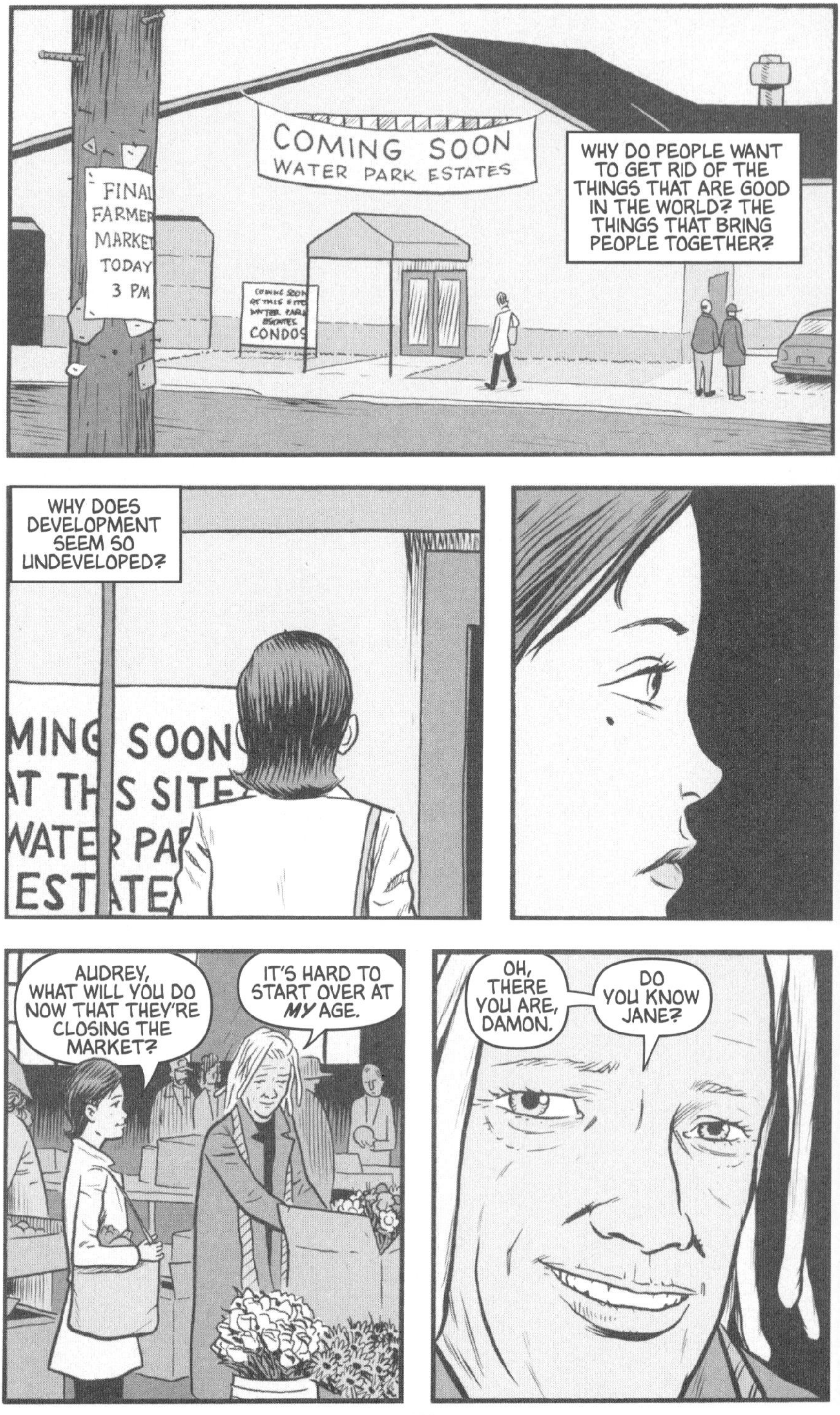
COMING SOON
WATER PARK ESTATES
FARMER
MARKET
TODAY
3 PM
CONDOS
WHY DO PEOPLE WANT TO GET RID OF THE THINGS THAT ARE GOOD IN THE WORLD? THE THINGS THAT BRING PEOPLE TOGETHER?
WHY DOES DEVELOPMENT SEEM SO UNDEVELOPED?
AUDREY, WHAT WILL YOU DO NOW THAT THEY'RE CLOSING THE MARKET?
IT'S HARD TO START OVER AT *MY* AGE.
OH, THERE YOU ARE, DAMON.
DO YOU KNOW JANE?

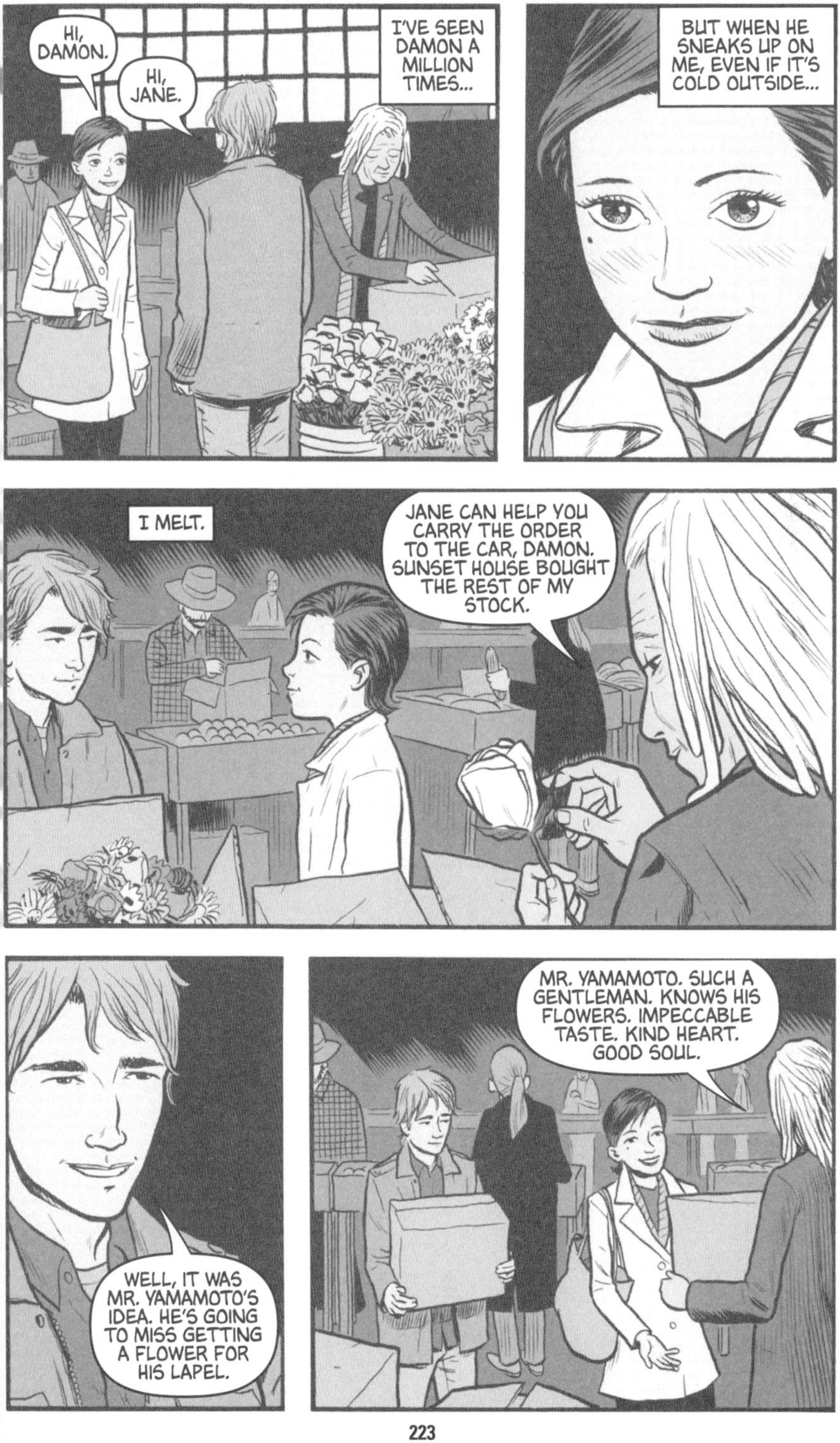
HI, DAMON.
HI, JANE.
I'VE SEEN DAMON A MILLION TIMES...
BUT WHEN HE SNEAKS UP ON ME, EVEN IF IT'S COLD OUTSIDE...
I MELT.
JANE CAN HELP YOU CARRY THE ORDER TO THE CAR, DAMON. SUNSET HOUSE BOUGHT THE REST OF MY STOCK.
WELL, IT WAS MR. YAMAMOTO'S IDEA. HE'S GOING TO MISS GETTING A FLOWER FOR HIS LAPEL.
MR. YAMAMOTO. SUCH A GENTLEMAN. KNOWS HIS FLOWERS. IMPECCABLE TASTE. KIND HEART. GOOD SOUL.

JUMPSUIT OR UTILIKILT?

DEPENDS. AM I ON AN ADVENTURE? OR AM I JUST BEING CASUAL?

TIME TRAVEL. GO TO THE FUTURE OR THE PAST?

FUTURE. I WANT TO WEAR SILVER.

COMING SOON THIS SITE WINTER PARK ESTATES CONDOS

FINAL FARMERS MARKET TODAY 3 PM

IF MOMENTS COULD BE PLUCKED, FROZEN, AND SAVED, I'D PICK THIS ONE.

SO, DO YOU WANT TO HELP ME DELIVER THE FLOWERS? I COULD DROP YOU OFF AT HOME AFTERWARD.

SURE.

COOL.

THE SMELL OF FLOWERS IN THE CAR.

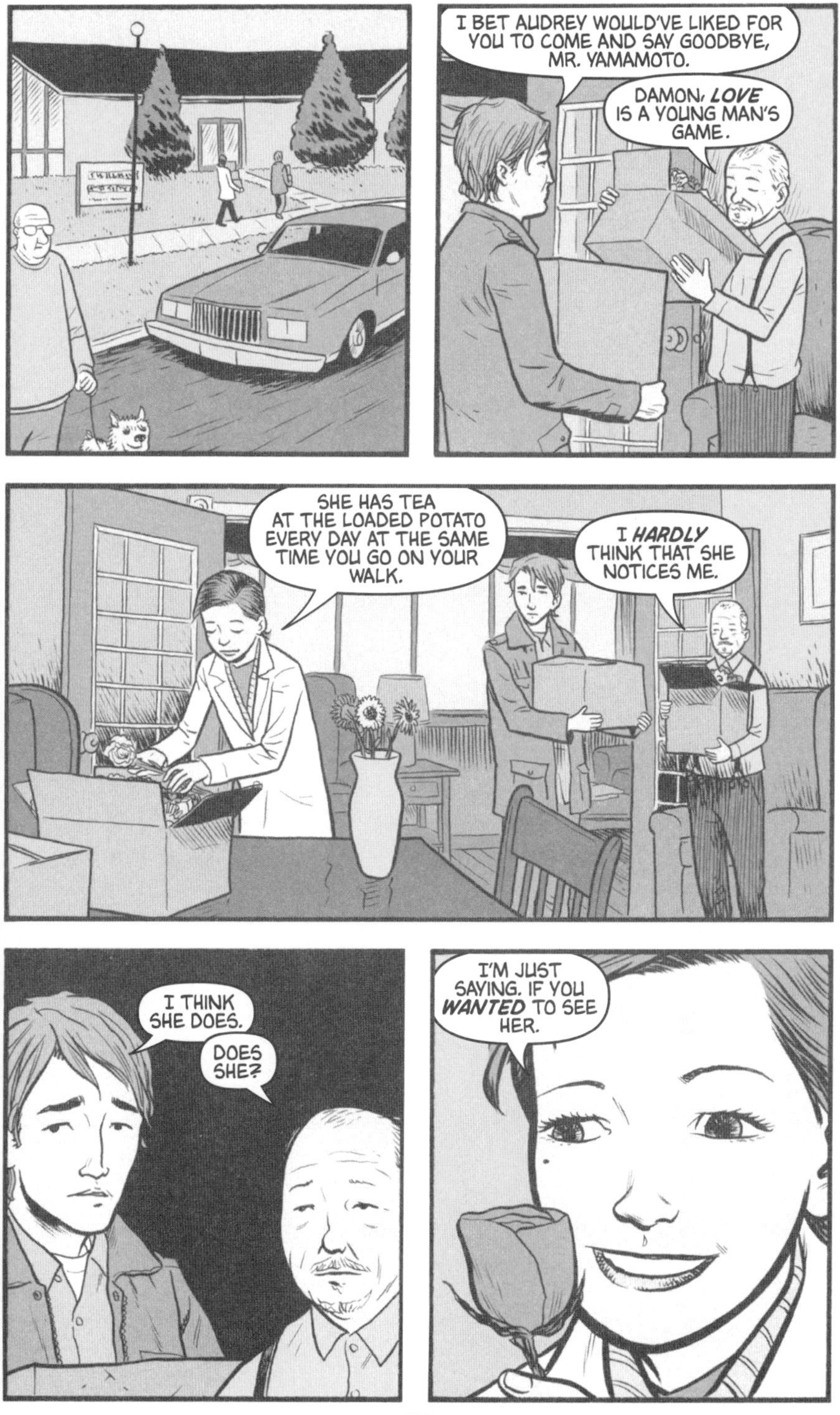
I BET AUDREY WOULD'VE LIKED FOR YOU TO COME AND SAY GOODBYE, MR. YAMAMOTO.
DAMON, *LOVE* IS A YOUNG MAN'S GAME.
SHE HAS TEA AT THE LOADED POTATO EVERY DAY AT THE SAME TIME YOU GO ON YOUR WALK.
I *HARDLY* THINK THAT SHE NOTICES ME.
I THINK SHE DOES.
DOES SHE?
I'M JUST SAYING. IF YOU *WANTED* TO SEE HER.

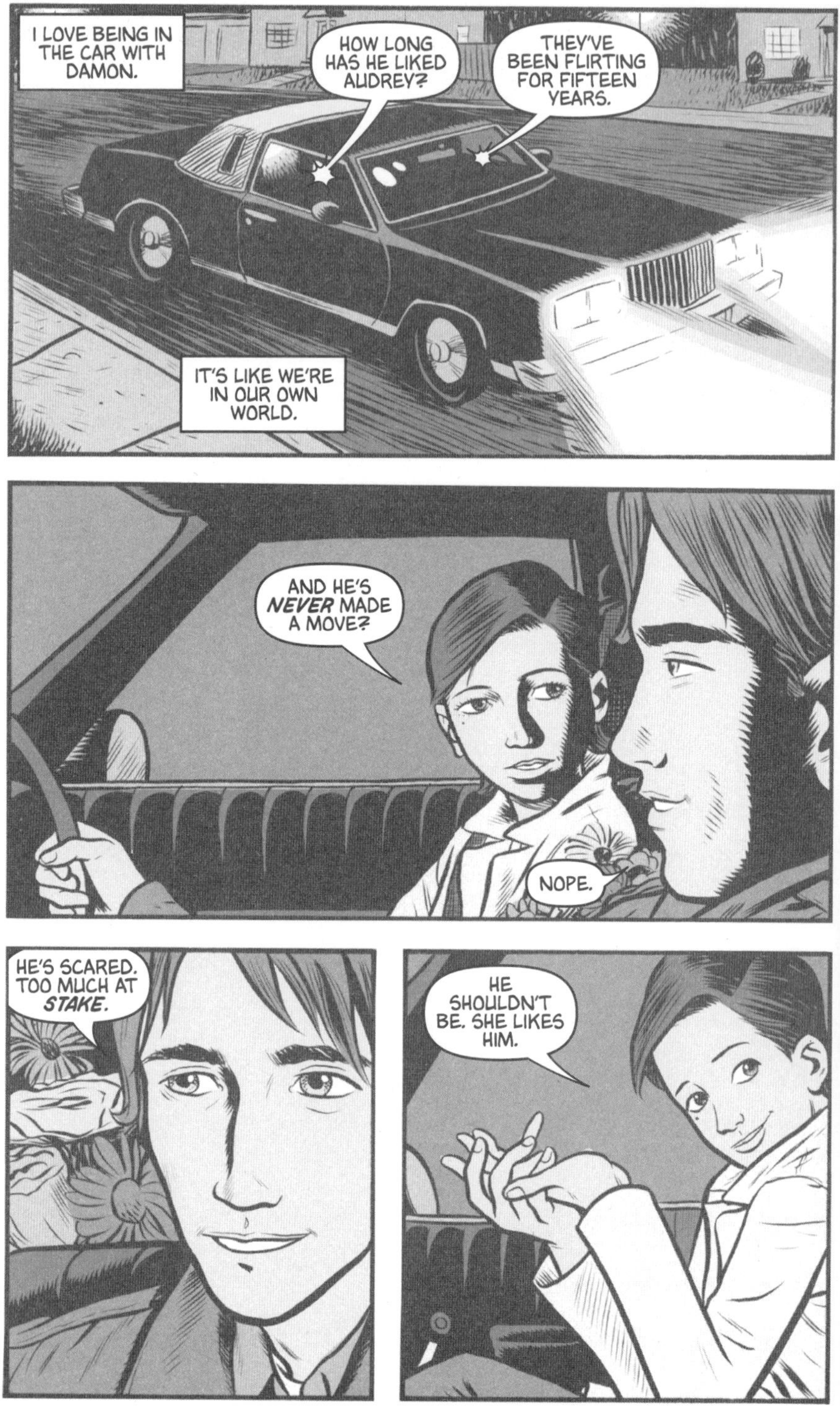
I LOVE BEING IN THE CAR WITH DAMON.
HOW LONG HAS HE LIKED AUDREY?
THEY'VE BEEN FLIRTING FOR FIFTEEN YEARS.
IT'S LIKE WE'RE IN OUR OWN WORLD.
AND HE'S *NEVER* MADE A MOVE?
NOPE.
HE'S SCARED. TOO MUCH AT *STAKE*.
HE SHOULDN'T BE. SHE LIKES HIM.

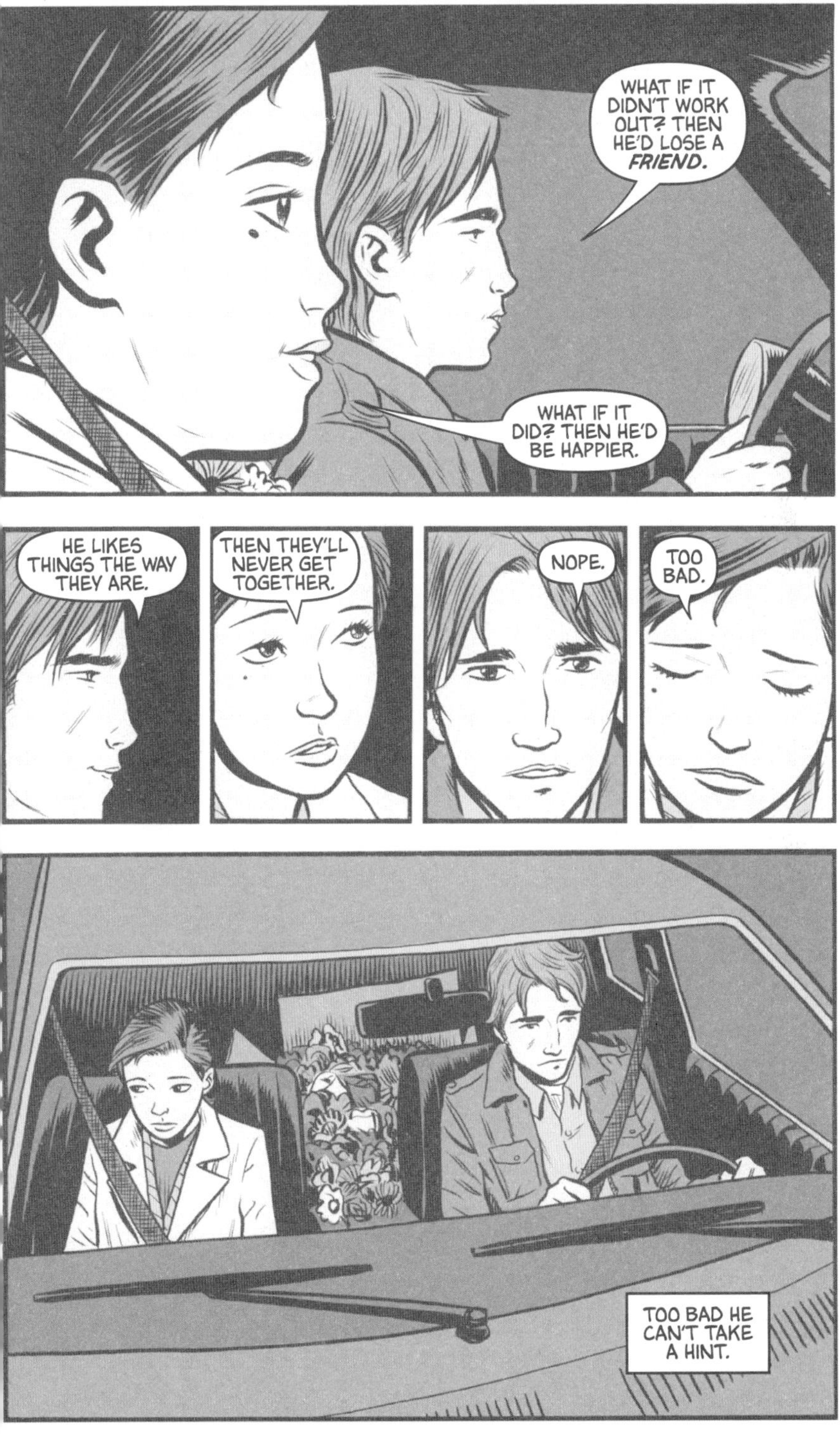
WHAT IF IT DIDN'T WORK OUT? THEN HE'D LOSE A *FRIEND.*
WHAT IF IT DID? THEN HE'D BE HAPPIER.
HE LIKES THINGS THE WAY THEY ARE.
THEN THEY'LL NEVER GET TOGETHER.
NOPE.
TOO BAD.
TOO BAD HE CAN'T TAKE A HINT.

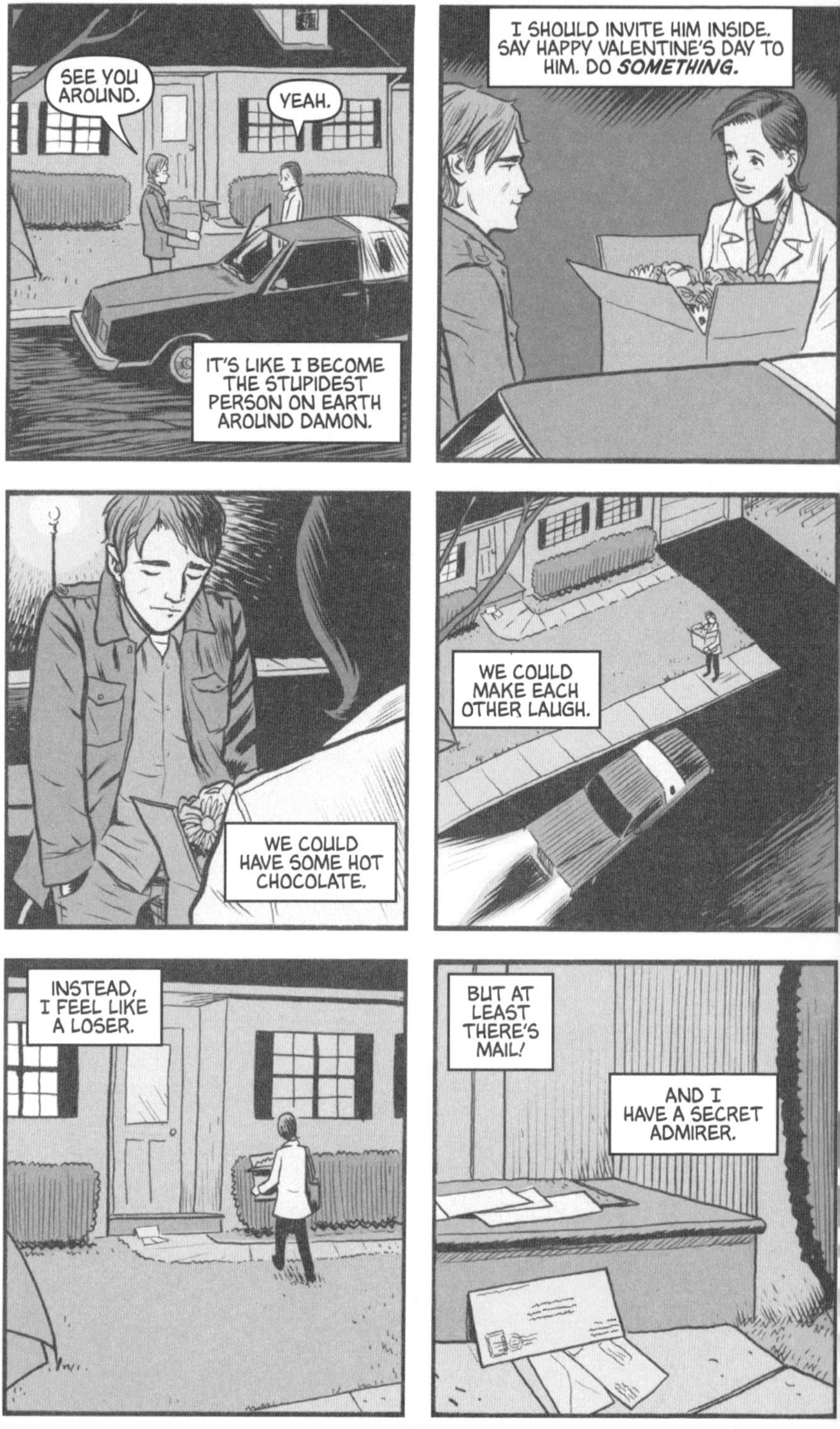
SEE YOU AROUND.
YEAH.
IT'S LIKE I BECOME THE STUPIDEST PERSON ON EARTH AROUND DAMON.
I SHOULD INVITE HIM INSIDE. SAY HAPPY VALENTINE'S DAY TO HIM. DO *SOMETHING.*
WE COULD HAVE SOME HOT CHOCOLATE.
WE COULD MAKE EACH OTHER LAUGH.
INSTEAD, I FEEL LIKE A LOSER.
BUT AT LEAST THERE'S MAIL!
AND I HAVE A SECRET ADMIRER.

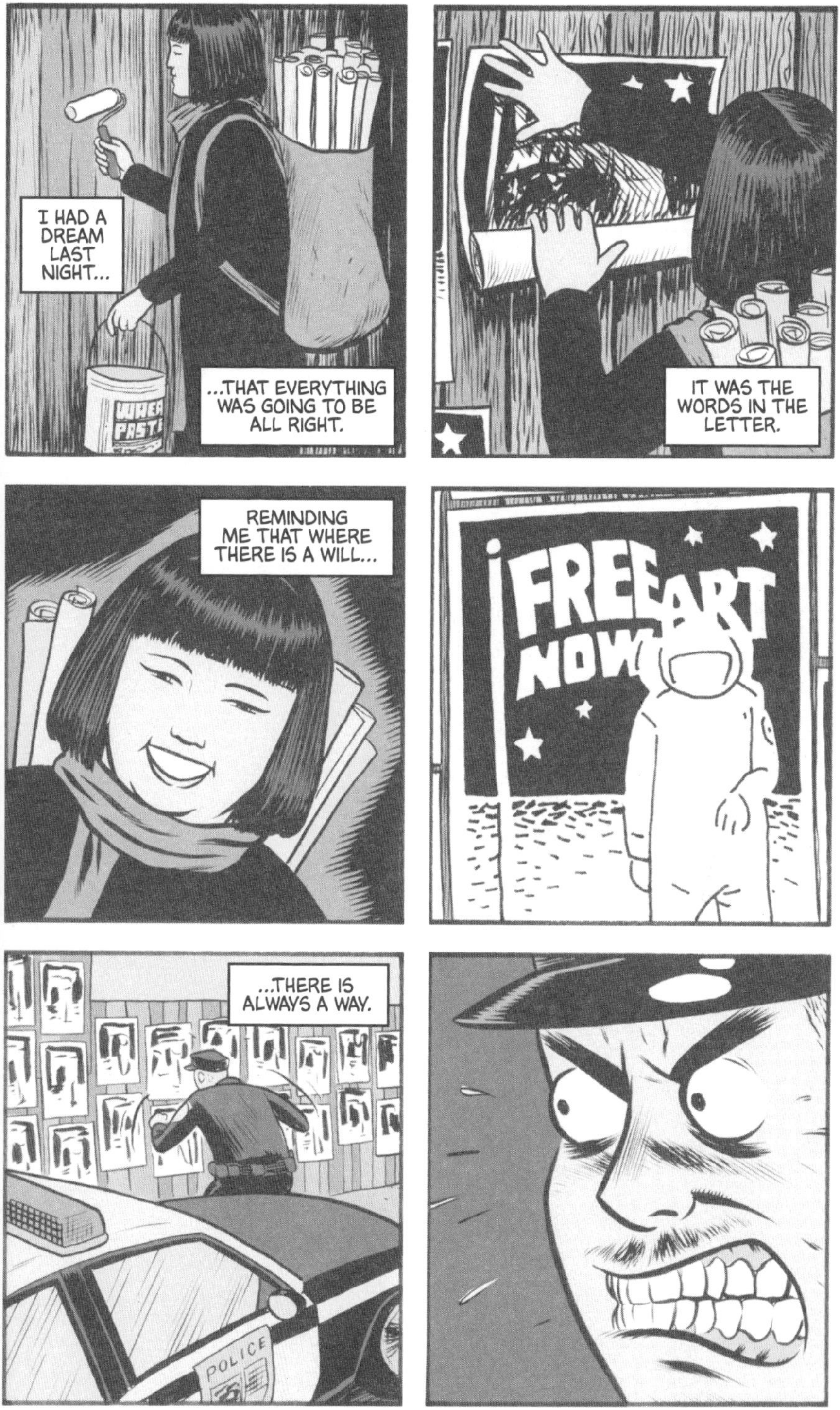
I HAD A DREAM LAST NIGHT...
...THAT EVERYTHING WAS GOING TO BE ALL RIGHT.
IT WAS THE WORDS IN THE LETTER.
REMINDING ME THAT WHERE THERE IS A WILL...
¡FREE ART NOW
...THERE IS ALWAYS A WAY.
POLICE

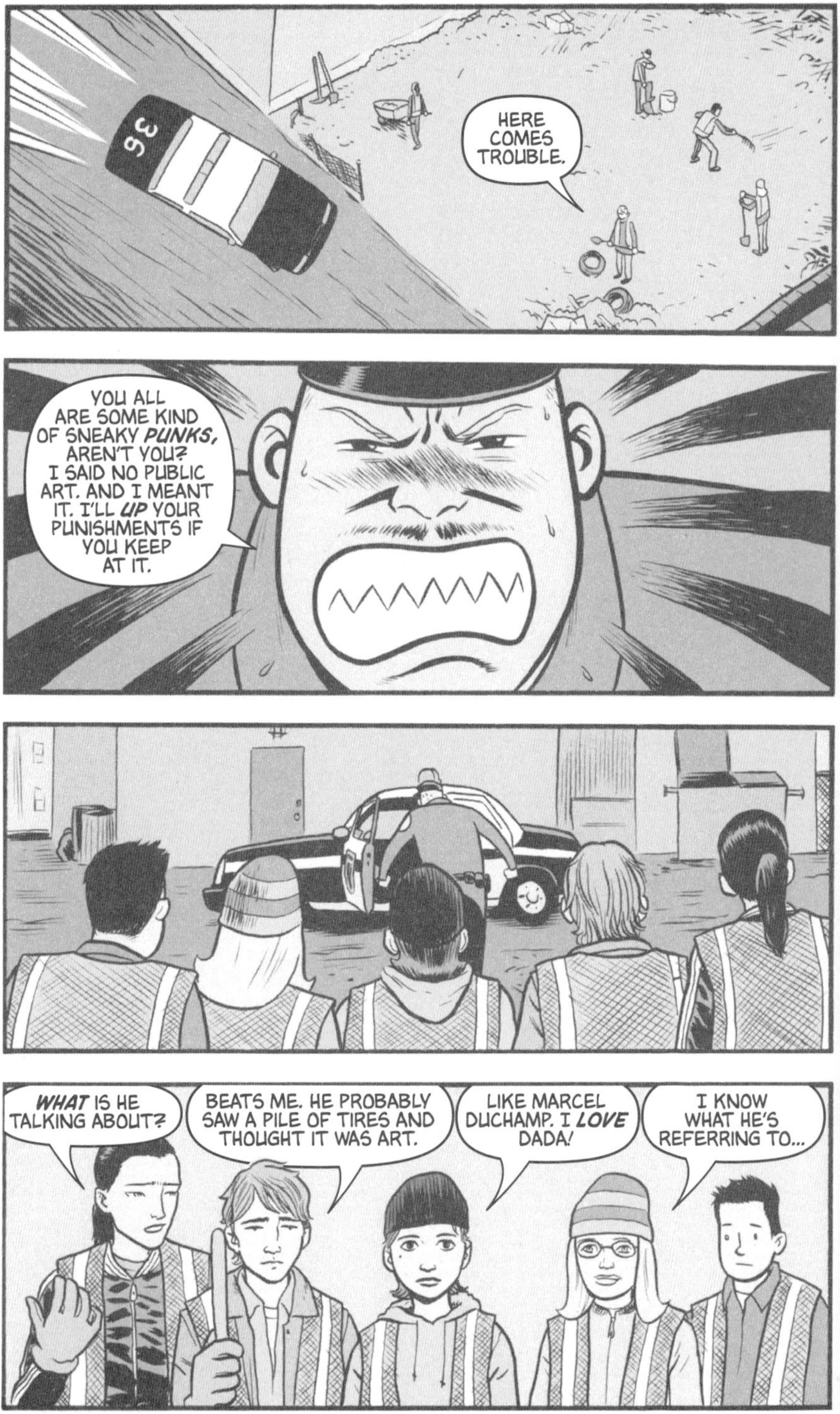
36
HERE COMES TROUBLE.
YOU ALL ARE SOME KIND OF SNEAKY *PUNKS,* AREN'T YOU? I SAID NO PUBLIC ART. AND I MEANT IT. I'LL *UP* YOUR PUNISHMENTS IF YOU KEEP AT IT.
WHAT IS HE TALKING ABOUT?
BEATS ME. HE PROBABLY SAW A PILE OF TIRES AND THOUGHT IT WAS ART.
LIKE MARCEL DUCHAMP. I *LOVE* DADA!
I KNOW WHAT HE'S REFERRING TO...

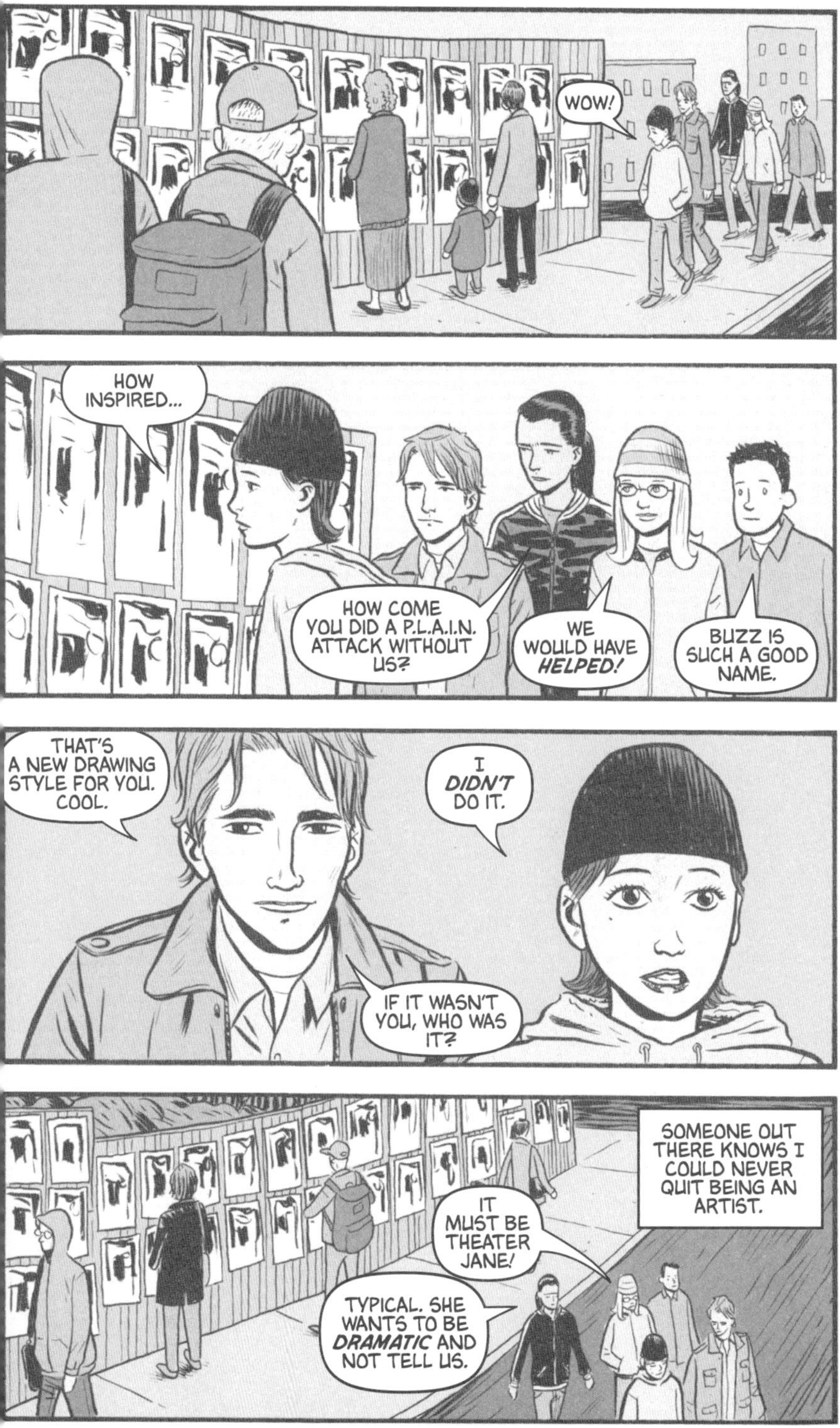

WOW!
HOW INSPIRED...
HOW COME YOU DID A P.L.A.I.N. ATTACK WITHOUT US?
WE WOULD HAVE *HELPED!*
BUZZ IS SUCH A GOOD NAME.
THAT'S A NEW DRAWING STYLE FOR YOU. COOL.
I *DIDN'T* DO IT.
IF IT WASN'T YOU, WHO WAS IT?
SOMEONE OUT THERE KNOWS I COULD NEVER QUIT BEING AN ARTIST.
IT MUST BE THEATER JANE!
TYPICAL. SHE WANTS TO BE *DRAMATIC* AND NOT TELL US.

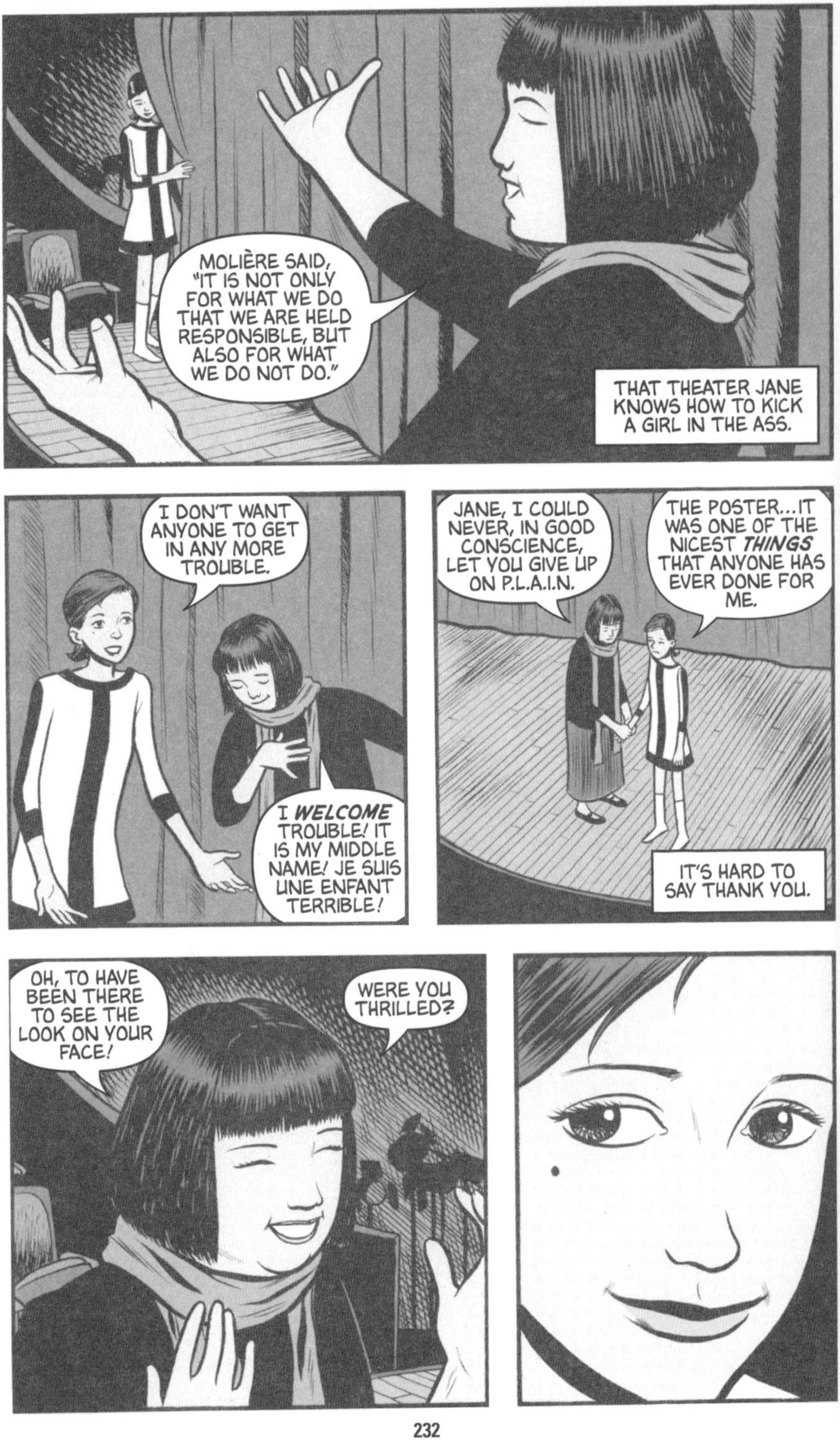
MOLIÈRE SAID, "IT IS NOT ONLY FOR WHAT WE DO THAT WE ARE HELD RESPONSIBLE, BUT ALSO FOR WHAT WE DO NOT DO."
THAT THEATER JANE KNOWS HOW TO KICK A GIRL IN THE ASS.
I DON'T WANT ANYONE TO GET IN ANY MORE TROUBLE.
I *WELCOME* TROUBLE! IT IS MY MIDDLE NAME! JE SUIS UNE ENFANT TERRIBLE!
JANE, I COULD NEVER, IN GOOD CONSCIENCE, LET YOU GIVE UP ON P.L.A.I.N.
THE POSTER...IT WAS ONE OF THE NICEST *THINGS* THAT ANYONE HAS EVER DONE FOR ME.
IT'S HARD TO SAY THANK YOU.
OH, TO HAVE BEEN THERE TO SEE THE LOOK ON YOUR FACE!
WERE YOU THRILLED?

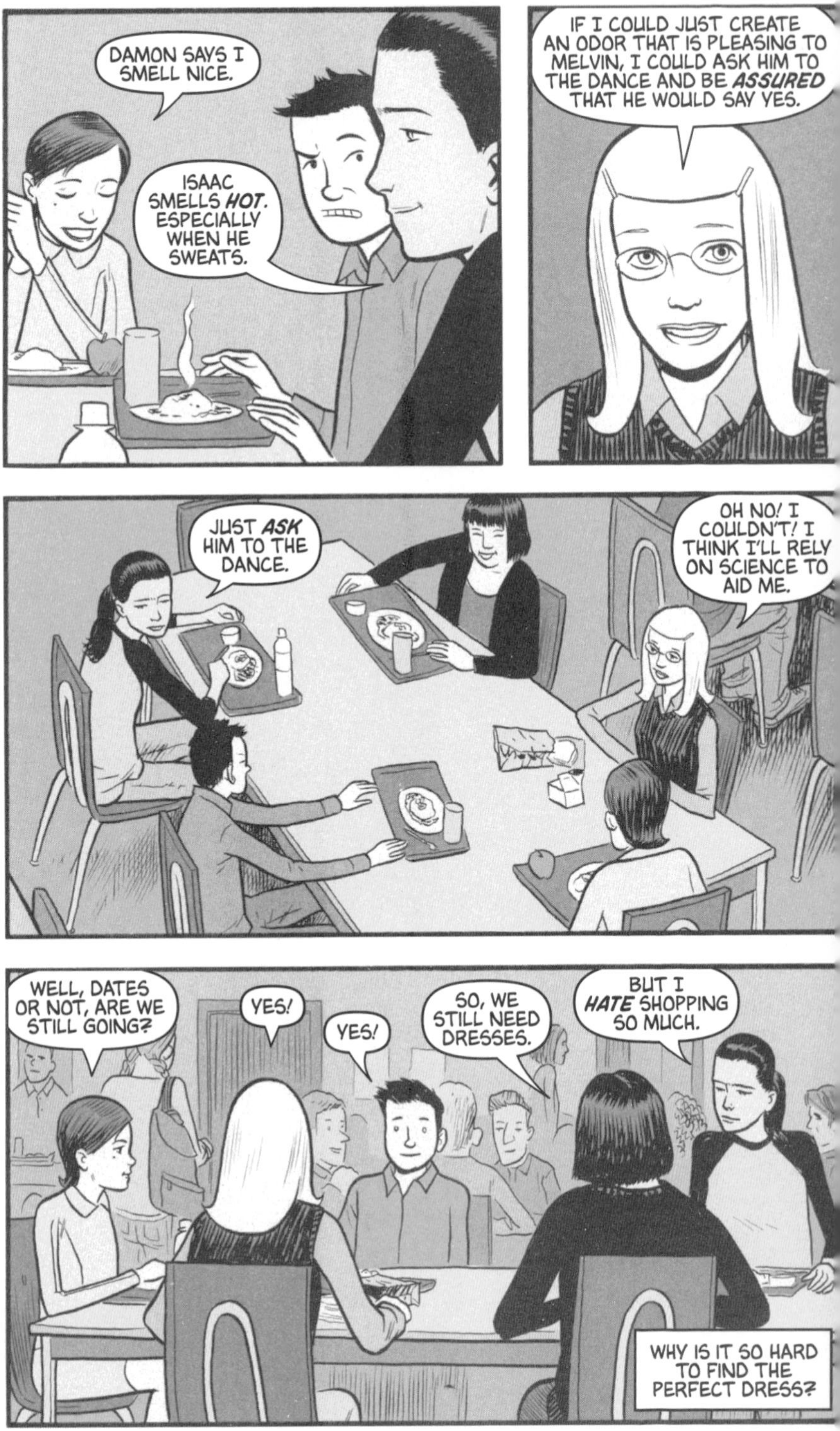
DAMON SAYS I SMELL NICE.
ISAAC SMELLS HOT. ESPECIALLY WHEN HE SWEATS.
IF I COULD JUST CREATE AN ODOR THAT IS PLEASING TO MELVIN, I COULD ASK HIM TO THE DANCE AND BE ASSURED THAT HE WOULD SAY YES.
JUST ASK HIM TO THE DANCE.
OH NO! I COULDN'T! I THINK I'LL RELY ON SCIENCE TO AID ME.
WELL, DATES OR NOT, ARE WE STILL GOING?
YES!
YES!
SO, WE STILL NEED DRESSES.
BUT I HATE SHOPPING SO MUCH.
WHY IS IT SO HARD TO FIND THE PERFECT DRESS?

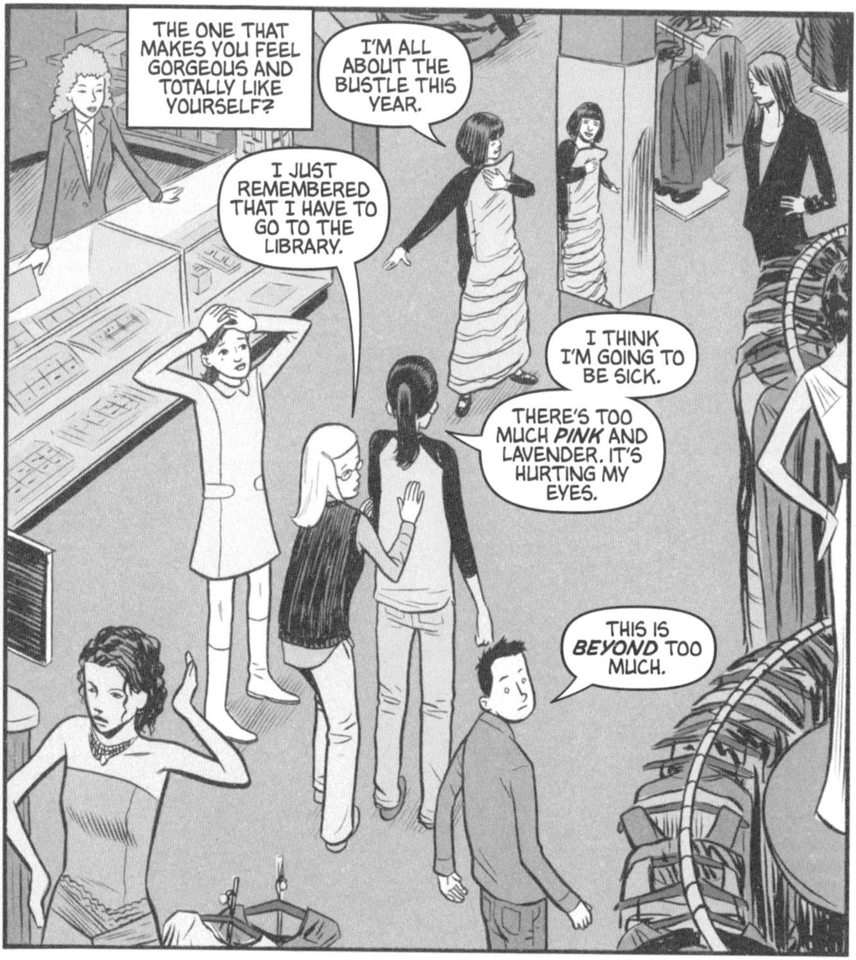
THE ONE THAT MAKES YOU FEEL GORGEOUS AND TOTALLY LIKE YOURSELF?
I'M ALL ABOUT THE BUSTLE THIS YEAR.
I JUST REMEMBERED THAT I HAVE TO GO TO THE LIBRARY.
I THINK I'M GOING TO BE SICK.
THERE'S TOO MUCH PINK AND LAVENDER. IT'S HURTING MY EYES.
THIS IS BEYOND TOO MUCH.

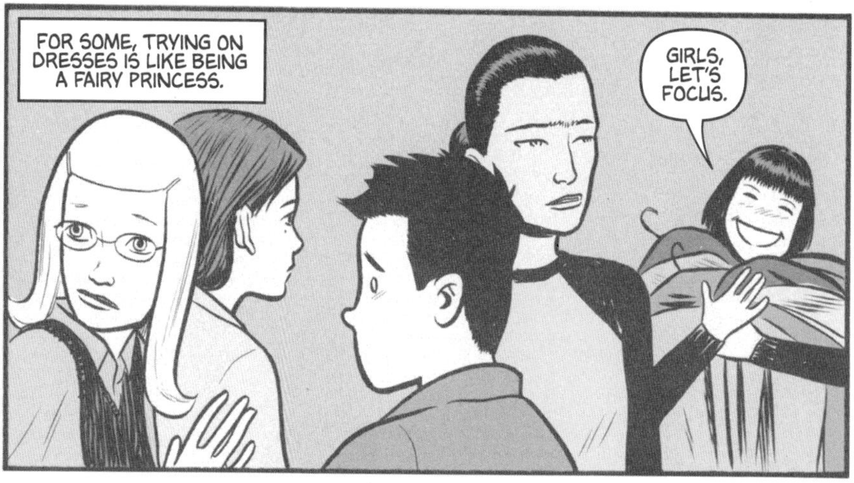
FOR SOME, TRYING ON DRESSES IS LIKE BEING A FAIRY PRINCESS.
GIRLS, LET'S FOCUS.

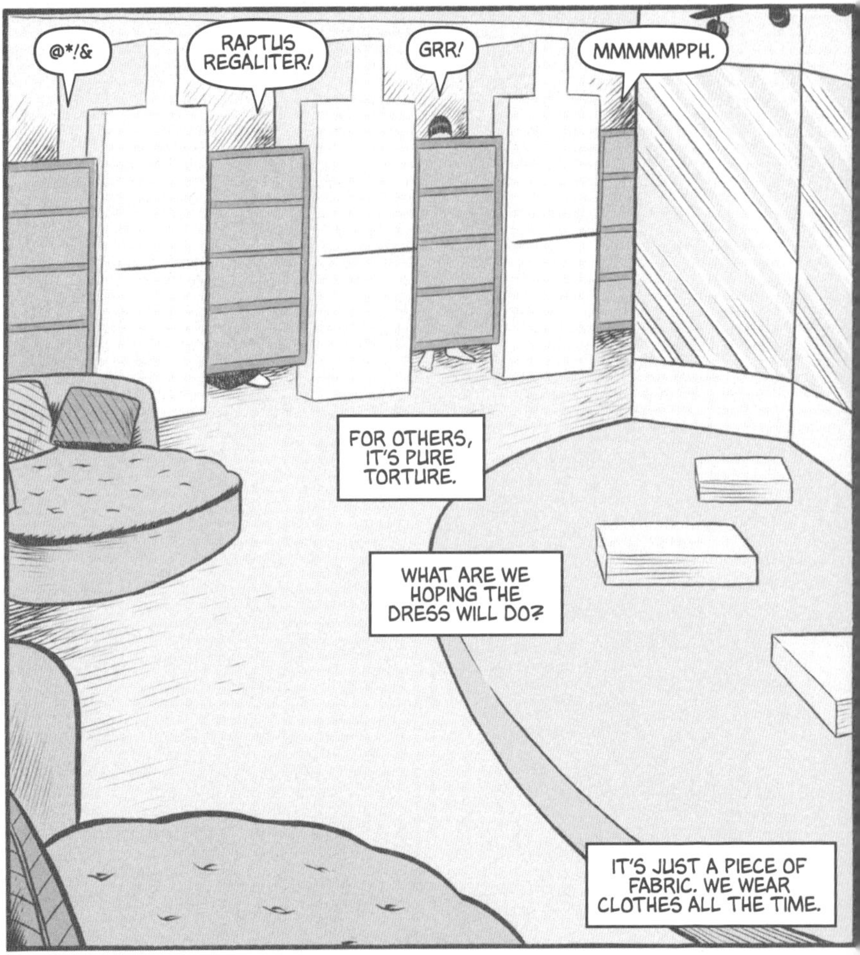
@*!&
RAPTUS REGALITER!
GRR!
MMMMMPPH.
FOR OTHERS, IT'S PURE TORTURE.
WHAT ARE WE HOPING THE DRESS WILL DO?
IT'S JUST A PIECE OF FABRIC. WE WEAR CLOTHES ALL THE TIME.

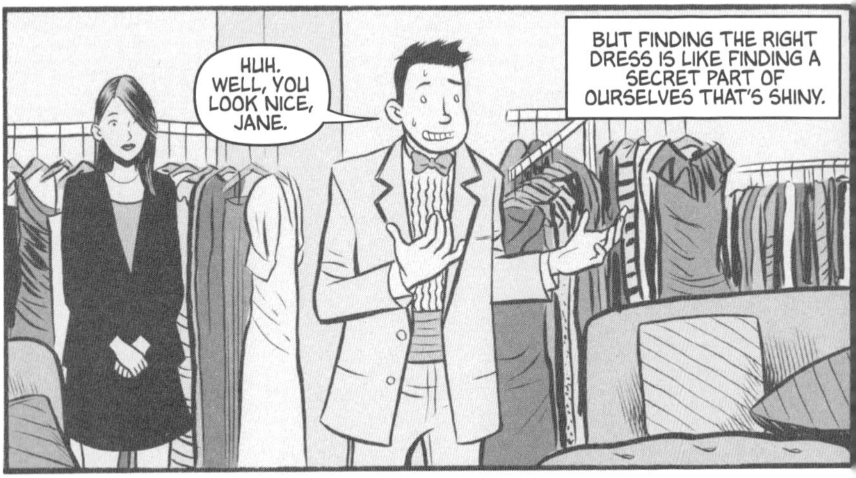
BUT FINDING THE RIGHT DRESS IS LIKE FINDING A SECRET PART OF OURSELVES THAT'S SHINY.
HUH. WELL, YOU LOOK NICE, JANE.

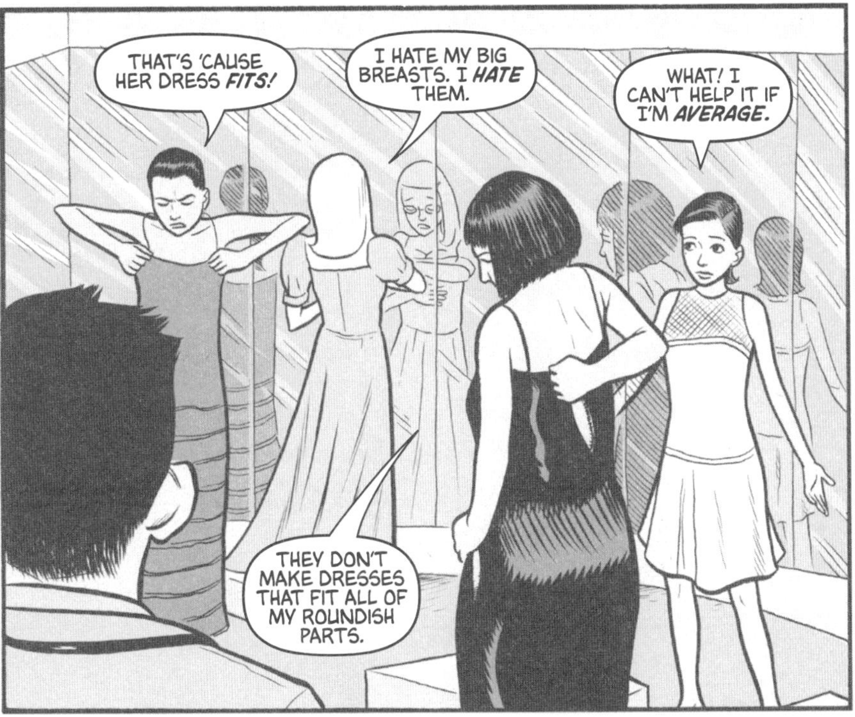
THAT'S 'CAUSE HER DRESS *FITS!*
I HATE MY BIG BREASTS. I *HATE* THEM.
WHAT! I CAN'T HELP IT IF I'M ***AVERAGE.***
THEY DON'T MAKE DRESSES THAT FIT ALL OF MY ROUNDISH PARTS.

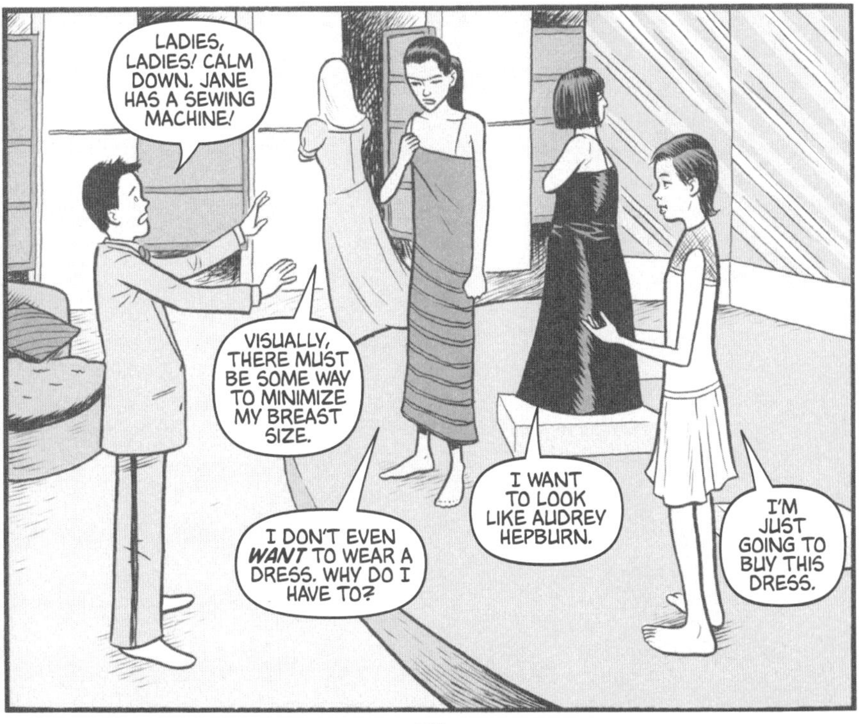
LADIES, LADIES! CALM DOWN. JANE HAS A SEWING MACHINE!
VISUALLY, THERE MUST BE SOME WAY TO MINIMIZE MY BREAST SIZE.
I DON'T EVEN ***WANT*** TO WEAR A DRESS. WHY DO I HAVE TO?
I WANT TO LOOK LIKE AUDREY HEPBURN.
I'M JUST GOING TO BUY THIS DRESS.

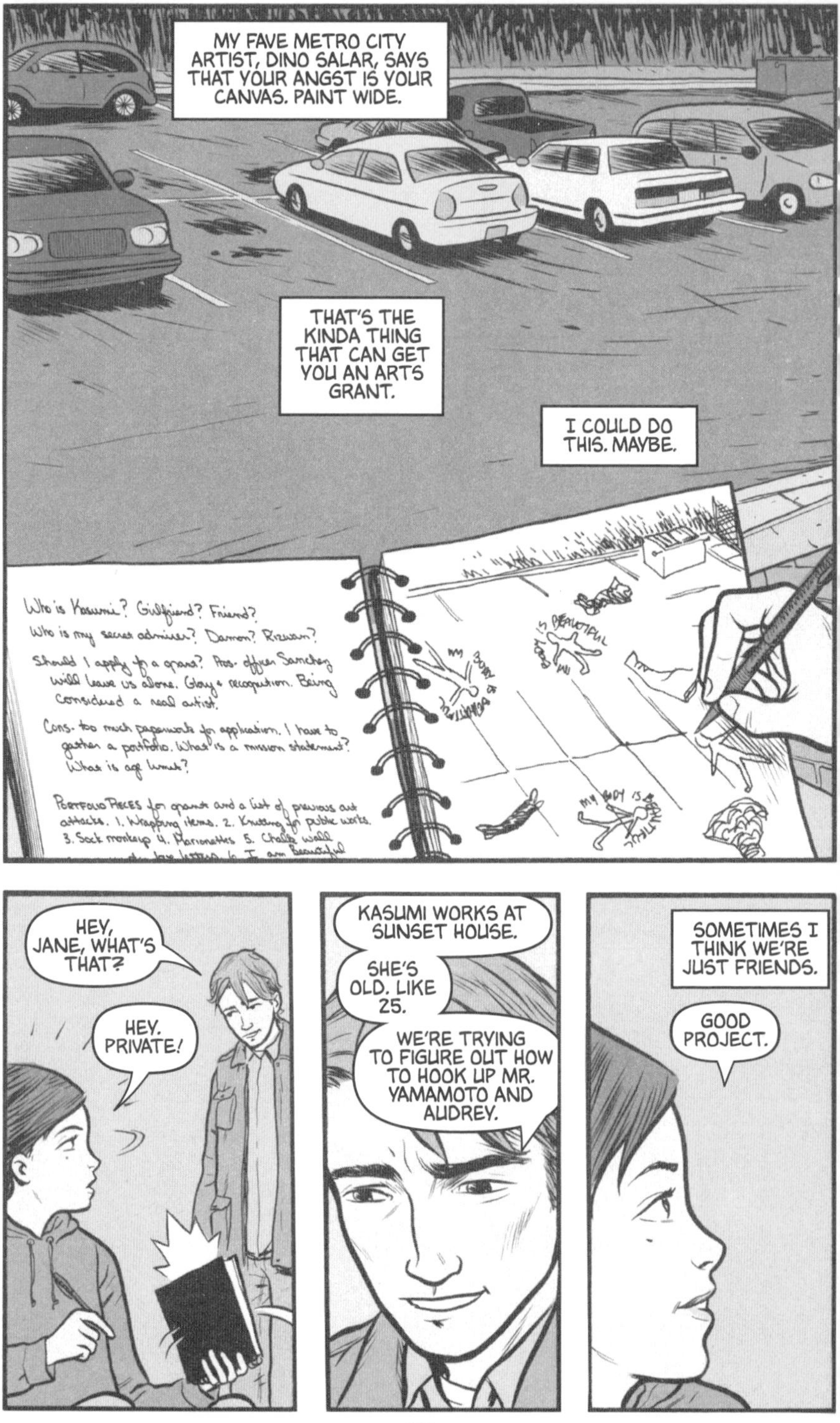
MY FAVE METRO CITY ARTIST, DINO SALAR, SAYS THAT YOUR ANGST IS YOUR CANVAS. PAINT WIDE.
THAT'S THE KINDA THING THAT CAN GET YOU AN ARTS GRANT.
I COULD DO THIS. MAYBE.
Who is Kasumi? Girlfriend? Friend?
Who is my secret admirer? Damon? Rizwan?
Should I apply for a grant? Pros- officer Sanchez will leave us alone. Glory + recognition. Being considered a real artist.
Cons- too much paperwork for application. I have to gather a portfolio. What is a mission statement? What is age limit?
PORTFOLIO PIECES for grant and a list of previous art attacks. 1. Wrapping items. 2. Knitting for public works. 3. Sock monkeys 4. Marionettes 5. Chalk wall
HEY, JANE, WHAT'S THAT?
HEY. PRIVATE!
KASUMI WORKS AT SUNSET HOUSE.
SHE'S OLD. LIKE 25.
WE'RE TRYING TO FIGURE OUT HOW TO HOOK UP MR. YAMAMOTO AND AUDREY.
SOMETIMES I THINK WE'RE JUST FRIENDS.
GOOD PROJECT.

239

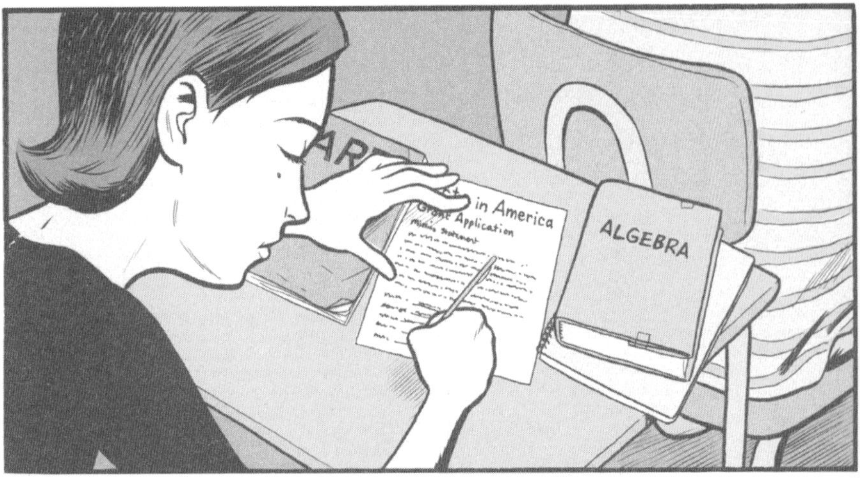
ART
in America
Grant Application
ALGEBRA

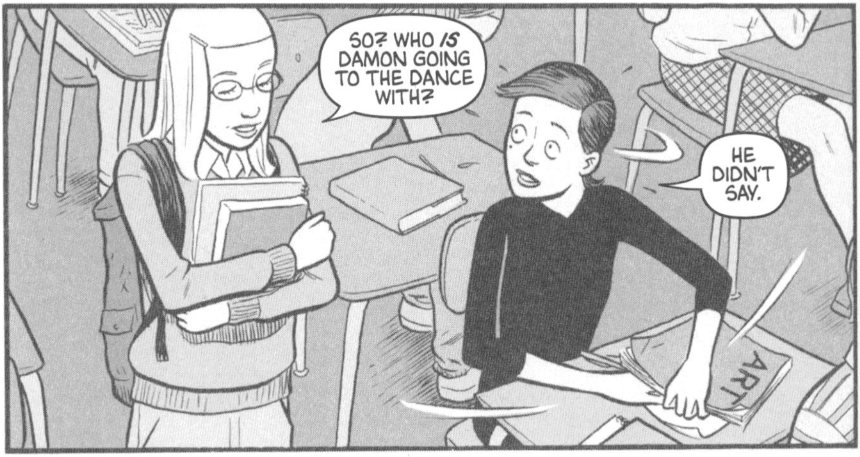
SO? WHO *IS* DAMON GOING TO THE DANCE WITH?
HE DIDN'T SAY.
ART

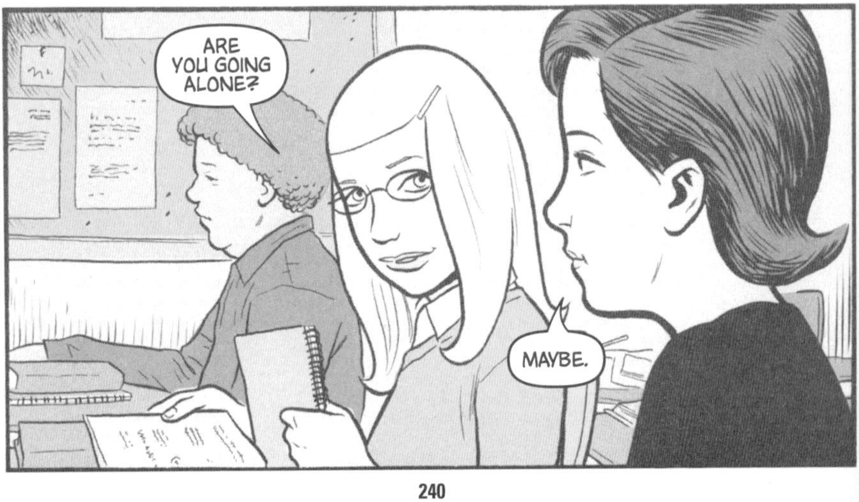
ARE YOU GOING ALONE?
MAYBE.

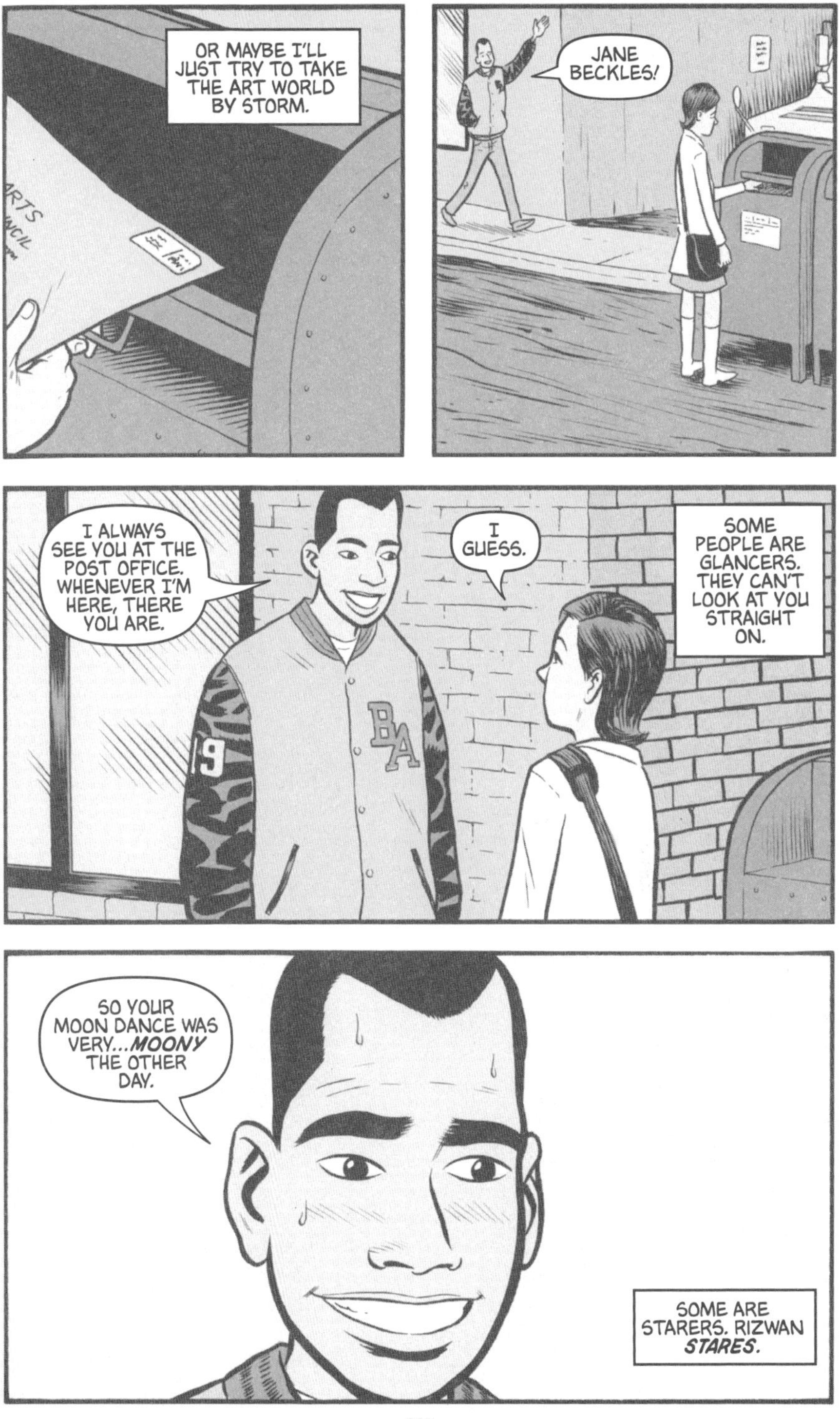
OR MAYBE I'LL JUST TRY TO TAKE THE ART WORLD BY STORM.
JANE BECKLES!
I ALWAYS SEE YOU AT THE POST OFFICE. WHENEVER I'M HERE, THERE YOU ARE.
I GUESS.
SOME PEOPLE ARE GLANCERS. THEY CAN'T LOOK AT YOU STRAIGHT ON.
SO YOUR MOON DANCE WAS VERY... *MOONY* THE OTHER DAY.
SOME ARE STARERS. RIZWAN *STARES.*

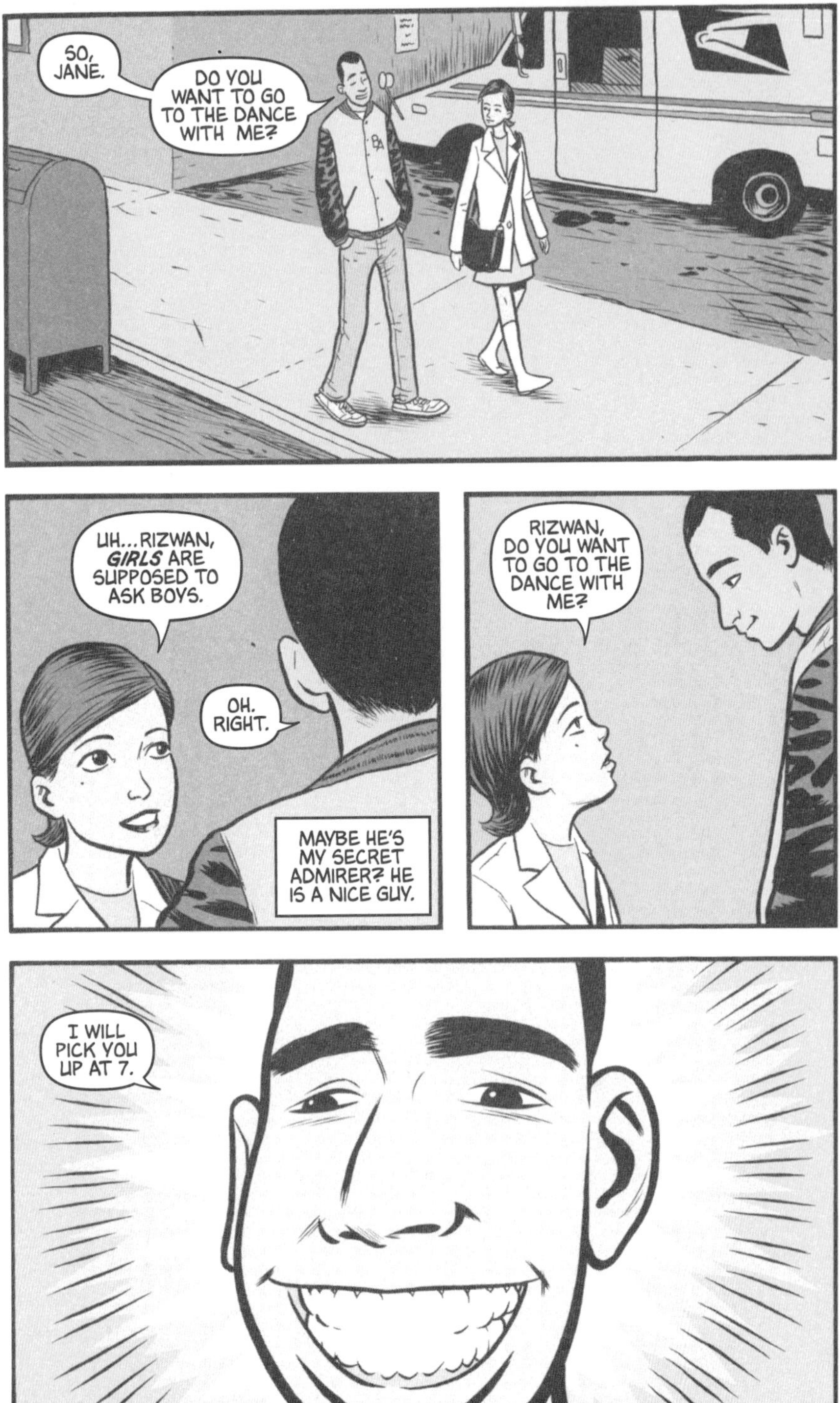
SO, JANE.
DO YOU WANT TO GO TO THE DANCE WITH ME?
UH...RIZWAN, *GIRLS* ARE SUPPOSED TO ASK BOYS.
OH. RIGHT.
MAYBE HE'S MY SECRET ADMIRER? HE IS A NICE GUY.
RIZWAN, DO YOU WANT TO GO TO THE DANCE WITH ME?
I WILL PICK YOU UP AT 7.

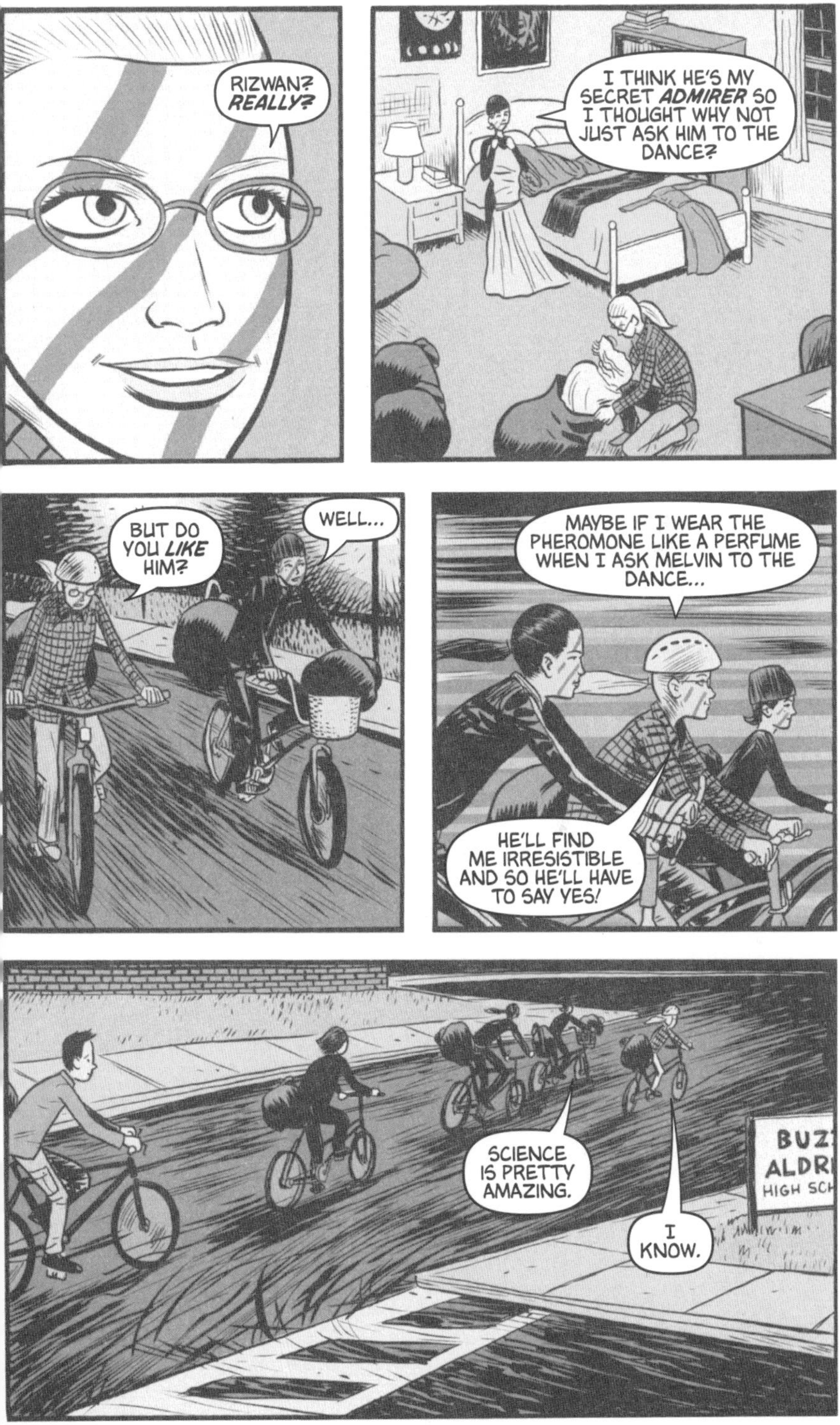
RIZWAN? REALLY?
I THINK HE'S MY SECRET ADMIRER SO I THOUGHT WHY NOT JUST ASK HIM TO THE DANCE?
BUT DO YOU LIKE HIM?
WELL...
MAYBE IF I WEAR THE PHEROMONE LIKE A PERFUME WHEN I ASK MELVIN TO THE DANCE...
HE'LL FIND ME IRRESISTIBLE AND SO HE'LL HAVE TO SAY YES!
SCIENCE IS PRETTY AMAZING.
I KNOW.

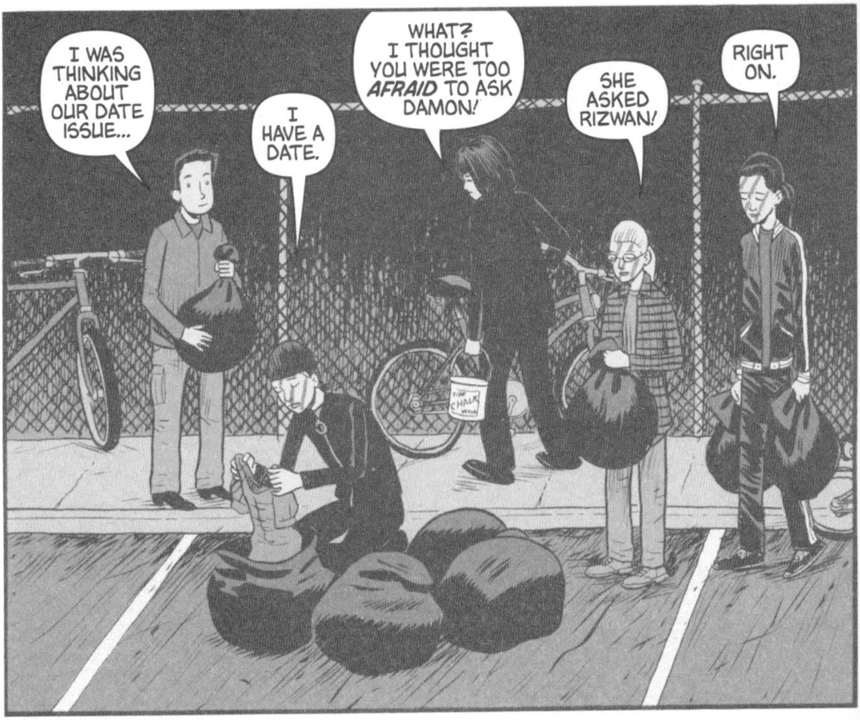
I WAS THINKING ABOUT OUR DATE ISSUE...
I HAVE A DATE.
WHAT? I THOUGHT YOU WERE TOO *AFRAID* TO ASK DAMON!
SHE ASKED RIZWAN!
RIGHT ON.

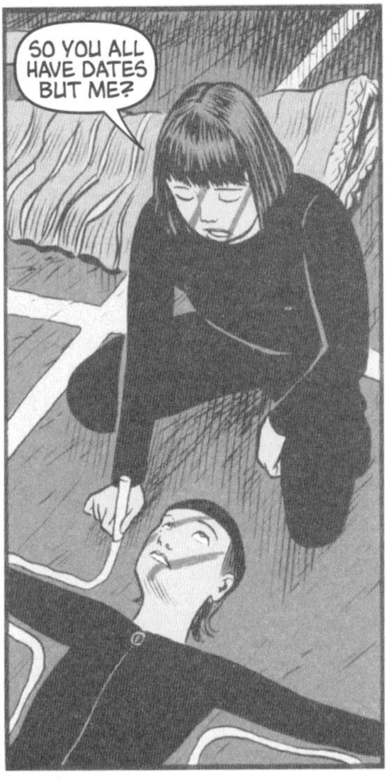
SO YOU ALL HAVE DATES BUT ME?

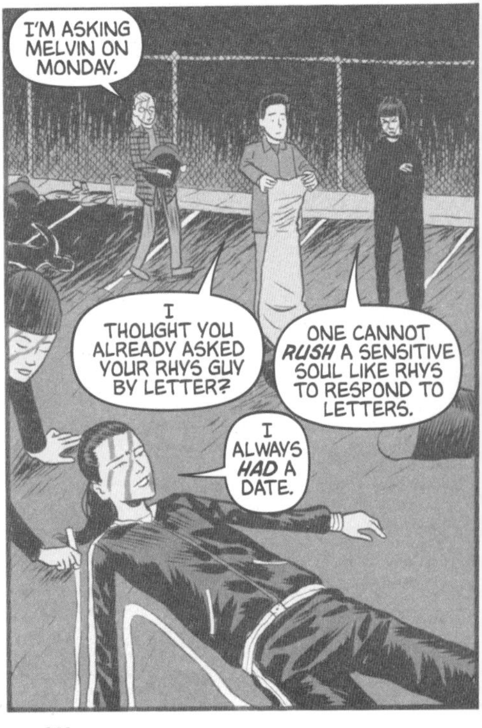
I'M ASKING MELVIN ON MONDAY.
I THOUGHT YOU ALREADY ASKED YOUR RHYS GUY BY LETTER?
ONE CANNOT *RUSH* A SENSITIVE SOUL LIKE RHYS TO RESPOND TO LETTERS.
I ALWAYS *HAD* A DATE.

Dear Miroslaw,
I've pulled off my biggest art attack ever. And I put together a portfolio.
my b
my BODY IS BEAUTIFUL
my body i
Can you keep a secret?
my

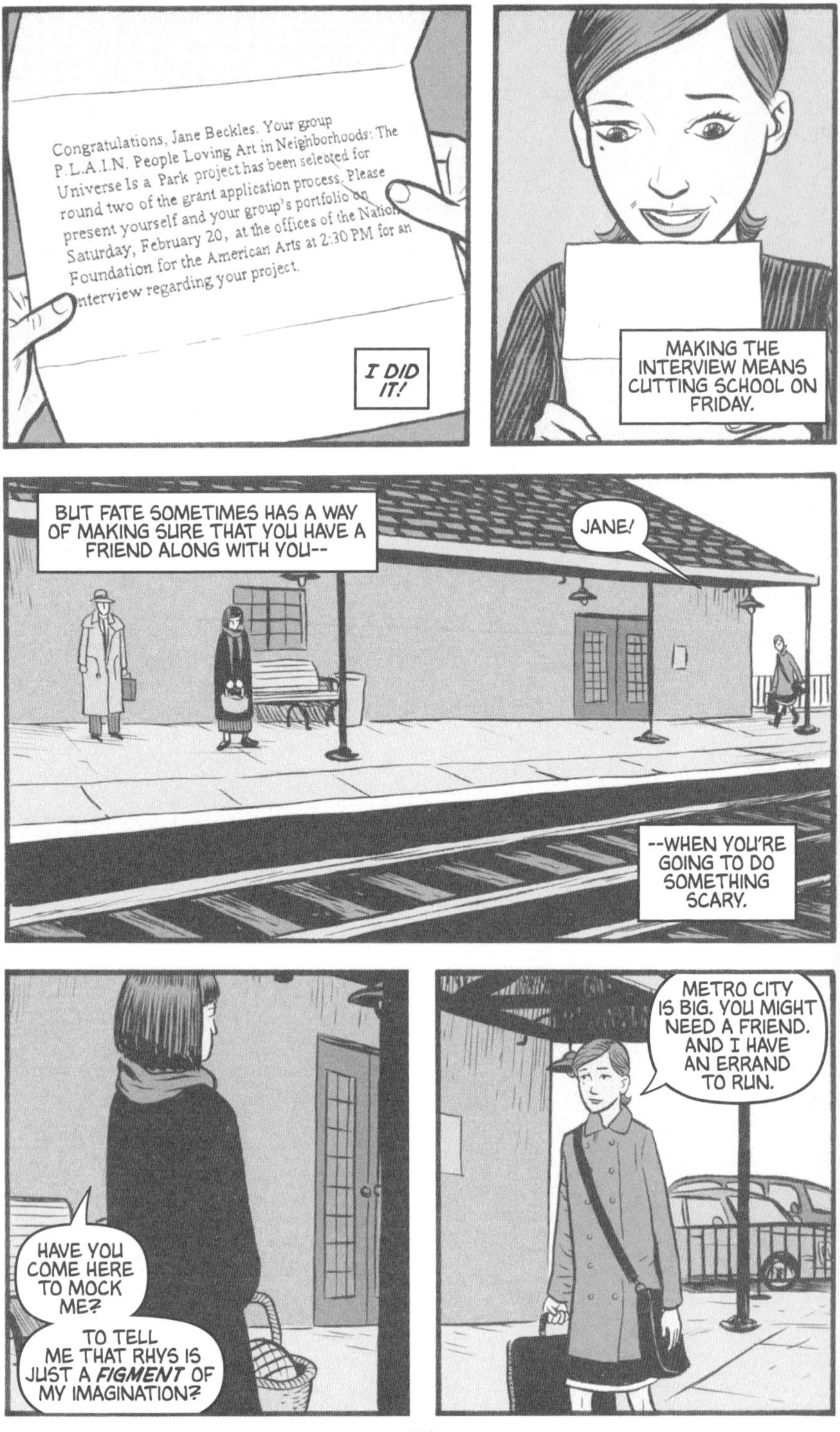
Congratulations, Jane Beckles. Your group P.L.A.I.N. People Loving Art in Neighborhoods: The Universe Is a Park project has been selected for round two of the grant application process. Please present yourself and your group's portfolio on Saturday, February 20, at the offices of the National Foundation for the American Arts at 2:30 PM for an interview regarding your project.
I DID IT!
MAKING THE INTERVIEW MEANS CUTTING SCHOOL ON FRIDAY.
BUT FATE SOMETIMES HAS A WAY OF MAKING SURE THAT YOU HAVE A FRIEND ALONG WITH YOU--
JANE!
--WHEN YOU'RE GOING TO DO SOMETHING SCARY.
HAVE YOU COME HERE TO MOCK ME?
TO TELL ME THAT RHYS IS JUST A FIGMENT OF MY IMAGINATION?
METRO CITY IS BIG. YOU MIGHT NEED A FRIEND. AND I HAVE AN ERRAND TO RUN.

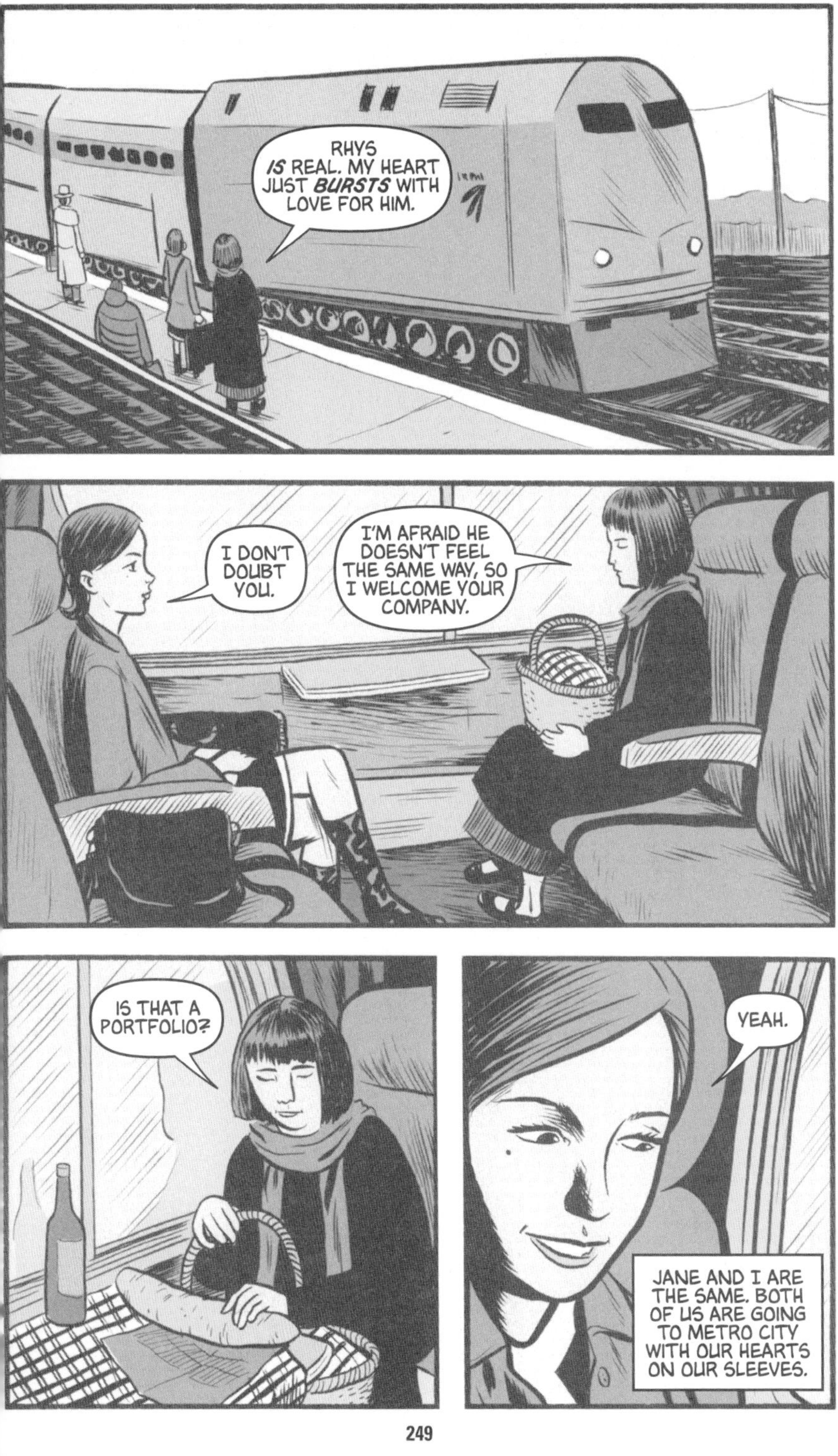
RHYS *IS* REAL. MY HEART JUST ***BURSTS*** WITH LOVE FOR HIM.
I DON'T DOUBT YOU.
I'M AFRAID HE DOESN'T FEEL THE SAME WAY, SO I WELCOME YOUR COMPANY.
IS THAT A PORTFOLIO?
YEAH.
JANE AND I ARE THE SAME. BOTH OF US ARE GOING TO METRO CITY WITH OUR HEARTS ON OUR SLEEVES.

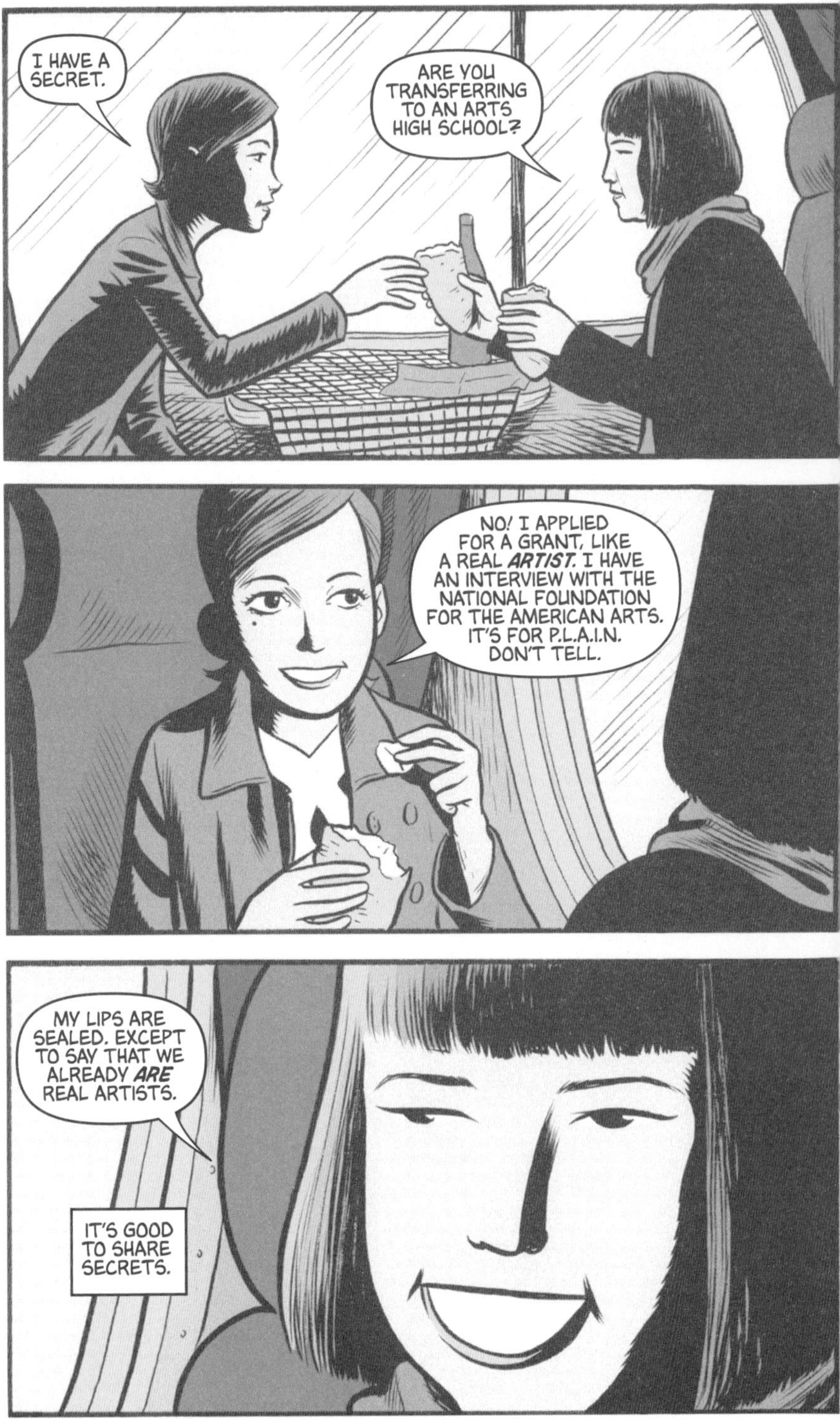

I HAVE A SECRET.
ARE YOU TRANSFERRING TO AN ARTS HIGH SCHOOL?
NO! I APPLIED FOR A GRANT, LIKE A REAL *ARTIST*. I HAVE AN INTERVIEW WITH THE NATIONAL FOUNDATION FOR THE AMERICAN ARTS. IT'S FOR P.L.A.I.N. DON'T TELL.
MY LIPS ARE SEALED. EXCEPT TO SAY THAT WE ALREADY *ARE* REAL ARTISTS.
IT'S GOOD TO SHARE SECRETS.

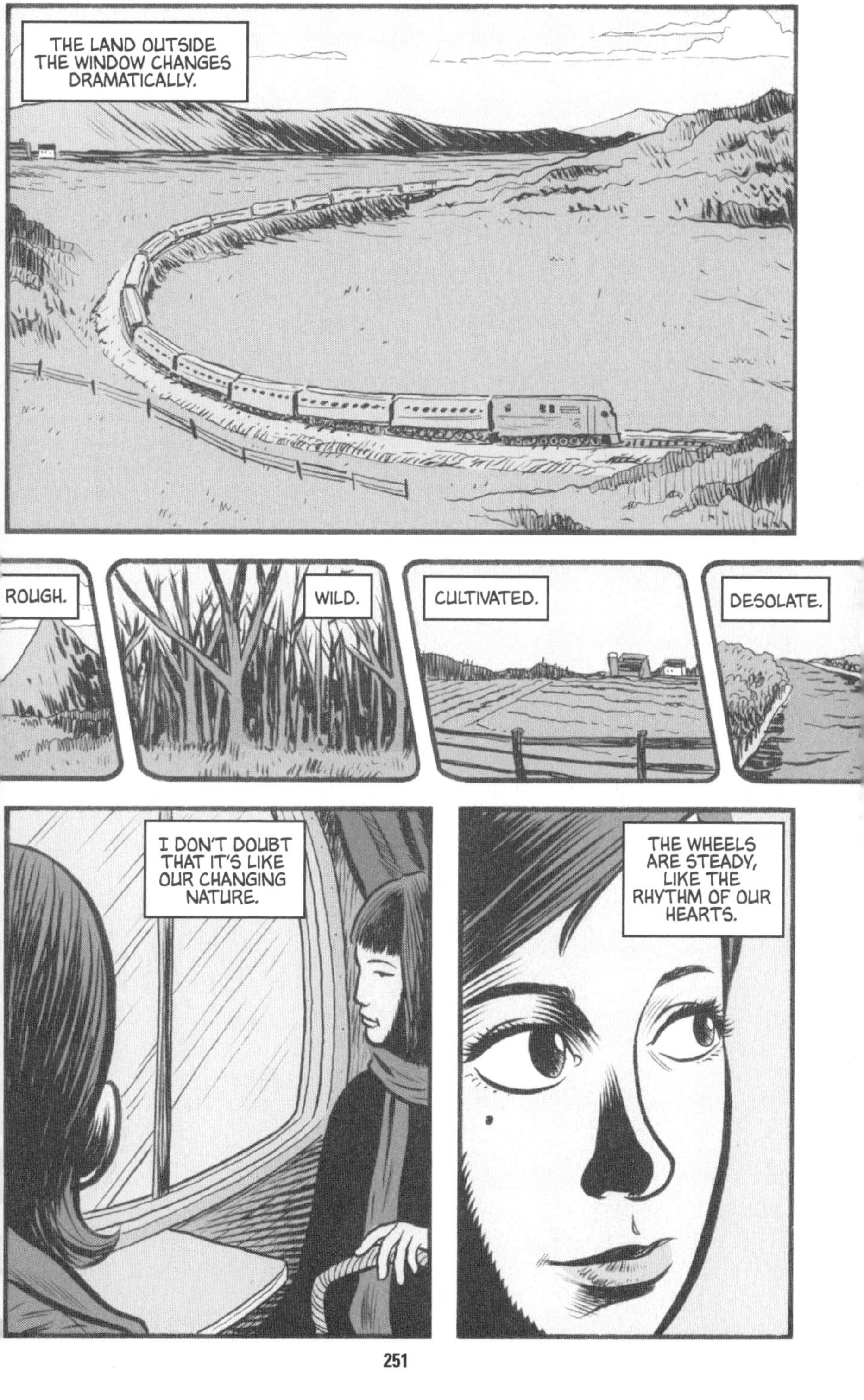
THE LAND OUTSIDE THE WINDOW CHANGES DRAMATICALLY.
ROUGH.
WILD.
CULTIVATED.
DESOLATE.
I DON'T DOUBT THAT IT'S LIKE OUR CHANGING NATURE.
THE WHEELS ARE STEADY, LIKE THE RHYTHM OF OUR HEARTS.

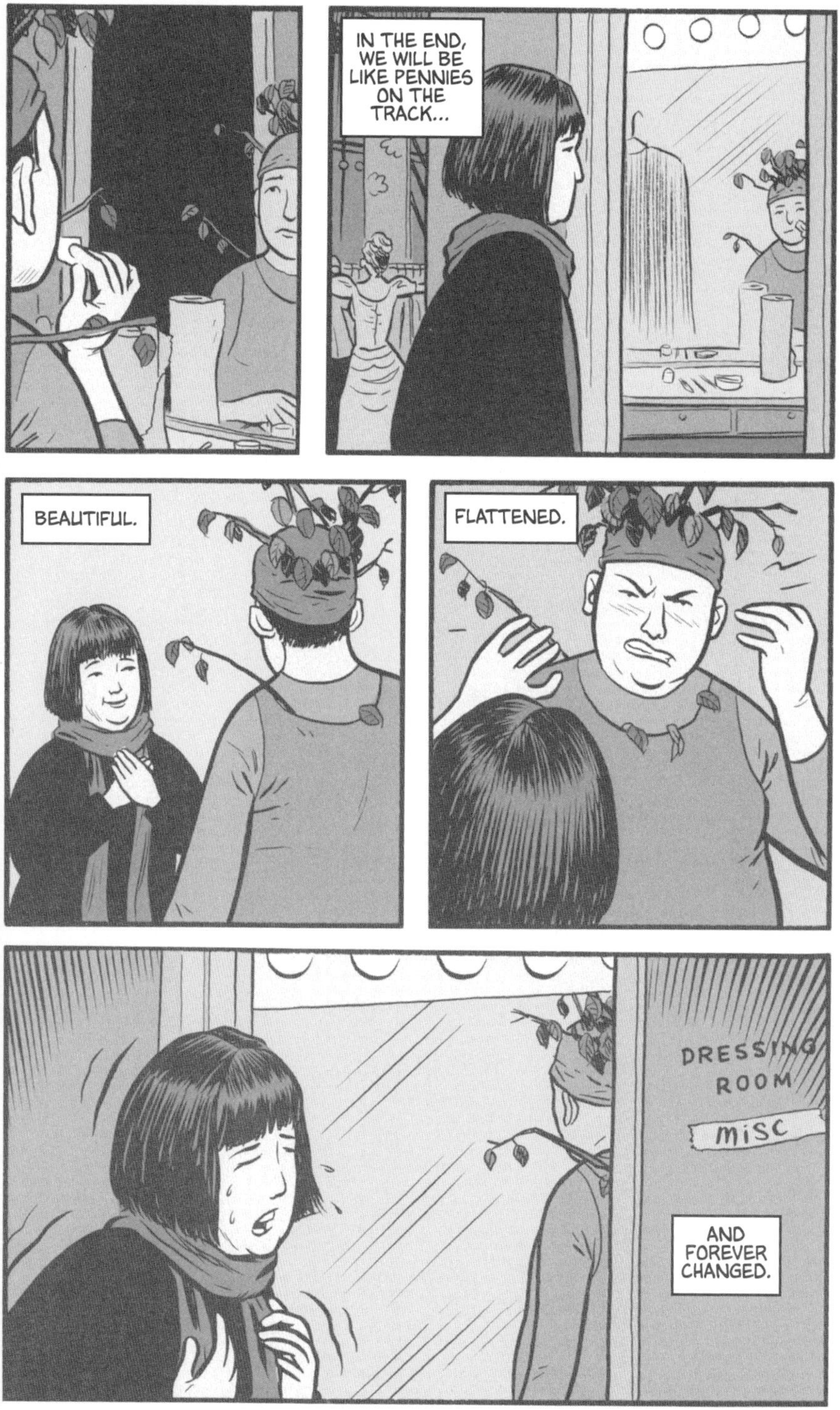
IN THE END, WE WILL BE LIKE PENNIES ON THE TRACK...
BEAUTIFUL.
FLATTENED.
DRESSING ROOM
misc
AND FOREVER CHANGED.

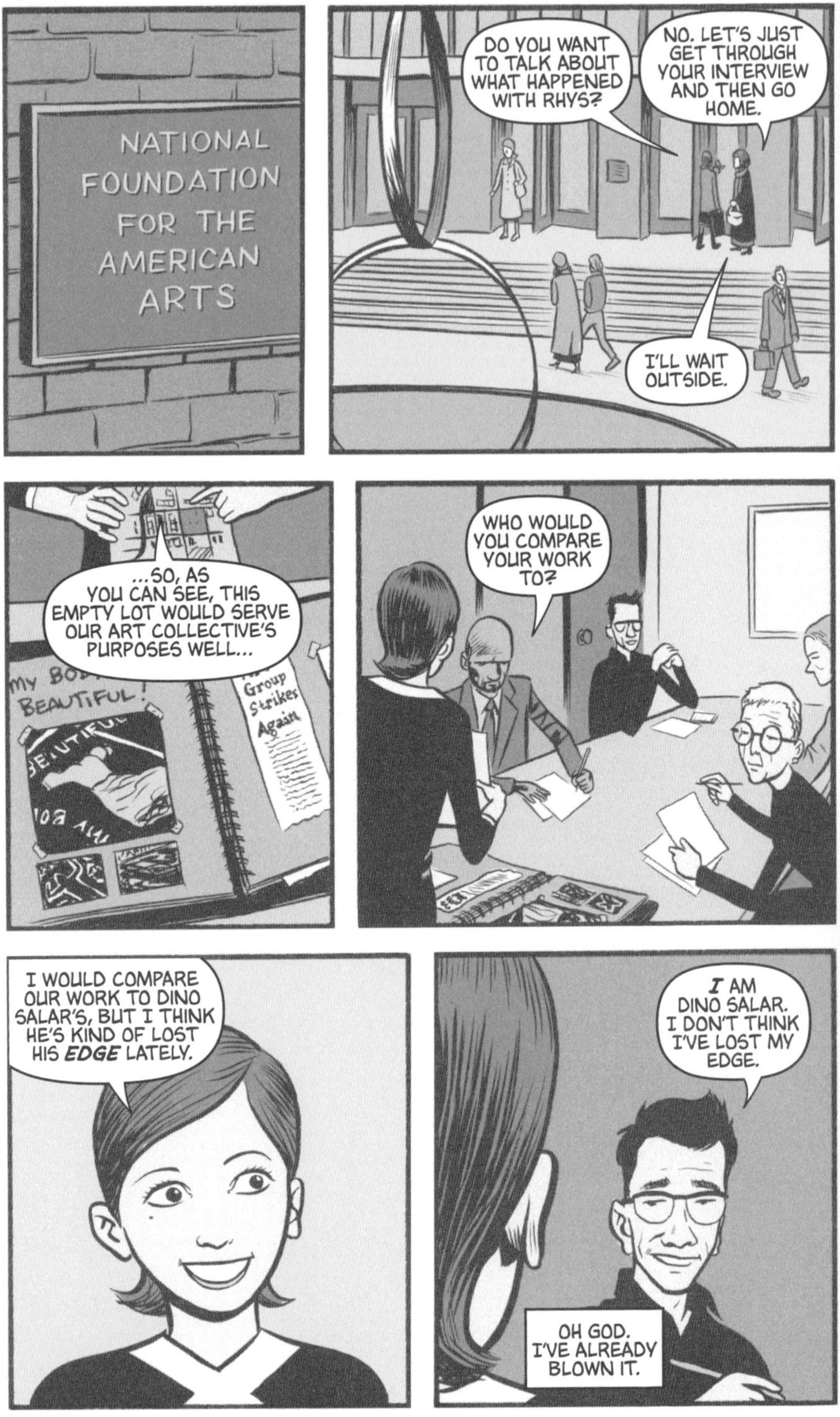
NATIONAL FOUNDATION FOR THE AMERICAN ARTS
DO YOU WANT TO TALK ABOUT WHAT HAPPENED WITH RHYS?
NO. LET'S JUST GET THROUGH YOUR INTERVIEW AND THEN GO HOME.
I'LL WAIT OUTSIDE.
...SO, AS YOU CAN SEE, THIS EMPTY LOT WOULD SERVE OUR ART COLLECTIVE'S PURPOSES WELL...
MY BODY BEAUTIFUL!
Group Strikes Again
WHO WOULD YOU COMPARE YOUR WORK TO?
I WOULD COMPARE OUR WORK TO DINO SALAR'S, BUT I THINK HE'S KIND OF LOST HIS *EDGE* LATELY.
I AM DINO SALAR. I DON'T THINK I'VE LOST MY EDGE.
OH GOD. I'VE ALREADY BLOWN IT.

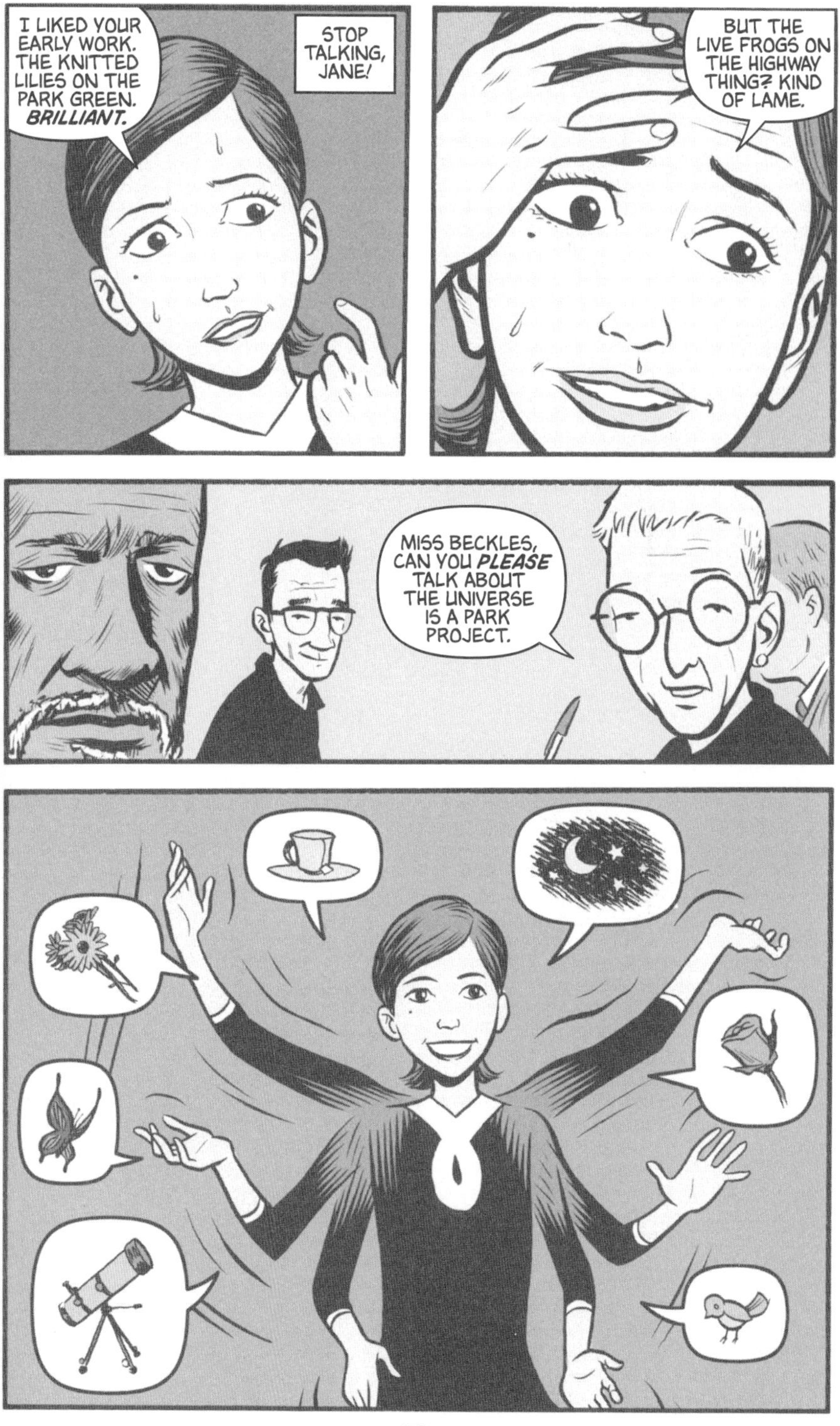
I LIKED YOUR EARLY WORK. THE KNITTED LILIES ON THE PARK GREEN. *BRILLIANT.*
STOP TALKING, JANE!
BUT THE LIVE FROGS ON THE HIGHWAY THING? KIND OF LAME.
MISS BECKLES, CAN YOU *PLEASE* TALK ABOUT THE UNIVERSE IS A PARK PROJECT.

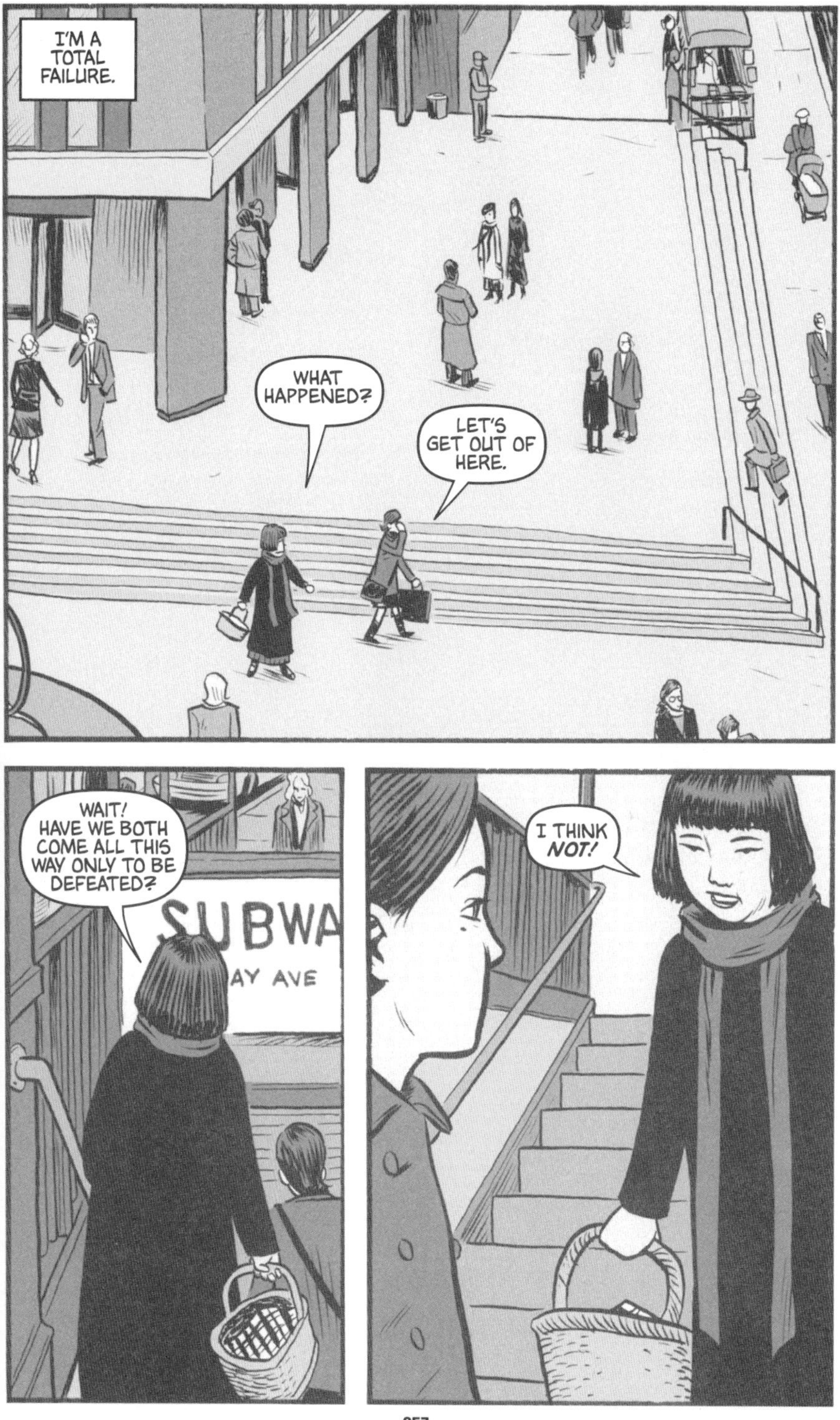
I'M A TOTAL FAILURE.
WHAT HAPPENED?
LET'S GET OUT OF HERE.
WAIT! HAVE WE BOTH COME ALL THIS WAY ONLY TO BE DEFEATED?
SUBWA
AY AVE
I THINK *NOT!*

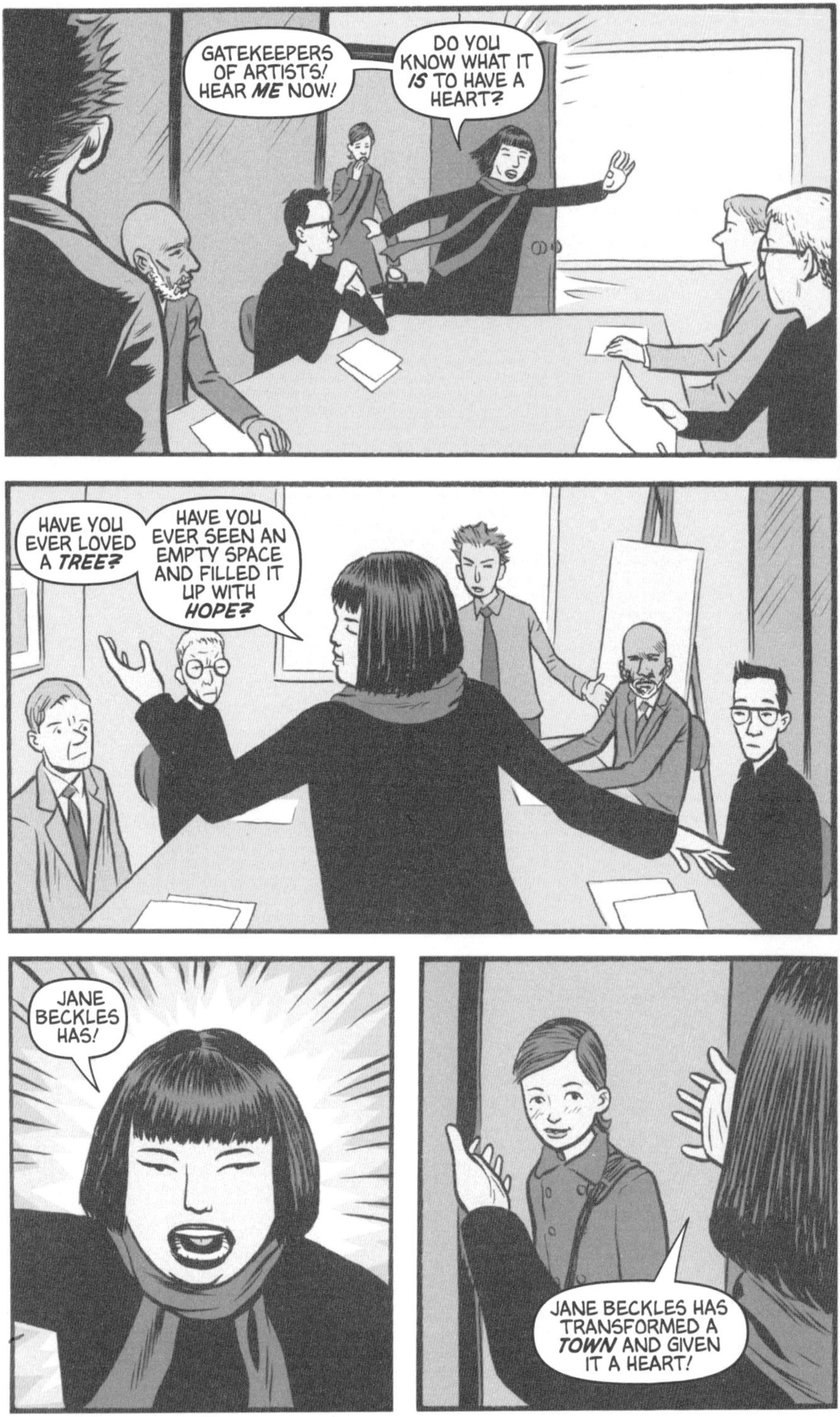
GATEKEEPERS OF ARTISTS! HEAR *ME* NOW!
DO YOU KNOW WHAT IT *IS* TO HAVE A HEART?
HAVE YOU EVER LOVED A *TREE?*
HAVE YOU EVER SEEN AN EMPTY SPACE AND FILLED IT UP WITH *HOPE?*
JANE BECKLES HAS!
JANE BECKLES HAS TRANSFORMED A *TOWN* AND GIVEN IT A HEART!

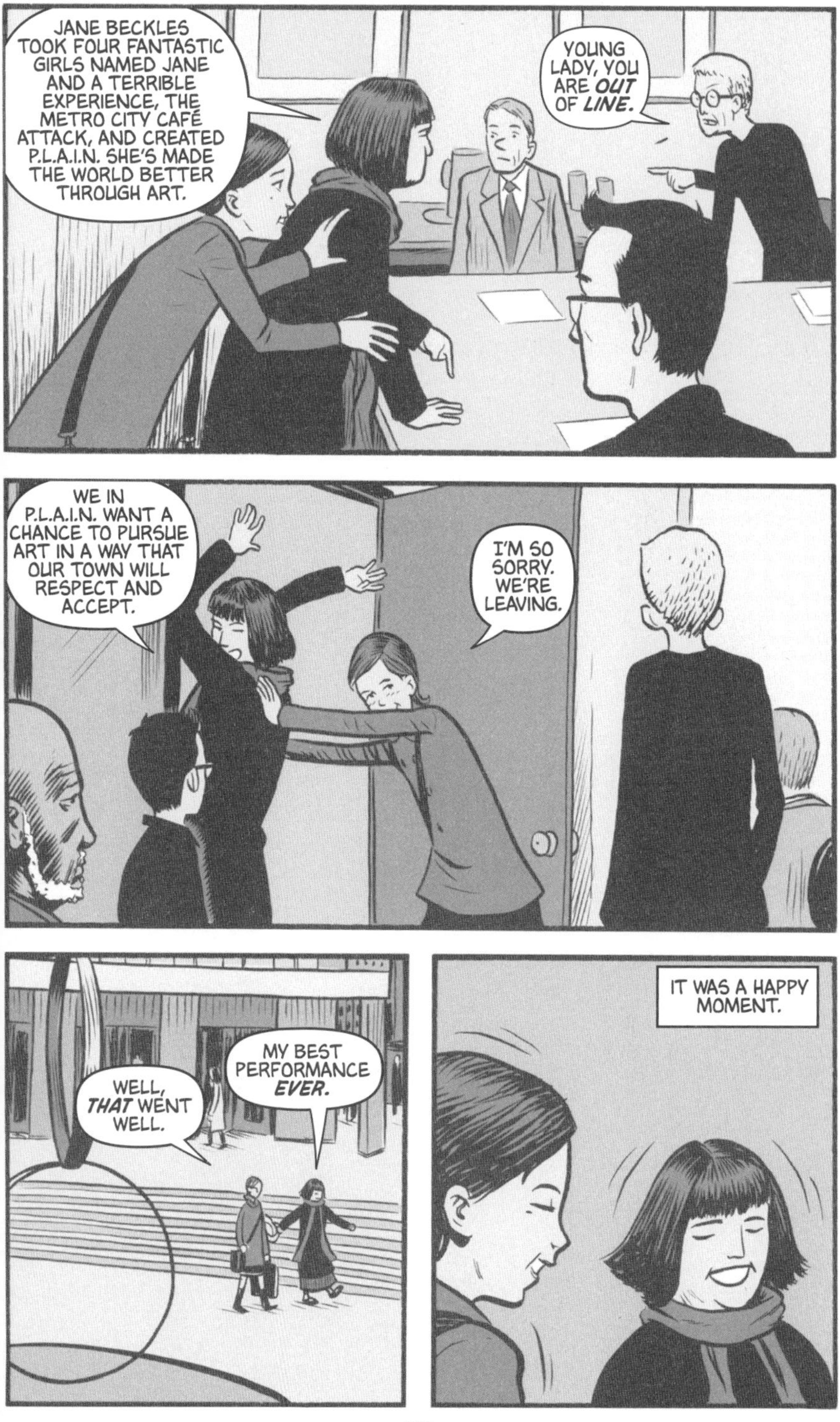
JANE BECKLES TOOK FOUR FANTASTIC GIRLS NAMED JANE AND A TERRIBLE EXPERIENCE, THE METRO CITY CAFÉ ATTACK, AND CREATED P.L.A.I.N. SHE'S MADE THE WORLD BETTER THROUGH ART.
YOUNG LADY, YOU ARE *OUT* OF *LINE*.
WE IN P.L.A.I.N. WANT A CHANCE TO PURSUE ART IN A WAY THAT OUR TOWN WILL RESPECT AND ACCEPT.
I'M SO SORRY. WE'RE LEAVING.
WELL, *THAT* WENT WELL.
MY BEST PERFORMANCE *EVER*.
IT WAS A HAPPY MOMENT.

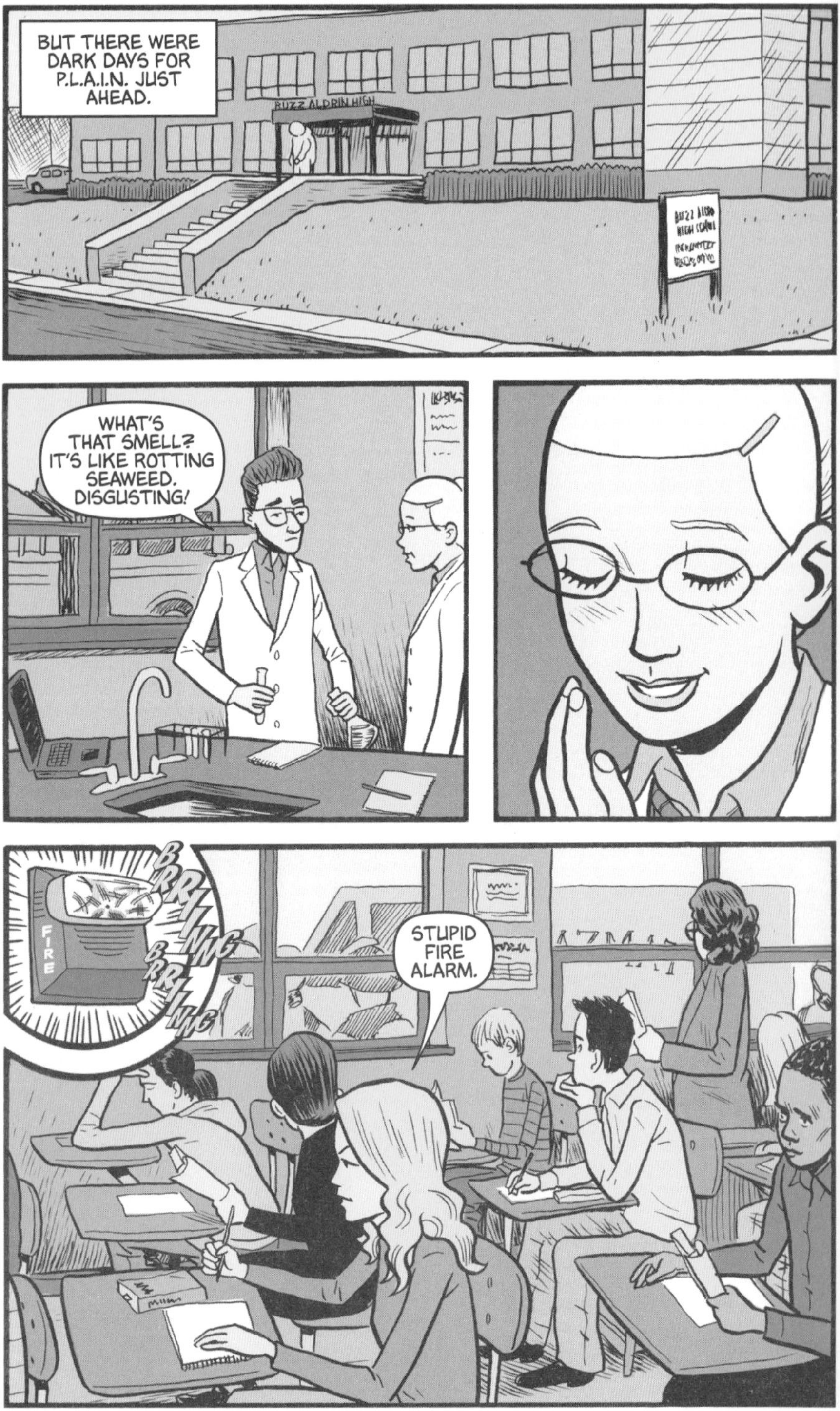
BUT THERE WERE DARK DAYS FOR P.L.A.I.N. JUST AHEAD.
BUZZ ALDRIN HIGH
WHAT'S THAT SMELL? IT'S LIKE ROTTING SEAWEED. DISGUSTING!
FIRE
BRRIING BRRIING
STUPID FIRE ALARM.

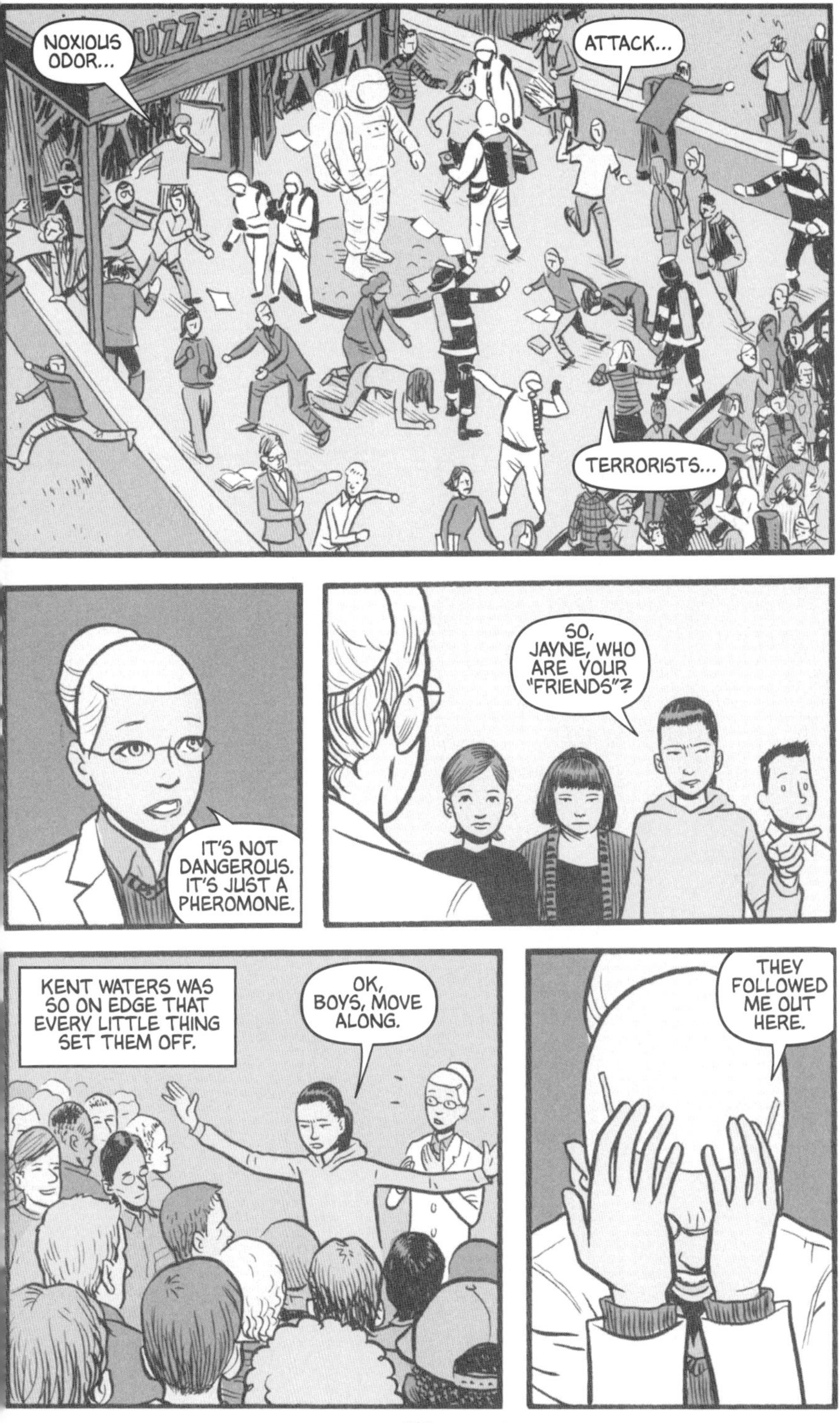
NOXIOUS ODOR...
ATTACK...
TERRORISTS...
IT'S NOT DANGEROUS. IT'S JUST A PHEROMONE.
SO, JAYNE, WHO ARE YOUR "FRIENDS"?
KENT WATERS WAS SO ON EDGE THAT EVERY LITTLE THING SET THEM OFF.
OK, BOYS, MOVE ALONG.
THEY FOLLOWED ME OUT HERE.

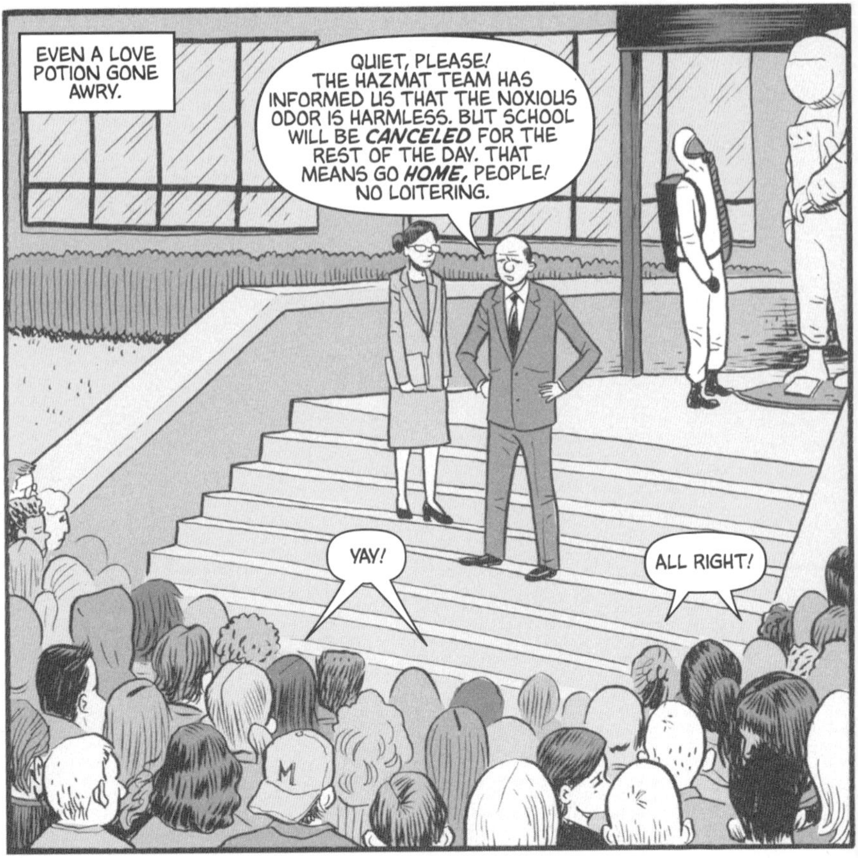
EVEN A LOVE POTION GONE AWRY.
QUIET, PLEASE! THE HAZMAT TEAM HAS INFORMED US THAT THE NOXIOUS ODOR IS HARMLESS. BUT SCHOOL WILL BE *CANCELED* FOR THE REST OF THE DAY. THAT MEANS GO *HOME,* PEOPLE! NO LOITERING.
YAY!
ALL RIGHT!

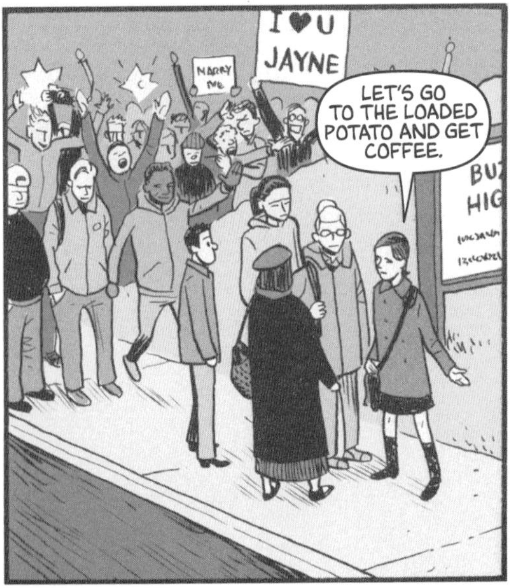
I ♥ U JAYNE
MARRY ME
LET'S GO TO THE LOADED POTATO AND GET COFFEE.

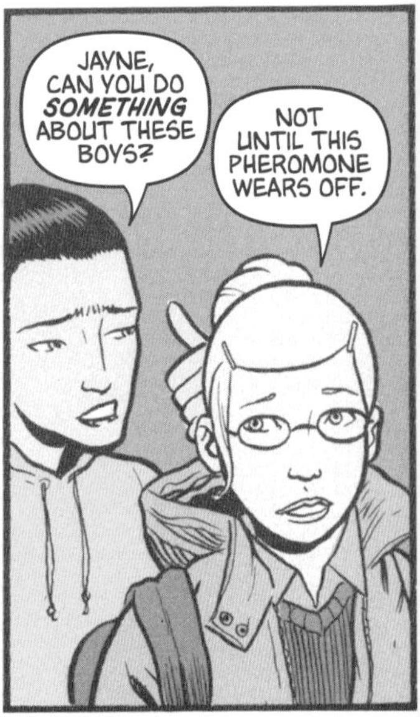
JAYNE, CAN YOU DO *SOMETHING* ABOUT THESE BOYS?
NOT UNTIL THIS PHEROMONE WEARS OFF.

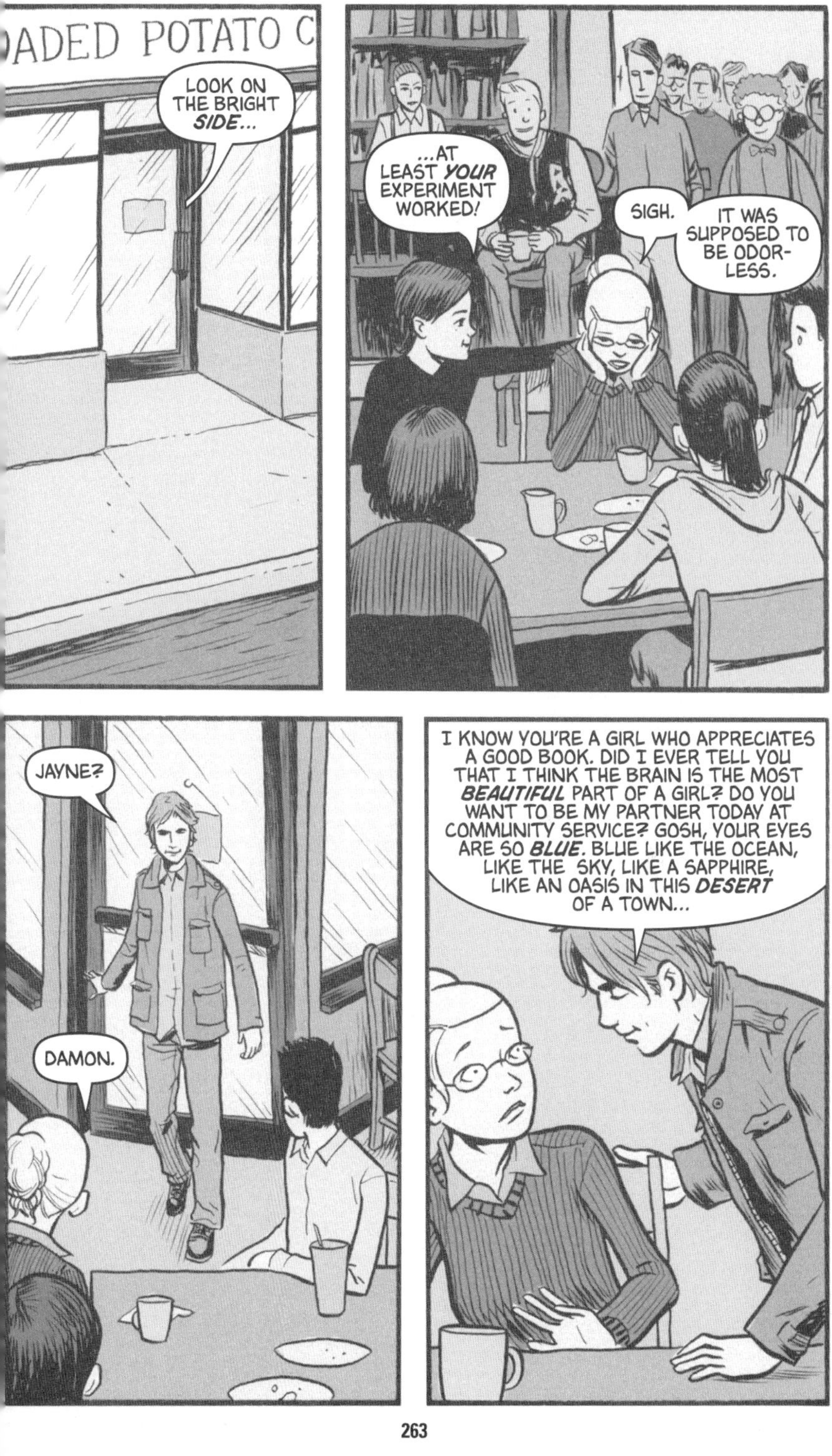

OADED POTATO C
LOOK ON THE BRIGHT SIDE...
...AT LEAST YOUR EXPERIMENT WORKED!
SIGH.
IT WAS SUPPOSED TO BE ODOR-LESS.
JAYNE?
DAMON.
I KNOW YOU'RE A GIRL WHO APPRECIATES A GOOD BOOK. DID I EVER TELL YOU THAT I THINK THE BRAIN IS THE MOST BEAUTIFUL PART OF A GIRL? DO YOU WANT TO BE MY PARTNER TODAY AT COMMUNITY SERVICE? GOSH, YOUR EYES ARE SO BLUE. BLUE LIKE THE OCEAN, LIKE THE SKY, LIKE A SAPPHIRE, LIKE AN OASIS IN THIS DESERT OF A TOWN...

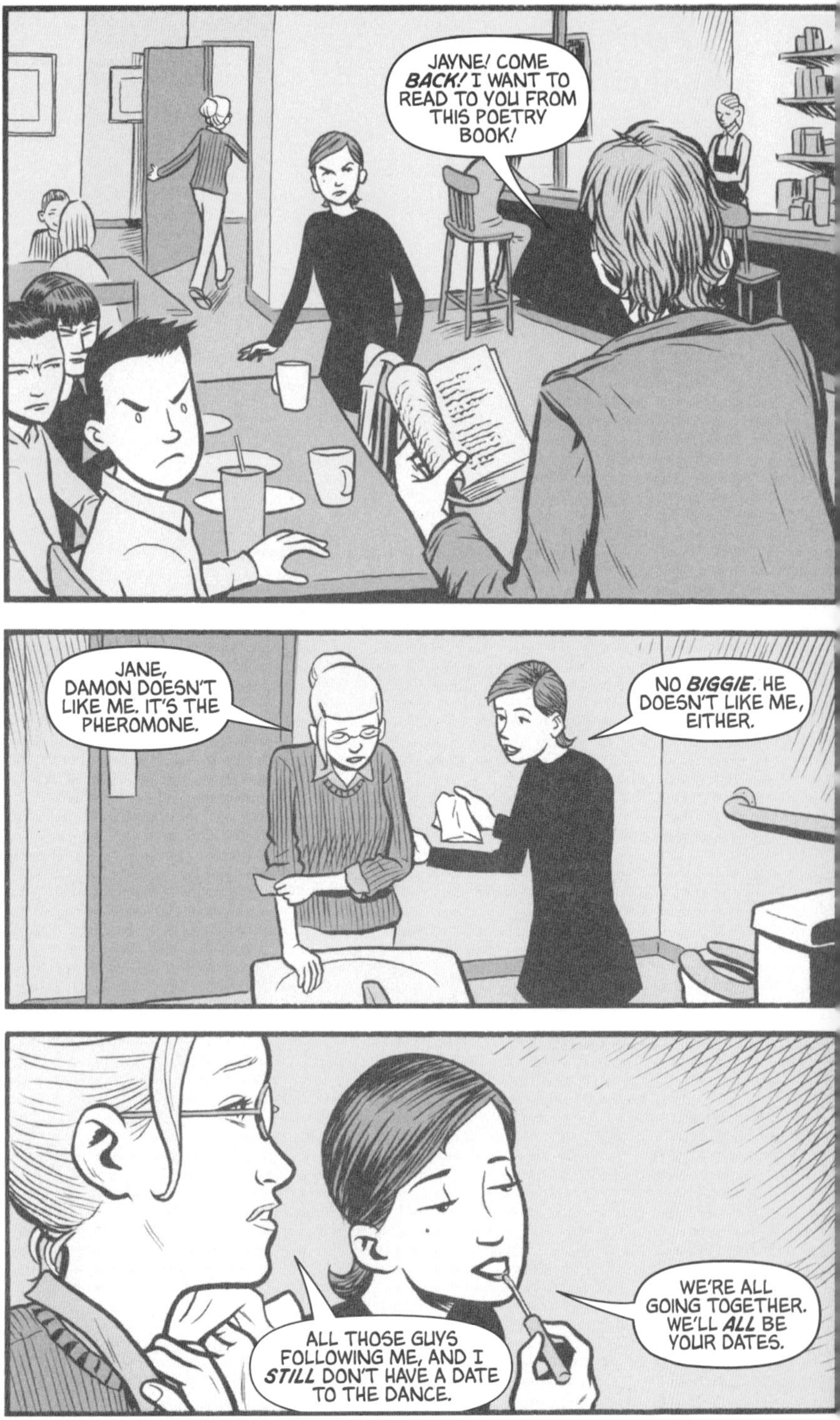
JAYNE! COME *BACK!* I WANT TO READ TO YOU FROM THIS POETRY BOOK!
JANE, DAMON DOESN'T LIKE ME. IT'S THE PHEROMONE.
NO *BIGGIE*. HE DOESN'T LIKE ME, EITHER.
ALL THOSE GUYS FOLLOWING ME, AND I *STILL* DON'T HAVE A DATE TO THE DANCE.
WE'RE ALL GOING TOGETHER. WE'LL *ALL* BE YOUR DATES.

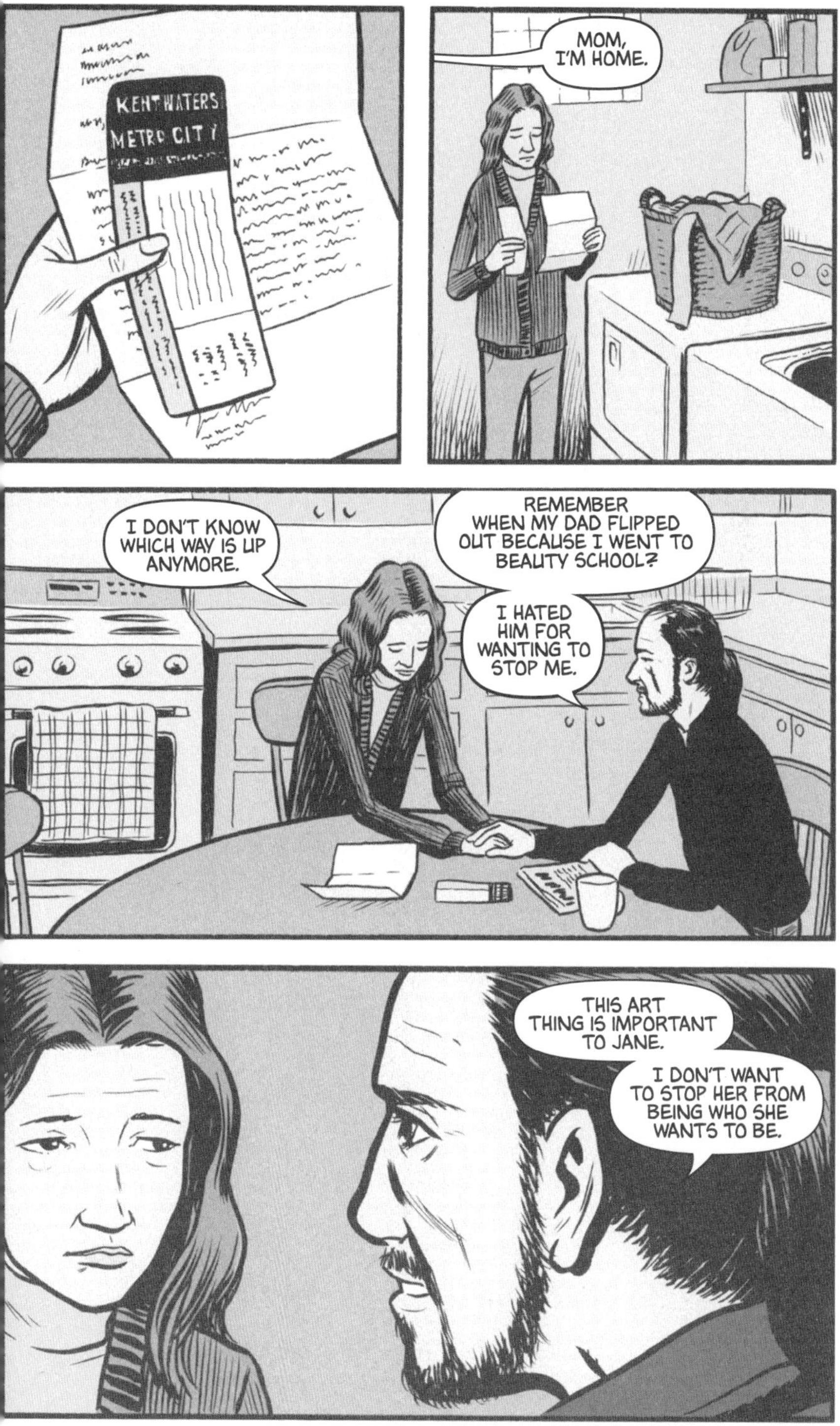
KENT WATERS
METRO CITY
MOM, I'M HOME.
I DON'T KNOW WHICH WAY IS UP ANYMORE.
REMEMBER WHEN MY DAD FLIPPED OUT BECAUSE I WENT TO BEAUTY SCHOOL?
I HATED HIM FOR WANTING TO STOP ME.
THIS ART THING IS IMPORTANT TO JANE.
I DON'T WANT TO STOP HER FROM BEING WHO SHE WANTS TO BE.

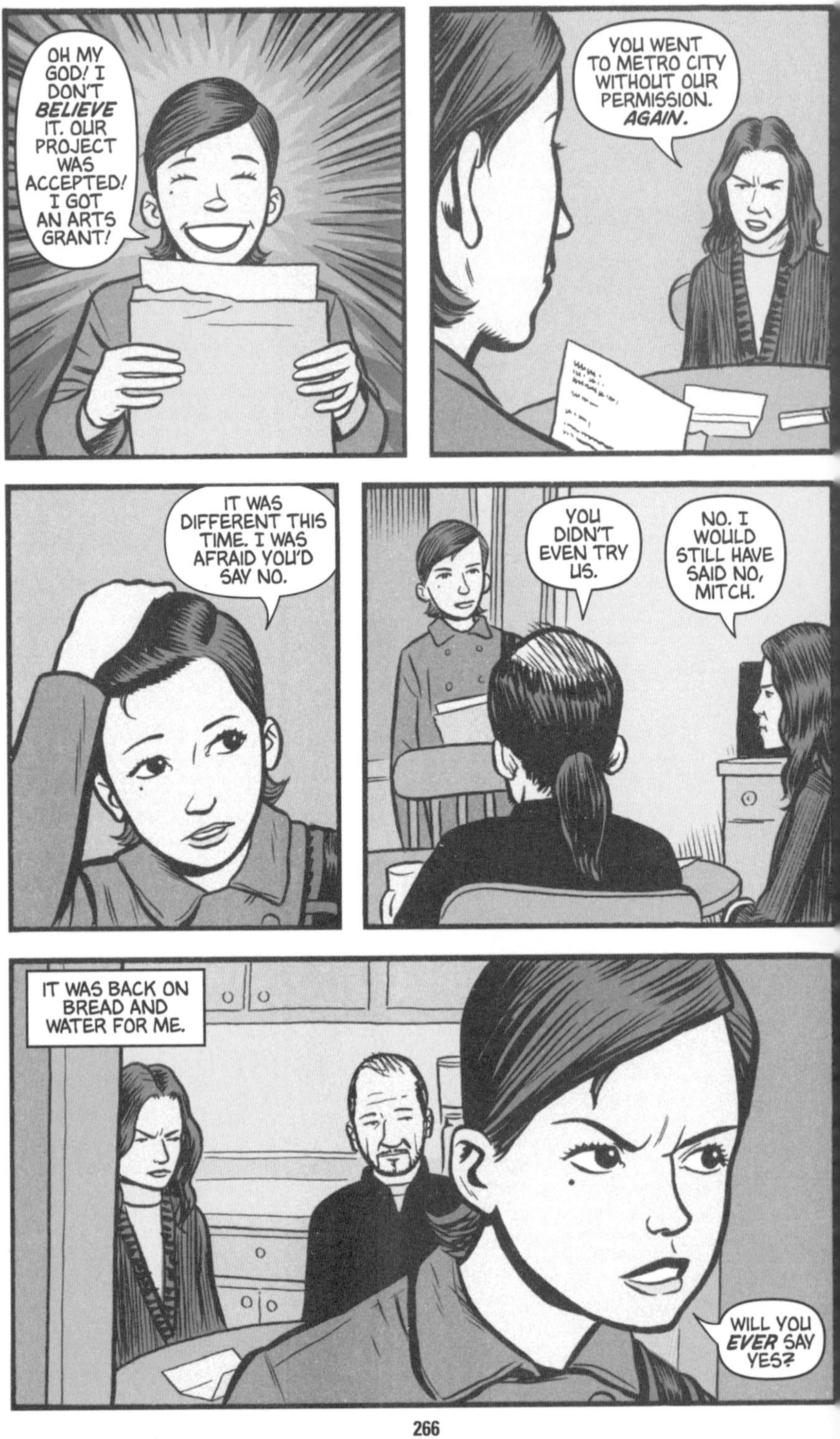
OH MY GOD! I DON'T BELIEVE IT. OUR PROJECT WAS ACCEPTED! I GOT AN ARTS GRANT!
YOU WENT TO METRO CITY WITHOUT OUR PERMISSION. AGAIN.
IT WAS DIFFERENT THIS TIME. I WAS AFRAID YOU'D SAY NO.
YOU DIDN'T EVEN TRY US.
NO. I WOULD STILL HAVE SAID NO, MITCH.
IT WAS BACK ON BREAD AND WATER FOR ME.
WILL YOU EVER SAY YES?

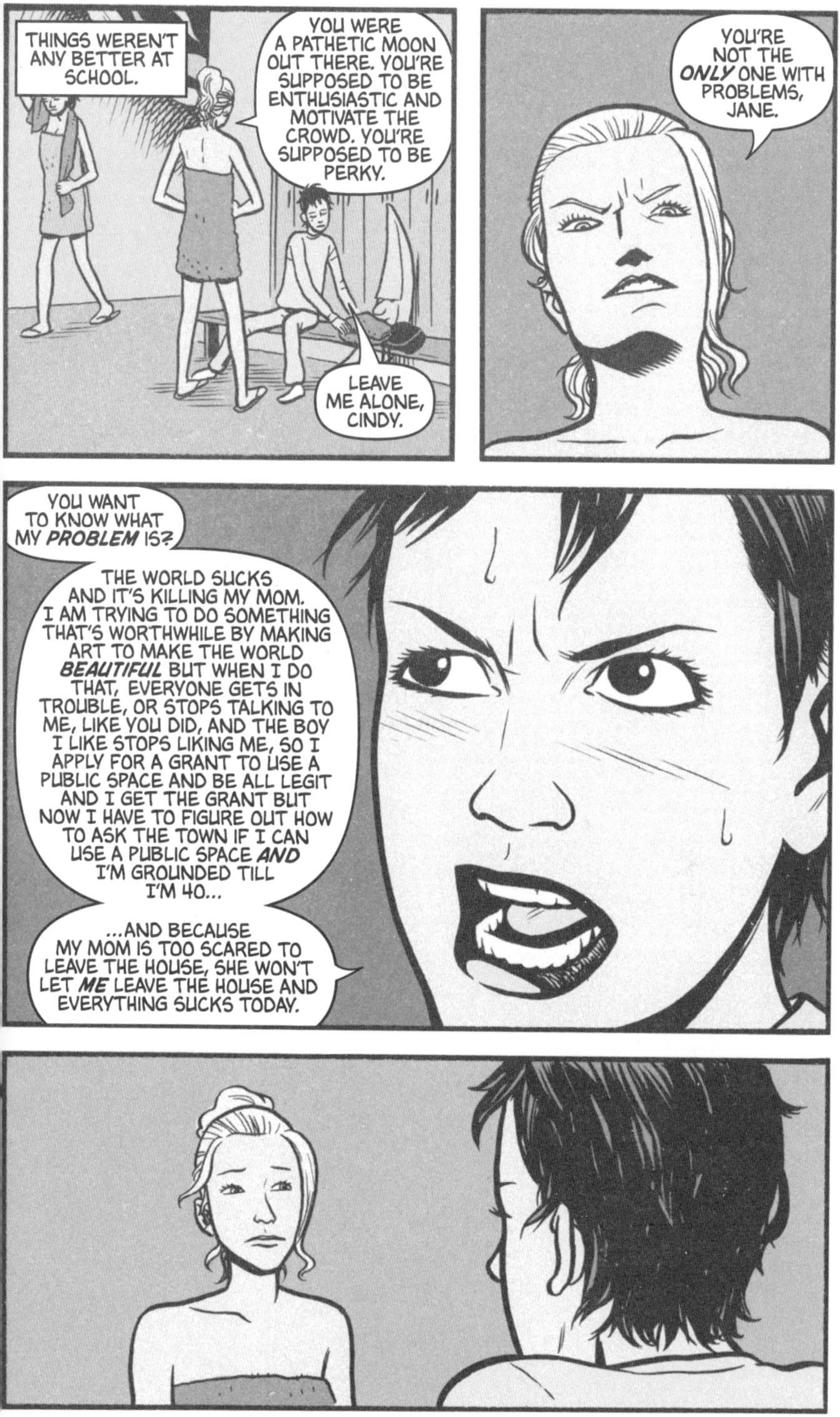
THINGS WEREN'T ANY BETTER AT SCHOOL.
YOU WERE A PATHETIC MOON OUT THERE. YOU'RE SUPPOSED TO BE ENTHUSIASTIC AND MOTIVATE THE CROWD. YOU'RE SUPPOSED TO BE PERKY.
LEAVE ME ALONE, CINDY.
YOU'RE NOT THE *ONLY* ONE WITH PROBLEMS, JANE.
YOU WANT TO KNOW WHAT MY *PROBLEM* IS?
THE WORLD SUCKS AND IT'S KILLING MY MOM. I AM TRYING TO DO SOMETHING THAT'S WORTHWHILE BY MAKING ART TO MAKE THE WORLD *BEAUTIFUL* BUT WHEN I DO THAT, EVERYONE GETS IN TROUBLE, OR STOPS TALKING TO ME, LIKE YOU DID, AND THE BOY I LIKE STOPS LIKING ME, SO I APPLY FOR A GRANT TO USE A PUBLIC SPACE AND BE ALL LEGIT AND I GET THE GRANT BUT NOW I HAVE TO FIGURE OUT HOW TO ASK THE TOWN IF I CAN USE A PUBLIC SPACE *AND* I'M GROUNDED TILL I'M 40...
...AND BECAUSE MY MOM IS TOO SCARED TO LEAVE THE HOUSE, SHE WON'T LET *ME* LEAVE THE HOUSE AND EVERYTHING SUCKS TODAY.

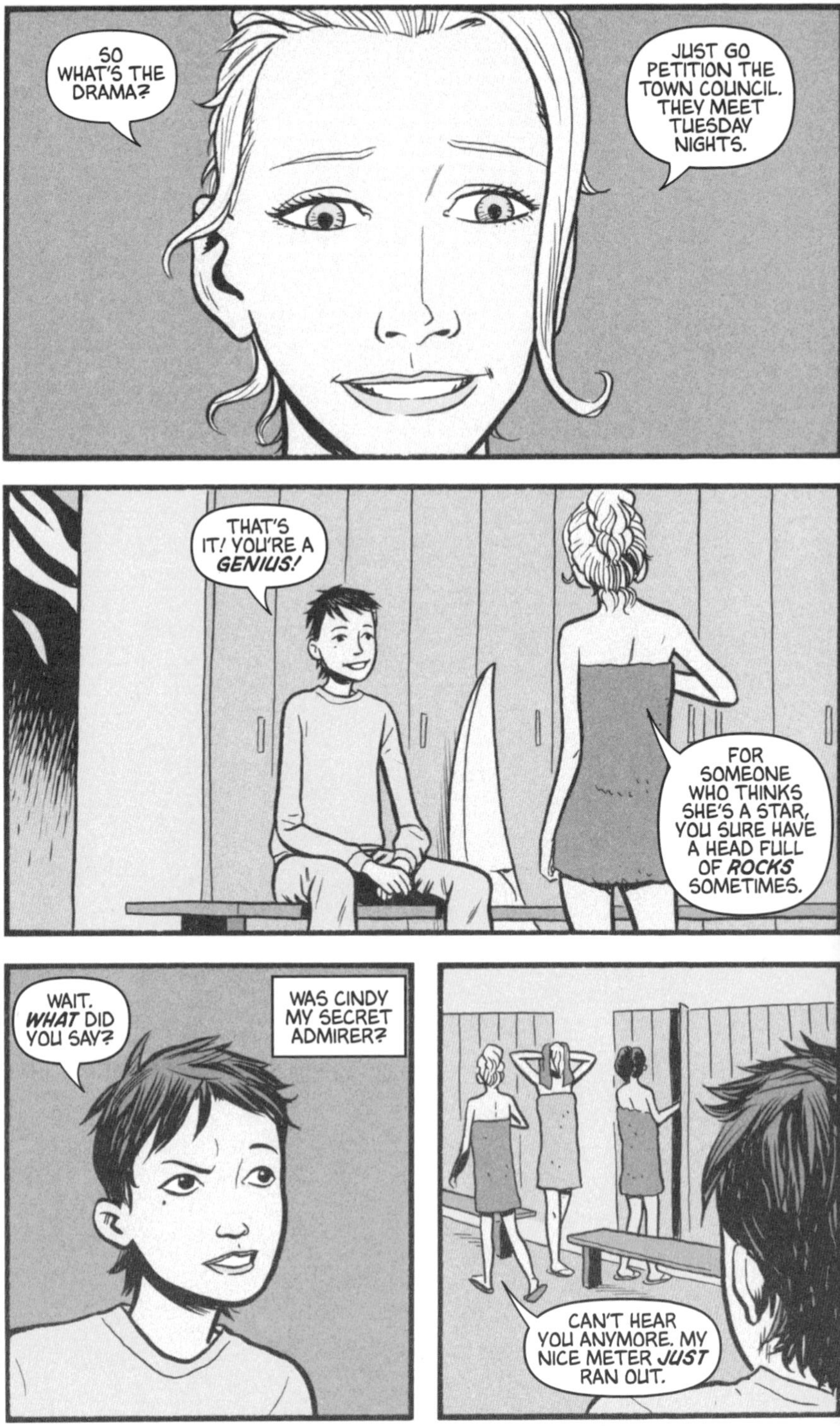

SO WHAT'S THE DRAMA?
JUST GO PETITION THE TOWN COUNCIL. THEY MEET TUESDAY NIGHTS.
THAT'S IT! YOU'RE A *GENIUS!*
FOR SOMEONE WHO THINKS SHE'S A STAR, YOU SURE HAVE A HEAD FULL OF *ROCKS* SOMETIMES.
WAIT. *WHAT* DID YOU SAY?
WAS CINDY MY SECRET ADMIRER?
CAN'T HEAR YOU ANYMORE. MY NICE METER *JUST* RAN OUT.

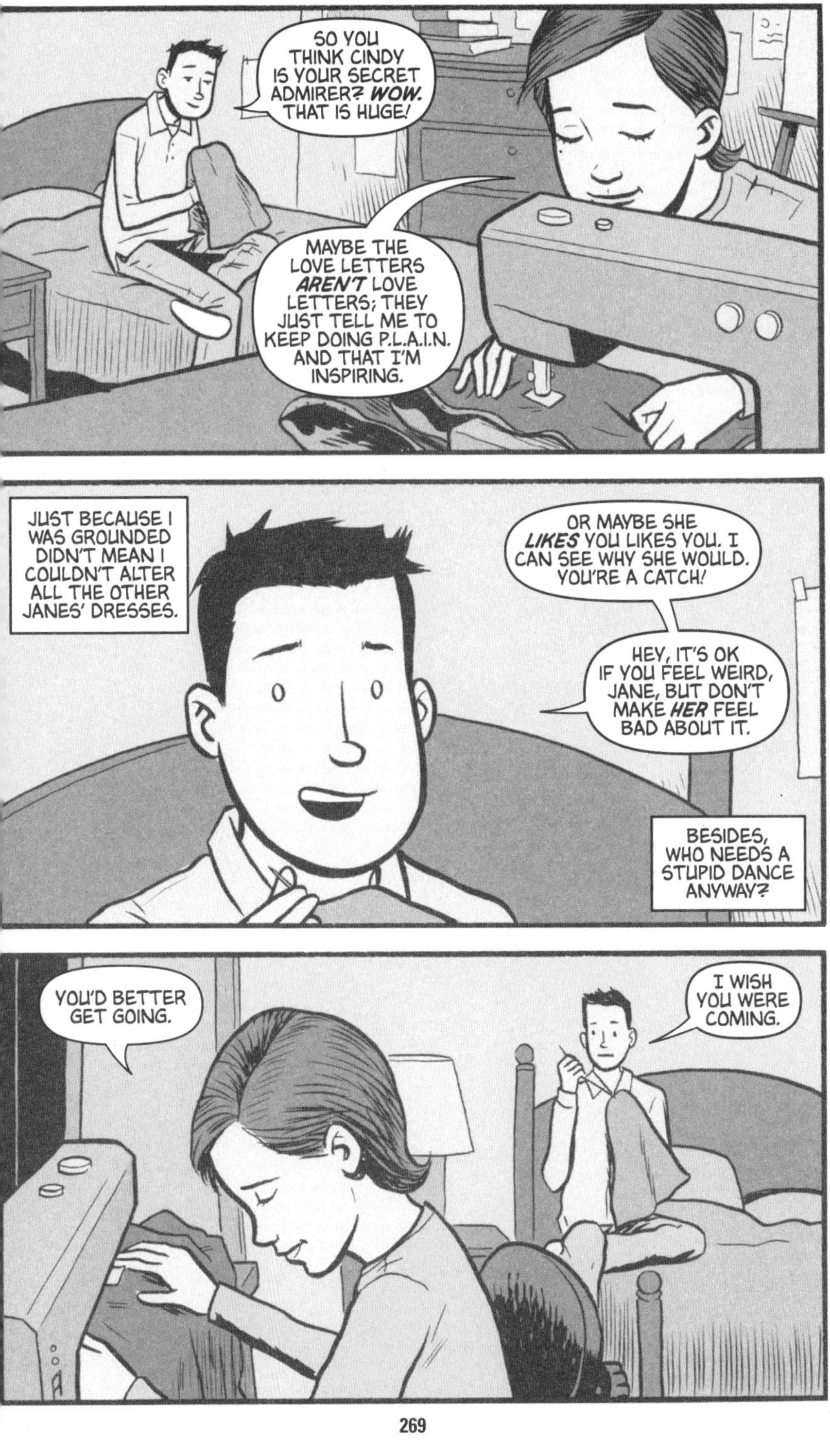
SO YOU THINK CINDY IS YOUR SECRET ADMIRER? WOW. THAT IS HUGE!
MAYBE THE LOVE LETTERS AREN'T LOVE LETTERS; THEY JUST TELL ME TO KEEP DOING P.L.A.I.N. AND THAT I'M INSPIRING.
JUST BECAUSE I WAS GROUNDED DIDN'T MEAN I COULDN'T ALTER ALL THE OTHER JANES' DRESSES.
OR MAYBE SHE LIKES YOU LIKES YOU. I CAN SEE WHY SHE WOULD. YOU'RE A CATCH!
HEY, IT'S OK IF YOU FEEL WEIRD, JANE, BUT DON'T MAKE HER FEEL BAD ABOUT IT.
BESIDES, WHO NEEDS A STUPID DANCE ANYWAY?
YOU'D BETTER GET GOING.
I WISH YOU WERE COMING.

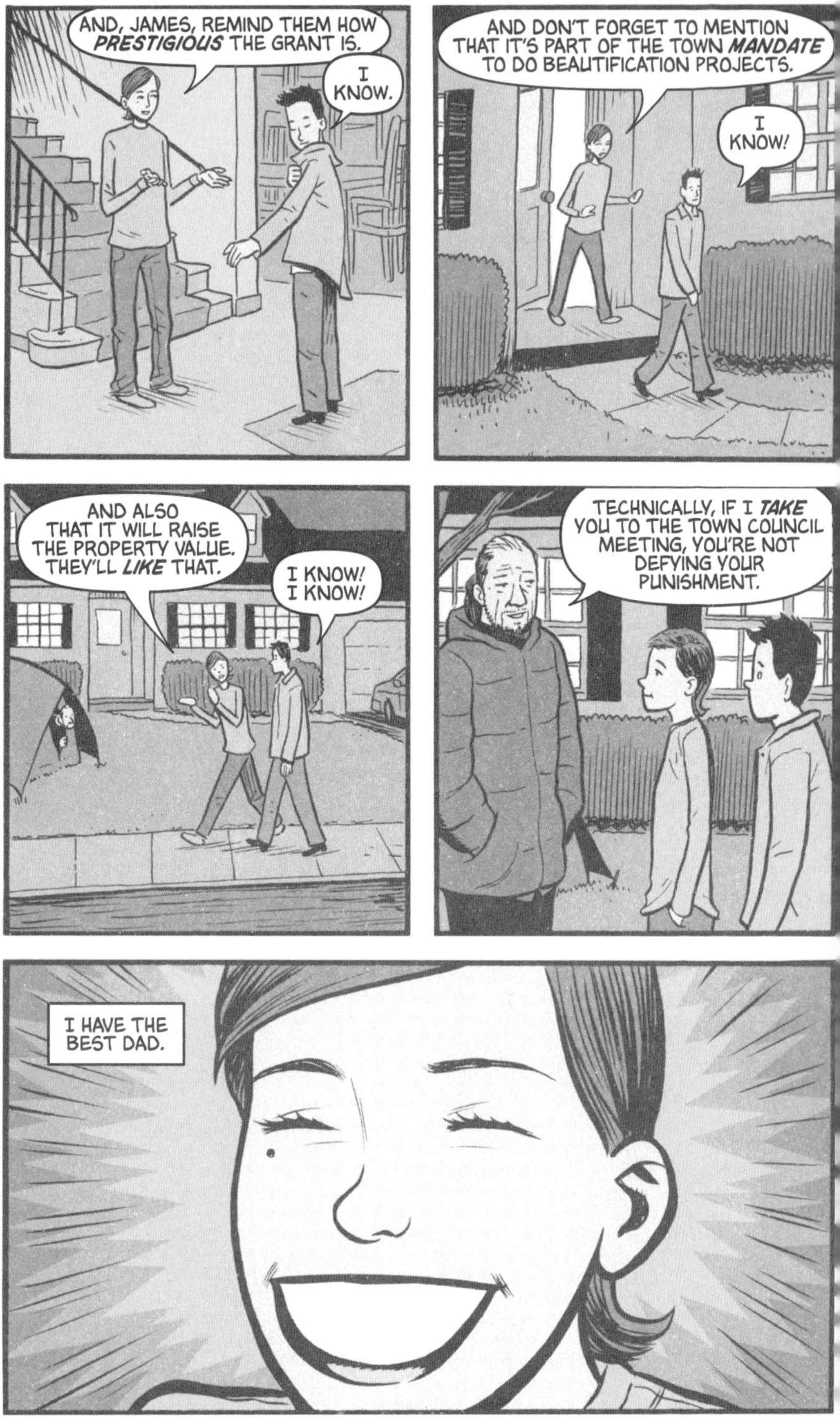
AND, JAMES, REMIND THEM HOW PRESTIGIOUS THE GRANT IS.
I KNOW.
AND DON'T FORGET TO MENTION THAT IT'S PART OF THE TOWN MANDATE TO DO BEAUTIFICATION PROJECTS.
I KNOW!
AND ALSO THAT IT WILL RAISE THE PROPERTY VALUE. THEY'LL LIKE THAT.
I KNOW! I KNOW!
TECHNICALLY, IF I TAKE YOU TO THE TOWN COUNCIL MEETING, YOU'RE NOT DEFYING YOUR PUNISHMENT.
I HAVE THE BEST DAD.

272

273

It's amazing how your parents can totally come through for you when they can see how hard you're working for something.

No parent wants to see their kid lose the good fight.

I FOUND US ALL TRENCH COATS. THE SIZES MIGHT BE A LITTLE WONKY BUT THEY'LL DO.

I'LL TELL YOU HOW IT GOES.

Love, Jane

DO I *REALLY* HAVE TO WEAR THIS?

IF YOU STILL WANT TO DATE ME, YOU DO.

ALL RIGHT, THEN.

I'LL TAKE CARE OF THE D.J. HE'S ON STAGE CREW WITH ME.

SO COATS ON UNTIL THE SONG COMES ON. THEN WE DO IT.

THIS IS GOING TO BE THE BEST *DANCE* EVER.

281

282

283

284

285

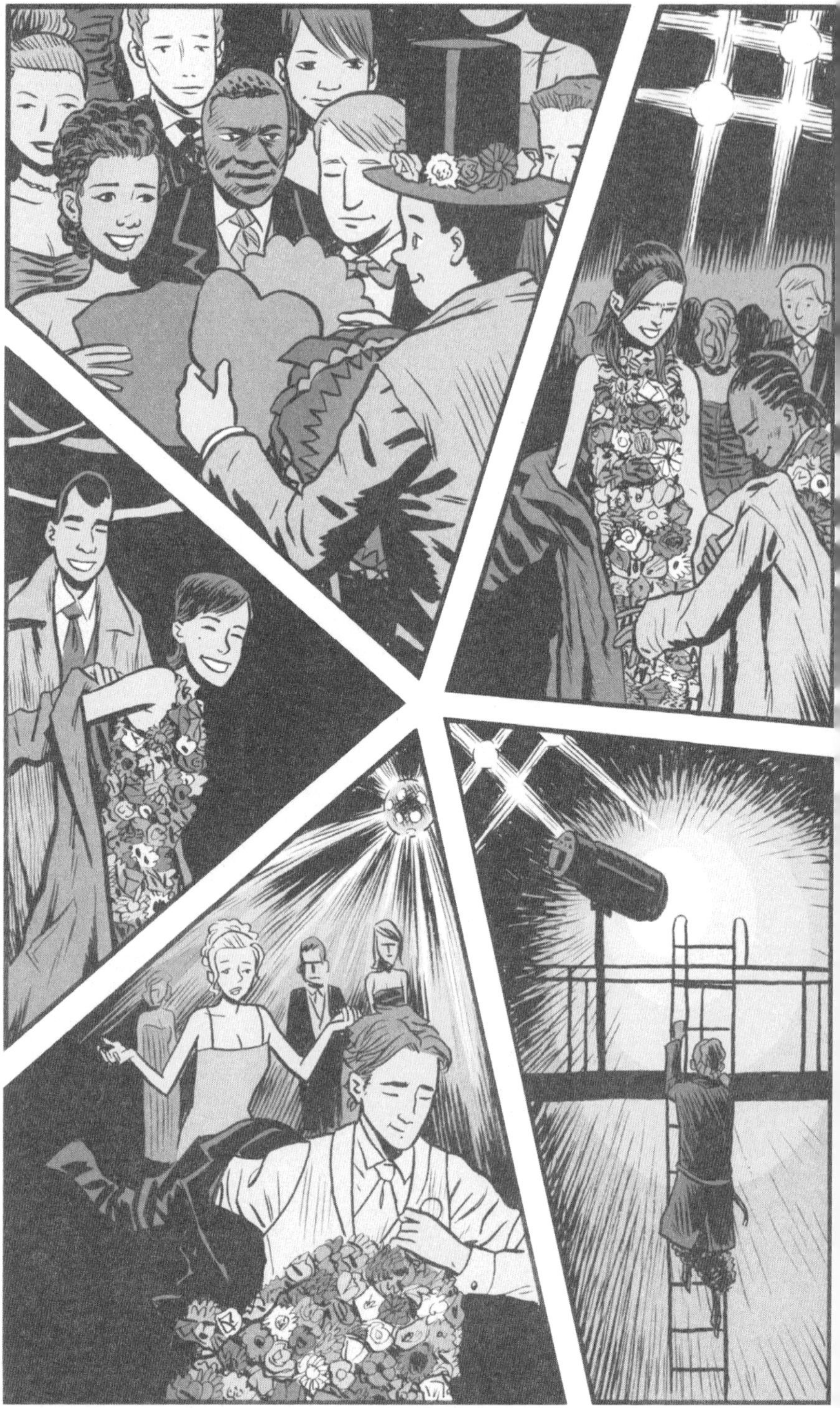

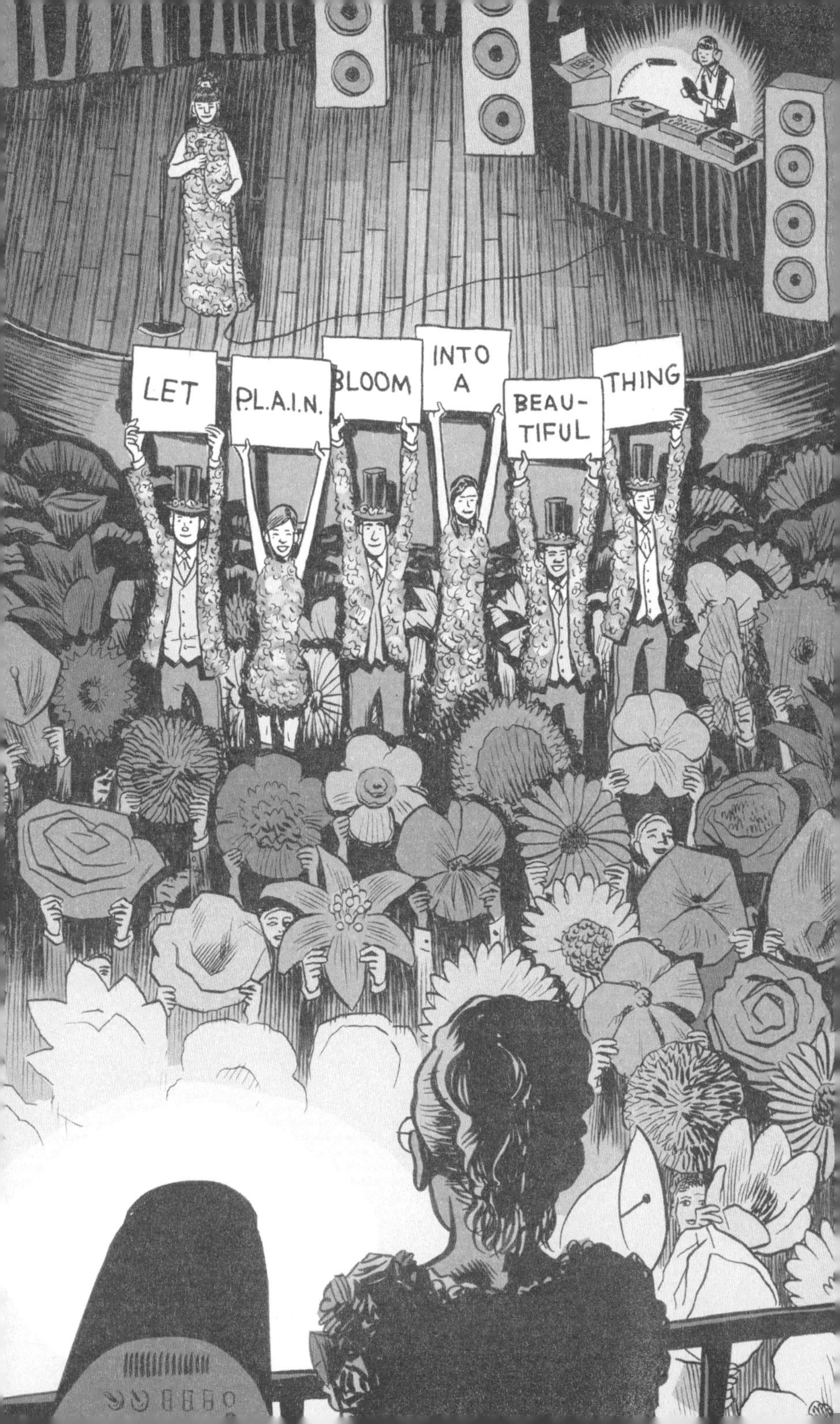
LET
P.L.A.I.N.
BLOOM
INTO
A
BEAU-
TIFUL
THING

289

290

291

293

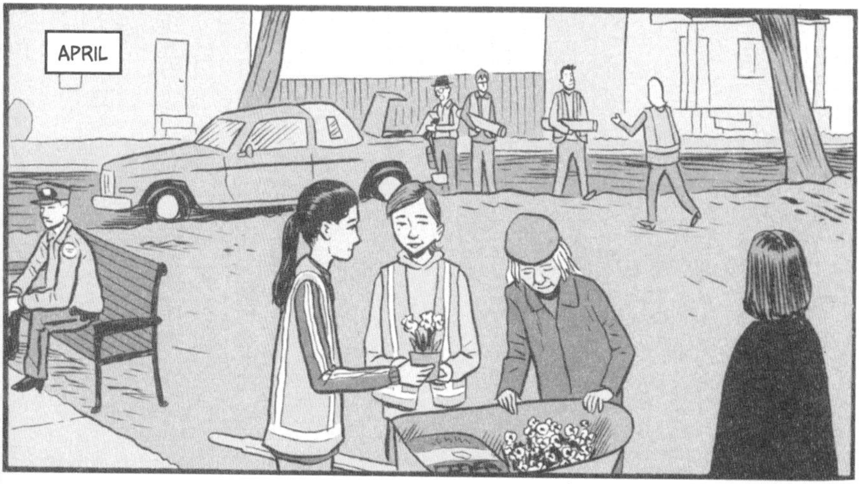
APRIL

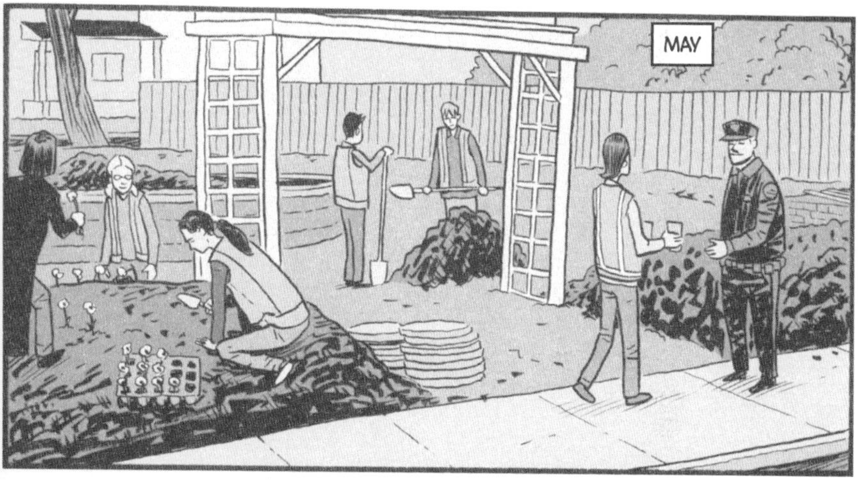
MAY

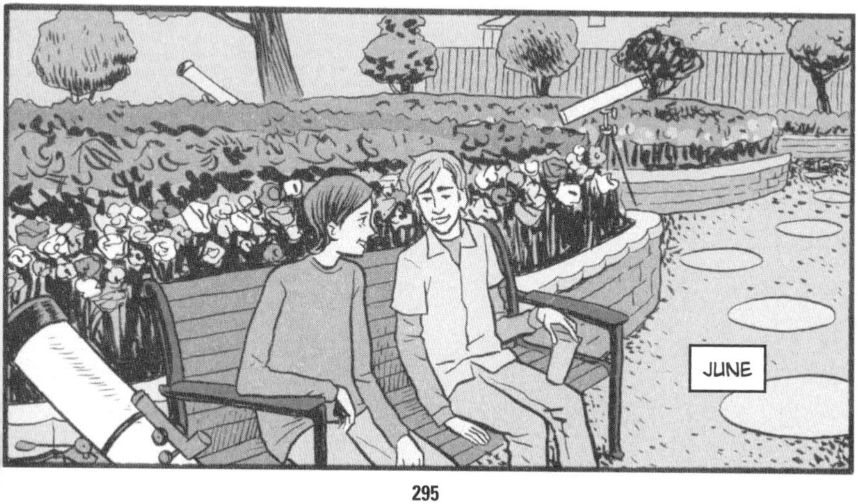
JUNE

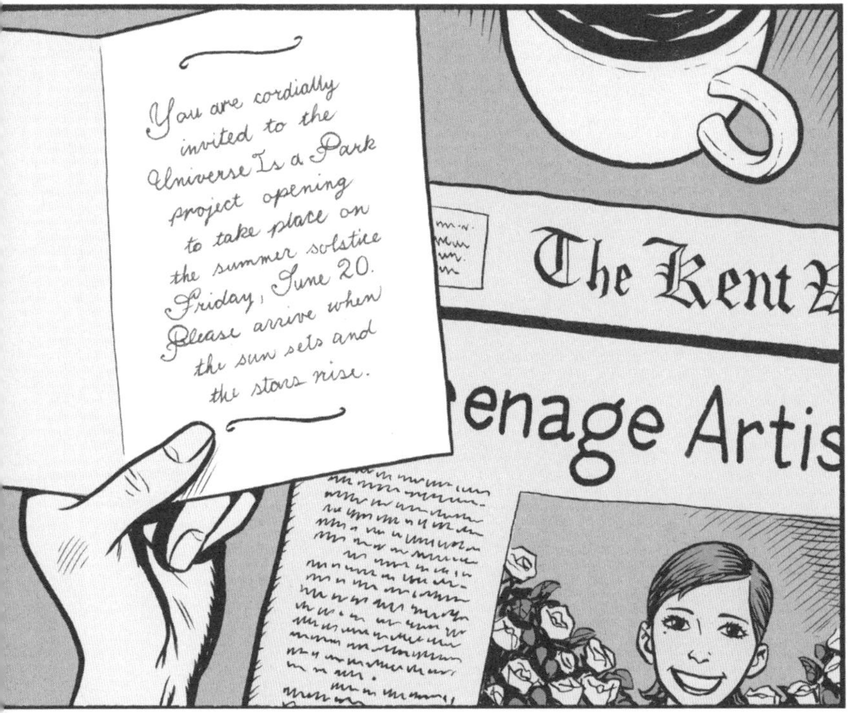
You are cordially invited to the Universe Is a Park project opening to take place on the summer solstice Friday, June 20. Please arrive when the sun sets and the stars rise.
The Kent
enage Artis

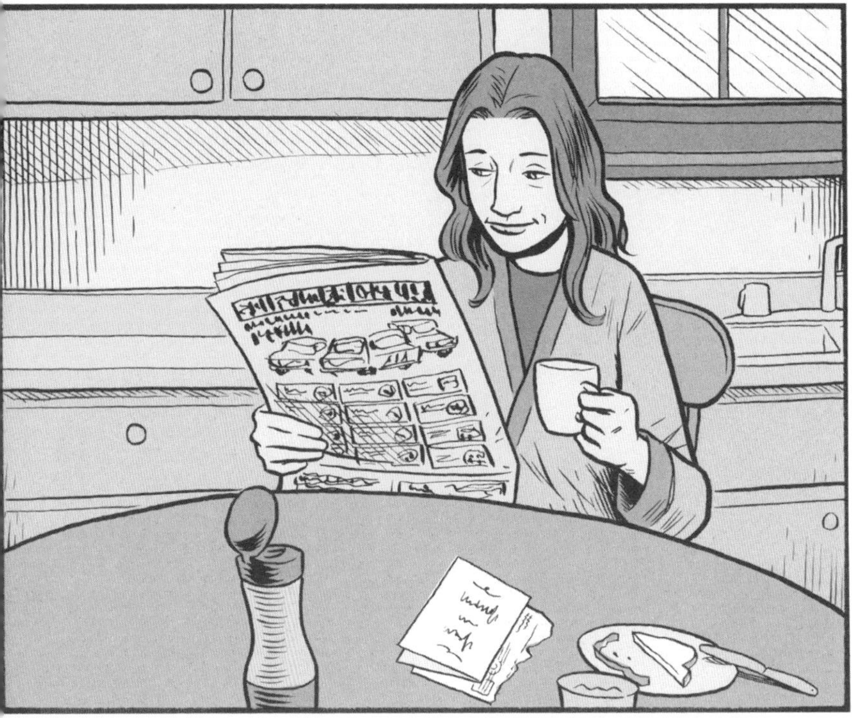

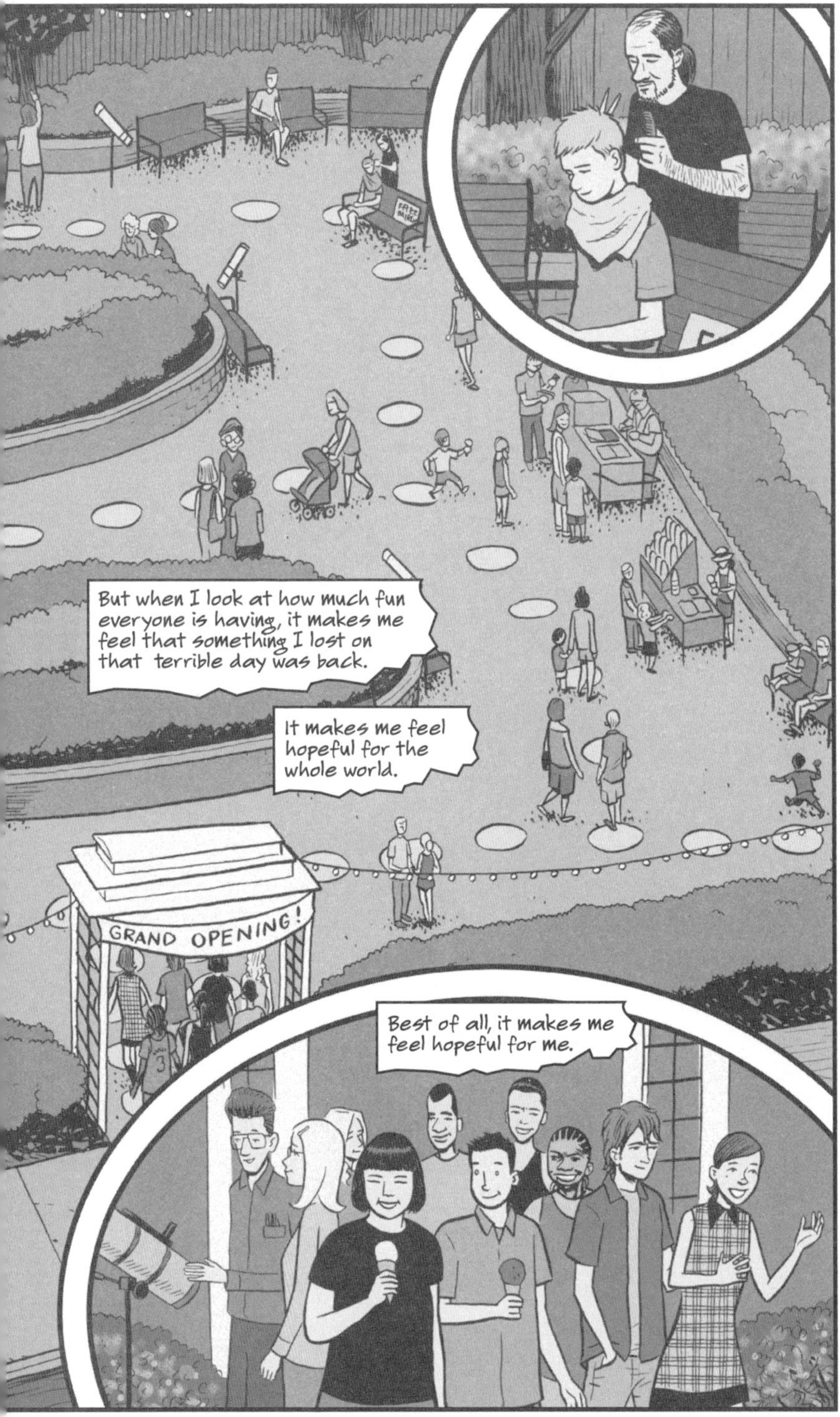
But when I look at how much fun everyone is having, it makes me feel that something I lost on that terrible day was back.
It makes me feel hopeful for the whole world.
GRAND OPENING!
Best of all, it makes me feel hopeful for me.

300

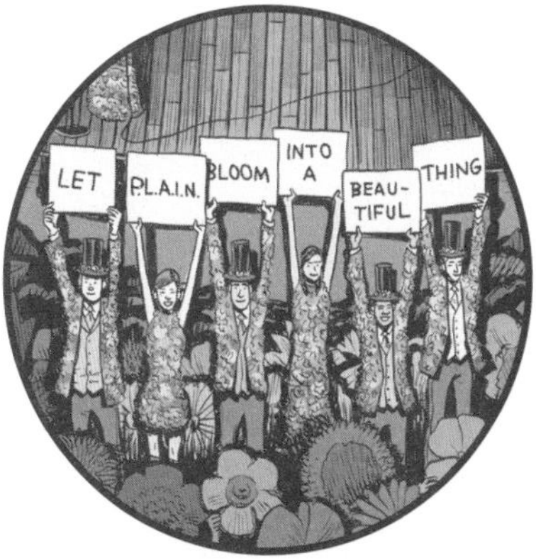
LET
P.L.A.I.N.
BLOOM
INTO A
BEAU-TIFUL
THING

The Evolution of a Graphic Novel
Step 1: The Manuscript

JANES IN LOVE – pgs 1 -40   3/12/07
Writer: Cecil Castellucci

CAPTION: Dear Miroslaw,

Making Art is a like my love letter to the everyone.

Panel 2

Long and skinny, we see that there are the puppets hanging beautifully from street lamps along the street.   A sign taped to the pole. There are many of us. We're PLAINly here to stay.

CAPTION: This is my world. I know it's not Metro City.   But that doesn't mean I can't make Kent Waters interesting.

Panel 3

Jane is in bed she's smiling. One of the marionettes she's saved, is hanging above her or maybe it's on the night table next to her.

CAPTION: I want to make it as surprisingly beautiful as possible.

It's still worth the effort.

Don't you think?

Panel 4

Jane is outside of her parents salon on her way to school, she's waving goodbye.   Her dad is looking up at one of the marionettes. He's smiling. Jane's Mom is in the window of the store hanging up a poster that says "New Salon Rules for Valentines Day Season: If you've just broken up with your boyfriend / girlfriend / significant other we will NOT CUT your hair."

CAPTION: Art is no trouble at all.

Love, Jane

| Page 6 |

Panel 1

Jane outside of Buzz Aldrin as all the kids are spilling into the building. It's the first week of January.   Pretty much, I think here, we should see each of the Jane's sort of standing together looking sadly at all of their crushes. (James has no crush, poor guy. He's bummed about that.) So, that is Isaac, Melvin, Damon. Theater Jane is holding up a postcard from Rhys (from a Midsummer nights dream).
This should be the biggest panel on the page. It's also still winter.

JANES IN LOVE – pgs 1 -40   3/12/07
Writer: Cecil Castellucci

CAPTION: It's a brand new year.   That always means just one thing.   Valentines day is
coming up.

Everyone's hearts is on their sleeves.

Panel 2

Theater Jane is taking up the center stage. She's very excited. Polly Jane is probably,
like eating.

THEATER JANE: Janes! I've had a note! In February Rhys is going to be in
Midsummer Nights Dream in Metro City in an off off off Grandway Theater!!

POLLY JANE: So what?

Panel 3

Close up of Theater Jane. She's kind of swooning. She's in the romantic theatrical zone.

THEATER JANE: Wouldn't it be romantic to surprise him and go to the city to see him
in the show?

Panel 4

Polly Jane is rolling her eyes. She is standing next to Jane. Who is having romantic
thoughts of her own.

CAPTION: I'd like to surprise a boy.

Go to Poland.   Meet Miroslaw.

Or down the street. Hang out with Damon.

Panel 5

Back to Brain Jayne. She's being as scientifically romantic as she can. Of course James
is very interested in boys. Theater boys.

BRAIN JAYNE: Oh that would be romantic.

JAMES: Does Rhys have any cute friends?

Panel 6

On our Jane again.

Step 2: Thumbnail Sketches

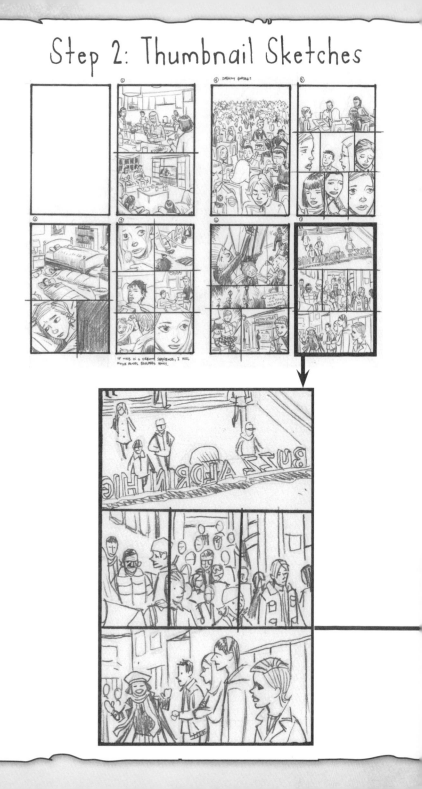

Step 3: Inked Sketches

Step 4: Final Art

Original Cover Sketches for *Janes in Love*

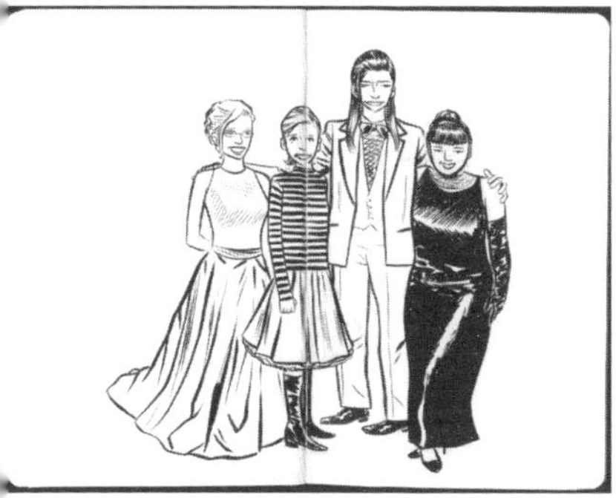

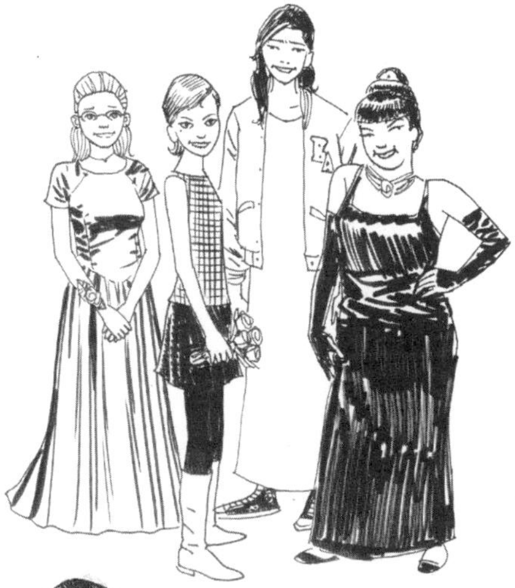

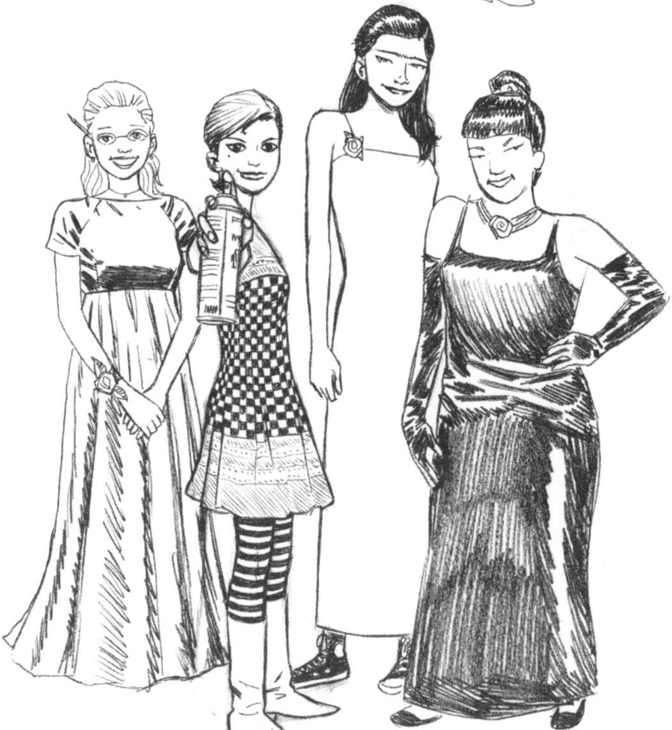

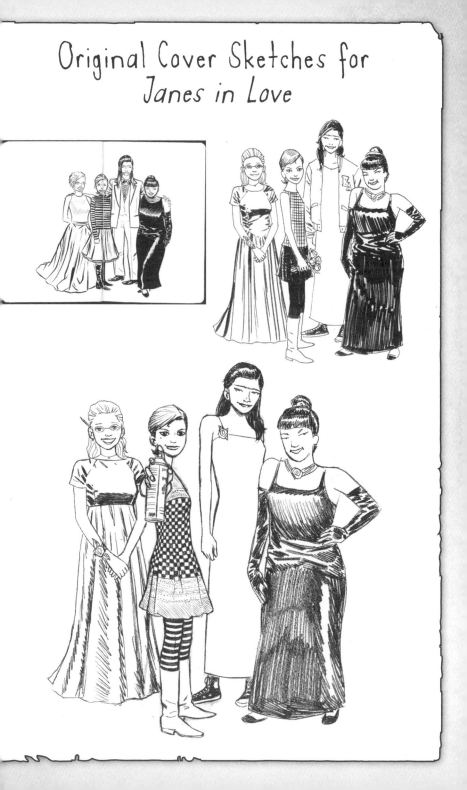

Cover Options

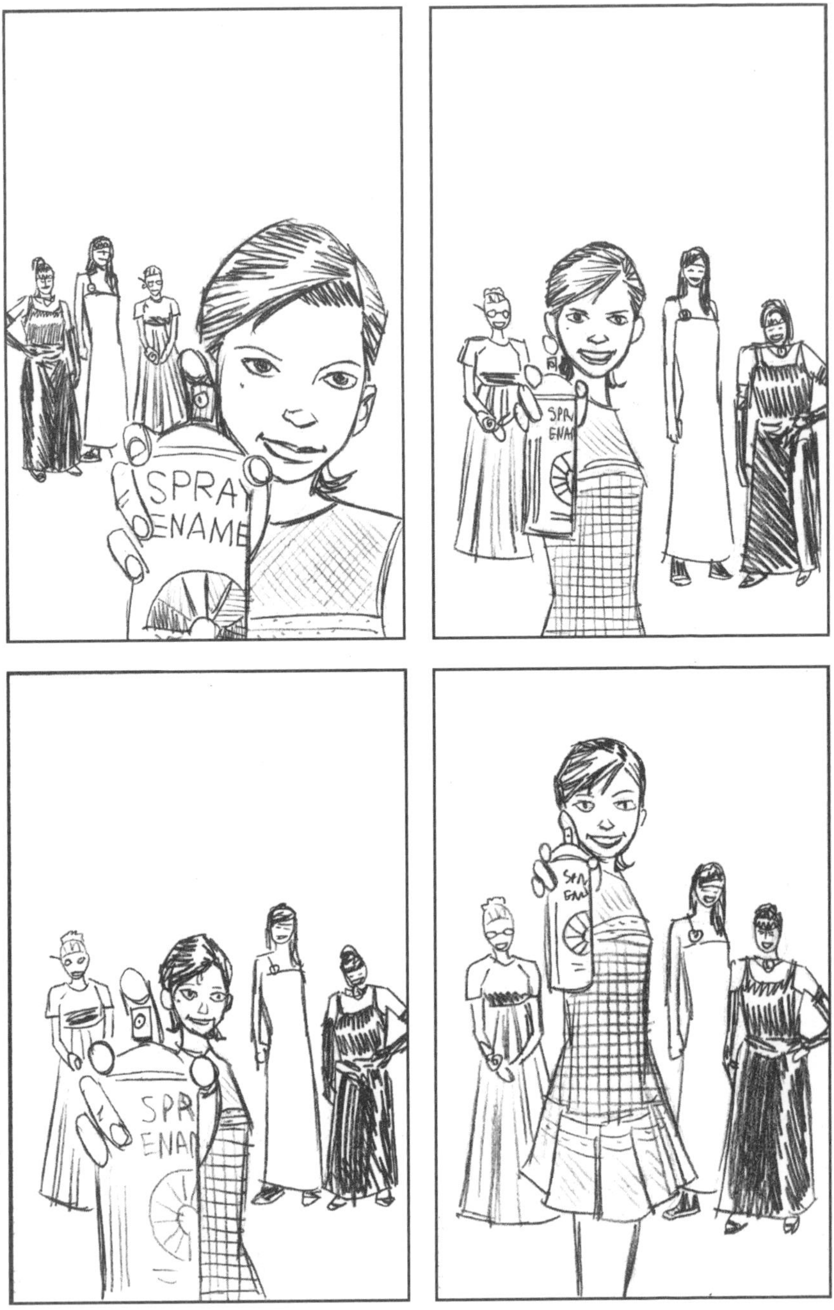
SPRA
ENAME

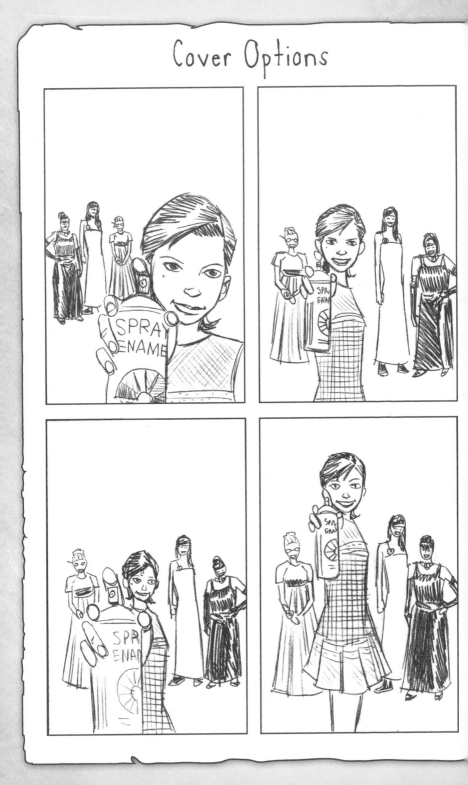

More Cover Options

Part 3
Janes Attack Back

317

320

323

324

330

332

333

I'D STARTED THIS BEAUTIFUL THING AND NOW I WAS LEAVING ART TO THE FATES.

FOR A MOMENT, ART WAS THRILLING AGAIN.

WE'D ALL GO OFF TO OUR SEPARATE CORNERS BUT STAY CONNECTED THROUGH THIS ONE PIECE.

AND THE WORLD COULD WATCH IF IT WANTED.

337

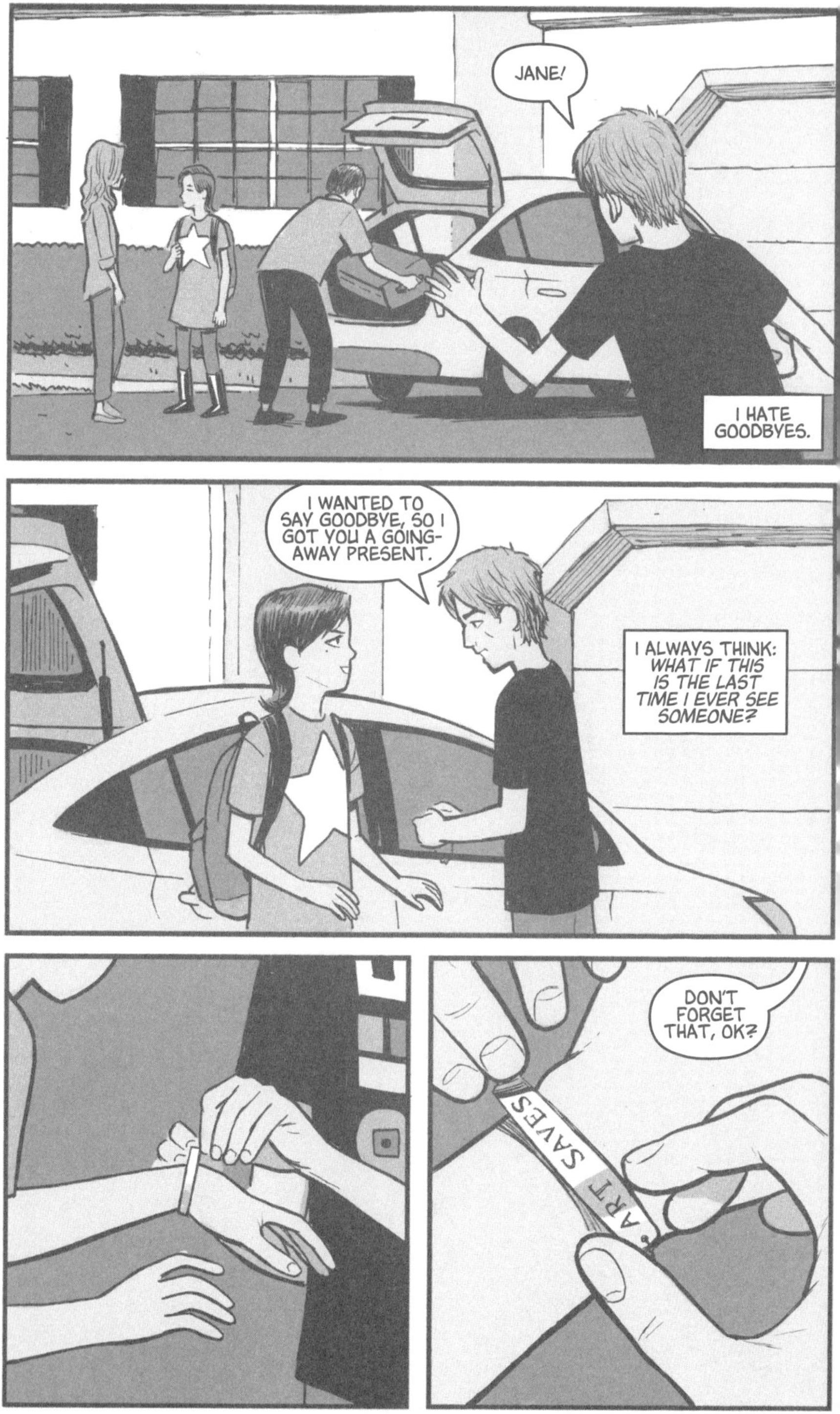
JANE!
I HATE GOODBYES.
I WANTED TO SAY GOODBYE, SO I GOT YOU A GOING-AWAY PRESENT.
I ALWAYS THINK: *WHAT IF THIS IS THE LAST TIME I EVER SEE SOMEONE?*
DON'T FORGET THAT, OK?
ART SAVES

339

345

346

351

353

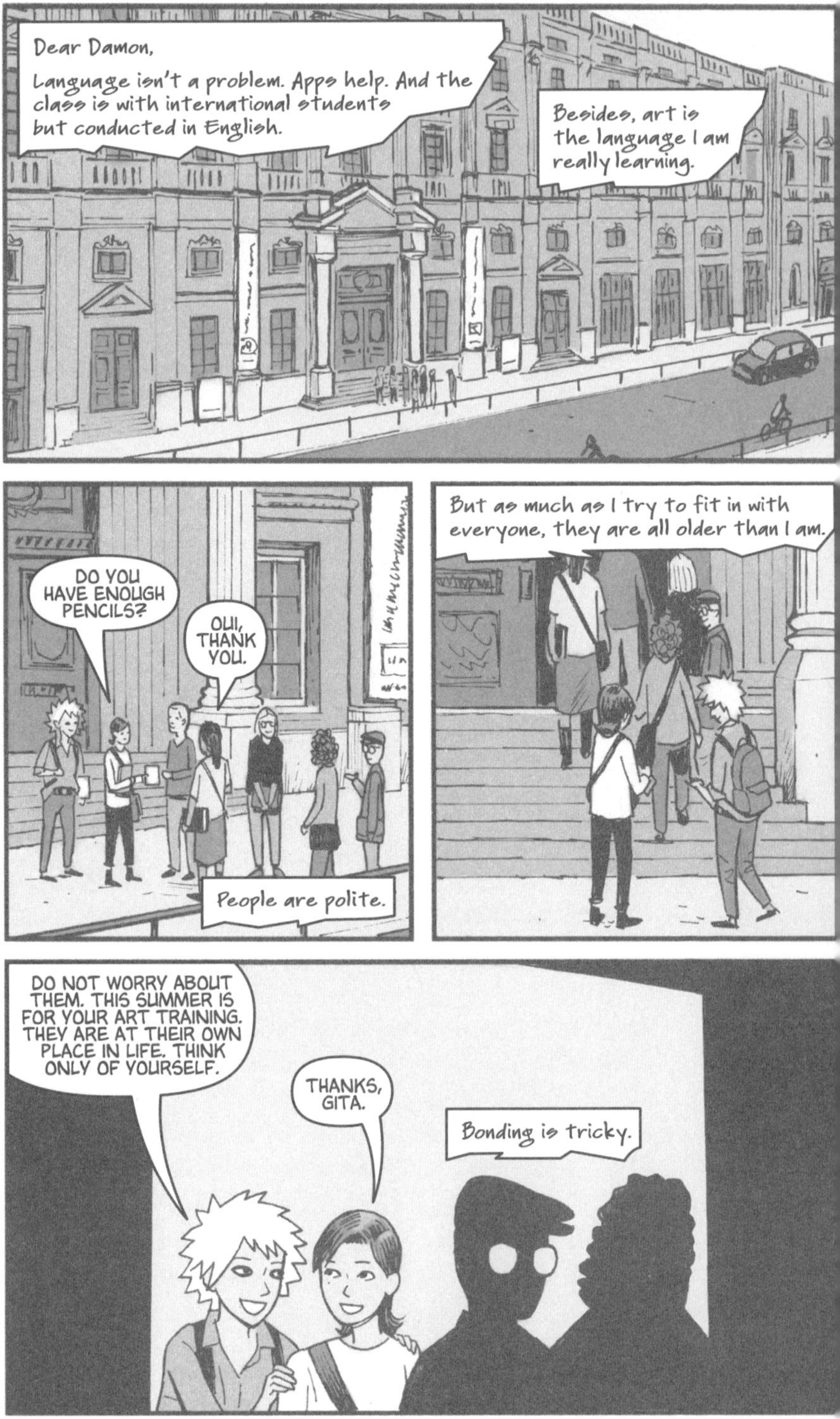

Dear Damon,
Language isn't a problem. Apps help. And the class is with international students but conducted in English.
Besides, art is the language I am really learning.
DO YOU HAVE ENOUGH PENCILS?
OUI, THANK YOU.
People are polite.
But as much as I try to fit in with everyone, they are all older than I am.
DO NOT WORRY ABOUT THEM. THIS SUMMER IS FOR YOUR ART TRAINING. THEY ARE AT THEIR OWN PLACE IN LIFE. THINK ONLY OF YOURSELF.
THANKS, GITA.
Bonding is tricky.

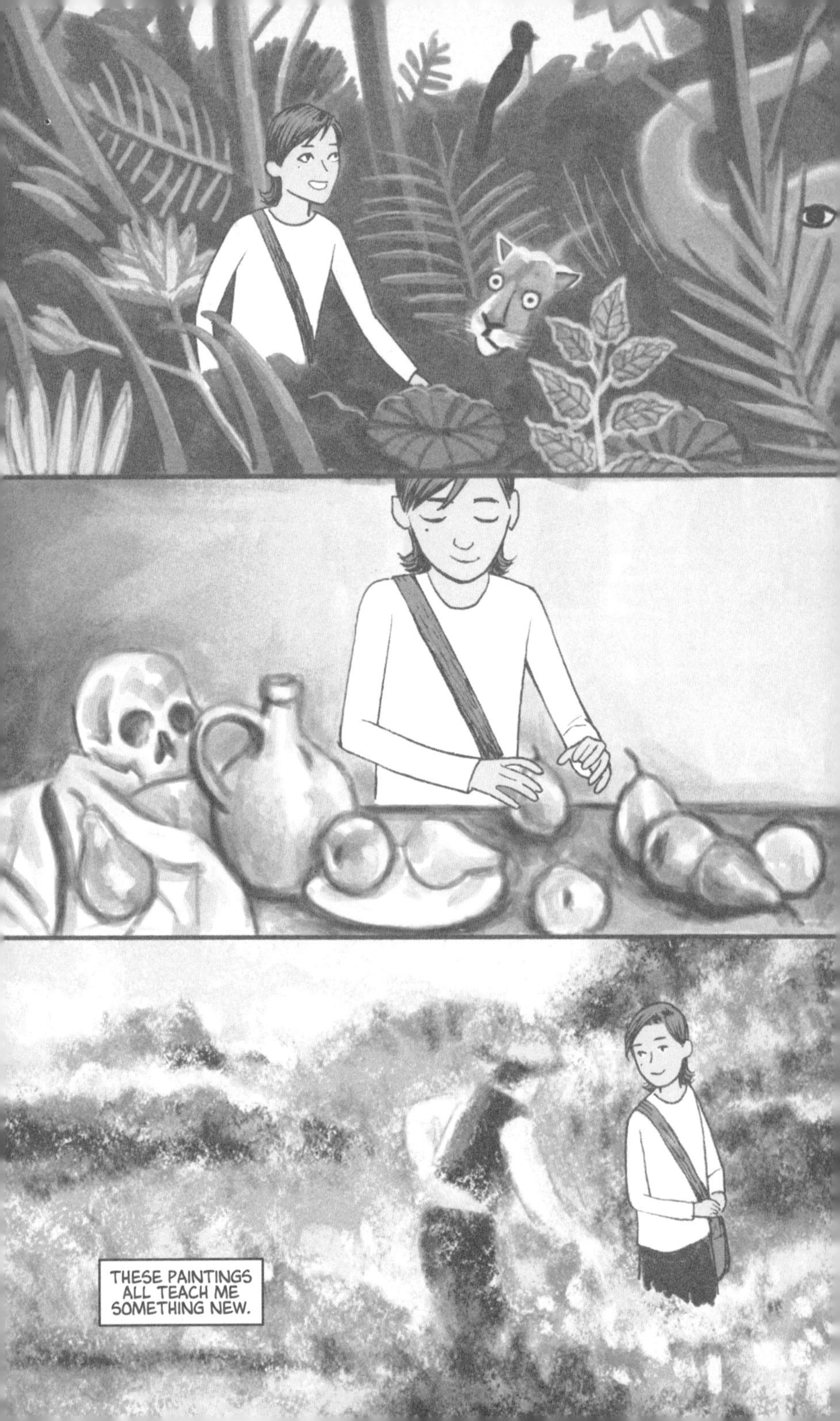
THESE PAINTINGS ALL TEACH ME SOMETHING NEW.

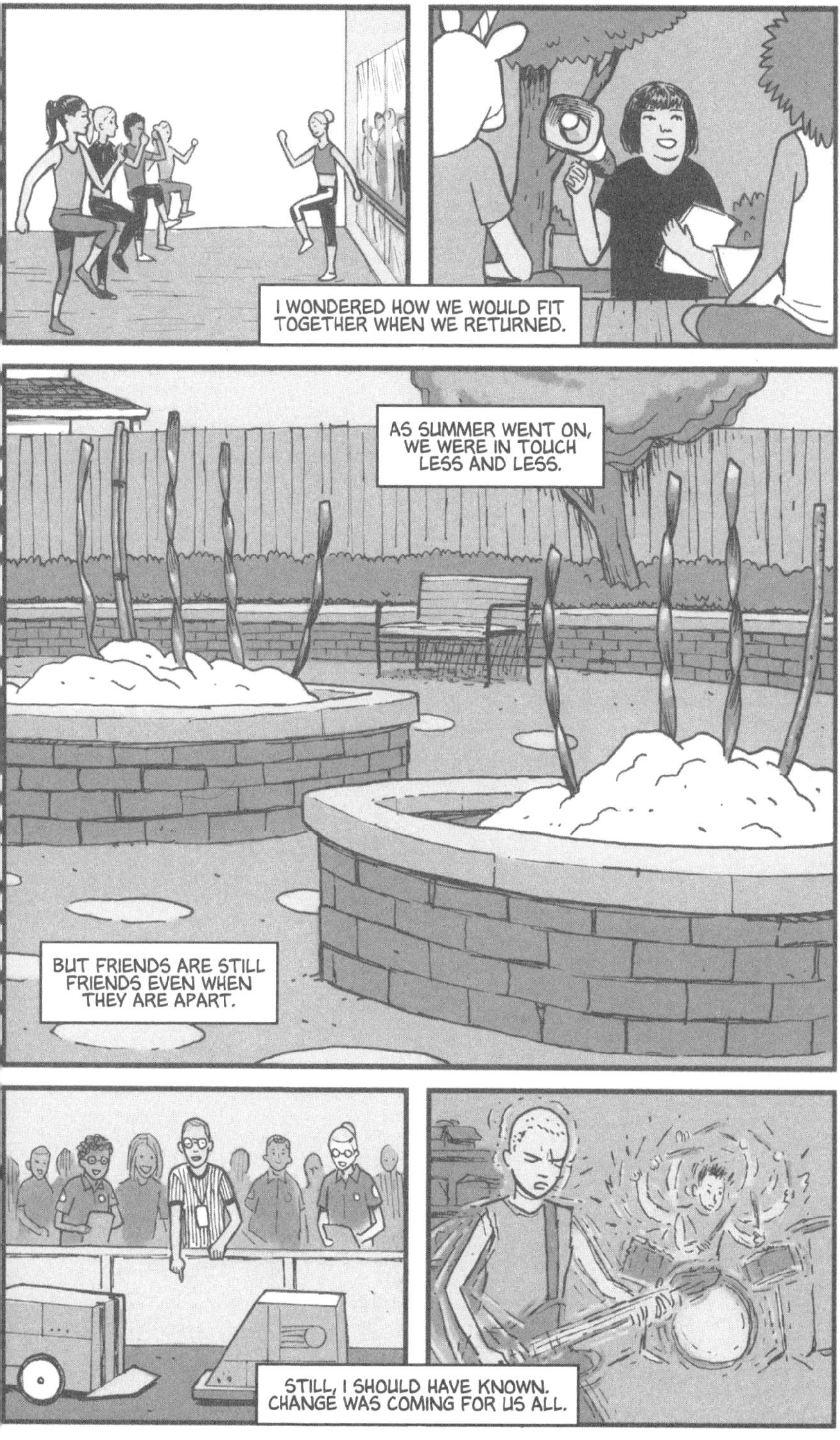
I WONDERED HOW WE WOULD FIT TOGETHER WHEN WE RETURNED.
AS SUMMER WENT ON, WE WERE IN TOUCH LESS AND LESS.
BUT FRIENDS ARE STILL FRIENDS EVEN WHEN THEY ARE APART.
STILL, I SHOULD HAVE KNOWN. CHANGE WAS COMING FOR US ALL.

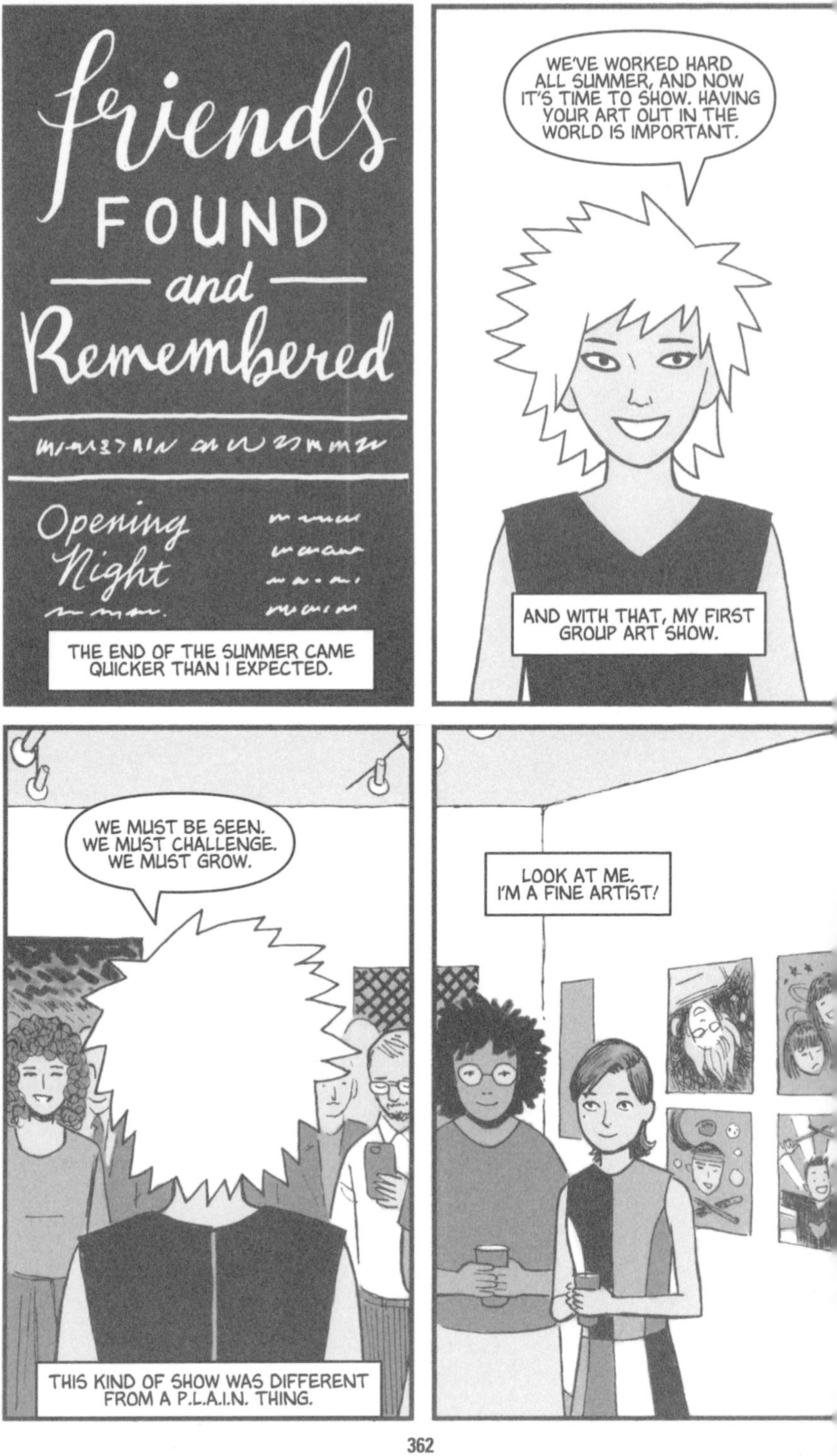
friends
FOUND
and
Remembered
Opening
Night
THE END OF THE SUMMER CAME QUICKER THAN I EXPECTED.
WE'VE WORKED HARD ALL SUMMER, AND NOW IT'S TIME TO SHOW. HAVING YOUR ART OUT IN THE WORLD IS IMPORTANT.
AND WITH THAT, MY FIRST GROUP ART SHOW.
WE MUST BE SEEN. WE MUST CHALLENGE. WE MUST GROW.
THIS KIND OF SHOW WAS DIFFERENT FROM A P.L.A.I.N. THING.
LOOK AT ME. I'M A FINE ARTIST!

368

371

375

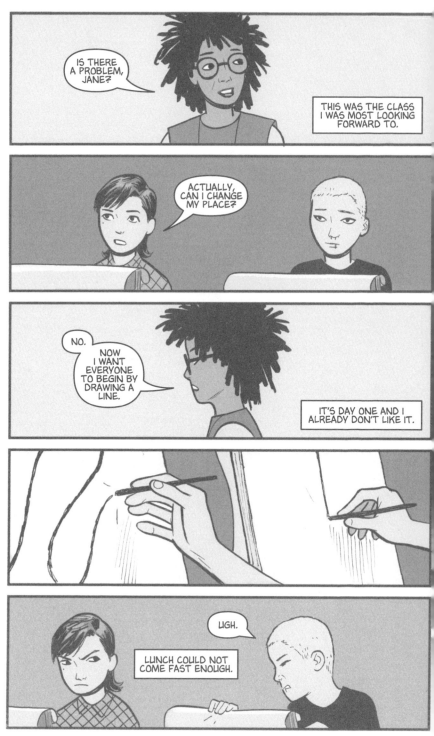

383

384

386

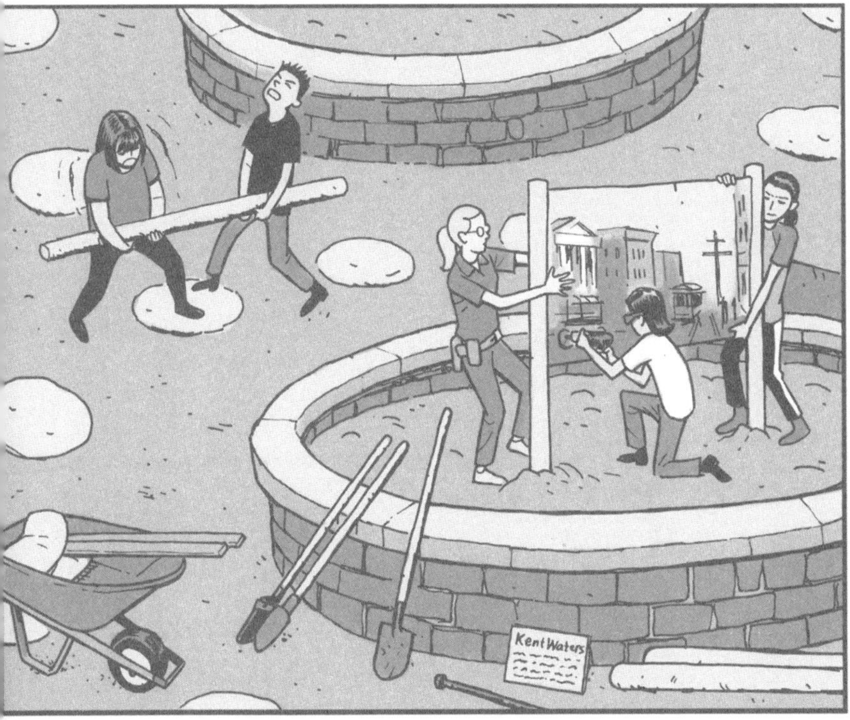
Kent Waters

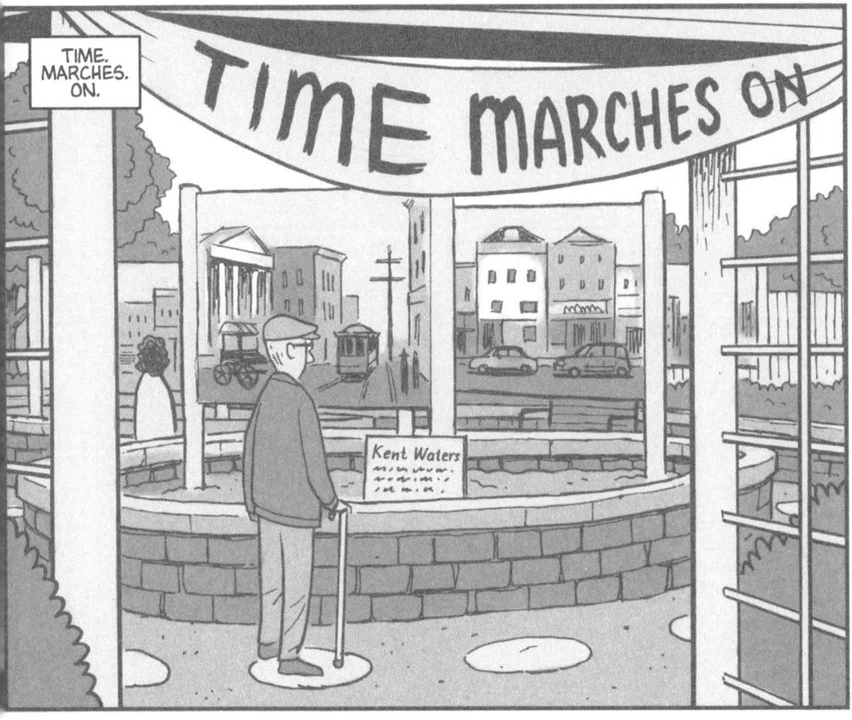
TIME.
MARCHES.
ON.
TIME MARCHES ON
Kent Waters

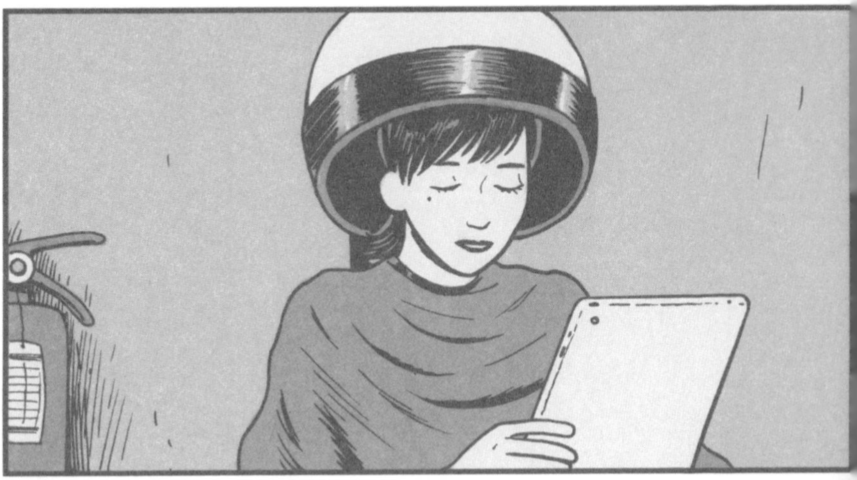

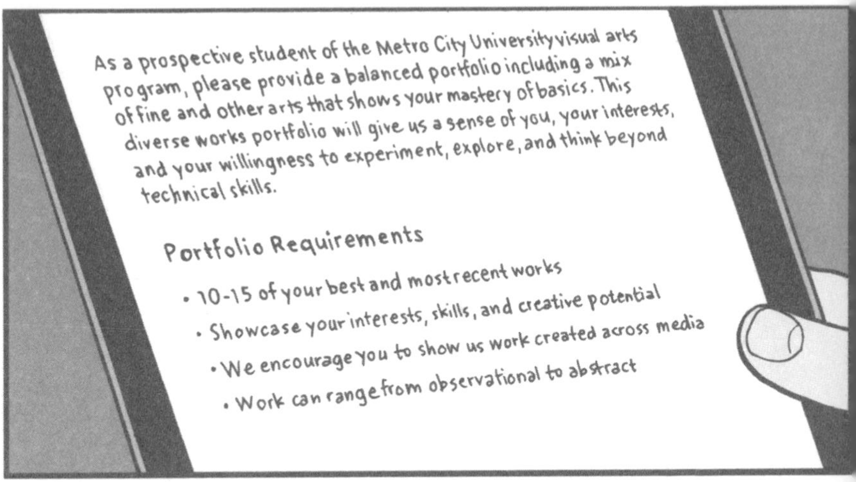
As a prospective student of the Metro City University visual arts program, please provide a balanced portfolio including a mix of fine and other arts that shows your mastery of basics. This diverse works portfolio will give us a sense of you, your interests, and your willingness to experiment, explore, and think beyond technical skills.
Portfolio Requirements
• 10-15 of your best and most recent works
• Showcase your interests, skills, and creative potential
• We encourage you to show us work created across media
• Work can range from observational to abstract

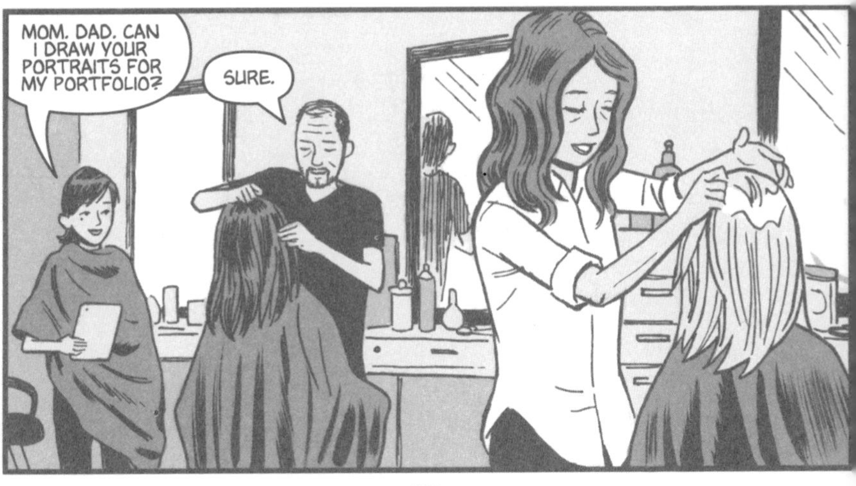
MOM. DAD. CAN I DRAW YOUR PORTRAITS FOR MY PORTFOLIO?
SURE.

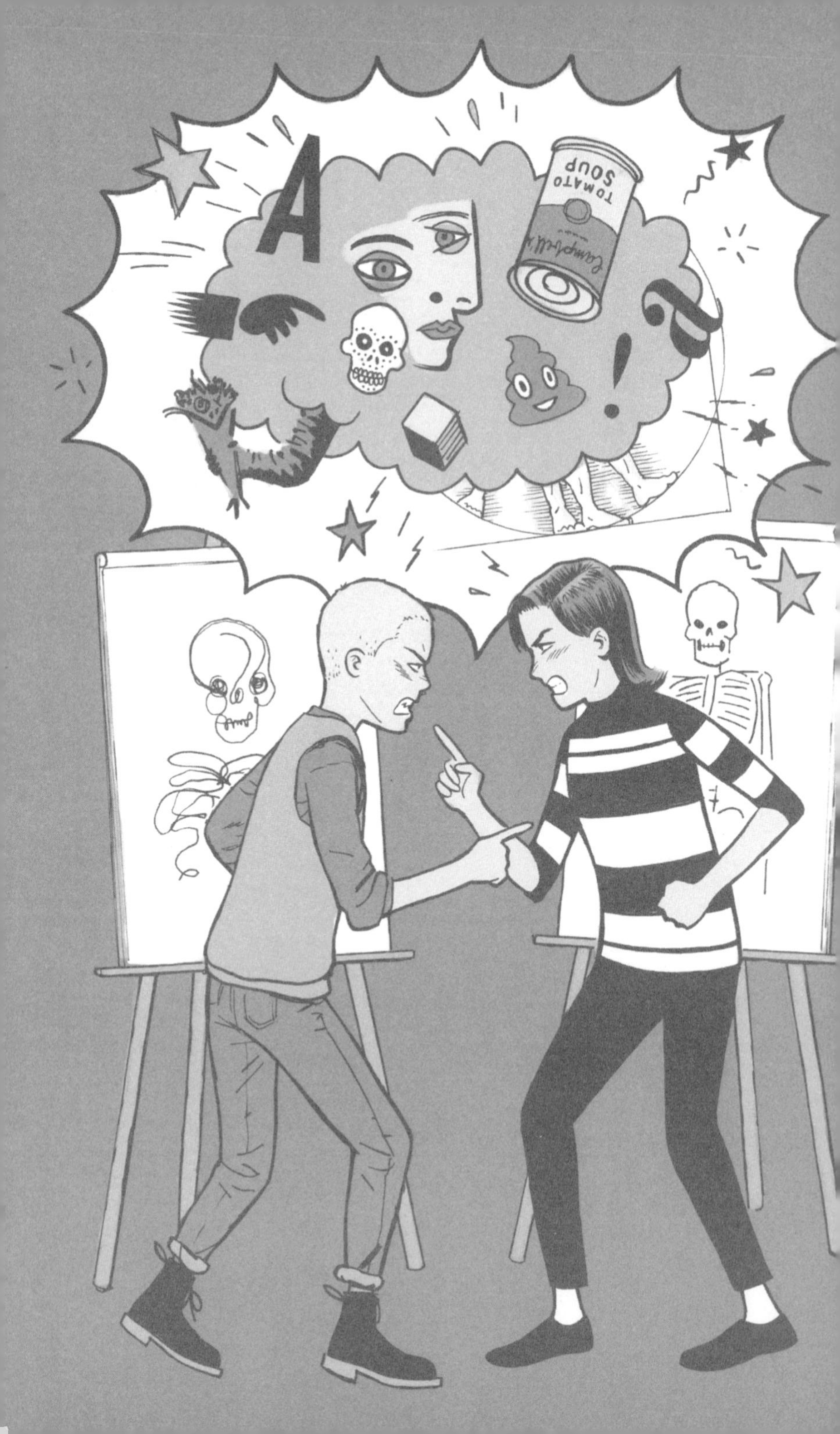
TOMATO
SOUP

395

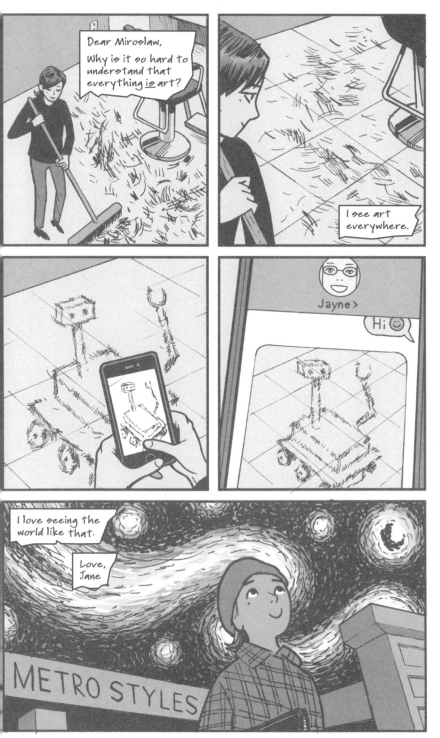

400

401

402

403

405

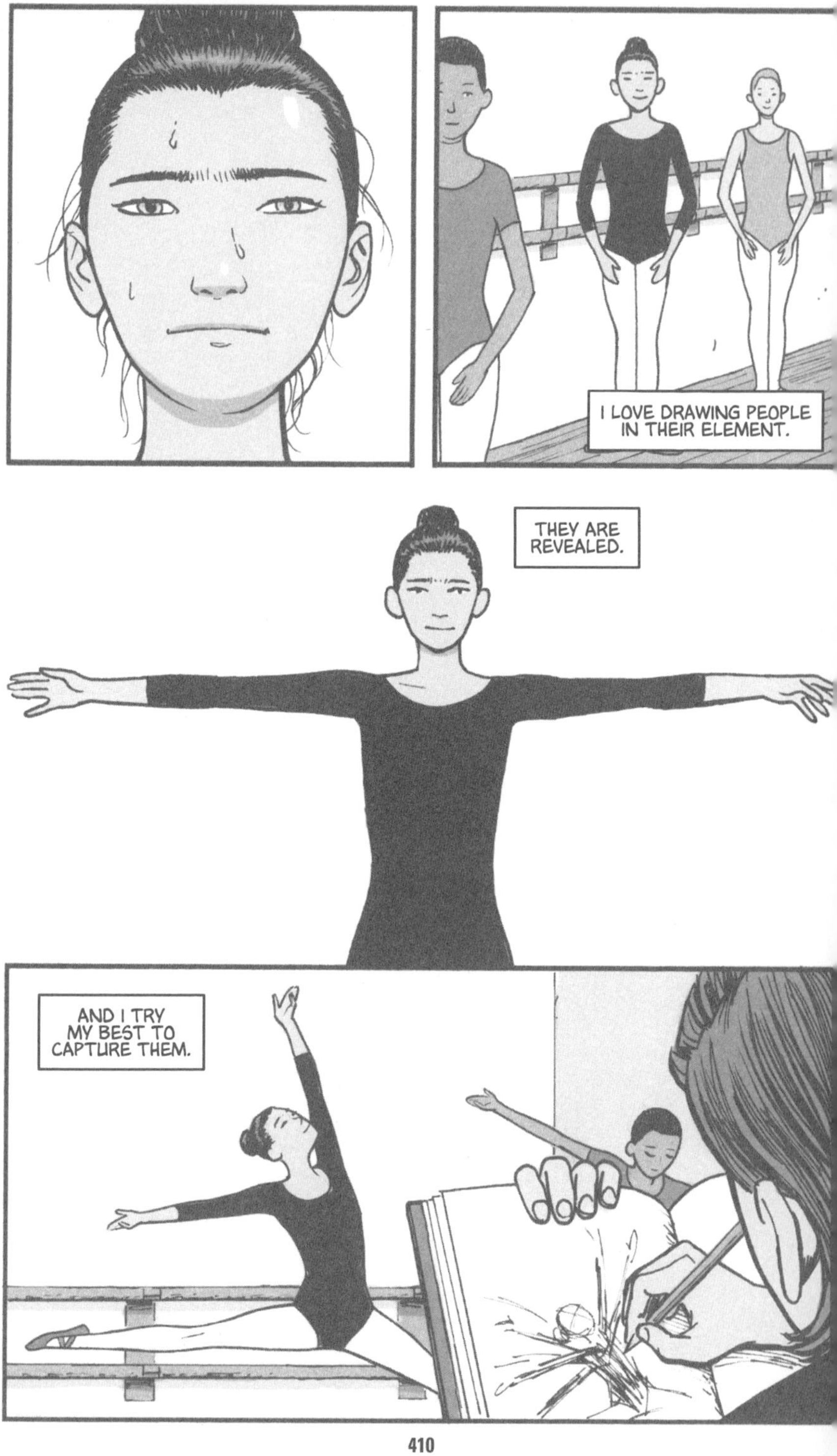
I LOVE DRAWING PEOPLE IN THEIR ELEMENT.
THEY ARE REVEALED.
AND I TRY MY BEST TO CAPTURE THEM.

411

413

416

419

420

421

422

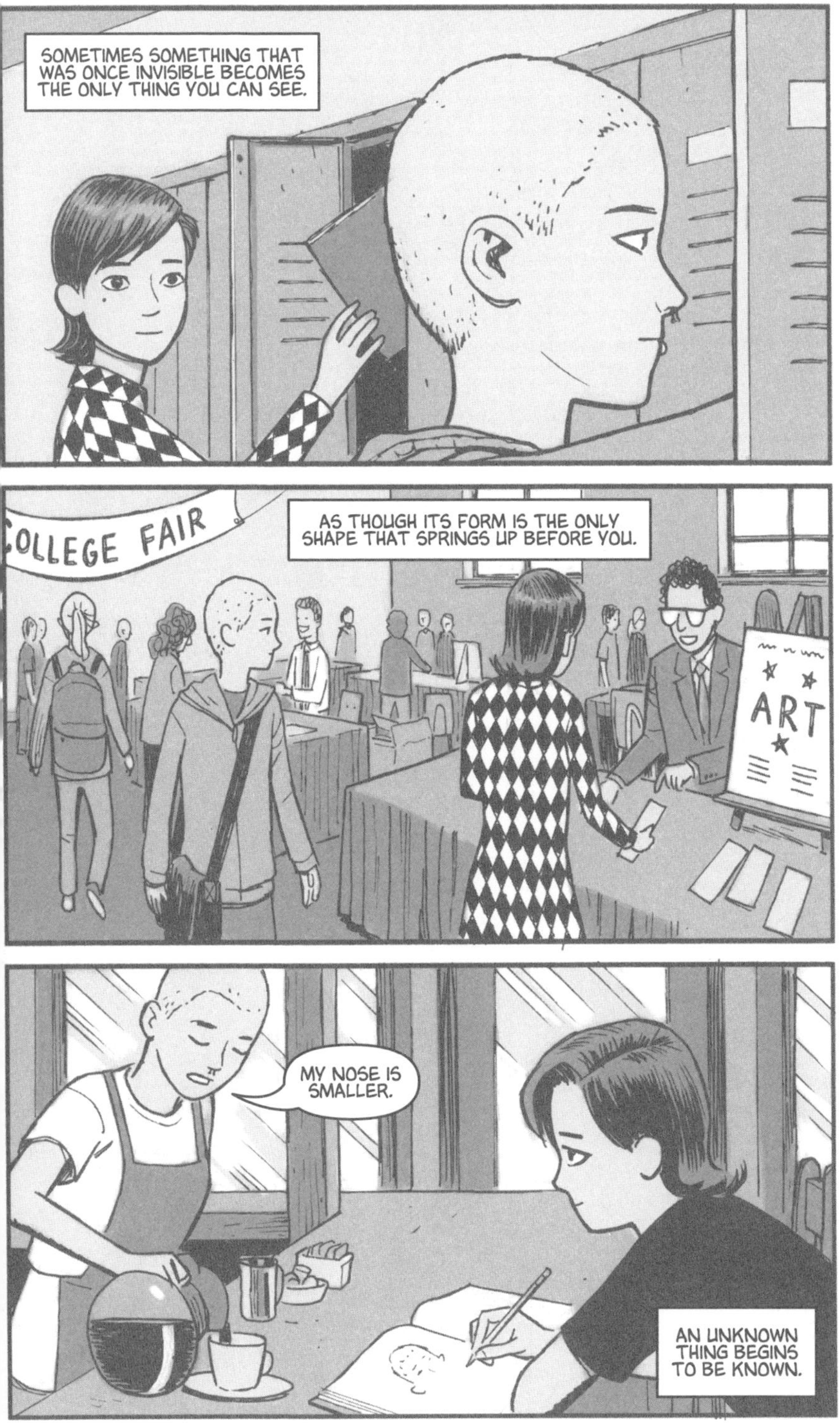
SOMETIMES SOMETHING THAT WAS ONCE INVISIBLE BECOMES THE ONLY THING YOU CAN SEE.
COLLEGE FAIR
AS THOUGH ITS FORM IS THE ONLY SHAPE THAT SPRINGS UP BEFORE YOU.
ART
MY NOSE IS SMALLER.
AN UNKNOWN THING BEGINS TO BE KNOWN.

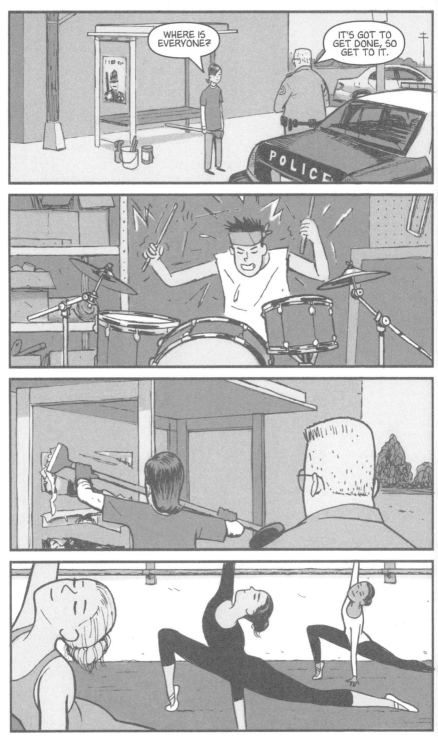

426

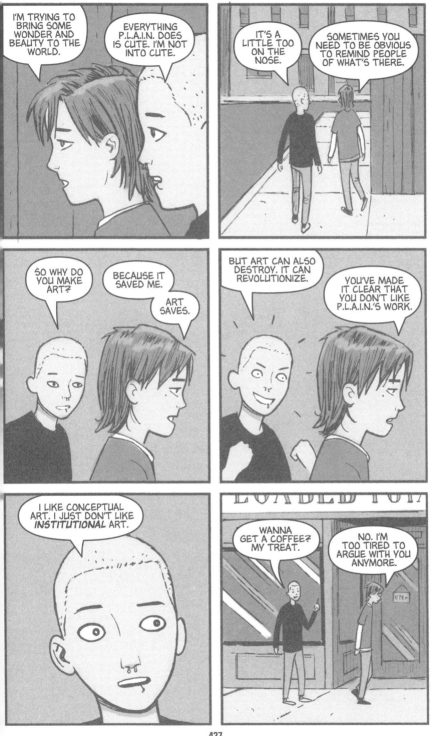

429

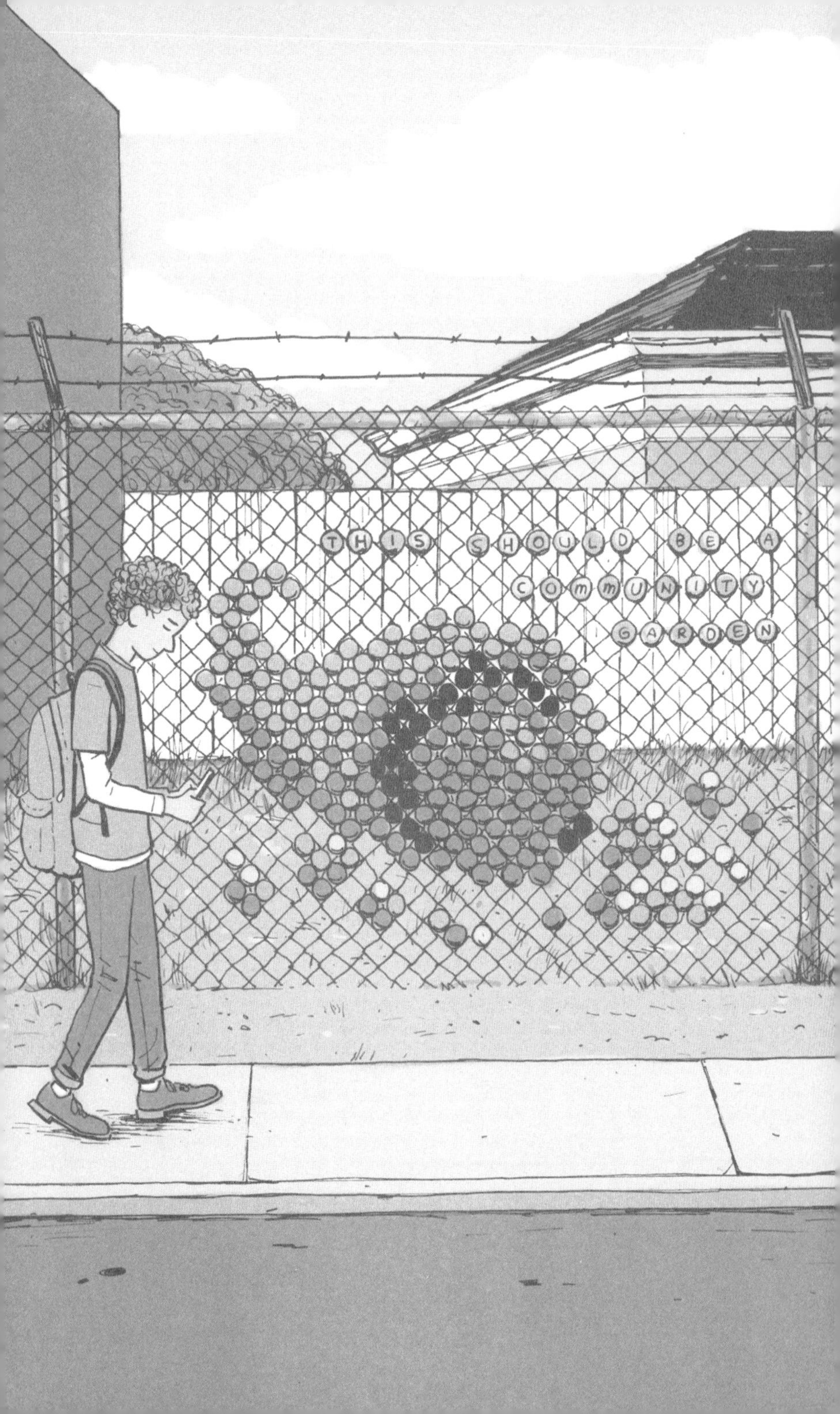
THIS SHOULD BE A
COMMUNITY
GARDEN

437

438

439

441

443

SAVES
WELL, OF COURSE SHE'S SCARED TO GO TO SCHOOL. WHO WOULDN'T BE THESE DAYS?
WHAT KIND OF WORLD ARE WE LEAVING OUR KIDS?
08:41
MESSAGES 1m ago
Damon
You ok?
MESSAGES 11h 32m ago
Damon
You around? You alive?
MESSAGES 13h 5m ago
Damon
Hey. Going to the movies tonight. Wanna join?
11 more messages...
WHAT ARE WE GOING TO DO ABOUT HER INTERVIEW AT METRO CITY UNIVERSITY?
IF SHE CAN'T GO, SHE CAN'T GO. HOPEFULLY SHE CAN RESCHEDULE.
I'M CONSTANTLY REMINDED THAT THE WORLD CAN BE DANGEROUS AND THAT THINGS CAN CHANGE IN AN INSTANT.

446

447

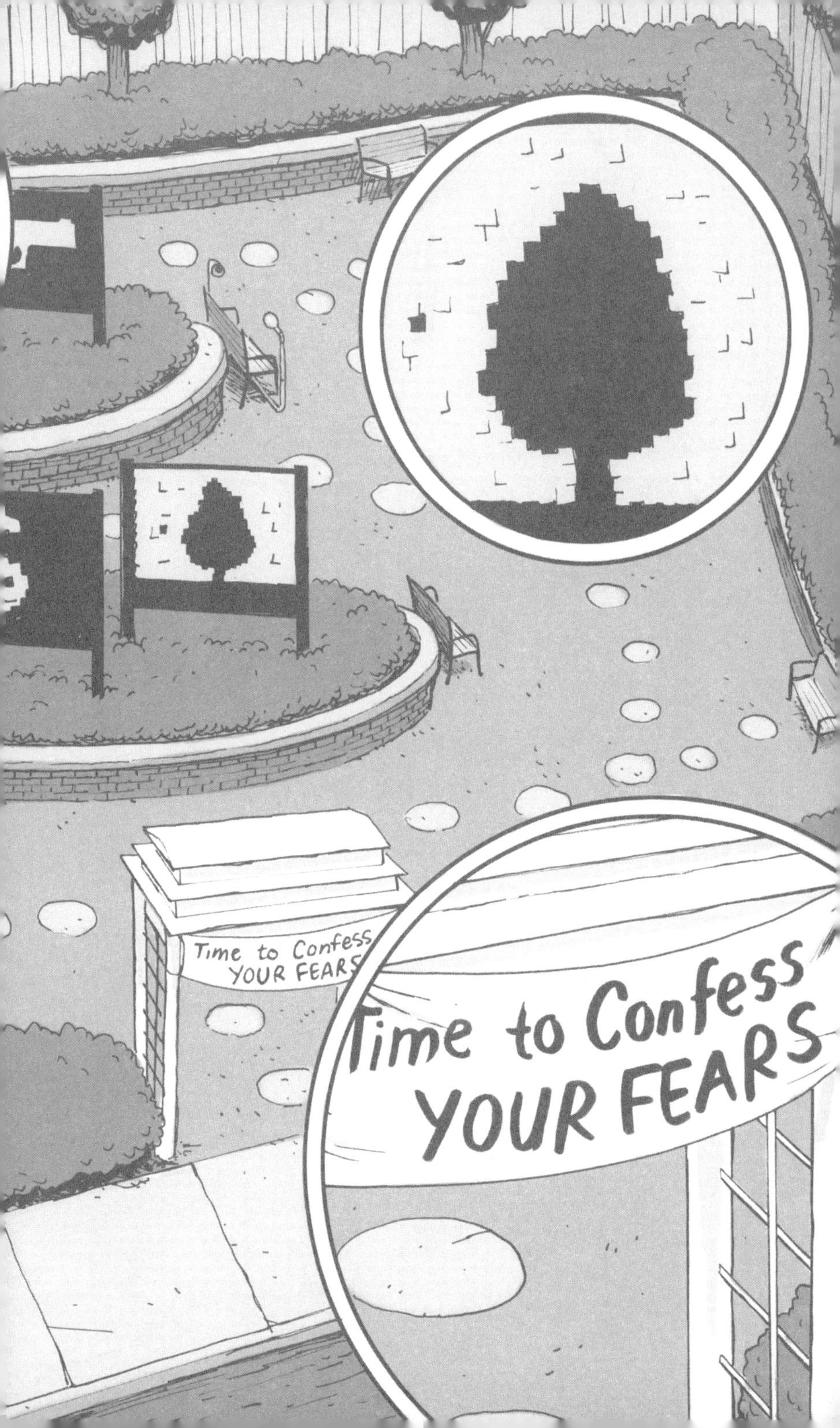
Time to Confess YOUR FEARS
Time to Confess YOUR FEARS

452

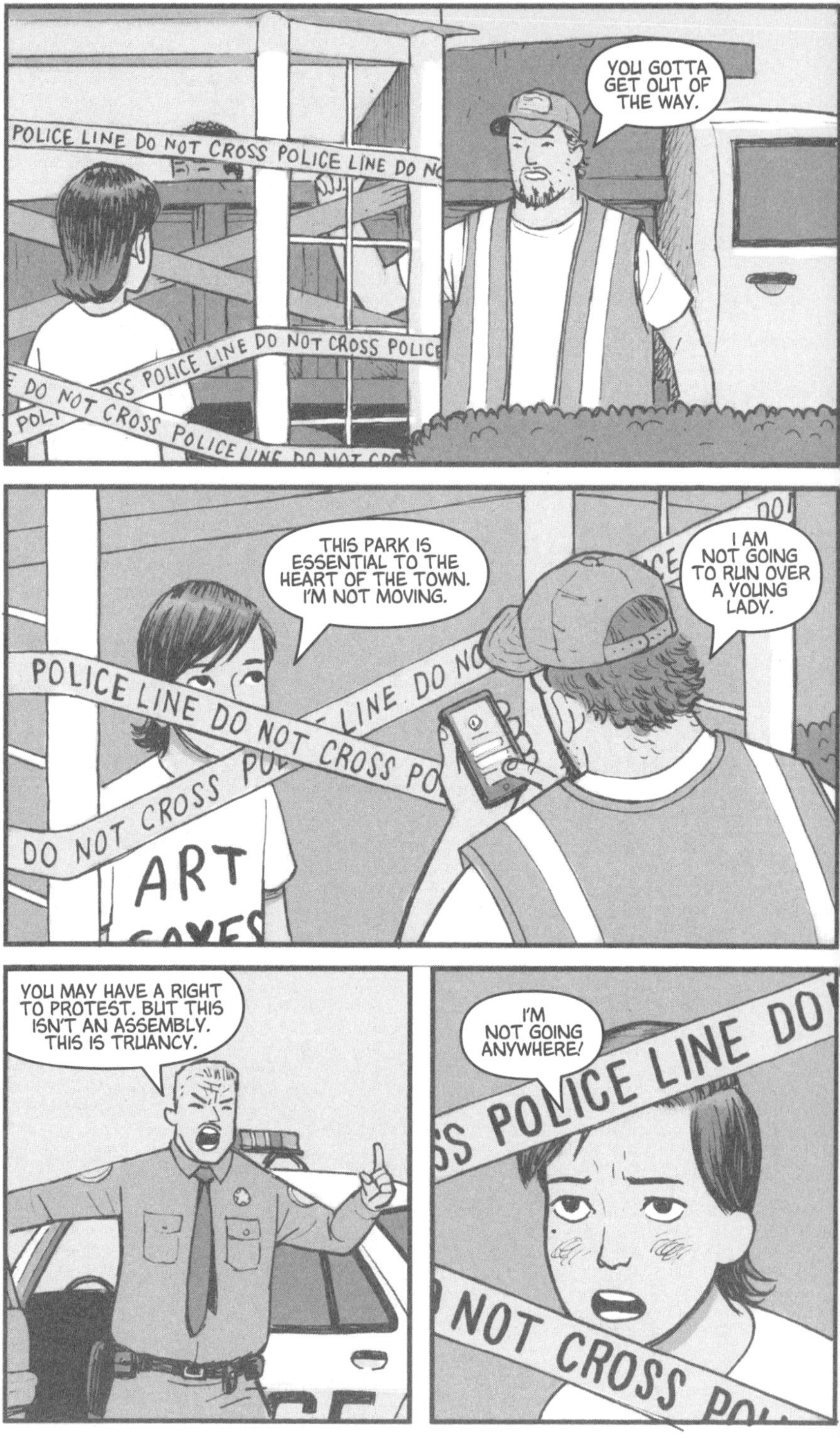
POLICE LINE DO NOT CROSS POLICE LINE DO NO
YOU GOTTA GET OUT OF THE WAY.
THIS PARK IS ESSENTIAL TO THE HEART OF THE TOWN. I'M NOT MOVING.
I AM NOT GOING TO RUN OVER A YOUNG LADY.
POLICE LINE DO NOT CROSS
ART
YOU MAY HAVE A RIGHT TO PROTEST. BUT THIS ISN'T AN ASSEMBLY. THIS IS TRUANCY.
I'M NOT GOING ANYWHERE!
POLICE LINE DO
NOT CROSS

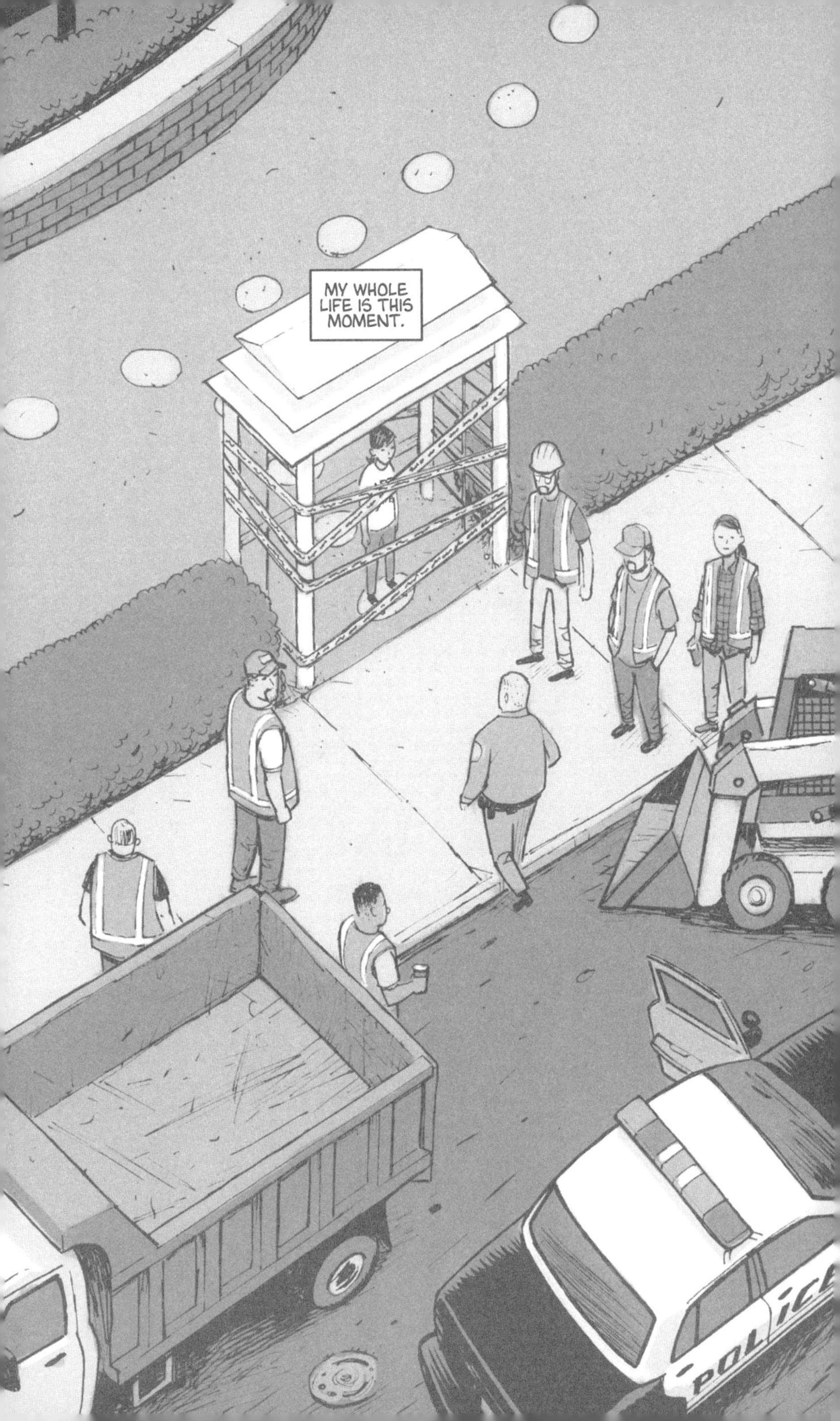
MY WHOLE LIFE IS THIS MOMENT.
POLICE

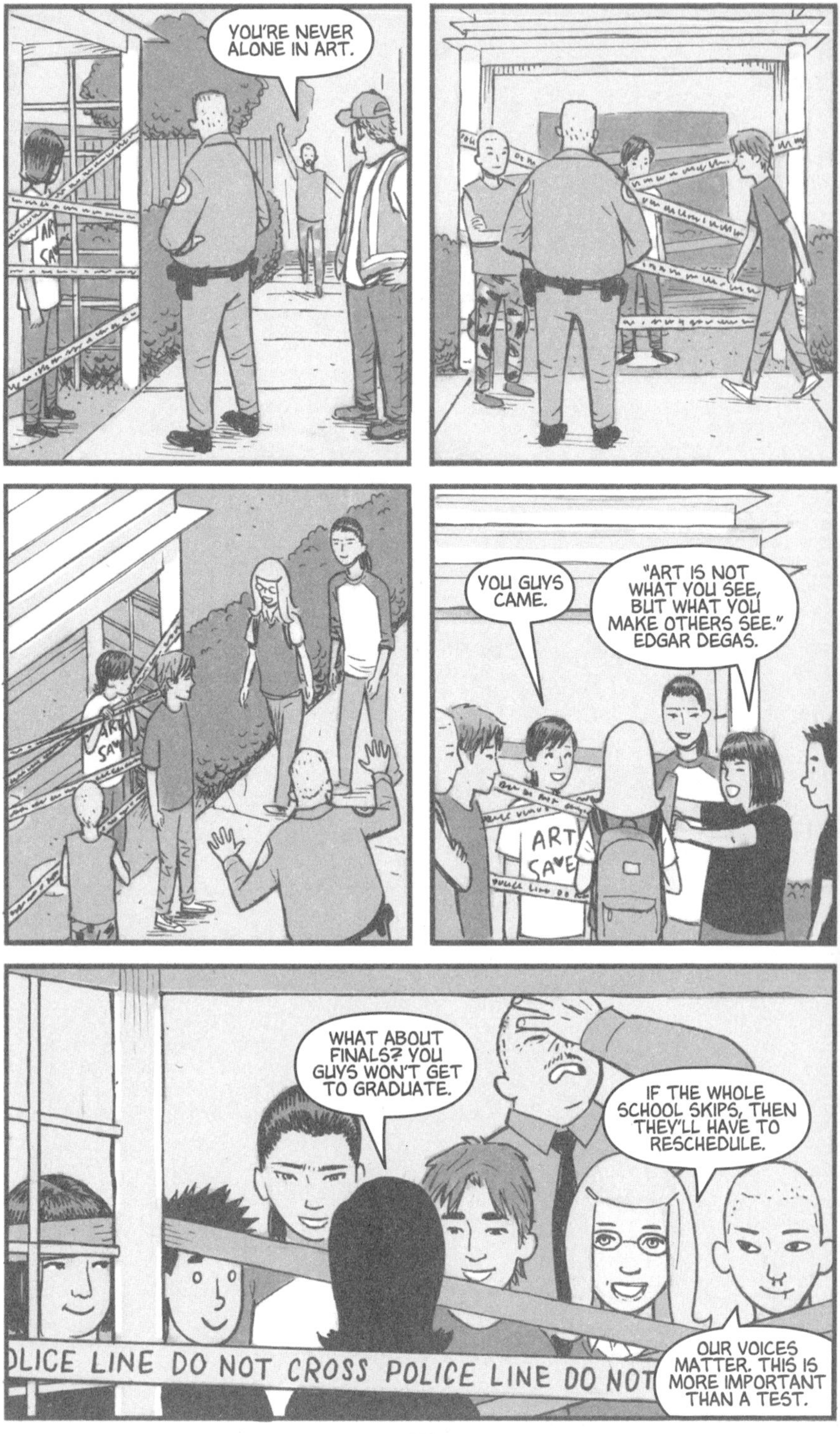
YOU'RE NEVER ALONE IN ART.
ART SAVE
YOU GUYS CAME.
"ART IS NOT WHAT YOU SEE, BUT WHAT YOU MAKE OTHERS SEE." EDGAR DEGAS.
WHAT ABOUT FINALS? YOU GUYS WON'T GET TO GRADUATE.
IF THE WHOLE SCHOOL SKIPS, THEN THEY'LL HAVE TO RESCHEDULE.
OUR VOICES MATTER. THIS IS MORE IMPORTANT THAN A TEST.
LICE LINE DO NOT CROSS POLICE LINE DO NOT

461

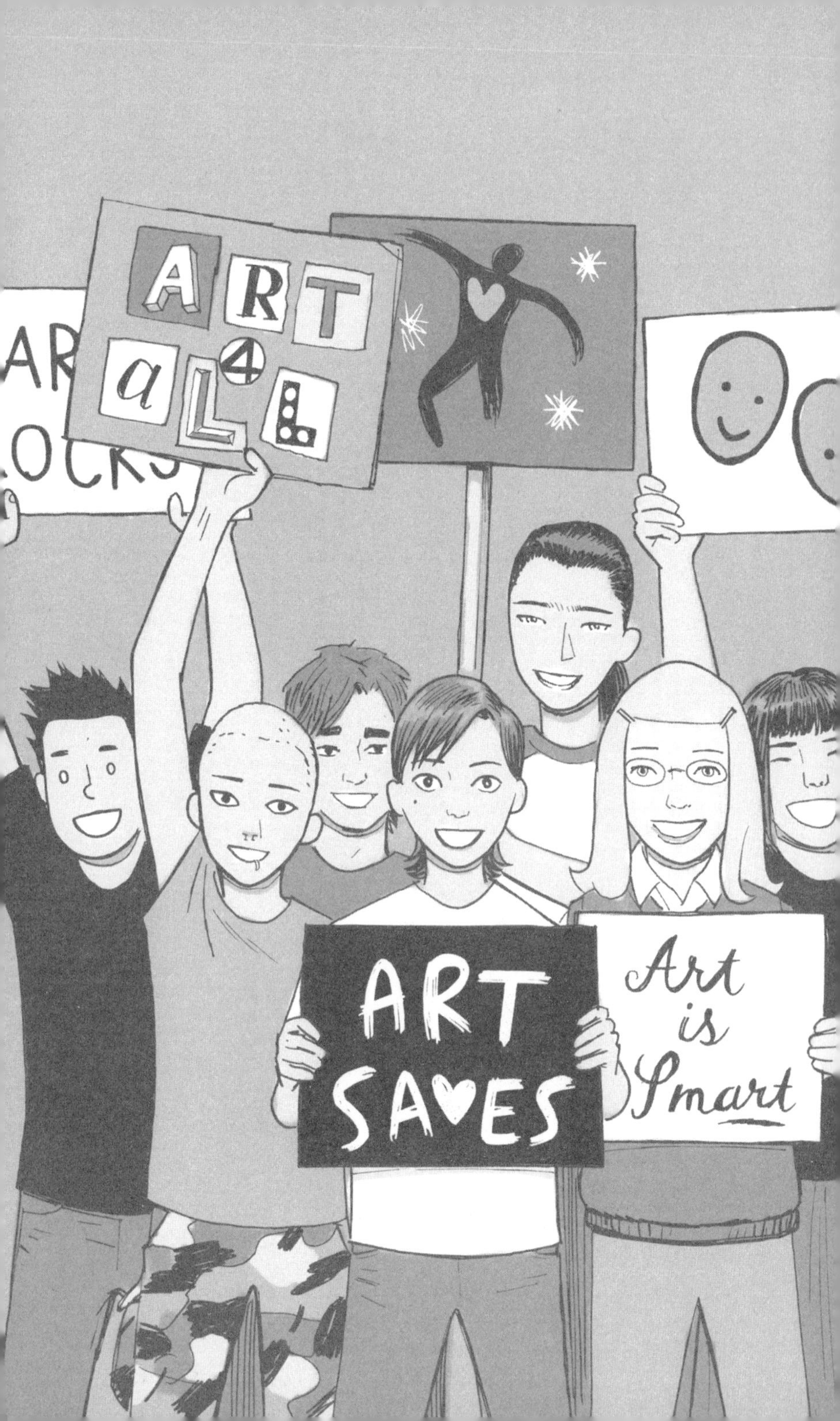
ART 4 aLL
ART SAVES
Art is Smart

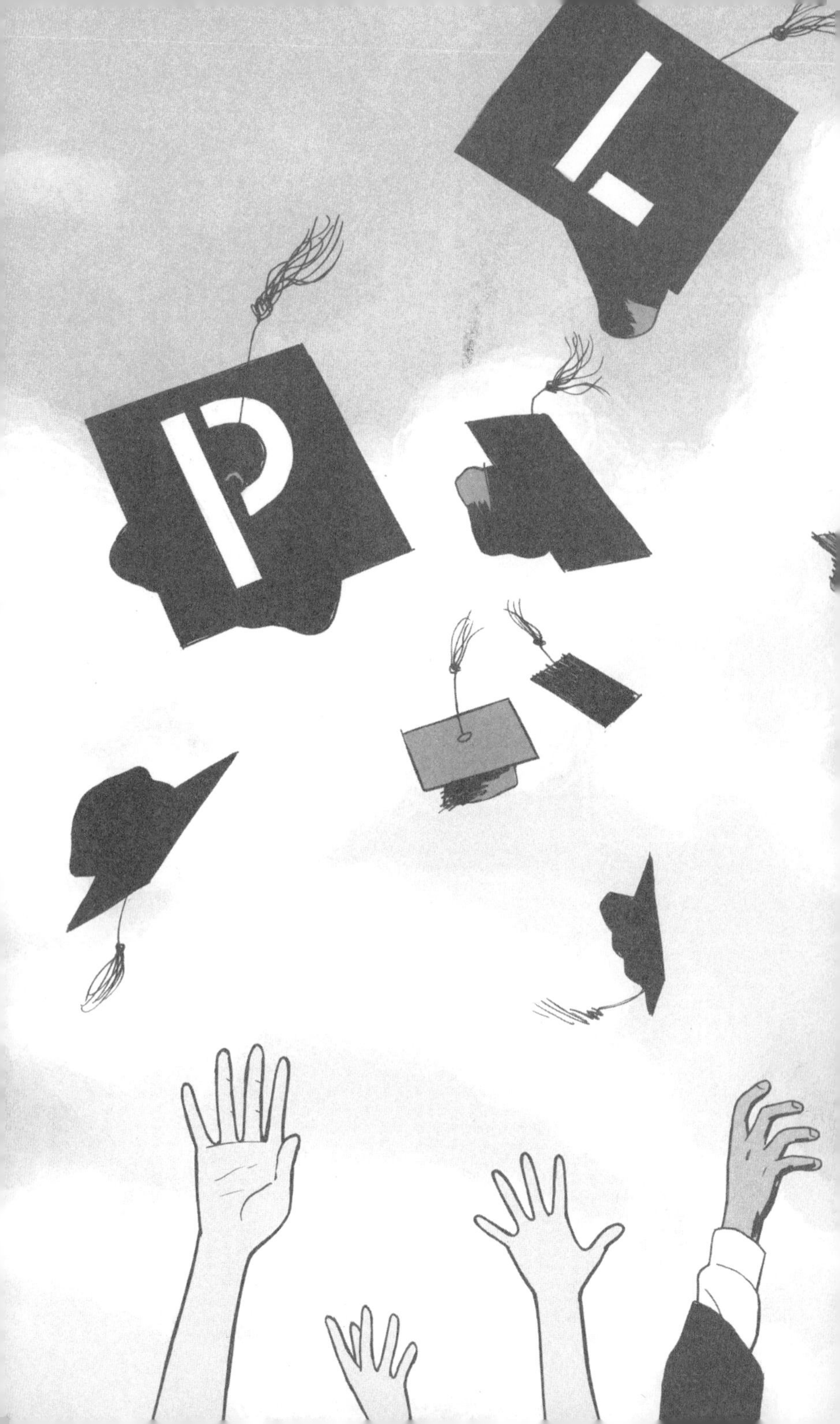

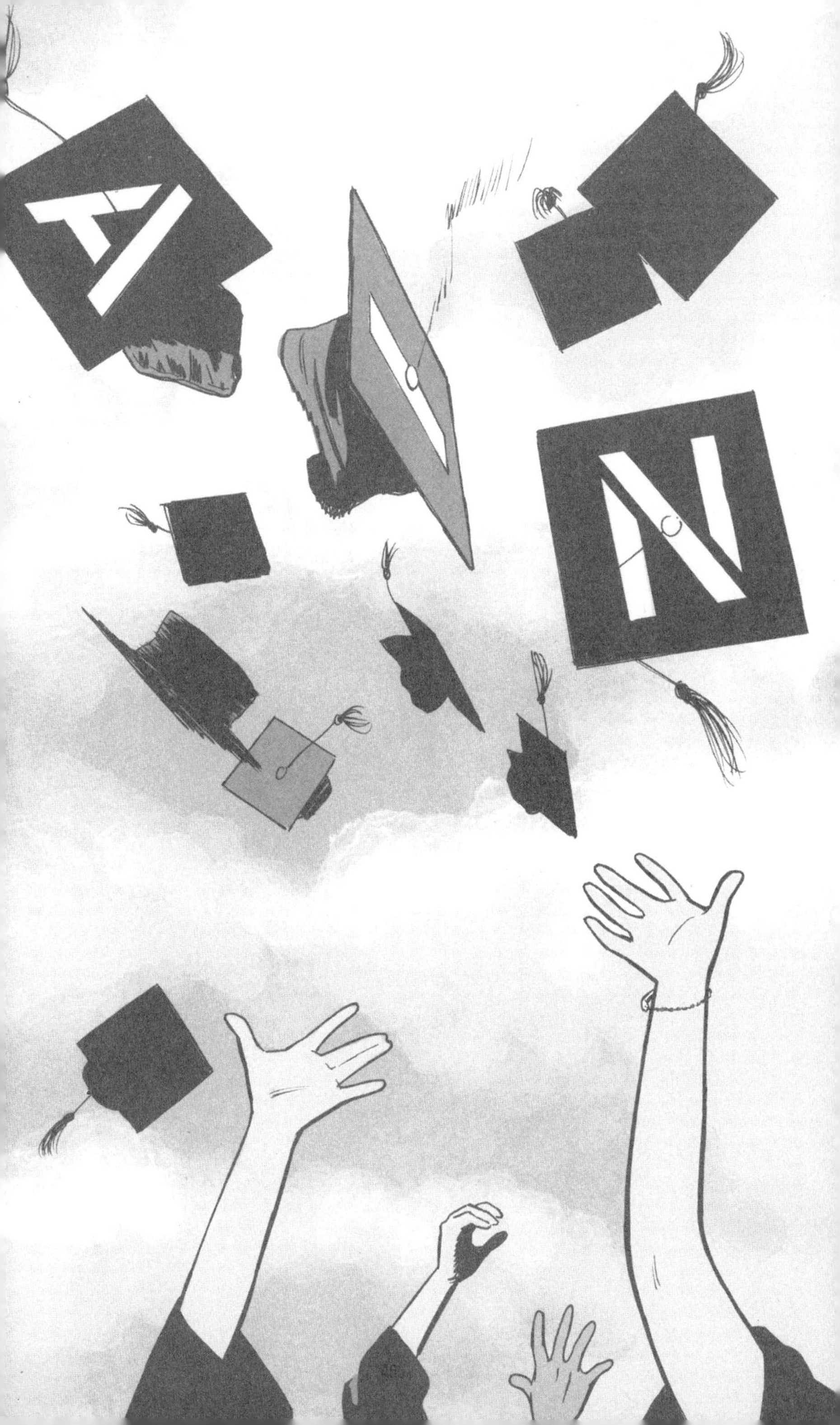

Other Artists Draw the Janes

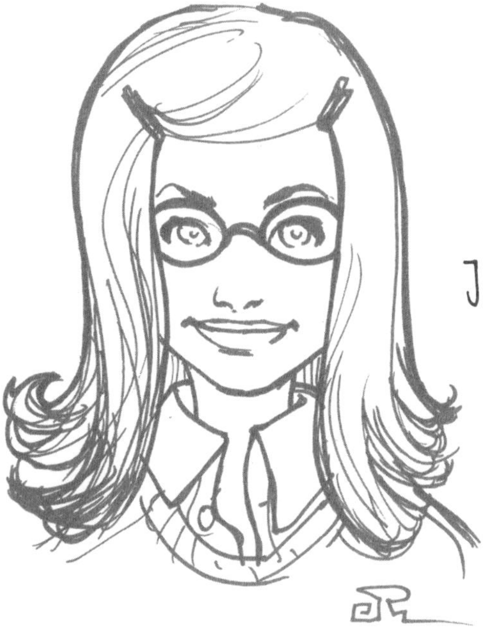

Art by
Joshua Middleton

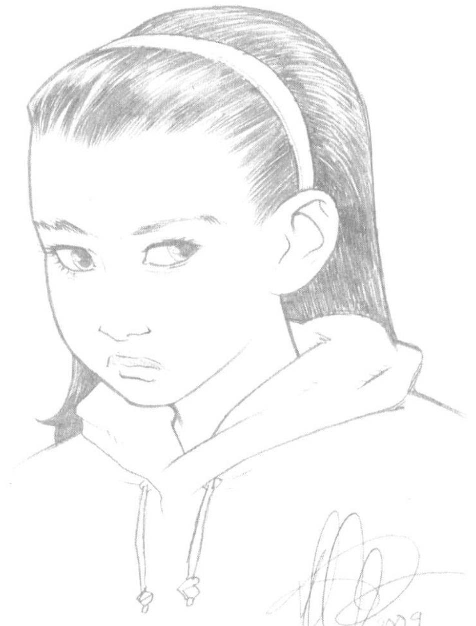

Art by
Sophie Campbell

Art by
Becky Cloonan

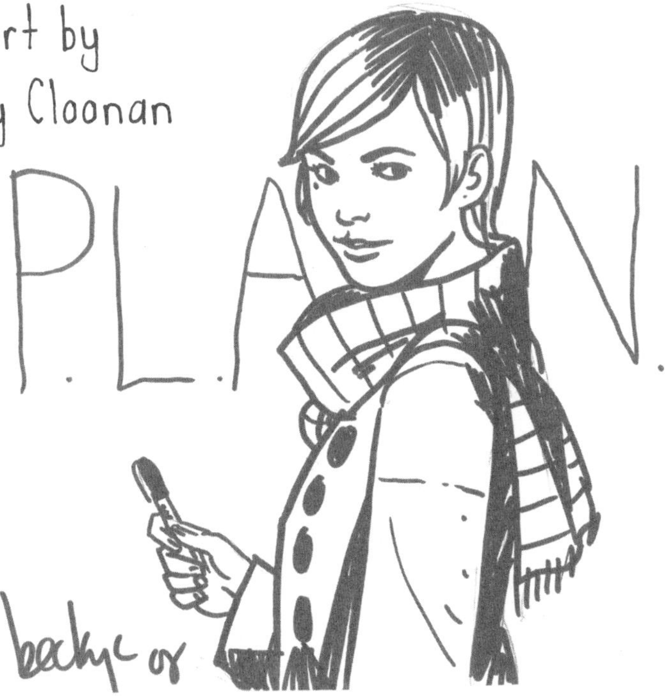
P.L.A.N.
beckyc 08

Art by
Cliff Chiang

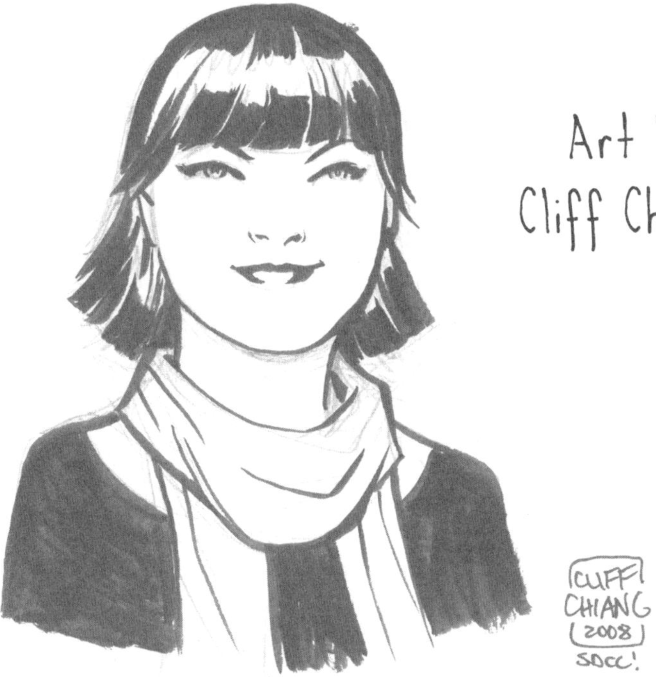
CLIFF
CHIANG
2008
SDCC!

Art by
Tom Scioli

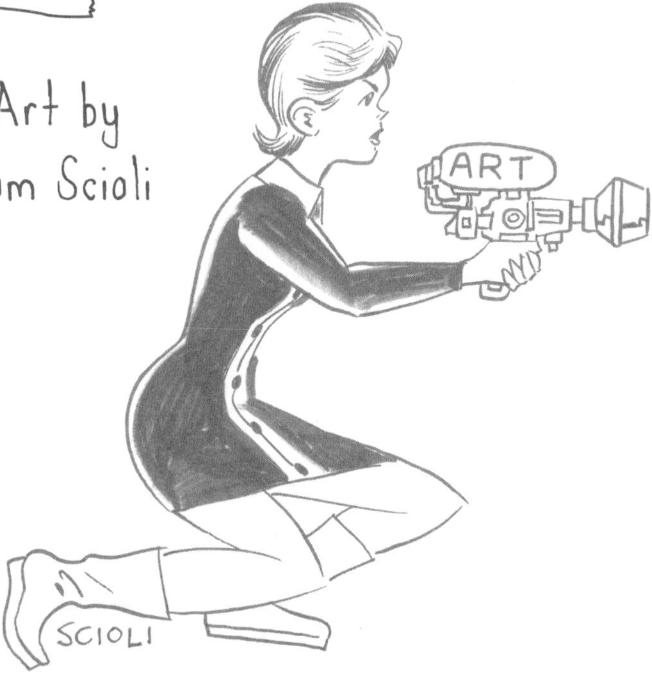
ART
SCIOLI

Art by
Philip Bond

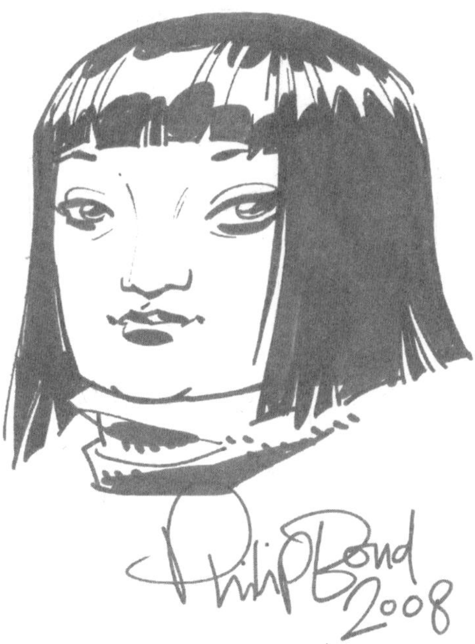
Philip Bond
2008

Acknowledgments

Thank you to:

Shelly Bond

DC Comics, Dan DiDio,
and Jack Mahan

Kirby Kim

Jared Fletcher

Pam Gruber and Little, Brown Books
for Young Readers

Street Art Everywhere

Photograph by Eric Charles

Cecil Castellucci is an Eisner, EGL, and Harvey Award-nominated, *New York Times* bestselling author of books and graphic novels for young adults, including *Shade, The Changing Girl, Soupy Leaves Home, The Year of the Beasts, Tin Star,* and *Odd Duck.* She has also written for DC Comics, and her short stories and short comics have been published in many literary journals and comics anthologies. In a former life, she was known as Cecil Seaskull in the '90s indie band Nerdy Girl. She is a two-time MacDowell Fellow and the founding YA editor at the *Los Angeles Review of Books.* She lives in Los Angeles.

Photograph by Natalie Rugg

Jim Rugg is a comic book artist, book maker, illustrator, designer, and cat dad. His books include *Street Angel, The PLAIN Janes, Afrodisiac, Notebook Drawings, Rambo 3.5,* and *Supermag.* He is the winner of an Eisner Award and an Ignatz Award, and he was recognized as part of the AIGA 50/50. His YouTube channel, Cartoonist Kayfabe, will make you love comics even more!